Only after he'd mov...
Clutching them in...
backwards until the...
then, his eyes holding encou...
of nerves. I forced myself to g... .... smile...right before I took a deep breath and turned my head to look through the organic window.

Revik's back rested against the furthest wall from the hatch, his chained hands in his lap. Legs sprawled in front of him, he tilted back his head, as if staring at the ceiling. In the sudden lack of talking among the seers outside the tank, the audio reached my ears, until it eclipsed all other sounds in the room.

He was singing, I realized. Softly, under his breath.

Not only that, but I'd heard the song before.

It was a seer song, but modern. Wreg played it sometimes, during sparring drills, or by the pool, where he often wanted music. As I listened to Revik though, I realized I'd never really paid attention to the words woven into the somewhat off-kilter tune.

"Never fire and back to earth...
Some days I submit, some I won't...
They always break me, inside, out...
They kill me, smash me...
Leave me without...
Family, friends, all lovers end...
I'm broken inside, but here I am..."

The words in Prexci melded together, forming a kind of whispered prayer.

"My heart was broken long ago...
Too far back, the elders know...
The books are dust, the prophets dead...
Our time won't come before the end..."

I felt emotion try to creep up around my light, inexplicable in its intensity, since I only understood the allusions in about half of the words.

Maybe I just remembered Wreg, and the others in his charge, who I'd led to slavery and death. Maybe I was remembering Nikka.

Taking another breath, I shook it off, forcing my eyes off his face.

"All right," I said to Balidor, glancing at Vash. "It's time to start."

Books in the Series

Rook: Allie's War Book One

Shield: Allie's War Book Two

Sword: Allie's War Book Three

Shadow: Allie's War Book Four

Knight: Allie's War Book Five

War: Allie's War Book Six

Bridge: Allie's War Book Seven

Prophet: Allie's War Book Eight

Prequel Books

New York: Allie's War Early Years

Revik: Allie's War Early Years

Terian: Allie's War Early Years

Birth: Allie's War Early Years

Other Books by JC Andrijeski

The Culling (Alien Apocalypse Part I)

The Royals (Alien Apocalypse Part II)

The New Order (Alien Apocalypse Part III)

The Morph (Gate Shifter Book 1)

Crash Morph (Gate Shifter Book 2)

SHADOW
Allie's War Book Four

JC Andrijeski

White Sun Press

SHADOW: ALLIE'S WAR
BOOK FOUR

Copyright 2012 by JC Andrijeski
Published by White Sun Press

Fourth Edition

ISBN-13: 978-1478265368
ISBN-10: 1478265361

Cover Art & Design by JC Andrijeski

http://jcandrijeski.com

This book is licensed for your personal enjoyment only. All rights resevered. This is a work of fiction. All characters and events portrayed in this book are fictional, and any resemblance to real people, organizations or events is purely coincidental. This book, or parts thereof, may not be reproduced in any form without permission.

White Sun Press
For more information
about any book published by White Sun Press, please go to
www.whitesunpress.com

Printed in the United States of America
2014

Dedicated to
Kathyrn

Acknowledgements

This is the first novel I've written entirely in India, working as a full-time writer, so I'd like to thank everyone who helped me get over here, including my good friends Sanja and Terri who gave me the most wonderful send-off I've ever received, as well as Tamela, Lizzy, Monica, Bryan, Dannie, KP, Cheryl, Niki, Emily, Jeannette, Gianina, Jennifer, Cindy, Susannah and Kara. Most of all, a huge thanks to my sister Kathy and my brother Steve and their families for helping me with the transition, and my parents for being so supportive even when my choices probably make them nuts. Thanks also to Cindie for providing me a buddy and fellow seeker almost upon arrival in the land of monkeys and Buddhas and stomping Lord Ganeshas. Many thanks as well to Kathy, Amelia, Tamela and April for their genius minds in helping me edit and improve all of my books and the Oregon Writers Network folks for all of your wisdom, insights, knowledge and skills that have so vastly improved all aspects of my writing and publishing that the difference really can't be calculated. Thanks especially to Kristine Kathyrn Rusch and Dean Wesley Smith for all of their invaluable help and guidance. To the beautiful people living in the town of Sidhpur, H.P., as well as McLeod Ganj, I say a warm thank you for such a soft and compassionate landing, especially Dolma, Ani-La, Linda, Sonam, Jon, Amala, the folks at Tushita and of course His Holiness the 14th Dalai Lama.

One
Demonstration

THE CROWD SURGED, SHOUTING IN MORE THAN ONE LANGUAGE BENEATH THE running marquees lining the downtown Hong Kong streets that converged at the office building.

Signs on metal poles and even some wooden stakes waved and jostled next to VR signs flashing on shirts programmed with the same words in multiple languages. The characters danced across chests as the signs bobbed in the hands of the onlookers. The yells grew louder when more seers appeared at the front of the glass doors. Humans stood beside seers in the crush of bodies, barely seeming to notice one another; the same anger etched in lines across their faces, although their reasons may have been different. A number of them threw pieces of cement and gravel from the nearby construction pit on one side of the store-lined road.

Balidor stared around at the growing numbers, feeling his trepidation worsen.

With it, his anger returned, too.

How had they all arrived here so quickly?

But he didn't have time to think about that, either.

"This is madness!" he shouted to Cass over the raised voices. "Suicide, at the very least! Why in the name of the gods did she want to come here?"

Cass only grabbed his arm, tugging hard on his sleeve to surf the motion of the crowd that surged again, now crushing them on either side. Secretly, she agreed with him; he felt her agreement in her light, but she didn't say it aloud. Nor did he bother to comment on it, nor probe her further.

He looked around them instead, wondering why they had not gone directly to the rendezvous site like they'd initially agreed.

They'd only taken a different route to ensure the safe transport of

Dehgoies Revik. Dehgoies, or Syrimne, or "The Sword," as he was better known, was the reason for the crowd of angry protesters they faced now. As Allie's former...or possibly current, Balidor honestly couldn't tell most of the time...husband, he'd been trouble enough.

As an international figure, he was a disaster, even before Allie had taken it into her head to kidnap him. She'd done it to get him away from Salinse and the rest of the rebels working for the Dreng...to try and extricate him from their ideology and their insanity, if she could.

Balidor hadn't been able to talk her out of it, or even argue the point really, not at the time. Then again, he'd been too happy to see her alive. Now he wished he'd drugged her, and left Dehgoies collared on that plane for his people to find.

But that would have caused problems too.

Maybe worse than the ones they faced now.

To the rest of the world it looked like Allie had betrayed her own husband in the worst way imaginable. Worse, she'd done it right after he'd run a major op to free a large number of seers from the institutionalized work camps that ruined so many lives.

That she'd been with him on the op was immaterial now. Clearly, none of the seers or humans present gave that much credence, since most of the signs identified her as a race traitor and an adulteress. Most assumed she'd only done the op to win his trust. In the aftermath at least, they figured the whole thing had been staged to bring him and his followers down.

Which, really, as far as theories go, wasn't entirely devoid of truth.

Given Dehgoies' notoriety, getting him out without anyone knowing where they were moving him, or even what condition he was in, had to take security precedence. They couldn't have anyone follow them to the debriefing site, given what was at stake. Dehgoies was a fully trained manipulator, or telekinetic, and probably the most dangerous man alive.

For him to get free now would be an unmitigated catastrophe...even without the hordes of religious fanatics who would rally to his side, pledging their loyalty to him and worse.

Luckily, the Lao Hu understood this, too.

The Chinese seers weren't looking to invite a murderous revenge spree from a telekinetic seer, either...particularly given their role in the overthrow of the rebel stronghold. Balidor had thought everyone understood the danger... *especially* Allie. He knew she was pissed off that the Lao Hu had exceeded their agreement and attacked the Rebel stronghold with force, taking prisoners. He knew she was especially upset over the deaths that had occurred, and the fact that most of the rebels had been forced to swear allegiance to the Lao Hu in the aftermath of their surrender, or lose their lives.

Balidor also knew, although she hadn't said it in so many words, that Allie had grown fond of many of the rebels themselves. The death of one of the females, in particular, seemed to have hit her pretty hard. The seer in question reportedly took her own life to avoid capture by the Lao Hu.

Balidor knew Allie felt responsible. She wouldn't talk about it, but they all knew.

There were a lot of things she wouldn't talk about these days.

Even so, regardless of personal feelings, he thought Allie understood the danger they were all in. Looking around him now, Balidor could scarcely remember how he'd gotten talked out of taking that circuitous route to its end, without stopping along the way. But he already knew how.

As angry as he was at her, he still couldn't bring himself to refuse her. That fact alone infuriated him as much as anything.

Allie snapped out of her stupor long enough to insist they make the stop. She made the decision not long after they got the invitation from the delegation in Hong Kong.

Balidor suspected she'd wanted to throw the rebels off Revik's trail even more than splitting routes would have done on its own. She seemed, in particular, to be nervous of Wreg, Revik's second in command. And yet she'd refused to kill him when the opportunity presented...for reasons Balidor still didn't fully understand.

Allie seemed to think that, of all of the seers who wanted revenge and wanted Dehgoies back, Wreg would be the most difficult to shake. In fact, Allie seemed to think Wreg would die before he stopped looking for Dehgoies.

Balidor reluctantly agreed, given what he knew of the militant seer.

But she didn't voice any of that to the others, when she brought up the Hong Kong thing.

As per usual, most of her real reasons remained fairly close to the vest. Balidor honestly found it hard to believe at this point, that she still had no formal training as an infiltrator. Half the time, she acted more like an infiltrator than those he'd trained in the arts himself.

He couldn't help wondering how much the marriage to Dehgoies played into that, too. Since the two of them shared light, Allie would have picked up a fair number of his skill sets, in addition to his emotional issues, mannerisms and whatever else.

The thought didn't exactly lessen Balidor's anger at her any.

What Allie told the others had been more political, of course. She said she needed to show her face, if only to let them know she wasn't afraid. She'd also wanted, as she put it, "to at least try and stop some of the stupidity before it gets completely out of hand."

Looking around where they stood, Balidor felt confident they had only made it worse. Whether they'd accomplished her real goal, he could only guess.

Humans and seers slammed up against the barricades that the Adhipan and local police had quickly put in place to deal with the crowd. The majority of the protesters seemed oblivious to the uniforms on either side of the racial divide, fighting their way forward despite the long line of infiltrators wearing the hanfu clothing and black sashes of the Lao Hu...or the uniforms of the Hong Kong police. The calming influence that the Lao Hu and Adhipan seers attempted to descend over the bulk of the crowd shook under multiple hits from seers interspersed in the same rolling crush...as well as those watching through the feeds, most likely.

The mob didn't want calm, and unfortunately, they had numbers on their side. The constant shaking of the construct rendered its effects close to zero, even with over a dozen infiltrators working, trying to keep the threads intact.

Anger surged higher in the crowd...high enough that Balidor could feel something had changed. Looking up, he caught a glimpse of his own face filling one of the image capturing devices. The anger intensified as his face flickered on more than one screen, rising in a sharp wave that told him that either the news of his role in the Sword's capture had spread, or more free seers among the rebels remained un-identified than even the Adhipan and the Lao Hu supposed. Ironic, really, that he was hated for destroying the Sword's marriage.

Especially considering how things had turned out for him.

"She cannot come out!" he yelled. "They will kill her on the spot!"

Cass nodded, looking grim.

She didn't take her eyes off the crowd. She clutched the strap of the automatic rifle around her shoulder in one hand, gripping his sleeve in the other as she looked around where they stood. Balidor glanced behind them.

He noticed the giant Wvercian, Baguen, watching her minutely from a few yards away. Everyone instinctively gave the Wvercian a wide berth, even the angriest in the gathering mob. Wvercians, an ancient ethnicity of Chinese seer, stood at around eight feet tall on average, and usually had the girth of two regular seers.

Cass spoke up, her voice a near shout. "They're losing control of them."

Looking around, Balidor found himself agreeing with her.

Signs shook more violently over the shout of chanted slogans.

Balidor tried to feel Allie through the secondary construct they were slowly losing control of as well, the one that housed most of the rooms in the Hong Kong office building where they set up shop. They had arrived only the day before and already Balidor's team had been forced to respond to two bomb threats, a number of skirmishes with seers trying to sneak into the protected zone with weapons, most posing as domestic help or security staff, and more death threats via the net and feed channels than they had received collectively in the six months previous.

It didn't help, of course, that representatives of the Chinese government, meaning the Chinese *human* government, were known to be visiting Hong Kong that very week.

That fact only solidified Allie's race traitor status in the minds of the majority of Western seers. There was no way in the Barrier they would be convinced that their joint arrival had been merely a coincidence. Hell, Balidor wasn't even sure that he believed it himself.

For all he knew, Allie had planned that, as well.

In any case, any but those seers under the direct influence and control of the Lao Hu considered Allie public enemy number one. Ironic really, given that she'd been the darling of those same seers only a few weeks earlier, due to her role and visibility in the Registry job. Those recordings of her using her telekinesis on Black Arrow security had gained her hero-worship status with just about every seer not directly aligned with one of the human governments...including, Balidor suspected, many among the Lao Hu.

Her face had been plastered all over news feeds. She'd been called public enemy number one by the humans. At the same time, the very mention of her name or Dehgoies' elicited shouts of joy among most seers, many of whom had lost family and friends to the camps.

When the survivors began trickling back, the emotionalism around the Registry job only intensified. Loved ones, families, friends and even mates had been reunited, and continued to be as the weeks passed. Stories and images of these emotional reunions, some of which had been several decades in the waiting, had been plastered all over the underground feeds run by seers. Allie had been toasted in every continent where seers lived...more so in settlements heavily raided for the work and slave camps that had been liberated.

But really, Dehgoies had been credited with the jail break itself.

The fact that Allie had been involved, that they'd done the op as husband and wife, only heightened the emotional reaction to the event.

Seers liked nothing more than a story about the devotion of a mated pair...particularly when that mated pair appeared to be working for the benefit of the race. The fact that they were believed to be the Bridge and the Sword, intermediary beings famous for both their allegiance to their race as well as to one another, only drove the mythologizing more.

But everything changed after that raid on the Rebel Headquarters, north of Ladakh.

Truthfully, things weren't even all that clear among the Chinese seers. Balidor had listened to their thoughts carefully over the past few weeks. It was obvious that most of them had mixed feelings about Allie's actions towards Dehgoies, as well.

Those who knew of the imprisonment of Syrimne, along with the disablement of the rebel army, generally viewed her warily at best. Even those who had been directly involved in the raids themselves hadn't all been in favor of the move.

They, too, were believers of the Myth.

Many also had relatives in the recently liberated slave camps.

The humans, of course, were doing their best to capitalize on the chaos within the seer community. Luckily, they didn't know enough about the historical basis for the rift to take real advantage. They instead made an attempt to reach out to the various factions using their own, human-centric incentives...offering them economic and political concessions that meant little or nothing to either side of the warring tribes.

Most, thankfully, did not bother to research why this approach didn't work. Instead, they continued to try clumsily to negotiate at the fringes, embarking on not-so-subtle ploys meant to widen the fissures between the largest of the competing groups.

Sadly, those fissures were plenty wide without the humans.

Allie herself seemed to still be struggling to place herself within these competing contexts –despite the fact that, from the outside at least, she served as the main figurehead for the forces representing the downfall of Syrimne. Given the backgrounds of the majority of seers, that wasn't a popular stance in the rank and file of the seer community. In fact, it marked her for death among the most dangerous of them.

The humans seemed equally unwilling to embrace her.

Whatever she'd done to bring him down, Allie still reminded them a little too much of Syrimne. Few would forget anytime soon the images captured of her using telekinesis to throw armed guards forcibly through the organic windows of the thirty-five-story Registry building in São Paulo. Or the fact that she blew up the top floor of that same building moments later.

"Where is she?" Balidor yelled through his VR link. "Do you have her, Tenzi?"

"She's on the other side...with Dorje..."

"Keep her in the goddamned room!" he yelled. "We're bringing the transport to the rear entrance, but we'll go up top if we have to...I don't want her moving until I get there. Trank her if you have to, but keep her indoors..."

Shots rang out.

Balidor dropped as seers around him instinctively hit the deck.

Gunfire being more common in seer versus human-only communities, reaction times were more swift among those of his own race. Many humans continued to stand or half-crouch over the sidewalk, screaming. Their visibility doubled when the seers dropped.

On the plus side, it probably gave Balidor the most accurate seer to human count since the crowd initially gathered.

He ducked lower with the rest of the bent heads as bullets whizzed dangerously close by their small group. Yanking Cass down alongside him when her head remained too high, he turned when he heard another series of screams. Before he could shove Cass back towards the doors, another pattering of gunfire erupted, loud in the confined space between buildings.

That time, it seemed to come from both sides of the velvet ropes.

It occurred to Balidor that the Lao Hu were firing back.

A bullet came close enough to his head then that he dropped entirely, realizing he was being targeted. He landed on his hands, face down on the pavement. As he still clutched Cass' sleeve, she landed with an 'Oof' noise beside him; he felt a ripple of pain from her when her weight fell hard on her palms into the cement. The gun knocked her head in the same instant, bringing another gasp of pain.

He slid an arm around her body, holding her to the ground and doing his best to act as a shield. It occurred to him in the same instant that he was thinking of Allie, even as he did that.

The thought brought back another surge of anger.

Why couldn't he purge his mind of her, in that way at least? She was his *job*, goddamn it. She'd made it clear enough that she would never be anything more than that, not again, not to him. She could say all she wanted that she was in love with her husband still, the man she'd originally married, but Balidor knew the truth...he'd seen it in her eyes.

She didn't just love Dehgoies. She'd fallen for that prick, Syrimne, too, while she'd been staying at the rebel base. She'd let herself fall in love with this new version of her husband, no matter how evil the son of a bitch was... or how many people he'd butchered. She'd rather stay married to a soulless pawn of the Dreng than try to build a new life with someone else.

Anyone else. Even him.

Balidor knew all of this. He'd told himself all the same things before.

But he thought of her anyway, as he shielded Cass.

The truth was, no matter how angry he was at her, he was worried about her, too. Whatever else happened at that rebel base, it had taken its toll on her, as well. If she lost another person close to her, she might crack for real.

Or worse, shut down to the point where they couldn't reach her at all.

He threw up a cloak with his light, disguising their appearance from those standing nearest. Pulling his face off the sidewalk only a few inches from the curb, he sent up a brief thanks to his Ancestors that his enemies' aim hadn't been better, then grabbed the human's arm to drag her along with him. He kept low, pulling her towards the glass doors and the armed contingent he saw standing there, rifles cocked at their shoulders, their faces grim.

Feeling Baguen behind him, along with a surge of the Wvercian's irritation at him, he glanced at Cass and saw why. Blood ran down the side of her face where the gun had smacked the back of her skull.

Feeling a faint flicker of guilt, he pulled harder on her arm, as if to compensate.

He heard and felt the local human police in the fray now.

Gunshots echoed in the small space, right before he heard the lower thunk of gas being expelled from metal canisters. Screams erupted soon after the gas hit, echoing against the glass buildings, and Balidor felt a kind of tiredness mixed with grief come over him as he felt the fear and anger expand out of the crowd behind him.

It was familiar, but not so much that he didn't dread what it meant.

The seer world was once more ripping itself apart.

He didn't let these thoughts slow his progress to the glass doors. Instead, feeling the heat of emotion ripple out behind them, he pushed his way through the crowd more aggressively, fighting his way towards the lobby of the glass-walled business building. Cass remained with him, but he felt her stumbling to keep up with his long strides. Balidor only tugged harder on her arm, keeping her as low as possible without slowing their pace.

It occurred to him again, that Allie had wanted to come through the front door.

Gods almighty.

He'd managed to overrule her without the usual back and forth, but it had been hell getting her to agree to stay inside while a smaller procession of Adhipan showed their faces out of doors with the Lao Hu acting as security.

He assumed Cass snuck out on her own, Baguen in tow.

The crowd must have been waiting in nearby buildings, connected through VR or some other networking device. In any case, the normal street traffic swelled in seconds to a parade-sized crowd. Balidor also noticed a lot more diversity in faces and heights than he normally would have expected in that part of the city.

Even with the efficient dispersal of the Lao Hu, it grew apparent within a few steps out of the building that things would quickly get out of hand.

Another gun went off, seemingly right by his head.

Balidor ducked. He turned reflexively, meeting the gaze of a seer he recognized from the ranks of the Rebels. The female disappeared back into the crowd before he could get a lock on her amongst the bodies pressing in from all sides.

Even so, he sent her image to the Lao Hu commander, who acknowledged it with a pulse of thanks. He sent it to the others before he'd withdrawn from Balidor's light.

Whoever she was, she'd been strong enough to see through his shield.

Ute, his mind supplied. *Her name had been Ute.*

He sent that to the Lao Hu guard, as well, though he doubted it would be much help here.

Ducking into and through the crowd with Cass, thanking the gods he'd chosen to *not* come in uniform, he finally reached the glass doors. He flashed a Barrier structure at the Lao Hu security detail for entry. He didn't pause but pushed Cass in front of him even faster once they were free of the crush of bodies.

Seconds later, all three of them stumbled past the main lobby desk.

The doors shut behind them, noiseless in the melee and seemingly well after they'd passed through their bullet-proof organic panes. The deafening sound of screams and distant gunshots instantly muted, leaving the three-story lobby strangely silent.

The chaos in the Barrier didn't lessen, however. The urgency Balidor felt there kept his fingers tight on Cass' arm, and his legs moving in a near jog for the corridor housing the suite of elevators that led to the upper floors.

The lobby itself was empty of anyone apart from security. The military must have evacuated the building when they realized what was going on. Either that, or they'd restricted them to the upper floors until the disturbance could be contained. The only people Balidor saw, in fact, were their own people standing watch over the elevators.

Flashing those guards a second Barrier signal as he passed, he ignored a few curt nods of greeting. Instead he sent a packed missive to their leader that Allie and her protection unit would be leaving within the hour.

Seeing the man acknowledge this with a seer's gesture of 'yes,' Balidor didn't wait, but pulled Cass in after him once the first set of elevator doors opened.

He prayed no one had deviated from protocol as he hit the button for the upper floors, motioning Baguen to hurry up as he shuffled his considerable weight in after them. Allie could be damned persuasive when she wanted... and stubborn. If she'd decided to leave the protected space of the secure construct, they'd all be at risk. Hell, there were seers who wouldn't hesitate to blow up the whole building to get at her.

Leaning against the brass rail inside the elevator, he released Cass only after it began gliding up floors on smooth rails.

Cass looked dazed, her brown eyes partially out of focus as she glanced at the mirror opposite the elevator doors. Baguen loomed over her within seconds, using a cloth from his pocket to wipe at the blood on her forehead, dabbing where it had started to roll down into her eyes. Balidor watched them without speaking, wiping sweat from his own forehead with his sleeve, only to find that at least some of that was blood, as well.

Touching his face more tentatively, he glanced back at the mirror, too. His fingers and eyes marked the length of the long graze by one ear and over one cheek. He couldn't help marveling that he hadn't felt it...or how close he'd come to seeing his own end out there. Likely the closest he'd been since the last world war. No one had taken a shot at his head since then, anyway, at least not gunning for him specifically...not that he could remember.

He used those same fingers to comb the sweat-stuck hair from his forehead.

Glancing at the other two, he was rewarded with a scowl from Baguen, who clearly blamed him for the state of his girlfriend's head.

Clicking at the Wvercian mildly, Balidor chose not to remind the giant seer that he might have saved her from being killed, as well. He supposed he might not have appreciated it much either, if their positions were reversed.

"Are you all right?" he asked Cass instead.

Still dazed, she nodded, looking at the cut on his own face. When Balidor reached for her, Baguen hit away his hand, grunting in irritation.

"Don't touch," he said in accented Prexci.

Glancing at Cass, Balidor raised an eyebrow, and she laughed. Reassured, he leaned back against the brass rail, closing his eyes.

They reached the correct floor a few seconds later.

Balidor's eyes opened with the doors. He felt something in his chest relax when his gaze immediately found the second security detail out in front of the correct room. Nothing amiss so far. He noted their raised weapons with approval even as he flashed the third Barrier countersign, walking out in front of Baguen and Cass.

It was protocol of course; the two seers at the door knew him.

He bowed only enough to acknowledge theirs, then pushed against the heavy, dark wood of the conference room doors.

He stopped dead in his tracks when he saw her, half in relief and half in frustration.

She still had that effect on him, even now.

Allie and Jon looked up from where they huddled together on the further end of the long, polished oak conference table. The table itself took up most of the center of the wide room, surrounded by high-backed, rocking swivel chairs.

Allie appeared dwarfed inside the dark brown leather, and out of place in her jeans, clinging t-shirt and laced combat boots.

Her face held an almost unnerving focus though.

She looked away from Balidor's face after barely looking at him at all.

He followed her gaze to a large monitor on the far wall, depicting the mob scene outside. Shots were still going off. He flinched when he saw a body fall as the crowded rippled backwards. The mix of seers and humans ducked and dove behind cover, but the majority scattered and shoved backwards in a panic.

The image capturing devices swiveled, zooming in on the faces of several humans and a few seers. One collapsed right there in the street, the gunshot to the head caught on screen as it happened. The avatar of the seer wavered, then showed his true face, once it was clear he was dead. His eyes stared upwards, half of his temple exploded into bone shards.

For a moment Balidor could only watch with Allie and Jon, equally silent.

The crowd surged again, tramping over those wounded even as screams filled the room from the conference room's built-in speakers. More shots went off. The chants grew louder in the pause, and Balidor realized that they'd never really stopped.

Kill the Bridge! Kill the Bridge! Kill the Bridge!

Vengeance for the Sword! Death to the race traitor!

Give us the Sword! Give us Syrimne d'Gaos!

Some sang an old seer song in a separate group by one building, led by a woman carrying a megaphone. Balidor didn't bother to try and make out the words. He knew the tune from the original protests, back in the 1920s, when the first set of racial purges took place.

The Evolutionist Movement.

Gods, Balidor thought. That was one movement they didn't need rising up again. They'd almost been worse than the overt racists, with their deification of seers, and those voodoo-like blood rituals they enacted. They seemed to believe the seers could save them somehow, rub their mojo off on them like a virus and save humanity the trouble of having to advance themselves, mentally or spiritually. They never understood why most seers didn't feel all that 'honored' by their attentions.

They were such fans of seers, after all.

Thinking about this, and what it had led to the last time, in terms of both World Wars and the racial purges of the fifties, Balidor felt his anger worsen.

"Are you satisfied, Bridge Alyson?" he found himself saying. "Are you ready to abandon this fool's errand at last? Or would you prefer to be dead, as well as despised?"

It came out harsher than he intended.

She only stared at him though, her pale green eyes flat.

Looking at her face, he found his anger draining away, replaced by something closer to frustration, maybe even grief. At times, she looked more like her husband than he felt comfortable acknowledging, even to himself... even when alone.

Lately, that tendency had been worse.

Whatever she'd done at the end, to get him out, she'd spent months with him there. She'd spent months entwined with his energy, with the light and energy of his people. She'd spent months as one of the pawns of the Dreng. Dehgoies had gone out of his way to strengthen that connection...to grow it, in fact.

Since she'd come back, she'd been different. Colder somehow.

Even what she'd done to Dehgoies himself had a flavor of that cold. It wasn't that she'd gotten him out, or even that she'd kidnapped him. There was something else in what she'd done, something that didn't entirely sit well with any of them.

She'd lied to him, yes. But it was more than that...she'd managed to deceive him at a far greater level. She'd done it with a ruthlessness that Balidor wouldn't have thought her capable of before all of this. The very fact that she *had* been capable of it made him uneasy, to say the least. She'd used Dehgoies' own devotion to her against him, and his trust of her, as his mate.

She'd used sex against him, too, in a way that most seers didn't do to one another...mainly due to the vulnerability of all seers in that area. That vulnerability was multiplied exponentially in bonded mates.

It was like kicking someone in their achilles' heel.

When Balidor really thought about it from that perspective, the whole op made him uncomfortable. More uncomfortable than he could fully admit to her, or to any of the others...even though he'd been the one to train her for it. In a way, he almost understood the outrage in the seers protesting below.

She'd gone after her own mate.

Balidor himself was a seer. He fully understood how the seers protesting outside would view that as evil...or at the very least, heartless in the extreme. The fact that he hated her husband didn't change that really. It only made him wonder about her, as well.

He knew he wasn't alone in feeling the Dreng seethe through the edges of her aleimi, or living light. Truthfully, he'd felt the change long before she'd left with him for that Rebel stronghold in the mountains. He'd felt it since her husband had turned back into Syrimne.

But it was worse now. A lot worse.

When she answered him, he even imagined he heard the Dreng in her voice.

"Yeah," she said, still holding his eyes with that empty gaze. "I'm ready, 'Dori."

Feeling his anger deflate still more, Balidor just looked at her, at a loss.

He glanced at Jon. After the barest pause, he realized the human felt it, too.

Even though he was human, Jon picked up on a lot. He knew something was wrong with her. Balidor felt it in Jon's light; he could see the understanding in the other man's gaze. He also saw it in the tautness around his mouth, even before Jon reached out, squeezing his adoptive sister's arm with his fingers. Balidor stared briefly at the human's mutilated hand, the place where two of his fingers had been severed by Terian with a jagged knife.

"What about you, 'Dor," Jon said, glancing up. "Are you ready?"

Balidor met his gaze. Seeing the creases in the human's forehead, he saw that Jon had been noticing the expression in his face, too.

Nodding a little to the human, Balidor forced a sigh, clicking.

He would have to talk to Jon...and to Vash. Maybe one of them could get her to see reason. Balidor himself certainly couldn't. Maybe it was his own fault; he couldn't exactly separate out his own feelings in a way that made sense these days.

Maybe Jon really could reach her.

If any of them could, it would likely be him.

For a long moment, Balidor only looked between them, watching the human look at Allie with that understanding in his eyes. Somewhere in that pause, her eyes returned to the wall screen; but Balidor discerned nothing in that empty stare as it followed the jerking and flickering images on its surface.

As the seer watched, Jon took her hand. He gripped her fingers tightly, as if trying to reach her behind that flat gaze, but Allie didn't seem to notice.

Just when Balidor was about to give up, to usher both of them out of the room and to the waiting helicopter, he saw Allie stiffen, her eyes riveted to the wall-length monitor.

Jon seemed to be staring at the same image, equally mesmerized.

"What the hell?" the human muttered.

Balidor followed his gaze. It occurred to him only then, that the crowd had gone silent. It was as if the monitor had been muted, but no one had touched the controls. The chanting stopped. So did the gunshots, and the screams.

A group of men wearing all black had formed a line in the middle of the main street in front of the office building. They stood perfectly still, directly between the barricades protecting the police and the Lao Hu on one side and the demonstrating crowd on the other.

Balidor frowned, stepping deeper into the room.

Something was definitely wrong here.

He glanced at Allie, but she was frowning too. He saw no emotion there, but the same puzzlement stood in her eyes as she watched the row of men on the screen.

Realizing she was trying to see them with her light, Balidor did the same, dipping into the Barrier to try and get a better look at the row of people in black kevlar. When he focused his aleimi on them, however, he hit a solid wall. He couldn't see past it, even after repeated tries, using a number of different sight tricks to get around any Barrier shields. All he could say for certain was that the shield was being reinforced from somewhere else.

Somewhere not in Hong Kong...or even Asia.

Which meant that the black-clad soldiers were likely seers themselves; humans couldn't be guarded effectively from such a distance. Their lights were too difficult to pick out of a crowd, and their aleimi lacked sufficient structure to support a full shield without physical proximity.

If the soldiers *were* humans, then they had guards on the ground as well, facilitating the shield connection...but Balidor doubted it.

In any case, the shields he could see surrounding them in the Barrier space were impressive. He could get past most of the low-grade stuff. Even some of the professional shields often had chinks of one kind or another that allowed Balidor some glimpse inside.

These completely blinded him.

"Sweeps?" Allie asked him.

Balidor split his aleimi so he was still halfway in the Barrier, glancing at her. "No," he said. He knew that signature well enough. "It's not World Court at all."

"Could they be rebels?" Jon said.

That time, it was Allie who shook her head. "No. I don't think so."

"Can you get through?" Balidor asked her.

After a pause, she shook her head again.

"No," was all she said.

The men in black kevlar raised heavy weapons, aiming them at the crowd. They didn't carry regular rifles, Balidor noticed, but dark green, semi-organics with stubby, thick barrels, too wide for normal bullets. Before he could say anything, Balidor heard the lower-pitched *thup* sound of the guns going off, a heavier and somehow slower sound than that of regular gunfire.

Once again, Balidor saw gas canisters bouncing on the pavement.

They exploded into clouds at once, obscuring faces of avatars, as well as the buildings and street kiosks closest to the largest crush of people. But the clouds didn't remain. Nor did Balidor hear the screams he would have expected with most nerve agents used on crowds, or see anyone in the range of the gas coughing, or rubbing watering eyes. The gas dissipated quickly into the air, so it hadn't been designed to create a diversion, either.

"What is it, then?" Allie said.

Apparently, Balidor's thoughts had been louder than he realized.

"I don't know," was all he said.

Just then, the first person collapsed onto the pavement.

Balidor watched in a kind of numb disbelief as the camera panned sickeningly, following the body to the ground. The woman's avatar faded, revealing the face of a twenty-something girl with black hair and a heavily made-up face. Trails of blood streamed from her eyes and ears and nose, obscuring her features, making trails through her foundation and lipstick.

The camera left her face in time to show the next body fall.

Within seconds, however, there were too many for the camera to capture.

Balidor watched it happen, unable to tear his eyes away, but a part of him still couldn't believe it. He was aware of the feed reporter's voice in the background, rising to a near hysterical pitch as more bodies fell. He heard more reporters reacting as the bodies seemed to domino down faster...but even with that, the silence remained in the background, making it impossible to understand the reporters' words.

It all happened too fast for Balidor's mind to catch up...yet so slowly that it seemed like an eternity before it was over. Half the crowd seemed to have collapsed on the pavement before Balidor became aware of another sound, something that also seemed to creep only slowly into his awareness.

It was screaming.

That time, the screaming had a different sound to it, though. It wasn't the sound of an angry mob, high on adrenaline. Or even the sound of people afraid of being shot.

Instead, it was a high-pitched, irrational sound, like a rabbit caught in a snare. It was a sound Balidor associated with what they used to call 'battle fatigue,' or 'shell shock'...the sound of pure, unbridled terror, terror that ripped a person out of their moorings, sending them spinning totally out of control. It was while the sound penetrated his awareness that Balidor noticed something else. Only one group of people in the crowd were screaming.

It was the seers.

Seers backed away from fallen, falling and swaying bodies, screaming in disbelieving horror as more and more people slammed unceremoniously into the pavement. Most of those falling were already unconscious or dead by the time their limbs gave out. They landed flat on their backs or directly on their faces. Few even had time to throw up their arms or fall to their sides. Some fell to their knees first, and a few were knocked into odd positions by the surging and fleeing crowd, but most fell like a tree falls...straight down, no resistance at all.

The seers watched it happen.

They tried to move out of the way only to trip over and run into more bodies, more bleeding faces, more death. So they screamed, caught within a maze of corpses. Once they started, they didn't seem to be able to stop. It took Balidor a few seconds more to understand why only the seers were screaming.

Then he realized the awful truth. The seers were the only ones left.

The humans were all dying, too fast for any of them to utter a sound.

Two
Caged

REVIK. DEHGOIES. NENZI. SIMON. ROLF. EWALD. SWORD. SYRIMNE.

There had been others...other names, other people.

The names blended now, grew meaningless.

He knew himself now as she knew him. He knew himself in her eyes, even when she'd tried to gouge his out...to kill everything he was, everything he had been.

He sat chained to the floor and wall of a green organic-metal room.

Revik stared up the high walls, feeling his chest start to hurt again. His head and body throbbed, pulsing a slow, nausea-laden heat as he took in the dimensions of the space.

Something felt off in the room, above and beyond the heavy collar he wore on his neck. Thick binders imprisoned his wrists and upper arms. But it wasn't just his physical restraints.

He felt cut off, alone.

Not just alone.

They'd broken him. He didn't know how she'd done it, but he knew it was her. She was the only one he'd let close enough. She was the only one who *could* do this to him, who would know how to hurt him so badly.

He'd always known that, but he'd thought...

He'd thought she wouldn't.

He'd thought she wouldn't hurt him.

His head throbbed, forcing his eyes closed against the overhead lights. They weren't bright, but everything hurt. Everything hurt so he did whatever he could to shut it out.

He had to remember.

He couldn't cower in here forever. He had to get out.

He had to find a way out, somehow.

But she'd crippled him. She'd smashed something that held together the pieces of him, that gave him internal order...coherence. Separation sickness didn't explain it. Separation sickness didn't break his mind until he got lost in the fragments, half dead in the spaces between thoughts, terrified of falling into a black pit that held nothing but pain and dread and a smothering feeling that wouldn't let him go.

Whatever it was, it wouldn't let him go. It strangled his light, even beyond the collar. It choked his mind, submerged him in dark coils.

He hated her. He hated her for making him feel like this.

He hated them all.

They'd chained his ankles as well. Protocol, perhaps. Perhaps she told them to, out of fear...or because her boyfriend, the Adhipan leader, advised her to do it.

He wondered, almost at a distance as he fought back the rage wanting to linger, to spiral higher and hotter in the forefront of his mind, whether it was the same room they'd used to simulate his wife's death less than a year previous.

He couldn't hold onto that thought, either.

Nothing remained. Nothing.

He fought it, even as he stared down through it...inside it. A seething pit below, a darkness glimpsed only with his light, knowing it without being able to touch it, without being able to feel any of it. It terrified him. He teetered on the edge, watching it, fighting not to fall deeper within. He knew what lived there. He couldn't articulate it to himself, but the feeling that lived in those spaces between spaces felt older than he...older than the stories he used to explain to himself who he was. The feeling was beyond familiar...

It felt like the truth.

The truth guarded, watched over. Lured.

Something else lived there.

He knew that thing as well, but it terrified him, even more than the dark.

Whatever it was, it lived. It had a consciousness all of its own.

It had hungers.

A demon, perhaps. A demon crouched behind all the shifting masks.

He could see it now. Recognize it as his. It wanted him. He wanted to eat the flesh off his bones, to crunch his bones in its sharp teeth, to knead his skin under its razor-like claws. Stripped of life support, the easy civilization he wore like a second skin, there was...nothing.

It wanted that, too. It would eat all of him.

He felt it waiting. It was patient, too...especially now, with him broken like this.

His arms ached from where they'd been wrenched into odd angles behind his back. The two sets of dead-metal organics – one at his wrists and the other at his upper arms – had been braced with a bar behind his back. They couldn't give him organics, of course. If he broke the collar, it wouldn't make much difference, but he understood the logic.

Safety net after precaution, redundancy with initial...backup and primary.

He'd been unconscious when they attached those, of course.

He'd become an animal to her. An animal that had to be put down, locked away in a pit.

But he always got free. Sooner or later...he always did. Even when he didn't want to be freed, he was, by someone or something. This wouldn't be any different.

He'd never escape. Never.

Arendelan ti' a rigalem...destiny is harder.

His uncle told him that; his uncle taught him the meaning behind what he'd become, what he'd been called to do.

The hard path. He'd heard it even from his mother, even before...

But his mind couldn't stay there, either.

Isthre ag tem degri...to lead is sacrifice.

He opened his eyes. The lights flickered back to life, sensing his returning consciousness, and he blinked...unsure if he'd slept, or if he'd simply lost more time.

He didn't move as he looked around.

He felt it then, the drug. He could feel the sedative wearing off.

He was already being hunted.

He tensed, but a part of him was relieved, too. He could fight what he could see. What he could smell, even taste. It wasn't his mind...it wasn't the demon lurking in the dark. His senses wove around him keenly, telling him all he needed to know, even with the collar.

He'd been trained for this. He'd been trained...

They would be watching him. She likely stood on the other side of that glass, watching him with her jade-green eyes. Studying him. Maybe reading him, since the collar made sure she could do so with impunity...without him knowing her in his mind, or feeling her.

Even now, after everything, the realization hurt. Wanting lived there...a wanting to touch her light, to weave back into hers.

Anger tried to assert itself, to live in the spaces between breaths.

He let it. He welcomed it...needed it.

As the realization sank in, the anger turned colder.

It held the demon in check, made it easier to breathe.

He bit his tongue until he tasted blood, and control lived there, too. He could hurt himself. He could hurt them, sooner or later. He wanted to feel something...even pain. Even from her. He knew how to lessen the call of that black pit. Anyway, he always operated better with concrete goals, with a puzzle to concern the parts of him that continued to fight that darkness.

He sidestepped the fear and the confusion from the broken fragments, and wondered again how she had done it to him, how she had destroyed his mind.

She was the Bridge. Perhaps that was all he needed to understand.

She lived to destroy...to break things.

Even so, he hadn't thought it could happen again. He'd fixed himself. He'd been whole once more. She even helped him in that.

Unless it was another lie, another key to get at that darker place...that place where eventually, everyone wanted to go. It drew them like a drug. It called to them, made them want to experiment on him, to feel it through him.

They all wanted what lay buried beneath his feet.

Perhaps that was the demon's song, too.

He fought to control the emotions slamming through his light, sparking currents in the sight-restraint collar around his neck.

He still fought them...

...when the door to his cell abruptly opened.

He looked over. He turned before he could stop the reflex and found himself staring at the seer standing there, unable to look away.

His eyes locked there, frozen.

The other male gauged his expression. His own gaze remained clinical...wary.

His clothes were neat, Revik noted. Pressed. His chestnut brown hair had been artfully combed. His black boots looked polished, straight out of the box. His gray eyes held the gravity of a man sure of his own righteousness, a man prepared to be generous to his inferiors. He looked like...what did Allie call him?

An aging movie star.

A timeless handsome, his friend, Kuchta, would have said.

The thought spun him helpless briefly, sliding him closer to that night-blackened pit.

Kuchta.

A name he'd forgotten.

Lives lost...*laughter in the sun, a field overlooking a valley rimmed by diamond waves...*

He'd seen her dead, too.

The gray-eyed man continued to study him, eyes wary. After what may have been a calculated pause, he walked closer with deliberate strides.

Revik felt his whole body stiffen, even as something in him grew entirely still. Gods. It was something simple at last. Something pure. They could torture him. They could do whatever they wanted. It wouldn't matter.

He would kill this motherfucker if it was the last thing he ever did. It was a goal worthy of the sacrifices that would come before. Of the training.

...Training.

"Hello, Dehgoies."

The older seer stood over him, but Revik hadn't shifted his gaze upwards. He found himself eye-level with dark-armored pants and the heavy, semi-organic boots the other man wore, that looked so polished he might see his own face in them, at the right angle. He felt his jaw harden as the brief flash of clarity slid away, leaving him in the flickering lights.

He could feel the dark again, that wavering space below.

The knees in front of him bent smoothly, bringing the gray eyes level with his.

Revik stared into the face of Balidor, the leader of the Adhipan.

He studied him, thinking about where he might start. Perhaps he would start with the face. The face seemed appropriate, given Kuchta's thoughts on the matter. She could help him...tell him what made that face so special, so much better than his own. She could give him insight into the female mind, human and seer.

She could tell him how to take those things away, one by one.

"Are you going to talk to me, Dehgoies?"

Emotion slid forward. He stared at his own feet, feeling the darkness creep forward, entangling him.

Kuchta. What had he been thinking just now? She couldn't help him. She was dead.

He frowned, trying to pull back the threads of his mind. His uncle would have beaten him bloody by now, for being such a sniveling child. He would have had his jaw broken, if he'd been in training...maybe one of his hands. His uncle never would have tolerated this. Never.

He would have put him back in the hole.

Tied his hands to his feet. Starved him. Given him to Merenje to play with. He'd survived that. He could survive this.

His uncle prepared him well. He'd been weak, but his uncle helped him with that, too. He taught him to be strong...forced him to be strong. That strength had saved his life, more than once. It would save him now.

Revik met the other male's gaze. The heat in his chest grew difficult to breathe through once he had. He stared at the other seer, taking in the lines of his chiseled, almost-human features.

His wife had thought this man handsome. He had felt that on her, too.

"Ah, yes." Balidor smiled, his eyes still level on Revik's. "...She told me that." The other man paused, still studying his eyes. "Does it bother you, Dehgoies, such a trivial thing?"

Revik didn't lower his gaze.

When he didn't speak, the older man rested his arms on his thighs. After another pause, he cleared his throat, gesturing lightly with one hand, his voice casual. He spoke Prexci, the seer tongue, framing his words in a precise, almost scholarly accent.

"This is childish, you know...this blaming of me for your domestic concerns."

Revik felt his breath fight its way through his chest.

"Frankly," Balidor added. "...I don't see how *this* is what concerns you, given the predicament you are now in. Or how the blame for these circumstances falls on me."

When Revik still didn't speak, the older seer clicked a little to himself.

Revik followed the motion of his jaw with his eyes.

Balidor sighed. "...She wasn't terribly difficult to seduce, Dehgoies," he said. "Nothing like what I would have imagined, going in. So things at home couldn't have been all that stellar, yes?"

The light gray eyes studied Revik's, flicking briefly from one to the other.

"...I let her think it was her idea, of course," he added. "...That wasn't particularly difficult, either. Your wife is a bit naïve, you know."

Revik could not take his eyes off his. He kept his expression still; even his gaze didn't move from those mild-appearing gray eyes.

The other man continued to appraise him, hands loose where they hung from propped arms on his thighs.

"...I don't suppose she told you why she agreed to fuck me, did she, Rook?" he said then.

Revik flinched.

He couldn't help it.

Pain whispered around his light, throwing it off its neat rails. Darkness tried to cover it, but the pain lived there too, so much older than...

"Ah, yes." Balidor's eyes remained grave. "You do not like the blunt accuracy of my words. But I do not cater to your sensitivities, Dehgoies. For we must all be men some day, yes? And you are getting older now. You cannot continue in this way...even for a Rook, it is undignified, to be such a child. Do you not think?"

He paused for another lingering set of seconds.

"...But you did not answer my question. Did she tell you why? Why she did it?" When Revik didn't speak, the other man's smile widened a bit more. "No, she wouldn't have. It was part of the infiltration, you see. Part of her deception of you. Given that, you can hardly be angry at her for not explaining her reasoning..."

Revik bit his tongue. It hurt, but not as much as he needed it to.

The collar prevented him from holding back the anger that rippled his light, doubtless sparking where Balidor could see it.

He would lose. He would lose everything, if he didn't...

Gods. His uncle would kill him.

Or worse. He wouldn't kill him.

He would kill someone else.

"...I trained her for months for that op," Balidor added. "I pretended to fight her on it, of course, to disapprove. I argued over every detail of her proposal, but still I trained her...I fed her everything she needed to know in order to deceive you, Dehgoies." Pausing, he gestured fluidly with one hand. "Then," he said, sighing a little. "When she was well and truly invested...I helped her to realize that it was the only way to be sure."

Balidor smiled, his eyes carrying a faint steel.

"...I told her it was the only way to know *for certain* if she could shield from you well enough to infiltrate you. We had to be intimate. If she could keep *that* from you, then she would be ready." He spread his hands. "Given that, she really had no choice..."

Revik felt his heart stop in his chest.

He stared at the other man, unable to hide his reaction entirely.

At the same time, he remembered. He'd been obsessed with why he hadn't felt it...why he hadn't known the instant his wife let another man touch her...

He still didn't understand.

How had Allie done that to him? Why?

What had happened to her? What had this man done to his wife?

Pain flickered off him once more, a grief so unbearable that he really thought it might kill him. He wanted it to kill him.

The Adhipan leader gestured towards him, an affirmative in seer.

Revik followed the motion, uncomprehending.

"Simple," Balidor said thoughtfully, studying Revik's face. "Deceptively simple. She really was an easy mark. So desperate for any means to get close to you..."

The dagger slid into his chest, hitting its mark.

He fought to keep the pain of it from his light as well, but he couldn't. He knew the Adhipan leader felt it hurt him...it hurt him so badly...

He would lose. He was going to die here. He would finally die.

The thought brought a near-relief.

"Then it was just a matter of using my light..." Balidor paused, smiling faintly into Revik's eyes. "I admit, I was unprepared for how much it would affect me. She whimpered at the end. Actually *whimpered*...like a child. Does she do that for you?"

Revik lunged against the chains.

They caught before he made it more than a few feet. His whole body strained forward, as if trying to rip off his own limbs. The posture hurt like hell within seconds, and the collar kicked in as his light fought to reach the older seer, too...but he didn't back off.

His mind didn't work. He couldn't think a single coherent thought. The chain caught when he was less than a foot from the other man's face, but he couldn't close the gap. A string of words came out of his lips that he barely heard, that didn't penetrate his mind until later, and even then didn't come close to expressing what he'd felt in that moment.

"...rip your goddamned heart out of your chest...feed it to you..." he finished, fighting to breathe. "...give me time...give me time, you fucker..."

The collar let off a higher pulse, nearly blinding him with pain.

In some backwards part of his mind, he realized it was cycling upwards as he tried to reach the other man with his light.

He gasped when the pain worsened, turning to fire under his skin.

He barely felt the metal cutting into his arms, into his wrists, closing off his chest. He stared into that face his wife had wanted hanging over her, and his mind fell into such a blackening rage it passed through him briefly that he might never get it back.

For a long moment, he and Balidor only stared at each other in that space. He hung there, sweating with pain, staring into those gray eyes.

Eventually, the collar did its work.

Revik slumped back against the wall. He landed there in a heap, muscles twitching. He stared at the other seer still, fighting to stay conscious, his mind shifting into a blank, lightless space. The fragments churned, leaving him desolate, lost in that dark, watching it wait for him. Adrenaline hurt deep in the abdomen, shaking arms and hands, even his fingers. Vulnerability washed over him, fear...of being lost, of insanity perhaps...but it felt deeper than mere madness. The physical pain didn't come close to touching it.

But the training remained there, too.

Parts of him assessed, calculated, catalogued...even now.

Even now, when he wanted to be dead, his uncle's training kept him alive. For example, he knew something about the collar now. Even in those moments of blank near-death, he noticed that the pain wasn't as bad as it could be, with collars of this kind. The light muzzle they had on him was thick, but it concentrated mainly on the structures used to perform telekinesis.

The device did little to nothing to moderate emotions...they seemed to have left that part of his light raw on purpose. While a liability in some ways, the opening would cut two ways, leaving room for vague impressions of emotional reaction or even thoughts from them, if they thought loudly and consistently enough around him.

He might be able to use that. He might.

He would be able to feel her.

For a moment he could only lean there, panting. Even in the midst of assessing of his predicament, emotion continued to flare in his chest. When he blinked, he realized tears ran down his face...although what they were from, he could no longer tell anymore.

The older seer nodded, still staring into Revik's face.

"Yes, my friend," he breathed, softer. "Yes, I understand. I surely do."

For the first time, the gray eyes actually smoldered with anger.

"Despite what I said, I regret very much that I let her go with you."

Balidor spoke low; so low, Revik doubted it would be picked up by surveillance.

"...I knew it was a mistake," he whispered, softer. "It is one I will not repeat. Not ever. Do you understand me, Rook?"

He stared at Revik, as if willing him to speak. Willing him to say he understood.

Revik did understand, but kept it off his face.

Finally, Balidor sighed, clicking a little in irritation.

"I don't think it will be an issue for long, Rook," he said. "She will see your true face now. She will understand what you really are, under that costume they gave you..."

Revik didn't move his gaze, even when the other averted his, a frown on his lips. The knees straightened, bringing the older seer gracefully back to full height.

"So we each have made our promises to one another...yes?"

Revik couldn't form words, but he felt it through his entire body.

Pain wrapped into grief, leaving only that darkness...the demon below.

Promises.

The Adhipan leader could phrase it to himself however he liked.

He would be free one day.

He would be free...in one way or the other.

She would be waiting for him there, on the other side.

And this time, Revik would be ready.

Three
Hope

I SAT AT THE TABLE WITH THE REST OF THEM, SILENT WITH THE REST OF THEM.
No one spoke until the recording finished playing, and even for a time after it ended.

I felt Jon's eyes on me as I slid fingers through my hair.

My adoptive brother Jon was the only human in the room. As I continued to watch his face, he clasped my fingers in his, using the hand that had lost two of his fingers. He never used to touch me with that hand, I thought, staring down at it. He seemed to have gotten over being self-conscious of the deformity. Lately, he touched me with it all the time.

He'd lost the fingers to the first seer he'd ever knowingly met, after my husband. Jon and Revik had been held captive together in a similar cave in the mountains, and tortured along with my best friend, Cass, for months.

Before that happened, my brother had been a pretty normal guy, at least for San Francisco. He'd been a jock. He had a lot of friends, male and female. He'd always been a little shy on the dating front, but I understood why. He was a gay guy in San Francisco who didn't like to swing. He never came out and said it, but I always figured he kept the whole dating and romance thing low-key, given how many guys would have tried to get into his pants if they'd known his orientation.

Anyway, he was always too philosophical for most of the jet set crowd in SF, gay or straight. He'd always been political, too, even a bit of a conspiracy nut at times, or so I'd liked to tease. He'd worked full time as a kung fu instructor in the Richmond District, and probably 90% of his students, male and female, had a crush on him.

He'd laughed all the time back then.

He looked so different these days, at times I barely recognized him.

Jon had regained most of his muscle tone from dedicated work in mulei, the seer martial art. He'd even gotten involved in politics again, with his boyfriend, Dorje. He sated his philosophical leanings by sitting in on teachings with Vash and his monks, and by studying these dense seer tomes that frankly would have bored me to tears. He was even meditating again, maybe more than he had when he lived in California.

But his face would never be the same as it had been back then. His features had hardened. Something in his hazel-colored eyes carried an intensity that hadn't been present before. Sadness lived there too, even when he smiled. Even when he seemed otherwise happy.

His hair had grown out a dark blond in the past few months, the same color as our human father's. He wore it in a clip at the base of the neck, seer-fashion.

I wondered if Dorje had given him the clip, too.

I felt him staring back at me. I felt the worry in his human light as he studied my eyes. I knew my face showed something, although I didn't know what.

I couldn't get past the image that hung frozen on the screen, of my husband, Revik, staring coldly at the man in front of him. Eyes vacant of any expression, of anything I recognized. I saw nothing of the man I'd originally married in that stare.

I didn't even see anything in it I recognized from Syrimne...the man I'd grown to know in the past six or so months I'd spent being his wife in that rebel stronghold in the Southwestern mountains of China.

I'd grown to love that man, too. Maybe not as much as I had my original husband, but I grew to care about him a lot, to respect him.

At times, I'd wanted to forget the whole reason I'd gone to him in the first place. I'd wanted to just stay there with him...be his wife. Pretend the rest never happened. Above all, never let him find out the real reason I'd agreed to live with him again.

I'd wanted that so badly it kept me up for nights. I barely slept at all after the Registry job, and I was on the fence right up until the very minute everything went down.

The sad truth was, I'd wanted to stay with him. Even given how he was. Even knowing how bad it was for both of us, for me to pretend, to leave him there like nothing was wrong.

Even in spite of things between us being a bit of a charade.

Not like everything was perfect, living there with Syrimne. We never reached that true depth of intimacy I'd had with him before he changed. There had been a forced quality to some of it...even the sex. Maybe especially the sex, at least when we were both using it to try and tie ourselves to one another. In some ways, his attempt to make the marriage work with me had also been an attempt to make a mythology of our relationship, one that didn't always leave room for the actual people behind it.

One that didn't always leave room for me. Certainly not a version of me capable of telling him the truth about what I saw happening between us.

I'd found myself doing things with him, as a part of that charade, that I never would have imagined myself doing for anyone else. In some respects, he'd been like a child...like the boy he'd been as Nenzi, before he turned back into Syrimne.

He'd been an exhibitionist. He'd been insecure and enthusiastic and he hadn't seen me clearly. He'd been too wrapped up in the myth of who he believed me to be.

He'd been too wrapped up in the myth of us.

We'd done things together that were borderline degrading, really. I knew that was more about his insecurities though, too...as well as attempts by both of us to solidify that hold we had on one another. I did it because I was terrified of losing him. I was terrified of losing him to Salinse, to the Dreng, so I'd wanted to have more of a hold on him than they did.

I don't know why he did it exactly, but I can guess.

I'd already left him once before. We'd called our months together a 'trial' period, and he didn't want me to leave him again at the end of it.

As Syrimne, he harbored no qualms about putting that stamp of ownership on me, even in quasi-public settings. At times, it was crass, embarrassing, overly rough.

And I let him do it. I even encouraged it at times, in an attempt to get him to trust me...to view us as being on the same side.

But still, even beyond all that, I'd found myself caring about him. As Syrimne, he could be incredibly tender and compassionate...even beyond the masks I sometimes witnessed. I saw kindness towards his people; I saw that kindness aimed at Terian, too, as his prisoner. When we were alone, he seemed almost to see me as a person again, as something other than his mate, the Bridge, who'd been promised to him since before he was born.

I'd forgiven a lot in him, knowing how much had been pushed on him growing up. I'd forgiven a lot, knowing his mind had been broken, that he'd been beaten and brainwashed until he hadn't really been able to grow up properly at all.

I'd forgiven a lot also because even under all that, I felt the man I'd married, so strongly at times it hurt to know I couldn't really be with him, despite everything.

The person in the security feeds, I didn't recognize.

I didn't know that person at all...and while they'd explained it all to me, numerous times, I still didn't understand.

Maybe I didn't want to understand.

We all sat around a heavy, semi-organic table housed in a conference room underground. I'd been in this particular underground structure once before. For weeks, in fact. But that time, I'd been unconscious through most of it. I'd also been screaming and wishing I could die during the periods I'd been awake...so I didn't remember the furniture, size or layout too well when we arrived a few days earlier.

I certainly didn't remember this room, which the Adhipan had been using as a strategy planning area for the past week or so. I'd never seen the kitchen that first visit, either, or any of the bunker-like residence rooms...or the library or other common areas.

The whole place felt old and futuristic at the same time. The rooms combined an odd mix of seer tech and furniture that looked to date from the late fifties or early sixties. I'd even found a stack of records in one of the lounge areas, with singers like Dean Martin, Ella Fitzgerald, Buddy Holly, a few of Elvis and Johnny Cash. I think the newest thing they had was Bob Dylan, which kind of jived with the dated feel of the caves in general.

We'd brought Revik here because of the tank.

The organic holding cell, which we'd all come to start calling "the tank," was the only thing we knew of that was strong enough to cut Revik's light off from the light of the Dreng.

Hopefully.

It had been designed by Galaith to remove a seer from the Barrier entirely.

The Barrier proper that is, meaning the space from which seers derived all of their powers, and where over half of their consciousness normally lived. Since the Barrier also housed pretty much every connection seers had to one another and other beings, removing a seer from it entirely was no mean feat.

Most devices that claimed to do it, only accomplished it at certain levels or frequencies, by housing them in a shielding construct of some kind.

The tank was different.

Galaith, while human, hadn't been above experimenting on the light of both seers and his own race. He'd also been interested in finding ways to both enhance and control seer powers...as well as grant similar powers to humans.

The tank had been designed to remove a seer from the greater Barrier totally. Not part of the way removed, like a sight restraint collar or sight-inhibitor drugs, or even one of the Dreng's own constructs. *Entirely* removed.

It meant, in theory at least, that the Dreng couldn't reach him in there.

It meant he couldn't reach them, either.

It also meant that *I* couldn't reach him, not from outside the tank's walls.

It meant no seer could find him, anywhere in the world, even those who had a strong personal connection to him. That same tank might be killing him, if I could believe what these seers were telling me. And not from his separation from me.

Maybe it just hurt that he actually did need the Dreng more than he needed me.

"You're sure that's what's wrong with him?" I said, looking at Vash.

"Yes." The old seer's expression held compassion. "...I am sorry, my dear."

"Have you done anything else to him?" I said, turning to Balidor. "Since I tranked him on the plane. Did you give him anything? Anything at all?"

"We stabilized him in transport..."

"I mean since he got here."

Another seer answered, speaking up from the other side of the room. Poresh, one of the seer infiltrators working under Balidor in the Adhipan, made a line in the air with his finger, a seer's no. He'd been overseeing the care of Revik's physical state, and now he looked me directly in the face, his voice falling into the cadence of a formal report.

"There have been sedatives a number of times, Esteemed Bridge," Poresh said, bowing to me in deference. "Those have merely been attempts to help him deal with anxiety...and the overt irrationality and aggression that accompanies this state. Nothing we have given him would cause the effects you are witnessing. In fact, the drugs have mitigated those effects... marginally, it is true...but they have kept him from hurting himself several times."

"Is he being fed?" Jon said. "He looks like he's lost weight."

"He is fed...he does not always eat. He is fed a lot, Esteemed Bridge," Poresh said with added emphasis, taking in my more pointed look. "Three meals. Sometimes more. As much water as he can drink..."

"Is it seer food?" I said.

"Seer food only, Esteemed Bridge. You had told us he would be unlikely to eat anything else. We also supply him with specific items, when he asks... including hiri..."

"He likes curry," Jon said. "It's about the only human food he'll eat a lot of."

Balidor gave Jon an openly disbelieving look, one laced with irritation.

I'd watched the Adhipan leader change, too, since I'd first come to know him.

Really, since I'd left the Forbidden City with Revik, a little more than six months earlier, he'd seemed like a different person. We still called it an op, the two of us, when referring to my time with Revik in those mountains. We acted like it was just work, just part of getting Revik away from the Dreng... but both of us knew it had been more than that. It had been the tipping point for me, I guess, in the decision of what I would do about Syrimne.

As in me, personally, in terms of my marriage. I'd made my choice.

I think Balidor could handle that I'd fallen in love with, and married, Dehgoies Revik. He'd liked that Revik. He'd even tried to recruit him to the Adhipan, and more than that, to become his friend...even mentor him as an infiltrator for the Seven. He'd supported us as mates, and during a time when a lot of the more traditional seers didn't.

So it wasn't the fact that I'd married Revik in the first place.

Or that I'd accepted him, despite his past.

What Balidor couldn't comprehend is how I could choose to remain married to *Syrimne*, an agent of the Dreng. Nor could he really wrap his head around the fact that I'd chosen Syrimne over him, the leader of the Adhipan, and supposedly one of the good guys.

I couldn't really explain it to him, either.

Revik, in all of his guises, still managed to trump any relationship I formed with anyone else, no matter how much I might care about that other person...and no matter what Revik did, to me or to anyone else. I'd done things I never thought I'd do, trying to help him. I'd done things that would probably make him hate me, when all was said and done, but I still couldn't say I regretted them...not truthfully.

I'd told Balidor all of that, of course. He'd known how I felt about Revik from day one. But like most people, even seers, he only heard the parts that made sense to him.

Since that scene on the plane, when Balidor saw me choose Syrimne over him yet again, despite everything, things had been pretty cold between us.

He didn't bring up the thing with us again, though. He seemed to have accepted, finally, that any kind of romance with me was a dead end. Since that time, he'd held me at arm's length in a way that made it clear that while he may have *accepted* it, he certainly didn't forgive me for it. He also didn't let me be alone with him much more than a few minutes at a time, even though we used to hang out all the time as friends, before all this.

But truthfully, I couldn't care about that either.

My mind was caught in a loop, and I couldn't get out of it. I stared at Balidor, but not for who he was to me. I stared at him because he was still the best infiltrator we had of all the seers, and because I needed him to help me fix Revik.

"'Dori?" I said. "I need you to explain this to me. He wasn't like this. Even on the plane. He was angry at me, and harsh. He even threatened me... but he wasn't like this..."

It wasn't the Adhipan leader who answered my question.

Vash spoke up instead, from the other side of the long table.

He had arrived in the compound only that day. The presence of the oldest seer in the Council of Seven...hell, perhaps the oldest of all seers, *anywhere*, for all I knew...had been a large part of the impetus for the meeting.

The decision to wait for him before having this little pow-wow had been mine. He still had the best sight of anyone I knew. He also provided a voice of reason and moderation when it came to the more militaristic approach of the Adhipan...especially when it came to Revik.

He cared about Revik, which to the others made him biased.

To me, it made him an ally, someone I could trust.

Now he sat on the far side of the rectangular table, wearing his trademark, sand-colored robe. His long, white hair tied loosely back in a clip, he'd sat there quietly through most of the discussion so far, his expression unmoving as they played the surveillance footage of Revik collared in that tank. I could tell by looking at him that he hadn't been unaffected by what he'd seen. Vash's narrow, smooth face almost always appeared to be smiling in some form, whether at his sculpted lips or at some level of depth in his dark, fathomless eyes.

But not today. Today he looked tired, sad, even somewhat at a loss.

And, well...old.

His voice, when he spoke, reflected all of those things, too.

"Alyson," Vash said. "We warned you of this."

"You did?" I said, biting my lip.

He went on as if I hadn't spoken.

"...I myself told you, way back at the beginning, when we first spoke of these things, what the Dreng do to those who work for them down here."

"You said they got addicted to being in their constructs, yeah," I said, nodding to acknowledge this. "You said they got addicted to the power, the endless supply of light...the pool of skill sets. You didn't say they'd go *crazy* if they left!"

Vash only clicked softly at my outburst.

"I told you of the ways in which they strip their servants of the ability to utilize their own light," he said softly, his dark eyes shining that compassion again. "I explained to you in detail what happened to him the last time, when he left the structure of the Pyramid. I told you of the work that had to be done to rebuild his aleimic structures, to make him self-sufficient once more. I told you what we had to do to him as Syrimne, once he'd been disconnected from Menlim and the Dreng. In all of these situations, a deep dependency had been created..."

"But this was different," I said, looking around at all of them again. "He wasn't *in* the Pyramid this time. He wasn't *with* Menlim..."

Balidor coughed.

I glared at him, then returned my eyes to Vash.

The older seer merely clicked again, his voice mild.

"It is much the same, Alyson," he said quietly.

Balidor spoke up from closer to where I sat. He stripped his voice of sarcasm that time, keeping his voice a subdued as Vash's.

"Allie," he said, giving me a level look when I turned. "He lived, full-time, in a construct of a Dreng stronghold. It functions in much the same way as the Pyramid. It may not have been as sophisticated...but it served very much the same purpose."

"But *I* lived there!"

"You lived there as a *guest,* Esteemed Bridge," Balidor said, bowing towards me politely. I heard the edge undercutting his words, though. "No offense is meant when I say...to compare these two things is beyond meaningless. His light operated as a part and function of that living construct, in a state of full or partial symbiosis. He was leading them, *na*?"

Inclining his head, he didn't wait for my response.

"...As a result of that leadership status, he became one of the construct's primary pillars. One of those holding and maintaining it for the others who lived inside. To do this, he had to be *completely immersed* in the functionality of the construct, as well as in its power sources, at all times. That means a direct line to the Dreng, Allie."

Pausing, he tipped his hand towards me again, another gesture of respect, according to the old forms, but one still tinged with anger.

"...You, Esteemed Bridge, did not."

I looked at him, at all of them.

"I was connected to him..." I began.

"Not enough," Balidor said. His voice grew into a mutter. "...Although that was changing, too." At my hard look, he shrugged, keeping his face expressionless despite the tension I saw in his eyes. "...You told me as much yourself. You would have noticed the changes more, had you remained with him there."

"But he doesn't even seem to be the same *person*."

Balidor's voice sharpened, this time carrying an open anger.

"He is *exactly* who he always was," he said, the edge rising in his light. "Only it is visible to you now, Esteemed Bridge. The illusion was this man, 'The Sword,' who you knew in those hills. Without the crutch of the Dreng, and the construct propping him up, you see past the illusion perpetuated by the Rooks. The illusion that he was a wholly integrated, stable being acting autonomously, according to his own wishes..."

"As opposed to what?" I said.

"As opposed to a puppet of the Dreng," Balidor replied, blunt. "Which is what I have been telling you for at least a year now that he *is*, Esteemed Bridge..."

From beside him, Dorje raised a hand, trying to calm Balidor, but the Adhipan leader ignored the gesture, staring only at me.

"You claimed that you understood, Allie...but clearly you did not. Once his light was reunited with the parts of him that were Syrimne, he became entirely incapable of functioning on his own, without the assistance of the

Dreng in some form..."

"But what does that actually *mean*, 'Dori?" I said, hearing anger reach my own voice. "I need more to go on than that. I need you to explain to me what *happened* to him...what's wrong with him." I swallowed. "And how we fix him..."

Balidor rolled his eyes, seer fashion, making a dismissive gesture with one hand.

"'Dori,'" I began angrily.

But Vash broke in before I could get any further. The old seer's voice held patience, and a compassion that Balidor's did not.

The softness emanating from his light forced my eyes back to his.

"Balidor is essentially right, Alyson," he said gently. "It is why your husband returned to them in the first place."

"Meaning what?" I said, swallowing. "You mean after DC?"

Vash gestured a yes with one hand.

"He needed them, Allie," he said. "...He could not handle the reintegration on his own. If such a brutal process can be called something as neutral as 'reintegration,' given the state he lived in as Syrimne..."

Clicking softly, he shook his head sympathetically before adding,

"...I cannot imagine the depth of his terror when he was reunited with that part of himself, Alyson. You had asked me once, why he did not find you right away, after what occurred in DC. I think now that it is likely he simply wasn't capable of it. He likely wasn't capable of doing much of anything but finding his masters once more, and asking them to help him put the pieces of his mind back together..."

He sent me images along with his words, clearly enough that I had no response at first. For a moment I could only sit there, digesting what I'd felt, staring at the table between my splayed fingers. Despite what I'd said to Balidor, nothing in me felt angry...even before Vash spoke.

The anger in me had petered out. I wasn't sure the hollowed-out feeling that replaced it was much of an improvement.

Even so, I knew what Vash was trying to tell me. I knew what he was reminding me of, too.

I remembered the boy.

When I married Revik, I hadn't known about the Syrimne thing at all. All of that had been excised from his light body by a group of seers back at the end of World War I...a compromise of sorts...orchestrated by Vash and

Galaith and some of the other ancients in the Seven.

They'd created a fiction, instead of killing him outright.

They created Dehgoies Revik.

The parts of him that made up Syrimne...the deadly, telekinetic seer my husband had been as a child, and then as a young man...were the same parts the old seers excised. They attached that part of his aleimi, or light body, to the body of a dead seer boy. Then they housed that reanimated corpse in a dungeon where they hoped no one would ever find him. At least not before the original body died, and the boy along with it.

I think they'd really hoped that would be the end of it. They'd hoped to wait out the long lifespan of Syrimne and, in the process, give him back at least part of the life that had been stolen from him. They saw that as justice, of a sort.

Or perhaps compassion.

I'd slowly pieced together maybe about half of his personal history since the death of the boy, with the help of Vash and even Revik himself. When I stayed with him in those mountains, he told me pretty much whatever I asked him about what he could remember about his life. He even told me things he remembered about his childhood...parts of it anyway.

He told me less about Menlim and what Menlim had done to him.

I'd heard from Tarsi, his only living blood relative, that he'd had a family once, who loved him. The Sword, the version of Revik I'd grown to know in those mountains, had nothing to tell me about them...not even their names.

Vash told me that the Dreng had likely restored his memory only selectively, despite Revik's claims that he remembered all of it after the boy died.

He'd been six years old when they'd taken him.

A few decades later, my husband became the most hated and feared seer to ever have lived. To the seers, *Syrimne d'Gaos* remained a legend, some kind of avenging angel.

To humans, especially those who encountered him when he first surfaced during World War I, he was more like the angel of death.

Clicking softly, in the cultured, older style of seer verbal cues, Vash raised a long-fingered hand, making a regretful gesture.

"...Under Menlim," he said, as if he'd been listening to me think about all of this. "From the very beginning, Alyson, he was being groomed for this type of dependency. They did this so he would be less likely to fight their plans for him...so he could not leave them, when he grew to be a man. The Dreng and Menlim broke his mind...then held the splintered pieces of his personality in place. Your husband was incapable of living independently, Alyson. He truly was broken...in a very real sense. While he was being trained as Syrimne, they deliberately fractured his mind, giving him situations he could not handle..."

"Situations he couldn't handle?" I said, swallowing. "Like what?"

"I do not know the specifics, my dear friend," Vash said gently, his dark eyes softer on mine once more. "...But whatever they were, they forced him to split himself, to create personalities that could cope. The process made him pliable. It also made him entirely dependent on the Dreng for the integration of those personalities...for the stability required for sanity."

Pausing, he gave me another regretful look.

"He *needs* them, Allie...quite literally. It is why, when we brought him down the first time, following the war, we compromised. We removed the parts of his personality that we knew to be unstable and put them in the vessel of the boy. We knew of no other way to give him back the ability to govern his own life. It was that, or leave him a slave to the Dreng..."

I tried to think about the old seer's words, to make sense of them. I tried not to feel like I'd murdered him again...like I'd somehow murdered the man I loved wholesale while trying to help him get free. I'd wanted more than anything to get him away from those people, especially Salinse, who was blood cousin to Menlim and seemingly cut from the same cloth.

I wanted him away from the Dreng, from the influence I could feel they had over his light, and increasingly, over his mind. More than anything, I hated how subservient he was to them, even when he pretended he wasn't. I hated how he made excuses for them, for Salinse, for his own behavior when he was following orders.

And I hated how Salinse treated Revik, the one and only time I ever met the fossilized seer in person. The smug attitude of propriety made me want to punch him in the face, bare-knuckled, about twenty or so times.

I didn't really realize until later why it made me so angry.

Then it hit me. Salinse treated Revik like a pet.

A prized one, sure...maybe even a beloved one. But a pet, nonetheless.

"So is he stable at all...?" I looked only at Vash.

"Right now, no."

"Will it get worse than this?"

"I do not know, my dear. If he follows the same pattern as before, it could get worse, yes. But essentially, he will shift personalities as he needs, to evade our attempts to reach him. It will seem worse at times than others, as some of these personalities are more benign than others...but essentially his condition will remain the same."

I bit my tongue, hard enough to taste blood.

Shaking my head, I tried to focus back on the problem at hand.

"Do we need to provide him the same kind of structure somehow?" I scanned my own light, trying to think of ways this might happen. "...How do we do that?"

Balidor clicked at this in irritation, but Jon snapped at him.

"Hey, man...why not stop the petty crap and help her with solutions?"

I glanced at Jon, swallowing. I'd forgotten he was there.

He loved Revik, too.

Balidor gave him a level stare. "I'm not in the habit of pretending there are solutions to problems that have none, young cousin."

"Or looking for one when you'd rather none existed, apparently," Jon shot back.

"You can go ahead and help your sister maintain her delusions," Balidor said. "Or you can be a *real* help to her and assist her with embracing reality..."

"You can give up if you want, man. We all know your stake in this..."

Balidor's lips pressed together, tightly enough to form a white line in his face.

Before he could speak, I held up a hand to silence them, looking at Vash.

"Can we help him?" I said. "What can we do? You have some ideas, right?"

After a long pause, the old seer purred another of those clicking sounds, leaning back into the high-backed chair. Gazing solemnly at my face, he folded his hands over the front of his robe, lacing long fingers.

"I honestly do not know, Alyson," he said. "I would have said no before...I would have agreed with Balidor, that he cannot be helped, not in this form. It is, in fact, why we split him. The breaks were too severe...the insanity too great. He viewed us all as his enemies. He did nothing but try to thwart our every attempt to reach him. We tried to show him compassion... and even affection..."

Vash sighed again, clicking softly.

"He was like, how is it you say in America...a broken record? Stuck on the same groove. Unable to get off of it, to position himself objectively...to see himself or us in any but the one way. We were the enemy in his eyes, and he fell back on his training, on what Menlim taught him to do when in the hands of the enemy..."

"And what is that?" I said, not sure if I wanted to know.

"To kill us all," Vash said, smiling faintly. "Or, perhaps more accurately... to defeat us, in any way he could. Even if it meant his own death. He was taught to never give in, Alyson...to never cooperate, never show weakness, to never surrender an inch of ground, no matter what was being done to him. His ability to withstand coercion in any form is remarkable, really...I don't believe there is anything we could do to him physically that would make the slightest bit of impression on him..."

"You mean torture," Jon said, his voice angry again.

Vash didn't respond immediately, but his dark eyes shimmered at Jon in a kind of pained silence. He looked away just before he shrugged with one hand.

"Not entirely," he said. "But yes...in part."

"You'll never beat him that way," Balidor added, giving Jon a dismissive look. Folding his rougher hands across his own broad chest, he sighed as well, but his held more anger.

"We tried to break him. Numerous times." He looked at me. "We tried everything. It was not a short project, our attempt to resurrect the man who had been Syrimne. We tried every tactic at our disposal, gentle and hard, to reach him. Including torture..." He gave Jon another level stare. "At times, that seemed to be the only language he understood. Unfortunately, it was also the least effective, as Vash says...I wondered at times if he even enjoyed it..."

Jon looked away, face flushed with repressed fury.

"It made no difference, cousin," Balidor told him, raising his voice. "Nothing we tried did, and we tried many more soft methods than we did hard." He glanced again at me. "He shut us out so completely that we were forced to admit defeat."

"But he can't," Jon blurted. "Not anymore."

Seers from around the table swiveled their eyes in his direction.

"Can't what, cousin?" Dorje said, from his right.

Jon looked at me. "He can't keep Allie out. He can't..." He looked at me, his eyes faintly pleading. "That's right, isn't it, Al? With the bond between you, he has no choice but to let you in..."

Before I'd really processed his words, every eye in the room had turned to focus on me. Still staring at my splayed fingers, I replayed Jon's words.

Once I had, hope bloomed in my chest.

It was a small hope, so small I found myself scared to believe in it at all, scared even to acknowledge it. But it wasn't nothing.

"Yeah," I said, clearing my throat. I glanced around at the rest of them, seeing the forbidding look that had already risen to Balidor's eyes.

"Yeah, Jon," I said again. "That's exactly right."

Vash surprised me then, maybe surprised all of us.

He chuckled. Still looking at me with his dark eyes, he broke out in a warm smile from across the table.

I was still staring at that smile, trying to decide if it was real, when he chuckled again.

Four
First Contact

I WATCHED WITH HELD BREATH AS BALIDOR WALKED OUT OF THE ORGANIC CAGE.

It was only the fourth time I'd watched him go in, although I knew he'd been in there a lot more times than that. His face looked about the same as it had the three times I'd seen it before.

He didn't look at me before turning to shut the door to the tank. I watched as he locked it methodically, activating the main lock with the keypad to the right of the organic hatch and twisting the wheel that activated the pressurized seal with the outer wall.

The door looked more like something attached to a bank vault than a prison. The organic material alone, even without the dead metal locks, measured over three feet thick on each side. I estimated it at closer to five in the center, where most of the mechanics lived.

I had deliberately stayed away from the security station, where I could have seen, and even heard their interaction.

Now, looking at Balidor's face, I wished I hadn't.

I watched the Adhipan leader approach where I stood, feeling my whole body grow colder when I saw the anger underlying the grim look on his face.

I knew he hated Revik. I knew he might not even care all that much, whether Revik survived this whole thing, even if it meant my death, too. For a number of reasons, I'd assigned him parts of our task anyway.

I'd already been told by a number of the older seers that I'd made the right choice.

Balidor was an expert when it came to deprogramming Rooks. He'd been doing it since the Rooks first appeared, in the period before World War II. He'd been fighting the Dreng even longer than that. He understood the difficulties we were facing.

When it came to various corruptions, symbioses and dependencies that could damage a seer's light, he knew what he was doing.

But I hoped like hell he understood his role.

I still worried he was running his own game alongside mine. I already knew he was capable of it. If he thought my judgment was compromised, for example, he wouldn't hesitate...and he could easily argue it was, considering who Revik was to me.

Really, what was an infiltrator, if not a professional liar?

He reached a space within a few feet of me, still not quite meeting my gaze.

I swallowed, touching his light cautiously with my own.

"Well?" I said.

"He cannot get free," Balidor said. "The collar will hold."

I felt my hands curl into fists at my sides, but my whole body hurt. I had to get used to that pain. Chances were, I might have to get used to it for the rest of my life. I stared at the pressurized door, avoiding the thick, organic window with my eyes.

I hadn't caged him, I told myself. I hadn't done this.

But I had. I had done it...and a lot worse.

"I knew that already," I said brusquely. "Unless you were lying to me earlier?"

"We are still conducting tests, Esteemed Bridge," he said politely, but by the formality of his tone, I knew my remark cut at him, too.

I'd learned a lot, in the weeks I'd been back from my months on assignment. Meaning my months at that rebel hideout in the mountains.

Most of what I'd learned hadn't been pleasant.

Most of it, in fact, still made me physically sick to think about. Before I'd even gotten all the way here, I'd already heard and seen details of the raid by Voi Pai and her "Tiger People," the Lao Hu. I saw it from the Barrier, and on the few recordings they provided us in the aftermath, likely to rattle me, if I judged Voi Pai correctly. I knew how many she'd killed. I knew how many had died in the gunfight, or trying to escape.

I knew how many of the rebels had committed suicide, thinking I'd sold them as slaves to the Chinese humans. One of them had been a friend of mine. Someone I'd risked my life for, and who'd done the same for me.

I also knew how many had fought to the death for Revik...and even for me.

I knew they knew the truth by now. Those who survived to hear my role in the attack hated me worse than they hated the Lao Hu. I was the worst kind of race traitor...and a traitor to my supposed role in history and my reincarnation status, which never used to mean much to me, honestly. It did now, if only because I knew it made all of this a more bitter pill to swallow by so many. Whatever I believed, they believed it...and to them, it was as if the gods themselves had turned against them, sending someone like me as their protector.

From Balidor, I knew that new bounties appeared on the black market feeds all the time. The Bridge's days of being a symbol for peace and freedom from human slavery for the seer race were over.

But I wasn't sure if I could think about all that yet. Mostly because I wasn't sure what I could do about it. I kept ops going in the background, sending out most of the Adhipan and the Seven to continue looking for seer refugees and bringing them back to the ancient seer strongholds in the Pamir. At first, I tried making public appearances to mollify both the humans and the seers, but from the way my comments were cut and pasted together in the feeds after each of my appearances, it seemed I was doing more harm than good.

Whatever I symbolized now, it seemed only to incite riots in my wake, so I decided to stop waving the red flag in front of the armed bulls.

Anyway, I needed Revik. I needed him whole again.

Whether he hated me or not.

After spending the last four weeks in training with Vash on how seers handle this kind of thing, I knew now, what it would take...what I would have to put Revik through to bring him back. To free him from the Dreng.

The truth was, he wouldn't ever really be "back" for me at all.

The Revik I'd married was gone. Really gone.

What would come out the other side would be a Revik I'd never met. Assuming he came out the other side at all, and the process didn't kill him.

But I had to try. If nothing else, because it still felt like the right thing to do.

Whatever else I was sure of, Revik didn't deserve what had been done to him. Whatever he'd done as a result, sure, yeah, maybe he was responsible for that. But he'd been taken by those people as a child, and he hadn't deserved what they'd done to him.

I studied Balidor's face, wary at the infiltrator's mask I saw there.

"What else do you have to tell me?" I said. "...About Revik, I mean."

"That is all for now. His restraints seem to be holding." He paused, giving me a level look with his clear, gray eyes. "It is no small thing, Esteemed Bridge...we have never attempted to cage a telekinetic seer before. Not without heavy sedation..."

"Are you absolutely sure, 'Dori?" I said. "He wasn't faking?" I felt my throat close, even as my fingers gripped the edges of the long kurta-style shirt I wore. "Vash said the room alone might not be enough...to keep the Dreng out, I mean. The collar has to work. It *has* to..."

Balidor's eyes slid back up to mine.

He looked tired, I noticed that time. Exhausted really, as if he carried a weight somewhere just out of view. As I looked at him, a thin smile formed on his lips.

"He wasn't faking," he said.

I felt my skepticism worsen at the flat certainty in his voice.

"How do you know?" I said.

Balidor shook his head, clicking at me, seer fashion.

"I have done this before, Alyson," he reminded me. "...I have, in fact, done it to this being before. I know him a little, you see..."

My jaw hardened. I tried to ignore the reminder that a small circle of my supposed trusted friends had known exactly who Revik was...and well before we were married. Balidor was one of them. So was Vash...and Tarsi. All three of them knew Revik and Syrimne were the same person, but had collectively decided not to tell me.

Hell, even Galaith knew.

He hadn't told me either...not even to taunt me with the information. Some secrets were more important than grudges between mortal enemies, I supposed.

In a certain way, I even understood their need for secrecy.

For one thing, I would have overreacted, no question about that. And given that Revik didn't himself know the truth about his past, I probably would have let the secret slip, given that we were married, intentionally or not. Terian already knew about the boy, so it probably wouldn't even have made any difference.

It still bugged me.

Even now, it bugged me...when it was sort of a moot point.

When I refocused on Balidor's face, I saw a vague sadness in his expression, gone before he startled me again, reaching up to caress the hair off my cheek and neck with one hand. I stiffened a little, but he removed his hand just as simply. The gesture startled me more in the tenderness I felt behind it than the fact that he'd done it.

His voice softened.

"Trust me on this, Esteemed Bridge. If he could get free, we would not be having this conversation right now."

I met his gaze. That time, I saw something more in his eyes. More than anger, I mean.

It might even have been regret.

"What do you say to him, 'Dori?" I said, my voice thick. "When you go in there? What do you talk to him about?"

"Does it matter?"

"Yes...it does. To me it does."

Balidor's expression grew blank once again, indecipherable.

"Then you'll have to ask him yourself, Esteemed Bridge," he said.

I saw that more complex emotion there again, briefly, but he had already turned away.

"...But not now," he added. His voice grew businesslike. "...You are not to go in there alone, Allie. Not for any reason. I would prefer if you did not go in at all, truthfully, so please do not try to coerce someone into accompanying you until we have completed all of our tests." I saw his expression harden as he stared at the far wall. Still looking at nothing, he folded his hands, seer-fashion, at the base of his back. "...Despite what I've said, I don't want you taking any chances. We'll give it a few more days with this collar configuration. Test it a few more times to be sure I'm right, along with the construct boundaries of the tank itself. We will ensure it meets Vash's specifications before we do anything more, yes?"

He looked at me again.

Despite the politeness of his tone, I saw a threat in his eyes.

"...Until then, stay away from him, Bridge Alyson. Even with gas as back up, we'd be foolish to risk putting you in there with him. We have absolutely no idea how he'll react..."

I thought about arguing.

Seeing the expression harden into anger on his face, I didn't.

There would have been no point.

I simply nodded to his words instead, my arms curled tight around my upper body. When he saw I wasn't going to fight him on it, the tiredness began to leak back out over the rest of his posture. Still silent, I folded my arms, keeping my expression blank as I studied his.

But he didn't remain long enough for me to draw any real conclusions.

Turning away from my gaze, he made his way stiffly down the corridor. I watched him make a right at the fork, following the larger of the two passageways leading to the next set of underground tunnels and the kitchen and common areas.

I wondered when he'd last slept, then pushed that from my mind, too.

Only when he was well and truly gone did my eyes return to the heavy green door.

Jon found himself in the segment of tunnel leading directly to the giant, organic, fishbowl of a cage where they were keeping Revik. Even with its touches of the past, like that Old West bank vault type door, the tank still managed to look retro-futuristic, like something from *20,000 Leagues Under the Sea*, or maybe an early movie about space travel.

Like the seers, he'd begun to think of the enclosure as "The Tank."

Jon had aimed his feet in that direction almost unconsciously.

Meaning, he'd been thinking about going there for days, but hadn't quite mustered up the courage to make it into an actual decision. He'd tried to justify both his wanting to go and his reluctance to actually see Revik in that place. He knew Allie felt responsible, but the truth was, they'd all done it, more or less. Jon hadn't exactly given Revik a call to give him a head's up on what she'd been planning...and while he hadn't known she intended to kidnap him, exactly, they'd all been more or less on board when she explained her reasons.

Well, all of them except Balidor maybe.

Jon had nearly reached the first security checkpoint before he'd fully admitted to himself where he intended upon going.

Even after he had, he still told himself that he'd only gone to visit the seer assigned to watch over the surveillance feeds for the room.

Because the seer on the console that night, monitoring the tank's feeds, happened to be Dorje, the lie was almost a convincing one.

But he knew the real reason he was going.

He also couldn't help thinking the visit overdue, given who Revik was to him, and the fact that he'd been there for Jon in the worst period of Jon's life. In that bunker under the Caucasus Mountains where Terian held them captive and tortured them, Revik had been a lifeline for him and Cass. He was the only reason either of them made it out remotely sane...much less alive.

So Jon had his own reasons for wanting to talk to Syrimne, the scourge of humanity. Truthfully, his reasons didn't have a whole lot to do with all the back and forth with him and Allie, although he wondered if either of them would see it that way.

That being said, he supported Allie, in terms of what she was trying to do.

He couldn't say he fully *understood* all of what she'd been trying to do, especially in terms of the op to pull Revik out...but he definitely supported the concept behind it. He'd met his brother-in-law in the flesh one too many times as *Syrimne d'Gaos*. He knew Revik had lost his soul somewhere in the change back to that older, more mythic identity. Still, the whole thing had been such a crazy nightmare from the beginning, with Revik being one person who had been split into two, returned to one again so abruptly and brutally.

It barely seemed possible that so much could have happened to one person in a single life. But then Revik was a seer, like Balidor...and Vash. They lived a long time.

In fact, their lifespans often stretched to ten times the length of a human's.

It was weird to think Allie might live that long herself.

But then, at the rate she was going, the chances of that were pretty slim.

From what Jon had been able to piece together, Vash and the other Council elders tried to save Revik from the Syrimne thing once before. They tried cutting out the parts of him that had been brainwashed and beaten and twisted into a weapon by seers with some crazy, anti-human political agenda. Vash and a couple of other seers had taken those removed parts...including the parts of Revik's seer light body that allowed him to kill people with his mind...and hid them in the body of a dead seer boy.

A dead seer boy who just happened to be the *real* Dehgoies Revik... meaning the child seer whose identity they stole to create the new Dehgoies Revik.

Pretty twisted, in a way.

Allie seemed to agree with him.

Jon caught her wincing a few times, when the other seers talked about the logistical problems of trying to split him again. They all seemed to agree it probably wouldn't work, and it might even kill him. They also talked about how it might have made his condition worse in the long run, particularly given how the boy had been treated for those 80-odd years, locked in a dungeon Allie said should have killed him.

Then again, maybe she just felt guilty...for the part of her that must have at least been *tempted* to make him back the way he was before, even if it meant being married to only half of the man. Or maybe knowing him as Syrimne, when she lived with him and the rebels, changed her mind about a lot of things.

Jon had that same twinge himself, once or twice. He hated the part of him willing to do that to another person, and for purely selfish reasons.

Not that he wouldn't prefer his *friend*, Revik, back...the seer he'd originally known in that body. Hell, Revik had been one of his best friends before Syrimne took his place.

More than that, he'd been family...above and beyond his marriage to Allie.

Jon missed him.

He missed the reticent seer with the dry sense of humor who'd managed to make him laugh even when they were being tortured by Terian. The person who taught him the seer language, Prexci, who kept him and Allie's best friend, Cass, from despair and madness in that same prison. The man who later taught him how to clean and load and shoot a gun, how to make seer *ingrat,* a kind of muddy-tasting spiced dish, and who patiently taught him about the Barrier and the myths, mulei and sign language...who saved his life.

That seer, despite his eccentricities, insecurities and prejudices, had been a good guy, with a good heart...and without a good percentage of the completely terrifying parts that had made him Syrimne.

Syrimne, on the other hand, contained all of them.

But Jon agreed with Allie's assertion that there was something off about the whole idea of trying to split him again.

Cutting a person up to get at the "good bits" just wasn't right.

Further, she loved the dangerous psychopath. Jon suspected she loved him as Syrimne, too. Jon also suspected she felt responsible in some way, for what had happened to him. More than that, she wanted to help *all* of him... not leave parts of him behind to rot. Vash agreed with her.

So did Dorje and a fair number of the others.

Balidor even seemed to agree...although Jon suspected it was for different reasons.

Balidor wanted Revik dead, or at the very least, completely neutralized. He thought cutting him up into multiple-personality Revik was a potential security risk...and one that would fail a second time, given enough years, even if Balidor himself didn't live to see it. He'd confided to Jon that he had no intention of leaving that burden on future generations of his people, or on future generations of humans, for that matter.

From Balidor's perspective, Revik was still relatively young.

But then, Balidor couldn't exactly maintain objectivity when it came to Revik. He'd fought Syrimne twice now, and nearly died both times. He'd seen him kill indiscriminately, turn seer against seer, human against human. He'd seen him cause death and mayhem wherever he went. He wouldn't let it happen again, he told Jon.

As a result, he agreed with Allie's proposal to eradicate the problem at its root.

But more than anything, Jon suspected, Balidor hoped the process would kill Revik. Or at the very least, that it would kill *Syrimne*...the being that Revik more or less truly was.

As far as objectivity and Revik went, Balidor had another problem. Jon strongly suspected that Balidor was more than a little in love with his sister.

Really, though, most of the fears around Syrimne and what he might do hearkened back to World War I. The more recent incarnation of Syrimne hadn't really had the time to do much damage. Anyway, he'd been a little too busy courting his wife to go full-fledged serial killer on the human race. Jon would even argue...hell, Balidor himself might even concede to this...Revik had done a fair bit of *good* as Syrimne this time around, despite the mayhem and the bombings.

Only a few months before they captured him, Revik and his rebels knocked out a Registry mainframe that held implant codes and registration keys that enslaved over a million seers on at least four different continents. Seers around the globe still bowed when they said his name as a result of that little caper.

They also spit at the mention of Allie's name, for the same reason.

Allie, who had been the darling of the seer world herself, had risen to the role of the seer Archangel of Bad Times when she trapped and imprisoned her own mate following the op.

For one thing, seers *never* betrayed their mates. It was a seer thing, and had to do with biology almost as much as custom. In fact, to do so fell so totally outside the reality of most seers that it almost made Allie a *non*-seer in the eyes of many of her race.

For another thing, she was blamed, rightfully and wrongfully, for the destruction of Revik's rebellion, which had pulled off the Registry job in the first place.

But the truth was, Allie was furious about what the Lao Hu had done.

Pushing thoughts of *that* mess out of his mind, Jon sighed, resting a hand on Dorje's shoulder where he slumped in a leather-backed chair. Dorje, who'd had his feet propped on the security console in front of him, jumped violently, only then ripping off the headset that Jon had failed to notice under his straight, black hair.

"Criminy, Jonathan!"

Jon stifled a laugh, holding up his hand in apology.

"Sorry. Didn't see the headset..."

Seeing Dorje still recovering, cursing a little as he tossed down the organic wire, fingering his longish hair behind his ears, Jon couldn't help but smile a little wider.

"...Criminy, Dorj?"

"I lived in England for awhile..."

"Really?"

"Yeah." Dorje glared up at him. "Really."

"And?"

"And, so...stuff it, cousin Jon!"

Jon laughed for real, slumping into the padded seat next to him. He smiled affectionately at the Tibetan-looking seer, kissing him on the cheek. After a bare pause, Jon turned his head, looking through the one-way pane of organic into the greenish bubble of the tank beyond.

He wasn't sure if he was disappointed or relieved when he didn't see anything but curved, blank walls at first.

Then his eyes found Revik.

Even that didn't dispel the feeling of unreality.

Revik looked smaller than usual, almost childlike with his forearms propped on his knees. More accurately, the tank was a lot larger inside than Jon had realized from hearing the seers talk. Nothing like a cell at all, it stretched out large enough to be a common room, or maybe a workout room for weights and mulei.

An irregular black shape of body and crossed arms over planted feet, Revik barely seemed to take up any space at all against the organic tiles. He leaned against the curved wall without moving, his dark head pillowed in his arms, possibly in sleep. Unable to see his face, Jon found himself left with the same inability to react to his imprisonment.

It almost felt like watching him on the feeds or something.

Jon couldn't even see the collar, given the way he sat, and the fact that the floor of the tank started a good six feet above the security console. He wondered how Allie felt, seeing him in there, chained to the wall of that giant, fishbowl-like space.

As he thought it, something in his mind clicked.

No wonder they called it 'The Tank.' It looked like an aquarium pen for dolphins, or some other large sea mammal.

"Any more news on what happened in Hong Kong?" Jon said. "Those gas canisters? Did anyone claim responsibility?"

Dorje gestured a seer's no with one hand, without looking up. "Balidor said he's got someone working on it. I'm sure he'll let us know when they find something..."

Jon watched Dorje fiddling with one of the instruments on the panel.

"Anything else exciting?" he said casually, glancing back at Revik's leaning form.

"No, Jon," Dorje said.

"He hasn't said anything?"

"I said *no*, Jon."

Jon gave him a wan smile. "No need to get testy about it."

"You know what I mean. I mean no...you can't go in."

Jon raised an eyebrow at him, frowning a little. "I thought we talked about this?"

"About you befriending murderous sociopaths in your spare time?" Dorje looked up from the panel. "We have. I believe I said...don't."

"No," Jon said, feeling his irritation spike a little. "About you reading me for things without asking. About you knowing things I should be telling you instead."

"I don't have to *read* you, Jon. Not when you sit right next to me and think like a loud American in my ear," Dorje said grumpily, pointing at his own ear, the one facing Jon. "Not reading. It's *listening*. An inability to shut out a loud sound that is *right in my ear...*"

Jon laughed, unable to help it. He swatted his arm. "An American, huh? Sure that's not code for worm?"

"Not all worms are so loud."

Jon swatted him again, smiling. "And what is that supposed to mean?"

Dorje looked him square in the eye. "*No*, Jon. Absolutely not."

Jon deliberately thought about sex, about the night before, when...

"Stop it." Dorje glared at him. "I mean it, Jon...it won't work."

Jon grinned. "You sure about that?"

"Yes, I am sure!" Dorje's eyes grew serious, almost pained. "Look, cousin...my love. This isn't about your annoying friendship with that waste of space, Feigran..."

"Come on!" Jon said, exasperated. "Feigran is getting better. Even you said so. And anyway, this is totally different!"

"I know it is different!" Dorje snapped. "That is *exactly* what I am saying to you!"

"And Feigran was pure pity on my part. Revik is my friend. Or was, anyway."

Dorje shook his head, clicking in irritation.

When he looked over again, his dark eyes held a denser emotion.

"Listen to me," he said. "I know he was your friend. But he is a fucking *killer*, Jon. Not like Feigran...not even like Terian. You have no idea what you're dealing with in him."

"He saved my life, Dorj."

"That was a different man."

"Not completely."

"Yes, completely!" Dorje said, his voice rising in exasperation. "Listen to me. He is different even than what you met as the *Sword*, Jon. Different from the man you met in Delhi...or in China. He is not any of those things anymore..."

"So what is he, then?" Jon said, not hiding his skepticism.

"He is completely lost in what they made of him!" Dorje said. "*Nothing* is cushioned, Jon. Nothing is left to keep any of his feelings in check. He cuts from one thing to the other without warning, without reason...and all of it is broken, disconnected. The trauma and hate, what they did to him...it comes to the surface and there is nothing he cares about...nothing, Jon! These parts of him have no regret, no conscience. I watched him, when Balidor was in there with him. He is like an *animal*, Jon..."

Jon held up his hands, letting them fall to his thighs.

"Okay, look," he said. "I get it...he's mondo scary. But he's still a *chained* animal, right?"

"Chains break, Jon."

"Yeah...and I heard from Balidor that the collar is holding just fine. He said that he tested it. A bunch of times."

"Yes," Dorje nodded, interrupting him with a sharp gesture in seer sign language. "*So far*, yes. *So far* it is working. He still wants to run more tests."

"Yeah. Okay. But if Revik was going to break the chains, do you really think he would waste it to get at *me*? Lowly, loud-brained, brother-in-law? Don't you think he'd try to get at the bigger fish...? Like Balidor?" He swallowed, shrugging with one hand.

"...Or Allie?"

Dorje didn't smile, or even look over. He only clicked to himself, staring into the tank.

"He won't hurt me, Dorje," Jon said, quieter.

"Bullshit." Dorje's eyes grew angry as he turned. "What the hell kind of shit are you trying to sell me, Jon? Not only are you human, but you are her *brother*. Why *wouldn't* he see you as an extension of her...even of Balidor? If nothing else as a human bug. Worthy of extinction for that reason alone, especially with your loud mind..."

Jon hid a smile. "And that would be different from you...how?"

"You are *my* bug," Dorje snapped, refusing to soften. "Let it go, Jon! The answer is no!"

Jon smiled a little wider, in spite of himself.

Dorje didn't return it. He only shook his head, folding his arms tighter over the Radiohead t-shirt he wore. It had been Jon's favorite shirt once, but they both decided, by mutual agreement, that it looked better on Dorje.

Jon glanced at the seer's jeans, and realized those had been his, too.

"No fucking way," Dorje burst out again angrily in his heavily-accented English. "*No*, Jon. And if you ask me again, I'll have Balidor come down and have you removed from here. Permanently." He glared at him again for emphasis.

"I mean it, Jon. I'm not letting you in there."

Jon just shrugged, leaning back in the padded chair. Resting a hand on Dorje's thigh, he sighed, staring up at the ceiling as he massaged the muscle there slowly.

"All right," he said peaceably. "Whatever you say, Dorj."

"It's not going to work, Jon."

"I heard you, man. Chill."

Jon continued to massage the seer's leg, working on the muscles he knew the other liked. When he still hadn't stopped a few minutes later, Dorje leaned back, his arms still tense where they crossed over a chest that wasn't large, but muscular from mulei. Jon saw his eyes close after a few minutes when he continued to massage him.

Jon waited a little while longer, still working over the muscle in his leg. When he felt the other starting to give in, relaxing more, he slid closer to him. The seer winced, but didn't meet his eyes, or push his hand away. He sat there, silent, as Jon worked his way up his leg. After a few more minutes, Dorje made a low sound, even as his breath came harder.

"You're a bad man, Jon. Even for a human..."

"It didn't seem like you minded all that much."

"I mean it. Not cool, Jon."

Dorje's long fingers gripped the other man's shirt though, pulling him closer.

"I know," Jon said, grinning.

He kissed Dorje's neck, then his mouth. He lingered just long enough that the seer followed him when he raised his head.

"I won't forget this," the seer added, short. "It's taking advantage, Jon... taking advantage of what I am..."

"Like you do, with the seer super powers?"

"This is different. This is personal..."

Jon smiled. "Whatever you say, cousin."

"I mean it, Jon. Things will not be cool with us, if you keep doing this..." Dorje's voice dropped off as Jon reached for his belt. It grew husky as he closed his eyes, fighting to control his breathing. "...Goddamn it. I hate it when you do this. You know I do..."

"I know," Jon murmured, still watching the other's face. "You'll forgive me though, cousin." Kissing him again, he smiled a little, knowing he'd won when he recognized the glazed look he could see forming there.

"Maybe I won't. I won't forever, Jon."

"Yes, you will," Jon said. "...Forever and ever, cousin."

Despite what he'd said, Jon entered the tank cautiously.

Pushing his way through the heavy green portal, he waited until he heard the lock click as the seal set against the dense organic wall.

He knew Dorje stood at the console...that he probably ran there after he locked the door behind him with the keypad and the pressure-sealing wheel. Jon also knew he likely stood with his hand poised over the gas contingency, cursing both of them under his breath. The gas had been one of the first safety features Balidor had ordered installed. Anyone messing with the door who didn't have the right pass-key triggered it. Anything breaking the seal of any one of the chains around Revik's limbs triggered it...at least if the breach hadn't been authorized in the system through some elaborate Barrier and physical key process.

The collar malfunctioning triggered it.

The collar breaking its seal triggered it.

The chains breaking any element of their connection to the wall triggered it.

Every single person comprising the security team could also manually trigger it, either via voice command in their headsets, a VR trigger, or a Barrier impulse. They also had a sequence that could be hand-keyed into the console itself.

According to Allie, the gas released following the trigger was no joke, either.

If he did get gassed in there, she warned him, he'd likely sleep for a few days, and wake up with a hell of a hangover...at least once he'd finished barfing up whatever acid remained in his stomach and had recovered from the painful diarrhea.

It could even kill him, but she said it was pretty unlikely.

Pretty unlikely Jon thought to himself now.

Smiling at the phrase, he shook his head a little as he glanced around the inside of the tank.

It was such an Allie-esque type of reassurance.

But when it came to Revik and drugs, they didn't screw around. The guy had a tolerance of some kind that made drugging him almost impossible, at least using normal doses and mixtures. Balidor theorized that Menlim was behind that, too...that he'd done something to train Revik or fortify his immunity to resist any kind of drug that might incapacitate him.

Jon had a feeling all of their precautions would be moot if Revik ever really got free. He'd seen him fight from the verge of death before, and it had been terrifying.

Taking another step deeper into the green-walled space, Jon glanced around again briefly at the room's proportions. Despite the tank's vast size, Jon found himself reminded uncomfortably of the cell where Terian kept them in the Caucasus Mountains. Taking another breath, he fought to relax. Once he had his heart rate under control, he edged a little further away from the door.

Revik didn't seem to have seen him yet.

At first, Jon even wondered if the Elaerian was sleeping.

His head slanted sideways against the organic green wall, showing his profile in sharp, black and white relief. The jade green walls made his skin look paler, his hair blacker. Under their odd, shimmering glow, the chained seer stood out as the only thing that seemed to be sitting still. Jon studied that glow briefly, reminded of what Allie had said again, that the walls of the tank were somehow more alive than most organics.

They'd been feeding him...a lot, Dorje confirmed, to support Poresh... but Revik had lost weight. His features were taking on that more angular, hunted look that Jon most associated with his friend's face.

In fact, how he looked now was still how Jon saw Revik in his mind. That was in spite of the fact that Revik himself hadn't really looked much like that for the past year or so. While leading the rebels, he'd buffed himself out... made himself into a kind of walking muscle squad with Wreg, his second in command, and some of the other fighter seers he had working for him.

Jon even wondered, once or twice, if he'd done that in part to impress Allie.

Or maybe just to shake an image of himself he didn't like. Allie told him once, that despite his height, Revik had a bit of a thing about being small. He'd been small as a kid. He'd been teased for it, beaten up for it, bullied for it, ridiculed.

Jon could relate. His childhood had been pretty similar...and he'd started training in martial arts for almost identical reasons. The fact that he was gay only made the necessity more pressing. Even in San Francisco, he'd had to deal with idiots.

Wreg, who'd known Revik as he was still climbing out of adolescence, even called him "runt" occasionally...although always with affection, and despite the fact that Revik now had a couple of inches on him.

Allie said Revik flinched every time Wreg said it.

Jon didn't know Allie's own preferences, in terms of her husband's body type, but personally, he thought Revik looked better leaner. It suited his face, but it also suited what Jon suspected to be the more authentic expression of his personality. Revik always had a feral quality to the way he moved, even to his facial expressions.

Jon took another step, moving closer to the line that had been painted on the floor, several inches thick and encircling the place where Revik sat. He'd been about to clear his throat, to try and get the seer's attention in some way, when Revik turned his head.

Surprise flickered over the angular features, the pale eyes.

Right before he let out a coarse laugh.

"Gods. They're sending in the fucking worms, already."

Jon flinched, but more in surprise. He sounded almost exactly like the Revik he knew. The faint German accent in his English was thicker than Jon remembered, but otherwise, identical. He even seemed to have relaxed somewhat, seeing Jon standing there. Even as he thought it, Revik gave him a wry smile. He gestured at Jon's face, his long fingers draping down from his hands on his knees.

"What do you want, cousin? What's this game they've pulled you into?"

Jon studied his face. Once he had, he exhaled a breath he hadn't known he held.

So Revik didn't see him as a complete enemy.

Not yet anyway. Not until he gave him a reason.

Jon shook his head, his hands still on his hips.

"I don't want anything, Revik. Not like you mean."

"Are you here to speak reason to me, Jon? Help me to find my inner human...?"

"No, man."

"You want to fuck with me? Play with my head a little?"

Jon smiled, shaking his head. "No, man. You know who'd win that little contest anyway. Collar or no."

"Did Balidor send you?"

"No."

The seer's gaze darkened. Jon flinched a little at the hatred he saw there. "Did Allie?"

"No, again." Jon said. "Jesus, man...Vash is right. You're like a broken record."

"What the fuck do you want?" The Elaerian's eyes shimmered with a pulse of anger. "I don't want to talk to you, Jon..."

"Sure you do."

"You can go back to that bitch and tell her she can damned well come herself..."

"She'd like to. They won't let her...not until you chill out a little bit."

Revik laughed again. For the first time, though, Jon saw pain in his eyes. He hesitated, trying to decide if he should try to follow it.

"Yeah," Revik said. "Right."

Jon waited to see if he'd say more. He didn't.

Finally, Jon took a breath and walked the final steps to reach the edge of the line drawn on the floor...the same line that Dorje warned him emphatically that he must not, for any reason, cross. He lowered his weight once he had, sitting on the floor across from the chained seer, propping his upper body up with his arms.

For a long moment, Revik didn't look at him directly, although Jon caught a few glances at his face. Revik couldn't scan him, which Jon supposed was a good thing, all in all, but it also likely was making him even more paranoid. He looked for that instability Balidor and Vash warned him about. He saw glimpses of it, but nothing like what he'd expected. No frothing at the mouth, no death threats or even irrationality.

He did see a lot of emotion though.

Anger fought its way across the seer's features in erratic bursts. Some of these brought near waves of heat...an electrical-type charge Jon could almost feel.

He waited to see if it would pass, if the other would talk to him.

But Revik just sat there.

After a few minutes of silence between them, Jon realized he recognized that expression, too...from their time together as Terian's captive. Only Jon had become the interrogator now.

Revik was waiting him out, hoping to elicit a reaction maybe, or maybe just convince him to give up.

Jon could see why the other seers thought maybe he wanted to be hit. On a certain level, maybe it was easier for Revik to resist pain than attempts at conversation. It was clean, too. Simple. So easy to know who the real enemies are.

Jon exhaled, letting his gaze rest on the other's face.

"Well," he conceded, using a seer gesture with one hand. "...They might have given up on you chilling out by now. They might just wait until they've finished with all the security protocols. Before they let Allie near you, I mean."

When Revik glanced up, Jon shrugged, smiling a little.

"...They're realists, you know?" he said. "Infiltrators."

Revik frowned, but didn't answer. His eyes looked bored now.

But Jon had caught the other look there, too. Her name still got his attention. That was probably good to know.

He didn't know if it was necessarily a good thing in general, however.

As he sat there, watching him, Jon saw the anger in Revik's eyes flare again. For the first time, he also glimpsed what Dorje and Vash and Balidor had mentioned. A kind of disjointed, hard jerking pulled across his expression. Whatever it was, it seemed to throw him off-balance, leaving the emotions there intense but confused. Anger mixed with a kind of animal cunning briefly, only to be replaced by fear. Whatever lived in his clear, almost colorless eyes, it seemed to remain only long enough to be replaced by something else.

If Jon hadn't known better, he would have sworn the seer had been drugged.

The version of Revik he'd met in Delhi, the one the Dreng commanded, had been a prick in many ways, and definitely on the crazy side...but there hadn't been any confusion in his light, or any sense that his different personality components weren't all working, more or less, in the same direction.

Jon honestly couldn't decide if the change was an improvement or not.

Finally, Revik seemed to exhale.

His light stabilized somewhere, and his broad shoulders gradually relaxed.

Jon almost smiled when he heard him clicking softly, nearly under his breath.

"Do you have a cigarette, Jon?" he said. "A hiri?"

Pulling the pack he'd brought with him out of his pocket, Jon put one of the thin, dark, seer cigarettes to his lips. Jon himself didn't smoke. In fact he'd *never* smoked, in any of the human or seer variants. But he knew his friend. He bought the pack off one of the infiltrators on his way to the tank, knowing it might come in handy. Lighting the hiri he held in his lips with the single match he'd brought, he took a mouthful of the honey-tasting smoke to ensure the end would stay lit, coughed it out, then tossed the thin-papered weed towards the seer.

"Don't let it go out," he said, wheezing a little, holding his hand up for a final cough. "I've got more hiri...only one match..."

He was still waving smoke away from his face as Revik leaned forward, picking the stick off the floor delicately from between his cuffed ankles, and putting it to his mouth. He took a long inhale, leaning his head against the wall behind him.

After a few seconds where he held the smoke in his lungs, he opened his eyes, exhaling it out through his lips.

"Thanks," he said.

Hiri smoke smelled a lot less reprehensible than human cigarette smoke, but Jon found himself shaking his head a little anyway.

"You seers and your long lives," he said. "Makes you cocky."

"You think so?" Revik said, his voice a faint smile.

"You think you'll live forever."

Revik grunted a little, but Jon heard the humor in that, too.

For the first time, emotion reached Jon himself. For the first time, he saw his friend chained to a wall, looking depressed, a collar around his neck.

"How are you, man?" He managed a smile.

Revik's expression grew cold. He took another long drag off the hiri, his eyes narrow as he exhaled smoke in Jon's direction. Ashing it on the floor of the cell as Jon waved the cloud away, Revik paused another beat before glancing up.

"I'm great, Jon. How are you?"

"Revik. I mean it...are you all right?" Jon hesitated. "I heard...well, they said you're not eating."

"If I wasn't eating, I'd be dead, Jon."

"You look thin, man...you've lost weight."

"Some exercise wouldn't hurt." Revik held up the cuffs, smiling a little, but that predatory glint was back. "Want to help me out, Sporto?"

Jon swallowed a little. Terian had called him that, while they were imprisoned.

"I'd love to, man," he said sincerely. "But I can't trust you right now. You know that. You wouldn't trust me either...under the circumstances."

"Yeah." Revik lowered the cuffs. His eyes held that same hard shine. "I guess not."

"Revik, man." Jon swallowed. He continued studying his eyes, his voice cautious. "They said you're having a hard time. That being in here is rough on you. Cut off from the Dreng..." He shrugged a little, faintly apologetic. "They made it sound like you've been going through withdrawals...like DTs. Like you can't really function right on your own."

"Did they?"

"Something like that, yeah."

Revik continued to study Jon's face, his eyes predatory behind a thinner sheen of disinterest.

"Why are you here, Jon?"

"I'm worried about you, man. I wanted to talk to you...before they..." Jon hesitated again, gesturing vaguely. "You know. Before they do their thing."

"No, Jon," he said, taking another drag of hiri. "I don't know. Before they do what?"

Jon shrugged. "Before they start, I guess. On you." At the other's continued empty stare, Jon gestured towards him a little lamely. "...You know what I mean. You know more about that stuff than I do, Revik. I'm just a dumb worm, remember?"

"Before they start what, Jon?"

Jon just looked at him, perplexed. Propping his arms on his knees, he continued to study the Elaerian's angular face.

"Why do you think you're here, man?" he said.

Seeing those clear eyes turn cold, Jon cut him off before he could speak.

"...You know what I mean," he said. "Why do you think you're *really* here?"

For an instant, the disinterested look returned to the seer's face.

"You mean, besides the fact that my wife is a whore?"

"Revik..." Jon clicked at him softly, almost without knowing he did it. "...Don't even try it, man. I'm not Balidor."

"Is he watching us? Now?"

"No, man."

"Who's over there?"

"Dorje."

"Ah." Revik smiled. His eyes flashed with understanding. "Dorje. Sweet, sweet, little Dorje..." He turned towards the microphone embedded in the organic walls, speaking louder, and not to Jon. "Did you like your blow job, Dorje, my brother? I hope it was good...I hope it was really good...I am jealous, my brother...jealous..."

Jon shook his head, smiling faintly in spite of himself.

"Nice, man. Classy."

"Do you have another one in you, Jon?" Revik reached for his belt, his eyes clinical when he raised them in Jon's direction. Briefly, his hand rested on his crotch. "Somehow I don't think the missus will oblige...and it's starting to hurt..."

Jon shook his head again, but his smile faded even as he felt his cheeks flush.

Still, he managed to keep his voice casual.

"Don't get me in trouble with my man, cousin Syrimne," he said lightly. "I'm in the shithouse as it is, for talking my way into here..."

"Talking?" Revik's hand remained on his belt, but he raised an eyebrow, taking another drag of the hiri as he leaned against the wall. He kept his legs somewhat splayed, and Jon couldn't help but notice he had an erection. "Is that the slang the kids are using these days? How are your conversation skills, Jon? Must be decent, if he let you in here..." At Jon's averted gaze, Revik lowered his voice, letting it turn cajoling.

"I've been told I'm a really good talker, myself," he said. "What do you say? I won't hurt you, Jon. Promise. Not unless you want me to..."

"Whatever." Jon felt himself getting impatient. Realizing the seer was pulling a number on him, collared or not, he shook it off, meeting the other's gaze. "Don't you want to *talk* to me, man? Not even a little? Or would you rather sit in here all day, alone, chained to a wall, dreaming of eating Balidor's intestines or whatever?" His mouth hardened to a line before he added, gesturing towards the seer's crotch. "...Or playing at petty acts of revenge towards Allie, like pretending to seduce me...?"

Revik glanced up at him, and for an instant, Jon saw his friend in his eyes.

"What are they going to do to me, Jon?"

Jon sighed. "She's trying to help you, man."

"Really? Is that what this is about?"

"That's all this whole thing has ever been about. You must know that... somewhere in your fucked up, paranoid head..."

"Really?" Revik said. "So my wife's trying to *help* me? What a relief."

The kaleidoscope returned. Jon watched the seer's face warily, seeing the confused anger flash more intensely behind that cold gaze, eclipsing the grief he'd seen there, along with a heavier emotion that looked almost like futility. Revik shook his head, and the light behind his eyes seemed to change channels once more.

A humorless smile came to his lips.

"Now that you mention it, I think you're right, Jon," he said. "I'm sure that's what this is about. Riding that Adhipan's cock...getting all my people killed. Putting a collar on me and chaining me in a cage...it's all been such a tremendous *help* to me, Jon..."

"She hates you being in here."

"...So much she's probably blowing that fucker right now," Revik said.

"You know that's not what's happening." Seeing the Elaerian's flat look, Jon amended, "Well, you should. You *would* know, if you weren't bat-shit crazy..."

"Fuck you."

"We already covered that. I believe the answer was no."

Instead of smiling, Revik narrowed his gaze, his eyes hard. "She slept with him. She admitted it to me, Jon. Hell...I *felt* it on her. I felt him inside her. She liked it..."

Jon flinched a little, feeling that grief on him again.

"I'm sorry, man. I really am."

"Sorry doesn't mean shit, Jon. She betrayed me. Lied to me..."

"Yeah." Jon nodded, his jaw hardening. "She did a lot of things to get you out of there. She probably would have slept with a lot more people, if that's what it took...your whole damned regiment, if need be..." Seeing something flicker in the other's eyes, he hesitated. "Jesus, Revik. Are you telling me you don't get that she *risked her life*, pretty much every day...for months...to get you out of there? And, oh yeah, didn't you do something similar once? Like sleep with a whole room full of people to get her away from Terian in DC?"

He shook his head angrily, his eyes cold.

"Don't tell yourself it's not the same, Revik. It is."

"She *lied* to me."

"Yeah," Jon said, nodding emphatically. "Yeah, man...she lied to you. That's what you do when you're trying to talk a crazy person out of crazy land...you lie to them, pretend you're crazy, too. Otherwise, you're one of THEM, you know?"

Revik gave him an irritated look, taking another drag of the hiri. "That's not funny, Jon."

"And weirdly, here I am, not laughing."

Revik's eyes grew flint-like. His voice sharpened.

"What are they going to do to me, Jon?"

Jon hesitated, watching the pale eyes of the seer. The man shackled in front of him still seemed to be shifting in and out of moods, in and out of flashes of anger, but for the first time, Jon saw real fear join the whispers of other emotions clouding that still gaze.

"Is she going to split me again?" Revik said, blunt. "Is she going to bury me down in a fucking hole again, Jon?"

Jon's brow cleared.

"No, man," he said, gently. "No, she won't do that. A few of the others talked about trying something similar, but she said no. She was dead against it, Revik."

"You're sure about that? You wouldn't lie to me, Jon?"

"I wouldn't lie to you, man. Not about this."

There was a silence.

In it, Jon watched the male seer stare at the floor, the hiri burning down between his fingers. It occurred to him that the other man was breathing harder, having some kind of reaction that didn't show on his face, or in his eyes. Jon watched his shoulders gradually relax. It didn't diminish the more unreadable wariness of his face, but it seemed to coincide with a heavy, if almost invisible, exhale. As if a weight of...something...had just lifted off him.

A few seconds more passed.

Then Jon saw him nod, seemingly to himself. Looking up, he clicked his fingers at Jon then, gesturing that he wanted another hiri.

Jon threw him one from the full pack in his pocket. He watched Revik light it off the end of the first one he'd given him, as soon as he'd plucked it off the floor.

"Then...what?" Revik said, his voice business-like. He finished lighting the hiri and exhaled smoke. "What will they do?"

"I don't know the details, man."

"You know *something*...or you wouldn't be here."

Jon shook his head, but raised his hands in a gesture of defeat.

"I know she's going to try and undo it. That's *all* I know. Honestly."

"Undo it?" Revik stared at him. "Undo what?"

As he looked at Jon, the human found himself briefly caught there, in that stare. Revik's clear eyes showed a near openness, despite the confusion they held, that odd profusion of emotion and thought. In it, Jon was startled to see an almost childlike vulnerability. He wondered at first if it was a ruse of some kind, but looking at his eyes, he decided it wasn't.

It struck him again how afraid some part of Revik had been of that cave.

"Undo *what*, Jon?"

"Whatever they did to you, man."

Jon's voice grew gentle again.

"...They don't want to hurt you, Revik. She doesn't want to hurt you."

Revik stared at him, but didn't answer.

Looking at that young, open expression on the Elaerian's face, Jon had an urge to touch him suddenly, strong enough that he shifted in his seat, clenching his hands. Feeling overcame him in the same instant, a sharp wave of compassion strong enough to reach his voice.

"I won't let anyone hurt you, Revik. Not if I can help it."

He cleared his throat, gesturing vaguely towards him.

"...All I know is, she wants to help you undo whatever they did to your mind. She and Vash are working on some kind of plan to help you break free of them. For good."

There was another silence.

For a moment, Jon saw his friend in those eyes again.

Then the fragments shifted. Jon watched the openness vanish under a collection of darker masks, buried until it was hard to remember what it had looked like.

The new Revik shook his head, clicking in a humor that wasn't really humor. Jon saw that hard, metallic light in his eyes, dimming the softer light they'd held only a second before.

"That's bullshit, Jon. Propaganda."

"Propaganda?" Jon still stared at the other's face in disbelief. "Propaganda for what?"

"You're believing the Seven's lies. Just like she is." His eyes hardened briefly. "It's bullshit. Conformist crap. They want you to believe their way is the only way, Jon."

"Who does?"

"The Council of Seven. And their dogs, the Adhipan."

Jon just looked at him for a moment, his brow furrowed.

"So Vash is a diabolical mastermind?" he said. "Really? Because he seems an awful lot like a nice old guy in a robe. I've seen him laugh just staring at his own toes, Revik..."

Revik gave him a flat look. "I'm saying, it's an ideology. It's not real, Jon. Vash is victim to it as much as the rest of them are...even with his wisdom. I mean him no disrespect...I believe he is a good man...and a gifted seer. But he is a product of his generation."

"Really? His generation, huh?" Jon tried to wade through the seer's words, to understand the logic that tied them together in his mind. Oddly, he recognized that Revik was actually being friendly towards him. In his own way, he was trying to teach him something again, to let him in on the secret truth that he saw Jon as missing.

"Okay," Jon said. "So we're clear...all that good and evil stuff, right and wrong, treat others decently...it's just crazy, huh? Not real?"

"No," Revik said, looking at him. "It isn't."

"So everything you told me before...it was all bullshit, too?"

Revik's mouth tightened.

For an instant, Jon thought he might react, get angry once more. Then he seemed to shrug it away with his other hand, seer-fashion.

"If you mean before I got my memory back, then yes. I was brainwashed too, Jon."

"Uh-huh. Got it." Jon continued to look at him, pursing his lips. Then, as if conceding the point, he shrugged. "Fine. Okay. You were brainwashed. I could buy that. After all, that's what they're saying about you now...and if it's true, of course we'd believe *you* were the one brainwashed, not us, right?" When the seer didn't answer, Jon counted off with his fingers.

"Vash is brainwashed. Allie, too...and me, of course."

He laced his fingers together, gazing at the Elaerian's face.

"...I suppose it goes without saying that all humans are brainwashed? And any of the seers who follow Code? And any of the seers who *work* with humans...?"

Revik leveled his stare on him once more.

"I thought you weren't going to try and fuck with my head, Jon?" he said, exhaling another drag off the hiri. "Or did you imagine that my IQ dropped about 100 points, since they locked me up in here?"

"I'm not *fucking* with you, man," Jon said, exasperated. "I'm just trying to make a point."

"Little heavy with the hammer on that one, Jon...but yes, I take your point."

"Well, let me ask you something else then," Jon said. "Do you remember what you told me about the *Dreng,* Revik? When we were still in that prison... with Terian?"

Revik shook his head. "No."

"No?"

"I can guess, Jon."

"You don't have to," Jon said. "I remember exactly what you said. I remember it perfectly." His voice sharpened. "You told me the Dreng were soulless Barrier beings who couldn't produce any light of their own, so they were forced to steal it from others..."

When Revik clicked at him impatiently, Jon held up a hand, raising his voice.

"...You also told me that the functionality of the Pyramid consisted mostly of scraps they threw to their faithful seer-puppets down here. That they'd built the Pyramid mainly as a way to channel light effectively to *themselves*...that there were these large, feeding pools of humans, and that the Dreng pretty much just fed off them, 24/7. You also said they'd feed off their own seers happily enough, if they didn't need them to keep the humans in line..."

"Jon..."

"You said they were parasites, Revik. Soulless. Dead. Parasites."

Revik clicked at him again. "Symbiosis, Jon."

"What?" Jon said, his voice incredulous again. "What does that mean?"

"It means seers benefitted from the relationship, too." Revik's eyes met Jon's, holding a deliberate patience. "You want things to be black and white that just aren't black and white. The world is more complicated than you want...than most seers in the Seven want. Than Allie wants. Many seers were rescued by the Rooks. Many, many seers. They did a lot of good."

"Rescued?" Jon stared at him. "From what? *To* what?"

"You are talking about things you don't understand."

"I understand just fine. I just wish you'd just *listen* to yourself, man..."

Revik's anger sparked. For the first time, his control over it snapped.

"So you are saying I did *no* good, just now? No good at all?" His accent grew stronger again, harsher. "You are saying the Registry job...this is all bullshit? That I saved *no* seers? That *no one* has a better life because of this?"

"No, man." Jon shook his head. "That's not what I'm saying."

"Then what? I am the bad guy now? I do it the *wrong* way, saving lives?"

Jon gripped his own hair in frustration, then let it go with a noisy exhale.

"I'm saying that you can't live off another being's scraps," he said finally. "That's not free will, man. That's slavery. And there's no way you're going to convince me that a bunch of parasites like that have your best interests at heart. They'll reward you, like a good dog...no offense...but they'll shoot you just as fast if you do something that pisses them off. I don't think that kind of short cut ever pays off, Revik. Not in the long run."

Rather than being offended, Revik only smiled, clicking again.

It was an indulgent, condescending smile.

"You have learned well, Jon. Speaking of dogs."

"So," Jon prompted, refusing to rise. "You're going to tell me that beings like that...beings who *aren't alive,* strictly speaking...who are just looking for ways to suck light off humans and seers, and to do so permanently, with a bunch of seer lackeys and a few thousand all-human light smorgasbords to supply their bottomless light habit...you're telling me that every job *they* give you is going to be a Mother Theresa type thing?"

Revik turned on him, his eyes blazing. "You are missing the point, Jon."

"Am I? Enlighten me, O Mighty Syrimne..."

"The Registry job was *mine,* Jon!" he snapped, slamming a fist against the floor. "Mine! Not the fucking Dreng's! Not Salinse's! It was *my* idea! *I* planned it! *I* executed it..."

Jon flinched as the chains smacked the organic floor.

Then playing back his words, he shrugged, unimpressed. "So they let you plan your own ops? How nice of them."

"I'm nobody's fucking slave, Jon!"

"Bullshit. You're lying to yourself, man!" Jon said. "How do you explain how you ran back to them like you did? You abandoned your wife...your friends. You abandoned everything you claimed to care about. And for what? Allie told me Menlim *tortured* you. For *years,* he tortured you...he did everything but kill you in an attempt to break your will."

Revik shook his head, clicking impatiently. "She is exaggerating."

"Bullshit," Jon snapped. "Don't lie to me, man!"

"She doesn't know. She wasn't there, Jon."

"Yeah, so if anything she doesn't know the extent of it," Jon said. "I saw you with Terian. I *believe* her, man...I think you could have withstood ten Terians, after what those sadistic fuckers did to you. And you go to them for help? You decide to join *that* little army again?"

"Menlim wasn't there!"

"So you go to his family? How does that work?"

"You are a child, Jon," Revik said, his voice cold. "You want a child's explanations for things that are more complex...things that require more gradations in meaning. They had the resources I needed to make a difference. They were different people...under different leadership. They put me in charge. I'm not a goddamned *child* anymore, Jon! These aren't the people who did that to me! I know Allie never understood that, but it is because *she* is a child, too!"

Jon watched the anger worsen in the other's eyes, but he saw the confusion there again, too. Gradually, both began to recede behind one of the harder masks.

Finally, Revik shrugged with one hand, taking another drag of the hiri.

His voice grew calm.

"Even if any of what you are saying is true," he said, gesturing dismissively with his fingers. "...She can't help me, Jon. Not if I'm understanding your meaning of 'help' in this context."

He exhaled another plume of honey-scented smoke.

"In fact," he added. "...I honestly don't really know what that would mean. Before, the Council tried to do a number of things to me, and none of it – "

"Yeah, I know," Jon broke in. "I know all that, what they tried and what happened. But she's going to do it herself, man. That's why Vash thinks it might work. Before they couldn't reach you. They had no access to your light that time...but you can't keep Allie out. You can't, even if you wanted to. She's already a part of you."

There was a silence.

Revik only stared at him through it. Crouched over his chained ankles, he held the recently lit hiri in his fingers, forgotten as it burned down to only a single, glowing ember, like an eye in the dark weed.

"What?" he said then. "What did you say?"

Jon hesitated, staring at the Elaerian's face.

He saw the fear again in the other man's eyes. It wasn't a shadow that time, or a shimmer in the background, or hidden behind one of the Elaerian's many masks. It stood out on the other male's face like a shell, a hard visage that changed the set of his jaw, even the way his skin seemed to configure around bone.

Looking at him, in that moment, it crossed Jon's mind that no matter what Allie told herself about what she was doing, or how hard she thought it would be...it would be harder.

He recognized the set of the face in front of him.

Not from Revik himself.

He'd seen similar things before, though, in students of his when he'd been a martial arts instructor in San Francisco. From time to time, he got sent people who were recovering from traumas of whatever kind...war veterans, police injured on the job, or police who had shot people. He got mugging victims, rape victims...even someone from SCARB once, although he'd been human, not seer. Jon started to learn a few things, in terms of who he could work with, and who he couldn't, who might soften, and who would hold out, who would become a reliable fighter, and who needed a few years of therapy before they could be trusted in the ring.

Looking into Revik's face, Jon knew, from the very core of his being, that the Elaerian wasn't going to cooperate with her attempts to reach him.

Whatever lived there, it scared him worse than any desire he might have to get better. It scared him more than torture, more than being locked up, more than anything they could do to him.

He would fight her, every step of the way...to the death if he had to.

Jon had another grim thought, as he stared at the male seer.

There was no way in hell Allie would succeed with him until that changed.

Five
Chandre

Chandre wandered into the locker room behind the military-style barracks.

Without looking up, she stopped in one of the narrow aisles of the segmented room, unhooking the front of her vest and tugging at the heavy nylon tongue of her weapons belt.

Two other women, also seer, stood by lockers on the aisle across from her, each having just gotten out of the showers. Without looking over, Chandre listened to them speak with the back part of her mind even as she opened the metal locker in front of her.

"...The coup is still going on in the East," another seer was saying. "But it's skirmishes mostly, now. My guess is, the rebels are using whatever resources they have left to look for their leader. They don't have the numbers to go after the Lao Hu now..."

Chandre's hand halted in its path.

Hesitating only a heartbeat, she lay her gun belt on the bottom of the locker, glancing over at the seers only for half a breath.

"...The Bridge still hasn't surfaced." The woman gave a scornful laugh. "She won't, either, if she's got half a brain. She'd be lucky to live the day in a major city with any seer population at all. Especially after that debacle in Hong Kong. She hasn't claimed responsibility, but who else could have pulled that shit? Spraying the demonstrators with some kind of deadly nerve agent?"

Exhaling with a snort of disgust, she shrugged.

"...Anyway, she's bonded to the Sword, so the rebels won't kill her at least. They'd probably just torture her for a few years, then throw her in a work camp for the rest of her life, once they found her mate..."

"So you think he's still alive then?" The woman's companion said. "The Sword?"

That time, Chandre turned.

The first woman shrugged. "He has to be, right? Even if she's as cold as they say, she'd have to be suicidal to kill him outright..." She smirked. "No, she's probably got him locked away somewhere. Playing with him when she gets bored..."

Chandre frowned. She couldn't help herself.

As she did, she focused her dark red eyes on the two females sitting on the opposite bench.

The one who had spoken the most, a younger, willow-thin brunette, looked familiar to Chandre. She remembered her name as Draya, and knew her to be one of the agents who worked directly with Secret Service. She helped guard the White House shields. Not many seers were allowed free access within the White House walls since the incident with the last president, so Chandre knew she had to be well-connected within SCARB's hierarchy.

Even a seer like this would have human handlers, however.

Given that she was female, the likelihood that she also took human lovers within the hierarchy was likely. It wasn't a cause for accusation, or even disapproval, from Chandre's perspective...merely a statement of reality.

Anyway, the female seer was attractive. She also seemed to know it.

Draya turned her dark blue eyes to the side, shuffling through an identical-looking locker that stood opposite a narrow alcove. She wore only a bra and a short skirt that looked like the bottom half of a business suit.

"...Lao Hu against the rebels, *d'Gaos*! It should solve our problems here, yes? But nothing is so easy. And who knows what that bitch will do next? She seems to follow no codes at all, not of any of the affiliated seers...the hierarchy is going crazy, trying to figure out her strategy." Draya arched an eyebrow at her companion, snorting. "They don't seem to understand she simply may not *have* a strategy. Or perhaps her only real strategy is to look out for number one...the hell with whoever gets in her way, even if she happens to be married to them."

Chandre had frozen again, unable to hide her emotional reaction.

Feeling her chest constrict, she glanced at the woman's companion, a dark-haired, Asian seer named Talei. Talei's dress marked her as an insider, too. Neither of these women were running field ops, or jogging beside limousines.

Noticing her stare, Talei gave Chandre a warning look.

Draya clicked softly, a humorless sound that pulled Talei's eyes back to her.

"What do you think?" Draya said. "She still has him, right? It has to be her...his wife. She either has him, or has sold him to the Chinese. It has to be true, yes?"

"I don't know," Talei said, noncommittal. "Perhaps."

That time, when she turned, Chandre found Draya looking at her, too, having noticed the reaction in her light this time.

"Is our conversation entertaining you, kneeler?" she said, her voice faintly hostile.

Chandre didn't answer. Pulling the braids out of her face, she tied them with a scrap of cloth she'd left at the bottom of her locker, then sat down on the metal bench, unlocking the straps holding the high leather boots to her feet. She didn't glance up as Draya continued speaking.

Still, Chandre heard every word.

"...They think now the whole alliance was staged." Draya spoke more loudly, knowing Chandre was listening. "She infiltrated his compound, tranked him in his own bed..."

She snorted in low amusement, shaking her head.

"...I don't know if the cunt deserves a medal or the gas chamber. I suppose it will depend on who she sells him to in the end."

Talei frowned, her light gold eyes narrowing slightly.

Again, she glanced for the barest breath at Chandre.

"*Gaos*," she said. "That's cold. She did that to her own mate?"

Draya shook her head, clicking softly. "From what I hear, the Bridge isn't exactly a warm one with any of her brothers and sisters." Her blue eyes shifted to Chandre. "...She let that *Lao Hu* bitch clean up. They stripped the rebel fleet, took their weapons, all of the equipment they had assembled. The seers they took, they gave a choice...the high-ranked ones were offered a position in their infiltration teams..."

Chandre felt the woman's eyes on her back once more.

"...The low-ranked ones had to swear off their allegiance to the Sword." Her voice grew even colder. "She burned the tattoos off them, sister. The sword and sun, a sacred brand...she burned it right off their arms. The way they do those tats, they'd lose a good quarter-inch of flesh getting those off..."

Chandre felt her jaw harden, but she didn't look up, rolling socks over her feet. Standing, she threw a sweatshirt over the t-shirt she'd worn under the armor during exercises, then sat down again, picking up her lighter shoes.

"What about you, kneeler?" Draya's voice rose from the bench. "You must have seen her over there, when you worked for those hypocrites, the Seven?"

Chandre considered not answering. Tugging on one of her tennis shoes, she tied the laces, yanking them tight over her socks.

She conceded then, with a flowing gesture of her hand.

"I saw her, yes."

"Could she have done this?" Talei, the Asian with the gold eyes, asked.

It struck Chan that Talei's voice held shock, rather than anger...shock and genuine wonder. Thinking about her question, Chandre felt her jaw harden.

Keeping her thoughts shielded, she shrugged again.

"Yes."

Draya smiled, her indigo eyes knowing. "I told you."

Her tone set Chandre's teeth on edge.

She spoke up before she knew she intended to.

"She is the Bridge," she said, her words curt. "It is not her place to make the easy choices, simply to gain the approval of the masses she leads. The Sword belongs to her."

Draya rolled her eyes in the exaggerated manner of seers.

"Ah. So kidnapping and torturing her mate...or handing him over to those human-loving Lao Hu, who show nothing but contempt for the rest of us...that was a *religious* act, was it...?"

"Perhaps," Chandre said. "Perhaps it was an act of love."

The other two women looked at her blankly.

Then Draya laughed.

"If I were the Sword, I would be asking that she loved me less, then..." she smirked.

Tugging a brush through her long, chestnut hair, she didn't see when Chandre came up behind her. Before the woman could turn, Chandre caught hold of her shoulders. Gripping her with both hands, she slammed Draya's back into the locker door.

The woman cried out, giving a low squeal of fear when Chandre put the gun in her face.

"What the fuck are you doing? Crazy dirt blood – "

"Watch your tongue," the East Indian seer said, dangerously soft.

Chandre aimed the gun directly at the other seer's forehead, watching the woman's coppery complexion pale to parchment.

"...You are talking about intermediary beings," Chandre added, hammering each word. She swallowed, cocking the gun pointedly. "...And more than that, my friends."

"Hey!" From the side, Talei held up a hand, a peace gesture. "Hey... Chandre, right? She doesn't mean anything. It's just talk...no need for violence...just talk. We are all upset at what is happening over there, *na*? All of us sisters, yes?"

After a pause, Chandre flipped the safety and lowered the gun.

"I don't kill my sisters," she said coldly. "But I expect them to behave as such."

The woman Draya swallowed, eyes wide with fear.

"You're out of your fucking mind..." she muttered, as Chandre moved away.

"Be silent!" Talei shushed her. "She is a hunter...do you not see the marks?"

Chandre didn't bother to react.

Realizing she'd blown a chance at connecting with a seer who could have granted her access to the inner sanctum of SCARB, and in the capitol city no less, Chandre just shook her head, clicking softly as she shoved the gun back into her shoulder holster.

It didn't matter.

The woman hated her anyway. She would never have gotten over her connection to the Seven. Not enough to grant her real access.

Even so, it wasn't until Chandre had walked away, closing the locker and heading for the exit with her daypack, that she realized she was mostly angry at herself.

Chandre sat in a bar in Georgetown, nursing the same drink she'd ordered when she came in, almost two hours earlier.

She'd been approached, of course, as humans frequented the place.

It happened so often she hardly noticed anymore; she couldn't hide her race as well as a lot of the seers working in the United States. Anyway, a certain kind of human seemed to relish approaching seers who weren't conspicuously owned.

Chandre adjusted. She had no choice, not without opting for major surgery...which she refused to do. Even contact lenses over her red irises didn't help much, given her height and the overall shape of her face. She simply moved like a seer, as Dorje had chided her once, during one of their infiltration field ops under the Seven.

Chandre could shake all of that for deep ops, if the need was dire enough, but it usually required wearing prosthetics to soften her cheekbones and the shape of her eyes, as well as a retooling of all her mannerisms. So far, it hadn't been strictly necessary. No one contested her ownership papers here, given that they had the federal stamp. She'd stayed out of the seer ghettos at night, where most of the attacks occurred.

The humans still hadn't gotten over what happened when Dehgoies had gone after his mate inside the White House. The humans still acted like their capital city existed inside enemy territory.

The large seer ghetto circling a good percentage of DC didn't help.

Chandre was shielded from the worst of that paranoia, however. Working overtly for SCARB ensured that most humans would see her as one of the "good ones." It was enough protection that Chandre didn't bother with the effort of concealment.

Realistically, passing might not have kept the human males at bay anyway.

It might have kept them slightly more polite, however.

"How much?" a young guy in a suit smiled, his words slurred through his grin, his face flushed from alcohol. From the caliber of his rumpled suit, Chandre pegged him as an intern of some kind...possibly a congressional aide, or someone who worked for one of the many nonprofits dotting the city's core.

When Chandre ignored him, he seemed to think volume was the answer.

"How much?" he said, louder over the talking crowd. "You working, gorgeous?"

She didn't turn until he laid a hand on her shoulder.

Her knife was out of her boot and to his throat in a heartbeat. She gripped his arm, turning him so that the blade wouldn't flash in the bar lights, or get picked up by the surveillance feeds. Pulling his face near to hers, she met his gaze.

"Yes, I am working, worm. Do you think you'd still like to hire me?"

The kid, who probably had only seen twenty-five seasons, given that he was human and they aged more quickly, went white as a sheet, even faintly green.

"No..." he stammered. "No, no...sorry. My mistake."

"I think it was a mistake, yes."

She retracted the knife. Flipping it quickly in her hand, she reinserted it in her boot, glancing around to ensure no one who mattered had seen her do it. Then, without giving the human boy another glance, she turned her back on him, facing the bar. When she did, she found the bartender standing there, shaking his head a little.

He didn't look angry at her, though; in fact, she saw a quirk of amusement in his brown eyes. Smiling a little in return, she downed the last of her drink.

"Can I have another of these?" Chandre asked casually, lifting her rocks glass.

"On the house," the man affirmed, plucking it from her fingers. Leaning closer, he muttered in a lower voice, winking at her. "You have no idea how often I've wished I could do something like that to these little pricks..."

Smiling back at him, Chandre, gave him a finger salute.

"Much appreciated, cousin."

"Don't mention it." He set the vodka and tonic on the bar in front of her, but not before Chandre noticed he'd poured her the good stuff.

It was a much-needed reminder that some of these worms were worth saving.

That was what the Bridge came here to do, after all.

Help the worms evolve out of a need for all-encompassing war. Help those escape who she could help escape, if war ended up being inevitable... which it likely was.

Save as many as she could before the Displacement took them all.

At the thought, Chandre gestured in respect to her, long-distance, before taking a long drink of the vodka and tonic.

"...Esteemed Bridge," she muttered under her breath.

You might want to be careful where you make that sign these days, sister, a voice said in her mind. *Or you might end up with a knife at your own throat one of these nights...*

Chandre turned abruptly in her chair, in time to meet a hard look above a fatuous smile aimed at a human male. The seer held onto the human's arm, and he didn't appear to have noticed the exchange. She wore a backless, sequined gown, and he a tux, so they had likely come from a formal dinner of some kind, or perhaps were on their way out, to the opera. Her razor-thin collar barely showed at the base of her neck.

It must be a light one, indeed, if she could speak through it. Then again, it might only be for show. A lot of humans liked their seers uncollared, despite the regulations.

Chandre let her shoulders relax, taking her hand off the gun inside her jacket.

The woman meant it as a warning only...and an expression of anger.

She was right, anyway. Chandre had to be more careful. Half the women in this room could be cloaked seers...but Chandre guessed it to be more like a third. Unlike in Asia, where the exact opposite would be true, the vast majority of seers she encountered in the United States would, of course, be female. The split in Asia often ran about 90/10, with males in the firm majority.

Here it would be almost exactly the reverse.

In Europe, things tended to split a bit more evenly, but still leaning heavily towards females. Perhaps more like 70/30...or even 60/40, depending on the country. Japan was more like the United States. So was Germany. South America varied from country to country, seemingly with no noticeable pattern. Africa, like Asia, was predominantly male.

Chandre had never really figured out the discrepancies, but it made sense to her that Dehgoies would have chosen to live in London, rather than the New World, despite the added sexual potential of a predominantly female population.

One needed balance, after all...or a semblance of balance, anyway.

Even Chandre felt this over-abundance of female seers. This was in spite of her personal preference towards the company of females more generally.

Her thoughts drifted back to the Bridge, even as Dehgoies flashed through her thoughts. Remembering how she left them in Delhi, she frowned.

The Bridge, or simply "Allie," as Chandre couldn't help but think of her still, might not be thinking of her all that fondly these days.

Chandre pushed that out of her mind, though. She had more pressing things to think about right then. She still hadn't made much headway on finding the source of that terrorist attack in Hong Kong, or even an ID on the exact substance used in those gas cylinders.

Even with the few leads she had, finding time to chase them down had proven difficult. The Registry job still complicated Chandre's life, given her day job with SCARB.

That had been the thing to send a shudder...then a convulsing spasm... over the human intelligence and military community. The Bridge had been caught in live footage throwing members of Black Arrow security through the windows of a forty-five story building in downtown São Paulo...right before she detonated enough explosive to blow out the top four stories in a column of fire.

Of course, few in the seer community could do anything but applaud.

That operation had effectively removed most seers from the racial ident tagging system and resulted in the overthrow of at least ten work camps. It allowed political prisoners to escape and resulted in the freeing of enslaved children.

It had, in effect, been a giant jailbreak.

Chandre herself had at least four close friends who owed their freedom, and therefore their lives, to the Registry op.

Less dramatically, but probably more importantly, the entire tracking grid went down.

All seers who weren't under collar and the direct supervision of their owners became essentially untraceable. Alyson and her mate had single-handedly dismantled the system that controlled the movement and social interaction of seers, which also meant their sentience categorization and proportional citizenship.

Registration and implantation had been mandatory for seers since the decade after World War II. That system made it nearly impossible for seers to move under the radar without *some* contact with the human authorities.

It also comprised the method by which humans determined which seers were "owned" and which "free," as well as their relative docility. It determined whether they were permitted to congregate with other seers, and in what numbers. It tracked the nature of their interactions with the human population, where they were allowed to live, whether they owned their own sexual rights, whether they had the ability to contract out their sight. It told the security trackers whether a particular seer could travel without a collar. It essentially dictated the everyday lives of millions of seers.

Given all of this, Chandre, along with the rest of the seer world, assumed that Dehgoies had won the battle of ideology within his and Allie's marriage.

Clearly, they couldn't stay apart forever.

Barely a month later, while Chandre still worked twenty-hour-days as SCARB recovered from the hit in São Paulo...everything changed again.

Rumors erupted that the rebels had been attacked by the Lao Hu out of China.

Those same rumors put Allie at the head of that attack.

Given all of the chaos occurring in Asia and elsewhere, Chandre couldn't help wondering if Balidor ever told Allie what Chandre herself was doing, working for Dehgoies. The Adhipan leader placed her in the Rebel camp deliberately. He figured, due to her friendship with Dehgoies and her own militaristic background, that Chandre would make a believable mole. Hell, Chandre wasn't even sure if she disagreed with Dehgoies half the time, while he worked ops as Syrimne, so she supposed Balidor was right. It was less of a stretch for her to flip sides.

Yet Chan wondered if she'd ever truly fooled Dehgoies. She knew he wouldn't harm her, both because they were friends and because of her relationship to Allie. He also knew enough about Chandre's history in work camps that he considered her a sister in arms.

He just sent her away. He sent her to America.

Given that she hadn't been privy to the op they'd run against Dehgoies in Asia, Chandre had to assume that Balidor remained wary about her true loyalties, as well. Perhaps that's even why he sent her away in the first place.

Chandre also had to assume that Allie might not know the real reason she'd left.

Anyway, it had been Dehgoies' orders that initially brought Chandre here, to this place. It had been Dehgoies who wanted her to apply for a position within intelligence, and specifically the branch of SCARB operating out of Washington DC.

Chandre was a reasonable choice for that work, as well. She didn't advertise it...in fact, she couldn't be sure whether she'd ever told the Bridge... but Chandre had worked for Seer Containment before. In fact, she'd done so as a mole for the Seven off and on for a number of decades.

SCARB itself had been convulsing ever since the demise of the last American president, Daniel Caine. Created by Caine himself after World War II to control and regulate seer powers, the bureau solidified its hold on free and owned seers in the 1970s and 1980s. Until recently, nothing had checked their expansion into all aspects of seer lives.

Daniel Caine, a.k.a. Galaith, hadn't been anti-seer himself.

Rather, he had been a realist. He knew humans and seers would never live easily side by side, so he provided structure to human fear and prejudice. He knew that humans would never be content with a simple leveling of the playing field. To assuage their fears around seer psychic abilities, the illusion of absolute control was necessary. Prior to the hit on the Registry building, SCARB had even been moving towards mandatory collaring in any public place.

Some even wanted seers collared in designated seer zones.

Collars were getting more and more sophisticated too...with certain abilities being blocked while others remained untouched. Varying levels of negative stimuli were programmed into the collars as well, including simply cutting the seer off from the light of other beings. Early collars had relied much more heavily on pain to keep seers out of the Barrier.

Of course, for most infiltrators, pain still remained a necessary component. Yet, for the first time in over half a century, the power of the human racial police was being systematically rolled backwards. As a result, the races hovered on the brink of war once again.

Or, they *had*, at any rate...until the Sword disappeared.

With his absence, the fear of the humans had been assuaged, if only a little. Enough to keep them from nuking Asia unilaterally, for example... or starting an all-out war with the Chinese in an attempt to neutralize their exponentially larger population of seers. Although that respite would likely be temporary, too. Especially if Draya's intel was correct about Revik's infiltration team being forcibly recruited to the Lao Hu.

Hey. You're not asleep, are you?

The voice pulled Chandre swiftly out of her thoughts. Seeing the seer standing there, she frowned. She checked an imaginary watch.

"You are late, sister."

"I have good cause," Talei said, sliding onto the stool next to Chandre.

Chandre watched the Asian seer's gold eyes as she motioned for the bartender, pointing at the drink Chandre still clutched in her fingers.

Still lost inside her own light, Chandre found her mind wandering. Her eyes marveled at the woman's smooth skin, a pale beige in color, at least four or five shades lighter than her own. Her eyes and light took in the dark hair, replacing it with a deeper red. She remembered caressing a scar on a different face, the woman who wore it smiling at her, her light brown eyes sad.

Pain shivered in her light.

She clicked out. Fighting to keep her reaction invisible to Talei, she tried to push out the image of Cass and failed. She found herself remembering her last conversation with the human then, and frowned. Picking up her glass, she replayed Talei's words, if only to distract herself.

"What is this cause?" she grunted a beat later, taking another drink of vodka. She averted her eyes from the seer's questioning look, propping her elbows on the bar. "You should not look at me so much, Talei, when you are with lackeys like Draya. She will notice something is up."

The Asian seer frowned. "Don't be stupid. *What* is up? That I know you?"

"Yes, that you know me. What do you think?" Chandre motioned at the room, her mouth set in a grim line. "You pick a place filled with humans, where she is likely to be whoring, or meeting with one of her Washington friends..."

"What is your problem, sister?" Talei said. "I am not so late, am I?"

Before Chandre could answer, the seer slid a hand into her lap, caressing her hip.

Chandre bit her lip, fighting back the pain that rose in her light.

"Ah," Talei said. "I think I am understanding."

Chandre shoved off the hand. "Less than you think."

Talei frowned. Her voice shifted from coy to irritated. "No, I am getting it now. It is that human bitch, isn't it? The one who left you. The one I am increasingly beginning to think I am only here to replace. I have already seen in your mind that I look like her..."

"You don't look like her," Chandre said, her voice warning.

"Bullshit." Talei took a long drink from the glass the bartender placed in front of her. "Do you want to hear my news, or not?"

Chandre glanced at her, frowning again when she saw the humor twitching the other's lips.

"Depends on what it is."

Talei rolled her eyes, clicking softly with her tongue. "There are a few things. First, I have a source for you. Related to that mess in Hong Kong. He is human. Part of British Intelligence, and his name checks out. He claims that it wasn't gas in those canisters...not in the strictest sense. Even though they deployed it as such."

"Not gas?" Chandre frowned at the Asian seer. "What do you mean? I saw the feeds. We all did."

Talei shook her head, flipping her hair back. "It was a concentrated dose of some kind of synthetic disease. According to my contact, they must have modified it for use in the canisters. It was originally designed for administration via the water supply."

"A biological weapon?"

"Yes," Talei said, rolling her eyes a little. "And a damned deadly one. It seems this was some kind of demonstration..."

"A biological weapon that only kills humans?" Chandre stared at her in disbelief. "Why would humans create something of this kind?"

Talei shrugged. "The rumor is, President Wellington ordered it from the bio-tech units before he died. They say it was supposed to be used on China. Beijing, specifically...as a prelude to invading the Forbidden City, I imagine."

Chandre's frown deepened. But she found she understood. "They hoped to keep the seer population intact." Clicking softly, she shook her head. "Idiots. The Lao Hu would destroy anyone who tried a stunt like that..."

"Maybe." Talei sounded less convinced. "I hear this op was pretty well funded. Not only the United States involved. Not only humans, either. My contact at British Intelligence says that a secret alliance exists, created to combat the Chinese. A group of seers and humans, cooperating to restore the balance of power with Asia."

Talei shrugged with her hand, a seer's shrug.

"...According to my source, this group feels there is too much risk involved, letting the Chinese own so many of the world's trained seers. With the Seven's apparent alliance with the Lao Hu, that risk became unacceptable. My source says that this alliance feels that the Bridge must be forced to pick a side...that she cannot be allowed to pretend neutrality, or continue to work without aligning with a specific faction among the humans..."

Talei paused, letting Chandre absorb all of this. Then she added,

"Which brings me to the second thing, sister. Bounties. They've gotten high enough to hit the SCARB networks...high enough to make those that appeared in the wake of the destruction of that cruise ship seem like a porter's tip..."

Chandre looked at her, feeling muscles in her abdomen clench.

"For the Bridge?"

"Yes, for the Bridge." Again Talei rolled her eyes. "All of them want her alive, of course. In fact, anyone who kills her is likely to meet a horrible end themselves, from what I've seen. Seems there are a number of interested parties looking for her mate. Most of those who matter are reasonably sure he's not dead...that she has him somewhere, and is mistreating him."

Talei paused, studying Chandre's eyes.

"...My bosses wonder if maybe the Bridge and Sword have orchestrated this whole thing. They think maybe this is a trick, something concocted with the Lao Hu...a prelude to attack on Western soil. I am having some trouble persuading them of the risk to her..."

Chandre didn't answer, staring into the darkness of the bar.

"You are certain they are bonded?" Talei prompted.

Chandre felt her mouth firm, remembering. "They are bonded."

"In lifespan? She could not survive him?"

"No." Chandre gave her a flat look. "She could not survive him."

Talei looked between the other seer's eyes for a moment, as if scanning them for truth. Then she clicked again softly, raising her glass to her lips.

"That is bad then," she said, lowering her drink back to the bar. "The reports I read...these are not seers I would want after me." She gave Chandre another look, this one harder, showing more of her infiltration rank. "Given the size of some of the bounties, I also wonder who is sponsoring this thing... if it is really only the rebels."

Chandre's gaze sharpened. "You have someone else in mind?"

"Only rumors," Talei assured her. "There is talk of an underground network of seers, deeply funded...working with some in the human elite to bring the Bridge in alive. I have heard there is even some thought to breed her...although likely their primary goal is to keep her out of the hands of the enemy, now that she is displaying as a telekinetic. In any case, it is talk only, as of now." She made a smooth gesture with one hand. "But I wonder. It sounds too similar, doesn't it? A secret group of seers and humans making weapons against the Chinese. Now *another* secret group of humans who want the Bridge...?"

Chandre frowned. "You think this is a coup that is happening?"

"I think there is more going on here than is readily apparent," Talei said. "Don't you?"

Chandre thought for a moment, staring into the bar's back mirror without really seeing it. Finally, she said, "Yes. I do. Do you think this is really about the Chinese? About trying to destroy the power of the Lao Hu?"

Talei shrugged. "It is plausible. Is it not?"

Chandre once more stared into one of the darker corners of the bar.

"It is, yes," she said, feeling her jaw harden. She glanced back at the shorter seer. "Have any names come attached, with those bounties?"

"On the Bridge?"

"Yes," Chandre said, impatient. "Of course, the Bridge."

"Many names were hidden from me. I saw only one. But his name checked out as being one from the inner circle of the Sword's army."

"What is the name?" Chandre said.

"Wreg," Talei said, downing the last of her drink and motioning to the bartender for another. "No clan affiliation, although he's got a formal designation in the original SCARB files...some human name. No one uses anything but Wreg in any of the intelligence reports I've seen."

Noticing the look on Chandre's face, she paused.

"Do you know him?"

Chandre's mouth remained hard. "Yes," she said. "I had hoped he might be one who had died in that mess in the mountains. He has the single-mindedness of an angry dog...he also likely has Salinse with him, if that old bastard isn't finally dead." She shook her long braids, exhaling shortly.

"If he is on Allie's ass, there is going to be trouble, Talei...whether or not he is affiliated with your conspiracy group. Wreg is not one who will give up easily. Not ever, if he thinks there is a chance the Sword is alive. He is loyal like a dog, too..."

She paused again, speaking only to herself that time.

"...I wonder that Allie let him live. She must have seen this in him, too."

The Thai-looking seer smiled. "Perhaps she likes a good fight," she said.

"Perhaps," Chan said. She took another long swallow of the drink, her dark red eyes out of focus as she stared at the feeds playing overhead, the sound all the way down on a picture of a rippling Chinese flag. "...But Bridge or no, she will not be long for this world, with so many after her. If nothing else, she will end up in a cage herself."

Talei shrugged, but her eyes showed that she agreed.

"Perhaps it is good," she said. "The Bridge only brings war anyway."

Chandre frowned, feeling that pain in her light once more as she remembered the last time she'd seen the Bridge face to face.

But all she said was, "I think it is too late to stop that already."

Six
Ground Zero

I STOOD AT THE DOORWAY OF VASH'S NEARLY FURNITURE-LESS ROOM.
Meaning, apart from a bunch of round pillows and a low table, there was no furniture.

He did have a few personal belongings, if you could call them that. Blankets. A bag of what might have been clothes. Books he'd brought from the Old House, one of the few structures that remained in the rubble of Seertown. An electronic monitor sat on the low table, along with a small altar. Several tapestries hung on the walls, but I figured Balidor had seen to that, or one of his younger students. In any case, I had my doubts about how "personal" any of what I could see was, given that I'd seen Vash just as happy in a featureless rock cave.

He wasn't really a "things" kind of guy.

As I let my eyes roam over the symmetrical walls of his room, I had to fight back a wave of sickness once more. I stared at the old seer, and tried to smile.

I knew I was stalling.

I'd felt sick for days now, really for weeks...ever since I'd been locked up in that room in the rebel stronghold, waiting to be shipped back to the Seven. Waiting for the shit to hit the fan when the Lao Hu reached the Rebel compound. Waiting for Revik to wake up after I'd doped him using his own tranquilizer darts on his own private plane.

Sick with worry...sick with a kind of dread that I knew wasn't all dread at this point, but at least half anticipation, I could barely come up with a facial expression as the 700-year-old seer climbed nimbly to his bare feet and grinned at me.

He clapped his hands together as if to snap me out of my trance, fixing me with his dark eyes. When I met his gaze, his smile widened.

"Hello, my dear! You look lovely! Just lovely!"

I grinned, unable to help it.

"You're awfully chipper," I said. "Is it because you're sending me off to the guillotine once again? That tired of me, are you?"

"No. I am always thus, Alyson," he said, clapping his hands again.

"Mmm." I tilted my head, squinting up at him. "No...you are definitely chipper. More than usual, I'd say." His enthusiasm relaxed me a little, making my own smile creep out wider. "So you're feeling optimistic about this crazy plan of ours, then?"

"Somewhat, yes! Somewhat, I dare say."

"Well," I said, a little sourly. "You might be the only one."

"You are thinking of what Jon said," the old seer observed.

I nodded. No reason to elaborate. Not with Vash.

The ancient seer took my shoulder in one hand, and steered me easily out of the rectangular room he'd claimed a few weeks earlier. I needed him, of course...there *was* no plan without Vash...but I'd still felt an almost indescribable relief when I actually saw his face, and not only for the role he would play in our little endeavor.

When Vash agreed to live with us for however long the exercise took, I'd only half believed him. I knew he was a busy guy. Even with me nominally in charge of the Seven, he still had the Council to hold together. He had his students, and the work he did trying to document the oral histories of the seers, especially their religion and myths. I knew Vash carried nearly the entire weight of the original spiritual traditions of the seers on his narrow shoulders.

And those old Council seers really believed in the Myth of Three. They wanted their traditions to survive not only the humans, but the Displacement itself.

So I didn't think he meant it when he said he was there for the long haul.

It didn't sink in, in fact, until I walked out back to see him methodically moving every belonging I remembered him owning to that rectangular room...pretty much within two hours' time of his arrival by jeep.

Then Tarsi showed up.

I hadn't seen her yet, as she'd only just arrived, but I knew from Balidor that she and Vash had been locked up together almost from the moment she entered the underground bunker. I didn't know if that had all been Revik-related, but I suspected a fair bit of it was.

Now I followed the tug of Vash's fingers without question, unable to hide my relief that I wouldn't have to do this alone. It would be bad enough, I knew, even with the two most venerated and experienced seers alive helping me.

"Start at the beginning, Alyson," he reminded me.

"I know."

"...Or as near to it as you can."

"I know." I forced a sigh, shaking out my arms. "I will. I'll try anyway."

"Remember, it is all only resonance. Resonance is all we seers do. You resonate with your mate, with the beginnings of his life...and simply see what unfolds. Tarsi and I can help with the rest, once you are inside..."

"Assuming he *lets* me inside," I muttered.

"Assuming that, yes," Vash agreed, still cheerful. "Do not overcomplicate this, Allie. It will be difficult enough. Your job is only to get there, and then to help your mate with whatever is there. As I said..."

"...It's only resonance. Yeah, I know."

Forcing an exhale, I rubbed my upper arms, biting my lip against all of the thousands of things that wanted to come out of my mouth to refute the old man's words.

Because it wouldn't be that simple.

I knew that. Vash knew it, too.

"He will fight you, yes," Vash conceded. "But he cannot keep you out, Allie."

"Not if I force him," I said, a little bitterly.

"You are ready to try and establish a closer resonance with him again?"

I gave a short laugh. "How sanitary you make it all sound..."

His fingers tightened on my shoulder. "This is the part that worries me most, Alyson. He could kill you, you know."

"I know." I sighed again. "I know, Vash. But I don't think he will. Anyway, if he does, that simplifies things considerably for the rest of you, doesn't it?"

Vash clicked softly. It was the only time I saw the smile leave his face.

He was right, of course.

I had to remember that this whole thing could be over really fast.

But we'd discussed it a million ways from Sunday, and neither Vash nor I could think of another solution. The reality was, before I could even start on what Vash wanted me to do with Revik, I had to *reach* Revik. His light had changed too much, even since I'd known him as the Sword, for me to find a way in without that initial connection. Vash confirmed the necessity of that re-connection. I had to try to find him, under the mess of what he'd become. Moreover, I had to do that first, before we attempted anything else. The collar would make it nearly impossible to rely solely on the light structure we shared between us as mates.

I could find the structure in *me,* of course.

It was the Revik side we worried about.

"You may have to rely on that, at first," Vash reminded me. "Your feelings for him."

"I'll need more than that," I muttered, shaking my head as I walked.

"It would be ideal," Vash agreed, just as amiably. "Yes, indeed...it would hasten things immeasurably. Possibly even mean the difference between failure and success." He paused, smiling at me as he patted my back. "...I must say, however, I think your plan is very risky, Alyson." He cleared his throat, politely. "I am quite sure our dear friend, Balidor, would agree. Do you not think so...?"

I grunted, unable to entirely suppress the amusement in my light.

To say Balidor wouldn't approve of our plan was an understatement, to say the least. But it was too late to back down now. I doubted I'd be able to gear myself up for this again, in the event I couldn't connect with him later. It was now or never.

"I was afraid you would say that," Vash said, sighing beside me.

We'd begun walking down the second of the six hallways we needed to cross to get to our destination. I didn't have a lot of time left.

"If it doesn't work," I said, softer. "You'll give the others my note? The video I left?"

"Of course."

My mind kept wanting to go back to Jon. I couldn't help but run my mind around his description of his last conversation with Revik...really the *only* conversation anyone had managed to have with Revik since he'd been captured. Jon's assessment of Revik's mental state really had been the thing to decide me on going the more radical route with re-establishing contact. I knew Jon knew what he was talking about.

I'd already run scenarios with Balidor, with Vash, even with Poresh, who'd offered to help Vash and Tarsi with the back end of our little "project."

But it always came back to the same thing. I knew Jon was right. It wouldn't be enough. Not without actual contact.

First, I had to reach him. That was step one.

According to Jon, Revik's resistance was fear-based, so deeply irrational. That meant, I probably wouldn't even get close to the true source of it until we'd been doing this for awhile. Even beyond what the Dreng might have whispered in his ears over the years, Revik would probably fight to the death to keep certain truths away from his conscious mind.

I had no idea how early the edges of that would surface.

"Yeah," I sighed, shoving my hands in my pockets. "You know I'm right."

"Yes," Vash said, without hesitation. "But it worries me, Alyson."

"Is Tarsi ready to help you out? Once I do my bit, I mean?"

"I am," a voice said to my right. "Stop stalling, Bridge."

I jumped. Turning, I found the other oldest-seer-I-knew watching me from the doorway of one of the corridor rooms. She sniffed at my expression, folding her arms.

"You can't cater to the sentimentality of this old fool," she said, indicating towards Vash with her head. "...He's a big baby, this one."

I smiled. I couldn't help it.

"I'll keep that in mind," I said.

"No you won't," she said, sniffing again. "Never could listen."

I laughed a little, shaking my head.

Vash and I waited while she locked the door to her apartments, fussing briefly over what she called the "grade-school security" built into the organic handle. Then she turned, giving me a stern look as she brushed off the front of the long, gray tunic she wore. Her hair and face looked exactly as I remembered them, with her oddly long, black hair and clear, almost colorless irises like her blood-nephew, Revik. She was an odd collection of old and young, with perfect white teeth and finely wrinkled skin on her narrow, hawk-like face.

"Not flattering," she said in her pidgin Prexci. "You be old one day, too, Bridge...older than me on the inside now." Muttering, she added, "...I can see it, even if no one else can."

I laughed again. I couldn't help it.

Before I'd thought about it much, I enveloped her in a hug.

She looked more irritated than pleased, and pushed me away from her almost at once, but I saw a small smile on her face as she disentangled my arms.

"You hurt my nephew any?" she said.

I winced.

"Yeah. That's what I thought." She frowned at me, hands on her hips.

I just stood there while she eyed me, and probably my light, more openly.

"You going in alone?" she said finally.

It wasn't really a question. I saw her eyes sharpen as they met mine. Their clear irises were so much like Revik's they still made me pause a little.

"I think I should," I said.

That wasn't really a question, either.

"Yes," she said, nodding at once. "Absolutely."

I felt my shoulders unclench. I glanced at Vash.

"You know the plan then?" I asked her.

"Yes."

"You're okay with it?"

She gestured sharply in assent, as if that was a given. "Not 'okay.' But necessary."

"Good," I said, relieved. "You can help me browbeat Balidor into letting me go in alone. He's going to absolutely hate the idea...even without knowing the details."

Vash chuckled good-naturedly at this.

The three of us didn't talk again until we reached the security station outside of the giant green tank. I was a little surprised to see a small crowd standing there, around the low console. In it stood Jon, Dorje, Poresh, Yumi, Tenzi, Illeg, Vikram and a few others I knew from Seertown or the Adhipan. Balidor stood in front of course, over Garend, who sat at the security console.

I tried to head off Balidor when he started walking in our direction.

"...I'll have a headset, right?" I blurted.

"Of course."

"With control over the organics of the room?"

"Yes, yes," Balidor said, impatient. "You can trigger the gas yourself, if need be...you can also lock down the room. If that happens, we will collect you as soon as he is out. But we have tested the chains, the collars...everything is holding. There has been some reinforcement to some of the organic shields as well..." He gave a snorting kind of laugh, one he reserved for ironies that he couldn't quite believe.

"...Feigran gave us that advice, if you can believe it. From when he held Dehgoies in the Caucasus Mountains. He studied his light pretty extensively, from what we can gather..."

I winced a little at that memory, too.

Great. We were now taking advice from Revik's previous torturers on how best to keep him locked up in a cage.

Balidor might have read some portion of this on me. His smile faded.

"You're not going in alone, Allie."

"Don't be ridiculous," I said, brushing him off in the hopes my dismissal might help. "I have to go in alone, 'Dori. It's not up for discussion."

"No," he said.

Folding my arms, I turned on him, keeping my eyes steady on his. "Because you're going to join me in there, I suppose? Because things will go just swimmingly if we gang up on him, especially given that how he sees the two of us..." I gave a kind of outraged laugh. "No, Balidor. The matter is completely settled. Vash and Tarsi agree with me..."

Swallowing a little, since Vash hadn't exactly, verbally *agreed* with me, I glanced at Tarsi, who eyed Balidor with a pale eye. As she'd been the previous leader of the Adhipan before Balidor, and therefore his mentor and trainer, I figured her opinion held more weight with him than anyone's. Still, his face remained expressionless when he turned it back to me.

"Please, Allie," he said, quieter. "Not me. But go in there with someone. Don't go alone."

"What about Jon?" I said.

"Jon can't help you!"

"Really?" I raised an eyebrow, but I felt my face flush with real anger. "Gods save me from the arrogance of seers...Jon's probably the only one here who *can* help me!" At the light that came to the other seer's eyes, I cut him off. "'Dor, come on! He's the only one who's managed to get more than a handful of death threats and muttered curses out of Revik since we brought him here. He got Revik to actually *talk* to him. And Revik loves him. That's worth more to me right now than a dozen of your trigger-happy infiltrators..."

"I'm talking about if you get in trouble, Allie," Balidor said, gritting his teeth.

"I know what you're talking about...and I'm telling you, no!"

Realizing we were both on the verge of yelling, I forced myself to take a breath, to glance around at the others to give myself a pause to chill out.

Fingering the hair out of my eyes distractedly, I sighed, tugging a longer piece restlessly in my hand.

"...And anyway," I said, my voice more subdued. "I'd still rather have Jon out here. Revik will feel ganged up on, even if it's just me and Jon...and I don't want him turning on Jon, too. The last thing we need is him thinking the one person he can even *semi*-trust is working with the enemy. He needs at least one friend here, no matter what their race..."

But Balidor's eyes had followed the motion of my hands.

"You're wearing your hair down," he muttered.

"Yeah, I am...so?"

His eyes traveled from the loose but somewhat low-cut jade-colored blouse I wore, down to the darker-green harem pants that cinched both my waist and at the ankle just above my bare feet. The only jewelry I wore were teardrop earrings, also jade, and the silver chain with Revik's mother's ring. I also wore make up. Not a lot, but enough that Balidor seemed to notice the difference on my eyes, as well.

"Do you plan to seduce him, Allie?"

"I plan to try to get him to *talk* to me, 'Dori. Every little thing helps...you know that! You're the one who *taught* me that. What is it, one of the dozens of rules of infiltration: use every asset you have to disarm your target, no matter how trivial-seeming...?"

"That's a slight abuse of those words..."

"I'm not going in there in a geisha outfit! Or a bathing suit!"

"Perhaps you should have opted for hooker wear. He seems to have a preference."

I felt something in my breathing catch. That hit had been a little too on-the-mark to have been entirely about my clothes. My eyes narrowed to slits.

"Are you really going to get petty on me right now, 'Dor?" I said. "Because I don't have time for that. I really don't. This is going to take every ounce of my concentration as it is, if we have a chance in hell of succeeding. So if you're not on board, I need to know. I need to know now, 'Dori...so I can get someone else to spot me on this..."

Balidor flushed a little. Enough that I knew my words hit their mark, too. Hands on his hips once more, he muttered, "It just seems like you're taunting him, Allie."

"Well, I'm not."

"Confusing him, then."

"He likes my hair down, okay?" I said. "Get over it!"

In the pause after I spoke, I realized the rest of the room had fallen silent, and now stood staring at the two of us. Glancing around at the circle of faces, I felt my own warm slightly before I turned back to the Adhipan leader.

"Look," I said, taking a breath. "I'm telling you the deployment I need. I need Jon accessible...in my headset. The rest of you can watch and put up whatever security *out here* that you think is necessary. But I don't want you directly involved. I know I probably can't get him to trust me, but the only hope I have is if he doesn't feel played. Have whoever you want as close to the *outside* of the door as you think necessary, but I don't want them coming in unless one of three things happens: I ask for them, I'm unconscious, or I'm dead."

When Balidor started clicking at me, his anger growing more audible, I gripped his arm harder, forcing him to meet my gaze.

"Balidor! This is an order. This is a fucking *order*, okay? Pretend you remember what that means. And trust me on this...or if you don't trust me, then trust Vash. And Tarsi. They've okay'd all of this...all right?"

Balidor looked at them, his eyes hard. "Is that true?"

Tarsi gave him a level look, making the affirmative gesture in seer sign language. Vash gestured in assent, too. When Balidor continued to stare at the two of them, as if looking for a lie in their faces, I touched his arm. He jumped a little, but when he turned, his gray eyes remained the color of steel.

"Make sure they get whatever they need," I added, softer. "They'll be out here, too."

Tarsi chuckled a little. I don't know if it was because of what I'd said or how I was talking to her favorite pupil, so I didn't look over. I watched Balidor's face instead.

Anger reached his eyes. He was about to open his mouth again, but I cut him off.

"'Dori," I warned. "Stop. We're done here, okay? We're done."

Balidor looked at Tarsi again, as if for help, but she only shrugged, clicking. "She is a bit of a nuisance, your Bridge," she said. "But it'll be all right I think, Adhipan Leader Balidor."

"And she cleared this with you?"

"Yes. Her logic is sound. Moreover, it is an infiltrator's logic."

Holding the old seer's eyes for a beat too long, Balidor turned to me then, and bowed, curtly.

"As you wish, Esteemed Bridge," he murmured.

I was about to make an equally sarcastic response, but he'd already turned, walking quickly away from the three of us to join Garend at the security console.

Only after he'd moved away, did I realize my hands were shaking. Clutching them in front of me, I focused my light, counting backwards until the trembling stopped. I caught Jon staring at me then, his eyes holding encouragement that barely concealed his own thread of nerves. I forced myself to give him a reassuring smile...right before I took a deep breath and turned my head to look through the organic window.

Revik's back rested against the furthest wall from the hatch, his chained hands in his lap. Legs sprawled in front of him, he tilted back his head, as if staring at the ceiling. In the sudden lack of talking among the seers outside the tank, the audio reached my ears, until it eclipsed all other sounds in the room.

He was singing, I realized. Softly, under his breath.

Not only that, but I'd heard the song before.

It was a seer song, but modern. Wreg played it sometimes, during sparring drills, or by the pool, where he often wanted music. As I listened to Revik though, I realized I'd never really paid attention to the words woven into the somewhat off-kilter tune.

"Never fire and back to earth...
Some days I submit, some I won't...
They always break me, inside, out...
They kill me, smash me...
Leave me without...
Family, friends, all lovers end...
I'm broken inside, but here I am..."

The words in Prexci melded together, forming a kind of whispered prayer.

"My heart was broken long ago...
Too far back, the elders know...
The books are dust, the prophets dead...
Our time won't come before the end..."

I felt emotion try to creep up around my light, inexplicable in its intensity, since I only understood the allusions in about half of the words.

Maybe I just remembered Wreg, and the others in his charge, who I'd led to slavery and death. Maybe I was remembering Nikka.

Taking another breath, I shook it off, forcing my eyes off his face.

"All right," I said to Balidor, glancing at Vash. "It's time to start."

I didn't look at him when I walked in.

Keeping my expression flat, I walked directly to the raised platform that stood to my left and his right, a half-dozen yards from where he'd been chained. The platform itself rose only about five or six inches higher than the sloped floor, but Vash agreed it was likely the best place, at least until I could risk getting closer to him.

I felt his eyes on me as I walked over, watching me as I tossed down the blanket I'd brought, along with a longer cushion and one of the prayer mats the seer monks used for meditation. I felt reactions in his light when he first saw me, but he managed to mute them even with the collar.

Most of what I felt on him at first was disbelief.

I didn't let myself think about it too much. I had my doubts I could control things with him, especially at first. I knew from Jon he'd likely pull out the stops. The only advantage I had in that first session was surprise.

Well, and the collar.

Between the two, it would probably win me minutes at most.

I knew I wouldn't be able to beat Revik if I let him turn this into a game. I knew it even before Balidor voiced essentially the same thing, using different words. The only choice I had was to refuse to play, at least as much as possible. I had to assume Vash and Tarsi would agree.

I also hadn't brought up the fact that I was pretty sure he was about ten times smarter than I was. If nothing else, he'd been playing these games for decades before I'd been born. He'd also been mind-fucked by people with whom I probably couldn't even hold my own in a regular conversation.

I would never reach him that way. Never. He'd chew me up and spit me out, and I'd have to start all over, from ground zero. Which was where I was now.

Even though he was collared, I kept all of this in the back of my mind while I spread out the first thick blanket, then arranged the cushion over the middle of it.

"Planning a nap, sweetheart?" he said from the other side. "Or were you going to strip for me?"

I didn't look up.

It occurred to me I also felt something like relief ripple through his light in those first few seconds, which I'd been looking for, as well. So I wasn't the only one who'd been feeling the effects of our separation these past few weeks.

The room cut him off from the Barrier...completely off. That meant it cut him off from me, too. He likely hadn't been entirely bullshitting Jon when he told him he was in pain. He would have to be, from our being apart, regardless of how he felt about me. The bond couldn't be reasoned with. At base, no matter what our personal feelings, that separation would kill us, if we let it go on too long.

But with both of us in the green-walled tank, even with him wearing a collar, his light could connect with mine. Maybe not as much as either of our light bodies wanted it to...but enough to ease off the worst of that irrational tension.

At least the parts of that irrational tension caused by the bond.

The reality was, I would have to spend time with him in the tank no matter what approach we took with him. If we couldn't get him to come around, I would probably have to live in here with him, at least part of the time.

That, or find some way to hold him in a less restrictive cell.

Either option made my chest hurt.

I spent another moment arranging the blankets and pads on the platform, and taking off the backpack I wore. I didn't look at him as I gauged the distance between where he sat and where I'd positioned my makeshift bed. He felt far away to me. I knew distance didn't have to matter in the Barrier, but it mattered from my perspective.

Hopefully it would matter less by the time this started for real.

"Is this your big plan then, sweetheart, to silence me to death?" I heard him smile. "You could have done that from the other side of the wall, lover. Or am I supposed to feel slighted, when you do it in here?"

"No," I said, with a single shake of my head.

For a moment he just watched me. I felt him thinking, as the surprise of seeing me wore off.

"Did you bring any hiri for me, wife?" he said.

I bit my tongue a little at the way he said it, but I didn't let it reach my expression.

"Yeah," I said.

I fumbled into the backpack, untying the strings holding it closed at top. It contained water mostly, some food, but also a full packet of hiri and an organic lighter. Garend assured me the packet contained the best brand of hiri that seers made. Sitting down on the blanket next to it, I tugged out one of the dark sticks and put it to my lips.

"...Gods, you're giving me a hard-on already," he said. "I don't suppose you could hold it in your cunt after you light it?"

I didn't raise my eyes.

Instead I pulled the bag into my lap, digging around until I found the lighter Garend had also given me. Organic, it should only light with my hands, using my DNA. Of course, that wouldn't help me when Revik had me in a stranglehold, forcing my hands to light the damned thing for him. The thought was fleeting, then it vanished, like smoke.

I lit the end of the hiri, and threw the lighter back in the bag.

Getting up from the narrow pallet I'd created, I walked a few steps closer and tossed the hiri to him, so that it landed not far from one of his hands.

"Thanks, love." Winking at me, he leaned over, picking it up with his fingers.

I saw him looking at my clothes then, his eyes traveling lingeringly up to my hair. He completed his assessment and smiled again, raising the hiri to his lips.

"Casual fuckable," he pronounced, taking a drag off the hiri, then picking some of the weed off his tongue. "...I like it. A little more Indian than I usually see you in..."

"Yeah," I said neutrally. "They brought a bunch of clothes back from their last trip to Delhi. Ours were getting a little threadbare..."

"Will you take off the top?" he said.

I flinched a little, but his voice remained conversational, almost friendly.

"...It's low cut, which I appreciate, love, I do...but it's just making me want to see your tits."

"Revik." I looked at him for the first time, letting my eyes show my impatience. "This is going to get really old."

He smiled at me, then glanced at the end of the hiri to make sure it was still lit.

"How about a blow job?" he said in the same tone. "Jon wouldn't give me one, but now I'm almost glad I waited...I forgot how much I like your mouth, lover."

I averted my eyes as he smiled at me again, his clear irises cold.

"Come on, baby," he said, cajoling. "I'll do you, if you do me. I know you've got to be hurting a bit, too...even if you are getting it from that Adhipan prick..."

When I only clicked at him in annoyance, he smiled wider, tilting his head back to look at the ceiling. He took another drag of the hiri.

"That bond thing is a bitch, isn't it...?" he added. "I guess the racial compatibility thing is a bit of a nightmare at times, too. I know it was with Elise. There were times when I wanted to fuck her with the hard end anyway... so badly it took everything in my willpower not to go to seer prostitutes until I got it out of my system..."

I bit my lip, but didn't lower my eyes.

His expression still thoughtful, he tilted his hand with the hiri, a seer's shrug.

"...Still. She was pretty amazing, for a human. She could do things with her tongue that were absolutely unbelievable..." Letting his gaze drift back to me, he exhaled smoke. "...She let me do it to her in the ass, too, once she realized what I wanted. It was almost as good. Almost, but not quite..." He took another drag of the hiri, his voice growing lazy as he studied my face.

"How is he handling that? The fact that he just can't *quite* give it to you, not like I can...? Does he whine about it? Or just go to prostitutes?"

"I have no idea," I said, my voice bored.

Without looking up at him, I arranged my legs, sitting cross-legged on the mat and pulling out a bottle of water. I let my voice turn businesslike when I looked at him next.

"Revik, Jon told me that he talked to you about what I was going to try to do."

"Did he?"

"Yeah. He did. I'd like to hear your take on it, if that's all right."

"What else did Jon tell you about our little chat?" Revik glanced over, his eyes cold once more as they appraised mine. "Did he tell you I gave him a hard-on?" He chuckled a little, exhaling another lungful of smoke. "He actually got me going there for a minute, too. Picturing him persuading little Dorje into letting him in here. Jon's more devious than I gave him credit for... or a better fuck than I realized." He let his eyes shift back to mine. "But I had him panting there for a minute, wife. I saw it in his eyes. Bet that pissed Dorje off..."

"Probably," I said. "Look, can we get off this infantile crap? I don't need you to cooperate with me, Revik...in fact, I don't expect you to. But I wish you would. More than anything, I wish you would help me with this."

He raised his head off the wall, staring at me. "Help you?"

"Yes," I said, biting my lip. "I'm trying to help *you*. I would think you would want this..."

"That I'd want you toying with my mind? Implanting a bunch of garbage about 'good' and 'evil' and the right and wrong ways of keeping our race from being fucking annihilated? Is that what you think I'd want your *help* with, Allie?"

For the first time, I heard anger in his voice.

I kept the relief out of my light and off my face.

"Is that what you think I'll be doing?" I said.

He gave a humorless laugh. "No, I thought you'd be rubbing my feet, telling me I was your one and only...what the hell else does 're-program' mean, wife?"

I kept my eyes level with his. "It's not re-programming...I won't be implanting anything, Revik. That's not what this is."

He shook his head, clicking loudly. "Sure. You'll just give them access... then they'll go in and fuck with my light..."

"Jon told me you were afraid."

"Afraid?" Revik turned, staring at me. After the faintest pause, he laughed, giving me an incredulous look. "Afraid of *what*? That you might see something about my past? I offered that to you, Alyson! Back when I thought you were my *wife*, I offered to let you see anything about me or my past that you wanted..."

"This is different. You know it's different. This is about the things they helped you *not* to see. The things the Dreng helped you cope with...protected you from."

He gave another disbelieving laugh.

"You are so full of shit," he said, exhaling smoke as he shook his head. "I can't believe they turned you into a zealot so fast. How did they do it, Allie? Was Balidor's dick really that good? The woman I married didn't believe in any of this crap. Gods, Dreng, prophecies...old religions and their rigid, absolutist moral codes. You didn't even have a particularly rigid definition of right and wrong, as I recall. You had all of the theological sophistication of a twelve-year-old, of course...and never really knew what the hell you were talking about. But I at least respected you had your own mind..."

"This isn't about believing anything, Revik," I said. I bit my lip, feeling my cheeks flush, in spite of myself. "You know it's not."

"Really? Then what is it about? What exactly is it that made you decide to use my own goddamned marital bond against me...that you'd let them use *that* to get to me..."

"I'm trying to help you," I said. "I'm trying to find some way to give you back your own life, the freedom to make up your own mind about – "

"Freedom." He let out a harsh laugh, holding up his chained wrists. "You want to talk to me about *freedom*, love? Seriously?"

"They can't save you, Revik. They can't."

"*Who* can't?"

"The Dreng."

"Jesus Christ, Alyson." He shook his head, his voice holding disbelief again. "If you could just hear yourself. I honestly can't believe this. I really can't..." His clear eyes met mine. "I almost feel sorry for you, wife..."

"They're not helping you, Revik." I bit my lip again, trying to keep the reaction off my face, out of my light. "If you don't face this now, you'll have to face it later. And the more you live in their light, depending on them, the worse it's going to be..."

He rolled his eyes, seer fashion.

"So you're going to save me. The waitress from San Francisco."

"Revik, I'm not saying that, either. I'm trying to – "

"I don't *depend* on anyone, wife."

I just looked at him for a moment, feeling my chest tighten at his expression.

"Really?" I said. "You don't?"

"No." He looked at me, his eyes hard. "I don't. And don't pretend you weren't there, in the mountains with me. Or that you weren't side by side with me for the Registry job. I can forgive Jon for this crap...he wasn't there. But are you seriously going to look me in the eye and tell me I wasn't running things there? That I was manipulated into doing that...?" His mouth quirked in a humorless smile. "Come on, love. Tell me. I'm dying to hear you explain that...or were you too busy playing GI Joe with my people to remember?"

"I don't have to explain anything," I said, not dropping my gaze. "I remember you there. I remember you perfectly."

"And?"

"And?" I gave a seer's shrug, placing my hands on my knees. "Yeah, you were in charge. Absolutely. They would have followed you to their deaths."

He gave me a faintly surprised look. "So?"

"So," I said, feeling my jaw harden. "How have you been *feeling* for the last few weeks, Revik?"

His mouth curled into a frown, even as he averted his gaze, taking another drag off the hiri.

Seeing the dismissive look on his face, I felt my own jaw harden.

"Come on," I said. "Tell me. Are you feeling like the mighty Sword now? Because I gotta tell you, I don't see the man I knew at the rebel base. I don't see Wreg's friend. I don't see someone capable of leading other seers at all..."

He exhaled smoke, his eyes on the ceiling, his face unmoving.

Biting my lip again, I tried to read his expression, couldn't.

I hardened my voice. "...I watched the tapes, Revik. Every session. Every conversation someone's tried to have with you since you got here. I don't care how angry you are...I don't care how wronged you feel. Anger doesn't explain what I've seen."

Giving me a bare glance, he only shook his head again, smiling faintly. While I watched, he leaned his head back against the wall, blowing smoke rings with his lips and tongue.

"How long did you practice this speech, love?" he said.

Watching him, I felt a kind of tiredness fall over me. The posturing in my voice dropped in the same instant. Swallowing, I shook my head, clicking softly.

"Look, Revik," I said, softer. "I know you think you're holding your own with me in this conversation. I know you do. Maybe you even think that you're 'beating' me in some way, with the condescending jabs, or the fact that you can hurt me with Elise..." Feeling a pain briefly close my chest, I waited for it to pass before I added, "...But you're not winning, Revik. You're not winning because there's no way to win. You can hurt me all you want, but it won't do anything. And it only convinces me I'm right. You're not him anymore. You're not the Sword...if you ever were. The Sword wouldn't have needed to talk to me like this. He'd probably be trying to negotiate with me right now. At the very least, he'd be more worried about his own people than his damned ego...or who his wife slept with while she was trying to get him out..."

He turned at that, his eyes sparking with anger as they focused on me.

"Yeah," I said. "You heard me. This stuff isn't real, Revik."

He averted his gaze back to the wall, his expression flat once more.

"So?" I said. "Are you going to explain that, Revik?"

He exhaled in a sigh, his voice openly bored.

"Explain what, my dear?"

Fighting the anger that wanted to rise, I rested my hands back on my knees. Eventually I swallowed it again and shrugged, my voice level.

"Well, how about explaining why I've seen you sitting in here alone, talking to people who aren't here. Explain how you seem catatonic half the time, when you're not acting like a rabid animal. Explain how your light looks broken to me, even now, as I look at you. And then tell me again how you're not *dependent* on them."

For an instant, I thought I had reached him.

His jaw hardened as he stared at the far wall, ashing the hiri on the green tile floor. Then he seemed to bring whatever I saw wavering and jerking in his light under control. I saw him wince as the collar kicked in when he did it. But he kept his expression motionless.

Shaking his head, he only clicked at me, taking another drag of the hiri.

"You know," I said. "Right now, you're an awful lot like Terian, Revik."

I bit my lip once more, but the more I thought about it, the more true it felt.

"...You really are. I don't mean Feigran. I mean *Terian*...the guy who held me captive in DC. It's amazing the similarities..."

"You would know," he said sweetly. "...You fucked us both."

"Yeah," I said. "He would have said that, too, Revik."

His eyes changed. I watched them grow cold, then slowly darken.

I flinched from that look. I couldn't help it.

"So let's talk about it, then" he said softly. "That is, if you're done insulting me, wife?"

I swallowed, giving a seer's hard nod.

"Fine." I looked back into those empty eyes. "Let's talk."

"So this is your premise then?" He took another drag of the hiri, his voice conversational. "That I'm...what...possessed? Or just compromised in some way?"

"More the latter," I said. "You're always going to be vulnerable to them, Revik. Always. Unless you deal with this, you're going to either be stuck with them, or someone's going to have to put you down."

"Put me down?" He smiled.

"Yeah," I said seriously. "And I really don't want that person to be me."

Giving another disbelieving laugh, he looked away.

I watched him smoke in silence. As he did, that cold, glassy stare climbed the walls of the room, as if measuring them.

"How about we just settle this thing right now?" he said finally. "Unchain me, love. I'll break your pretty neck, and then we'll both be done for this world. Wouldn't that be simpler? Less of a time suck, too, for all of our friends out there..."

I managed to hold his gaze when he turned. Looking at what lived there, I felt something in my stomach grow cold.

"Go on," he said, softer. "Ask me if I mean it, love. Ask me."

"So it's a suicide pact, then?" I said, fighting my voice level. "We're to that already?"

"I might be okay with that. Yeah. If the alternative is having to sit here for the next however-many years, listening to you talk to me about myself..."

"Pretty sad, that you'd prefer that to my help."

"I'd prefer to be the sex slave of a human *leper* to your help, wife."

Biting my lip, I fought back my anger before I answered.

"So that's it, then. You want to do this the hard way?"

He gave a low laugh, shaking his head. "Gods, just kill me, will you? One more cliché and I think I might bite open my own wrist..." He faced me with another cold stare. "What I *want,* wife, is for you to come over here so I can beat you to death with my bare hands...since that seems like the only thing that might actually *shut you up...*"

Feeling my breath stop, I didn't move.

I just sat there for a long moment, my eyes closed.

Then I stood up.

My heart jerked in odd, sideways leaps in my chest. My whole body tensed as I regained my feet...but I did it anyway, sent the signal I'd programmed to the organics through the headset they'd given me. I could only hope Balidor wouldn't notice, at least not right away.

From the silence in my headset, I had to assume nothing showed up on their board.

Taking another forced breath, I walked directly up to the line around where Revik sat.

"You want to kill me, Revik?" I said.

He smiled up at me, his eyes those of a stranger.

"No, love. I want to make love by a fireplace and then cuddle, tell each other our secrets..."

I felt my face tighten.

We'd done something not dissimilar to that once. I'd almost forgotten that Revik at times, in the long months that had passed since he'd changed back into Syrimne. Looking at him now, I saw him again. I saw the Revik I'd met in San Francisco, the one I'd woken up next to in Seattle. The one I'd laughed with and become friends with and fallen in love with on the ship. I saw the one I'd married, really married, in that cabin in the mountains.

Still looking at that Revik, I stepped over the line Balidor had drawn around him on the floor, the one that dictated a safe distance from the range of his chains.

As I did, I heard an explosion of static as the audio came to life from the headset.

Balidor's voice broke over the line, as if he'd grabbed the mic away from someone.

"Alyson." His voice was a command, but I heard the harshness underneath. "Step back. Right now! Step the fuck back!"

"No," I told him.

"Alyson! I will break the damned door down, if you – "

I tore off the headset, tossing it behind me to the floor.

Taking another step, so that I stood right in front of Revik, almost close enough to touch, I held out my hands, almost a seer question.

I just stood there, my legs slightly apart, my arms at my sides. I braced myself, knowing it wouldn't do any good.

"You want to kill me, Revik?" I said. "So kill me."

He moved so quickly, I didn't even have time to tense.

"What is she doing, what is she doing..." Jon muttered under his breath.

He gripped his own upper arms. Tensing, he watched Allie walk calmly to the very edge of the circle drawn on the floor around Revik.

Looking at the expression on her face, he felt something in his stomach go cold.

They'd had the audio playing over the whole staging area outside the tank, cranked up so that her and Revik's voices could be heard, even if they whispered.

Jon doubted he'd missed a word since she'd entered.

He'd listened to their exchange with a mixture of horror and disbelief. He'd actually been impressed at Allie's ability to keep her cool, when all was said and done. Revik had thrown his ex-wife at her, talked to her like she was a prostitute, threatened to kill her, told her she was brainwashed, told her she was stupid, laughed at her when she tried to be honest with him. Jon could tell, just from some of her reactions, that he was hitting more personal buttons with her, too...likely things Jon himself didn't know enough about to pick up on.

He did pick up on a few though.

He knew Allie was insecure about her intelligence, especially compared to Revik's. He'd already jabbed at that button a few times, mostly by rolling his eyes at every other word she said when she was trying the hardest to talk to him. The Elise thing was a low blow too, given how sensitive Allie had been about the fact that he'd been married before.

Now Jon heard her voice come over the line clearly.

"You want to kill me, Revik?" she said, her voice strangely calm, if tinny through the 1950s speakers in the room.

"I don't like this," Dorje said next to him.

"Me either," Jon said, not looking over.

"No, love," Revik's voice came back.

Jon saw the look on the seer's eyes and his skin grew colder still.

"...I want to make love by a fireplace and then cuddle, tell each other our secrets..."

Dorje caught hold of Jon's arm, his fingers tightening.

Then Allie did what Jon had a sinking feeling she was going to do from the second she got up off that pallet. She stepped over the line drawn on the floor of the cage and walked slowly but deliberately up to Revik. Jon saw the cold anger in Revik's eyes bleed rapidly into disbelief, then an even more predatory stillness.

Balidor's voice rose sharply from by the security console.

"Alyson!" His voice came out as a harsh command, but Jon clearly heard the fear underlying his words. "Step back! Right now! Step the fuck back!"

"No," her voice drifted back through the loudspeaker. Quiet, almost distant.

"Alyson! I will break the damned door down, if you do not step back this instant...!"

Jon watched her unhook the headset from around her ear before he'd finished speaking and fling it behind her, a few yards outside of the drawn circle.

The circle she now shared with Revik.

"Goddamn it!" Balidor cursed, slamming his hand down on the console. He turned to Garend. "Hit the gas! Now! Knock them both out!"

"I can't," Garend said, disbelief in his voice.

"What do you mean, you *can't?*"

"It's been turned off...and the doors. She's locked herself in. I'll need to break the encryption code she's got on this, first..."

"Holy christ," Jon muttered. "She planned this."

He watched Balidor and several of the other seers try to access the failsafe through their headsets...then through the Barrier...and fail.

Jon glanced at Vash, who sat easily next to Tarsi on the floor. The two of them shared a mat not dissimilar to the one Allie had spread out in the next room. Both of the old seers appeared to be watching attentively, but neither of them seemed surprised.

Co-conspirators, he thought, even as Dorje gripped his arm tighter once more.

At the seer's nudge, Jon's eyes jerked back to where Allie now stood directly in front of Revik, her hands open at her sides. She gestured at him, a seer question. Jon couldn't help but think how small she looked, with her thin but muscular arms and legs, brown from the sun but feminine from the harem pants and ornate, pale-green blouse. Her dark hair hung down to the middle of her back, a thick, tangled mass of soft curls framing a narrow face with high cheekbones. Her light green eyes didn't leave Revik's face.

She looked so...female.

Jon didn't always see her that way, in her combat gear and with her hair tied back, especially when they were sparring in mulei.

But she looked vulnerable to him now, and small next to the man on the floor.

"You want to kill me, Revik?" she said, her voice quiet in the silence of the room.

Every set of eyes watched her. Every seer around Jon seemed to hold their breath.

"...So kill me."

He moved so quickly that even Jon, who was used to tracking takedowns with his eyes, barely had time to see it. Revik pulled her down by the ankle, tripping her with his legs in the same swift yank. Without a pause, he dragged her under him, rolling over her and catching hold of her wrist in one hand. The other, he clenched on her throat, using the same arm to pin her free arm even as he crushed her legs and body with his, sinking his weight.

In less than a blink, he had her immobilized, lying under him.

Her free hand grasped at his fingers on her throat, looking small beside his, seeking purchase on the metal cuff around his wrist.

Jon saw the fear in her eyes, the dazed look on her face, probably from hitting her head as she came down, or maybe from the hand he had on her throat.

Every seer in the place fell into dead silence.

Then Balidor turned, and Jon saw a look on his face he'd never seen before. Fury filled it, along with a foreboding command that seemed to charge the whole room.

"Break down the fucking door!" he said. "Now!"

Seers around Jon moved abruptly to comply, even as Jon's eyes returned to the view he could see through the transparent, organic pane.

"Don't," he heard her say. He realized in some incredulity that she was talking to them, not to Revik. She was talking to the organic wall, to the mic embedded inside, her free hand held out towards the seers on the other side. "Don't...break in...it's all right..."

Revik, looking down at her, smiled.

"I wouldn't be so sure about that, love..." he said softly.

His words seemed to echo in the small security room outside the tank.

I stared up at him, fighting to breathe, to get my equilibrium back.

My head hurt. The back of it throbbed; I knew I'd have a lump there from where I smacked it on the floor. I fought my way back through the daze that remained, trying to focus on the angular face hanging over mine, the clear eyes.

Already, his light was crashing into mine, sliding around it, into it.

I gasped as I felt the changes in him, in his aleimi...fighting to adjust.

I felt him doing the same, even as his face tightened.

His eyes winced from the collar as his light flared into mine. His aleimi coiled into me harder, pulling at me as if fighting to hold me in place along with his hands. Even under the anger and the deluge of grief and fear and frustration I felt on him, that need wound the furthest into me, stronger than I'd ever felt it, even on the boy. He pulled at me with his light, a deprived, half-starved urgency woven through the threads.

He hated me for it, but it didn't change anything.

I couldn't think past it...or even try to soothe either of our reactions with my own, un-collared light. There was nothing loving in it, or sensual. It was raw need...a need that would kill to be sated. I fought to adjust to having him back in my light, gasping against the hand that held my throat...and couldn't. I tried opening my light more, to let him in, and felt his light surge around me even brighter, hot against my skin.

He still held one of my wrists, his legs and body pinning me to the floor. My other hand gripped the metal cuff of the one he had around my throat.

After another few minutes, I gave up trying to pry his hand off.

"You really want to kill me?" I managed, fighting for breath. "Really, Revik? You'd really rather die, than live without the Dreng? Are you that afraid to be without them?"

He laughed. "Sticks and stones, love."

"This isn't necessary..." I said.

"Necessary?" His smile hardened, his face directly over mine. "I suppose that's all a matter of opinion, isn't it? I guess, from a certain perspective, it wasn't wholly *necessary* that you pretend to be my wife, infiltrate my military operation, drug me, kill half my crew, enslave the other half, and then stick me in a cage so you could use my marital bond to help your lover torture me...?" His smile turned cold once more. "Or was there some biological drive calling the shots on that one, wife...some condition I'm not aware of?"

I was still trying to regain my breath when he lowered his mouth to my ear, speaking in a murmur, his lips brushing my skin.

"Anyway, I don't have to kill you, wife," he said softly. "I can break every bone in your body...and then I can play with you for awhile."

I felt myself wince. Then anger asserted itself, hot in my light.

"Go ahead," I said. "I always knew it was bullshit that you'd never hurt me. Just the fact that you had to say it, over and over again..."

He broke into my words, laughing again.

Before I could react, he released my neck, sliding his hand down my body. He had it under my shirt and inside the pants I wore before I knew what he meant to do. The chain and cuffs were cold on my skin, but his hand and fingers were warm. I gasped involuntarily, trying to writhe away from him.

Then he slid his fingers inside me, and my whole body arched.

"Gods..." I managed. "...don't..."

He slid his fingers deeper, deep enough that my mind briefly stuttered. The urgency in his light worsened, until I couldn't see past it, couldn't breathe. My eyes closed, and I gasped, clutching the front of his shirt with my free hand. When I opened them again, he was staring at my face, his glass-like eyes clinical.

"You are hurting a bit, aren't you, love?"

He did it to me again, slowing deliberately to caress me until I gripped his hair, crying out. His touch grew slower still, sensual as he leaned his weight on me, sliding his fingers deeper once more, arching against me until I couldn't move. I felt his light pulling at mine, coiling into me, invasive as it dragged me into his. When I bit my lip, fighting not to cry out again, his eyebrow rose, even as his gaze flickered to my lips.

"You want me to fuck you, Allie?" he murmured.

"No."

He laughed. "Hell, I think I could have you begging me here in a minute..."

I shoved at his chest, and he smiled, sliding his fingers deeper again.

"Come on, love...ask me for it...ask me..."

"Stop..."

He seemed somehow immune to his own light, to what he was doing to me. Whether it was because of the collar or for some other reason, I saw no indication in his face. His eyes turned clinical once more, studying mine. When he groaned softly in my ear, he wasn't losing control...he used the sound to pull at me instead, his voice cajoling.

"Remember, Allie?" he murmured. "That time in the room? When you let me tie you up? I think you would have done anything I wanted by the end of that night...I had blue balls so bad by the end I almost did hit you..."

I felt my breath catch, right before his tongue grazed my throat.

"You said you loved me," he said, softer still. He kissed my ear, breathing words against my skin. "You said you'd never leave me, Allie...that you'd do anything for me..."

I met his gaze, directly that time, and felt my heart clench. His eyes were empty once more, his clear irises a shining cold that looked almost dead. I saw the Dreng in that stare, and it felt like they'd killed him. Like he was dead, and this was only the shell. I fought back the pain that tried to take over my light, holding that vacant stare.

He smiled, pressing against me. His light coiled deeper, until it felt like a part of him was already inside me, already forcing its way into my body through my light.

I let out a low gasp, unable to hold it in.

"Are you really going to rape me, Revik?"

He smiled. "Is that what this is?"

Raising his head, he shrugged, removing his hand. Sliding his fingers between his lips, he sucked on on them briefly, using his tongue. He smiled at me after he had, using the same hand to caress the hair out of my eyes.

"You came to me, love," he reminded me.

"I thought you wanted to kill me."

The glass-like stare met mine.

"Give me head, and I'll play your little game," he said. "I'll let you mindfuck me, or torture me...whatever you want, Allie...but I want a blowjob first. A good one. A really, really good one. I want you to make me black out when I come, wife..."

I clicked at him, shaking my head in irritation.

Watching his face warily, I tried to decide if he really had reconsidered hurting me, or if this was just him circling around the same game.

Then I decided it didn't matter. Trying to second-guess him was a waste of time, too.

His light coiled through mine, still pulling at me, sliding over my skin. I felt it winding around the light in my legs, moving through my abdomen to my chest, my throat, my hands. He gripped my wrist tighter as the pull grew more insistent, until I found myself wondering if it was affecting him, even through the collar. His weight grew heavier even as I thought it, and I found myself thinking that the coldness in his eyes had receded somewhat, shimmering more distantly in the background. His eyes shifted to my mouth.

I saw him focus there, right before they closed, longer than a blink. When he pressed against me that time, he was hard.

"Gods," he said. "Give me head, wife."

With him so close, looking at me like that, I felt my skin flush.

"Revik..."

"I'll turn my back," he offered with a faint grin. "Away from the window. So your boyfriend doesn't have to watch."

My eyes flickered back up to his. I gauged the smile on his face with some impatience.

"You can't possibly believe that," I said. "Even *you* can't."

"That he won't watch?"

"That he's my boyfriend."

The coldness cycled back up to the forefront of his gaze. "Give me head, wife, or I'll break your fucking mouth."

"Go ahead."

He stared down at me, his light eyes flickering from one of mine to the other. I felt surprise curl off his light, a near puzzlement.

"You want me to kill you, don't you?"

I shook my head. "No," I said. "I just want this part out of the way."

"This...part?"

"Yeah. You know." I blew out my cheeks a little, clicking. "You threaten me...tell me you want me dead, that I'm a whore, that I deserve to have my face carved up. The whole Dreng litany...'I'll play with your insides, kill all your friends' bullshit. I figure you have to get it out of your system...I'd rather just get it over with."

He stared down at me, his face unmoving, only a few inches above mine. Swallowing a little at his expression, I shrugged from where he held my arm.

"...I knew you wouldn't ever really be satisfied with threats alone. So if you want to punch me, rape me, break a bone or two, degrade me...go for it. It's better than having to listen to you go on about it for the next however-many weeks..."

He surprised me, bursting out in a laugh.

"But you won't give me head?" he smiled.

"Whatever." I rolled my eyes, puffing my cheeks again, seer fashion. "If it's absolutely necessary to make you feel like you're in control, I'll do it, Revik..."

He laughed again, and that time, I heard genuine enjoyment in it.

"Gods," he said, caressing my face. "I think I will fuck you...you can read whatever into it you like, wife."

I felt my heart break into a panicked hammering in my chest.

He caught hold of my other wrist before I could twist it away, pinning it with the same hand as the other. He moved methodically, almost businesslike as he unhooked his belt, sliding it from around his waist before he used it to tie my wrists together, his eyes briefly concentrated as he wove the leather between and around them and then pulled the strap tight, locking it with the silver tongue. I fought to writhe away from him, but he caught hold of the front of my pants, using them to pull me back towards him, then yanking the thin fabric down my body.

Through all of it, he didn't look at my face.

I bit my lip to keep from telling him to stop, trying to control my own reactions to what he was doing, even as I struggled against him. What I'd said had mostly been a bluff...but I couldn't quite keep my cool when he started unhooking the front of his pants.

"Revik, don't..."

"You said I could, love. You gave me permission."

"I know I did, but please. Don't..."

"You're only making my cock harder, love."

"Revik. Not here. Not in front of them..."

He only laughed, pushing the shirt up my body deliberately.

"Every seer in that room has a hard-on right now, wife. I guarantee it..."

Just then, there was a metallic clanging and the round hatch of the door opened. I turned my head as Revik did, and saw four of the Adhipan standing there, two of them holding electric rods. Whoever was behind them closed the door once they were inside, probably to keep up the Barrier shield, which only remained intact for a few seconds once the seal was broken.

"*Deghoies.*"

The voice came over the loudspeaker, echoing in the hollow walls of the tank. It was unmistakably Balidor.

I flinched. Still, my trick with the gas must have held, or they would have dosed us both by now. As it was, the four guards were walking cautiously towards both of us, three with electric rods held out. Poresh held a rifle instead, loaded with some kind of tranquilizer. Even as I thought it, Poresh fired, hitting Revik in the neck with a blue-tipped dart. Revik pulled it out of his neck, crushing the vial with his fingers. He laughed then, looking up at the four guards, even as he gripped my throat in his hand again.

"You willing to risk your precious Bridge?" he taunted them. "Come on Pori. Dart me again. How many, do you think, before I go down? Do you really think I'll pass out before I can crush her windpipe...?"

Balidor's voice rose over the intercom once more.

"Dehgoies...let her go."

Revik smiled, looking up towards the sound. He barely paused as he finished undoing the front of his pants, still holding my throat in his other hand. He barely seemed to notice my attempts to get my legs out from under his, to kick him off me.

"You're just in time, 'Dori," he said, pushing me to my back.

"Dehgoies, don't!" Tenzi said. He held up his hand, the one holding the electric rod. "We won't hurt you...just let her go..."

Rolling over with me under him, Revik used his weight and his knees and hand to force my legs apart. Positioning himself between my thighs, he paused long enough to yank at the top edge of my underwear, ripping it open down the front. Then he shifted his hold on my arms, using his weight to pin me before he rested a hand on my hip.

"Dehgoies," Balidor's voice echoed. "...*whatever she says, this will have a price tag attached you won't want to pay...*"

Revik hung there poised, pausing to smile again at the organic wall.

"You want to see her whimper again, my brother...is that it?"

"*We can beat you into a bloody coma, every day if we want...*"

Revik only laughed. "If you didn't want me fucking your girlfriend, 'Dori, you shouldn't have let her in here alone. You must have known she'd come to me eventually..." He grinned down at me. "Isn't that right, love?"

I didn't answer, but felt my jaw harden.

Poresh hit Revik with another dart. Revik removed it from his neck, crushing that one as well. Poresh aimed another that Revik tried to dodge, but it caught in his hand until he jerked out the needle, tossing it onto the organic floor.

"Just a few more minutes..." Revik said, panting. "Just give me a few more minutes with the missus, boys...then I'll behave, promise..."

I saw from his eyes that the darts were affecting him, but not enough. I could hear the four infiltrators in the Barrier. They were trying to decide if they could risk rushing him, or if Revik would hurt me before they could separate us.

Even as I thought it, Revik's light flooded into mine again, seemingly against his will. He let out another low gasp, even though I couldn't be sure how much he felt through the collar. I saw pain flicker over his features, just before it expanded like water into my light. I was gasping then, I couldn't help it. Holding my bound arms, then my throat, he pushed my legs wider apart. Briefly, I felt him lose control. I felt myself opening to him, and he seemed to notice that, because he let out another half-gasp. That one, he turned into a laugh.

"Tell me you love me, wife..."

"I love you..."

He laughed again, harsher that time.

Balidor's voice rose.

"I'll put you on wires, brother. I'll do it personally. For months if I have to. You won't be able to feed yourself. You'll beg us for the next fix..."

Revik glanced up at the camera again, smiling. As he did, he maneuvered his way into me, entering me all the way before my brain caught up with what he was doing. His whole back arched once he was fully inside. The hard end of him extended almost the instant he had, going so far into me I felt my aleimi flare out. I cried out, my back arching my hips further against him.

Briefly, his eyes closed.

"Gods," he said, looking up at the camera again. "I forgot how good this feels...you don't need me to tell you that, though, do you, brother Balidor? Even collared, I could come right now...I really could..." He slid into me deeper, closing his eyes longer than a blink. "You sure you're fucking her often enough, though, brother? She's awfully tight..."

That time, Balidor didn't answer.

I tried not to think about the seers on the other side of the organic wall.

Or my brother.

Just then, Tenzi rushed him.

He and Illeg closed the last yards while Revik's eyes were half-lidded over me. Revik still held my throat, but his fingers had loosened, resting at the base of my neck. He probably still could have crushed my windpipe, but instead he laughed when he saw them coming.

The next thing I knew, they'd hit and dragged him off of me.

I rolled under them and away, looking back even as I tugged up my pants. By then, Illeg and Tenzi were tagging him with the electric rods. I was on my feet and gripping the string ties of my pants before I knew how I'd gotten there, and then I was backing off, standing outside the painted circle on the floor. A part of me couldn't believe it had happened...another part couldn't believe it was over, that I was just standing there, watching them beat on him. I found myself staring, almost paralyzed as they hit him again and again, until he was pinned up against the wall, holding up a cuffed hand, protecting his head. He looked drugged now, only half-conscious. He was still laughing though, gasping as Tenzi hit him again with the metal rod.

I was still standing there, numb, when the hatch door opened behind me. I turned in time to see Balidor's face. He'd crossed most of the floor almost before I realized what he intended to do. Seeing the look in his eyes, I tried to get in between him and Revik.

"No!" I yelled, grabbing the front of his shirt. "Balidor...he's down!"

Balidor shoved me aside without looking me directly in the face. He barely paused to get me out of his path; his feet never changed course as he walked straight up to Revik. He was kicking him against the wall before I could think to do anything but yell at the others to stop him.

I watched, numb again, as Illeg and Poresh dragged him off.

Revik sat up once Balidor was off him. Pulling up his pants, he wiped the blood off his mouth with the back of a hand, smiling up at the Adhipan leader.

"Something bothering you, brother...?"

"You goddamned little prick!" Balidor snarled. He seemed too enraged to even speak clearly, to force out words. He kicked Revik again, hard, in the thigh, evan as Tenzi jerked him back. "You're out of lives, Rook," he growled, lower. "I'll see you dead if it's the last thing I do..."

Revik smiled at him again, leaning against the wall. "Temper, temper, Balidor," he said. "Remember, your girlfriend can't live without me." He winked at me, his eyes cold once more. "Isn't that right, love? Isn't that why you came to me...?"

Closing my eyes, I looked away, keeping my expression still.

"We're done in here," I said. I gave Balidor a hard look. "We're done, 'Dori. I want you and your people out of here. Now."

Balidor gave me a look that actually made me flinch.

Swallowing, I gestured a seer's shrug.

"It's over," I told him, trying to reassure him with my eyes.

It didn't work. If anything, the fury in his expression only worsened. Only when Tenzi started pulling him backwards did Balidor finally turn away. He walked out of the tank almost as quickly as he walked in, and I saw Revik smiling as he left.

"Be seeing you, brother..." Revik called, right as Balidor reached the door. "Thanks for the loan. It wasn't quite long enough though, brother...I might need to borrow her again..."

The door shut with a hollow clang, and Revik chuckled.

Biting my lip, I didn't look at him directly as I tied up my pants and pulled my shirt down over the top of them. Unable to think of a better time or way to exit, I finally just looked to Poresh and Illeg, signaling with my hand for them to leave with me.

"Come visit me anytime, wife," Revik said, smiling. "Anytime at all..."

I didn't look at him again, but walked straight for the round hatch. I managed to get outside without changing facial expression, but only just. Poresh and Illeg trailed silently behind me, locking the tank's door once we were all on the other side.

Then I found myself standing in the security chamber, facing a room full of seers...and Jon, who wouldn't look at me, at least not directly.

For a long moment, no one said anything.

Looking around at faces, I couldn't help feeling a little sick, realizing what they'd seen through that organic pane.

But it was too late to regret anything now.

I'd gotten what I wanted...more or less. Revik might not feel exactly like himself...like either of the men I remembered.

But I could feel him again. I could feel him in my light.

Seven
Beginnings

Listening to the other seer yell at me, I held my head and my tongue, watching him pace in front of the low mattress in my room. I tried to remind myself he was worried. In fact, both of the men standing in front of me were worried, upset, probably completely freaked out at what they'd just seen.

Even so, I wished Cass had been there. It would have bothered her too, but she would have listened to me at least. She would have understood why I'd done it.

More than anything though, I just wanted to be alone.

I wanted a shower. I wanted to change my clothes.

I wanted them to leave so I could collect myself back into some semblance of myself. I wanted about an hour to remember who I was, before all of this.

But they didn't leave.

Finally, after another ten minutes or so, my patience began to wear thin.

"You knew this would be ugly!" I said, breaking into one of his tirades. I looked up, meeting his gray eyes in frustration. "'Dori, we talked about this! You said yourself that this would bring out every ugly thing buried in him, that he would pull out the stops, trying to drive me away. Do whatever he could to make me hate him...'"

"I didn't expect to have to stand there and watch him *rape* you!"

I shook my head, clicking angrily as I folded my arms.

"Alyson...we heard everything. Everything you said to one another. Are you going to tell me you didn't provoke him to do this?"

I felt my cheeks grow hot.

I guess I didn't really expect them to spare my feelings around the fact that they'd all be watching, but I still felt my anger sharpen, mixed with a kind of bitter embarrassment.

It also brought to mind the last time Revik and I had been together in front of other people. That time, at his stronghold in the mountains, he hadn't wanted any of the other seers to even see me naked. It had still been embarrassing. It still had been very un-Revik, at least in terms of the man I'd known before all this...exhibitionist and possessive and almost a test in a way, as if he'd been worried I'd want the others if he opened that door. But he hadn't been trying to humiliate me, or to hurt me. He'd been loving and half out of his head with desire, and by the end he'd been so soft, it was almost –

"You let it happen, Allie!" Balidor burst out. "You walked right into it!"

"Yeah," I said tiredly, looking up at him. "I guess I did. Can we move on, please?"

"Why, Al?" Jon spoke up from the door.

I turned, meeting his gaze.

He'd said a lot less than the other man, but he looked greener than most of the seers when I walked out of the tank. He still looked upset. Almost like a pain lived somewhere in his abdomen, and he couldn't quite push it down.

Even so, his voice was calm, and it was a real question.

Sighing, I ran my fingers through my hair, shaking my head.

"I know you won't understand this," I said. "But I needed to."

"You *needed* to?" Balidor said. "For what possible reason?"

Glancing at him, I realized he'd been listening as intently as Jon for my answer. Hurt blazed at me from his eyes, but beyond that I saw fury. A kind of helpless, undirected fury that seemed to leak out the edges of his light.

"I needed him to let me in," I said patiently. "Sex is as good of a way as any. It's better than most, actually."

"That was *sex*, now?" Balidor said.

"It was close enough," I said, giving him a warning look. "It worked, okay? And it could have been worse. For a minute there, I really thought he was just going to beat me up. That might have worked, too, but I have my doubts..."

"So you're going back in there," Jon said neutrally. "Today, I mean."

Sighing, I looked up at him, vaguely pleading him with my eyes.

"Yeah, Jon. I am."

"Absolutely not!" Balidor said angrily. "Not after that! You can't just go in there, as if he didn't just *do* that thing to you..."

I turned to Balidor, holding his gaze as calmly as I could.

"'Dori, I can. Everything I did in there will have been a complete waste of my time if I don't. I don't know how long the connection will last..." Looking away from his expression, I clicked to myself again, tugging ruefully at the torn green shirt I still wore. "...I only came out of there to clean myself up. I'm going back in within the next two hours."

There was another silence, this one fuller.

In it, I could feel the two of them looking at one another, silently communicating with their eyes. I didn't bother to try to decipher what their collective verdict was of what I'd said. Looking up when I felt it finish passing between them, I motioned towards the door.

"A little privacy, please." I added politely, "...If you don't mind."

Jon only hesitated for an instant. Nodding, he took his weight off the door, and rested his fingers on the long handle. Pausing as he opened it, he glanced at Balidor.

"'Dori?" he said. "You coming?"

His voice held the faintest trace of warning.

The Adhipan leader looked at me for a moment longer, his gray eyes hard.

"If he rapes you again, Allie..."

"He won't," I said, shaking my head. "He won't get the chance. Not for a good long while, anyway...so don't worry about it."

"I'll beat him until he can't walk," Balidor said, his voice an open threat. "Whether you authorize it or not. I've half a mind to do it anyway, as soon as you've finished with him today...or maybe just let one of the Wvercians have at him..."

I lifted an eyebrow, but otherwise didn't let my reaction reach my face.

"'Dori," I said quietly. "It wouldn't help."

"It would help *me*."

"Well, it's childish," I said. "And anyway, it's probably what he wants."

For a long moment, the Adhipan leader only looked at me. Then, his eyes still holding that roiling anger, he bowed to me curtly and turned, leaving out the door in front of Jon.

Before he followed, Jon gave me a weak smile.

"Hope you know what you're doing, sis," he said.

I met his gaze, and for the first time, I fought a tightening of my throat that swiftly wanted to turn into something else.

But I wasn't going to let them see me break down. It wouldn't help anything...in fact, it would only confirm to them that I needed to stop this, or move slower, whatever. It had been hard enough to keep my composure in front of Revik afterwards, but I'd managed it.

Remembering his words as I walked out, I shook my head, almost to myself.

"Allie."

I looked up. I'd almost forgotten Jon was there.

"Allie," he said. "Just be careful, okay?"

I gave a humorless laugh. "Believe it or not, I'm trying to be careful, Jon. I don't actually want to die, despite what everyone here seems to think..."

"I don't just mean with Revik. At least not like that."

I gave him a sharper look. "Then what?"

"You were there, too, is all." Hesitating, he studied my eyes. "I know you think you had to do what you did, going after him...after the Sword, I mean. But it scares me a little, that you were *able* to do that, Allie."

"That I was able to do what?" I said, feeling my voice tense.

"What Revik said. He's right in a way. I totally get why you did it, I mean that...but you really yanked him around." He swallowed, gesturing at me a little lamely. "You pretended to be his *wife*, Al. You pretended to be his friend...and you made friends with of all of his people. More than that...you pretended to be his *partner*. I honestly think that means as much to him as the marriage...maybe more in some ways. He's always had to do all of this stuff alone. The idea of the two of you, working together...that was huge for him, Al. Then he finds out it was all a lie, that you were infiltrating him..."

At something he saw in my face, Jon left off.

Clearing his throat, he averted his gaze, shrugging.

"I just mean...he trusted you. You probably really hurt him, breaking his trust like that. Maybe more than you realize."

I felt my jaw harden.

I couldn't think of a good reply, though. The same thoughts had gone through my head, more than once...even before I knew what Voi Pai had done. I knew what I'd done was beyond the pale on some level. But I also knew that I'd probably do it again.

"So you think it was wrong, what I did?" I said.

"I didn't say that." Jon's voice held a thread of frustration. "I'm just saying...be careful. You and Revik...you share light. I guess I'm just wondering if maybe the Dreng are affecting you, too. Maybe more than you realize.

You used to care about means, Al...not just ends. You didn't have such an 'anything goes' approach to the people you love..."

I looked up, meeting his serious gaze. After throwing around things I could have said in response, I finally just sighed, running my fingers through my hair.

"I know," I said.

"You do?"

"Yeah." I looked at him. "I've known for awhile. I felt it...even in DC."

The surprise in his eyes turned to bewilderment.

"Have you told anyone?" he said.

Giving a short laugh, I threw up my hands. "Because I need more people telling me I should kill him. Deciding both of us need to die...as agents of the Dreng."

Jon flinched, but I saw him nod a moment later, as if thinking.

"Yeah," he said finally.

"I'll be careful, Jon," I said. "Right now, that's about all I can promise. Getting Revik well is the only thing that's going to help either one of us. And as for the other stuff...the stuff I did to him..." I hesitated again, gazing at the wall of my room without seeing it.

"...I'm trying to fix it. Some of it, anyway...the stuff I can fix..."

"Allie, I know you are." His voice sounded apologetic, almost pained. "I know you're trying. This isn't a lecture...I'm not trying to give you grief, I swear. I'm *worried* about you. Even what you did in there, today. On one level, he abused you...on another, you totally manipulated him. I'm not sure which one bothers me more, honestly..."

"Do the others know?" I heard the sharpness in my voice.

He shrugged. "I don't know. Obviously Vash and Tarsi know something, but I suspect that's not who you mean. Balidor knew what you did today. It's the reason he's so pissed, I think. He's scared you're going dark, Al...or I think he is. He's probably not the only one. You've gotten so...I don't know..."

"Yeah," I said. "I get it."

I didn't really want to know how he would have finished that sentence.

"So maybe tone it down a little," Jon said. "At least around Balidor. The guy's paranoid enough...especially about you and Revik." His voice turned joking, but there wasn't much real humor in it. "You don't want him shooting you again, Allie. Not for real."

Giving a half-smile, I nodded, still staring at the floor. After another pause that was longer than it should have been, I met his gaze.

"I'll be more careful," I said. "I promise I will, Jon...but I really need to be alone right now. I need to, you know...regroup. Take a shower."

He flushed a little. His eyes flickered down my body seemingly against his will.

"Yeah," he said. "Okay. Sure." He stepped through the door, and started to close it behind him, when he hesitated again, his voice low.

"Are you *sure* you're okay, Al?" he said.

I nodded, forcing myself to smile. "I'll be all right, Jon. When all this is done, everything will be fine. No more scary Dreng sister...promise."

He nodded, smiling back wanly, but his eyes remained unconvinced.

Still, he shut the door, which at that point was all I really wanted.

Once he had, every muscle in my body abruptly unclenched.

I rested my forehead in my hands, letting myself just breathe for a moment, to try and think past everything Balidor had said, and Jon...and everything that had happened in the tank less than an hour earlier. Once I'd pushed past the details of all of those things, I found that one thought kept wanting to repeat in my head, like some kind of mantra.

I didn't have much time.

I don't know how I knew it, but I did. I couldn't afford to wait a single day.

I'd just have to get better at holding it together around the rest of them. That included Revik and Jon and Balidor and whoever else might be watching. I had to get through this, or neither one of us would survive it. I'd kill us both if I had to, to keep us from the Dreng, but it wasn't a thought that exactly filled me with joy.

So I only nodded to myself, wiping my cheek absently with one hand.

"*Never fire and back to earth...*" I muttered, glancing up at the curved stone walls. "*...Some days I submit, some I won't...*"

For a long moment, I only sat there, staring at the bathroom door.

Just like the first time, I didn't look at him as I walked in.

Just like the first time, I felt him watching me, his eyes following my movements minutely as I crossed the floor of the green-walled tank.

He didn't talk.

I wasn't sure if his silence was because he'd decided to try something different with me...or if he was surprised I'd come back at all so soon. In any case, the quiet only lasted until I'd arranged myself once more on the blanket and prayer mat pallet.

"Hungry again then, pet?" he said.

Not looking up, I flattened the blanket around my feet.

"You're walking a little stiffly there, love," he said. "I didn't break anything, did I?"

Moving the longer cushion closer behind me, I sat on it, folding my legs. Reaching into the bag next to me, I pulled out the water bottle and took a long drink.

I heard his smile, the harder note woven underneath.

"You're not mad at me, are you, wife? You used to like it rough..."

He waited. I felt his eyes on my face, watching me.

"...Maybe next time I'll make you talk to me," he said, his voice growing softer, more cajoling again. "...Make sure I'm getting it right. I have to admit, it drives me crazy when you do that...I'm getting a little turned on just thinking about it..."

My mind pretty much just blocked his words out as I tried to focus on how to even start this next part. It occurred to me, as I did, that I hadn't done anything remotely like this in months, even years...not since I'd been on the ship with Revik, hunting for the man I'd thought was responsible for killing my mother. Later, I'd worked with Maygar and Vash to find Galaith, but that had been more of a coordinated, team effort.

I hadn't done it alone in a very long time.

Vash and I had talked about a strategy, of course.

He'd told me a lot, actually, answering just about any question I had, at least those he could. He told me what he knew about Revik's past and even gave me a fair bit of detail about the first and second splits they'd made in his light. He hadn't known as much about the specifics of his time with Menlim, not other than the bits and pieces they'd pulled out of the scans they'd done of his light following his capture. Despite how detailed those scans were, they didn't pick up much on his earliest years.

Vash assumed those memories were buried deeper...and possibly protected through a number of mechanisms in Revik's own mind.

We talked most about the splitting process itself.

I found myself replaying parts of that conversation in my head.

"...It was very crude, that first split we did of your mate, Alyson," Vash had said, looking at me from where he leaned against a virtual tree in the Barrier space he'd created for us.

His voice had been somber, almost sad.

For most of those talks, we sat in a Barrier field that seemed to replicate some locale in the high plains of Asia. Wherever it was, a real place of some kind, or a composite of several places, it felt almost familiar. Tall grasses waved across a bowl-like valley, dotted with trees and resting below a pale sun in a high, deep dome of sky. Drawing in the air with his fingers, Vash showed me a faint outline of an aleimic body that I recognized as Revik's.

Swallowing a little, I looked at the structures over his head.

"He's really got all of those again?" I said.

"Yes," Vash said. "You saw him use them, at least some of them, in Brazil."

"Yeah." I waved off my own comment. "I know. I just...you know. It's kind of unbelievable. I remember seeing them on the boy. They seemed almost unreal..."

"Your light could look the same one day, Alyson," Vash said, smiling at me. "Your mate has already structured it quite a lot...perhaps more than you realize."

I made a dismissive gesture to that, too.

"So you were saying," I prompted. "About the split...what you did to him the first time?"

"Yes." The old seer's smile faded. "It was quite crude, as I mentioned. Most of this was lack of knowledge on our parts...and perhaps too much haste, in that we were concerned with how long we would be able to successfully hold him captive. This was before collars were anywhere near as prevalent or effective as they are now, Alyson..." he added.

"So?" I said, staring at the model of Revik's aleimic body. "How did you do it?"

Vash clicked a little to himself.

"I am somewhat embarrassed to admit that we did the Barrier equivalent of taking a hack saw to him, Alyson. We essentially cut out every structure we could find that he used for performing the telekinesis. In effect, that also removed any memories associated with those same structures. But a wide gap remained, in terms of his memory and his actual abilities..."

Sighing a little with another set of low clicks, he explained apologetically, "It was the first time I had ever been involved in an operation of that kind, and there were concerns that it would kill him. We tried to be...restrained. And yet, we likely took far too much of him and far too little, if you get my meaning..."

I watched him replicate the process on the model that hung in the air between us under the shade of the Barrier tree. A thin line of bright gold light formed an incision towards the lower part of his aleimic structures.

I watched as that incision widened, systematically selecting and removing pieces of a number of the rotating geometries that spiraled above his head.

"...The second time, we tried to be more precise," he added, showing me the areas of his light that were honed under his time with Galaith and the Pyramid, working for the Rooks. Vash pointed at some of the darker structures.

"You see, here?" he said gently. "These broken parts of his light...the missing parts...most of these were put there by Menlim, too..."

I found myself following his train of thought.

"...So he was vulnerable to them," I said. "Before he got to Germany, and worked for Galaith...he already had the resonance in his light."

"Quite a bit of it, yes," Vash said. "More than we should have left there. If we'd known more about what we were doing, we may not have made that mistake."

"Is that why he had to go to those caves following the second split?" I said. "He told me he had years of light restructuring...that even after he was separated out from the Dreng, and his memories changed, he spent a long time working on his light."

"Indeed. That is exactly why. We did not wish to leave the same open door available to the Dreng. It was an attempt to rectify that original mistake, as it was clear they would try and bring him over to their side again..."

Vash conjured a new image, this time of an underground series of caves. I saw Revik sitting cross-legged on a mat, his hands on his thighs as he listened to someone...or something. He looked tired, thin, worn out. But the expression on his face had a kind of peace to it.

"...We were very afraid of killing him at that point, Allie," Vash added. "Or of taking so much of him that too little of the man remained. His time with Galaith spanned almost as many years as his time with Menlim. Together, his periods with the Dreng have taken up more than half of his life." Vash clicked softly, a lulling sound when it came from his lips.

"...He is strong, Allie. Most seers would have died with what he's been through, in either one of those lives. It is what gives me hope that this plan of yours might work."

"Why him?" I said, before I'd thought about it. "Why did you send *him* on that mission with Galaith...why did you have him become a friggin' *Nazi*? Couldn't you have assigned someone else to infiltrate the Rooks, given his past?"

I fought to keep the anger and accusation out of my words, but didn't succeed.

"...Putting Syrimne into that kind of danger again, when you knew who he was...what he'd been through. You had to have known it was a risk, even without knowing you'd left the door wide open to them. Hell, even just throwing him in with the Nazis would have screwed with his head, given that Menlim raised him in Germany..."

Vash's smile grew heartbreaking.

"He volunteered, Alyson." His voice was almost soft. "I could not refuse him. It is a mistake I will never stop regretting...never."

Closing my eyes, I shook my head, taking a deep breath.

Focusing back on the room where I sat now, I tried not to think about what had already been done to the mind of the man in front of me. Neither Vash nor Tarsi vocalized it outright, but I knew that was the biggest risk. Revik simply might not be able to handle having any more surgeries done to his light...even the relatively non-invasive kind.

When I closed my eyes the second time, I half-expected him to say something else, to try to break my concentration.

But he didn't. My last glimpse of him was a wary stare from the far wall, his arms crossed and resting on his propped up knees in front of his chest. But the image didn't stay with me for long.

Instead, I found myself immersed almost immediately in black clouds.

But that didn't last long, either. After all, this time, I knew who I was hunting.

And I knew exactly where he was.

...Light explodes into flickering shadows and bursts of brilliance as I find myself thrown into a movement of arms and legs and hands...

Beginnings live here, and the beginning is light.

So very, very light...

The lightness brings relief, an inhaled breath that nearly catches in my unseen throat...too light for me to take in. It has been so long since I felt so light myself. I find myself thinking of people, places, memories...things I haven't thought of in so long...

Revik laughing up at me from a blanket spread beside a river, horses tearing at grass from where they're tethered nearby...laughing harder as I show him the ridiculous jazz routine I did for one of my dance classes in college, until he is nearly crying, begging me to show him another...

My father grinning before the room-sized model of the planets and the stars...spinning them around on their brass rails, so that they sing to us...

My mother and Cass and me at the beach, wearing our bathing suits and sunglasses with the big rubber noses...giggling uncontrollably when someone asks us for the time...

Jon and I climbing rocks at Big Sur, singing at the top of our lungs...

This feels like all those memories, but it is lighter still.

So light I can barely stand how good it feels. I want to run and jump and climb and laugh...I want to be with him here, but I don't know how to be in such a breathless place...

He is happy here...so happy...

The thoughts cascade to me, a child's thoughts, settling like a butterfly's feet only to whisk away at the first whisper of wind, the first new smell, the first high-cheekboned face.

A woman with black hair and clear eyes. She smiles at him, and the love in her eyes makes it hard to breathe...fights to break my heart. I hurt for him, but he takes it in, and it washes over his small form, leaving him lighter than before. Even when she scolds him, I see that love there, shining at him, her light encasing his in warm, gentle tendrils that reach through every structure around his body. He rests there, without needing it explained, without questioning it or distrusting it or worrying about its permanence or when it might go away...

Another form stands in the doorway.

A simple thought enters his mind, and then his hands are outstretched, grasping at air.

"Up!" he exclaims. "Please up!"

I feel a dizzying thrill as larger, male hands grasp his middle, throwing him up in the air, making him gasp and choke with laughter.

"Again!" he shrieks, and I find myself watching him half-incredulously with the man, pulling my light apart from his to look around their three-roomed, tile-roofed home with the long, horizontal windows. The floors are wooden and clean. Thick rugs cover the polished planks, along with hand-painted, wooden furniture and the threshold of a stone fireplace, wide and smoke-blackened, so used for cooking and not simply warmth.

It reminds me of that other place, too, where we were married, and I wonder if that was deliberate...or simply the fragments of some repressed memory that fought its way to the surface, trying to be shared.

The woman smiles from that smoke-blackened hearth, watching as the man tosses the boy again, and her eyes are clear, slanted at the edges, almost entirely colorless. I stare at those eyes, still trying to get my footing in this new place, when the boy's feet return to the floor, and he runs from the room at top speed, darting through the open door and towards a sound it takes me a moment to identify.

Hoof beats. Horses, and they are coming closer, moving at a steady walk.

I am outside with him then, and a larger girl holds him back, grasping his shoulder in insistent fingers. She smacks his head a little when he squirms, whispering in his ear, and he laughs, butting into her with his back and head and feet.

She stands two heads taller than him, and she has the same colorless eyes, but her face is rounder, more like her mother's. It is a strong face, almost Asian, but with that same odd mixture that always made it so difficult to pinpoint her brother's exact ethnicity.

They watch the riders approach together.

His eyes are excited, and focus only on the horses.

Hers are worried, I notice, almost somber as she stares at the riders.

Older seers sit on the backs of tough-looking beasts who blow through their noses from the long, steep climb to the little wooden house. Four of those scruffy horses stand there, with four riders. The newcomers wear monk's robes, a pale amber color, and one the color of sand, and they are looking at the boy with great interest, smiling at him, speaking to him in a tongue that is like his, but so different he can barely make out their words.

They speak to him in his mind also, and there he understands them.

Syrimne d'Gaos...we honor you...most Illustrious Sword...we bring you blessings from the lower heights, most beloved intermediary...

Their words make him laugh.

They also make him hide behind the skirt of his sister, whose sun-browned face wrinkles in a frown. She grips his tanned arm in strong fingers, pushing him further behind her, away from the curious eyes of the monks.

"Go away from here!" she yells, motioning with her other arm in seer sign language. "He is not your holy man! He is a boy who still eats grass and snails!"

The boy laughs hysterically at this, still holding her shirt.

Grass and snails!

Elashi, his sister, is always funny.

His parents, who come to the door, are somber, though, and do not laugh at her words. They bow to the monks as the latter dismount from their horses and they shush Elashi, who is still complaining that they are messing up the stone footpath she mended only the day before.

Elashi is upset. The boy feels in her light that it isn't all about the stones. She wants to take him from there, away from the monks. She doesn't like them.

He grips her clothes tighter, trying to warm her with his own light, to reassure her.

He can barely tear his eyes off their horses, though. The black one blows out air from its nostrils, staring back at him with one large, liquid brown eye.

He looks up at his mother, then his father. He tries to understand the fear he sees in his father's face, the somber look as he listens to the monks speak in their odd tongues. His father's face is long and straight, with the angularity I know from his son's adult face, the same narrow mouth, and the broad-shouldered height and athletic frame. There is an easiness in those angles of his face, however, wind-worn and set differently with dark blue eyes that seem to be forever scanning the horizon. I see his arms and realize they are Revik's arms, just as the woman's eyes and smile and thick black hair are Revik's, too.

Something in the simplicity of their biological sameness clutches at my heart.

They leave gifts, these newcomers. Scrolls and fine fabrics, loops and coils of what look like organic chains, an urele, a tool I'd only seen once before, which Terian claimed had once belonged to Revik...and could even be this exact urele, from so many years before. Long, crystal wands cut in elaborate patterns, urele had been used for training young seers.

The monks give his father a rich-looking tapestry, bearing the symbol of the sword and sun. They give his mother and sister delicacies to eat and money from the people in the land from which they have come.

They praise him, again and again, and tell him they had seen him come, from very far away. They say they will be back soon, with even more riches.

After a time, the monks ride off.

The boy watches the black horse walk back down the slope, and wishes it was his.

Since the strange men seem to like him so much, he wonders if they will bring him a horse next time, if he asks. He wishes he thought to ask before they left.

When he asks his father though, his father doesn't answer.

No one speaks of the mysterious horsemen again, not at dinner, nor at breakfast the next morning...but the boy hears the adults talking, using the hand language and the longer words, that other dialect they think he does not know.

More will come, he hears his father say to his mother. *More now, that they know of him.*

She shrugs with one hand.

She hides it better, but her eyes reflect the same fear.

"It is too late, husband," she says, in that other tongue. She stares ruefully at the collection of gifts. Her pale eyes hold no attachment to anything in that pile of rich items sitting on the floor by their kitchen table. She looks at it almost like it crawled into their home and died there, and now she is stuck dealing with the corpse.

The boy watches her, puzzled. But he does not want them to notice him, so he doesn't ask.

"We could move," his father answers her, in the same tongue.

She shakes her head, her eyes holding a whisper of sadness.

They would only come again, she says.

His father sees him then, and pings her light. The two of them turn, and the boy watches them stare at him, thoughtful looks on their unusually serious faces. The boy is not made nervous by this...there is no fear. But something in those looks brings him into his mother's lap for a hug, right before he lets his weight fall into the cradle of her arms. Touching her hand, he plays absently with a silver ring she wears around her thumb.

"Go outside now," she says gently. "Go on, Nenzi...find your sister..."

Sliding off her legs, he pauses only to kiss her cheek and press his against it. Then he scrambles for the door outside.

As he hits the sunlight, something jerks me, and I fall...

Until I am lying on a thin pallet on an organic floor, fighting to breathe.

Tears run down my cheeks. I am choking, gasping for air, but I am still in the Barrier, still surrounded by sounds and that bright, blinding light, and I hear Vash's gentle voice, talking to me somewhere behind the shadows...

Go back, Allie, he urged. *Go back now...see it all, while you can...*

Before I make up my mind to obey his soft words...

I am already there.

Light erupts behind my eyes.

Blue sky. Tearing into the space above me.

It shifts, tilts...

The shadow morphs in wind over a broken world, tearing holes in the light, drifting deeper into the sun. Everything is jerking, moving wrongly...

The world spins too fast.

I am sick from it. I can't breathe. It is like a weight sits on my ribs, crushing me slowly.

I see trees around me. Grass on the ground, along with moss and ferns. It is green, so green everything washes into breathing soil and plants, water in quivering beads dotting every frond. Towering white clouds fill a distant horizon, visible through the tree-line to the valley below. The earth smells rich and mulchy, drenched in mold and mushrooms, dotted with moss-covered rocks and the water-soaked trunks of trees sprouting ferns like sharp green beards.

There is screaming.

Screaming fills the clearing, but not loud enough to cover a woman's agonized grunts, as if something is being torn from her, ripped from her insides.

It goes on and on. There is no end to it. He is lost there, in that moment that will not end, but they hold him off. He screams and screams, fighting to be free while the animals laugh...

And then, when there is no breath left, no time, no wind, no blue sky or winging birds...

It is silent.

Not a sound touches me, nothing but breath reaches me from the being sitting on the ground. He breathes hard, concentrating on each in and out breath. There are no words, no thoughts, no feelings. A blank slate rests there, holding his hands to her chest.

But the blood is cool now.

It is cool.

The world tilts faster still, bringing a gradual darkening, and alien sounds from the trees. The rain starts, but the boy doesn't notice. The monsoon season is only a few weeks away...but for now, it brings only spurts of thunder and rain, the threat of more to come. The rain drenches his hair, his clothes...and the woman...forcing him to blink and cough as he holds on.

He is alone.

He watches the water as it pools in the hollow at the base of her neck, pools at the corners of her eyes, in the dimples by her mouth and in her clothing. The rain washes her skin, washes her dress and hair and lips, but his hands remain on the front of her embroidered apron, feeling for a heartbeat in stiffening, hardening flesh.

The clearing lay in darkness but for a few lights swinging in a half-ring, obscuring shadowy forms. The sun has already disappeared. I don't remember it leaving and the rain hasn't stopped, but it has grown colder. I try to move...

And a shout rings out.

He is found. Someone sees him there, with the woman. They call to other someones, holding a lantern higher to illuminate a bearded face. Other bodies lay on the ground beside the boy, but it is to the woman that he clings. She is the one whose clothes he put back on, who he washed.

The others...

He looks at his sister's wide face, the boots of his father.

But they aren't real either, broken dolls.

He can pretend. He can look at them, not see them.

With the woman it is different...

Look away, Nenzi-la, she whispers. *Don't watch. Don't watch, my love...*

They hurt her. He doesn't understand what they are doing, but they hurt her, like animals. They rip at her, tear at her clothes, laughing. He sees her eyes understand, knows she is reading them, but they don't seem to read her, or understand the anguish in her high-cheekboned face.

He is screaming. He doesn't know this then.

He is screaming, and his father's boots already lay inert on the soil, and the animals, the beings with dense, cloudy light, with nothing but blank eyes and hungry mouths, they look at him, and they laugh again.

In the silence, he can pretend.

He can wait for them to return.

But now...the silence is invaded.

It's dark now and he's alone, lights swinging in the wind through the tunneling tress...and there's only one being left to rip and tear and laugh at. He doesn't run though, or let go of the woman lying in the rain-soaked ground still covered in boot-prints from the last set of trampling feet. He doesn't move, still kneeling at her side as the new danger comes to him in his clearing...for it is his clearing, now.

He watches them, trembling, knowing only that he won't run away. He won't...

He is sure it will be more of the animals, more creatures come to pick the bones dry. He is deathly sure it will be them...so when the tall, gaunt seer with the skull-like face appears out of the dark, a feeling that is almost joy floods his heart.

He begins to cry.

One of his people has found him. They will help him. They will bring her back.

They will find his father...

But the thought dies there, with nowhere to go.

He doesn't look at the boots that face him from the ground nearby, the man's crumpled body in the mud. He doesn't look at the girl lying beside him.

The aged seer walks over to him, his long face grave. It is not an angular face, like his father's, but one almost devoid of flesh entirely, with a small, strangely thin nose.

The boy sees the animals who are with him, but the seer is their master and he is the one who has come for the boy.

The seer whispers in his mind, a careful caress.

I am so sorry, nephew.

And now he knows that the old seer can't bring her back. He can't find his father. He can't reverse anything that happened all those hours below.

Elashi.

The name burns in his throat.

The boy can't answer the old seer. He tries. He fights to remember his voice, to pretend that none of this is real. His words come out in choked attempts at air.

The old seer speaks to him again, before he can make his voice work.

Where is your other family, my son? Are they near?

The boy is confused. He gestures a thank you to the seer, but it is not for his words.

He has no place to go. There is no one.

The thought is debilitating. Too foreign to be real.

I am so sorry for this terrible thing that you have suffered...so sorry, my son...

The boy tries again to speak to the tall seer with the skull-like face, fighting for words, even in his mind, using hand-language when he can't speak past the clouds in his mouth.

The seer seems to understand. His long fingers stroke the small, black head, tightening briefly on his narrow shoulders.

We will bury them, he whispers softly. *We will bury them together...*

The boy can't breathe.

He can't breathe.

But he can gesture yes.

At the tall seer's prompting, he reluctantly releases the woman's dress, clutching her silver ring in one hand as he moves his feet to follow...

I broke out, sweating.

The room felt deathly silent.

The floor under the pallet hurt my back; my muscles felt cramped into knots. There was no gentle transition, no period where I was half in and half out, floating in the ocean of light with Vash and Tarsi...or even with him.

The tank felt dead inside. Cold.

I still saw Menlim's skull-like face behind my eyes, those cold, urine-colored eyes. I knew now, that he didn't look as much like Salinse as Revik had told me.

I heard my own breaths, but they didn't penetrate that silence. It only deepened around me as I stared up in the dark. Aloneness trembled my light, a feeling of being lost...so profound I couldn't see past it. I wanted to cry. But whatever I felt couldn't come out through tears, or even through screaming. I felt sick enough that I broke out into a sweat and fought to breathe for a full minute, sure I would throw up if I tried to move.

My hand clenched the front of the cotton shirt I wore, sweated into a fist, nearly white-knuckled. I lay there, staring at the ceiling, feeling the nausea coil through my body, tightening my lungs, making my bowels loose.

That some of this was cold, naked fear only reached me afterwards.

It was more fear than I'd ever felt in my life, even when I'd been captured by Terian. Even when I thought he'd killed me. It was more fear than my body could handle.

Immobilized, I tried to move through it some way, to let it pass, even as it seemed to be crushing my chest.

I remembered this...tastes of it anyway.

I remembered the intensity of feeling from when I'd been in the cave with Tarsi. The same influx of emotion met me nearly every time we followed the boy's footsteps through that broken trail of memory. Tarsi had me study Syrimne, before I knew who Revik really was. I remembered the familiarity there, the lost feeling. I remembered wondering how any one person could feel so much, without going insane.

I knew now, how that was possible. The very thing that made him so happy as a kid had been the thing to destroy him afterwards. I'd loved my human parents...a lot. I know they loved me, and that Jon loved me...and Cass. But they'd never been capable of being as open and loving to me as Revik's family had been for him.

He'd been open in a way no human being could even comprehend.

Of course, I realized now that Tarsi had shielded me from that, too.

She'd protected me from the worst of it, probably to keep me going as we studied his past. It wasn't until after everything happened in DC that I realized the true purpose of her little exercise. She'd been introducing me to my mate.

After another long collection of minutes, I realized I felt him, too.

I heard him breathing.

I thought I imagined it at first, that it was some echo in my mind, some remnant from the place I'd just left, or even my own body's labored attempts to regain equilibrium.

Then I heard him in it. I heard his voice. He spoke through his attempts to breathe, as if reciting prayers, or repeating the same snatch of song lyric over and over...like I'd heard him do earlier that day.

This was different. Rather than some exercise in whistling in the dark, he was choking for air, as if fighting each breath past a thick weight sitting on his chest.

Realizing it wasn't coming from the Barrier, I turned my head.

He lay half on his side, his legs coiled in a strange crescent shape, close by his body, his arm over his abdomen. Still choking and breathing, he whispered more words while I watched, as if unable to keep them from spilling through his lips. He didn't look at me for a long time. He lay there, sweating, his eyes staring blankly ahead when they weren't closed.

He muttered quietly, reassuringly, as if talking to himself.

Then, all at once, he felt my stare.

His eyes shifted, meeting mine from the other side of the room.

The look on his face shocked me, bringing my heart to my throat.

"Revik." I couldn't find words to follow. An image of the boy slid forward into my mind and I had to fight not to burst into tears. "Revik...are you all right?"

"Stop..." he said. "Allie...please stop."

I continued to stare at him, fighting what I saw, what I heard in his voice. It crossed my mind that it was a trick, that he was imitating me where I lay on the blanket, but his voice was barely a murmur.

"Please," he repeated. "Stop this, Allie...please..."

"I can't," I said, almost helplessly, still lost in his clear eyes. I'd never seen so much emotion in his eyes. Never, not since I'd known him.

"Yes, you can...please...please, Allie...I'll do anything..."

His voice pleaded with me, pulling at me through the bond.

Tears came to my eyes, feeling him there, too, in my light. I couldn't stop them before they nearly blinded me.

"I can't. I'm sorry, Revik..."

"Allie...I'm sorry...I'm sorry for what I did to you..."

"That's not why. I'm not trying to hurt you."

"Please...gods, please...don't do this to me..." His voice broke. "What did I do to make you hate me so much? What was it, Allie?"

I found myself unable to look away from his pale face, at the look of anguish there, but more than that, fear...more fear than I'd ever seen in anyone's face, much less his. He looked lost in it, his eyes nearly wide in his narrow face, his chest still laboring for breaths. His hair looked sweated to his head; his fingers clutched his shirt in the same place I'd clutched mine, as if trying to crush his own heart, to keep it inside his chest.

"Was it DC?" he said. "Have you hated me since then?"

"I don't hate you, baby...I don't...I swear I don't...I'm trying to help you..."

He closed his eyes, shaking his head as if to push my words away from him.

Then I felt the other thing.

His grief expanded over me, bringing a low cry from his throat.

"Allie..."

A sob broke out of him, so young-sounding I flinched.

I continued to watch him, helpless, as he choked on another cry. He was talking again, murmuring words in a litany I'd never heard, that sounded foreign to my ears, even more than his singing had earlier. It struck me suddenly that they were prayers.

I'd never seen him pray before, although he'd hinted around to being religious, and I knew from Balidor that Syrimne left coded messages and spoke in scripture during the war.

I watched as his whole body wracked in another heavy sob. He looked like someone had just gauged his heart out of his chest and stabbed it over and over again.

I didn't want to look at him anymore.

I didn't, but I couldn't look away.

And somewhere in all that, I understood. Really understood. Vash and Tarsi weren't going to 'fix' him...not in any of the ways I'd told myself that they would, when they told me of their role. They weren't going to pour some magic Barrier juice on his head, and flush out everything horrible that had ever happened to him.

They were simply going to make him feel it.

There were going to make him face every excruciating frame. They were going to ensure that the line stayed open both ways, despite the collar. They would keep it open, emotions and all, as I looked for the source of the initial breaks in his light.

Swallowing at the look on his face, and a rising swell of guilt I couldn't think past yet, I finally tore my eyes off his. I didn't know if he understood yet or not, but I knew that if he didn't, he would soon.

In any case, I had been wrong. More wrong than I'd been about anything I'd tried to do with him, through all the mess of the past year.

I would be torturing him. Worse than anything Terian could have devised.

I was going to make him relive his own life.

Eight
New York

"WHO IS THIS?" THE VOICE REPEATED, STILL CARRYING A THREAD OF DISBELIEF. "I don't think I heard that right the first time..."

"It is Chandre, cousin Jon," the seer clicked impatiently. "...And please stop pretending that you have some form of worm-amnesia and do not remember who this is..."

"Oh, I remember my cousin Chandre, all right," Jon said, incredulity still in his voice. "I just can't believe you're calling me. Aren't you, like, one of terrorists now?"

Pushing out her lip in frustration, she clicked at him loudly through the line.

"Is Balidor there? Or not?"

"I told you, he can't come right now...he's busy."

"Fine. Then just give them the message. Tell Balidor, or someone else in the Adhipan..." She paused, barely a beat.

"...Or Allie. Tell them I have a lead on the occurrence in Hong Kong. I will do what I can to send updates, but for now I know very little. I will attempt to make contact with a new source in two days...after that, hopefully I will know more."

"Is that it?" Jon said, skeptical. "That's not much. In fact it's nothing, Chan..."

Chandre hesitated. Then she shrugged, seer fashion. If they were tapping this line, whatever she said wouldn't matter now.

"All I can tell you is that it could be a disease," she said, blunt. "Not a gas."

"A disease? What does that mean?"

Chandre ignored his question. "...Be clear with Balidor, also, that there is no doubt that they are looking for you...that at least one group is expending considerable resources..."

After a pause, Jon seemed to let it go.

"Yeah," he said, sighing. "So what else is new?"

"Well, if that is the case, I would think you would be glad I am keeping an eye on them for you," she said shortly. "...And glad as well of the information I am indirectly sharing with you, as to the inadequacy of your current security protocols..."

"What?"

Chandre sighed, clicking a little in impatience.

Then she indicated to her own person, holding out her hands, knowing her avatar would copy her visual cues if he had his VR option switched on.

"If *I* can find you, cousin..."

"Yeah, yeah," Jon said, seeming to have caught up. "Okay. I get it."

"Exactly *where* are you, cousin Jon?" she said. "...If you don't mind my asking?"

"Where?" He laughed. "You called me, remember? And yeah, I do mind you asking. Terrorist, remember? As in, last we knew, you worked for him..." He paused. "And just how *did* you know how to find us?"

"I found *you*, Jon...not 'us.'" She hesitated, but barely a beat. "...And I called the old secure line. The one from the Adhipan...the same one they used in Delhi," she lied. "They patched me to you. GPS is obscured to all but the rough area of continent, so you can tell Balidor that much is secure...but it is not a geography with which I am familiar..."

"Oh." Jon paused on this. A second later, his voice grew openly skeptical again. "You're telling me that *Balidor*, the most paranoid man in existence, didn't change that number, after you and Garensche and whoever else defected to Revik's camp?"

She bit her lip.

For humans, neither Jon nor Cass struck her as being quite as stupid as they perhaps should have been. Clicking again, more sharply that time, she told him the truth.

"It is satellite, Jon. I tracked you through your implant."

"My *what?*" he said.

"Your government chip. The one under your tattoo. I can get a basic location from that. Then I just scanned open lines in the vicinity until I found yours..."

"I don't *have* a chip, Chandre. I opted out of getting that when I was eighteen!"

She smiled. "Really? Then you tell me. What am I looking at on my screen right now?"

"How?" he demanded. "And since when?"

"Since always, little brother," she said, rolling her eyes. "You humans are so trusting. Believing everything your human government tells you, yes? Like when it says it removes an implant from your skin and replaces it with an ident tattoo, even though that implant provided them exponentially more valuable intel for their own internal security..."

She paused at the silence this produced, shrugging with one hand as she tossed the braids out of her face.

"...Most of the seers have theirs altered already, cousin. It might not have occurred to Balidor to do this for you, as well. I would look to that, if I were you...in case it occurs to one of the Sword's people." She paused again, feeling her jaw harden.

"...I would have Cass do the same," she added tersely.

"Cass isn't here," Jon said.

"Where is she?"

She felt the human's mind through the line, his reaction to the pointedness of the question.

"Forget it," she said in a clipped voice. "It does not matter...as long as she is somewhere other than where the Bridge is." After another bare pause, she added, "I would move whatever you are doing, though, cousin. In case they have already determined to track you through your implant. In any case, given the danger, it would not be wise to stay too long in one place..."

"Yeah, okay, Chan." He hesitated. "Look, about Cass..."

"I told you, it is not my concern," she said.

Before he could take another breath to respond, she added crisply,

"...Peace to you, cousin Jon. And honor to the Esteemed Bridge...as well as her mate, the Illustrious Sword."

Without waiting, she disengaged the signal.

Pulling the headset off her ear, she found she was still angry, however.

With a few key touches and a DNA scan, she erased the record of the call, replacing the log entry with a dummy call to a fellow seer in New Orleans that she had running simultaneously in the background. She matched the time signatures up exactly, using every trick she knew to make the trace signatures disappear, but still, risk remained, particularly if anyone were monitoring her communications already.

She hoped Jon spoke to Balidor as soon as the call ended.

Gazing out the window of her Maryland apartment, she stretched her arms, tilting her body sideways to get a kink out of her back.

So far, she had met with nothing but dead ends since arriving here. Of her three assignments, she had made concrete progress with only one, and that progress had not been as significant as she would have liked, given the amount of time she'd been in the United States.

One of those outstanding tasks, in particular, nagged at her.

Unfortunately, that was also the one with which she had made absolutely no headway at all.

She'd come to the United States with two initial charges.

Dehgoies wanted someone who could infiltrate the SCARB branch in DC for intelligence purposes, working their way as closely to direct White House access as possible. Her second task of course came from Balidor, and was pretty straightforward. Watch the Rebels *and* SCARB. Report back on the doings of both.

Once she'd established a stable identity with the Rebels and with SCARB, Balidor assigned her a third task. He wanted her to track down the whereabouts of an old female seer, a scientist who used to work for Galaith. All he'd had to go on were a few aliases, the seer's age, and the fact that she had strong backgrounds in both law and genetics.

What he hadn't come out and said, but what Chandre discerned from the intel he'd provided, was that somewhere, this old seer had connections to other, very powerful seers. Seers he wanted to know more about. In particular, he seemed very interested to know if she had connections to any seer colonies based out of South America.

The old seer's name was Xarethe.

Weeks after Dehgoies got custody of Feigran and Allie from the Lao Hu in China, the Sword contacted Chandre with a fourth task.

He wanted her to find evidence of a biological weapon that the Americans had developed. He had read intelligence off the schizophrenic seer, Feigran, from when he was president of the United States. During that time, he had apparently commissioned the design of a virus that killed humans while leaving exposed seers alive. The purported goal within the human defense community had been to potentially deploy this weapon against China in

Wellington's unfolding war with the East. They wanted to retain as many seer assets as they could, while taking out a significant portion of the urban population of Beijing.

Naturally, the Sword wanted her to find out where they were with the project.

Officially, he suspected it had been taken off the books...either by the CIA or its research arm when the president was assassinated. But Revik knew how such lists tended to operate. He suspected the project had merely been shifted into a different budget category, its funding buried under a paper trail of several other projects of its kind.

He also suspected the new president might not know anything about it.

"Perhaps," he'd joked with her over the VR link, "It is now labeled 'Experiment for the balancing of non-European populations to meet international livestock projections'..."

The Sword, like the Bridge, had a bit of a dark sense of humor at times.

She'd asked him if the opposite kind of virus might also be in development. Meaning one that would kill seers, leaving humans untouched.

He told her to let him know.

She had found nothing on the books, official or unofficial, regarding either type of disease. She'd pored through funding lists for the research tanks supplied with military contracts, looking for any individual or cluster of projects that might meet some portion of the description she'd been given. She used everything from keyword searches in databases with several hundred thousand projects that might be related, to actually visiting several of the labs in person and speaking with their administrators under the guise of being a SCARB investigator.

Even reading the humans, and pushing them with her light, she'd found nothing.

The closest she'd come had been in Los Alamos, New Mexico, where they showed her a family of tests they had been running to *combat* such a virus, were it ever to be developed elsewhere in the world. The paper trails and funding around those tests had been obscured under a number of different guises, mainly connecting them to vaccine projects to combat ebola and other dangerous diseases to which humans fell victim in the developing world.

Still, Chandre knew that not finding it did not mean it did not exist.

Then the Sword had been kidnapped, and not long after, the incident in Hong Kong occurred. The news feeds screamed about terrorism for a few weeks and there were memorials and paranoid rants on talk shows...but no real evidence surfaced, officially or unofficially, about whatever it was that had actually *killed* the humans. All of the connecting points in the different stories and fragments of stories kept trying to form a picture in Chandre's head, but whatever that picture was, it never came into focus.

She knew ways existed to bury such a thing, by splitting it up into enough components and giving each component a long, boring-sounding and obscure name that no one would tie to the actual intent. Still, at least one person would have to be on point for assembling those components, and ensuring that they, together, produced the desired results.

If such a thing *did* exist, Chandre would have to find that person.

Clicking softly to herself, she shouldered a leather coat over a white blouse and dark jeans, and pulled on her boots, stomping each heel individually to settle it. Grabbing a piece of toast off a plate on the kitchen counter of her two-bedroom flat, she holstered her sidearm in her shoulder harness and grabbed her keys from the hook by the door.

She opened the door, and instantly froze.

A seer stood there, holding a gun to her face.

She stared at him, unable to hide her disbelief.

Her eyes flickered to the gun only long enough to see that the safety was off, then she was looking at the seer's face again, studying his dark brown eyes.

"Hello, sister Chandre," he said. "I don't suppose you mind if I cut into your morning routine a bit?"

Chandre pursed her lips, looking him up and down, from the dark leather motorcycle jacket to the heavy boots on his feet. Then she gestured towards him hospitably.

"Brother Maygar," she said, tilting her head back towards the inside of her apartment. "If you wanted breakfast, you had only to ask..."

"Not here," he said, shaking his head. "I want you to come with me, Chan."

"Maygar," she said, impatient. "What is this about?"

"I can't tell you here. But I'm not here to harm you...I vow it, sister."

She quirked an eyebrow at the gun. "What's that all about, then?"

"Just a little insurance," he said. "Nothing personal, sister."

She gave him an impatient look. "Insurance? If I wanted you dead, I could have gone after you months ago. Sources tipped me off as to your whereabouts in New York before I even landed on U.S. soil..." Clicking at him in irritation, she added, "I am probably the only seer working for the Sword who would *not* inform him that I had received news of you. You should be grateful for that, at least..."

"I am not here to kill you, Chandre."

She folded her arms. "What a relief."

"Damn it," he snapped. "Will you just get in the car? I want to talk to you!"

"Why can we not talk here?" she said, gesturing fluidly with one hand, her eyes darting around the green lawns and white painted trim of the houses on her Maryland street. "I have food inside, if you really are hungry – "

"I'm not hungry, Chan," he said. Still, he seemed to sigh a bit in frustration, right before he holstered the gun back in his own shoulder harness.

"Look. I have something I want to show you. It won't take long," he said, looking back towards the car, motioning with one hand.

In that instant, she punched him hard, in the throat, with her fingers. When he choked, raising his hand to where she'd hit him, Chandre yanked her own gun out of its holster, flipped it in her hand, and slammed the butt into the side of his head.

Maygar crumpled on the steps of her apartment complex, dazed.

Reaching into his coat, she swiftly disarmed him, then pulled a small, metal cylinder out of her own pocket and pressed the flat end against his neck. Pushing a button on the organic syringe with her thumb, she released the entire contents into his blood.

Without waiting for the drug to take effect, she grabbed him under his thick arms. Using her hip to push the door open behind her, she dragged him back inside the red-painted door, dropping him unceremoniously once she'd cleared the arc of the door.

Walking around his body, she kicked her front door shut, locking the deadbolt after she'd done a quick scan of the windows and cars outside.

Maygar's eyelids fluttered for a few seconds before he opened them. His head lolled on his thick neck before he managed to raise it to more or less vertical.

Chandre sat across from him, perched backwards on one of her kitchen chairs as she sipped a mug of fresh coffee. After a second or two more where he seemed to be fighting to focus his eyes, he blinked at her.

She smiled at him.

Frowning, he tried to sit forward in the chair.

The bindings on his ankles and wrists stopped him. So did the organic wire she had coiled around his chest and waist.

"Would you like some coffee, brother?" she said, raising her cup.

Maygar frowned up at her again, his eyes still half-focused. He returned them to where he'd been examining his predicament with the chair.

"What the..." He squinted at her, blinking to clear his vision, his mouth still a puzzled frown. "Chan? What are you doing?"

"What am *I* doing?" She clicked at him softly, her expression hard. "You showed up on my doorstep, brother...holding a gun. You tried to abduct me. That's not very brotherly now, is it?"

"*Abduct* you?" The male seer's Prexci still came out somewhat slurred, but his disbelief sounded genuine. "Chan, *d'gaos 'le yilathre*...I'm trying to help you! Now untie me, goddamn it...my arm's starting to fall asleep..."

"Help me? By pointing a gun at my face?"

Clicking in irritation, Maygar averted his gaze, wincing a little as the hangover from the drug must have slid more to the forefront of his awareness.

Shaking his head, he said, "I didn't know how you'd react to seeing me. Last I knew, you were working for him..."

Chandre snorted into her mug. She shook her long braids then, clicking a little at his pained expression as she took another sip of the coffee.

"Well?" she said. "We have a predicament, then, yes? Because I do not like it when little baby Rooks show up at my door, brandishing pistols..."

"Rook? Me?"

He made a disbelieving noise, staring her straight in the face. She noticed his lip held more of that curling sneer of a frown she recognized. His expression reflected the belief that her remark had openly insulted him.

"This from *you*...a sister working for the head Rook himself?"

She shook her head with a laugh, taking another drink of coffee.

"Chan," he said angrily. "Just what do you think Dehgoies *is* these days? An emissary of the beings from beyond the Barrier? Some kind of good fairy, here to dispense justice and hope for all of his people? You can't possibly be that dumb..." He bit his lip then, his eyes showing a more complex flair of emotion, almost an accusation.

"...How could you leave Allie?"

Chandre stared at him, her dark red eyes clouding.

For an instant, the question angered her. She might have reminded him that he hardly treated the Bridge all that well in their last direct encounter... that he had, in essence, tried to rape her in an attempt to break up her marriage to the Sword. That he'd been involved somehow in her imprisonment under the White House, working with Terian. That he'd stood by and let Terian beat her and abuse her when she wouldn't submit to the Rook's wishes while he had her locked in that underground cage.

But even in thinking all of that, Chandre found herself turning over the question separately, thinking about it in terms of herself.

"I did not leave her," she said finally. "Not in the way that you mean. I needed some time apart from her...from her team. I thought I could better spend that time helping Dehgoies." At the other's angry tsking sound, she raised her voice. "...Who, despite the measure of truth in your words, is doing good works. You must know what he did for our people, dismantling the Registry system...freeing prisoners under the boot of Black Arrow and other slavers..."

"Dehgoies the Rook..." he muttered.

She made an impatient gesture. "I did not think that would last."

"That *what* would not last? Him being evil?"

She clicked in irritation at this, too, waving at him dismissively.

Still, she could not tell him about her dual role with Balidor. She had no idea where Maygar's own allegiances lay these days, and she hadn't yet made up her mind to leave DC, or to blow her cover with Wreg until it was absolutely necessary. For all she knew, Maygar would spill the beans to his Rook mother, intentionally or not.

Maygar frowned at her, as if trying to read past her silence.

"Chan, the guy's certifiable. How is it that I'm the only one who seems to see it?"

"You speak like a child does, Maygar," she said curtly. "And you know things are not so simple with him. He and the Bridge cannot remain separate forever. In the end, working for him is not so different from working for her. They will both go the same way eventually, either towards the light or towards the dark..."

"All the more reason to kill him," he muttered, shifting under the bindings on his arms.

"I simply have more faith in the Bridge than you appear to," she said, her voice sharp. "I have more faith in him, as well..."

"You must have more faith in him," Maygar said. "For I have none at all."

She sighed a bit, clicking, but her voice grew more patient.

"She will not let him go so easily, brother," she said.

"Yeah," he said. "Right."

"She will try to help him. To bring some of his excesses under control..."

"Until he murders her in her sleep," he grumbled under his breath. "Or forces her to join him as a puppet of the Dreng..."

But she talked over his sarcasm.

"...You must recognize that she has influence over him, at least. I thought I could work more closely with him, help him with the operations that they are in agreement on, at least in principle. I expected to be back with her in not too long a time...and I had..." She hesitated, shrugging with one hand. "...My own reasons. For needing time apart."

There was another silence.

Then Maygar snorted, inclining his head as he gestured with one bound hand.

"Yes," he said. "I heard about this, too."

"You heard about what?" Chandre said, a little shorter than she intended.

"Cass. The Bridge's human...and that Wvercian." He smiled at her, his dark brown eyes flat. "That's got to suck. I hear he's a walking throwback. Nothing like being replaced by the brawny but moronic model..."

"I do not know him," she said stiffly.

"Yeah," Maygar said. "Right." He inclined his head once more, his broad face tilted towards the window. "...Well, you should not take it personal, Chan." Readjusting his posture, he raised an eyebrow. "...You know those Wvercians just *have* to be hung like horses."

Chandre felt her fingers tighten on the back of the chair. She stared at him, biting back her fury with an effort. "I have tied you to a chair," she reminded him.

Maygar smiled. "Yes. I caught that, sister. Very tightly, too...it is a bang up job, as my American friends would say."

"I overpowered you without even trying," she said. "Like you were a Sark child...like you had no training at all whatsoever..."

"Yeah, I caught that, too." Frowning a bit, he sighed, looking down at the chains, then up at her, his brown eyes holding frustration. "Let me go, Chan. You know I didn't intend you any harm. I only wanted to show you something."

"Show me...what?"

"It's in New York."

"*What*...is in New York?"

He sighed in exasperation, clicking at her. "You are looking for a disease, right? Something that is supposed to kill off all the humans?"

Chandre's hand halted from where she'd been about to put a piece of toast to her lips. Completing the motion, she took a bite of the buttered crust, chewing it slowly before she answered him.

"How did you know that?" she said, lowering the hand to her lap.

"I was with them at the White House."

"Yes," she said. "I know this, too." Taking another bite of toast in the pause, she glanced up at him as she chewed, putting the remainder back on the plate and setting it on the table. "The Bridge said you helped them. That you held her captive."

"*Terian* held her captive. And that creepy kid..."

"But you were there?" she said. "How is that?"

"My mother."

"Your...mother?"

"Yeah," he said, giving her an uncomfortable look. "My mother. She brought me there. I didn't want to be there, believe me..." When Chan only stared at him, Maygar exhaled again in some irritation, clicking. "She pulled me out of Seertown...during the bombing. No one was watching me because of all the panic. After she helped Terian pick up Allie, she went back and found me. She took me with her to America."

"Why?"

"Why?" He gave a disbelieving laugh. "Because she's my *mother*, Chan. She knew Dehgoies would have me killed the second he got the opportunity... and she knew the Seven would only stand by and let him."

"Your mother the Rook," she reminded him.

"Yeah," he said, his face hard. "My mother the Rook."

Chan gauged his expression for a moment, gripping the back of the chair.

"So what is it, then?" she said. "What are you now, Maygar?"

He shrugged. "I'm nothing, Chan. I've been living in New York. Passing."

"And in your spare time...looking for deadly viruses that kill humans?"

"No, look...that came to me."

"Came to you how?"

"It's complicated."

"Complicated...how?" Chandre said, adding a bit of that warning back into her tone.

"I heard about what happened in Hong Kong," Maygar said. "I didn't think anything of it at first, but then I ran into a bunch of seers in New York. Underground types...you know. Work for hires, doing some of the less legal jobs for high pay..."

Chandre gave him a wry smile. "I thought most of those were ex-Rooks too, Maygar."

He gave her a surly look, clicking in irritation.

"The point is, we all got drunk together...and they let slip about their last job. They claimed they had the location of the lab where that virus was stored...that someone tried to pay them to break in and steal it. They also claimed it was the same virus used on that crowd in Hong Kong. They called it a 'demonstration' and said that their maybe 'client' told them that the disease would be deployed for real in the coming months..."

"Where?" Chandre asked, stiffening.

"I don't know, Chan." Maygar frowned at her, rolling his eyes a little.

"Did they tell you anything about this deployment? Anything at all?"

Maygar sighed. "I asked them about the deployment...if it would be water supply or something else, but they claimed they didn't know. They said it might even be somewhere in the United States, though..." Maygar frowned again, shrugging with one hand. "They were joking about it...saying I should ship out before things got ugly. They seemed to think no matter how many it killed, once it was really deployed there'd be total chaos..."

"And who hired them to steal this thing? This virus?"

He shook his head, his almond-shaped eyes slanting sideways.

"I don't know exactly."

"But you suspect?" she said, reading his light, as well as his face.

He conceded with a tilt of the same bound hand. "One of them let slip a name that I recognized."

"Which is what?"

Maygar sighed again, clicking in irritation. "I doubt you'd know her, Chan. There was this old seer my mom used to work with...or really *for*, I guess. I saw her at the White House a few times while I was there, and my mother told me that was her 'real boss'...she seemed to think of Terian as a bit of a flunky. She said that they both really worked for the old woman, whether Terian would admit it to himself or not. She seemed to think Galaith answered to her, too..."

"Old woman?" Chandre said, straightening in her chair.

"Yeah. She was like a fossil...scary, really. Face like a reptile. All of the humans were terrified of her..."

"What was her *name*, Maygar?" she said, impatient.

"She was going by some human name, impersonating the Chief Justice of the Supreme Court. They'd eliminated the real one, of course, to put her there..."

He hesitated, and she knew he was recalling it from the relevant portion of his light.

"...Novak," he affirmed, nodding. "That was it."

"Is that the name these freelancers told you of?"

"No," Maygar said. "They only knew her by her seer name."

"Which is *what*, Maygar?" she said. "The seer name?"

"The only name I ever heard my mother use was Xarethe. That was the name those black marketers mentioned. They said a seer named Xarethe hired them..."

There was a silence.

In it, Chandre looked at him, feeling her fingers curl around the wood of the plain-backed kitchen chair.

"Do you know where she is now?" Chandre said.

"Lizard lady?" he said. "No."

"What about your mother?"

He hesitated, his eyes growing more evasive.

Chandre smiled. "I will not hurt your mother, Maygar. I only wondered if I could speak with her. If she would talk to me..."

"She's in China, I think," he said finally. "Last I knew. She and that Lao Hu dragon lady are friends. You know...Voi Pai. She said they had some work for her."

"Would she speak to me, do you think? If you asked her?"

He frowned a little, looking at her. "Honestly? I doubt it."

Chandre nodded. Still watching his face intently, she took another drink of coffee, mulling over his words. Finally, curiosity leaked into her voice, almost without her willing it. "Why me, Maygar? Why did you bring this to me?"

He gave her a surprised look.

"We were friends," he said. "I thought we were anyway. I thought you might be the only one of that bunch who wouldn't shoot me on sight...and I figured the Bridge had to be interested in this..." He shrugged, his eyes turning more cold. "...Or her Rook husband, if not her. I wasn't sure which of them you were working for, honestly. I had some hope you were infiltrating him, working for her..."

Hesitating, he glanced at her, his dark eyes holding more of a predatory edge.

"Are you, Chan?"

She only laughed, rolling her eyes at him, seer-fashion.

"Well," he said, frowning. "Is it true then, Chan? Can you tell me that, at least?"

She felt her mouth tighten.

"Is what true?" she said, although she knew what he meant.

"What they say? About what she did to him?"

Chan shrugged, her eyes indifferent. "I have heard many things that she is supposed to have done with him. They cannot all be true."

"Did she really infiltrate his operation? Take it down from the inside?"

Chandre felt herself hesitate. Finally, she gestured a yes in seer sign language.

"That part appears to be true, yes."

"I don't suppose the rumors that she killed him are true?"

She rolled her eyes impatiently. "You and I both know how unlikely that is. If it were true, we'd be hearing about *her* death by now..."

"Does she have him locked up somewhere?"

Chan shrugged again, with the same hand. "Honestly, I do not know. That seems to be the prevailing theory. And the most likely of all the fictions I have heard."

"What do you suppose she's doing with him?" he said.

"*Doing* with him?" Chan smiled faintly, leaning her arm on the back of the chair as she raised the mug back to her lips. "I would not get my hopes up, brother Maygar. I have my doubts she is putting hot coals on his feet..."

"But things must have fallen out with them," he insisted. "They *must* have, right? She wouldn't have done this...not if they were still married. Not if they were still bonded to one another. She wouldn't have tranked him like a rabid animal...not from his own bed."

"Bonds are one-way, Maygar," she said, her voice warning. "It will never just 'go away,' no matter how much you might wish it to be so..."

"I have heard they can be broken," he muttered.

"Have you?" She smiled at him faintly. "From who? Another of your old lady Rook scientists? This is news to me, Maygar...I know of no such 'loophole' clause in lifelong mates..."

But Maygar smiled at her, shaking his head a little.

"I never said she was a scientist, Chan." Smiling wider at the irritated look that came to her face, he laughed. "You *are* interested in her. You are so interested, it is taking all of your willpower to pretend that you are not..."

"What is in New York?" she said.

"Untie me, and I'll show you."

Exasperated, Chandre clicked at him for a moment. Then, realizing she had already made up her mind to go with him anyway, she rose to her feet, setting the empty coffee mug on a cork coaster with an image of the Capitol Building stamped on the front. Walking over to him, she fished the keys to the cuffs out of her pocket.

"Remember how quickly I took you down," she said.

"I remember," he muttered, glancing up at her.

"Remember that I can do it again."

Standing by him, however, she could feel in his light that he had relaxed. She doubted he had developed such a skill at infiltration in the past year that he could feign compliance so thoroughly as to fool her, not when she was standing so close to him. Still, she gave his face a last warning look before she averted her gaze.

"You have a car?" she said.

"Yes. It's out front."

Chandre nodded. As she squatted down to begin unlocking the first cuff on his wrist, his eyes craned past her, gazing somewhat wistfully to the kitchen.

"I don't suppose you have any more of that toast?" he said.

She snorted a low laugh, reaching for the cuff around his second wrist after she had unlocked the first.

"We will make you toast," she said. "You can eat it while you drive. Or we will go to one of those horrible places with the food in boxes...the places the humans like..."

Maygar shook his head, clicking, but she heard the humor in it.

When she glanced up, he was looking at her, his brown eyes clear as he rubbed his unchained wrists. It struck her again that some of the piss seemed to have been knocked out of him in the past year or so since she'd last seen him. Maybe from his having been ostracized from the Seven and most of the seers in Seertown for what he'd done to Allie. Maybe from Allie herself nearly killing him with her telekinesis. Maybe from something he had witnessed while being forced to rely on his Rook mother for protection.

Either way, the arrogant, halfway-smirking look she normally associated with his broad, Chinese-looking features had changed somewhat.

Not quite softened, but perhaps lost some of its punch.

"You all right, Rook?" she said teasingly, slapping his back. "You look like you might cry."

For a second, he didn't answer. When he did, it was with the last words she would have expected from him.

"Thanks, Chan," he said. He looked at her again, his dark eyes serious. "You are a good sister to me. Even when I have not deserved it."

She glanced up at this, hiding her surprise with an effort.

Then she grunted, squatting back down by the chains at his ankles.

"I will tie you up any time you like, brother Maygar," she said, pulling out the second key on the ring. "...Just don't expect me to play with you once I have."

He laughed at this, the most genuinely she'd heard him since he'd arrived. He was still rubbing his wrist as she unlocked the first of two organic cuffs from around his ankle, cracking it open with a soft pop.

"I think you can be assured that I will never make that mistake with you, sister Chandre."

"That is good, Maygar...good," she said. "Perhaps then, you are learning after all."

It took them a few hours to get to New York.

Maygar seemed to know where he was going, she noticed; he drove without programming the GPS, and without seeming to be thinking overly about the details of his navigation. He barely seemed to be concentrating on the road at all, in fact, as he steered them towards the New Jersey Turnpike. Instead, his attention still appeared to be mainly focused on her...and on the sandwich he ate with an almost unnerving enthusiasm after they stopped at one of the human restaurants on the way to the highway.

She watched him swallow mouthfuls without chewing in some distaste, and not only because he kept spilling bits of the sauce on the front of his dark blue t-shirt. She'd often wondered how it was that some seers developed such a taste for human food...particularly of the most poisoned variety.

When they entered Manhattan through the Holland Tunnel and popped out on Canal Street, she found herself frowning.

She had forgotten about this place, about what it was like.

"What?" he said, nudging her arm. "Don't you like the Big Apple, Chan?"

"It is not a seer-friendly town, my brother."

"Sure it is," he said, grinning. He pointed at a marquee as they passed.

"Oh, I am terribly sorry," she said curtly, clicking at him and rolling her eyes exaggeratedly. "I had forgotten how much they would love me if I agreed to put them in a box and whip them for a few hours, calling them a naughty, dirty boy..."

He laughed, leaning back in the beat-up leather seat of the sedan.

Chandre noticed he'd relaxed however, and seemed oddly at home in the honking and aggressive traffic of the lower part of Manhattan. As she watched humans milling on the street, seemingly an endless parade of them in all of their varieties, mixed in with VR projections from the ubiquitous ads that followed pedestrians down the street, Chandre found herself glad she'd brought her ownership papers and a gun.

She also found herself reluctant to use her sight, at least not conspicuously, where it might make her visible to other seers occupying the nearby Barrier space. Unfortunately, that meant the only people of her kind she could identify easily stood and walked on the street like overgrown dogs, wearing collars. Many even appeared to be leashed, literally, with their human masters grinning and holding leads as if they'd stumbled upon the winning ticket in some grand, genetic lottery. She had heard about this on the feeds...a new fashion trend among the rich and ethically retarded. Watching one of these rich idiots yanking on the throat of a female seer who looked only a few years older than the Bridge herself, Chandre found herself thinking maybe she should have brought two guns. Or at least a few more clips.

They passed more fetish shops, and a clothing store for human 'sponsors' to buy apparel for their owned seers. Chandre found herself gripping the padded dashboard with one hand as she peered through the windows of the latter, waiting for the light to change, half-hoping it would before she could see much inside the fogged windows. She glimpsed more of those leads in different colors, however, as well as what could only politely be termed as costumes. The outfits ranged from elaborate period clothing from a few hundred years back, to pink taffeta, studded leather and VR-panel minidresses with nothing but suspenders on top.

By the time the light changed, Chandre found herself biting her tongue hard enough to taste blood.

"Explain to me again why you live here, Maygar?"

Glancing in the rearview mirror at the same store, he frowned.

"Come on, Chan," he said. "That shit is everywhere...it's just more blatant here."

"Which means more humans think it is okay," she retorted.

He conceded to her words with a vague gesture. "Maybe."

"There is no maybe, Maygar. *Look* at these worms..." Her eyes followed a human female wearing an expensive suit and yanking on a neon-pink lead attached to a young male seer, one of the few Chandre had seen. "...They have no regard at all for what they do," Chandre added angrily. "It is like our brothers and sisters are nothing more than shiny toys to them..."

Maygar grunted back, noncommittal.

Watching another female seer being led into an Italian restaurant by a twenty-something human wearing designer clothes and holding a metallic blue lead, Chandre felt her frown deepen. She turned, aiming a scowl at Maygar before her eyes drifted back to the window.

"Do you ever kill them at night, Maygar?" she said. "Walking the streets? Or are you too busy 'passing' at the local nightclubs, chasing human tail and trying to find ways to fuck it before they notice your cock isn't quite what they envisioned on the dance floor...?"

He gave her a thin-lipped smile. "Only sometimes, sister Chandre."

"Which part?" she snorted.

"Both."

She smiled humorlessly, clicking at him. Leaning back in her seat, she folded her arms, grunting, "I would love to bring the Sword here. Even for one day. I would buy popcorn and simply watch from a safe distance..."

He gave her a look at that, his light exuding an open annoyance.

"What?" she said. "Tell me you would not do the same. Then tell me again how he is always wrong...and that there is never any cause for the hard path..."

Maygar didn't answer that, either.

Chandre was still scanning faces and storefronts when he pulled the little green sedan into a side street just a few blocks east off Bowery, north of Canal. The amount of graffiti seemed to double within a block. She saw a few large paintings from the Myth archives, bordered by seer script, but most appeared to be English, and human. She supposed there weren't really enough seers with outing privileges for there to be much of a street-crime problem in the local seer community...if it could even be called that. Infiltrators and SCARB agents didn't generally tag, and house pets usually had other duties after dark. Thinking about this, Chandre felt her mood sour even further. She kept her thoughts to herself, however.

They passed a community garden bordered by a junk area, and a school that looked like it hadn't been repainted in about two decades. Chandre studied the buildings as they passed, most of them residences, until Maygar slowed the car, parking in front of a dilapidated apartment building that seemed to consist mainly of exhaust and pollution-darkened brick.

Scanning the area briefly with her eyes and her light, Chan noticed at once that the building stood directly across from what appeared to be a motorcycle shop filled with overweight and angry-looking human bikers.

"Charming neighborhood, brother," she said. "Is there a reason you've decided to live in a human armpit?"

He shrugged, pulling the keys out of the ignition. "You've got to learn to blend, Chan."

"I blend fine," she said, still watching the humans warily as they stood around outside the roll-top garage door, drinking beer. "...I simply prefer not to live in places where they view seers as rabid animals that need to be raped daily and beaten into submission..."

"Here," he said impatiently, thrusting a pair of sunglasses on her. "Stop staring and put these on...or with your bad temper, we *will* have a problem."

Without waiting for her, he slid off the long seat, snapping the latch to the car door and stepping out.

Shoving the mirrored glasses over her nose to cover her eyes, Chandre took another few seconds to tie back her braids in a loose bunch at the base of her neck and then followed him out of the car. She felt the stares as soon as she straightened to her full height, but a quick scan of their light caused her shoulders to relax a little.

They didn't know what she was. They just liked muscular women.

"Hey!" one of them yelled. "You with the braids!"

Another of his friends whistled, bringing a general laugh.

"Pretty woman!" another sang out. "Lovely lady! We're talking to you!"

"You with poser boy over there, honey? Hey! Dark and gorgeous! Over here!"

"How about you come for a ride with us?"

After hesitating the barest breath, Chandre didn't look up, but simply turned, following Maygar to a set of stairs badly in need of more rust-colored paint.

"Lovely lady legs...come on! Have a beer with us!"

Listening to them vie for her attention, she found herself remembering Allie in Berlin.

Chandre had been escorting her to Seertown and to Vash for the first time; the Bridge had been grief-stricken, barely able to stand, but she'd still managed to snap out of her coma long enough to scoff at what she called Chandre's "throwing a grenade at a gnat" in her dealings with the local male humans. Her advice to Chan had been to just do what the human females do, and blow it off. Unless they come after you, pretend you don't hear it, she said.

Chandre found herself remembering that advice with a thin smile now.

Her smile widened as she reached the top of the steep, creaking staircase that smelled vaguely like wino piss. The Bridge's advice seemed to have worked. The men forgot about her as soon as she made it clear she intended to ignore them.

When he turned back, Maygar gave her a puzzled frown.

"What are you smiling about? Thinking about taking me down again?"

"No," she said, clicking softly. "Never mind." Her voice turned business-like. "Where is this big surprise, Maygar? You have brought me a long way without telling me anything, and I still don't see why we couldn't have done all of this in VR...or in the Barrier..."

He stopped outside the front door to the building, his hands on his hips.

Ignoring the wrinkled brow look he developed as he stood there, Chandre glanced past him, to the door itself. Chipped rust-brown paint adorned the front of the wood, revealing an older, yellow coat of paint below. The effect mottled the front of the building, making it look like it had a skin disease. Finally, she met his gaze.

"What?" she said. "What story are you going to feed me now?"

"Look," he said, reaching into his coat pocket for a set of keys. "I know this will probably sound crazy to you..."

She clicked at him in annoyance. "...That is never how anyone wants to hear someone else start a sentence, Maygar..."

"...But I think I'm being followed."

"Followed?"

"By a pro, I mean." He hesitated. "Even before."

"Before what?" she said impatiently.

"Well, I did a job recently. It's part of why I brought you here...but this started before." He shrugged with one hand, giving her another nervous look. "...Before the job, I mean."

She raised an eyebrow, scanning the street beneath them. "And you bring me to your place of living? So that I will obtain this tail, as well?"

He clicked at her, unlocking the main bolt of the outside door.

"I don't mean *literally* followed, Chan....I mean in the Barrier."

"I still appreciate the favor, brother." Snorting a little, she shook her braids, walking in past him when he opened the door and gestured her forward. "Who is it that is following you?"

"I thought it was your people...before, I mean."

"*My* people?"

"You know...the Sword's. I figured I'd end up in one of his 'interrogation' rooms...a few hot pokers up my ass." Giving her a wan smile, he shrugged. "It could still happen. Knowing that asshole, he'll never get over his little grudge..."

She gave him an incredulous look. "His little *grudge*? You attempted to rape his mate...when they had not yet consummated...and knowing full well that he intended upon asking her. Then you appear in DC, as if somehow involved in her capture, where yet *another* seer abused her – "

"Yes, yes." He waved off her words, but she saw a bloom of color reach his cheeks anyway. "I know all that. I just meant, I didn't think it was for anything but personal reasons."

"Personal reasons are all we have," she said, her eyes hard. "You are seer. You should know that."

Running his fingers through his straight, dark hair, he sighed again, motioning for her to proceed up the stairs in front of him. She noticed for the first time that he wore his hair shorter than she'd ever seen it, a good few inches shorter than what he wore in Seertown. He'd grown taller, too, she realized, and his features had lost some of their roundness. She'd forgotten how young he was still, only a few decades older than the Bridge. The Bridge herself had aged rapidly in the past few years, but Chandre and most of the infiltrators of the Seven assumed that had to do with her taking an older mate and bonding with him.

She was still looking him over, noting other changes, when Maygar sighed again.

"I know, Chan. It's just..." Hesitating, he waved off whatever he meant to say as he began to climb the wooden steps after her. "...Anyway, I stopped thinking it was about that. I mean..." He gave her an apologetic look. "I've been watching you for awhile, trying to figure out what you were doing in DC. I kept an eye on a few others I knew to be working for him, too..."

"Why?" she said, more puzzled than annoyed.

Instead of answering, he gave another vague shrug.

"...Anyway, this new thing felt different," he said. "And it didn't add up with what you and the other Rebels seemed to be focusing on...so now I think it's someone else."

"Who?" she said, looking back at him.

"I said they were pros, Chan. I don't know."

She heard a glimmer of something else in his words. She scanned him with her light. "You don't know?" she said. "Or you don't want to say?"

"Well," he said, sighing again. "It could be more than one group. If someone's after me about the job I just did, it *might* be Varlan."

"Varlan?" Chandre clicked through memories in her light. "Who is that? Is he a Rook?"

"Yes. He used to work for Galaith...but he didn't stay with Terian when the Pyramid fell. There are quite a few who didn't, but who still work together occasionally."

Chan gave him a wary look, doing another quick pass over his light. Then she gave a low snort, but without humor. "You stole from him."

"No," he said. "Not exactly."

At her pointed look, he shrugged.

"Well...I didn't steal from *him,* but one of his people, maybe. They might have mentioned he was the head infiltrator on the job...the one working directly with the client."

"How many infiltrators on this job?"

"Four. Maybe five."

"Who is the client?"

"They didn't know." At her skeptical look, Maygar rolled his eyes. "I can't be absolutely certain, but they seemed to be telling the truth. The whole job seemed to be set up so that no one knew what it was really about..."

"And what was this job?"

"I'm getting to that," Maygar said, sounding a little annoyed with her questions. "It's why I brought you here. It's just easier to show you, Chan..."

Her puzzlement returned. "And this Varlan...he was one of Galaith's, but not Terian's?" At Maygar's gesture of yes, she pursed her lips. "Is he an infiltrator of high rank?"

"High, yes. Actual at ten. Eleven maybe."

She shook her braids a bit, exhaling in a sigh. "That is risky business, brother," she said, clicking. "Why would you go provoking a seer of that kind?"

"Yeah, well." Maygar shrugged. "I didn't really know who he was then. Anyway...you'll understand when you see it. It was a calculated risk..."

"Stupid, you mean," she snorted, louder.

Maygar didn't answer, but she saw his mouth harden.

Running his words over in her mind, Chandre continued to climb the steps, following Maygar's gesturing hand at the second landing towards a door with a brass number '17' nailed crookedly into the wood. She glanced down the hallway, noting the water damage on the walls and more peeling paint, this time of a sky blue color that had mottled almost to gray.

"And again I ask...why would you bring any of this to me?" she said, watching his hands as he fumbled with another key to open the locked door. "You know I am loyal to the Sword."

Maygar glanced at her. After a pause, he gave another shrug, but she saw his eyes harden a little. "I knew you could get it to Allie for me," he said simply.

Chandre's eyebrows shot up at this, but she didn't comment at first.

He swung open the door, and walked inside.

"Why would you want me to do that?" she said finally.

"Well," Maygar said, tossing down his keys. He gave her an irritated look. "Who else is left, who is actually *fighting* the Dreng, instead of 'compromising' with them in some way?" His voice grew somewhat bitter by the end. Glancing back at where she'd hesitated at the door, he narrowed his gaze at her slightly.

"Are you coming? I'm not going to hit you, like you did me..."

After the barest pause, Chandre followed him, still puzzling over his words.

"Anyway," he said, running a hand through his hair with a sigh. "I'm still loyal to *her*, even if I'm not that crazy about her mate. You must know *that* about me, at least..."

Chandre barely had a chance to glance around the cluttered space, when another voice spoke up, from the far side of the room.

"I would be very careful where you admitted that aloud, brother," it said smoothly.

The voice was deep, and carried enough of an aleimic pull that Chandre couldn't help being affected by it, lowering her guard almost unconsciously. It was also decidedly male.

"...But your loyalty is admirable," he added, softer.

Chandre froze. Even so, she nearly ran into Maygar's back when he also came to a dead stop a half-second before her. She reached for her gun even as, behind her, someone shut the door of the small, dim room they had just entered. Her fingers had only just closed on the handle when the same voice spoke calmly from the other side of the room.

"Put it down, sister." He paused, and she heard a long exhale, and realized she could smell hiri smoke, the dense, hand-wrapped kind that cost about twenty dollars a packet. The seer added, softer, "I hate to shed the blood of any of our race...at least when there is no need."

Chandre started to look for the voice in the darkness in front of her, but a ping to her light drew her eyes to her left.

Standing by the curtained window, a seer held a Mossberg rifle trained at her chest.

After the barest pause, Chandre released the handgrip of her gun.

Removing her fingers from her jacket, she raised the hand they were attached to along with the other one, keeping both visible on either side of her chest. She kept her eyes on the rifle, and on the seer holding it, trying to decide if she recognized him. Because most of his face remained in shadow, she could not be sure she didn't. Whoever he was, he wore a dark-colored tattoo that covered most of his face.

"Thank you again, brother, for this little vacation," she muttered to Maygar.

Maygar scowled in her direction, his own hands up at chest level.

The same voice rose again, but humor threaded it this time.

"Your friend here seems to have drawn you into his troubles, sister," it said.

Following the sound, Chan peered around Maygar's back to its origins.

"...Since you are here, perhaps you can do yourself a favor, as well," the voice added. "Help me to persuade him to return the property he stole from me..."

Chandre's eyes finally came to rest on the male seer who had spoken. Her hearing had not deceived her; he sat almost directly across from the door where they walked in. Looking completely relaxed, he lounged in a scuffed 1970s-style wooden chair with spoke-like decorations at its back. Next to the chair stood a roll-top desk, from roughly the same time period, and a map that covered most of the same wall of Maygar's rather cluttered studio apartment. The seer's gray-streaked hair had been pulled back in one of the old wooden clips, in a style the Adhipan used to wear back before the time of first contact.

That, and the lines in the long face and the depth of his eyes gave her some indication of his age, and it was not young. His deep-set, violet eyes gazed up at her, resting on hers briefly before flickering back to Maygar. He sat with his hands folded in the lap of an organic-enhanced black coat buttoned over his abdomen and chest. The scar that ran from his lips to below one of his eyes gave his face a serious, almost drawn look.

"I apologize for the inconvenience," he said emotionlessly, the light behind his voice once more causing Chandre to shiver. "...But I really need my property returned to me. At once. We can discuss the...repercussions...for your rashness, Maygar, once I have the materials in question in hand..."

Stubbing out a hiri with fingers stained by some dark powder, he clicked in a soft, rolling purr, carrying the Asian accent Chandre knew from other old timers she'd met in the mountains. He looked familiar to her somehow, but she couldn't place him, even with her seer memory. Whatever caused it, the impression was fleeting, and likely being distorted by the man who returned her gaze.

Maygar lowered his hands slowly.

"I would be very careful if I were you, brother," the man said softly.

"I'm going to get it," Maygar said, blunt. "I need my hands."

"Proceed."

Maygar walked over to the small refrigerator on the floor by a sink and a counter mostly taken up by a two-burner, electric coil stove with rusted iron brackets. Chandre watched, frowning slightly, as Maygar began prying off the panel on one side of the fridge, using a small instrument like a miniature crowbar. As he worked, she heard the crackle of minds around her, likely irritated that they hadn't found the hiding place earlier.

Chandre looked back at the gray-haired seer, swallowing right before she jutted her chin. "What is this thing he took?" she said, forcing her expression still. "If I'm to die for it, should I not at least know its significance?"

The older seer looked up at her, his eyes holding a kind of tired smile. She wasn't buying it though, not from a seer of his rank.

"No one need die today, sister. I have a few questions for your *friend*, though..." He smiled at her, saying the word 'friend' as if challenging her to disagree.

She didn't give him the satisfaction.

"I hear you are in the market for our quarry as well?" the older seer asked politely. "Is that true, sister Chandre?"

"Can I not at least know your name?" she said, holding that violet gaze with an effort. "Since you know mine, it seems only fair..."

The seer smiled, and Chandre saw genuine humor in it that time.

"I am Varlan," he said simply.

"And this means...what, to me?" she said.

"Who I am is immaterial," he said, dismissing her words with a subtle gesture of his fingers. When she didn't change expression, he sighed again. "What you really want to know, sister, is who I am working for...and what that job entails. You want to know why someone would need so many infiltrators, if all I am dealing in is intelligence..."

Chandre glanced at Maygar, who was now pulling something out of the edge of the refrigerator panel. It looked like an organic memory chip, now that her eyes had adjusted somewhat to the dim light. One that had been wrapped in plastic to protect it.

"And?" Chandre said, looking back at Varlan. "Do you intend to elucidate?"

Varlan sighed again, looking up at her. "You know of the weapon, sister.

As I said, we are aware that you have been working in this area, too. For the Bridge, correct?"

"Actually, no," Chandre said, folding her arms. "For her husband, the Sword – "

"You can sell that to the boy here," Varlan interrupted smoothly. "I know you are working as a double agent, infiltrating the rebellion. That your handler is Balidor of the Adhipan. You work for the Bridge, sister Chandre..." The smile touched his lips once more. "...Although it is unclear to me if *she* is aware of that fact. At least not yet."

Maygar had paused to listen to this exchange, and now his eyes widened, seeming to fill more of his face. They nearly glowed in the dim light of the room.

"Chan!" he said.

Chandre winced, unable to avoid hearing the happiness in the younger seer's voice. It was too bad he hadn't yet figured out that they were probably dead. Or why it might not be a particularly good thing that this Rook knew who exactly she really was.

"...I should have known," Maygar added, still grinning at her as he shook his head. "You're a sly one, Chan...I'll give you that. I actually believed you that you were loyal to that Rook..."

"I *am* loyal to that Rook," Chandre said through gritted teeth.

Maygar grinned wider. "Sure you were. I think I could kiss you, sister Chandre...I really could."

"I wouldn't, if I were you," she warned, holding up a hand. "And Varlan is right. It wasn't Allie, it was Balidor. I doubt Allie knows anything about it. He couldn't risk telling her, given who she is mate to...and especially not with what she has been up to this past year..."

Still smiling faintly, Maygar shook his head, whistling softly.

"Chan the man," he said.

Chandre couldn't help rolling her eyes, folding her arms in irritation. Varlan acted as though Maygar hadn't spoken.

"Do you deny you are seeking this disease?" he asked Chandre.

"No," she said. "I do not deny it."

"Then tell me, Sister Chandre. What do you know about it?"

She answered promptly, without any attempt to shield her light. "Only that it is said it kills humans very quickly," she said. "That it is supposed to be completely harmless to seers. It is also said that the last human president in this country, Wellington, commissioned to have it developed." Pausing, she added, "One of Terian's bodies...the only human of his personalities that we are aware of."

She trailed, watching Maygar as he handed the plastic bag with the memory chip to one of Varlan's people. The female seer took it from him, then promptly attached it to a portable VR monitor and laptop. Chandre watched as she brought up the file directory for the chip. Chandre's own eyes shifted to the screen as the female began scanning the chip's contents, including 3-D diagrams, what looked like government documents, at least one map, blueprints. The seer opened each of these in order and scanned them both with her eyes and her aleimi.

"It's the correct chip," she said, glancing at Varlan after a few seconds.

"Is everything there?"

"I'll know in a minute," she said, not taking her eyes off the screen.

Varlan's eyes remained on Chandre.

"Continue, sister," he told her softly.

Seeing the frown on Varlan's lips, Chandre gestured in acquiescence, using the deferential version. She already knew that full disclosure was her only real option, with a seer of his rank. Being honest might give him a reason to spare her, if only by avoiding pissing him off. And there wasn't much point in lying...he would get the information from her regardless.

"Terian...or Feigran, as he is called now...has since given Balidor some intel on this project he commissioned," she added, keeping her words concise, yet accurate. "But the original Terian, Feigran, is easily confused, and not often linear in his thinking. He is reasonably sure he commissioned this thing, but not who he told...or what would happen to this project in the event of Wellington's death. Information retrieved through scans is conflicting, and filled also with hallucinations and other false-memories..." She hesitated, giving a seer's shrug with one hand. "...My sources were unaware if his successor was ever made aware of the disease at all. They seem to feel the project may have been appropriated by other parties, and buried. If it continued to be in play in some form, then they believe that the research, too, has gone underground. I have conducted a search of the government files and relevant facilities, but I have been unable to find trace of it anywhere. At least not in any of the documented labs..."

Varlan nodded. His expression slid back into the blank mask of a highly ranked infiltrator, but she got the feeling she had satisfied him.

"The boy knows more than that," he said in that melodic voice, his eyes shifting back to Maygar. "...What of this new contact?" he said then, focusing his light back on her. "The one your friend told you about...in DC?" Varlan exhaled another cloud of dark smoke. "He is Mi5, is he not? British Intelligence...and human?"

Chandre heard the message behind his words that time, too.

"I was not withholding, brother," she said, again gesturing respectfully. "I haven't had a chance to follow up on that yet...I only heard of this last night. A contact of mine in SCARB told me of this. She is nominally SCARB, too, but someone I have been working with in an infiltration capacity. She is sympathetic to my employers, but as she often deals in rumors, I don't normally consider her data valid until I have the opportunity to verify..."

"By employers, you mean Adhipan Balidor?"

"Yes."

Varlan nodded again, his expression motionless.

Chandre found herself thinking that she preferred Balidor's less heavy-handed approach to his working infiltration rank...although she had to admit, Varlan's was more honest.

Balidor had mastered the art of appearing to know and hear far less than he did.

At her thought, she saw a smile touch Varlan's lips.

"Indeed he has," the seer agreed emotionlessly.

Chandre hesitated, then said, "Can I know these things, as well?" she said. "This information about the disease that brother Maygar seems to have?"

Varlan smiled faintly. "What motivation do I have to tell you?"

"A simple courtesy, brother."

Varlan nodded, his eyes showing indifference again when they met hers. "Very well. Your friend, Maygar, interfered with a drop-off in progress. In fact, he took intelligence meant for me in the conduct of a paid job...by pretending to be one of my people. The client's messenger has already been dealt with. I am here now for the intel he stole..."

Chandre turned, staring at Maygar in disbelief.

Maygar exhaled in irritation, glaring at the seer in the wooden chair. When Chandre clicked sharply at him, he rolled his gaze in her direction, his hands still in the air.

"I told you I had something to show you," he muttered.

"Did you do as he said?" she asked him. "Did you impersonate the contact for the drop?"

She was actually a little impressed.

Maygar sighed again. "Not exactly. I was playing poker with a few friends, and the courier, well...he mistook me for his contact." He shrugged a little, glancing at Varlan. "...I just let him, that's all. I didn't even know for sure what it was..."

Maygar indicated his head towards the VR monitor displaying the contents of the organic chip. Chandre watched as diagrams flashed across the screen, and again what looked like blueprints. She'd seen something like them before...

"You found the lab," Chandre muttered. She glanced at Varlan. "What will you do with this thing? This disease?"

"I am under contract," the seer replied. "I will do as I was contracted to do."

"Which is what?" Chandre said.

Varlan smiled at her thinly again, not answering. He kept his eyes on hers, exhaling more of that dark, sweet-smelling smoke towards the water-stained ceiling.

Chandre felt her jaw harden. She was about to try again, when the door to the corridor opened sharply behind them, banging into the wall.

Light flooded the dim room, momentarily blinding her when she turned at the sound. Holding up a hand, Chandre found herself looking at another seer, likely whoever Varlan had stationed outside to keep a watch over the building's entrance. The new seer was dressed the same as the others, at any rate, in that same organic armor, with the same modified Mossberg with the organic scope. He wore a long coat over the armor though, likely to remain at least nominally inconspicuous outside.

He held someone else with one hand, gripping his captive's collar tightly with his pale fingers. The man he held balanced precariously on his toes, looking rather like a frightened rodent. The effect was heightened by the human's small frame, as well as his old-fashioned glasses and thinning brown hair.

Chandre felt another ripple of surprise in her light when Maygar stiffened next to her.

She felt the familiarity he aimed towards the seer's captive even before he spoke.

"Eddard?" His voice grew openly disbelieving. "Eddard, is that really you?"

The human turned, his eyes confused, probably blind in the relative darkness of the room. One of the seers by the door leaned over and switched on the light, causing most of the seers to raise hands to shield their eyes from the abrupt change. The human seemed more at ease however.

He glanced around at faces, until he was staring at Maygar, too.

"Maygar?" he said. His voice held also bewilderment.

"Yeah, it's me," Maygar said. "What are you doing here, Eddard?"

"And yet," Varlan observed, speaking to the human. "You must have expected to find Maygar here." He glanced between the two of them once more. "...It *is* his dwelling."

The human glanced at Varlan, and then over at Chandre. His eyes traveled around to the other seers in the room, taking in faces, clothing and weapons. Then he pushed his wire-rim glasses up his nose with one finger on his free hand, swallowing nervously.

"Are you the contractors?" he asked. "...For the Shadow?"

There was a silence where every seer in the room stared at the human wearing wire-rimmed glasses. Maygar finally spoke, drawing Eddard's eyes back to him.

"What are you doing here, Eddard?" Maygar said again.

Before the human could answer, Varlan seemed to lose his patience. He focused emotionlessly on Maygar, clicking out from where he'd obviously been reading the human, Eddard.

"You know this worm. Explain."

"Well, yeah...I mean, sort of." Maygar looked between Varlan and Chandre. His jaw tightened right before he gestured vaguely towards the human. "He used to work for Dehgoies...the Sword. He was like his butler, I think...or maybe some kind of secretary. Dehgoies said the British military hired him partly to keep an eye on him. Before he *was* the Sword, I mean. He was there when we blew the place up, in London..."

Incredulous, Chandre looked at the man the seer held. "*He* is the human who aided you that day? With the explosives?" The captive looked more like a human tax accountant to Chandre than any kind of field operative. "Why would he be here now?"

"I don't know." Maygar shrugged. "He worked for British Intelligence. Didn't you just say you were looking for someone from British Intelligence...?"

Varlan nodded, smiling a little.

"Perhaps our Mi5 agent has come to find us," he murmured quietly. "Yes," he said, answering an unspoken question from the seer holding Eddard's collar. "Bring him here...but continue your scans..."

Varlan motioned to the seer at the door as he spoke, indicating for him to bring Eddard closer. The hulking seer at the door tightened his grip on the human's collar before pushing him forward, guiding him past Maygar's queen-sized bed in the middle of the room and to the desk. Chandre saw that the human was wearing what looked like a rain coat over an expensive-looking tailored suit and slacks with polished, Italian-made shoes. Not exactly a normal outfit for this neighborhood, she thought to herself...nor for British Intelligence.

"You helped Dehgoies and the Bridge escape from that building in London?" Varlan asked the human evenly. "You defied your human employers. Why?"

The man Maygar called Eddard looked around at all of them, his blue eyes wide behind the glasses he wore.

"Yes," he said after a pause.

"Why?" Varlan repeated.

Eddard shrugged, his eyes holding a faint embarrassment as he cleared his throat. "It seemed the right thing to do at the time," he said. "I'd worked for Dehgoies Revik for over a decade..."

"You were friends?"

"No." Eddard smiled a little at the thought, shaking his head in amusement. "Not exactly. But I knew him a little. I knew he wasn't a terrorist..." Thinking about this, he frowned. "...Well, he wasn't back then, anyway."

"What are you doing here?" Chandre blurted. "Who are you, that you would be here?"

Varlan glanced at her, raising an eyebrow as if to ask, 'who is doing the interrogating here?' But he didn't speak, and when Eddard answered her, he turned politely to listen.

"It's like he said." He motioned with his head towards Maygar. "I work for Mi5," Eddard added, his voice strained from the hand at his collar. He glanced around at their faces a second time. "...I've been looking for you. For all of you."

Varlan indicated for the seer to release him.

Once he did, Eddard rubbed the front of his throat, where the collar had dug into his skin. His face slowly returned to a normal color as he straightened.

"And?" Varlan said. "Answer our sister's question."

"I work for Mi5..." Eddard began.

"You said that. Who are you?"

"I thought you knew," Eddard said, looking around them. "I'm the one who's here to help put a stop to that disease. The one released in Hong Kong..."

"*You're* the contact?" Chandre said, bewildered. "The one Talei told me of?"

"Yes." Eddard turned, looking at her seriously. "I meant for us to speak directly in DC...but then news of the contract for the disease came to me. I got the name of the contractor," he added, glancing at Varlan once more. "...but not the client, at least not apart from the code name, 'Shadow.' I was planning to come to New York anyway, when I heard that Maygar had gotten possession of the materials instead..."

"You know a lot, worm," Varlan observed quietly.

If he heard the threat behind those words, Eddard's expression didn't show it.

"Not really," he said seriously, in his clipped, British accent. "I know only that you were hired...not by whom. Nor do I know the precise layout of the lab you intend to break into, although I do know of its existence and location. I also happen to know the name of the scientist who is running the project, although I do not know where *he* is currently, either..."

Varlan looked up at him, his eyes faintly amused. "Anything else?"

"I need to speak with you," Eddard told him, as serious as before. He glanced around at Chandre and Maygar, adding, "...To all of you, really. It's damned lucky I found you before you'd executed the contract. I'm here about the disease you plan to destroy..."

In the silence that followed, Chandre turned, staring openly at Varlan.

"Destroy?" she said in surprise. "That's what you've been hired to do? To find the lab and destroy the biological agent? Really?"

Varlan sighed again. Exhaling a cloud of hiri, he shrugged, seer-fashion, and said, "Does this bother you, sister?"

Chandre felt her jaw harden again. "It does not bother me."

"You would rather if I deployed the disease?" he said, still sounding tired. "...Caused a worldwide epidemic and pandemonium as the human race is rapidly exterminated?"

"No," Chandre said. "I do not wish that."

"Well, then...our interests seem to align," he said, shrugging. "As do those of my client...who thankfully is better informed than all of us, it seems, as well as being significantly better funded." He smiled at Eddard, his eyes openly amused. "Unless, of course, the human objects to our eliminating a human-killing virus...?"

"I do not," Eddard said. Hesitating, he glanced around at all of them, once more pushing the glasses up the bridge of his nose. "...In fact," he added. "I want to help you."

Nine
Torturer

He didn't beg me the next time I went in.

He didn't curse me, either...or try to bargain.

He watched me from the wall instead, his face and eyes expressionless. Looking at him, I couldn't help but be reminded of cornered animals I'd seen, those who had been hit one too many times with something hard and sharp. He looked thinner too, as if he'd lost weight even in those twelve or so hours since I'd last seen him. His expression still showed the remnants of his introductory tour down memory lane...meaning a lingering grief and tiredness that went beyond captivity and lack of sleep. But mostly what I saw behind his stare was anger. The war with me had begun, I suppose.

That had been over a week ago.

According to Jon, he hadn't eaten at all in the past two days. He drank water from the spigot on the wall, even stuck his head under the same faucet and splashed cold water on his face...but he pushed away the food they brought him without even looking at it. The sandwich from that morning's meal still sat on the floor in a metal plate, a few feet away from the stub of the last hiri he'd smoked, which Jon gave him when he delivered the food.

He leaned his back flat against the organic surface, his long legs drawn up in angles so that his forearms rested on his knees, hanging his hands over the floor.

From there, he stared at me, as if I were another animal.

Each day I entered, I braced myself for another back and forth with him, another series of taunts and attempts to provoke me or knock me off balance. But it never came. I didn't know if he was studying me, trying to decide on a new approach or simply taking a new approach by being silent...or if he'd given up trying to reach me at all.

I tried not to contemplate any of the things he might be thinking as I walked in and set my bottle of water on the floor. I told myself it was irrelevant, but I knew that wasn't entirely true, either. The truth was, I couldn't tell if what we were doing was even making a dent. I didn't know if him seeing these things, re-experiencing his past, was accomplishing anything at all, other than making both of us miserable.

I'd done what I could to strengthen the connection between us.

Even as early as that second day, I'd spent the night in the tank with him, leaving only for a few hours the next morning to shower and change my clothes and debrief with the others.

The decision to sleep in there with him had been pretty straightforward. I'd felt the connection between us strengthen significantly after those initial two sessions on that first day; but after a night spent apart, with him in the tank and me out in the barracks, that connection felt only about half as strong as it had by the next morning. The Barrier shield in the tank was just too strong for me to be away from him for long.

Vash had already warned me that I would need to develop a stronger connection to him, if I wanted to get at the memories he most didn't want me to see. So I'd resigned myself to the fact that I would essentially be living in the tank with him until that happened.

Balidor hated the idea, of course.

They'd gassed Revik not long after the first session ended. Partly to give him a shower and a change of clothes, and partly because I think Balidor wanted to silence his cries, which went on for several hours even after I'd left.

Everyone who'd been watching at the security station had been spooked.

No one said anything to me directly, but no one quite looked me in the eye when I came out, either. I read whispers off a few of them who thought I'd done something to really hurt him in the Barrier...some kind of revenge against what he'd done to me earlier that day, I guess. More than one seemed to think he deserved it, but they still gave me plenty of space when I came out, and looked at me as if appraising me with new eyes.

I had become his torturer.

The seers seemed to respect that fact as much as they feared it.

Only Jon followed me back to my room that first night, and he didn't come out and ask me anything. Instead he just hung around while I ate, making jokes every now and then when the silence got too thick...offering to spend the night if I didn't want to be alone.

Finally, when he couldn't coax me into going to the other room to watch an old movie with him and Dorje on the feeds, or play chess, or the seer card game *rik-jum*, or even just go to sleep with him there, he gave in to the fact that I wanted to be alone and left.

The days started to bleed together after that first one, just like they had in Tarsi's cave. I knew Revik and I were both likely overdue for another break and a serious hosing off, but I didn't want to do anything that might slow things down just yet. I also wasn't sure if I could make myself come back in as easily or as quickly if I stopped for too long without having made any noticeable progress whatsoever.

In that sense, it really was like Tarsi's cave all over again, only worse...a kind of sick voyeurism that both repulsed me when I let myself wonder about my own pulls and motives, and at times drew me like a drug, even made it hard to end sessions.

But I couldn't afford to think too much about that, either, or what this might be doing to me as well as him. If I was going to finish this thing, I was pretty sure it had to happen in one shot. Until that hard push was done, and I had some idea if any of it might work, I didn't have the luxury to factor myself into the equation much at all, really.

He'd begged me one other time, since that first session.

Lifetimes seemed to pass between the first time he asked me to stop and the second. In reality, only about six days had gone by...seven at most. Over the course of those days, we spent as much as seventeen hours in the Barrier in any one twenty-four hour period.

The gap between the two didn't make it any less horrible to listen to, or make me feel any better when he started screaming obscenities at me after I tried to talk him down.

I'd made myself sleep in there that night, too.

I laid there through most of it, not sleeping, but I didn't let myself leave. About three days in, I'd had the Adhipan set up a protected space so I could go to the bathroom in there, on the opposite end from where he'd been chained, so they wouldn't have to put me through security protocols every time I needed a toilet or to wash my face. Using the organic functionality, I could even take a shower if I wanted, have the wall barf out shampoo and soap...even a clean towel and clean clothes, if I wanted.

When I stopped answering his attempts to provoke me that second time, he just lay there, crying...which was worse.

I think what we were doing affected his dreams, too.

I know it did mine. I woke up unsure if my mind still lived solely inside the Barrier, feeling his light weaving through mine in erratic pulses as it looked for an escape, for any way out. I dreamt about caves and shackles that tied my wrists to my ankles. I dreamt of the smell of urine and blood, the sound of rats, the feel of insect legs and pinchers piercing my skin under my clothes...I woke up with weights crushing my chest, in pain like I was dying. I woke up screaming once.

I don't know if I scared Revik, but Jon told me that Yumi, who had been monitoring the security console, nearly jumped out of her skin.

The gaps between jumps got shorter, as sleep became more and more pointless for both of us. Some part of me was even trying to wear him down, I think, to make him so tired it was harder for him to fight me. I slept whenever I could, even when he lay there gasping...trying to save my own energy, hoping he would stay awake, hoping the pressure would force him to submit. Hoping he would do it before his mind broke totally.

A few times, I wondered if I might have a torturer living in me after all.

It was a terrifying realization, but one I didn't let myself get too close to, as I began to view him as a puzzle that needed cracking, a thing I had to open up from the inside out, and hopefully without breaking the overall design. I saw myself dancing on that line at times, even pushing on it, to see if it might bend, drawing back when the strain seemed to be moving him into a space I couldn't control.

Somewhere in the back of my mind, I wondered if I drew on his experience in that, too...one of the many shared skill sets inherited as a part of the bond.

I didn't really want to think about whether that made it better or worse.

...he screams, lying face-down on a heavy wooden table.

He is hoarse from screaming, deaf from it. He can't make himself stop.

Panic smashes into his light; he fights to get free, his left wrist shackled to the wood. The human works over him with slitted eyes, his mouth twisted in a half-smile as he raises the brand from his skin, looking at the end that still sizzles with fat and blood.

In here, I can't not be here...I can't not be him...

But I can look away.

I can't stop myself looking away, willing myself into some other part of the room, some other place where I can hear it and smell it, but at least fewer of the images are burned into my brain, making me feel like it's me that's doing this to him...

I see the old man watching passively, his long hands folded at the base of his spine, his skull-like face unmoving over the dark motionlessness of a gray cloak and hair a darker shade of iron. He wears human clothes. Riding breeches and a coarse cotton shirt. His hair is combed and the beard is trimmed down to a goatee, which only makes the skull-like shape of his head more prominent. His features blend strangely beyond their bone-like similarity; little stays with me but skin stretched tightly over that death-like skull and skeleton, leaving no other impressions than his deep-socketed, staring eyes...yellow eyes, the color of sickly urine.

He waits until the boy has literally run out of air.

"Nenzi," he says then.

His voice is cold, a command.

"Nenzi...you must be silent."

The boy gasps, choking on a breath that wants to become more than that. It is the only command his body can obey. He knows what will happen if he does not...and already, I realize, already Menlim's voice holds more sway than his own, even in this simple thing. Even so, he is choking, fighting for air, his thin arms and legs tensed to their limit where they've got him splayed over the table. He is brown from the sun, barefoot, and to my eyes, which still see age through the lens of a human, he looks about seven years old.

I can't stand it. I really can't stand it.

But I have to.

When the boy regains control over the sounds he is making, closing his eyes, his breath still a lunging fist in his chest, the old seer clicks at him in a rolling purr, gesturing with one hand.

"You can save yourself, Nenzi," he says softly.

"No." Tears fill the light eyes. "I can't..."

"You can kill this human. You can kill him as easily as swatting a fly."

"I can't...uncle, please..."

The old seer's eyes harden to slate. A frown touches the sculpted lips.

"Do not beg me, nephew. Do not grovel before me like some kind of craven worm. You are an intermediary being...one of the chosen..."

"No..." the boy gasps. He gestures 'no' with a shackled hand, tears in his eyes. "Mistake. It's a mistake. It can't be. I'm not him...I'm not Syrimne..."

The old seer's eyes don't move at first.

Then they shift from the boy's face, returning to the human.

"Again, Merenje," he says, emotionless. "We will do it again...and again...until my nephew realizes what a sacrilege he has performed with his own mouth...to refuse the honored position to which he was born...to scorn his parents, and his parents' lives, which they sacrificed for him..."

"No!" He screams, twisting his head around to try and watch the human. "No! Please! I'm not...I'm not refusing...I'm ready! I'm ready to be him!"

"When you are done," the old seer says. "Put him back, Merenje..."

"No!" the boy screams. "No! Please! Please don't!"

I stand somewhere in the shadows, flinching at every scream.

Even so, I know I only catch the barest taste, feeling it with him but not, watching the old seer as he turns to leave the underground room. I know already that there is a room below that, that a trapdoor lives in the stone below the table where the boy is chained. I know that down there is where the rats and other crawling things live, where he digs in the dark, fighting to breathe, suffocating in the dank air. I know the boy will be there again, his hands tied to his feet, and that they'll leave him there, possibly for days... possibly for longer.

And I look up as the Sark turns at the top of the stairs, the protruding bones of his face catching the light as he watches the boy again with hard, almost reptilian eyes.

I want to kill him. I've never wanted anything so much.

But I am not really here.

Menlim waits until the human pauses once more, until the screaming devolves back into broken gasps and softer cries.

"I'm doing this for you, Nenzi," he tells him, his voice almost quiet. "What I teach you can save you, my son..."

"Please!" the boy chokes. "Please, uncle. Please. I'm sorry..."

"Nenzi," he says, clicking quietly. "Nenzi, stop."

"Uncle, I..."

"Just stop, Nenzi. Stop. I want you to pray with me..."

For a moment it grows deathly silent.

All I hear is breathing in the dim room, a room smelling of blood and charred flesh. It is mainly the boy who fights to breathe, his head pressed against the wood, his hands clenched in fists on either side of his face. His body is still contorted in pain, his back bent where he's half arched off the wood, but I can tell from his face that he's heard the old seer, that he knows he must obey him in this, too.

Even the human pauses in his work, looking up at Menlim with a subdued look on his face, almost a reverent look.

"Nenzi?" the old man says. "Are you speaking with your Ancestors?"

I look at the boy, and I see his eyes shut tight.

His face is still pressed into the wood, but now his lips are moving, muttering words. I watch him, feeling a kind of despair creep over my light, a deeper nausea.

"Remember this moment, my son," the old Sark breathed, his voice a near caress. "Always remember who you are...how much you have given to the cause. You will look back on this, and know you can withstand anything. You will know you have given everything to save your people, Nenzi...that you are more than a man, you are an emissary of Light..."

It breaks off, like it does.

I am left sick, alone in a different place, no time to adjust, no place to go in my mind to rest, to even absorb where I've just left. There is pain here, everywhere, and my mind is too lost to see a cause. I am the boy once more, lost inside his physical vessel, and a voice is calling to him sharply, calling his name from another part of the room.

He jerks up his head, moving like an animal, expecting shackles to stop his movements.

When they don't, he moves too far, nearly falling out of his seat.

...and laughter erupts around him. Children's laughter.

But the other voice silences theirs, too.

"Ewald!" The woman says, her voice sharp.

With him, I try to focus on the face that called to him first.

"Ewald! Are you listening to me?"

He starts to use his hand to gesture, then remembers, stopping in mid-motion even as his eyes dart furtively to the giant boy crammed into a similar-sized seat two rows back. The boy with the shocking white hair and the deep-set black eyes smiles at him, the skin around his eyes crinkling faintly as he makes a kissing gesture towards the boy, tapping his temple.

Too late, he thinks, knowing the boy will hear it. *Too late, runt...*

"Ewald," the woman says. "I asked you a question."

"Yes, *Frau* Schlossing," he says, jerking his eyes back to the front. "I am listening."

"That is the final warning. You will wait for me after the class breaks."

Fear clenches at his abdomen. Abruptly, he has to go to the bathroom, but he can't ask her. Nor can he tell her that he can't stay, that they'll be waiting for him.

"Ewald! Did you hear me?"

With him, I refocus on the woman standing at the old-fashioned-looking blackboard.

He nods once he has, taking in her frustrated and perplexed stare with a glance that shifts sideways, that won't hold hers.

"Yes, *Frau*. I will wait."

Still, his eyes find the tow-headed giant once more, taking in the humorous smile on his thick lips as the pressure on his bladder worsens.

"...I need to go to the bathroom," he blurts, speaking before he knows he meant to. "I need the toilet...now, *Frau*..."

The other children laugh again at this, but Frau Schlossing only frowns. She seems about to refuse him at first, then something in his face appears to change her mind.

"Go, Ewald. Be back in a reasonable time."

He slides off the seat before she has finished speaking, stepping over tripping feet and pushing his way past arms and fingers that try to poke at his sides and back. He sees them without seeing them, obstacles between him and his goal, the door to outside. He knows he'll get a beating either way, no matter which way he leaves, but he doesn't care. In a place of no freedom from hurt, the only choice he has is in what form it comes.

He reaches the door to the hall, then the hall itself. The wooden schoolhouse is made of four rooms, arranged by age, but the outhouse is shared, and it's outside. He is in the final segment of corridor, looking at the back doors, nearly able to smell and taste the breeze outside...

When a voice calls to him from directly behind him.

"Ewald," it says.

He freezes in mid-step.

"Ewald...come here."

He turns before he can think about stopping himself, his nerves strung on edge, his mind bent only on escape. His hope plummets with that soft voice, even before he sees her face. He meets the eyes of the other teacher, his teacher from the previous year, when he was younger. Once he has, he can't force himself to look away.

She beckons him into her room.

Her classroom is empty now. The younger children have gone for the day, those under seven and eight, who finish their schooling early. The boy is small for his age, small even for a seer, smaller than some of those in the younger kids' classroom, but the humans think of him as eleven now.

Fighting himself for another few seconds, he follows her beckoning finger into the room. When the door closes behind him, the pain in his abdomen worsens.

She walks back to the front of the classroom, moving one of the small chairs so that it sits only a few feet from the teacher's chair, behind the desk.

Unlike *Frau* Schlossing, she is young, perhaps only in her late teens or early twenties. Her long, blond hair hangs braided down her back, and she wears a heavy but light-colored dress, practical, but form-fitting enough that her figure is shown in all its curves.

She is pretty, and her legs are strong. He cannot help but look at her, his eyes taking her in almost guiltily from across the desk.

"Ewald," she says, looking up in puzzlement. "Come here."

"I am not supposed to be here," he stammers. "*Frau* Schlossing..."

"I will make sure you do not get in trouble with *Frau* Schlossing," she says, smiling at him in a friendly way. Sitting in the chair behind her desk, she looks pointedly at the one she has placed so that it is sitting across from her.

"Come here, Ewald."

Unable to think of a reason to refuse, he obeys the summons reluctantly.

"Sit here," she says, patting the other chair.

"I cannot be here," he says again, looking at the door.

"I won't hurt you, Ewald..."

"I know, *Fraulein*, I just – "

"Ewald." Her voice becomes her teacher's voice. "Sit down."

Reluctantly, he closes the gap between them, sitting in the wooden chair next to hers. "I didn't do anything..." he says.

"I know you didn't. You're not in trouble, Ewald. Please. Just try to relax."

He sits there, feeling his heart hammering in his chest as she looks at him critically. Her eyes take in the length of his body, then pause longer on his face.

"You have a bruise," she says after a moment, indicating the place on her own neck. "Where did you get it, Ewald?"

"I don't know."

"It is a large bruise, Ewald. It looks painful."

"I don't know where I got it, Miss."

She continues to look at him, as if waiting for him to go on. When he doesn't, she nods, as if to herself. He watches her lips purse, a look of concentration come to her blue eyes.

"You were limping, Ewald...when you walked in here. Did you know that?"

"No."

"Well, you were."

"No. I wasn't limping, Miss."

"You were." Her voice is gentle though, understanding rather than accusatory. "It's all right. You're not in trouble, Ewald. You're not..."

He doesn't have an answer for this, so he looks away.

"Will you show me your back, Ewald? Under your shirt?"

His eyes shift upwards, even as his ears catch up, as his heart hammers harder in his chest. A kind of dread takes hold of him, mixed with that blackening fear, strong enough that he can't answer her at first. When she reaches for his shirt, he jerks back.

"No!"

He half-stumbles to his feet, nearly toppling the chair, then doesn't move further. Clutching the edge of the desk, he just stands there, holding his own shirt, not quite able to run away. He has to go to the bathroom again...so badly he can't think straight. He's afraid suddenly that he'll lose control, that he'll void his bladder right in front of her.

"Please," he says. "I'm sorry."

"Why are you sorry, Ewald?"

"I have to go. I really have to go. I told *Frau* Schlossing I would be back... that I wouldn't be gone too long. I need to go to the outhouse..."

She hesitates, but as she looks at him, he doesn't see any anger. Concern still stands out in her eyes, a concern that is almost pity, perhaps even more than pity. Moving closer, she touches his arm, and it is a reassuring touch, taken away the instant he flinches, as if to persuade him it won't remain there if he doesn't want it to.

"I won't hurt you...I promise you I won't, Ewald. I promise. I'm trying to help you..."

"Please stop...stop doing this..."

"I know someone is hurting you. I know you are being hurt..."

"You have to stop," he says. "Please, Miss. You have to..."

"Stop what, Ewald?"

"Stop talking about him," he blurts. "...Please."

She stares at him, and for an instant, he is lost there, in her young, pretty face.

"Who, Ewald? Who do I have to stop talking about?" She frowns, but it doesn't feel like it's aimed at him. Her eyes have a flicker of charge in them now, and he knows, he can feel in her light that she knows exactly who he means.

"Your uncle? Is that who, Ewald?" She bites her lip in anger, and it only makes her look prettier. "Did he tell you to say that? Did he tell you to threaten me? To stop asking questions about you?"

"It's not safe," is all he can say. "Please. Please...just please stop."

"If I help you, then he can't hurt you anymore, Ewald."

"You can't." He shakes his head. "You can't help me...you don't understand..."

She frowns at him, and for a moment he sees real grief in her eyes.

"Ewald," she says, her voice gentle again. "Don't you want him to stop hurting you? Don't you want to live with people who care for you? Who don't do that to you?"

Pain slivers through his light. He stares at her, and for a moment, he struggles not to touch her, not to slide his arms around her neck, even just for a moment. But the feeling worsens along with the pain, the knowledge that they might already know, that someone is probably watching their exchange, even now. He hears voices in the hallway as he thinks it, wonders if Gerwix has already noticed the time has been too long, that he's been gone longer than he said.

The giant boy with the white hair would be waiting for him, even if he got out on time.

"I have to go," he says.

"Ewald. Please. Please let me help you." She is upset, pleading with him. "It's not right what he's doing. You must know that...you must know it's not right..."

As he looks at her face, he realizes he has to do something.

It's too late.

His uncle will kill her.

He knows it without having to think about the reasons why. She's already filed complaints with the township authorities. His uncle asked him questions, asked him who she was, what she'd said to him...what he'd said to her. Then the boy changed grades. He managed to convince his uncle that she wouldn't see him anymore. But they would know if she said something again...they would know that she'd seen something, that she'd said something to him.

He can push her. He can push her into forgetting about today.

But it won't be enough. He's pushed her already, three or four times, and she keeps coming back, keeps asking him the same things.

He has to make sure they never believe her.

He has to make her go away.

As the thought forms, and an idea behind it, his pain worsens.

His light whispers out before the plan has fully solidified, taking over hers. He acts before he can second-guess himself, knowing it may be his only chance before she says something again, before something happens to her. He uses his aleimi to push on her mind, until her face slackens, growing still. Keeping his light in hers, he coaxes her to relax, to lean back in her teacher's chair. He takes over her mind, and he holds her there, waiting as he looks at the clock.

He needs an audience.

But the timing is right for that, too.

Ten more minutes until the bell.

Then eight.

Then six.

When it is five, he looks at her, feeling another whisper of fear. Her face is as smooth and expressionless as one of the cows in the pasture behind the school. Her hands sit folded neatly in her lap.

She looks younger to him suddenly, not like a teacher at all...and it occurs to him again that they are roughly the same age, although she would never believe him if he told her.

She sits in the chair like a posed doll, her blue eyes vacant as they stare off towards the door, a faint smile on her lips.

"I'm sorry," he tells her in German, his voice a whisper. "I'm so sorry Miss Pirna..."

Moving closer to her, he kneels between her legs, pushing the pale blue dress up tentatively past her knees. Pain reaches him before he can think about whether he should really do this, and then he's got her partway undressed and he's working on her, closing his eyes as he pulls on her with his light and his mouth. By the time the bell goes off, he lets go of his complete control over her light. He is so far in hers by then, it is easy to coax it where he needs it to go.

Even so, she is half-fighting him, and he feels horror on her, a near terror.

"Ewald, no...no..."

He doesn't stop though, and her hands aren't forceful enough to make him.

In minutes she is clutching his shoulder in one hand, her back half-arched in the chair, her legs further apart. He hears voices in the corridor behind them, even lost in the woman's light, and he ignores her feeble protests until she is moaning.

He feels his light respond, coiling more deeply into hers, until he is hard, his eyes closed, nearly at the point of losing control. He wants her then, wants her for real...wants her badly enough that it seethes off his light, a pulse of dense frustration. He sends her that too, sliding his fingers into her, and feels her light open more.

She cries out weakly, and at that moment, the door to the classroom opens.

"Pirna," a familiar voice calls. "I wonder if you would lend me a hand with – "

The voice cuts itself off in mid-sentence.

In the silence, he worries briefly that she hasn't seen, that she's left, when...

A scream makes him jump violently, falling backwards when he loses his balance. He slams his already tender back against the thick leg of the desk, letting out an involuntary cry.

The woman at the door screams again.

He turns, feeling shame, despite why he's told himself he's done it, and the shame is worse when he sees her face. Then she is shouting at him, and the words penetrate, reaching his mind even as he ducks instinctively, backing away and low down by the tables as if to avoid the missiles of her words.

"Filthy animal...filthy, disgusting *beast*...!"

She throws things at him then, real missiles, in the form of books from a nearby table, an eraser from the blackboard beside it, and he winces as he ducks. But once he reaches the edge of desks by the windows she aims her fury at the woman in the chair. The woman who is fighting her way back into the room, pulling down her dress, trying to understand what just happened, color blooming so bright over her cheeks that she looks like a different person.

"You whore! You filthy whore!" Frau Schlossing stands in the middle of the room, her face a dark shade of purple. "To a child...a *child!*"

When he looks back, not only Frau Schlossing stands there, but children's faces peer through the doorway, seeing Miss Pirna clutching the folds of her dress, her face flushed bright as her eyes follow the boy. Frau Schlosssing tries to keep them out, but the children point and laugh as Ewald runs away, marking his progress past the row of windows, as one by one he tries the iron handles. He looks for one that might be unlocked, where he thinks he might escape.

In the back of his mind the faint hope remains, that he still might be able to make it first to the lawn outside, pelt his way into the forest and disappear before Gerwix and Stami get ahead of him. He knows they will be outside soon, if they aren't already.

But Frau Schlossing seems to realize what he is doing.

She moves with surprising speed, cutting him off, grabbing him by the collar of his shirt and his hair and half-lifting him off the floor. The shirt cuts into his arms and back where the whip cuts still lay open. His hair hurts as she tightens her fingers and he screams and can't stop screaming even as she shouts in his face.

"You little disgusting *vermin*...where do you think you're going?"

I broke out, without preamble.

Unlike the drifting in and out state that accompanied a lot of these jumps, I found myself out, truly out. I lay there, aware long enough to find myself physically sick, holding my stomach, half curled on my side on the sweat-soaked blanket.

It took me a few beats longer to recognize the feeling as separation sickness, bad enough that I could hardly breathe...bad enough that I couldn't control the nausea that spiraled up in waves from my belly to my chest and then my throat.

It wasn't the first time it had come up in these sessions.

At times it was bad enough that I wanted to die, that I could barely hold on to rationality. Something about the complete lack of affection at that age twisted any normal desire to be touched into a despair-blackened need, a kind of pit that could never be sated. I lay there, unable to move, even to look at him.

But eventually I had to. I had to look at him.

When I did, he lay in a similar position as I did, only with his back pressed against the organic wall, his face pressed to the floor...as if seeking sensation anywhere he could, in any form. He didn't move, or meet my gaze.

I wanted to talk to him.

I had no idea why, or even what I wanted to say...but I wanted to so badly I had to bite my lip to keep from saying his name.

I honestly couldn't even tell if he was aware of me. His eyes were closed, his face slack, almost as if he were somewhere else again, somewhere that the collar and my light couldn't reach. I might have thought he'd passed out, but I could see his lips moving again, reciting words with a uniformity that made them seem closer to a chant.

Remembering the boy doing the same, I closed my eyes, feeling the nausea worsen.

I had just started to look away, when his eyes opened. He stared at me from where he lay with his cheek against the floor, and I felt the pain in his light, worse than I felt it in mine. I saw him looking at me through it, maybe because he couldn't refuse contact with anyone at that point, even me. I still didn't expect him to talk to me, so when he did, I jumped.

"They got me Gisele after that," he said.

I couldn't look away, but his words made no sense to me at first.

Then the name clicked, and I found I understood.

"The prostitute," I said.

He nodded, closing his eyes again. I saw pain on his face, and it didn't disappear in the intervening seconds. I spoke before I knew I intended to.

"Did she get fired? Miss Pirna?"

There was a silence. Then he let out a choked laugh.

"Of course she got fired."

"No more inquiries?"

He shook his head again, his eyes still closed. "No more."

"Gods, Revik..."

He looked at me, and for a moment, I saw a glimmer of that shame.

"I don't mean that." I shook my head, feeling my chest hurt. "That you would even think of that, of doing that to get her fired, to discredit her, at eleven..."

"I was closer to twenty, Allie."

"I know. I know, I just..." I shook my head, closing my own eyes. I lay a hand on my forehead. "You were just so..."

"Small. I know. Gisele thought so, too."

"I was going to say young," I said, turning again.

He didn't respond right away, but I saw him settle against the floor again, holding himself tighter with the one arm. The pain remained etched in his features, but he seemed to be breathing easier, maybe just from stabilizing somewhere within it. I couldn't help but wonder if it was different for him, feeling it now, compared to how it must have been back then. As if he'd been reading me past the collar, he spoke up once more.

"I wonder sometimes, if I did it more for the sex," he said.

He rolled halfway to his back, grimacing a little as he closed his eyes.

"I wanted her," he added. "I had a crush on her, the whole time I was in her class. I used to fantasize about her..."

Glancing at him, I returned my gaze to the ceiling, biting my lip before I'd thought about why. After a pause, I shook my head.

"You did it for her. I saw you, Revik. I felt what you felt."

"You felt what I told myself at the time," he corrected me. "That might have been me lying to myself then, too, Allie."

He closed his eyes again, settling his head on the floor.

"I went to find her, you know," he said. "When I was older."

Flinching a little, I found myself turning my head. When I looked back at him, he was frowning, his eyes still closed as he lay on his back.

"...She'd moved," he said. "To another town. She was married. I tried to thank her...for trying to help me. I tried to apologize. She couldn't even look at me. She couldn't look me in the face..."

Feeling another pulse of shame off him, I couldn't answer him at first, lost in his light as I glimpsed an image of her older face.

The image faded quickly though, leaving me with nothing.

Taking another breath, I looked at him.

"If you wanted her to touch you, you can't exactly blame yourself for that," I said. "Whatever age you were exactly...I remember those years. I remember what it was like, and I had a family, Revik. I had friends. I had a brother."

He raised one of his shackled hands, gesturing no in seer.

"Allie. I don't want to hear the Jon story again."

I felt my cheeks burn, even as a flush of my own shame hit my chest.

"That's not what I meant."

"I know." He shook his head. "Forget it."

But the sick feeling in my stomach wouldn't dissipate. I bit my lip.

"Why does that bother you so much?" I said after another moment, turning towards him again. "Is it because he was my adopted brother? I *knew* he was gay, even then, and I was scared. There were these guys at school..." Thinking about it briefly, I shook my head, realizing I didn't want to explain that, either. "Never mind. I know it was wrong. I know it was stupid. I just...I had my reasons for asking him."

"I know."

"And anyway, there's nothing I can do about it now..." Feeling my jaw harden, I looked at him again. "I wish I'd never told you..."

He stared at me from the floor, his clear eyes on mine.

I saw what might have been an apology in them, or maybe just understanding. After another pause, he just nodded.

"I know. I get it, Allie."

"I know you get it. So why does it bother you so much?"

"It bothers me because he's my friend."

I just stared at him for a moment, stuck on his words. Then, thinking about them, I stared back up at the ceiling, turning them over again, finding I understood even more than I'd thought.

"Balidor was your friend," I said, quiet.

Silence filled the space between us.

It expanded out of him, hitting at my light. I didn't move as it reached for me, didn't look over as I felt him replay my words. I regretted them already, even as it occurred to me that Revik had been talking to me...actually talking to me...for the first time. I returned his hard gaze, feeling my chest tighten when his eyes finally shifted away, focusing on the ceiling.

"Why, Allie?" he said.

I felt my breath stop. I think I reacted more to the feeling coming off him than the words; for a moment I couldn't even make sense of the question. When I turned my head, he was looking at me again, his clear eyes cold.

"Why?" he repeated. "I don't mean me...I'm sure you had your reasons with me. I mean them."

"Them?" I said.

"Yes, *them*...I thought you loved them. Wreg and Nikka. Jax, Holo, Gar... the others you went in with. You acted like you did. You knew what their lives were like before, what it would mean for them to become slaves again..." He paused, swallowing as he looked at me. "Why, Allie? How could you do it? How could you just throw them away like that?"

I couldn't move.

Thoughts seemed to rise to answer him, then just die.

Finally, I shook my head, wiping my face with one hand.

"I didn't throw them away, Revik."

Anger pulsed off his light. "Balidor told me they belong to the Lao Hu now. He said you authorized her to raid the place...gave her the damned map coordinates. He said almost none escaped...that they were forced to swear allegiance to her then and there, or be faced with a Chinese work camp..."

I felt pain in my chest again, even as my anger at Balidor flared.

Well, I'd wondered what he'd been saying to Revik for all of those days.

Even as I thought it, the anger dissolved, breaking up around me like salt in water. Guilt nearly crippled me instead, and a grief I couldn't keep out of my light, even as I fought to keep it off my face. I couldn't handle that right now, and I knew it. I didn't have the luxury to wallow in any of it, not until I'd finished what I'd started here.

"I didn't authorize that," I said finally, hating the words, hating them probably more than he hated hearing them, but unable to change them. "She broke our agreement."

"Voi Pai?"

I nodded, gesturing yes in seer.

"What was your agreement?"

I stared up at the ceiling, knowing he would hate this, too, but realizing I wanted to tell him the truth anyway.

"I needed them distracted," I said, clearing my throat.

My voice came out stronger, almost business-like.

"...I needed them contained until I had you somewhere safe. I knew your people. Well enough to know they'd send everything they had after us, once they figured out I'd taken you. Voi Pai was to keep them there, and that was all."

"And she accepted that, the leader of the Lao Hu? A job as errand runner to the Bridge?" His voice was openly sarcastic. "Are you really that naïve, Allie?"

"I offered her payment," I said angrily. "Tribute was in cache...in weapons. Not in people. Not even in planes. I offered her what you had in those crates, in the main hangar." I paused, feeling my jaw harden again. "...And I offered her Salinse. She seemed to think he might be useful...for intelligence purposes, she said..."

"You gave her Salinse."

"I offered him," I said angrily, turning. "You're damned right I did. She was welcome to him, as far as I was concerned. She's *still* welcome to him. But he's the only one of your people that bitch managed *not* to capture..."

Revik stared at me, his eyes showing a faint surprise.

Then he clicked at me, and I saw the surprise dissolve back into a colder anger.

"You're pretty fucking arrogant these days, Allie," he said. "Being the Bridge seems to have gone to your head, if you think you can take on the Lao Hu single-handed and win."

"I didn't try to 'take her on.' I offered her what I thought were fair terms."

"Well," he said, shifting to his back. "Clearly she disagreed."

I felt my jaw harden again as I watched him settle his weight on the organic floor, his hand covering his face. But there wasn't a lot I could say to his words.

For a moment both of us just lay there, not speaking.

"Wreg," he said then. "Is he dead?"

I shook my head, folding my arms tighter with a sigh. "No."

"You didn't kill him on the plane?"

"No." I looked at him in bewilderment, angry again. "I didn't kill *anyone* on the plane. Why would I? And why would I kill Wreg?"

"How did you keep him from stopping you?"

Clicking to myself in irritation, or maybe at him, I folded my hands over my ribs, still fighting the anger out of my voice.

"I threw him...with the telekinesis. When that only slowed him down, I shot him. In the leg." When Revik didn't speak into the silence, I shrugged with the same hand. "I had him cuff himself to one of the seats before I tranked him...using the same stuff I used on you."

There was another silence.

"He was alive, Revik," I said. "He wasn't even in danger. I had him fixed up before we left him on the plane. They were *all* alive when I left."

Again, he didn't answer.

I felt him thinking as he lay there, even as another pulse of grief left his light. Remembering the Barrier images Vash shared with me in the aftermath of Voi Pai's attack on the rebel headquarters, I felt sick again, unable to tear my mind off of what I'd let her do...what I'd helped her do. I hadn't even told him about Nikka yet, but now I couldn't help wondering if Balidor had, or someone else maybe.

I didn't even want to admit it to myself. The idea of talking to him about it, especially if he had to hear it first from me, made me feel physically sick. I knew it was cowardice...and that it wouldn't probably even make a difference at this point, in terms of how he viewed me...but I didn't want to be the one to tell him, anyway.

He was right. I'd been stupid to think I could trust Voi Pai.

Especially me. She made it clear she hated me, and hated the authority I had over her as Bridge, pretty much from day one.

At the time, I'd told myself I didn't have to trust her. I'd trusted Balidor, and he and Voi Pai seemed to have an understanding of their own. He told me that she would honor their agreement, and I believed him.

But for all I knew, Balidor had been in on it with her. He certainly thought my approach towards the rebels and their stockpile of weapons and planes in the mountains had been lenient, to say the least. He'd accused me of being naïve, too. And of being overly sentimental with a bunch of terrorists who happened to be "nice" when they weren't out murdering people in the name of their gods and ancestors. The part that frustrated me most was that both of them were right, in a way.

The truth was, I couldn't trust any of them anymore.

Balidor, Tenzi, Yumi, Poresh, Illeg, Farador, Garend, Jared, Vikram... possibly even Dorje. The Adhipan infiltrators all saw me as having been compromised by Revik. They thought I was tainted. I wasn't sure if they'd picked up on what Jon brought up with me that first day, about the Dreng being in my light, or if they just thought I was incapable of being objective where Revik was concerned. Either way, I had to concede they were probably right.

And Revik's team, well...they pretty much thought I was the Antichrist.
I fought back the pain that tried to rise, shaking my head at the ceiling.

"You're right," was all I said.

"About what?"

"About everything," I said.

"Meaning what?"

"It was stupid," I said, biting my lip. "...I was stupid. It doesn't help either of us, knowing that. But I don't want you to think I'm not hearing you. I am."

I felt another coil of his light, a faint whisper of confusion that tried to turn into anger and only halfway succeeded.

"If it comforts you," I added. "Pretty much everyone agrees with you... and not just the seers on your side. The Seven, too. They all think I've lost my fucking mind."

When feeling started to strengthen around him once more, I turned on my side, facing him directly. His eyes met mine immediately that time. I paused, watching him look at me, the running lights at the base of the far wall reflecting in his clear irises. I didn't let myself read anything into his expression, and I kept my voice toneless, leached of inflection.

"You know," I said. "I probably don't have to be the one to do this anymore. Not now that we're this far in. If you want Vash to do it...or Tarsi...I think the connection is strong enough now. It doesn't have to be me."

There was another silence. In it, he only stared at me. I saw his expression change somewhat as my words sank in, as his surprise filtered deeper into his light. Then he was looking at me again, his focus flicking forward as he studied my face from across the space between us.

"No," he said, startling me. "No, I want it to be you, Allie."

"Why?"

"Does it matter why?"

"Yes."

Settling his face back on the organic floor, he closed his eyes.

"I just want it to be you."

I struggled through my own confusion at his answer, not letting myself read anything into his words as I studied his resting face. I almost thought he might be going to sleep, when he spoke up again, his eyes still closed.

"Don't worry, love," he said, softer. "It's not a present." Clearing his throat, he resettled his shoulder on the ground. "If you don't hate me now...

you will by the time we finish this."

I bit my lip, looking at him, but he didn't open his eyes.

"You're so sure about that?" I said, fighting my voice.

"I'm sure."

I nodded, feeling my anger turn into something heavier, a feeling that slid briefly into a kind of depression.

"Then you're stupid, too, Revik," I said.

Before he could answer, I rolled to my back again, exhaling shortly as I resettled on the thin blanket. Tugging it around me, I closed my eyes.

He didn't look up, or speak to me before either of us slipped off to another uneasy bout of sleeping and dreaming. But before I drifted away, I felt another coil of confusion leave his light, whispering through mine right before he pulled it back again.

Ten
Emissary

Cass stood under a leafless cherry tree that grew partway inside the wooden pagoda where she and Baguen had been left to wait, over an hour earlier. The tree's dark brown branches extended jointed arms towards a gray and low-hanging sky, somehow providing a contrast that made that sky look even more bleak than it did.

The beginnings of winter had transformed the gardens so radically that Cass may not have recognized them at all, if it weren't for the high walls and the few buildings that stood out more starkly against the leafless trees. The trees themselves, which had all been in bloom when she last stood in this place, now had sticks for arms and twigs for fingers. They stood in muddy slots surrounded by stones and yellowed grass, cropped low to the ground and covered in dark moss and, in some cases, a thin layer of ice.

Most of the warmer-weather bushes had been covered, or moved into one of the long greenhouses that took up one whole segment of the open space between the Tian'anmen and the Meridian Gates. Now, with fewer trees to obscure those, too, Cass realized that an entire complex of such greenhouses existed, lining almost a third of the high walls. Movement around their lit doors and walls told Cass that work continued inside the greenhouses themselves, even at this time of night. Someone maybe even worked around the clock caring for the plants, or harvesting for meals that would be cooked and served inside the secondary set of walls.

The ponds and wells were covered. Bird cages had been moved indoors, and many of the trees were wrapped at their bases, to keep them warm and cushioned from the worst of the snow and ice. The sheep, cows and horses had all been moved to indoor stables as well; Cass saw only a few horses huddled together under trees in one of the paddocks further back beyond the hot houses that glowed in the dimmer light of heavy clouds.

It felt like the entire of the several acre gardens had gone into hibernation.

In any case, Cass certainly lost track of the majority of her landmarks and reference points from when they'd been staying there in the spring.

Exhaling in frustration, she shivered in the late November chill, wishing she'd forgone the elaborate silk outfit for a decent fur coat and one of those Russian-style hats.

It was starting to get dark.

Cass blew on her hands to warm them, then blew her choppy bangs out of her eyes. Her hair, though still bright red at the ends, had started to transform under the inevitable creep of her naturally straight, black hair. Still on the fence about whether she wanted to go back to the shocking red she'd worn for years in San Francisco, she hadn't bothered to do anything with it for this trip. She knew to the Chinese seers, it wouldn't have made any difference, anyway. Unlike a lot of seers, the Chinese ones didn't disparage her because she was human, per se, but because she was from one of the 'lesser races' of Asians, and a mutt to boot.

She hadn't figured that out on her own.

Baguen told her, in his choppy and heavily accented Prexci-English.

One of the servants who'd attended them told her it was supposed to snow in two days. Glancing around the empty courtyard, Cass wondered if it would snow before the leader of the Lao Hu would agree to grant them their requested audience.

In any case, she knew it was likely a lot warmer *inside*, where their host presumably waited, likely smirking at them from behind the walls of the Inner City while she drank hot, imported rice wine. Meanwhile, Cass and Baguen remained locked outside of the Meridian Gate, in a ceremonial pagoda in one of the gardens, freezing their respective asses off.

Of course, Voi Pai hadn't refused them outright in their request.

In fact, every message they received was polite to the point of being a mockery of subservience. As emissaries of the Bridge, they'd been given a tour of the entire outer premises. They'd been taken to several different gardens, greenhouses and tea houses. They were given presents of hothouse flowers and embroidered sashes. They were recited poetry, sung songs and given a demonstration sword fight in the ancient ceremonial forms.

At one point, there'd been puppets.

The seer overlord of the Forbidden City stretched out the preliminaries and the honorifics to the point of teeth-grinding madness, both to avoid letting them inside and, Cass suspected, to make them feel as humiliated and disrespected as possible.

After hours of seemingly endless processions of bowing and poem-reciting and pointless gift-giving, Cass found she was losing her cool. A part of her wondered if she should just take the letter from Allie and shove it into one of the guard's hands before flipping them off collectively and making her own way back out to Tian'ammen Square.

Instead she sat in the cold, looking at Baguen, the Bridge's letter to the leader of the Lao Hu rolled up inside her brocaded jacket.

Why Allie sent her, of all people, on this little job, was beyond her.

She might not be seer, or Chinese, but she knew full well when she was getting the raspberry.

Baguen seemed to agree. He looked at her with his dark eyes, shrugging with one hand. It was almost a human shrug, and she couldn't help smiling a little when he did it, tugging on his sleeve.

"This sucks," she said, clutching his hand.

"Not going to see us," he said in his accented Prexci.

"You think she'll blow us off altogether?" Cass said, frowning. She gestured at him, using seer sign language. *I thought she would see us because of Balidor, at least.*

He shrugged a little at that, but she saw the eye roll, knew it wasn't aimed at her.

He didn't like Voi Pai. In addition to the historical stuff between the Lao Hu and the Wvercians, he thought her actions repeatedly disrespectful to the intermediaries...Revik and Allie both. He felt the same way about Balidor, more or less.

Cass didn't exactly disagree.

What should we do? she signed at him.

Send her a warning, he signed back.

She smiled, laughing a little. *With what to back it up?*

He gave her a puzzled frown, even as he signed a response. *With the Bridge to back it up. With the Sword...Syrimne d'Gaos.*

Thinking about this, Cass nodded.

Caressing his broad cheek with a hand, she kissed his mouth when his eyes closed in response. When they parted, she motioned towards the guard standing at the bottom of the steps below the raised platform of the pagoda.

"Can you talk to him?" she said in English, knowing it was less likely to be overheard. "...Just to start out, I mean. Get him to come over here. You're a bit more...impressive than me, Bags. I'll do the actual threatening."

Nodding once, seer-fashion, he straightened to his full height, pulling the long, Chinese-style shirt back on his shoulders a little so that it lined up with his broad frame and cracking the knuckles in his massive hands. Winking at her, he glided easily over to the edge of the pagoda.

Cass watched, shaking her head with a grin.

She watched Baguen take the stairs with a grace that always surprised her a little. He landed with a crunch in the cut, frozen grass. Walking closer to the seer standing there in ceremonial garb, Baguen fixed the smaller male with a hard stare, moving so that he stood right up in his face. Glaring down at him with his black eyes, he slid a few inches closer, emphasizing the gap in height between the two of them, which was maybe as much as two feet.

Cass grinned a little wider when the sentry paled.

She kind of had to love Baguen's sense of humor.

Staring up at the shocking white face, the yellowish braids that cascaded down the Wvercian's back, woven through with leather thongs and even some feathers, the Lao Hu sentry bowed, using the sign of the Bridge to indicate respect.

Cass laughed a little again. She teased Baguen that he was her Viking, but she was never sure if he got the reference, and anyway, he looked too Chinese in his features for the comparison to be wholly accurate.

In any case, she couldn't suppress a rush of feeling for the big lug.

She knew Allie thought it was weird, the thing with her and Baguen. Jon didn't say much, but she got the impression he thought it was mostly about sex. And maybe that had been a lot of it at first. Remembering what Chan said about the whole thing when they last spoke, Cass frowned. Then again, Chan wasn't exactly coming from an objective place.

Anyway, Chandre was just so...well, *intense* about everything. Truthfully, it had started to make Cass nervous. Balidor even warned her, in an offhand way. He'd told her that Chandre didn't get involved very often, especially for a seer of her age. Cass heard the underlying message there, too, that she should be careful not to assume that just because she was seer, Chan would be okay with keeping things casual. In fact, Balidor said at a later point, she should assume that unless it was explicitly stated that the arrangement was sexual only, she should assume *any* seer was potentially interested in her for more than that. He said that with the light component in sex for seers, they could get very attached, even when no bond or other formal tie was involved. They could also get possessive.

She should have listened to him.

Sooner, that is.

As it was, Baguen and her had been a bit of an accident. Cass hadn't really intended to get involved with someone else, but he'd been unflaggingly persistent...and he'd saved her life in those woods behind Seertown.

Truthfully, she liked the simplicity of being with him, after the complicated headache that had been her and Chan. Chan wanted more from her. Chan wanted to know things...about Terian and whatever else that Cass didn't really want to share. And when she got paranoid about Cass' unwillingness to talk or open up in some other way, she got way too invasive with her light.

Baguen didn't do any of that.

Maybe it was something to do with him being a Wvercian. Or maybe seer males weren't as different from human males as Allie kept telling her.

But it could be the Wvercian thing.

Wvercians, unlike the Lao Hu, actually originated from China. And, unlike any other type of Sarhacienne, or Sark, the vast majority of Wvercians couldn't pass for human at all. Generally, they stood at least a foot above other seers and weighed about three times as much. Since seers on average stood taller than most humans already, this made Wvercians positively frightening to the vast majority of their human cousins.

To add to the oddity of their size, Wvercians' hair and skin usually displayed as nearly albino in coloring, contrasting with their broad Asian features and thick noses.

Only their eyes didn't fit. Coal black in color, so dark that they appeared to be without irises, their almond-shaped eyes stood wide in high-cheekboned faces, slanted at the edges so that they looked somewhere between Mongolian and Southern Chinese.

Baguen had been the first Wvercian Cass had ever met.

She suspected he was one of the first...if not *the* first...who had ever tagged along with an entourage that included the Adhipan.

He'd also told her she was his first human girlfriend.

From what the other seers told her, Wvercians were viewed a bit like pirates. They often lived outside of Code. They didn't take much interest in the factional struggles among the other Sarks. They flat-out refused to join the Lao Hu, and killed humans whenever they ventured too close to one of their enclaves.

They also refused to join the Rooks, at least in any significant number.

The combination of lawlessness and flagrant dislike of rules or constrictions of any kind made some of them revolutionaries and rebels, but the vast majority of them thieves and smugglers. The lack of Code also meant they were often associated with a number of other shady practices, including selling or trading children and females, both human and seer, and providing seer slaves for the work camps and organic tech.

It didn't *necessarily* mean they did these things, though.

According to Baguen's own take on it, Wvercians followed whatever or whomever suited them in the moment, and didn't let any one person or system make the rules. From what Cass could tell, most of them believed in the Myth, however, and deferred to the Sword and the Bridge.

She couldn't really make sense of the whole mishmash, frankly.

According to Dorje, no one had actually ever been able to document the make up or location of an honest-to-gods Wvercian settlement. If one stumbled upon a large group of Wvercians, one was usually lucky to get out alive. Even if one did get out alive, Wvercian practice was to abandon any living space penetrated by outsiders. As a result, no one knew exactly where any one Wvercian stronghold might be based, or even if there was a single Wvercian township anywhere on the map big enough and permanent enough to be noteworthy.

Dorje figured the vast majority were nomads, like some of the earlier seer tribes. They lived off the grid, trading with one another and banding together when it made sense, but for the most part living and working in small or large family units.

Even bonded mating seemed rare among the Wvercians. Dorje claimed to have only ever seen one such pair himself; he told Cass they were so psychotically possessive that he'd been warned not to speak to either of them, for any reason.

In any case, no one wanted to mess with a Wvercian.

Not even a member of the Royal Guard of the Lao Hu.

Cass inched a little closer, trying to listen to their conversation. Baguen spoke so low and deep, she couldn't make out his words, but she caught a few from the sentry.

"...most honorable..." (she missed some of what came after this) "...of course, she will. I will of course relay the message that..." (again, she lost some of it) "...will be most dismayed that the reception was not to your..."

Cass folded her arms tighter, smiling involuntarily.

"...right away...yes..."

Cass watched the sentry bow, right before he motioned to another of the Royal Guard. After a short exchange in sign language, which Cass noted was a bit different from what she'd learned from Baguen and Chandre, the second guard ran off, aiming for the Meridian Gate.

Cass wondered again why they bothered doing everything by foot, when they could just use the construct to talk to one another.

"For show," Baguen said, walking back to her after vaulting up the stairs. "More time."

Cass nodded, shivering against the cold. "Are they going to let us in?"

"This time, I think...yes," he said. "I tell them we leave otherwise. Come back with the Bridge. And with the Sword. Come back with more of us."

She smiled, clutching his fingers briefly. "Thanks, Bags."

"You talk to Lao Hu...the female...?"

"Yeah," Cass sighed, clicking a little to herself.

Refolding her arms in an effort to keep warm, she gritted her teeth against another gust of freezing wind. It was definitely getting dark out now.

"Yeah," she said. "Don't worry, Bags. I'll talk to the scary old bitch."

Smiling, he coiled his arms around her, pulling her up against his warm bulk. As she snuggled up against him, her eyes never left the trail of footprints in the half-frozen ground left by the runner who'd disappeared through the Meridian Gate.

Still, she'd nearly dozed off by the time another form came crunching back over the lawn.

He yelled out something in Mandarin to the other sentry, who immediately motioned politely for Cass and Baguen.

"Come," he said. "You will come now."

He smiled, showing all of his teeth, but Cass didn't smile back.

Giving Baguen a look and an exaggerated eye roll, she climbed out from between his arms and made her way to the wooden steps.

Baguen followed behind. A low grunt left his lips as he did, letting her know in the simplest way imaginable that he felt exactly the same way.

"I apologize if you felt your greeting was overly...traditional..." the seer purred, laying sideways on a low couch embroidered with red and gold silk. Her mouth was a perfect red, the color of blood; Cass couldn't see a single flaw in the Lao Hu leader's seamless make up.

"...I am not accustomed to unannounced visitors," she added, ashing a hiri from a long, ivory holder. "...Even those as auspicious as the emissaries of our Esteemed Bridge..."

Cass forced herself to smile back, but had a feeling she looked more like she was baring her teeth.

Voi Pai, the leader of the Lao Hu, looked pretty much exactly the same as Cass remembered her from however-many months before. She still wore her raven black hair in a high bun with hand-painted wooden clips. Her traditional hanfu dress appeared deceptively simple under its elegant lines, dyed a bright yellow to match her eyes and with the black sash of the Lao Hu knotted expertly around her waist.

It was her eyes, however, that always forced Cass to stare. Those same eyes sometimes made it difficult for Cass to view Voi Pai as quite as much of a person as she did the other seers. Their vertical, cat-like pupils held a distinctly predatory glint, narrowing and widening seemingly at the will of their owner, not due to any changes in the lighting of the room.

She looked like an animal with those eyes. Like some kind of freaky genetic hybrid.

Further, those eyes didn't seem to hold emotion the way most human and seer eyes did. They had a flatness that went beyond the normally inscrutable infiltrator's expression...venturing into pure alienness, a reminder that she truly was a different species.

"Yeah," Cass said after a pause. "I'm sure that's true. Except that we weren't unannounced. Allie told you we were coming...days ago. So did Balidor."

"I received no message...?" the seer said innocently, raising an eyebrow and looking to her left, where a male and a female seer stood by the sliding door to the outside gardens.

"Yunes? Maiwan? Did you see any such message?"

"No, Lady."

"You are quite sure?"

"Quite sure, Lady."

The two seers standing there also wore the badge of the Lao Hu, but Cass couldn't help but roll her eyes at their response.

"You see," Voi Pai said, smiling sweetly at Cass. "I am so sorry, but it seems to have been missed. Can I please offer you some more tea?"

Cass glanced at Baguen, who clasped his hands at his sides. She could tell from his posture that he wanted to fight. She wasn't sure which one of them he wanted to fight, but she had a feeling it was Voi Pai herself. She still wondered that he'd let them take his sword at the gate.

"Tea," Cass muttered. "Sure. Can't have too much of that..."

She shifted her butt uncomfortably on the hard wooden chair.

Baguen had refused to sit. He stood behind her, his dark eyes fixed on Voi Pai.

"Look," Cass said, barely giving the servant a glance as her tea cup was refilled. "You know I'm here as a spokesperson for Allie, right?"

"Of course," the woman smiled, gesturing in the respectful sign of the Bridge.

"Then you know what I want?"

The seer sighed, once more throwing up her hands in a kind of confused dismay. "I am afraid I have no idea what the Esteemed Bridge would want from me, dear cousin."

"Okay...fine."

Distracted, Cass glanced up suddenly, meeting the gaze of the seer who had just served her tea. When she did, she started violently, realizing she knew him.

The seer was just as large as she remembered, but next to Baguen, he seemed almost normal-sized. His dark brown hair was tied back in a ponytail, like that of all of the servants she'd seen, and he wore the same dark-blue hanfu clothing.

"Garensche," she whispered.

He winked at her, but she saw a taut look on his face.

Gritting her teeth, Cass turned to face Voi Pai.

"Since you got no message," she said angrily, yanking the scroll out of her jacket and cracking the seal with her fingers. "...And since you clearly didn't bother to read the request sent to you by the Bridge, then I'll just read it for you..."

"No, no," Voi Pai waved, clicking her fingers to the two Lao Hu standing behind her. "That is not necessary, cousin. Please. Just hand it to my brother, Maiwan..."

"Oh, it's no trouble at all," Cass said, biting back her anger. "I'm happy to do it, most venerable Voi Pai. And I would hate so much for another of the Esteemed Bridge's messages to get lost in what must be an impressively large stack of mail..."

Behind her, she heard Garensche snort just a little.

Baguen was staring at him now, too, frowning below his hard, black eyes.

Before Maiwan could move towards her from the wall, or Voi Pai could argue with her again, Cass unrolled the scroll that Allie had spent a full day transcribing so that it would be in the ceremonial format.

"*...With Respect to You, Voi Pai, Leader of the Lao Hu...*" she began reading shortly.

She gave Voi Pai a hard look, silently promising herself Allie didn't need to know all of her hard work with the ceremonial stuff might have gone to waste.

"Respect this...respect that..." she said, skipping over the second paragraph, her voice bored. "...Title, title, ceremonial crap...I think you can fill in the blanks on all of the formalities, right, cousin Voi? I mean, we don't want to waste *your* time now, do we?"

The Lao Hu leader's eyes narrowed to slits.

Without waiting for her response, Cass picked up reading again a few paragraphs down.

"*...I know that this message will receive a fair hearing from you,*" Cass continued, reading Allie's actual words again. "*...for I know from the hospitality of my short stay in your City that you are a seer who honors the old forms, and whose manners are exceeded only by the generosity of sharing your beautiful home with a stranger in need of her assistance...*"

Hearing Voi Pai sniff a little at this, Cass raised her voice.

"*...That being said, I must tell you that I am very displeased with you, sister,* *and with the actions you have taken against our brothers and sisters who are loyal to my husband, Syrimne d'Gaos. Although I am sure you are treating them with the same hospitality afforded me during my stay, it is my strong opinion, based on intelligence that I have received, that you are holding them against their will. Further, I have had numerous reports that the way in which you compelled them to return with you to Beijing did not accord with treatment befitting our free peoples, no matter what your intention. I have since heard that you even placed some in other facilities outside Beijing...*

Cass felt her jaw harden at the last, knowing it was Allie's polite way of letting Voi Pai know she knew about the seers she'd already sent to work camps.

Baguen seemed to want to punctuate that point as well, grunting angrily behind her and laying his hand on her shoulder as she read.

Cass didn't look at Garensche.

"...I do not wish to debate the veracity of any particular set of circumstances I have laid before you. Nor am I interested in punishing you for these crimes against our race. I would instead like only to determine what terms you would require for the release of my husband's loyal friends, as well as their safe transport back to their homeland...

"That being said, please be aware, venerable Voi Pai, that I will be most displeased if you do not provide reasonable terms to me, in writing, before my emissaries leave Beijing. Further, I will consider any such refusal an act of war between us...one to which I will not hesitate to respond. Since your taking of these brothers and sisters of your Intermediaries blatantly violated the terms of our original treaty, you should consider it an extreme courtesy that I have not declared such a state between us already..."

Cass heard Garensche clear his throat behind her.

Pausing, Cass glanced up at his face.

The ex-Rebel's expression held a faint shock, but she saw something else on his face too, an emotional reaction he seemed to be trying to mute in some way, maybe even to disguise as something else. Looking at his large-featured face, she realized suddenly that he was close to tears, and that at least part of the look on his face was relief.

Smiling at him briefly, she turned back to the note.

"...I would like to leave you with a final caution, sister Voi Pai. This is not a process I would like drawn out in any way. I am aware that your favorite game is to toy with the ceremonial forms to delay the delivery of agreed-upon goods in legal contracts with your allies and enemies. Without postulating which of these categories I may fall into of late, you should know that my patience these days is increasingly thinned from my increased responsibilities to our people.

"In short, I am unwilling to play this game with you, as far as my people are concerned. If that requires a difference in payment, then do not be coy about outlining any stipulations in your terms to that effect. I am willing to provide any settlement that is reasonable to see this accomplished...but I warn you that I expect it to occur within a timeframe appropriate for the reconciliation between our two peoples. For there will be no peace with us, Voi Pai, as long as you hold a single of my brothers and sisters captive...

"Further," Cass added, giving the Lao Hu leader a hard stare.

"...I would like to request, as a sign of your good faith, the release of five of these seers at once, to return with my emissaries, Cassandra and Baguen. As I said before, fair and mutually agreeable payment will be made for the return of all of my brothers and sisters to me. As you clearly did not view our previous agreement as acceptable in terms of the payment originally agreed upon, I would like an honest answer as to what you would require to make this trade with me complete within two weeks' time...

"Any failure to do so," Cass read. "Will also result in a assumption that you wish war with me, sister Voi Pai, and with the seers under my command..."

Rolling up the scroll in her hand, Cass gave the Lao Hu leader a flat look, still speaking as if reading from the letter,
"...Yadda, yadda...sincerely yours, hugs and kisses, Esteemed Bridge."
At the Lao Hu leader's faint smile, Cass raised an eyebrow, leaning back in the wooden chair as she picked up her cup of tea.
"Oh, and then there's the postscript she forgot to include," she said. "Would you like to hear that, as well?"

Voi Pai stared, her predatory eyes fixed only on Cass' face. She seemed to have forgotten Baguen, and even Garensche. When Cass simply returned her look, expressionless, the seer smiled more widely, motioning with one hand as she poured herself more tea.

"Please do, continue, most honorable emissary to the Bridge."

"Okay. It goes something like this," Cass said. "...The Sword is feeling better. In fact, both of them are feeling better...and the two of them might just decide to come kick your ass and light your fair City on fire if you continue to piss them off."

Voi Pai's eyes narrowed slightly, but her porcelain face did not change expression.

"The Sword is her prisoner? You admit to that?"

"*Was* her prisoner, yeah."

The female seer only stared at her. Cass found herself quite sure that the other woman was reading her light, and likely every word in her mind. Feeling Baguen move closer to her in the pause, she realized he'd felt it, too, and likely was trying to shield her.

She didn't care. She'd known that would happen coming in; so had Allie.

"You believe this," the Lao Hu leader said. "You believe he will come here."

"You're damned right, I do," Cass said, gritting her teeth. "And you might be forgetting...he's not the only telekinetic seer on the block anymore. Even if he doesn't, Allie *will* come here. You can bet on it. And she won't be alone. She's really pissed off at you...and she knows what you've done to those seers who worked for Revik..."

Voi Pai smiled again, but Cass saw the wary look in her eyes, the hardness that seethed through the yellow irises around their long, oval pupils. After another long pause where she seemed only to be looking at her, Voi Pai averted her eyes, clicking softly.

"But of course we will accede to her wishes," the seer purred. "There was never any question of that. We all live to serve the Bridge..."

Turning to the two seers behind her, Maiwan and Yunes, she clicked her fingers once more, speaking rapidly in Mandarin. Cass looked up to Baguen, knowing he would understand their words. When he gave Cass a reassuring look, touching her shoulder with one hand, she relaxed somewhat.

Voi Pai returned her gaze to Cass.

"You may have this one, too..." she said, gesturing at Garensche. "He is next to useless to me, even as a trainee..."

When Cass grinned at Garensche, he grinned back, stretching his face around the scar that slid up by one of his ears. He had moved away from them somewhat, but Cass figured it was more ceremonial crap, since he stood in an alcove by the wall, a servant's station. She had no doubt he had heard every word of the note as Cass read it, though.

"...But of course, you cannot leave here," Voi Pai added, her voice still a silky purr.

Cass turned, the smile leaving her face.

"What?"

"...Not until I have spoken to the Bridge personally," Voi Pai added. "...and apologized to her for the wrongs she feels I have done to her..."

"Are you kidding me?" Cass said. "No way. That's not part of the deal... we're going *back* with your terms. In writing. With five of the rebels. Allie said so, in the letter..."

"But I'm afraid that won't suffice," Voi Pai said silkily, her expression showing a theatrical kind of grief as she held up her hands. "For you see, I simply cannot bear the thought that I have offended one of the revered Intermediaries. I must apologize to her in person...and to her husband, if he is 'feeling better,' as you say..."

Cass clenched her jaw, keeping her voice low with an effort.

"Then you'll have to come with us, I guess," she said. "To meet with Allie in person."

"I'm afraid that's not possible. Although I would very much like to visit the Bridge in her own home, I'm afraid that the duties of my position will not permit me to leave the City at this time. I have masters much nearer to her, you see..."

"She'll see this as an act of war," Cass said tersely.

"An act of war?" Voi Pai said. "My attempt to apologize, an act of war?"

"Holding us against our will," Cass snapped. "Making us your prisoners."

"I sincerely doubt that," Voi Pai said sweetly. She gestured to the guards who appeared in the doorway, motioning with one hand lazily towards Cass and Baguen. "...Since your mistress has such an appreciation for the hospitality of the Lao Hu, she must only see this as the highest compliment, honorable emissary of our Bridge. Our desire to keep you here, with us, is meant only as a gift to you...as well as to your most impressive escort, who was *obviously* chosen for his familial ties to our nation, as a representative of one of its most ancient tribes..."

Cass swallowed, looking up at Baguen. She'd heard the threat towards him, too. Most of the Chinese seers viewed the Wvercians as throwbacks. Little more than animals.

Baguen returned her look, his eyes hard, a deep black in his head. She knew he was ready to fight them off, if they came near either of them. She also knew that the Lao Hu would probably kill him without a second thought, especially given his race.

Clutching his fingers with one hand, she gave him a warning look, right before she rose to her feet.

She looked at Voi Pai, her voice hard.

"Fine. You heard the note. You know what you are doing."

Voi Pai smiled again, her eyes glass shards. "We will pamper you and your consort well, cousin. Please follow my guards, and they will show you to your quarters."

"Fine," Cass said again.

Baguen stiffened when the seer sentries approached, but Cass touched his hand once more, forcing him to meet her gaze.

"No, Bags," she said softly in English. "Allie wouldn't like it. We'll just have to play her little game."

Looking down at her, he frowned, his dark eyes displeased, but not at her.

"Bridge come," he said, after another pause.

It wasn't a question.

"Yeah," Cass said, looking again at the Lao Hu leader. "Bridge come."

She stole another glance at Garensche, who still stood in the shadowed alcove behind her.

When she did, the look on his face startled her somewhat. His eyes were trained on the Lao Hu leader, and for the first time since she'd known him, she didn't see the jovial, good-natured seer in that look. He looked at Voi Pai like he intended to kill her.

"I think she might have some help, Bags," she said softly, still tugging on the Wvercian's hand. "I think she might have more help than she thinks..."

Without another word, Cass followed the Lao Hu guard through the doorway into the garden.

As they made their way down the stone path towards the guest area of the Inner City, Cass saw the first, thick flakes of snow drifting down from the sky, reflecting in orange lamplight before they stuck to the trees or the ground.

Looking up as the flakes began to thicken, she found herself wondering just how long it would take before Allie realized they were overdue.

"Bridge come," Baguen repeated, his voice a grunt in English.

"Yeah," Cass said, frowning a little. "Yeah. I just hope she doesn't come alone."

Eleven
Kuchta

"I don't want to talk about it," he says. He smiles at her, shoving his hands into the front pockets of the coarse work pants he is wearing, leaning back on the bale of hay. "You are a pervert, you know? Wanting to talk about this all the time..."

She smacks his arm, shoving him on the blanket until he laughs.

"...I am *not* a pervert! You are one to be calling me that anyway, with a reputation like yours." When he shakes his head at her, pretending annoyance, she shoves at him again, forcing him to look over at her. "...You know there are girls who say you have bewitched them...that you put them in a trance to get their clothes off..."

When he looks away, reddening, she snorts, taking a bite out of her sandwich.

"Look at you, shy suddenly! I will have to tell the other girls it is true."

"Kuchta..." he begins. "Don't."

"I am only teasing you, Ewald," she says, leaning back on her arms. Still gripping the sandwich in one hand, she closes her eyes against the sun, sprawling out her legs in the work dress she wears. "I have kept your secret. No one knows about our little outings. But I have to have some fun... especially since you will not do this bewitching thing to me..."

"You are my friend."

"So...you do not bewitch your friends?"

"No," he says, turning to look at her again. "No, I don't."

Seeing the serious expression in his clear eyes, she smiles, resting her head back on her arm. She takes another bite of the sandwich, chewing as she gazes up at the rafters.

"Then I will consider myself fortunate," she says, laughing a little. "...

To have evaded your snare. I will have enough trouble marrying, with my father being the old drunk he is..." Her smile widens, right before she prods him with one foot.

"...Right, my friend? If I have to explain my lack of virtue due to bewitchings, it will only be the harder..."

He smiles at her, pushing back at her booted foot with one hand. "You won't have trouble marrying, Kuchta. Men like bossy women...and long, dark hair..."

"So he says...the one who tries to bed every girl in town but me." Seeing his mouth tighten again, she grins at him, motioning towards the blanket. "...Eat! You complain you are hungry, then you won't eat!"

He picks up the other sandwich, the one she brought for him, frowning at it a little before he takes a bite. Grimacing briefly, he forces himself to chew, fighting the ripples off his light as he tries to eat it as seer food, and can't.

"You don't like chicken?"

"It is okay."

"Okay, only?" She lies back on the hay, closing her eyes. "Why do I invite you on these picnics of ours? You hate my cooking, you will not bewitch me, or help me with math or science, or even tell me if the rumors about you are true..."

Feeling her words, part of them anyway, he looks at her, his clear eyes serious once more.

"You should not, Kuchta." He frowns again. "You should not invite me on these things. We should only talk on the retreats...where it is safe."

"Only retreats? But those are only once every month...I would never see you if I waited until then! And you would get very lonesome, Ewald." She smiles, her dark hair wound into a bun behind her head. She tugs on his playfully, and he lets her, leaning into her arm "And anyway," she says. "Why shouldn't I? Didn't you just say we are friends?"

"We are friends," he says. "That is why you should not."

She prods him again with her foot. "What is this sudden concern? Are you worried about my prospects? That I might get a reputation as bad as yours?"

"No." He frowns again at the sandwich. "But they will find out...sooner or later. And then it will be bad for you. You know what happens."

She snorts, taking another bite of her sandwich. "Do you mean Gerwix and his band of idiots?" she says. "I am not afraid of that white mutant, with the brain of a horse fly."

He gives her a narrow look, his face suddenly hard, devoid of humor. "They are no joke, Kuchta. You have never had them angry with you."

"I have seen them plenty. I have known them longer than you, Ewald."

"It does not matter what you have seen!" he says, fighting anger for real. "You don't know him. He may seem stupid to you, but he is not. And he knows things, Kuchta. If he finds out we are friends, it will go badly for you...I promise you that..."

"Knows things," she mutters angrily. "He knows I will cut out his eye, if he tries anything with me again..."

When he looks at her in surprise, he sees a frown on her face. She stares up at the rafters, a wrinkle over her nose, between her eyes, like she's caught a bad smell. In that moment, he sees the look behind her smile, and realizes she knows more than she is pretending.

"He liked me, you know...Gerwix." She glances at him, that sharp look still behind her gaze. "He wanted me to go with him to the dance. This past winter he asked...and tried to steal a kiss even. He is lucky my brother was nearby..."

The boy only looks at her for a moment, a little stunned.

It has never occurred to him that Gerwix would like any girls, much less that he'd approach his friend. Looking at her, he realizes again that she really is quite pretty. Her honey-colored eyes are wide and laughing atop a heart-shaped face. Her sensual mouth is often smiling, and instead of silence, like the boy, she uses laughter to cover up what she sees. Her long hair is wound in braids, stuck now with straw, but he has seen it down before, and knows it is thick and dark.

Uncomfortable with his own appraisal, he looks away, shrugging. It is a human shrug.

"All the more reason," he says. "He will assume it is something else. That we are more than friends." He gestures vaguely, reddening again. "...He will think I am courting you."

"*Courting* me?" She laughs, looking up at him once more from under her hand. "He'll think you're bewitching me, Ewald...not courting. He'll think you're talking me out of my clothes whenever we are alone. It is what all of them think about you. No one thinks you are looking for a wife, Ewald...or even a steady girl."

"Whichever," he says, biting back a flush of irritation. "He won't like it."

"We will not get caught eating sandwiches, Ewald. Your uncle does not watch you as closely now. Perhaps he trusts you more...or has decided to bully you another way..."

He stiffens, unable to keep his expression still as he turns his head.

He stares at her face where she lays on the hay, but she only smiles at him, her eyes knowing, holding that intelligence that unnerves him somehow, that feels almost like being read by another seer.

"What has my uncle to do with Gerwix?" he says.

She rolls her eyes, again causing a reaction in his light, even though she does it as a human does it, not like a seer. Giving him a disbelieving look, she lays back on the grass.

"You know he *pays* them, right?" she says. "...He pays them to do that to you. I heard Gerwix bragging about it once, after he bought that horse. The Granger stallion...the one that his elder brother wanted and could not afford." She looks up, squinting at him against the sun. "Do not pretend you do not know. You must know."

He continues to frown at the sandwich, not answering.

His chest hurts, in a way that actually surprises him. Somehow he never thought he'd feel so humiliated, having Kuchta know so much. But that is not the real problem, and he knows it.

She touches his arm, and it is almost a caress. It pulls him out, enough that he moves away from her fingers, forcing the emotion out of his light.

"Did I offend you, with what I said?" she says.

"No." He looks at her, biting back his worry. "You know too much, Kuchta."

"I pay attention," she says. "That is all. I've watched you since that day in school." She sighed, holding her face up to the sun. "...Well, before that, really. We all wondered about you. Not just because of Gerwix and his army of rats. You were always sleeping in school. You bled through your shirts sometimes...and you didn't walk right..."

Fighting another jolt of that embarrassment, he shakes his head, closing his eyes. It's not only embarrassment this time. He doesn't want to hear it, doesn't want to remember, so he goes back to the other, to where she started.

"Which day?"

"You know which day."

He shakes his head again, staring at her. "No."

"The day you got Miss Pirna fired," she says.

He blinks, only just managing to keep his expression still. He considers things he might say to her to deny it, or to pretend it wasn't him that had done it, but he realizes it won't matter...not unless he pushes her to forget.

And he doesn't want to push her.

"You did it on purpose, didn't you?" she says.

He looks away, feeling a sharper pain in his chest.

He won't look at her through it, and he feels emotion whisper off her light, a pang of regret that she spoke. He feels ambushed too, like she held all of this in, hoping to get him to confess to everything at once.

He feels her thinking about this, realizing she has gone too far... wondering what she can say to pretend she hasn't said it. He feels her wondering about him still, wanting to know why he is so sad. He pushes her light from his when he gets to that point, forcing himself to focus on the shafts of sunlight through the hayloft door, the birds winging just outside the edges of the glare. He watches the swallows spin and chase one another in the air outside the barn before darting back inside its shadowed folds.

The darkness wavers there, a blackness under his feet.

"Eat," she urges, pushing at him again with her foot. "You are too skinny, Ewald."

Pain slides through his light. He fights it, until she pushes at him again.

"Eat," she says. "Or I will never cook for you again."

Sighing, he forces himself to take another bite, chewing it slowly. Remembering Miss Pirna's face, he feels it stick in his throat, and he can't look at her until it passes.

It has been a few years.

He is sixteen to the humans, twenty-three in reality. It has been five years, and everything has changed for him, but he can't entirely push that day from his mind.

He thinks about what Kuchta says, about him bewitching females, and another pain hits at him, catching in his throat. His uncle encourages it, tells him it is all right, that he needs to learn, that human whores aren't enough... but hearing Kuchta talk about it, and remembering the blank face of Miss Pirna, he feels it differently.

"Yes," he says slowly. "He trusts me more now."

"Who does? Your uncle?" she says.

"Yes, my uncle." He takes another bite of the sandwich, forcing himself to chew without tasting it with his light. "I understand him better...I understand

218

what he is trying to do. He doesn't need to watch me as much. He never wanted to hurt me..."

"Really?" she says dryly.

"Really," he says, giving her a warning look.

"How the poor man must be suffering, then."

Ewald feels his shoulders clench. "You don't know him, Kuchta. He is a great man. You would need to understand his work to realize it."

"And is that a requirement?" she says, her voice still flat. "Must one 'understand his work' to earn the privilege of food as a child? To avoid being beaten? You are right, Ewald. What a fine man this uncle of yours must be..."

He looks at her, feeling another hard pain in his gut. "You talk about things you don't understand..."

"Do I?" she says tartly. "Perhaps I need a beating too."

He flinches a little at her words, then looks away, into the sunlight streaming through the square hole cut into the wooden walls.

"You are not alone, Ewald," she says. Touching his arm, she makes her voice quieter. "You don't need to be his slave forever. You can leave this place."

He shakes his head. "I can never leave."

"Why not? I do not see any chains."

"Yet they are there."

"You are not a coward, Ewald," she says angrily. "So do not pretend to be one with me!"

He looks at her, his clear eyes serious. "I cannot explain this to you, Kuchta," he says after a pause. "Not as you would like. But one day I will. You will understand that I have a job to do...that he was the only one who could prepare me for this."

She does not argue with him that time, but she looks at him warily, her eyebrows slightly raised. He sees her studying him with that scrutiny of hers, and he can see she does not believe him. Worse, he can see that she thinks his uncle has done something to his mind.

"What kind of job?" she says.

He shakes his head. "I cannot tell you."

"Why not? Did he say so?"

"Yes," he says, looking at her. He sighs a little. "He did...but he didn't have to, Kuchta. He is right. This job is important. And I need to try and do my best at it." He glanced back out, towards the sun. "It will not matter one day, that I had to sacrifice for this. It will seem trivial."

"Trivial?" she snorts. He hears real anger in her voice. "I wonder. I wonder what your wife will say, when she sees how 'blessed' you have been by that frightening uncle of yours with the skeleton for a face..." Biting her lip as if to take back the words, she looks away. When he doesn't speak, she prods him again with her foot, trying to smile. "...Or are you really too busy bewitching girls to want to be married, Ewald?"

"I will be married one day, Kuchta."

She smiles, sitting up on her arms. "Will you, now? You sound very sure."

He nods, feeling his face redden even as he hugs his knee to his chest. "Yes. I am sure."

"You will have to go to another town to find a wife, or she will never trust you to be faithful to her..."

Pain hits him, hard enough that he turns on her. "Will you stop with that?" he says. "I am tired of it, Kuchta!"

She blinks at him, startled. "I'm sorry."

Biting his lip, he shakes his head. "I would never be unfaithful to her. I would never touch anyone else once I had my wife with me..."

"Promises, promises..." she murmurs, resting her back on the hay.

He bites his lip harder, but doesn't answer her. When she breaks the silence, he nearly jumps, having lost himself in the flight of the birds once again.

"You are one of them, aren't you, Ewald?" she says.

Her voice is cautious, quieter even than her murmur from before.

He doesn't answer, or touch his light to hers.

Still, a coldness reaches him as he replays her words. It seeps past his skin to his blood, despite the heat of the sun streaming through the square window.

"You are one of those others," she prompts again, quieter still "The ones whose eyes glow...the people they found in the mountains..."

For a long moment he just sits there, holding the sandwich in one hand, his leg with the other. He thinks at first he can brush it off, pretend he doesn't understand, or that she is being ridiculous. But he knows it would not convince her. He fights back and forth in his mind, knowing what his uncle would say, what his uncle would want him to do. He would want him to erase her...to make her forget they were ever friends, to make her forget everything she knows about him. He would want him to never see her again.

"Do you like me, Kuchta?" he says finally.

There is a silence while she sits up slowly, looking at him in genuine surprise.

"Of course I do, Ewald. You are my best friend."

Meeting her gaze, he swallows, studying her light with his.

"Then don't ever talk to me about that again," he says.

For a long moment, she doesn't speak. He waits for her to think about his words, to see how much he means them. She studies him back, her honey-colored eyes reflecting in the sun from where she sits. Finally she nods, her eyes almost afraid as they look at his.

"Okay," she says, nodding. "Okay, Ewald."

"Thank you." He continues to look at her, still feeling that tightness in his chest, but now it is not only fear. "Thank you, Kuchta..."

She grabs his boot, using it to slide over and put an arm around his shoulders. He is surprised when she kisses him on the cheek, her eyes holding compassion now, and the kind of fear he knows isn't for herself, but is for him.

Then she puts her mouth right against his ear.

"Be careful, Ewald," she whispers to him softly. "You have to be more careful...with the girls. I won't be the only one to wonder..."

Hearing her words with more than his ears, he nods to her, fighting that tightness in his chest once more, even as he recognizes it as love, as feeling he hasn't permitted himself with anyone, not in longer than he can make himself remember. It isn't romantic love, or even a crush. It is something else, and he feels a kind of protective rush of feeling before he raises his eyes to hers again. Once he has, the feeling worsens as he scans the worry on her face.

She is afraid for him. He doesn't scan her to know why, but it touches him.

"I will." He looks up at her again, wanting to say more, to comfort her in some way. Hesitating, he catches hold of her arm instead, studying her face seriously.

"If I ever ask you to leave here, Kuchta...if I tell you it's life or death... would you do it?"

The worry flickers in her eyes, then leaves, replaced by surprise.

"Leave here? As in this town? Or Bavaria?"

"Either," he says. He doesn't smile when she does. "Would you do it?"

Sitting back on her heels, she smiles more humorously, rolling her eyes.

"Only promise you will ask it soon," she teases. "Before my father marries me off to some wild boar from the valley with a fat ass and bad breath..."

"I mean it, Kuchta. Would you do it? I would give you money."

"Enough money for Paris?" she grins, throwing out her arms.

He smiles back; he can't help it. "Enough money for New York, if you wanted," he says. "And a new dress every week...and champagne..."

"Then you most certainly have a deal, Mr. Gottschalk."

They are shaking hands on it, both faces solemn despite their youth, when a wind comes, blowing straw in and around the open window. It makes her laugh first, and he can't help but join her as golden strands swirl around where they sit...

The wheel spins again, leaving me in a space between spaces, a time between times. Pain reaches me there, a kind of crippling hurt that I can't identify, can't place. I feel him in it, and feel myself there, too. He is ashamed, lost inside a realization that I have seen what she saw, what Kutcha saw in him and understood. Somewhere in that, he feels his own rationalizations, but the blackened hole beckons, self-hate mixed with something else, a terror...a dread of the feeling she brought up in him, a dread of being left alone...

I can't go to him here, not really.

But I can let him feel me near, with him in that lost space.

I like her. I know he feels that, too...that I like her, and like that she saw more than she told him, and loved him anyway...

I feel it confuse him. I feel it confuse both of us, because even in all of that...

But I don't have time to complete that thought either. Even in this place of no-time, there is no space left for us before we move off to the next fragment where...

...He is sitting again. Alone, at a wooden picnic table.

Around him, other kids in his class at the human school laugh and talk, and sit together in clusters around other tables. He is alone, as he has always been alone; he hardly notices anymore. He doesn't mind. He doesn't understand them, or their social games. He finds it easier to be alone, to listen from afar, to pretend to be somewhere else in his mind.

He eats self-consciously, carefully. It is an old habit, one that cannot help but stay with him. Although the memories themselves are not forefront in his mind, their effects remain in the background, dictating many of his moves...memories of beatings for eating like a seer, for not just chewing and swallowing and grunting like the others among the humans.

He eats an apple because it is easy, potatoes because they are relatively plain. He chooses his own foods now, so it is not so hard as when he was younger.

But he still feels eyes on him that are no longer there, that no longer bother to watch him.

He hears them though.

He is aware of where they are, where they eat, what they talk about, their thoughts, opinions, flares of emotion, indifferences...when they are silent. It is another habit that cannot die, even though they have not chased him from the schoolhouse in over a year now. Gerwix is bigger now, even bigger than before, and he is loud where he sits with a group of other kids circled around him. He still has his 'army of rats' as Kuchta calls them, but he no longer is tasked with setting them on the boy just to keep him in line.

He knew his uncle paid them.

He wonders why he didn't admit it to Kuchta.

He hears pieces of the blond-haired giant's dialogue, even follows some of its tangents, but mostly he uses his light to feel for any change in the other's mental currents, any movement outside of his usual ebb and flow. He lets his light touch theirs from the Barrier, a scarce touch, in case other eyes are watching...eyes who might block him from knowing if another test is coming...but he feels no differences in his light.

Not until she walks by him.

She smiles at him, a bare look, but he cannot help but give a small smile back. Her honey-colored eyes close in a quick blink, an acknowledgment of him, but she doesn't break stride, or change expression. She has agreed, long before this, to follow his rules.

Still, she passes too close, and the blond boy is watching her, too.

"Hey, Kuchta!" he calls out, stopping midstream in one of his soliloquies. "Kuchta! What are you doing out here? Not inside, like a little book worm as usual?"

The smile in her eyes evaporates. She rolls her eyes at him instead, continues to walk.

But the giant doesn't give up. "Will you come to see me race, Kuchta? I am riding my new horse in the township race this weekend...I am sure to win, with the nags they show!"

The boy feels a curl of her disdain, a disgust she does not hide in her voice.

"I'd sooner clean the school outhouse with my mouth," she tells him. "... As spend a second with you without a gun to my head..."

"That could be arranged," Stami yells, while the blond giant is still digesting what she's said. The others sitting around the table laugh.

The silence of the blond-haired one makes the boy nervous, though.

He doesn't want to look at first, but when the silence deepens, he turns his head.

It is a mistake.

The dark eyes fix on him. They grow hard as coal as they meet his.

"You can't make the races, Kutcha?" he says then, loudly enough that most in the yard turn to look at him. "I suppose you are busy, eh? Too busy rutting with runt boy over there?" He lets the silence grow louder, as other conversations in the yard die. Then he speaks up again. "If you're to be had by that little cock, maybe I'll take some for myself one of these evenings, Kuchta..."

"You might lose something if you try," she retorts, but this time, her face is bright red. "And it might be too small for you to notice, but it'll burn if you pee..."

The others at the table burst into a laugh.

Even Stami lets out a low snort, covering it over with his hand when the giant swivels his head to glare at him. Gerwix's eyes are back on the girl though, quickly enough that the boy feels his body stiffen from the other table. The giant's pale skin is flushed, blotchy with anger when he focuses on her.

"You little whore..." he growls.

He leaps over the table and reaches her in two strides.

...But the boy finds himself on his feet in the same breath of time, until he stands between them. Gerwix towers over him, his eyes as emotionless as a doll's.

"Out of my way, runt."

"Leave her alone."

"I'm only going to ask you once..."

"The teachers will be out here in a minute," the boy says. "If they see you picking on a girl, they'll suspend you...you won't graduate..."

Gerwix laughs, his eyes incredulous. "Listen to him! The little kiss-ass doesn't want me to miss out on my schooling..."

The boy starts to speak again, but she touches his shoulder.

He jumps, but doesn't turn his head, or take his eyes off the giant in front of him.

"Ewald, don't..." she whispers near his ear. "He won't hurt me...don't do this..."

The giant's laugh grows harsh. "Yes, she likes you, runt. She likes you a lot..."

"Shut up, you idiot," Kuchta says.

"You know where he learned to give head so well, little girl?" Gerwix says. Stepping closer, he lowers his voice, so that it's softer than a whisper. His eyes never leave the boy's face. "Have you told her, runt?" he says, smiling. "Have you told her how much you liked practicing, before you finally tried it on a girl...?"

He feels her react behind him, before his mind has wrapped around what the giant has said. She squeezes his shoulder in her hand, tight enough to hurt. He feels her panic, a pulse of horror off her light as she hears Gerwix's words, and he realizes she hasn't missed the crack, or its meaning. Nausea rises in his gut, a hatred that makes it hard to see clearly.

"Did you tell her, runt?" Gerwix says, his voice still soft. A kind of contentment rises in his eyes as he sees the boy's face at his words. "Or should I? Should I tell her just how many cocks you had in your mouth before you tasted your first pussy?"

Before he can find his voice, he feels the fury on her expand outwards, bewildering his own.

"You bastard!" she spits. "You goat-fucking son of a bitch!"

The boy jumps a little, shocked in spite of himself.

Gerwix only laughs. "Goats were a step up for us after that, my lovely..."

"You aren't fit to touch his boots! You complete and utter *bastard*...I hope you die *choking on your own vomit*, being pissed on by that *damned horse*..."

Gerwix laughs again, looking to his friends. The others watching from the table he'd just left laugh, too; Stami's voice is louder than any of them.

But most of them hadn't heard Gerwix's words before hers. Stami walks up behind Gerwix, clapping him on the back.

"She's got a mouth on her..." the taller, thinner boy remarks, nudging Gerwix's shoulder with his. "Maybe we should all give her a run...teach her some manners."

"In your dreams," she retorts. "You're as worthless as he is, *Stami Gunter*. You're nothing but a thieving drunk, whose father only has land because he *stole* it..."

Stami's eyes glitter at her, just before they find Gerwix's.

The white-haired boy shrugs, smiling.

"Can't really argue with that," Gerwix says.

"She's a little trash talker, that one," Stami says. "We really do need to find something to stuff in that mouth. Something bigger than runt-boy's cock..."

The boy glances back at her briefly, willing her to be silent. Despite how quickly he looks at her light-brown eyes, it is still for too long. Before he turns back to look at the giant, the knuckles of his massive fist are already most of the way to his jaw.

The blow knocks him sideways and off his feet.

Half-stunned, he stumbles, catches himself with his hands before he goes all the way down...and pivots his body without thought.

He sweeps the giant's legs with one of his own, throwing his weight back to compensate for the other's, which is easily three times his own.

He's been training. For years now, he's been learning to fight.

He learns by fighting humans...then by fighting other seers. His uncle throws him into the ring with three against him, then four, then five. He learns to fight long before he is allowed to use it...long before he is allowed to tell anyone what he can do.

It is why the boys don't bother him anymore. His uncle tells him that he has no need of such tests anymore. His uncle tells him he could hurt the other boys now, that for him to use his skills could call too much attention to him, that it might make people ask the wrong questions.

How much of this Gerwix knows, the boy doesn't know.

But he isn't expecting a fight.

He was relaxed, standing with his feet too close together, his balance off slightly to one side. He is caught totally unawares, and so he goes down hard, hitting his head in the packed dirt. The boy turns his head in time to see him struggling to get up, a fury in his eyes that is almost inhuman, clouded in a daze of having hit his head.

"Run!" he yells to Kuchta, pushing at her behind him. "Get the teacher!"

Stami lets out a scream, catching hold of his hair.

Before the boy can turn, the other sticks him in the side with the hand-blade he keeps shoved into a band around his wrist, under his sleeve. He knows about the knife, of course...it's been used on him before, more than once, but he barely is able to move back enough to keep the blow from seriously hurting him.

Crying out, he feels it slide between his ribs before he wrenches his weight backwards, straight away from the blade, kicking out and down with all of his weight, aiming his boot for the side of the other's knee. He feels his heel connect, feels the joint give, moving hard in the wrong direction. Before he can know if it will drop him, he leaps to the side, avoiding the right cross of another of Gerwix's followers, a heavyset boy named Troy.

Jerking the knife out of his own side, he lets out a gasp.

Staring at the bloody blade though, rage settles over his light.

He steps back from all of them, moving fast now, light on his feet as he keeps his hands and the knife clutched in front of him. He buys himself seconds as they stare at the stained blade. He finds himself focusing on Gerwix in that pause, who is still only halfway up, still holding his head where it cracked against the ground from the sweep.

"I'll kill you," the giant bellowed. "I'll kill you with my bare hands..."

Without thought, the boy jumps at him.

His feet land on his chest before the brute is fully sitting up. His fist comes down hard on the other's face, hitting him where his eyes are still half-focused. Using his weight to slam Gerwix's head against the ground, he worsens the wound on the back of his head. Feeling the giant's light shift into a deeper confusion from the blow, he hits him again...harder than before.

And now, out of nowhere, feeling flows through his arms...a rush of adrenaline that brings all of his strength forward in a hard pulse.

He is bigger now, still more than a head shorter than the giant, but his muscles are hard and his shoulders broad from the nonstop work he does at his uncle's command.

Feeling a rush of that power, he hits him again and again, half out of his mind with fury as he continues hitting him even after his hand feels broken, his knuckles swollen where they are covered with blood, only some of it his.

Thoughts don't reach him, but images do. He remembers knives they'd used on him, along with switches, sticks, and pieces of metal. He remembers pain as they took turns on him, forcing him to beg, forcing him to do whatever they asked. He remembers what Gerwix told to Kuchta, too...being forced to do that to them when he was done, Stami holding a knife to him, threatening to cut his throat if he didn't, or break his teeth in his mouth...

He remembers doing it in front of all of them, on his knees, like an animal.

The fury turns into a black hatred, a wanting to kill that takes over his mind, that leaves nothing but silence, a throbbing, single-minded need.

He hears screams behind him, shouts to stop, but he discovers the knife is in his hand, the same hand he's been using to punch the giant in the face, and the realization twists the rage in his light into something colder, more sure.

Without leaving that no-thought space, he shifts the angle of his hand...

...and slices the throat of the white-haired boy all the way through the artery.

He watches blood pump through the hole, a warm liquid flow, and a kind of peace falls over his mind, a silence that fills him with relieved quiet.

He is still sitting on Gerwix's chest, holding the bloody knife in his hand, when someone hits him from behind in the head.

They hit him with a rock, hard...

...and everything disappears.

...but I am not outside of this, not even for a second.

It is dark, and the wind is blowing.

It is night, and I can feel that weeks have passed, enough that the late summer has shifted into a new season, or the cusp of one. The ground feels colder, and he is huddled in the dark, his back to the outside of a barn, his fingers close to numb.

Still, he waits.

He has been there for hours, waiting, but he does not move, or make a sound.

As I watch with him, a light trails out from the back side of the house, and he watches it, too, squinting against the wind. He thinks at first it is one of the others, a brother or sister, or her mother perhaps. He walks closer as she disappears into the outhouse, but remains in the shadows, in case someone might see him from another window. He is still unsure if it is her when she opens the door and exits the small wooden shack, but then she raises the light and he sees her face.

"Kuchta!"

He calls to her in a whisper, rising to his full height on stiff legs. He pulls the coat tighter around his body, walking fast, low to the ground, watching her face. He sees her eyes go wide, sees the terror in that look, and holds out a hand, a peace gesture.

"Kuchta! Do not be afraid...it is me!"

She blinks, staring at him in bewilderment. "Ewald?"

"Yes. It is me."

"Ewald." She stares at him like he is a ghost. "What are you doing here? I have not seen you since..."

"Since I left school, I know."

She stares at him, bewildered, and seemingly without words, or maybe with too many of them. While she looks at him, he does the same, realizing that he's missed her in the past few months. He sees that she is wearing only a robe and a long nightgown of heavy cotton under what looks like a long work coat. Letting his eyes drop all the way to her feet, he sees her bare legs disappear inside the frayed tops of leather boots that are likely not hers...that look like her brother's, or perhaps her father's.

She grabs the sleeve of his coat while he is looking at her, and drags him back towards the barn, out of sight of the windows of the house. He watches her face as she pulls him deeper into the darkened doorway, sees the determination in it, the lack of fear.

"What is it Ewald?" she says, once they are out of sight. She touches his hand and flinches, staring up at his face. "You are freezing! How long have you been out here?"

He shakes his head. "It does not matter."

"It does," she says. "What is wrong? Why are you here?"

He looks at her, helplessly, as she stands before him in her family's clothes. Guilt seizes him, an awareness of the total unfairness of what he's come to ask her to do. But the words come out of him anyway, all in a rush as he remembers his uncle's face, the look in his eyes when they last spoke.

"Kuchta," he tells her quietly. "Remember what I asked you? In the hay loft that day?"

She frowns. It puts that pit between her eyebrows he knows. He is about to remind her of what he means when she speaks, her voice suddenly serious, and all-business.

"Of course I remember," she says. "You never wanted me to talk about them, those other people. You asked me not to – "

"Not that." He catches hold of her hands, flinching a little at how warm hers are, next to his. "I asked you, remember? I asked would you ever leave here, at once, if I told you it was life and death. You said you would, Kuchta. You said you would do it even without knowing why..."

Her eyes widen slowly as she stares up at him.

"What has happened?" she says. She touches his face. "What has happened, Ewald?"

He shakes his head again, clicking at her without realizing he is doing it.

"I cannot tell you." Seeing the look on her face, he squeezes her fingers tighter. "I can't, Kuchta. I'm sorry...please. You have to trust me on this. Please..."

She stares up at him, her eyes flickering between his.

"Please," he says again. Fumbling in his pocket, he pulls out the other things he has brought for her. "I've written out what to do," he says, knowing how it sounds, forcing himself to continue speaking anyway, to get it out. "...If you follow this, they will leave you alone. You have to follow this *exactly*, Kuchta. Do not deviate from it at all. I will cover for you here. I will give them reasons not to go after you..."

She stares at the bound pad of paper he gives her, filled with careful neat print in German.

"Please, Kuchta," he begs her. "Please...I've got money. A lot of money..."

He hands her everything he has, everything he has made from the fighting he's been doing over the past year, and even from before that, when he got money from his uncle and hoarded it. She stares at the pile he hands her, her eyes showing disbelief.

"It is enough for Paris," he says. "Maybe not dresses...or champagne... but you could get work there. You could go to school. You wanted to be an artist, yes?"

He waits for her, watching her face.

He waits for her to catch up, to hear what he is saying to her. He waits, holding his breath, hoping he won't have to coerce her, that he won't have to push her into doing this thing. He stands there in the cold, holding her hand with one of his, clutching the coat over his chest, realizing suddenly that he is taller than her now, by almost two inches. He grips her hand tighter as he waits for her to look at the money, as she takes the notebook from his other hand.

When she looks up, her eyes study his once more.

There is fear in hers, but he sees something else there, too, something that causes his breath to expand in his chest.

"When?" she says, when she finally speaks. "Tonight?"

He nods, restraining himself from kissing her in his relief.

"Yes, tonight."

"All right. Will you wait for me?"

"Yes." He smiles, nodding as he holds the jacket tighter. "I will wait."

He releases her arm, watching her as she walks back up to the house.

He doesn't have long to wait.

Even so, by the time she returns he is beside himself with worry, nearly sick with it. His mind churns through scenarios as it occurs to him that she could be telling her parents, that she could have decided he was dangerous, or that he'd lost his mind. She might have told him yes just to get away from him, to fool him into letting her back in the house.

He is still thinking about this when she returns.

She is fully dressed this time, wearing a work dress and a thick cloak, and carrying a satchel over her back. He sees a second bag coupled with the first, and realizes she's packed food as well, and water. He watches her in a kind of disbelief, barely able to think straight when he realizes she is really going to do this thing, and without asking him why.

When she reaches him, he doesn't think.

He kisses her, pulling her to him.

She doesn't fight him, but kisses him back, sliding her arms around his waist as he pulls her between his. He kisses her for a long moment, holding her tightly against him. By the time he draws back, she is breathless, her cheeks flushed.

"What was that for?" she asks, smiling at him.

"For trusting me," he says.

He doesn't smile as he says it.

Then he is handing her the money and the book, telling her that there is a wagon waiting for her, pointing directions as he looks up the road. He doesn't kiss her again before she leaves, but squeezes her hand a last time, looking at her face with a love he doesn't know how to feel, that he doesn't know what to do with.

"Goodbye, Ewald," she says, smiling at him.

"Goodbye," he says, feeling the word catch in his throat. "Be safe, my friend." Once she is out of earshot, he says, quieter, almost as a prayer.

"I'lenntare c'gaos untlelleres ungual ilarte...y'lethe u agnate sol.."

The Gods love and keep you my most beloved sister. It is for you that I am here...

He doesn't cry until she is gone.

He is sure he'll never see her again.

"Allie!" the voice was frantic, almost yelling. "Allie! Wake up! Come on!"

I fought to open my eyes, but it felt like weights were on them, like I was being pulled from deep inside a well of ice-cold water. I felt pain there, but more than that, the feeling of loss almost overwhelmed me, brought a sickness that made it hard to see.

"No..." I managed, pushing at his chest. "No...leave us alone..."

"Allie!" The voice, the light behind it, flooded with relief. "Thank God. We couldn't wake you...we couldn't wake either one of you...it's been three days...Revik's a mess, Allie...he's dying...we have to get him help..."

But I was beating against him, hitting my fists against his chest.

I couldn't stop the sob that built in my throat, tearing out of me, like an animal trapped inside my chest. I fought to get free of him, struggling against his hands, but I was still back there, still lost in that other place, where I saw her face...

Rough hands hold him, gripping his collar and his hair, holding his bound wrists behind his back. They've seen his face, and he's with others, so he can't do anything. He can't fight them, not even with his sight...

He looks at the dirty faces across from him as they are pushed across a hillock-covered field. He sees the others from his unit then. He sees three he knows right off, and a half-dozen who are wearing his uniform. More than twice their number push and pull them along, including the French soldier holding him by the artillery belt he knows they will strip from him as soon as they are someplace where they won't have to carry it.

Likely after they've put bullets in each of their brains.

His body is hard from days in the field. He is hungry, almost starving, but barely feels it as they march him hard across the grass. He sees a house up ahead, a normal farmhouse, like he would see back home, and there are lights on upstairs. Whoever they are, they are awake, but likely getting ready for bed, as they have vacated the main living space on the lower floors.

It must be their field they are crossing, their animals they walked among earlier, trying to find cover. There is something strangely familiar in this scene.

He could die here. It would be like coming home.

The man behind him grunts as one of the others in his unit stumble.

He turns and stares at the dirty face, seeing near-black eyes in Chinese-looking features, tattoos on the hands which are visible beyond his uniform sleeves. He looks at this other one, a brother of his, and he thinks to himself that his face is too unusual here.

They will know what he is. They will know him, and all of them will be caught.

He can't kill them though...his own people. He won't. Even beyond his uncle's orders.

They push him and the others through the door of the house and yell at the occupants in French. He can't understand French, but he reads the bulk of the meaning off their minds as they yell, waiting expectantly for an answer.

They want these people to keep them here, bound and guarded.

He relaxes a little, exhaling under his breath. They will get free. As soon as these soldiers are gone, he can push their captors. He can push the humans in his unit, too, convince them he is appealing to their captors' hearts, not manipulating their minds. Wreg might even help him. The others of his kind accept him because of who his uncle is, but the humans who fight alongside him don't know what he is, either.

Usually they fight in separate units, the seers and the humans. He wonders why they deviated from that on this day, of all days...then decides it doesn't matter. They will get out of this. He has to. There is only the easy way, and the hard way.

He is still thinking this when there is an answering call from upstairs, and a man comes down, disheveled, with brown hair and a large nose. The man, presumably the owner of the house, is thin but wiry, tall with eyes that are large in his face and that carry a surprisingly gentle light. Despite the lack of meat on his frame, his shoulders are broad, and he has a worker's hands.

He barely looks at this human though, before the farmer is motioning them back out the front door, past the windows along the side of the house, and towards a green-painted cellar door, whose frame stands in solid earth.

He follows along with Wreg and the others, stumbling first among the group down the wooden stairs, with the French bastard's fist still in his back. He lets himself be shoved into a corner of a cellar filled with wooden shelves holding jams and jellies, even butter and cheese.

Staring around at all of it, he feels his stomach cramp, wonders how much they can carry with them as they leave...

Then a light follows the farmer down the wooden steps, and a woman is with him.

He stares at her, stares at her face.

For a moment, he is transported somewhere else. Thoughts of how he will get away, how much food he can steal and how many he will have to kill, leave his mind...

He stares at her, and he cannot stop staring.

But he forgets another of their classmates is among them.

"Kuchta..." Stami breathes, from two bodies left of his. He stares at her, too, then his eyes find Nenzi's, holding a kind of condensed hate. "You little fucking *bastard*..."

A French gun hits him in the head, silencing him before he can speak any further. Nenzi is relieved when he sees Stami hit, but his eyes cannot help but return to the woman's face. This time, he finds her staring at him, too. Her eyes wide in her face, she looks him over, taking in the size of him with a kind of disbelief before returning her gaze to his face, and finally his eyes.

She looks at the French soldiers then, biting her lip.

They are staring at her, their eyes openly wary.

He is in their minds before the thought is fully formed. Within seconds, their expressions grow slightly blank, right before they look away, focusing back on the farmer.

"You will watch them," their leader tells him. "Keep them here."

"*Oui*," the man replies, looking at the prisoners with a pained expression. He says in French, "We will lock them up in here...bolt the doors on top, and use a chain..."

The head of the French unit, the pigs that have taken them, nods, giving a last hard stare over the group of them. He does not pause on Nenzi's face.

"Give us any trouble, and we'll shoot you all dead," he says then, in broken German. "We will line you up and shoot you, and say you fought back..."

"Or say nothing at all," another adds darkly, his voice deeper than that of the first.

Nenzi doesn't look up at their threats, afraid he won't be able to keep his eyes off the woman. He holds Stami's mind now, too, and forces him to forget what he's seen, hoping it will work until the woman leaves the cellar and returns to the upstairs rooms.

In what feels like a long time, they all do leave. The cellar goes dark, and he is in there, with the others, breathing hard the smell of mold and butter.

"Who is she?" asks Wreg. He is the oldest of the seers there with him, and the one Nenzi had been looking at earlier, the one who is too obviously a foreigner.

Keeping his mind blank, Nenzi turns on him.

"Why did you not take them?" he hisses instead, his voice openly angry as he speaks in Prexci. "They had no seers! What chickenshit game are you playing at, *Commandante!*"

Wreg blinks at him in the dim light, his eyes shifting from curiosity to irritation. It is dark in the cellar, too dark for the humans, but not so for the seers' more sensitive eyes.

"Orders, runt," he says. "Pretend you remember what that means. Then pretend you remember that you're still under my command...and that I can have you beaten until you piss blood if you do not do as I say..."

"But to what purpose is this? We could be out there now...going after them..."

"They wanted us to scope out the area."

"From a fucking cellar? Was that the request? And who made it?"

"Watch your tongue, you little prick, or you might get it cut off when we're out of here." The older seer's voice hardens more, even as those black eyes meet his. "You wouldn't dare speak to me that way, if your uncle was someone other than who he is. Maybe you should think about what kind of man that makes you, runt..."

"I'm not such a runt now," he retorts back. "I'd caution you to remember that, too..."

The other laughs, looking up and down his body in disbelief. "You want to duel with me, little Nenz? I would gladly take that challenge...see if a good long trip to the hospital helps you to grow up a little. Or at the very least gives me a few weeks' peace..."

"You're on, you arrogant cocksucker. Any day...just give me the time and place..."

He is about to say more, when sound, and then light pull his eyes upwards, towards the trap door as it opens over them. He feels a sinking feeling in his gut, even before he sees her face glowing behind the lamplight.

"Ewald?" she whispers. She peers down through the hole in the ground, scanning faces to find his. "Ewald, is that really you down there?"

"No," he says, glaring at Wreg when the other pings him insistently with his light. "Go away, woman. Go back to your farmer."

"He is out with the soldiers now. They asked for him to come and help them with some of his equipment...to move things...bring them supplies..."

"You should not be telling us this," he says angrily. "We are enemy soldiers, remember?"

She laughs, and the familiarity of it closes his throat.

"You are hardly in a position to do my husband harm," she says.

"Go back to sleep, *Frau*..." he growls at her. He does not realize he is speaking German until then, or that she has been using the same.

Who is she? Wreg asks him in his head. *How do you know her, runt?*

He ignores the other seer, his attention focused on the woman in front of him. She looks so much the same it catches his breath, makes it hard for him to think clearly, much less pretend he does not know her. Her face is slightly thinner, her cheekbones more prominent, but otherwise, it is the same face, and the same honey-colored eyes staring down at him, holding a kind of wonder as she looks at him, too.

He is still watching her warily when she pulls out a long kitchen knife.

"No...Kuchta..." he whispers fiercely as she approaches him. "Don't! We can get away. It is all right..."

"So you do know me?" she smiles.

"Kuchta! This is serious! Leave me here...I don't need your help..."

She gives him a puzzled smile, then bends down over and behind him, sliding the knife between his wrists and sawing at the heavy rope.

"Who says I am doing it for you?" she retorts, in the voice he remembers well. "Do you think I will miss my one and only opportunity to question the man who sent me away all those years ago? The boy who once said he was my friend?"

He glares up at her, gritting his teeth. "What will you tell your husband?"

"Absolutely nothing. There will be one less prisoner when they return. By then, they will likely be so drunk they will not notice." At his raised eyebrow, she smiles, cutting through the last of the rope around his wrists. "...Their very *first* request was wine, *Herr* Gottschalk. And we are blessed with an abundance. I imagine my husband will be gone quite some time. He knows how to handle these swine...they pillage our stores regularly these days."

When his hands come free, he rises to his feet, catching hold of her arms.

"Kuchta...go back upstairs."

"Only if you will come with me."

He stares at her, half out of his head with relief that she is alive, joy to see her, and fury at her for being so completely unreasonable.

"No. I won't," he says.

She folds her arms, looking up at him without changing expression. Despite her surprise in seeing him before, she seems undaunted by the differences in their sizes now.

"Then we will have to talk down here. Shall I start asking you questions now?"

"Kuchta..."

"You are a soldier now, Ewald? Why? What is this stupidity to you?" she says, staring up at him. She unfolds one arm, pointing at where Stami lies on the ground, his head bleeding. "What are you doing with that sack of shit, like he is your brother now?"

"It is complicated, Kuchta."

"Complicated? That you pal around with your tormenters now? Explain to me just how complicated that is, Ewald..."

He looks at her, then at Stami's face, and cannot help a curl in his lip.

"He won't live out the war," is all he says.

Stami starts to speak, but Wreg elbows him, hard, to keep him silent. He is staring between Nenzi and the woman, his black eyes wary. Nenzi takes this in, then turns back to the woman, feeling his jaw harden again.

"You have to go, Kuchta," he says.

But she acts as if he hasn't spoken.

"Shall I ask you the other question now?" she says pointedly. "The one about why you sent me away all those years ago? What the real reason was?"

He looks at Stami again, sees the death threat in the other's eyes, and the way he stares at Kuchta in her dress. He won't remember this though. He won't remember any of it. Nenzi will make sure of that, no matter what he has to tell Wreg to convince him to go along.

"Ewald?" she says. "Are you coming? Or not?"

Seeing the stubborn look on her face, he thinks about pushing her. Then, on impulse, he doesn't, grabbing her arm instead as he steers her towards the stairs.

"One hour," he tells her. "We will talk. Then you will bring me back down here, and tie me up..."

Brother, what are you doing? Wreg asks him in his mind.

Piss off, he returns shortly. *Getting laid...what the fuck do you think I'm doing? I'm sure you don't mind, given that you're sitting on the ground in your own shit, just like you wanted...*

He closed off his mind before the other could answer, following her up the wooden stairs without looking back. But he feels a ripple of the other's anger even through his shields, continues to feel him seething down in that dirt-floored room, even after Kuchta shut the double doors to the cellar and locked them with a thick chain.

"Why are you doing this, Kuchta?" he asks her, once they are inside the house.

They are upstairs and she is sitting on the bed, looking up at him with a half-smile on her face. He glares at her when the expression doesn't change, looking around the small room in spite of himself, taking in the wood floors, the curtains on the windows.

"You are doing well for yourself," he grunts finally. "Is he a good man, your husband?"

He turns to look at her, and she laughs, right before she gets to her feet. She envelops him in a hug before he understands what she intends, and he can only stand there, holding her back. After a moment, she separates herself from him, wiping her eyes. He sees her fingers holding tears and is frozen for a moment, unable to make himself speak. He is still standing there, when she slaps him hard on the shoulder, just like she used to.

"You are enormous!" she laughs. "What the hell have you been eating?"

He smiles, he can't help it. "Baby goats," he says.

"Well stop it, you're like a mountain."

"I'm not so large."

"You are! You are..." She holds her hand up, until it reaches the top of his head. "You are so tall, Ewald...how did you get so tall?"

"Nenzi," he says, without thought. "My name is Nenzi now."

"What kind of name is that?"

He hesitates, then shrugs, looking her directly in the eye.

"You know what kind," he says.

She frowns at him a little, but it is a frown that is almost a smile. He realizes she is pleased with his words, if only because he told her the truth. He feels an odd rush of pride on her as she sits back on the bed, patting the mattress next to her with one hand.

"Sit! Talk to me! Tell me all about how you became this scary soldier..."

"No, Kuchta..." He shakes his head, feeling his frustration rise once more. "Put me back with the others! I did not send you here to get you shot by the fucking French..."

"They are my people now," she says, indignant.

"Which is why you would be a traitor for helping me!" he returns angrily.

"Ewald..." Seeing his face, she smiles, amending, "...Nenzi. Come here. Please. I have not seen my friend in so long. Please, just let me talk to you. Please."

Seeing the clear look in her eyes, the genuine affection in her light, he cannot refuse her. Sighing in frustration, as much at himself as at her, he walks over to her, and sits beside her.

"They cannot know how I know you...they do not know me, Kuchta."

"The French soldiers? How would they?"

"No," he says, shaking his head. "Not them. The ones with me. They know me differently...as someone else. Someone you would not like..."

She frowns at him, studying his eyes. "The foreigner down there...the big one, with the paint on his arms. He is like you, isn't he?"

"Yes."

"And he thinks you are someone else?"

He sighs, still drinking in her face in a kind of wonder. "Yes."

"And why is that?" she says. Seeing him frown, she laughs, but there is a bitter edge to it. "I know...you cannot tell me. You have not changed at all, Ewald." She clutches his hand impulsively, kissing his fingers. "And you are still with him, too...your uncle?"

He feels his jaw harden, right before he looks away. "Yes. You know I am."

She hesitates a moment, then her voice grows more pointed.

"And you know of this being they talk about?" she says. "The one they call Syrimne? Syrimne d'Gaos? Is he with your uncle, too?"

He turns, staring at her. Feeling his heart pound in his chest, he can only look at her for a moment, doubting his ears.

"Kuchta," he says then. "I don't know anything about that."

She snorts. "Sure you don't." Shaking her head, she shoves at his shoulder again with her hand. "...Do you know, Ewald, you were always the most terrible liar? I've meant to tell you that for years, but I never had the heart to do it. You are positively the *worst* liar I know..."

"Kuchta..." he begins.

"Don't. I know. You can't talk about it." She looks at him again, and he is shocked to see more of her tears. "Is he treating you better at least?"

He stares at her eyes, at a loss. "He treats me fine."

"Sure he does," she says, wiping her face. She gives a short laugh, but there is no humor in it. "By fine, I assume you mean he no longer beats you until you can't walk..."

He reaches for her arms, tugging on them. "Stop, Kuchta. Stop. That is all over now. I'm not a child anymore..."

"No, but you are still his. I can see it on you. I can see it in your face."

He frowns at this, but he doesn't argue with her. He is trying to decide if he should push her, if he should just blank out her mind and free the others from the cellar, when she speaks up again, wiping her eyes with her fingers.

"Did you get married, Ewald? Like you said you would?"

He swallows, looking at her. Then he shakes his head. "No," he says.

"Why not?"

"She is not here," he says. "My wife. She has not come yet."

She laughs again at this, looking up at him. "What kind of wife is this?" she says. "An arranged marriage?"

He smiles at her attempt at humor, still worried at the grief he feels in her light, that seems to be emanating all around her.

"Something like that," he says, shrugging a little.

"Something like that?" She tugs on his hair. "You need a haircut."

He watches her distract herself with his hair, but he can feel the grief on her still.

"And you?" he says finally, smiling when she turns. "You are happy here? With your farmer?"

She smiles, and he is relieved that it is a real smile, one with warmth.

"You are happy," he says.

She nods. "Yes. He is a good man."

"So no Paris, then?"

She laughs, wiping her eyes. "No. I never made it to Paris, not back then. I stopped here, first, and never really left..."

"You made it later?"

"For my honeymoon," she smiled, pushing at his shoulder. "If you really must know."

"Did you see the dancing girls?" he asks, smiling back. "And the Eiffel Tower?"

"And the cafes and the river and Notre Dame and the Louvre...yes, I saw it all."

"And you came back here," he says, looking around the room once more.

"Yes," she sighs, following his eyes around the same space. "I came back here."

"It is very nice," he says, giving a nod of approval. "Very nice. Do you have children?"

"Yes," she smiles again, wider that time. "Two. They are with their grandparents. The front was getting too close to here...we will join them probably in a few days. My husband wanted to get most of the harvest in first, if he could..."

"I understand," he says, gives another nod of approval. Her husband is not a coward, either. And he is providing for them, even in wartime.

Watching him look at her, she hesitates again, then tugs at his hair.

"And you, Ewald? Are you still as lonely as I remember?"

"Lonely?" He frowns at her, genuinely surprised. Then he thinks about her words, and a kind of heaviness settles on him. "I am fine, Kuchta. Busy."

"Yeah." She snorts. "I'll bet."

For a moment she only watches his face, as if assessing him all over again.

Again, he wonders if she sees through his skin somehow to his mind, if she sees more of him on the other side than he ever seems to credit her. Even as he thinks it, she moves back on the bed, indicating for him to follow her. At first he is alarmed, thinking she wants something of him, that the look in her eyes means something else. Then he reads her, and realizes he understands.

"No, Kuchta," he says anyway.

"Come on," she coaxes. "Let me be an old married woman. I can do this, now, and it doesn't mean the same...it doesn't mean you have to bewitch me..."

"And if your husband comes in?" he retorts. "Will he see it the same?"

"He will not come in," she says, rolling her eyes. "And anyway, he trusts me, Ewald...and he knows all about who you are. He already wondered, and asked me if you were one of the men under the house. He offered to take the wagons, to give us time to talk..."

He frowns at her, clicking softly. "He is a good husband. But you should not have told him, Kuchta. They have our kind, too. The French. Not many, but some..."

She only rolls her eyes again, holding out an arm to him.

"Come here," she says. "Or I will make a fuss, Ewald. I will yell and yell until my husband hears, or the soldiers come running...or your friends burst out of the cellar..."

"You are a brat still, too," he grumbles.

"I still get my way, if that's what you mean." Her voice and hand gestures grow impatient. "What...are you afraid of girls altogether now?"

He hesitates, still wanting to refuse her, but wanting more not to.

After a bare pause, he does what he always did with her, and doesn't let himself think. Without meeting her gaze directly, he rolls to his side, and lays next to her on the narrow bed. Her arm circles him in a tight hug, holding him against her body. He lets himself relax into her arms as she starts stroking his hair.

After another moment, he feels his light open, and it is a relief.

It hasn't been open in a long time, longer than he lets himself think about. Hers is open, too, as open as he remembers it, maybe more so from having a family and children now. He lets her hold him in her light and he pulls impressions off her, feeling her husband, her two girls. He sees smiles and honey-colored eyes and bow-shaped lips stained with berries.

It is a good feeling, this family.

He finds himself relaxing more, even as he leans into her.

"You don't know how badly I wanted to do this for you," she says, as he closes his eyes against her arm. "...The whole time I knew you, I've never met anyone who needed affection more than you, Ewald. It was hard not to touch you sometimes..."

"So why didn't you?" he says.

"Because I couldn't then, Ewald," she says. "You know that."

He feels her words catch in her throat, so he does not answer.

Letting his weight fall even deeper into hers, he closes his eyes once more. Her fingers in his hair are lulling, even without the arm she has around his chest, caressing his shoulder. He lays there, and realizes it is all right. There is nothing wrong with what he is doing. Something about that simple thought is a tremendous relief.

"You used sex for this, didn't you?" she says then. "To be touched?"

He nods against her arm, feeling the truth of her words. Feeling another layer in his chest relax, he nods again, squeezing her arm.

"You knew that," he says.

"Yes, I knew. I wonder if some of them did, too."

Remembering Gisele, the last time he saw her face, he closes his eyes. Forcing the image out of his mind, he clears his throat, shaking his head.

"I don't know," he lies. "I did not know any of them."

"Do you now? Know any of them?"

He feels his throat tighten, and tries to smile.

"Why do you always want to talk about my sex life, Kuchta?" he says, glancing up at her. "Does your husband know what a pervert you are?"

She pulls at his hair again, laughing. "He knows."

"That is good," he says, leaning back into the curve of her body. He feels a reaction in his light, but ignores it, forcing himself to relax. "You married the right man, then."

"I married the right man."

He smiles, unable to help it.

It is the last thing he remembers, before he falls asleep.

Darkness finds him, a blank terror that holds him against a wall, half broken with chains. He feels pain in his body...pain in his back, in his legs. He fights to get free...

And chokes, forced awake by a pitcher of water to his face.

His head hurts, feels swollen out of proportion on his neck. For a long moment, he can't move, not even to open his eyes. But he does get them open, eventually.

The face of Wreg hangs over him. He is frowning, staring down at him as if trying to decide if he should kick him, or throw more water over his head.

"What happened..." he manages in Prexci. "Where am I?"

"We are in the woods. Two miles from your precious farm wife..."

"Where is she...?"

He looks around, half in a panic, feeling a dread in his body that is physical, that makes it hard to breathe. He grabs the other seer by the front of his shirt.

"Where is she, Wreg?"

"The wench?" Wreg looks surprised, taking in the expression on the other's face. "I left the boys to take care of her...Stami seemed to have a particular wanting. He clocked you pretty good when he saw you in her bed...I thought he'd killed you, honestly. I figured it was payback for what you did to him in that cellar..."

Nenzi stumbles to his feet, lurching in the direction that Wreg indicated with his light. Wreg gets in his way, blocking him easily, but Nenzi fights the other seer, tries to force his way past his broad body. He still can't move right, and the other forces him to stop, gripping him tightly with strong hands.

"Where are you going?" he says in bewilderment. "The girl is dead, Nenz...Stami and the others had their way with her, then they cut her throat..."

For a moment, the words hang in the air, broken, like so many pieces of light.

Then he sees her face, watches her look at him, and something in him breaks open.

He fights out a sob, choking on it.

The other seer stares up at him, as if he can't believe his eyes.

"Nenz..."

He screams into the night, unable to hold it back. He screams again, even as the larger seer wrestles him to the ground, clamping a hand over his mouth.

"Nenzi...gods...what is the matter with you? There are still French fucks out there..."

But he can't stop screaming, he can't...

"Nenz...Nenz...what is the matter with you? Brother...calm yourself..."

The other seer sounds almost afraid, his voice trembling even as he tries to comfort the other with his light, to calm him down.

But the younger seer is inconsolable.

He screams again, behind the other man's hands, unable to stop the feeling sliding through his light, the dread and black emptiness that breaks something, somewhere inside his mind. He is still screaming when the other uncaps a syringe of something, sliding it into his neck with a practiced jerk of his wrist.

He is trembling as he does it, shaking with adrenaline from holding the other down, from keeping his hand over his mouth, but he pushes the stopper all the way down, and pins him to the forest floor while he waits for it to work.

Nenzi is still sobbing when the drug takes effect.

He can only hold the shirt of the other, crying as he lies under him on the grass, unable to stop. He wants more than anything to be dead. He tries to get the words out, to ask the other seer to do it, to just shoot him, but he can't speak, can't get anything past his throat.

Wreg continues to stare at him, the shock deepening in his dark eyes, reflected in the features of his broad face. He stares at the other seer like he doesn't know him, like he can't believe he's the same person.

It is the last thing he sees before he sees nothing at all.

Twelve
Opening

I woke up and didn't know where I was.

I lay on a bed I didn't recognize, in a room I didn't know.

As soon as I moved, I felt presences around me, faces I only just recognized in the fog behind my eyes. One of them remained over me, seemingly for a long time, until I couldn't help but focus on it, try to make sense of it.

I finally realized I knew who it was.

Jon sat by me on the bed. He wiped my forehead with a damp cloth while I blinked harder, fighting to pull my mind out of the cement in which it seemed determined to stay.

Gradually, it got better. My thoughts still felt mired, stuck in quicksand, but I could almost...

Memory hit me, cutting my breath. I found myself gasping, in a state of full-blown panic. I sat up, hard enough and fast enough that I nearly blacked out. I still managed to grab the front of Jon's shirt. My balance wasn't right, but I didn't let go. I pulled on him with my fingers, nearly falling into his chest when he let me tug him closer to where I sat.

"Where is he?" I said.

"What?" Jon stared at me, his eyes showing his concern, and a kind of frustrated bewilderment. "Allie," he said, looking from one of my eyes to the other. "Jesus, Al. Are you all right? You look like hell still..."

"Where is he, Jon?"

His frown deepened. "We had to take you out," he said. "We had to, Al. You were practically in a coma. You hadn't eaten in days, either one of you. It took us hours to even decide what to – "

"Is he still in there? In the tank?"

"Well, yeah. Of course. What else would we do with him?" Seeing something in my expression, he took my free hand, clasping it in his. "Allie, the doctors have been in there for hours. They're taking good care of him. They've been feeding him, trying to clean him up..."

I bit my lip, hard enough to taste blood. My fingers tightened to fists in Jon's shirt.

"You left him in there? Alone?"

"He's not alone, Al. People are checking on him..."

I gripped Jon harder, fighting not to cry. "Gods, Jon. Take me back to him. Please..."

"Allie." His voice grew openly alarmed. "Jesus, Al...calm down. He's all right..."

"Please, Jon...please bring me back to him...please..."

He stared at my face. I kept begging him. I couldn't seem to stop, or stop the tears that started running down my face.

"Please, Jon..." I whispered. "Please...please..."

He just looked at me, holding my hand against his chest. Then I felt him exhale a long breath, and it felt like worry. Something softened in his light in the same moment. He touched my face, pulling me into the curve of his body in a hug.

For a long moment I just clung to him, letting him hold me as I fought to breathe out the rest of it, to feel anything but that desolate hole under my feet. I couldn't quite get there. I couldn't stand the thought of leaving it, of leaving him alone. I don't know how I knew, but I did.

It was over. If not the end, then maybe the beginning of it.

But I was terrified it would kill him.

"Please, Jon..." I fought back more tears, clinging to him. "Please..."

"All right," Jon said, holding me tighter. "Okay, Allie. I'll take you."

He lay on the floor, curled on his side, much like how I'd found him when I woke up the last time. But his light felt different. The difference hit me, as tangible as a physical blow, almost the second I entered the tank with enough of my light to feel him at all.

He opened his eyes as the door closed behind me.

When he saw me, I saw relief and pain in his face, both in such quantities it made me pause, but only for a second.

I walked straight up to him, ignoring the line drawn around him on the floor, and the lecture Balidor had given me just minutes before entering the room. Sliding under and around him so that his head and most of his upper body was in my lap, I sat on the floor, leaning my back against the wall. I was caressing his hair and face even as he lifted his hand, pushing at my thigh with his fingers.

"Don't," he said. "Please don't, Allie..." His voice broke. "Please..."

I ignored that, too.

After a moment, I felt the resistance go out of his limbs. His hand clasped my leg instead, his fingers tightening above the cuff on his wrist.

I fingered it with my other hand.

"I want them to take them off," I said. "I asked them to, Revik."

He shook his head. "No."

I smiled, but it was humorless. "You're agreeing with Balidor now?"

He gripped my leg tighter. "Allie. Send Vash. Send Vash for the rest."

I felt tears come to my eyes. Nodding, I held him tighter, gripping his shoulder with one hand. Letting my back soften against the wall, I caressed his hair. My other hand, the one that had been holding his shoulder, began to massage his back when he didn't move away. I felt his body relax against mine almost reluctantly, his fingers loosen on my thigh. Closing his eyes, he swallowed, merging his light into mine, even through the collar.

We didn't talk for what felt like a long time.

I was still caressing his hair, using my fingers to massage the back of his neck, when he finally broke the silence.

"I don't want you to see the rest, Allie," he said.

I nodded, sliding my fingers back into his hair.

"I know."

"I know what I said. But I changed my mind. I don't want you to hate me."

"I won't hate you, Revik."

"Yes, you will." His voice broke, even as tears came to his eyes. "Allie, you will."

I gripped him tighter, fighting to swallow what couldn't get past my throat. I continued to touch him, caressing his fingers where they lay on my leg. I watched his face, saw the pain return to his expression, even as he began caressing my calf, then my bare foot.

"Allie..." he said then. "I still want it to be you."

"I know."

"I don't want it to be...but I don't know if I can do this with anyone else."

"I know," I said, caressing his face. "I know, Revik."

"Do you still love me?" he said.

His voice was so low I barely heard him.

Before his words had fully penetrated, before I'd heard them all the way with my ears, I hugged him against my lap, tightly enough that he closed his eyes, gripping my leg in return.

"Yes," I said. "More than anything, Revik. More than I ever have."

He looked up at me, his eyes holding pain again, a near reluctance.

"And you still want to do it?" he said. "You still want to see this?"

"Yes."

"Why, Allie?"

I stroked the hair back from his face. It was soft again, clean from whatever the Adhipan had done to him while I was out. Looking him over more critically, assessing his long form, I realized his cheeks had drawn in more since I'd last seen him. They'd fed him, of course. Jon said they'd even put an IV drip on him for awhile, giving him vitamins and hydrating him and whatever else, but he needed to eat more before we went in again.

Hell, we both probably did. He looked and felt clean though, and he wore a fresh set of clothes. He also looked exhausted. Leaning down, I kissed him on the mouth.

I studied his eyes after I had, raising my head as he caressed my jaw with his fingers.

"You're sure, Allie?"

"Yes. I'm sure." Tracing his cheekbone, I felt my throat close as I shrugged with my other hand. "I think you need me to see it, Revik. I don't think you'll ever believe me if I don't. I don't think you'll ever believe anyone..."

Gripping my hand in his, he met my gaze. While I looked at him, his eyes grew bright once more, even as he fought to smile.

"I still might not believe you, Allie," he said.

Looking at him, at the serious look in his eyes, I smiled back.

Then I laughed a little, wiping my own eyes. Laughing again, I gripped his hair tighter, watching his expression relax as he studied mine.

"Yeah," I told him, still smiling. "Yeah...I know, Revik. I know."

We started only a few hours later.

He picked the time. We got some push-back from the techs, who wanted to give Revik another 24 hours, let us both build up his strength, but Revik was adamant.

I got him to eat more first. They brought us food, a lot of it, actually, once they realized we were serious about going back in. We did our best to make a good dent in it, but both of us had to work at it. The last month or so had cut both of our appetites quite a bit, from our stomachs shrinking to just being constantly in the Barrier.

Balidor threw a fit when I dragged my blankets and pallet over to lie with him, but even he let it go when he saw us eating together.

I didn't know if it would be harder this time, to go back in. I didn't know if it would be one of those three steps forward and two back things, or if we'd end up somewhere in the middle of World War I, or some other timeline I hadn't yet seen. So far, he'd taken me to see very little about the actual war, so I had to assume that was probably next.

But there was no transition.

We laid down together, my head on his chest, his arm around my back.

We slid into the Barrier together, our light already entwined.

And then, with no preamble...

...he is standing in the field behind his uncle's house, holding a gun.

The others linger around the fence near the back of the house, watching him.

He feels their collective presence like a pack circling, waiting for a signal from the alpha on what to do. He feels Merenje's breath by his ear, almost a caress, and he flinches from the stink of it, unable to take his eyes off the woman in front of him.

"Don't do it," he whispers. "Don't do it, Nenz...please..."

The boy flinches, tries not to hear him, but he can't help it.

Merenje smiles, exhaling more fumes from the whisky he's drinking in a laugh.

"*Please* don't do it," he says. "Please...you little cowardly fuck...please.

You have no idea how badly I want you *not* to do it..."

The boy swallows, fighting to hold the gun in one hand, fighting not to meet her eyes, or the eyes of his uncle standing nearby.

"...We'll have so much fun with her, boy," the human laughs, tugging at his ear. "So much more fun than you could ever have. We'll play with her until she's dead...smash out all her teeth...cut off her tits, her fingers..."

The boy closes his eyes.

Biting his lip, he shakes the images out of his head.

The one that remains is the girl kneeling in front of him, naked and bound, her hands tied behind her back, a gag in her mouth, sucking inwards against her breath. Tears are running down her face, and she's shaking her head at him, pleading him with her eyes.

"What is the delay, nephew?"

He turns his head.

Silence envelops the field.

The tall seer stands by the door to the back of the house. The deep-set, yellow eyes bore into his face, as if trying to see past it to his bones. He feels the faintest flavor of disgust from the old seer's light, a darker whisper of disapproval.

He looks at the boy, and the boy sees nothing forgiving in that face.

"Are you attached to her, Nenzi?" he says.

"Uncle..."

"What did I tell you about that, Nenzi?" he says. "About getting attached to these creatures? Haven't we spoken about this?"

The boy looks at Merenje, seeing the smile on the human's face.

"Nenzi!" the seer commands, forcing the boy's eyes back to his. "Why is this hard for you, of all people, to understand? Do you not see? It was relatives of hers...creatures *just like her*...who killed your parents." His voice grows quieter, more intense. "Do you know how many seers died in the last year at human hands, nephew? Do you?"

The boy grips the gun tighter, looking at the old seer.

"No," is all he can say.

"They kill them in their labs, experimenting on them...they sell them as slaves, as whores, tear them from their mates, rape them with impunity..."

The boy stares back at the girl, feeling his stomach go cold.

He remembers...he remembers the first girl they gave him. Before Gisele, there was another. He never knew her name. Even so, he lost his virginity to her. She had dark hair, eyes the color of new leaves. She was quieter than Gisele, almost shy. He lay with her, and then Merenje came in with three of the others, and they raped her in turns in front of him.

When he tried to stop them, Merenje shot her in the head, his cock still inside her.

She died without making a sound.

He still remembers her face though.

He sees it sometimes, her eyes staring up at the ceiling of the stone cellar.

Merenje only looked at him after he did it, his mouth quirked in a half-smile as he studied his expression, trying to determine if the message had penetrated.

It had. He didn't fight them when they wanted Gisele.

He watched her take it from them. He watched her enjoy it sometimes, her back arched as their more adult cocks drove into her, forcing her to feel.

Pain grips at his heart, hurting his chest.

"I thought I taught you better," his uncle says, that disappointment prominent in his voice. "I thought you understood, Nenzi...why it is important you do not become attached to these things. They cannot *feel* sex, nephew. They are not like seers...they have no awareness in their aleimi. To them sex is purely an animal act, devoid of feeling. They use only their bodies, Nenzi..."

He purrs in a series of disdainful clicks.

"...You might as well be using your hand."

The boy looks at him, the pain knotting once more in his chest. He tries to think past his uncle's words, to find other, better words for why he can't do this. He fights to bring a voice to the dread that rises in his chest, the pain that lives there, but he can't.

His uncle's voice pounds past whatever logic lives in his mind.

"...You think this female cares for you, nephew?" he asks, his voice a cold splinter in the air. "For all the time you have spent with her, with her body, do you think she thinks of you at all? That she would not betray you without a *second's* hesitation...at her very first opportunity? Do you think she desires *anything* of you, nephew, other than her own survival...?"

"And I can't give her that?"

He blurts it out, a half-plea.

His uncle's eyes narrow, once more boring into his.

"It is one thing, uncle," he says, subduing his voice. "A trivial thing...as you said."

"You would jeopardize our entire goal here? Our purpose, by letting her live? You would leave her as a witness to what you are? To what we are doing?" He clicks in admonishment. "Nenzi...must we always come back to this? To the greater good?"

"She can come with us," he says. "She can come with us, Uncle...I'll keep her..."

The old seer shakes his long face, gesturing 'no' in seer.

"Please, uncle...I won't let her get away..."

"You are too old to keep humans as pets anymore, Nenzi."

"I've done everything you've asked of me. Everything..."

"This is not a punishment, nephew. You must let her go. You are becoming a man now. It is time to put away childish things...to make your own way in the world, including in this..."

The boy can't think. He holds the gun, and it trembles in his hands.

The only word in his mind is no. He looks at the girl, and tears catch in his throat as he looks at her face under the sodden gag, the tangle of her light brown hair. He hears the truth in the old seer's words. He knows she never cared for him. He knows she never did anything but try to stay alive, doing what she had to with him to make herself valuable. He knows she looked at the other humans with as much longing as him...more, probably. She knew they had the power of life and death, and he only had it in words, in his pleading with them.

"I will let him, Nenzi," Menlim cautions, his voice a lull. "I will let Merenje dispose of her in any way he pleases. I will let him and his friends take as long in that process as he likes..."

He pauses, motioning with one long, white hand.

"...And if that happens, you will watch, Nenzi. You will watch, and when he is finished, we'll bring another girl, and we'll do it all again...from the beginning. And again, if you need the lesson a further time. And again. This will go on, nephew, until you learn...like every other lesson you are given..."

The boy looks at Merenje. The tall, lanky human was a teenager when he first met him. He is almost thirty now. He stares back at the boy, his dark eyes holding a dull spark of intelligence buried in a confident and almost comfortable cruelty.

He would enjoy it, the boy knows.

The human's shoulders are broad, almost a wrestler's shoulders. His hands are large, but they can be subtle, almost dextrous when he desires them to be. His arms are strong, corded with muscle. He looks at the boy's face, as if reading him in his assessment, and he smiles, the spark in his eyes flickering in pleasure.

"Don't do it, boy," he jeers. "Be the little girl that you are...tell daddy uncle no, you can't hurt the tart who sucks your cock...that you want me to do it for you..."

The boy bites the inside of his cheek, hard enough to taste blood.

His eyes leave the human's face, focusing back on the gun in his hands.

"Go on, then," Merenje calls out, louder. "Let me have her, you little prick...you know you want to. I've watched you...you get off watching me do it. You can pretend all you want, you little *fuck,* but I know what you are..."

He doesn't look over at the human, and Merenje laughs, raising his voice.

"Go on. Little fucking pussy...kiss her one last time. Tell yourself you're doing her a favor...that you're 'good' and I'm the one who's 'bad.' Then go brainwash some other bitches to lick your cock...tell yourself how 'good' you are then...all the while imagining what I'm doing to your little friend here while you spill your seed in their mouths..."

The boy's fingers clench. His anger turns cold, to a deeper fury.

It builds until he considers turning the gun on the male, on blowing a hole in him right then...no matter what his uncle says.

Merenje sees the change in him, and gradually, his smile transforms, turning to a colder leer. His dark eyes shift in a blink, holding an expression and intensity the boy recognizes. He sees the hunger in them, a near desire. He stares at the boy, as if willing him with his eyes. Willing him to aim the gun at him, to give him an excuse.

"Come on then," he says. "Be the big man...show uncle Merenje how big your little cock is now..."

Nenzi's fingers tighten on the gun. His jaw hardens.

But the other voice rises, forcing his eyes back towards the house.

"You could do that, too, Nenzi," his uncle cautions, softly.

Taking a step down the stone staircase, the old seer folds his hands in front of his robe, inclining his head in a half seer's shrug.

"...You could kill the hired help, certainly," he says, gesturing vaguely with one hand towards the humans by the wall. "...But it would not be the lesson, nephew. It would not teach you what I need you to learn. That would be vengeance...not clarity of purpose. I would only acquire another human like him, and we would start again..."

The boy looks at the old seer, his voice defiant.

"He is human, too," he says.

"He is," the uncle concedes with a gesture. "But he is of use to us, Nenzi. Like a pack horse, or any other beast of burden. You do not kill what has use, Nenzi...not out of anything but childish motives. And that, above all else, is what I need you to learn."

"She is not useless." He looks at the girl. "She has use to me."

Menlim smiles at him.

It is a small smile, a bare wrinkle around the fleshless lips, but it stretches the skin further around the bones of his sallow face.

"Does she?" he muses. "Despite the crudity of his remarks, Merenje is not entirely wrong, nephew. From what I hear, you are doing quite well with the female humans of the neighboring townships on your own..."

"That's different," he says. "You *told* me to do that...to get better at pushing them..."

"And you are doing remarkably well," his uncle says, his voice final.

His voice holds the thread of a compliment, though, unusual enough that the boy looks at him again. At his stricken look, Menlim waves a hand dismissively, clicking again in that soft purr.

"No, nephew. Do not lie to me. You do not need this female anymore. And we will be changing location soon. We need her disposed of. Now, before we begin making preparations..."

He meets his gaze, his voice gentle.

"...You are only prolonging the inevitable, my boy."

The boy looks at Merenje. He sees the leer on the human's face, the broader smile only half-covering it.

He knows what he has to do. He knows.

Before his mind can fully grasp it, before he can second-guess it once again, he shifts the gun back to the girl, aiming without thought, using his light to align the points and then firing before he's taken another breath.

There is a silence after he shoots.

In it, he sees smoke, feels the kickback of the gun, into his shoulder.

He's been practicing for months. Using the grid his uncle showed him, using his light to pinpoint targets with a deadly accuracy, again and again, until he rarely misses.

He sees her waver, for the barest breath, her body suspended.

Then she is thrown unceremoniously to her back. She lands with a dull thud. The hole in her head looks small to him, a mere dark spot on her pale skin.

He doesn't see her eyes close. He doesn't see her expression change at all.

Then he is just standing there, the gun aimed towards the ground.

It takes another few seconds before the sound returns to his awareness, before he hears anything but his own breaths, hollow in his ears. The echo of the gun continues to linger in the valley, just like the smoke that dissipates in the cold air.

Then Merenje lets out a half-laughing whoop.

He jumps up from where he's been leaning against the wooden horses set up to hold the saddles for his uncle's small herd. Merenje laughs again before the boy turns his head, his voice holding a thread of disbelief even under the alcohol.

"Holy damn! The little shit actually did it!"

He is laughing again when Menlim's voice pulls the boy's head in his direction.

"Very good, nephew."

He nods in approval when the boy turns, but his eyes are hard, still focused on his face with a scrutiny that sees through the lack of expression on the boy's face.

"...But I think the lesson is still not there," he adds softly. "I think this is a compromise for you, yes? That you are still missing the point of this little exercise..."

The boy feels his hands go cold.

He looks down at the gun he still holds, unable to make his eyes go to the body of the girl.

"You want me to do another," he says dully.

The uncle only motions to Merenje, clicking to him as he gestures, speaking to him in that other language, the one from Merenje's place of birth.

"Bring her," he says. "We will do this now. Get it done." He looks again at the boy. "I can see he is ready. That he understands the need for it, at least..."

Merenje grins, pushing off from the saw horse as he whistles, pressing two of his fingers against his lips, on either side of his mouth. The whistle is loud and two of the others, two who are newer than Merenje, but cut from the same cloth, bring the next one.

The boy doesn't know their names. He barely looks at them as Merenje's men drag another human into the clearing from behind the stone wall, this one bound as well, her face bruised along one side, her eyes wide in her face.

He understands the point of the drinking now, though.

They came for the show.

None of the understanding in Gisele's face lives in the face of the second. Fear explodes over her features, eclipsing all else.

There is no begging, no comprehension. She sees the dead body of Gisele and screams behind the gag, fighting the men holding her in a writhing, mindless panic.

The boy blanks out his mind.

They've barely got her kneeling on the ground before he raises the gun, using the grid behind his eyes to aim at her heart.

He fires before anything penetrates that fog.

The girl crumples.

He looks at his uncle, and knows the meaning of the expression even before he speaks.

"Again," his uncle says, motioning to Merenje.

The human laughs, making a circular motion over his head to the other two, telling them to bring another, jerking his head towards the space behind the stone wall.

Looking down at the gun, the boy only clenches his jaw, checking the bullets in the round chamber before pushing the wheel back closed. Cocking it, he is ready when they bring up the next one. He barely notes the face, other than to see that this one is older. A man with graying hair, and blood on the front of his shirt.

He shoots that one in the head, like Gisele.

"Again..." his uncle says, as the smoke clears.

The boy is no longer there. A part of him is gone, drifting up above the clearing behind the gray stone house, watching from above as he empties out the gun, then fills it again, his fingers steady, his eyes vacant as he watches from that other place.

He hears only one thing after every pull of the trigger, sees only one thing.

It is the low purr of his uncle's voice, the steady look in his yellow eyes.

"Again, Merenje..." he says, his eyes never leaving the boy's face. "Bring the next one."

The boy raises the gun, waiting for them to arrange them inside the kill zone in front of him.

His mind is relaxed now, almost at peace.

...and it is dark. He is alone, and it is cold.

The ground it hard. He digs with a metal shovel at first, sweating in the cold, his back aching with the strain. It seems to take forever, he wonders if he is in the right spot...if he somehow got confused in the dark...when his shovel tip hits the first of them. He has to use his hands then, working as fast as he can, excavating only with the edge of the shovel where enough space lives between torsos and limbs...and then only to save time.

He doesn't have much time.

He finds her after what feels like hours, after he is covered with dirt, surrounded by the stench of death, the smell of decay filling his nose until he feels like he is one of them.

It is only the first part of what he needs to do.

Uncovering the body carefully with his hands, he eventually clears enough away that he can lift her, throwing her over the saddle of one of the horses he has with him. After he fills the hole, making it look as it had before he started, he ties her down, fighting not to breathe, wincing at the stiffness of her limbs as he ties cords around her hands.

He feels sick briefly, fights nausea, his hand over his mouth.

Then he remember his uncle's voice, the words he spoke to him only the day before, and his hands steady, even as he grits his teeth.

He finishes lashing her down and leads the horse back to the tree. He mounts the other horse he brought with him. He has a few hours' ride, and it is well past midnight now.

He has to hurry.

The sunlight swirls, showing a gaunt face looking at him from across a wooden table.

In the morning, especially on a day like this one, his uncle always looked older.

A human cooks for them, and the boy drinks coffee, grimacing against the taste as he wipes his mouth. He has never liked coffee, but it is the norm to drink it here, so he is teaching himself. He avoids the seer's stare until his uncle addresses him directly.

"She is dead?" he says, his voice holding a faint lilt of surprise. "You did this on your own, nephew?"

"On my own?" The boy looks at the old seer, his mouth a hard line. "You told me to."

"I told you it might be necessary," the old seer concedes. "Yes."

"So? Is that not the same thing?" Nenzi's eyes dropped to the table once more, even as his jaw hardened. "...Since when have your 'suggestions' been anything other than orders, uncle?" Hearing the edge creeping sharper into his voice, he fell silent, frowning at the plate of eggs placed in front of him. Pulling apart a roll to butter it, he ignored Merenje's eyes from the other side of the kitchen, where he sat in the window box, smoking a cigarette.

"I took care of it," he muttered. "You said we had to move soon, didn't you?"

"Yes," the seer clicks softly, glancing at Merenje. "Yes, I did."

The boy catches the look between them.

"And her body is where, nephew?"

"I told you. Under an oak tree. In the old forest...behind where it forks for Ruchnell."

Merenje raises an eyebrow at the old man, but the seer is looking at the boy again.

"...When did you do this, nephew?"

The boy pauses, as if thinking. He frowns. "Not long after you said it. Maybe a day or two after. Not longer."

His uncle doesn't answer, but continues to stare at his face.

The boy forces his eyes to his plate, then his fork to capture some of the eggs lying upon it. He eats silently, without letting his mind think about what he puts into his mouth, without looking at the food, or using his light on it.

"Does her death distress you, nephew?" the old seer asks.

He feels his jaw harden. "Yes."

"Why?"

"She was my friend."

His uncle clicks at him softly. "We have spoken about this, nephew."

"I know." He digs his fork back into the plate, letting his expression harden. "But Kuchta was different. She was my friend...I don't care if she was human. I don't care if that means I was 'attached.' She was my friend."

His uncle clicks at him softly, faintly sympathetic.

"Your heart does you credit, nephew," he says softly. "But this self-delusion must be corrected, if you are to fulfill the whole of your work here..."

"It is not heart," he says, giving the old seer a warning look. "I observe. I see who she is, and I respond. She was a good friend to me...better than any I have had..."

"She was human."

"I do not care."

"You should care, nephew...for it could mean your death if you don't. You cannot ever trust them, nephew. Not really. Not in the way you would clearly like to believe..."

The boy doesn't answer him. He stares out the window of the stone house, holding his fork in one hand as he watches the birds in the trees outside.

"Their minds are so weak," his uncle reminds him. "...They will betray you even without meaning to, nephew. Any seer can push them into betraying you, without them even knowing they have been pushed. They could be pushed into putting a gun to your head, pulling the trigger. They would betray their own children...their own spouses and parents..."

"I know. You have said all of this."

"You have seen it, nephew. You have seen it with your own eyes...with your light. You see it weekly from what I hear, in the humans in town." He smiles faintly. "You have seen it with the humans you have coerced into your bed..."

The boy doesn't look up, swallowing another mouthful of eggs, right before he reaches for a piece of the thick toast.

"I took care of it, didn't I?" He glares at the old seer. "I did as you asked. Don't ask me to like it. Don't, uncle...not today. I'm not in the mood to lie."

The old seer's eyes continue to study his face.

The boy's expression doesn't change as he eats.

After another pause, his uncle purrs again, clicking softly, as if to himself.

Then, he dismisses their previous conversation with a wave of his long, white fingers, leaning back on the wooden bench.

"Very well," he says. His eyes return to the boy's face, but holding a calmer scrutiny now. "Are all of the loose ends tied up? With your human school?"

"Yes."

"Then we can train tonight? You and I?"

The younger seer hesitates, then looks up at the seer.

"I had thought we would train today," he says, his voice cagey.

The man in the corner of the room laughs. "Busy tonight, pup?" When the boy only gives him a hard look, still chewing his bread, the human laughs louder. "Go on. Tell him. Tell him what you've been doing at night, lad..."

When Nenzi looks up, the old seer is watching him, his dark yellow eyes incurious. One of his eyebrows rise on his long forehead, pulling up the skin.

"Is there something you'd like to tell me, nephew?"

When Nenzi only shakes his head, gesturing negative, the human laughs again.

"He's fighting at night. On the street. Winning not a small amount of change, too, from what I hear." Hopping down off the window seat, the human walks to the stove, pouring himself more coffee from the saucer on the stove. "Where's our share of it, runt? Seeing as how it's our training you've got under you, helping you win...?"

Menlim doesn't take his eyes off the boy's face. "Is this true, Nenzi?"

The younger seer shrugs, chewing bread without looking up.

"So what's the money for, runt?" Merenje laughs. "You want to buy another girl of your very own?"

The younger seer doesn't look at him. His eyes return to the window instead.

Menlim watches him for another moment, then sighs, clicking softly.

"We will work today then," he says. "Is that agreeable to you?"

Fighting not to let his surprise show, the younger seer nods. "Yes, uncle."

"Good." He steeples his fingers, resting them against his chest. "And you have been practicing? For the exercises today?"

A shadow crosses the other's eyes, but he nods. "Yes."

"Any progress?"

Nenzi doesn't look at him for a moment. When the seer's light darts out, touching his, he flinches, turning his eyes to face his uncle across the table.

"No."

"Nenzi." Menlim watches him, his eyes pensive where he leans against the bench. "We are running out of time. The pre-manipulatory work is finished. I have taught you everything I can...done everything I can to try to induce it in you..."

The boy gestures dismissively. "I know you have. I will spend more time with it, uncle."

"There can be no more delays with this, nephew."

"I understand."

The old seer continues to stare at him, his eyes motionless.

"I know you do not want me to seek out further motivations," he says, softer. "Things that might speed the process..."

The younger man looks at him, his mouth hard.

"No, uncle. I don't."

"Then we will pray for success together, yes? The two of us?"

Nenzi's eyes are hard when he looks up, almost as hard as those of the human who watches them both from a darker corner of the room. Nenzi sees the ember of the human's cigarette glow from that same corner, lighting his dark eyes; he feels the human's stare, but doesn't return it. His expression doesn't move as he meets the motionless gaze of his guardian.

"I will pray with you, uncle," is all he says.

His voice, when he speaks next, even carries feeling in it, whispers off the stronger pulse of his light. The uncle feels it, and his eyes narrow slightly, as he scans the light of the younger seer.

When they begin to speak, even the birds outside seem to grow quiet.

Iltere ak selen'te dur Hulen-ta
Isre arendelan ti' a rigalem
Ut isthre ag tem degri
Y'enj balente ut re mugre di ali
Isre rata s'u threk Ralhe t'u rigalem
Isre arendelir d'goro anse vikrenme
Isre l'ange si nedri az'lenm
Isre ti'a ali di' suletuum...

The One God oversees his steps
Knowing the destiny of the one is harder
For to lead is sacrifice
Lost in the tides of time and meaning
He follows unto the Bridge's first light
A spark, in darkness...
When he learns that hardness overcomes
And that all what he has done

He has done for the greater good...

When he reaches the part about her, something in his voice catches. But he doesn't lose the words.

Their voices echo together in the morning air as they finish. He manages to recite every word along with the old seer, and when they are done, Menlim is still staring at him, his dark amber eyes motionless. He doesn't move as the boy resumes eating, doesn't turn his gaze from the younger, rounder face.

The boy feels it, but he pretends not to notice.

He is crying.

I am with him this time, so lost in him I can't feel anything else...I can't even see him. I see his hands, our hands, in his lap. I see the coarse coat he wears, the splatter of blood on his off-white shirt. He holds the gun in both his hands, cradling it almost, the barrel on the lap of the dark spun pants with the holes in the knees.

He looks up at the rusted warehouse, and he can't see past its broken walls.

He's come out here.

He's come out here before...when his uncle isn't around. When he isn't being watched.

It is one place he uses to be alone.

He sits there and I feel what he wants to do. I feel him wrestle with it, and a part of me fights him, even though the time is past...even though this moment has already happened. I cannot reach him, cannot reason with him.

I can only be there, inside of him, when he first puts the gun to his head.

He holds it there, cocking it. His finger trembles by the trigger, and I feel the thoughts on him, the pain in his light. He remembers his parents, but that is dim now too. He remembers Gisele.

The pain worsens, until he can barely breathe. He has let the gun drop in the pause, but he raises it again, placing it against the side of his head.

He closes his eyes...

"Nenzi!"

He lets out an exhale, and anger replaces the other. He lets the gun drop to his lap once more, but he doesn't uncock it, or take his finger off the trigger.

"Nenzi, what are you doing?"

"Go away!" he says. "Leave me alone."

But the old seer only stands there, silent in the waving grass. How he came upon him without being heard, without being seen...but the boy doesn't care about that either. He isn't a boy anymore. He is old enough to decide to die.

"Are you so sure of that, nephew?" Menlim asks.

Nenzi doesn't think about his words; he doesn't want to. His voice comes out angry, a near snarl. A voice he never uses with the old seer.

"You won't have any reason to do it anymore," he says. "You'll stop killing them, with me gone. You won't have any reason to *do* it anymore..."

There is a silence.

Then the old seer clicks softly, sitting gracefully on a stone not far from where the younger seer sits. His eyes hold no anger, only a kind of thoughtful patience.

"You missed your lesson today."

"Fuck the lesson!" His eyes rose, meeting those of the other seer. "I'll never be able to do it! It won't matter what you do! And you'll have killed them all for nothing!" He raised the gun back to his head, pressing the end against his temple.

"If I do this, it stops. It...all...stops!"

The old seer folds his hands, clicking again softly as he shakes his head.

"No, brother," the seer says simply, using the designation of equals for the first time with him. "This war will come, with you or without you. There will be many deaths, with or without you..."

"We're *not at war!*"

"We *are* at war, Nenzi...only you are too far away from it still to feel the effects of it." The old seer's eyes narrow, growing harder. "Right now, as we speak, your brothers and sisters are being butchered in Asia...relocated... enslaved..."

"I don't care." He puts his finger by the trigger once more. "I don't... fucking...care..."

"The war will happen, whether you are here or not," the old seer repeats heavily. "But if you are not here, Nenzi, then we will lose. The seer race will cease to be."

Nenzi shakes his head, his jaw clenched.

But the old seer clicks at him, louder.

"We are not ready for this fight, Nenzi," he says, his voice sharp.

When the boy only shakes his head again, Menlim speaks louder.

"...We have spent too many centuries in caves...praying to our Ancestors. Telling ourselves that our ability to see into the Barrier will protect us from what happens down here. Our brothers and sisters are superior beings, Nenzi...and they are being *slaughtered* right now, for the simple reason that they do not have the kind of mental strength that allows them to fight back. It simply does not occur to them...it does not occur to them to defend themselves..."

"I can't change that..." he says.

"But you *can*, Nenzi! Don't you see?" Menlim leans forward, clasping his long hands between his knees. "You can teach them. You can teach them to fight. You can teach a whole generation how to fight back...how to survive..."

Nenzi holds the gun in his lap again, but he shakes his head, looking at it.

"Maybe we aren't meant to survive, uncle," he says.

The old seer frowns mildly, shaking his skull-like head.

"We are meant to lead humans into their next evolutionary state, my friend," he says, his voice matter of fact. "Your wife will do that...and you must be ready for her. You must prepare things for *her*..." His voice grows more gentle still. "Will you abandon her here? Will you let her come here...expecting to find you, only to find herself alone? Would you do that to her?"

Pain clutches at his chest, tightening his hands on the gun.

"Gods," he says, his voice a near cry. "I can't do this...not even for her."

"You can, Nenzi," the other says. "And you will. I can see it in your light. You are so close now, you have only yourself in the way..."

"But I try. I try every day...even more than I tell you. I try all the time..."

"Then stop doing it for me," the old seer says, his voice stern for the first time. "Stop doing it to avoid *pain*, Nenzi! Stop doing it to make your life *easier*. Do it because it is what you are meant to do...do it so you can fulfill your purpose! Do it for her!"

The younger seer's jaw tightens again, but he doesn't answer. He stares at the gun in his hands, and doesn't move when the old seer regains his feet.

"I cannot help you with this, Nenzi," the old man says. "If you choose to end yourself...to take the coward's way out, when you are so close..."

"I'm not a fucking coward!"

"Then prove it to me!" the old man returns shortly, his voice impatient, carrying an edge of contempt. "Prove it to the gods! Be a man, Nenzi! If you do not like the direction your life is going, change it. Do not whinge about it like a broken animal...do not expect someone to come along and *hand* your power to you. Men with lesser powers than you...with lesser *potential* than you...have fought harder for what meager lots they were given..."

The young seer feels his jaw clench harder, hurting his face.

He doesn't look up though, or respond to the seer's words.

He doesn't move, in fact, as Menlim leaves him, walking away through the thigh-high grass covering the hill. He sits without moving, holding the gun in both of his hands, staring at it. It isn't until the old seer is well and truly gone that the boy realizes that he meant what he said. Even after everything, his uncle is not coming back.

He will let him end his life.

Clenching his jaw, he rises to his feet.

He doesn't want to think about his uncle's words, but he can't seem to help that, either. His uncle is right. He is weak. He has always been weak.

Aiming the gun at one of the remaining panes in the wall of rusted metal, he fires. The rectangle of glass explodes, breaking into larger shards and a circle of powdered glass. Fighting to breathe, he is still staring up at the building, holding the gun. He considers firing again, then lowers it, so that it is pointed at the ground by his feet.

He finds himself thinking about the old man's words again, repeating them in his mind.

But his mind rebels, too.

He *has* tried. He has tried everything...he has endured everything. For years, he has swallowed his anger, his want of revenge. He obeyed even when it meant beatings, even when he didn't understand why. He took all of it, did everything they told him to do. He didn't run away, didn't kill himself. He did everything they asked of him...every *single thing*.

But he is done. He isn't following orders anymore.

He isn't following the scripture, or his uncle, or Merenje. He isn't listening to any of them anymore. If he is really meant to do this, then the gods would want it of him. They would tell him how to do it. They would tell him what he is supposed to do. But the gods are silent for him. They have been silent for years.

They abandoned him, like everyone else, when his parents were murdered by humans in those mountains. The world behind his eyes is flat and empty, made of dead walls and smoked gray glass. There is nothing for him here...no purpose. He does not know what he is doing here. He doesn't feel anything. No matter what his uncle says, he feels none of it. It has no meaning to him...not anymore. It is gone. All of it...gone.

For nothing. He did all of this for nothing. He endured all of it...let them kill everyone around him, all for nothing. He can't do what everyone tells him he must do.

He is weak.

Anger fills him.

"Fuck you, Bridge." Raising his eyes to the clouds, he raises his voice. "Fuck you! Come here, if you want me! Come here and fucking *help* me!"

He stares up at a blue sky patterned with darker thunderheads. Pain fights to break open his chest but he can't breathe past the anger. He can't feel anything but that hard pain...the shell that wants to fight or fuck or hurt something...to keep hurting it until he's broken something with his hands, smashed it until he can't feel any of it.

Light ripples through his aleimi, making patterns he can't see...that he might only be able to see through his uncle's urele. He's tired of parlor tricks too, though. He's tired of using his light to win at fights against humans, to mind-wipe teachers and town authorities, coerce blank-eyed females to lie down with him...

Pain hits him harder, along with another realization.

He'll never do it. Never.

They'll never give him the ability, because every ability he has he's only abused.

He's not just impure...he's corrupted.

The anger turns into fury, a pulse of grief he briefly can't control.

It bursts out of him in a hard, bright stream of light. Somewhere, in the midst of all of it, his grief reaches up, feeling for something familiar... for anything he used to know. He looks for himself at first, that presence he used to know...some hint that the person he barely remembers still lives there, somewhere. But that is gone too, whispered away like so many dead leaves. That hadn't been him, either. It had only been a covering, something to wear when the sun shone on him, when nothing lived there to tear it away from the bones of whatever remained.

In the briefest, most futile moment, he surrenders.

He gives in to death, to meaninglessness...to the hopelessness of his life.

He gives in to his own worthlessness, to how little power he really has.

He gives in to having been left alone...left to die.

He feels something in his light open, like the breaking of his heart.

He glimpses a golden valley, filled with red clouds. An ocean lives there, made of diamond light, and he is there, briefly, surrounded by liquid warmth. The sky is crimson and gold, the water and waves filled with so much light he can barely hold it in himself...

He knows this place. Gods, he knows it...it is so familiar to him it hurts.

The pain changes, turning into something closer to love.

He isn't alone. He was never really alone.

The certainty comes from nowhere, but he cannot shake the feeling it leaves behind. Atoms vibrate the air around him...a pulse of living light he can feel in his fingers, electric currents that raise the hairs on his arms. He lets out a low gasp, feeling another presence there, a presence so familiar tears spring startled into his eyes. His throat closes as his chest catches, as his light expands, rippling outwards, stuttering in its rhythms...

And then he hears it.

A sound like the swell of an ocean wave.

He knows this. He knows this, too. It is familiar to him.

He knows that light from the golden valley, he knows it from other times, other places. He knows it so well it worsens the pain in his chest, and then his light is moving, flickering, changing, coursing down trails so familiar they bring tears to his eyes.

A folding sensation starts over his head, a feeling like a part of him collapsing inside, and it fills him with so much he can't hold it all; he can't feel even a portion of it. A jolt of hot light floods him without warning, forcing another gasp, and he has to let it out, he can't hold it, can't begin to want to hold it back...

He lets out a cry, a near scream as he looses the fist around his light...

There is a silence where every bird in the sky holds its breath.

Until above him, the sound of breaking glass fills his ears.

He opens his eyes, unable to see for the light...there is so much light, he is blind with it, but still he sees somehow, looking beyond it, looking past it and through it, through those vibrating strands...

...and he laughs. He laughs...

...as every glass pane in the rusted building in front of him bursts outwards in the same instant. Shards fly from the rusted metal frames. They cascade down around him in a rippling arc, raining down and out like a glass umbrella with the strength of his light. He watches them float, filling the sky like the calls of a thousand birds before bursting, one by one, into a shroud of fine powder, whiter and finer than sand...

And he is laughing, laughing...

Light fills every pore in his being. He can't express all of the joy he feels... it bursts out of him in another ripple of light, a love that he wants to share, that he pushes out and away from him, to reach anyone it might touch.

In it, he finds himself...a feeling of belonging, or rightness that is so strong he cannot help but see it as divine...

He is who he is. He is who he was always meant to be.

He is alive, and the world has not left him alone.

And in that moment, he loves her so much.

She answered him...she answered his call when he needed her most.

He will wait for her. He will wait forever if he has to. All the rest of it feels trivial. All of it feels like nothing, a short path filled with muddy ruts before the longer highway stretched out before them...

Thirteen
Laboratory

"You are sure this is it?" Chandre said, unable to keep the skepticism out of her voice. "It does not look right, to be a complex like you are suggesting..." Her frown deepened. "...The security protocols are almost nonexistent. Apart from that fence..."

Varlan barely looked up. "You are missing things, sister," he murmured. "There is more here than it appears at first glance..."

Faintly, Chandre could see in his eyes that Varlan was mostly in the Barrier, likely coordinating the final surveillance with the three seers across from them. They all stood on the same side of the low concrete wall bordering the hills around the substation nestled in a green, tree-filled valley. The wall itself likely marked the edges of the government property.

Their real barrier was the high, metal fence located a few hundred yards below. It stood at least twenty feet in height and surrounded the actual lot and grounds of the substation itself.

Inside that heavier fence, an additional row of lower fences surrounded the parking lots and buildings, but they didn't have security codes or an electrified field surrounding them. They were topped with razor wire, however, and locked with heavy chains.

"Organics?" she said.

He shook his head, still staring down at the fence. "Look closer."

Despite Varlan's use of the Barrier, Chandre chose to remain outside of it. She spoke aloud to him as a result, if only to minimize the number of Barrier presences projected by their small team in the immediate vicinity. She did not know for sure if someone was watching, but under the circumstances, it seemed wise to take precautions.

Anyway, Chandre wasn't a rank 11 infiltrator.

Chances were, if anyone *was* listening, it wouldn't be Varlan they overheard.

"I appreciate your silence, sister," Varlan said quietly, answering her thoughts. "...it is most helpful. And the complex is designed to look this way," he added. "We are supposed to think it is nothing but a electrical power substation, not something the military is protecting. We are not supposed to see the secondary structures at all..."

He gave her a thin smile, that whisper of elsewhere still visible in his dark eyes.

"Were you expecting a sign, sister...?" he joked in that flat voice. "One that reads 'Human-killing virus to be found here,' perhaps?"

Chandre's frown deepened, but she didn't answer.

When Varlan handed her one of his organic rifles, she took it, examining the touch controls to make sure she was familiar with all of them.

It bothered her when she realized she wasn't.

Again, before she could ask, Varlan sent her the gun's schematics in a single, packed thought. She accepted the gift with a nod of thanks, but couldn't quite return the Rook's smile.

He'd been friendly to her, more or less, once Eddard got him to agree to bring all of them along on his job. The fact that Chandre wasn't interested in a cut of his contract probably had at least something to do with his cheerfulness, and his overall willingness to include her in his plans. She'd increased his team by two mid-ranked infiltrators, both of whom were cleared and licensed for full firearms use...and completely free of charge.

But there was no possible way to trust his motives. He was too skilled of an infiltrator for her to be able to trust much of anything he said, really.

She studied the scar on his face, recognizing the mark.

He was one of the ones who survived the camps run by the Germans. About halfway through the second world war, after collars had been developed and produced at high enough numbers, the Nazis began rounding up seers, not just killing them wholesale. They began by collecting them for training and use on the battlefield, but their interest soon shifted to include medical experiments, as well. Once they started housing them in Auschwitz and the other large camps, they also began cutting their faces.

As a result, a lot of seers had those diagonal scars.

The marks served as brands, so there would be no mistaking who was seer and who was not. Of course, for the few humans with similar facial scars, this could have had unfortunate results...but for the most part, the system had been effective in identifying the seers out of the humans, and a lot faster than the collars did alone. The Nazis designed a different set of ident tattoos for seers, as well...but the facial scars were immediate, impossible to hide.

Chandre knew Garensche had such a scar. He told her once that an SS dagger bearing the words *Blood and Honor* had carved it across his face. He got it while standing in a line of other seer prisoners, waiting to be assessed for use in medical tests.

Terian had branded Cass in such a way, too, only as a human.

Chandre had never told Cass about the significance of the mark, but she had heard via intelligence reports that Terian lost many of his family in the camps. She often wondered if the mark had been deliberate...to brand her like cattle, as had been done to so many of the Second Race. She kept these thoughts in the back of her mind, however, as she watched Varlan signal to one of his seers to keep an eye on the road.

"Five minutes," he told her, his voice lower than a whisper. "The human says they usually change shifts on the quarter hour, and that the guards arrive twenty minutes before that..."

Chandre nodded, not speaking.

By the human, she knew he meant Eddard.

Eddard, who had designed this approach, to save them time. Who had provided them with the employee schedules for the site, and a frontal approach strategy that shaved weeks off the plan initially drafted by Varlan and his people.

Varlan, like most infiltrators, was conservative. He'd wanted to infiltrate the structure first...and if possible, find a way in down below, that bypassed primary security systems altogether, particularly anything involving imaging or DNA scans.

Of course, that approach would have taken months of surveillance at the site, and probably required a few death to replace current employees with some of Varlan's people. Eddard claimed none of that was necessary. Somehow, he convinced Varlan of the same, although Chandre still didn't know how precisely.

Looking over the gun she held and comparing it to the schematics Varlan sent, Chandre couldn't help but remember Dehgoies' scathing remarks about the antiquated equipment in use by the Seven...and even that used by the Adhipan. Varlan's toys seemed to put proof to Revik's words, in that everything she'd seen him use so far had been pretty much state of the art. Although she understood the funding differences between the Rooks and the adherents of Code, she couldn't help conceding Dehgoies' point. Really, how could they expect to win at anything if they weren't even competing at the level of basic equipment? She understood why Revik would have found it necessary to secure other means of funding the Rebellion...other than selling books on the seer religion and relying on donations from philanthropic humans, that is.

It always came back to the same problem...Code.

In their purest form, the Sark Codes eschewed violence of any kind... particularly that against what the Code considered 'less-evolved' beings. The basic tenets of Code instructed that seers could not use their powers in anything but a defensive manner, either in defense of themselves or of the race as a whole.

Those definitions had often been stretched, of course, under seer leaders less peace-loving than Vash. The Rooks themselves believed they were working in defense of the race...even for its very survival. The direct followers of the Dreng were, on the whole, even more dogmatic about that point than most of those who had lived under the Pyramid.

Chandre's own feelings on how she interpreted Code had gone through a number of changes of late, as well. In terms of the Dreng and the Rooks versus the Seven, she felt significantly less strongly about the tactics than she used to. In fact, all she really cared about anymore was what lights each aligned with behind the Barrier.

She wondered how many in Balidor's army might even feel the same way.

Dehgoies' light had always confused her the most. Perhaps because of Allie's influence...or perhaps simply because of something pertaining to his intermediary status. Supposedly there were those among the Seven who'd entertained similarly conflicted feelings about Galaith, even though he'd been the head of the Rooks' network.

In any case, the loss of Dehgoies to the Dreng was a significant one indeed.

Even beyond her own feelings about him, the voice of the Sword was one that many seers listened to...as much if not more than the Bridge herself, even under normal circumstances. It didn't help that Allie had been raised human, and thus was often viewed as brainwashed even by seers loyal to her. That Allie espoused the same basic peaceful doctrine of Vash didn't help, either. The seers had grown tired of hearing those words in the past decade. Nowadays, such sentiments actually angered a lot of seers, particularly after the destruction of Seertown.

The successes Dehgoies claimed by following a more offensive approach worsened the rift, even in his short time of leading the rebels.

Varlan nudged her arm, pulling her mind back to the present.

It was almost time.

He sent her another packed set of schematics, this one of the layout below the substation itself. She'd already received those of course, the night before, along with the rest of them. Eddard had supplied much of that intel, as well. Even so, she nodded to Varlan once he'd sent it, refocusing her attention on the task at hand, which had been his real intent.

They were in California, a few hours inland from San Francisco.

Chandre couldn't remember the last time she'd been in California. It was strange to think that the Bridge had grown up only a few miles from where she now stood.

She looked down the oak and scrub-covered hill to the fenced clearing housing the substation. She looked for the details she had missed, what Varlan had alluded to when he said she was missing things. She had to assume, from his words, that the clues as to the station's real purpose were subtle, but present, even for someone of her own infiltration rank.

It wasn't long before she began to realize what he'd meant.

Most of her attention up until then had centered on the largest of the structures behind the fence, a two-storied complex of green buildings. Electrical towers and transformers with criss-crossing wires filled most of the air behind the tallest of the green-painted office buildings, but they'd already decided the night before, while looking over the schematics, that most of that area probably constituted a real substation, either for the complex below ground, or for cover.

The largest of the green buildings had a high wall in front made of glass, a security terminal for entry and what looked like bullet-proof, organic doors. The front windows were bordered by landscaped trees and even some parking spaces for higher-paid workers. Only three cars stood there now...a black SUV, a European sports car, and what looked like an antique American car that had been refurbished to run electric. Not the sort of cars one would normally expect to see in front of a substation complex for run of the mill engineers and low-level techs. Maybe the occasional project manager or higher up making the rounds would drive a car like that, but it struck Chandre as sort of unlikely.

Of course, there was the detail of the cars in general. Eddard walked them through that part the night before, when he'd shared the surveillance photos his team at Mi5 had collected. The main, covered lot filled most of the area behind the acre or so of dirt housing rows of transformer towers. Eddard's Mi5 team already knew from x-ray images that over half the parking slots were taken during weekdays, despite the fact that most substations were almost fully automated.

On weekends, like now, the parking lot still contained over a dozen cars. Yet none of the people driving those cars walked in or out of the organic doors to the main building.

Varlan's team had been in place since dawn, and they'd only seen one person, period, and that had been the gardener watering the landscaped trees and bushes rimming the main office complex.

High, razor-wire barriers stood around the entire structure, including the two-story building, the parking lots and a low equipment shed on a lower service road. A checkpoint let cars in and out...automatically, it appeared...but still, Chandre had to admit it was strange. Not exactly high-grade security, but more than was usual for a structure of this kind.

Further, where did the people go? Were those cars in the lot simply company cars? Or did some of the techs actually sleep somewhere in the complex?

Chandre had already picked up the hum of current from the fence, as well.

"Look closer, sister. That's not just an electrified fence," Varlan murmured beside her, sliding the gun up to his shoulder on its jointed harness. He gave her a level look. "How many electrical substations do you know of that have OBE fields protecting them?"

Chandre didn't answer, but she extended her light briefly to confirm his words.

Once she had, she clicked out, frowning.

He was right. She'd missed that, too.

OBE, or organic binary electrical fields, were generally only found around military bases...and often not even around those. They had been designed and implemented by Black Arrow Industries, the same group that collected most of the big ticket defense contracts involving sophisticated seer tech. They designed and manufactured most of the organic tech contracted for by the government...and not only the government of the United States.

"You still think it's underground?" she said, just as soft.

He gestured a 'yes' in seer. In the same instant, she felt him ping the seers on the other side to let them know to be ready.

He'd felt something. Likely in the security station.

Chandre glanced down the line of the cement wall, wondering again what possessed her to come along on this little jaunt, even though she hadn't been able to clear it with Balidor. She managed to catch Maygar's gaze from where he stood beside two of Varlan's people. Eddard was with that group, too, standing on Maygar's other side and showing the other female infiltrator something he had on a portable monitor. It had been agreed to split into two teams, with Varlan on one and Eddard on the other, since they were the only two who seemed to have detailed information about the existence and layout of the facility.

Even though he was human, Eddard provided not only the basic plan, but also the majority of the input into organizing this little outing. He convinced Varlan, with not a small amount of money, that it would be better if they all did it together, and not only because they all shared essentially the same goals.

He also convinced them to do it sooner rather than later. According to intelligence he had from his superiors in England, the disease would be deployed again soon...although whether as another demonstration or for real this time, no one knew.

Eddard was convinced that he could help them on the inside, as well. His only price had been to collect at least a sample of the antiviral for the disease, as well as a sample of the disease itself. He said the antidote would be replicated back in England once he returned, mostly as insurance, in the event that another supply of the virus existed elsewhere.

Why he'd been so insistent that Chan and Maygar come, she could only guess. She'd tried to read him to determine if he was working for the Seven, too, but there were blocks on his light that felt like military. Even Varlan admitted to her that Eddard was well shielded...which likely meant he hadn't been able to fully penetrate those shields, either.

In any case, Varlan seemed content to be paid.

The whole arrangement made Chan nervous...and not only because a frontal assault on the compound was a lot riskier for all of them.

She also still had her doubts about who hired Varlan in the first place... much less what their true motives were in wanting to destroy a disease that only seemed to kill humans. Eddard called Varlan's client 'Shadow,' but that name could mean anything, since it was obviously fake.

Moreover, Varlan was a Rook. Chandre could feel it in his light as tangibly as she could feel it on any of her brothers or sisters who had worked under Galaith. The Dreng seethed through his light...so did traces of the Pyramid. In fact, it felt like such a part of him she had trouble distinguishing Varlan's own aleimi as a separate vibration. Varlan may not have followed Terian after Galaith's demise, but he had not lost any of his allegiance to the cause...nor to the Dreng.

The idea of conducting a joint op with one like him made her nervous.

The realization that she could disappear out here and no one would know where she had gone, or who she had gone with, made her nervous as well.

Varlan gave her a sideways smile, but Chandre brushed it off, unapologetic.

"Do not pretend such sentiments surprise you," was all she said.

"I do not," he said, his voice low. "But I do wonder at the loyalty you feel towards the Sword, in spite of this aversion..."

"I don't know what you mean," she said stiffly.

"Of course you do." Varlan smiled. "He is, after all, my master, too."

Chandre didn't answer. She knew Varlan didn't work for the rebels, not directly anyway. So he must be religious then. That, and he clearly viewed the Sword as the new Head of the Rooks network down on Earth.

"Who else did you imagine held that spot?" Varlan asked, his amusement plain once more.

"Salinse," Chandre said at once.

Varlan gave her a dismissive look, but didn't comment.

"So you really think Eddard's plan will work?" Chandre said. "With only six of us...and a human...you think we have enough to succeed with a frontal assault?"

"He claims he can shoot straight," Varlan mused, smiling at her again.

"You know what I mean, Varlan."

"I do," he conceded. "We planned this op initially with only four infiltrators, sister Chandre...and no human Mi5 agent. It was not a frontal assault, true, but I could find no fault with the plan the worm laid out...and it shaves months off my operating time." He glanced up from where he'd been surveying the charged fence, smiling at her faintly once more. "...Besides, blind or no, a worm who can shoot is still an asset. You have worked with humans yourself over the years, have you not, sister...?"

Chandre heard the faint dig behind his words. Her face hardened, but she acknowledged his comment with a gesture, holding the harnessed rifle close to her body.

Varlan hunkered down, once more in a waiting posture.

Chandre knew he was monitoring time from the Barrier.

Since she had gone over the plans with all of them the night before, she knew also that they were now waiting for the shift change for the outside security guards to occur. She still couldn't see the guard of course; supposedly the booth lived just inside that green-glassed structure that stood between them and the substation transformers. The building, despite its relatively tall windows, was as bland and featureless as a military barracks building, and looked like it hadn't been painted in at least a decade. It also, despite the expensive organic doors and the cars parked in front, seemed to be entirely uninhabited...and more than a little shabby. Browning trees dotted the entrances, all the way down to a long and even more featureless shed in the lower driveway, where trash barrels stood in rows next to a yellow dumpster and a hill of rusted scrap metal.

In all the time they'd waited, not a single person had walked between those buildings or out into the substation itself.

Chandre was watching the main doors to the green building, checking her own watch periodically, when a dark blue pick up truck grew visible in the distance, bumping down the long service road to the fenced main gate. The road was paved...barely...but the truck's massive tires still kicked up a thin cloud of dust when the truck swerved, making the final turn before the substation's main driveway. Slowing as it reached the perimeter gate, the truck came to a full stop beside a stand-alone terminal located directly outside the line of the OBE.

"Do you have him?" she asked Varlan.

He didn't answer her at first.

Looking away from Varlan, Chandre watched the man in the truck. He only sat there for a minute, engine idling. Just when she was beginning to think the pause was too obvious, that they'd know something was wrong on the surveillance feeds, she saw the truck driver lean over to roll down his window. The truck was old enough that he had to crank the window down by hand...but like the antique parked in front of the glass doors, it also looked refurbished. She wondered about the obsession with antique cars, and then it clicked.

Non-organic components. The military often used older models in their civilian-based fleets, to keep them from being hijacked. The station probably logged every kilometer they traveled.

"Do you have him, Varlan?" she asked again, feeling her pulse rise a little.

Varlan gestured an affirmative. His eyes clicked back into focus, even as the gates opened in front of the truck's grill.

Neither of them moved or spoke as the driver threw the vehicle into gear, and drove through the OBE. Chandre found herself watching Varlan's face. By the time the driver was steering the truck down to the lower lot, where the long storage shed lived, the tautness in the older infiltrator's eyes had relaxed. Glancing up, he nodded to her, and she felt herself relax a little, too...but not much.

The truck parked next to a number of other less-expensive vehicles, just to the left of the long shed. The security guard got out a few seconds later, holding his uniform jacket over one arm and what looked like a lunchbox in his other hand. Even from where they crouched, Chandre could see his gun belt and shoulder harness. He began walking leisurely back towards the shed's main entrance, sipping from a paper coffee cup.

"Well armed for a rent a cop," she commented.

Varlan didn't answer, but continued to focus on the guard.

In order to get through the OBE and the secure Barrier construct, they needed someone on the inside. Rather than doing the usual and getting their own person hired with clearance, Eddard proposed they wait until the shift change and establish a tap with the new security guard on duty. It was risky, of course...something they couldn't have even attempted without Varlan with them. A lower-ranked infiltrator couldn't have pulled it off without being seen by whoever held the lab's construct.

But the main risk for that part had been overcome already. Varlan had gotten to the guard and established the link before they entered the construct. Given the short window they had, that initial tap had been the difference between success and failure. Anomalies in a seer's or a human's light wouldn't be noticed as easily if they entered the construct that way. Once inside, however, any changes in an individual's aleimi...especially a human, especially a human working in a high-grade security capacity...would show up like a flare in an otherwise predictably gray backdrop.

"You're sure you have him?" she repeated, rearranging her hands on the gun.

"Yes."

"They didn't notice you in the entrance scan?"

"No."

"You are *sure*, Varlan?"

Giving her an amused look, he clicked softly. Then he glanced down the wall, making a series of hand gestures to the other seers. He looked up at Chandre again once he had, his eyes serious. "Down," he said, pointing to the lower level of the fence, the part by the long shed and surrounded by trees. "I read him while I arranged the tap. He can open the OBE for up to fifteen second intervals. Any of the guards can...to run perimeter checks...but only within certain intervals. We have five minutes before the next. There's an access tunnel there..."

He pointed to a gate she could just see in the trees below the long shed.

Following the direction of his fingers, Chandre nodded.

When he began making his way soundlessly past the gap in the wall and through the trees, she followed, moving as quietly as she could. Behind her, she saw the other seers following. As they did, something else occurred to her.

They would all be entering at a single point now. Riskier if they got caught, but it would make it easier to communicate without using the Barrier. Once they were inside the construct, there would all have to maintain Barrier silence. Even as she thought it, she saw Varlan hand-signal to one of his people, a female seer with another of those Nazi scars across her face.

Chandre caught the gist of his signal and stared at him in surprise.

"We need one on the outside," he said softly. "We can spare her now. Maygar will take her place, bringing up the rear."

Hesitating, Chandre nodded, watching as the female disappeared into the trees.

Seconds later, they reached the edge of the OBE by the outer fence.

Chandre's eyes scanned upwards, taking in the dense metal mesh fence, and the top covered in glass shards and razor wire. If anything went wrong, they weren't getting back out that way, even without the OBE in place to fry them when they tried to get through.

Rather than speak, Varlan used sign language.

Two teams, he signaled to the remaining six of them. *Three and three. Don't risk the fifteen second gap...go straight through. We reconvene after the second fence...*

Chandre saw nods and gestures of acknowledgement.

You're with me, he signaled to Chandre.

Swallowing, she was about to answer, when he grabbed her arm.

"Now," he murmured, pushing her forward towards the fence.

Chandre felt herself tense, instinctively reacting to the current she could feel from the OBE...but she didn't fight him. The current dropped dramatically as she reached the edge of the trees, and disappeared just before she and Varlan and a third seer broke cover. She crossed the remaining yards and felt something in her chest relax.

She'd seen what OBE fields could do to a person...

Before she could complete the thought, they were through.

Within a few seconds, she stood on the other side of both fences as well. She crouched in the trees with Varlan and the other seer, looking back at the remaining three, which included Maygar, Eddard, and a hulking giant of a seer that Chandre had heard called Rex. He, too, had the Nazi scar on his face. It hadn't really occurred to Chandre until then, but all of them did, with the exception of the tall, thin seer who'd come through the OBE with her and Varlan. He appeared to be a few centuries younger than the others and had unusual coloring for a seer, in that he looked like a human of African descent, both from the color of his skin and from the texture of his hair. Chandre knew that seers like him went for a cool couple of million Euros on the black market. They were virtually impossible to visually detect as seers, so high ranked ones could cost as much as twenty-million once they were trained. It was the rarest ethnic coloring seers could be born with...even rarer than the blond hair and blue-eyed variety, which only showed up in something like one in a million as well.

Chandre watched the human security guard, who stood behind them, as if looking casually out into the trees while he enjoyed his morning coffee. His blank-eyed stare remained peaceful as he worked the controls of a standing terminal just outside the second fence. He acted like none of them were even there, like he was just testing to make sure the mechanism was working.

All six of them waited for the next interval, five minutes after the first. Then, abruptly, Varlan gestured urgently to the other three still outside the fence.

Now! he gestured. *Fifteen seconds! Move it!*

They didn't wait. Within five of those seconds, the three of them bolted out of cover and across the line of the switched off OBE. They joined them after the second fence, and then the six of them were moving, staying low behind the cover of trees overlooking the long shed.

Varlan turned to Chandre once more, using hand signals.

The entrance is through the shed...

Surprised, Chandre only nodded. So the green building was cover, too.

The security guard, still moving casually and whistling now, walked back to the long, featureless shed in front of them. Instead of going through the main entrance however, he walked past it to the other side. Hanging a left, he followed a cement path that ran between the shed and a high, cylinder-block wall. The seers followed cautiously, but at the edge of the path, once they were shielded by the wall, Varlan raised a hand, indicating for all of them to stop.

The guard walked directly to a featureless segment of the shed's wall. Chandre watched as he laid his hand on the bare-looking metal. There must have been a disguised organic panel there, because seconds later, the guard entered another elaborate code into a terminal that revealed itself from behind a panel that slid open in the dirty gray surface.

A few more seconds after that, a larger door smoothly retreated sideways into the wall. There was another pause while the guard went inside.

He's disengaging the image recorders... Varlan signaled. *Be ready to move. We can't keep them off for more than ten seconds without it being noticed in the control room...*

A few seconds later, the infiltrator motioned sharply for them to head for the door.

Following Varlan's hand gestures, they darted from cover to the opening in the shed wall. Chandre, since she was just behind Varlan, was one of the first to make it through the new door. Inside was a surprisingly small, squarish room with high walls.

Every segment of those walls reflected a pale, organic green. Chandre barely glanced at the mirror-like tiles, though, focusing more on remaining silent while the other seers joined them one by one inside the shed walls.

She watched the security guard re-engage the outside imaging the instant Maygar entered behind Eddard. It wasn't until they were all there and the outer door was closing that Chandre looked around at where she stood, and realized she knew exactly what the small room was for. Once it hit her, her brow cleared.

Whatever else might happen to her here, they were definitely in the right place.

She was standing in a decontamination chamber.

It took about twenty minutes for Varlan, Rex, Chandre, Maygar, Eddard, the human security guard and the dark-skinned seer to make it through all of the decontamination protocols.

Chandre emerged on the other side feeling a bit light-headed from the two chemical baths she'd been forced to endure, as well as the high oxygen content of the air on the other side of the chamber walls. Now she found herself staring at a long, low-ceilinged space. It took her another few seconds to realize that it was larger than the shed had been. The decontamination chamber had also been an elevator...while it sprayed them off, it also brought them underground.

Now, from what Eddard told them the night before, it was really a race with time. Someone would notice that the camera had been turned off outside the lab at the next feed scan...which should be in about one hour, if Eddard's intel was sound. But long before that happened, someone would likely notice that six unauthorized persons had just gone through decontamination protocols. No matter what else happened, they couldn't go back out the front door...but supposedly, Eddard's plan had that end covered, too.

Once they entered the secure portion of the lab, their presence would be picked up by construct security. They could try to delay it, using Varlan's tap to the security guard wherever possible, but regardless, they had to be in and out before anyone could show up to stop them on the ground. But that should give them the time they needed to get through the secure doors below ground, which was where the virus was located. The security protocols would focus on locking them inside, which should also delay any team making it downstairs to intercept them.

Even as Chandre was thinking all of this, Varlan was gesturing in a swift arc, signaling them to move for the next set of doors. She found she was jittering somewhat on her heels as they waited for the guard to open the next set of secure doors for yet another elevator.

This floor's mostly storage, Varlan told them with his hands. *According to the worm, labs are below. Along with residences for several of the scientists. DNA and retinal scans to get through the last set of doors. We'll have to blow those in any case...but we need to get there before the construct seers know we're here...*

The security guard was disengaging the camera for the elevator. Chandre watched him, her mind whirling around the next set of steps they would be taking to destroy the lab...

When out of nowhere...she felt it.

Before she could make sense of the feeling, Varlan turned to the others.

Construct alarm, he gestured sharply.

"What?" Maygar murmured aloud. He signed, *...How is that possible?*

Varlan gestured for all of them to remain silent.

Focus, Varlan signed then. *Nothing's changed. They'll try to pinpoint our location first. We have four minutes before the elevators lock down. Mark time,* he added, looking at Chandre, who immediately looked at her watch. *And keep Barrier silence until I say so...* Turning, he gave Eddard a hard look. *...You'd better be right about this, human...*

Eddard looked paler than usual, but he nodded, his eyes decisive.

"Four minutes," he confirmed, his voice lower than a whisper.

Chandre jumped a little. Not many humans understood seer sign language.

She truly hoped he was as confident as he sounded.

The human security guard had the cameras turned off by the time the elevator doors opened. They all got inside the car and the doors closed. By then, Chandre's eyes were locked on her watch face. She noticed Varlan and two of the others looking at time pieces as well.

Three minutes, she signaled.

The elevator kept descending.

Two minutes, she signaled a minute later.

Weapons ready, Varlan gestured. He pulled his rifle down on its harness, so the muzzle faced the elevator doors. *Four of them, waiting for us. I've got a tap on their leader. Be ready to fire when the doors open...I'll do what I can to delay them...*

He looked at Chandre. *I need you to monitor the construct, but wait until we're out of the elevator...if they pinpoint us now they could just shut us down. Once we're out, coordinate the shield with Rex and Stanley...* He pointed at the two seers he meant, then his eyes shifted to meet Maygar's. *...I want you looking for additional security while we locate the merchandise...and the way out. Bring Eddard with you, and make sure you find it before we finish setting the charges...*

But Eddard shook his head, adamant. *I need to go with you,* he signed. *I need to get samples of the disease...and its antidote. We'll need that...all of us. Your client, too...*

Varlan frowned. He thought about the human's words, but for scarcely a heartbeat.

Fine. He looked at Maygar. *You have any trouble finding our exit, I want to know within three minutes. Three...do you hear me? Any more than that and I'll kill you myself...*

Maygar scowled, but nodded once, seer-fashion.

Varlan's eyes shifted to the African-looking seer, who Chandre now realized must be Stanley. *Take over the tap on this worm...* he signed, indicating the human security guard.

...And all of you, pull down your guns! Now!

The rest of them yanked rifles down on their harnesses, aiming for the elevator doors. It hit Chandre in the same set of breaths that this wasn't going to be bloodless. They were already off the parameters for the job. They should have gotten control of the lower security gates before the broader construct had been alerted. Now they would have to shoot their way through, and hope like hell that Eddard's exit wasn't on the main security grid. Or worse, rigged with another OBE field.

Chandre hadn't been in a hot op since the bombing of Seertown. Now she found her hands shaking, even as she aimed the rifle at the elevator doors. She blinked sweat out of her eyes despite the air conditioning in the elevator, squinting past the yellow security light as it continued to rotate overhead, disorienting her eyes. She considered aiming with her aleimi instead, then remembered Varlan's instructions to stay out of the Barrier and felt her shaking worsen as it occurred to her she could have gotten all of them killed with that slip.

What the hell was the matter with her? Her infiltrator training seemed to have gone out the window. It hit her suddenly that she was having what amounted to a PTSD reaction. It couldn't be from Seertown...she'd mostly been helping rescue survivors with the Adhipan. She hadn't been involved with any of the on the ground action during the bombing in Delhi, either...in fact, she'd been two hotels over, looking for Revik and Allie, when the main explosion took place.

It hit her then. She hadn't seen any real action since that fiasco on the cruise ship with Allie. That fiasco that killed nine seers directly under her command.

Just then, the elevator car landed with a jerk and a shudder on the bottom floor. After what seemed like an interminable pause, the doors slowly slid slowly apart.

As soon as they had, the sound of alarms filled the small space of the elevator. Chandre winced against the noise, looking for it with her eyes... when a voice shouted out, forcing her gaze down again.

Five guards stood there, armed with organic weapons.

"Don't move!" the man in front yelled. He held up a hand. "Hold your fire!" he said to the guards standing behind him. "We need them alive..."

The guards behind him looked startled by this, but they hesitated, fingers poised over triggers as they followed orders.

The pause wasn't long, but it was enough.

Varlan immediately opened fire.

Chandre followed suit before her brain caught up with her hands, and she heard the echoing bang as Stanley and Rex and Maygar did the same. Even Eddard was firing when Varlan finally held up a hand, signaling for them to stop.

At another gesture from him, they all exited the elevator, even as the alarm began to beep on Chandre's wrist. Their four minutes were up.

Maygar leapt out through the closing elevator doors, barely squeezing through before he landed on the other side, looking winded.

The five guards who'd been waiting for them, including their leader, who Varlan had pushed into delaying their fire...were dead.

"Charges," Varlan hissed at once, walking for the security checkpoint. Chandre stared at the thick organic walls of the station. On the other side, she could see men and women in lab coats, shouting to one another. Obviously they'd seen the shooting, either on the interior security feeds or through the transparent panes or both. In any case, there was no mistaking the panic on their faces as they backed away from the reinforced organic doors.

"Wait!" Eddard said, as Varlan began to lay charges over the doors' locks. "They might not have shut it down yet! Use the guards!"

Chandre found herself moving almost before her conscious mind had understood his words. She picked up the leader of the guards by the arms, and started to drag him towards the security console, when someone else picked up his other arm to help her. Chandre looked over and found the seer, Rex, gripping most of the human's weight.

They dragged the guard to the console and stuck his finger on the blood prick for the DNA scanner, then held his eyes over the retinal scanner for the console.

"Is it working?" Varlan shouted from the door.

They'd all given up on being silent, maybe because of the alarms.

Chandre adjusted the man's face over the retinal scanner, and then she saw the light pass over his open eye.

"I need an answer, people," Varlan said. "We're out of time..."

He trailed when the scanner turned green, right before all four sets of locks slid out from between the organic door and the thick frame.

The seer Stanley laughed aloud, clapping Eddard on the back.

Varlan didn't wait. Wedging his body against the door, he ushered the others of them through quickly. Chandre and Rex dropped the human unceremoniously, and ran for the opening. Chandre reached it last, and Varlan nearly shoved her through before following behind her.

They didn't have time to wait and see the door close behind them.

Chandre found herself in another long, narrow and low-ceilinged room filled mainly with narrow lab tables that stretched the length of the two longest walls. Staring around at the machines and the equipment, she found herself studying the white, terrified-looking faces that lined the shadowed wall near the back, as far away from the main door as they could get. Looking to the sides she saw more of those thick, organic doors, these ones leading to pressurized vaults of some kind...or perhaps freezer units. She didn't want to know if they kept test specimens in there as well.

"Disperse!" Varlan said. "You know your jobs....Chandre, Stanley, Rex... with me."

Chandre exchanged a fleeting look with Maygar, who smiled at her grimly, winking at her in a way she found oddly cheering. Somehow, having him in this with her made her feel better, if only for a few seconds. He was a little shit in some ways, sure...but she realized suddenly that he was right, too. He was her friend, in spite of everything. Even if she never could quite forgive him for what he'd done to Allie, he was still her friend.

She was still thinking this when he turned on his heel, jogging for the corner of the room that was supposed to house the entryway to the air duct system that would allow them passage into the coolant exchange...and finally the gray water runoff tunnels that should afford them a way out of the complex altogether via the main sewer.

She didn't know at the time, that it was the last time they would see each other...for a very long time, at least.

Fourteen

GRADUATION

HE STANDS OVERLOOKING A LONG FIELD DOTTED WITH HILLS, SURROUNDED BY mountains. A river winds down there, but that is not what draws his eyes. It is the humans he feels, more humans than his eyes can track, although their movements are clumsy by seer standards, obvious in terms of their tactics...and their attempts to conceal their numbers. Still, he sees them moving with military skill, here and there...and a few brighter lights live within that gray. He can feel what is coming, what vibrates their light. He has not yet seen his first battle, but the promise of it runs adrenaline under his skin until he is trembling slightly, unable to stand still.

He is to remain concealed for this fight.

The others who trained under Menlim will fight on that field, but not he. He can no longer see or feel any of the other seers with whom he has been running exercises for months, albeit in a different set of hills, in a wetter countryside far to the north.

The old man alone fills the empty space beside him, a silent specter hovering as he gazes down on the same unfolding scene under the stars. Both watch, silent, as the humans' numbers gradually increase, filling the fields below. The younger seer feels the old man watching him, expectant, perhaps even wary of what he might do, but for the first time he can remember, he doesn't feel intimidated, or afraid.

A difference lives there, somewhere.

Some change in identity and purpose that allows for a real effort to understand. More than simply understand...to be better. To push himself in ways he never contemplated pushing himself before. To be a different kind of being entirely.

He wants to learn now. He spends every spare minute practicing. He dreams about practicing, about exercises he might try...things he might do with his light if he pushed it into more and more subtle gradations. Pushing humans, even fighting hand-to-hand...all of that has lost interest for him now. It is shadow-play, distraction...nothing more. It bores him because it no longer taxes any part of him he values.

He is no longer able to pretend it is enough.

As he thinks of that, the woman drifts into his mind.

He frowns, remembering her face the night before, the eagerness in her light as she looked at him. But she doesn't see him...no more than any of the worms see him. That's not enough for him anymore, either...even now, when his conquests no longer require him to use his light.

He wants more. He wants something real.

His mind and eyes return to the reason he is here; his concentration sharpens. He is not content now, to simply do as he is told. He fights to understand every structure that lives within his light, to find new ways to combine those structures, to get them to work together. He reads the old texts, trying to find hints and knowledge between their words.

And sometimes, to try and discern how much longer he might have to wait for her.

He throws himself into his work, looking for anything that might force him to improve, to push his limits. He practices even when the old man is not around...he practices whenever he is not forced to other duties, such as the increasingly strenuous military training he's also now receiving from the seers and humans in his uncle's employ.

He's exhausted now; he barely sleeps. He runs on adrenaline and purpose, and a kind of fevered hope that if he accomplishes what he is here to do, if he succeeds in this thing, then she will find him all the faster...

But now...a test.

The first test. The first real one.

He is nervous. He stands on the grass, wearing a dark shirt and dark pants, just enough in the shadow of nearby trees that he won't be visible from the valley below.

His uncle is still speaking inside his mind, but he only half-hears the words.

...*This is a demonstration only, nephew,* the old seer sends softly. *We have no stake in who wins the wars the worms wage against one another...we have only to help them go where they already desire to go. To do that, we must seem to align with those who most need us...who are desperate enough to think us their allies...*

Nenzi's eyes held still on the field below. He gestures in assent to the other's words.

He has heard all of this before of course, but it still provides a kind of background comfort, a story with which he can frame what he is about to do.

It is an exercise. Like any experimental weapon, he must be tested.

...As a result, it would be expedient that we gain the attention of the Austro-Hungarian forces, his uncle adds softly. *...and win their favor through something suitably dramatic, for which they have no reasonable explanation. We wish for the patronage of this group of humans at the outset...if only so they can aid us in weakening some of their rival human powers. In particular, we mustn't underestimate the threat of Russia to the east. They cannot fight this bear, not if they are divided, and forced to fight in the south, as well...*

The younger seer nods again, gesturing his understanding, but he is not really listening.

His own concerns are more immediate, and more personal.

How will I know when it is right? he asks. *I cannot see all of them...*

When the two armies are about to meet, the time is right, his uncle responds easily. *Just as we discussed. Just begin as close to that point as you are able to reasonably estimate...*

What if I cannot control it?

His uncle only looks at him, his dark amber eyes glittering faintly.

"Does it matter all that much, nephew?" the seer says aloud, in old-tongue Prexci.

Looking up at him, the other swallows. After another pause, he shakes his head, clicking a little to himself with nerves.

"No," he answers in the same language. "It does not."

"Then begin, nephew. When you are ready."

Nenzi's eyes return to the field beside a river. Under the moonlight, he sees the humans massing from either side, moving swiftly but surely across the uneven ground. Some look ready to dig into defensive positions, readying themselves for the onslaught from the north, but his eyes remain with those in the rear, who carry the ammunition and the fuel. He focuses on guns, on other areas they discussed him using to target, even as he begins to feel for the different places he needs in his light, the structures he will use above his head.

Then, he feels it.

A shift in the air, as a command is given, somewhere below.

He watches the lines begin to converge...

And then he is inside his light.

A symphony erupts over his head, that now-familiar feeling of an almost sensual loss of control. The folding starts then, and he feels it like the unclenching of a fist he's held so tightly he's forgotten the reason for its grip. He fights to hold onto the map that seethes through his light, telling him where he must aim those flames, what to do with them once they are free... but then there is that merging into everything, into light and air and other living flames...and the vibration of living things, swimming around him, lifts him out of his body altogether until he is lost in the world of meaning in those shifting particles...

A kind of collapse occurs, between himself and the rest of the world. His heart opens in the same breath...and then he feels them, all around him...

The light of the worms, rolling into and between the guns they carry, the clothes they wear, the trees they hide behind, the earth on which they stand. He feels them there, a sea of heart and striving and need, and he wants so badly to give them what they want, to reunite them with the light from which they were born...

Pain slides through him, but it's almost that of love, a kind of repressed grief he can barely feel in its entirety. He slides through them, and the practicing he's done, the training he evokes, it only helps him pull back a little...and then, not for very long, not for more than a breath or two before it explodes out of him again, a wave of heat that he uses to try to connect with them, to connect with all of them, to liberate them, give them the peace they so desperately want...

Tears are running down his face as he directs the course of that folding arc.

He feels bones crack, ammunition light up, and he's already moving out of the rear lines, and into the mass of them...the sounds are those of a stage play, not real, only incidental.

He feels their confusion, their fear as their comrades fall around them, as he twists spines, breaks necks, stops hearts. He tries to ease their suffering, even in this, annihilating their fear by extinguishing their lights before it can fully blossom...

He sets them free.

He moves into the other side of the line without thought. There are no borders that make sense here, no uniforms, no sense of justice that either side can claim...

He continues through the sides until he is lost, and time disappears...

When he comes to, the sky is lightening, but it is cold.

He feels pain in his head, a throbbing in his light and heart he doesn't recognize, even as his limbs tremble from lack of light. No...not lack of light, from new light, supplied from somewhere else. He doesn't know its source, feels half-sick from the amount of it. His aleimic structure bears the influx, reluctantly, but it leaves him off-balance, dizzy and unable to focus.

The light doesn't feel like his own, not yet anyway.

He hears laughter, foreign and loud-sounding in his ears.

Voices echo from nearby, and they are loud with sound, boisterous in emotion. He can hear drink in the cadence of their words, the clink of bottles or glasses and what sounds like utensils scraping the bottom of metal dishes.

He tries to remember how he got here, finds his mind shifting backwards, moving into the darkness behind his eyes, until he feels...

"Hey! The runt is finally awake!"

A strong laugh brings his eyes upward. A face hangs over his, dark eyes and a heavy mouth crossed lightly by an age-white scar. The Chinese-looking seer looks down at him, holding the curtain to a bunk that he realizes only then had cut him off from the rest of the room. The older seer grips the fabric in one hand and stares down at Nenzi with a bleary and at least partially drunken grin.

He understands now, at least, where he is.

He is back in the tents, with his unit.

Fighting to keep his eyes open, he holds up a hand to shield them from the light. Remembering who he is to them, he forces his voice lower, into a surly cadence that is matched only by the obscene hand gesture he gives the older seer in the pause.

"Fuck off," he says, to emphasize the point. "Leave the curtain closed, will you?"

"Do you intend to sleep for the next two days, little Nenz?"

"I will if I want," he says back, his voice close to petulant. "What the hell did you give me, anyway? Or did you just bash me on the head when I wasn't looking, to keep me out of the fight?"

"Give you?" Wreg laughs, but that time, a harder edge touches his voice. "You knocked yourself out in the first hour of battle, runt. Jonas barely dragged you out before the Hungarians mistook you for a Serb and shot you just for the hell of it. They had to house you in here, like an old woman, while the rest of us fought in your stead..."

His smile widens then, turns more genuine. The next words that come from him seem to come from another man almost, bursting out of his lips in his excitement.

"You missed it, my young brother!" he says, clasping Nenzi's shoulder. "You missed seeing Syrimne wipe the dirt with their human asses!"

"I missed...what?"

"Syrimne, my brother! You missed seeing our Syrimne take on the humans and teach them what it means to fight our people!"

"Were they fighting our people?" Nenzi asks dryly. "I thought they were trying to kill one another, brother Wreg. This hardly seems like a victory for us..."

"It may have started that way, but they know *exactly* who they are dealing with now, runt! You can be assured of that!"

Nenzi battles to sit up, forcing his arms under his shoulders.

At once, his head starts pounding again, until it feels as though the pulses might splinter his skull. Reaching up, he feels the bandage someone has wrapped around his forehead, and the stickiness of blood in a lump at the back of his skull.

"What are you drinking, Wreg?" he says. "Whatever it is, spare me a glass, won't you?"

"Did your uncle not tell you? Syrimne was to do his first test on this day..."

"He mentioned it, yes."

"Mentioned it?" Wreg says in disbelief. "And did he 'mention,' you little prick, that our intermediary single-handedly ended the battle of Cer in under an hour's time? That he did it before the humans themselves had managed to exchange more than a dozen shots between them?" He grins wider, as if unable to help himself sharing the news, even with a young seer he dislikes. "...Did he tell you *that*, runt? Did he?"

Nenzi forces his eyes up.

He blinks into the light once more, wincing against the pain. That part, at least, he doesn't have to fake.

"Did you see him?" he asks only. "Syrimne. Did you see what he looked like, Wreg?"

"Only from a distance, my young brother."

"And what *did* he look like?" Nenzi says. "From that distance?"

"He was older than you...and younger than me," Wreg replies. "He had dark skin, and looked Asian to me...only with light brown hair. I could see little else, at the distance..."

"He sounds like a fairytale," Nenzi says, his voice a grumble.

"A fairytale? That fairytale killed almost 60,000 humans today, and in under an hour..."

"60,000...?" Nenzi stares up at him at this, not able to hide his bewilderment. "Sixty *thousand*...? That number cannot be correct. How is that even possible?"

"He is *Syrimne d'Gaos*...that is how it is possible!"

"But the Serbs," Nenzi says. "They barely had that many in troops..."

"He did not only kill Serbs, my young friend." Wreg smiles, obviously enjoying the reaction he has finally managed to wrestle from him. "He started with the Serbs...but then he moved into the lines of the Austro-Hungarian army, once he had decimated most of their enemy. Both sides were running before they knew what was going on. We intercepted calls for surrender from the military leaders of both armies...almost within minutes of one another!"

Wreg's eyes shine now with a kind of fevered light.

"...I have never seen anything like it, brother Nenzi," he says, raising his hand in the signal of an oath. "No seer on that field has ever seen anything like it. The day of the human is over! Our slavery is over! They will not dare to imprison and rape and torture our people anymore, not with Syrimne there to stop them!"

But Nenzi cannot answer. He stares at the floor under his feet, his mind lost in a haze of moving particles and half-remembered light. He fights it out of his aleimi, keeping the cloak around him that his uncle has instructed him to wear around the other seers. He knows there is a good chance that they will discover his identity eventually...but his uncle is adamant that he remain anonymous for as long as it is remotely possible to do so.

So he only nods at Wreg's words, frowning.

"Can I have that drink, brother Wreg?" he asks then.

The other seer smiles, grabbing his arm. The mood of celebration is infectious in the small tent, but Nenzi cannot help but be bewildered by it all, lost in the triumph he feels in the lights of the other seers. They hand him a bottle, which turns out to be from the Austrians, and open it for him before he has managed to focus his eyes on the fire they have burning under the hole at the center of the tent's roof.

Later that morning, there is singing. Nenzi can only watch, smiling a little as they begin to howl like wolves and sing off-key the old traditional songs that he only just remembers from his childhood. It pleases him, to see them like this...flying on adrenaline and regained hope...even if he cannot fully share it with them. He listens instead with a kind of wonder, unable to feel the freedom they feel, or the triumph...or even any real sense of accomplishment.

Instead he watches them, more pleased that he has pleased them than the reasons for their laughing and their affection with one another.

As he does, he thinks to himself about the flaws in what he has done, the loss of control...

But he can't yet force himself to dwell on that, either.

So he simply sits there, by the fire, his head bandaged as he listens to them laugh and exchange stories of what they saw, and he can't quite believe they are speaking about him.

Still bleary-eyed, fighting exhaustion, I listened to Balidor with a barely-suppressed frustration. Biting my lip, I met his gaze, keeping my voice as even as I could.

"I understand all of that," I said, when he paused long enough to take a breath. "But I want you to untie him...to take the chains off at least." I motioned at the tank. "He'd be collared still...he'd still be locked inside. I just want you to let him move around like a person...not some kind of animal we have tied to a tree."

The older seer looked at me, his gray eyes faintly incredulous.

"Do you even *know* your mate, Allie?"

I felt my jaw harden. Looking at him, then at the man on the other side of the transparent organic pane, I folded my arms.

"Meaning what?"

"Meaning...absolutely not," the Adhipan leader said. "I don't even like having him in there with the same chain configuration for as long as we have. To have his hands and legs unsecured, even in a locked room...it is completely out of the question, Allie. Completely." He looked at me with flat eyes. "You should know this by now. You should take your sentimentality out of this, and look at who he is..."

"But he's better now," I said, fighting to keep my anger down. "You said so yourself!"

"He has not attempted to *rape* you lately, it is true," he said, emphasizing the word a little harder than necessary. "...But I would hardly consider that fact alone a measure of his overall stability. And in any case, he is a prisoner, and prisoners, by nature, attempt to get free."

"He's through the worst of it. He shouldn't even *be* a prisoner for much longer..."

"Through the worst of it?" Balidor gave me another of those incredulous looks. "Allie. What makes you think he will get through this at all?" When I felt my fingers curl into fists under my arms, he caught hold of one of my hands, looking me in the face. "You have gotten him to feel some of these things, it is true...it is making him different, we have all seen it. But Alyson, you still have absolutely no idea what he is going to do with this information..."

"*Do* with this information?" I said.

"Yes," he said, emphatic. "Do you think any of what he is seeing is significantly more palatable now than it was back then? He will need to determine some way to exist past this point...or not. You have no idea what he will do..."

Tugging on my hand, he softened his expression. Somehow his empathy threw me more than his anger, maybe because I was tired enough to let it in. Or maybe because I was so used to him angry these days that when the anger vanished, I didn't know how to fight him.

"Allie, he could eat a bullet when this is over," he said, his voice soft. "He could go fanatical religious again, like he did in the past...he could decide he needs a few more decades in snow caves." His eyes hardened to a faint steel. "...Or he could decide everything that happened to him and everything he did was fate...that his uncle was right, all along. He could go back to being bent on avenging the seer race...only this time, do it with a greater sense of logic and purpose..."

"Or he could decide to just *deal* with it, 'Dori."

"Meaning what? Go away, live in the mountains somewhere? Resume his daily penance ritual for the next four hundred years? You do not know what you are *saying*, Alyson...you have never had to face a life debt of this kind! The truth is, you have *no idea* what he will do to incorporate this information...assuming he *can* incorporate it..."

I shook my head at him, biting my lip.

"You're right," I said. "I don't. Because he could also decide to let us help him. He could decide to let Vash help him, and Tarsi. He could decide to try and leave all of that other crap behind, and just be who he is now..."

"Which is what, exactly?" Balidor said.

"My husband," I felt my face tighten at the pitying look that rose to his face. "...And more to the point, *The Sword*, Balidor...Syrimne d'Gaos! You talk like a human, as though that name were synonymous for evil, but it's not. We could *use* him, 'Dori. In fact..." I swallowed, looking back at the tank before I faced 'Dori again. "...We need him."

"We need him?"

"*I* need him," I said, giving him a warning look. "...And so do you, whether you'll admit it or not. We can't do this without him."

Seeing the anger returning to his expression, I lowered my voice, stepping closer.

"I know you think this is all personal for me, 'Dori...and I get that, I really do. It is personal for me, but that's not all of it. When I say we need him, I don't just mean the old Revik, the guy I married. I mean the *real* guy, Syrimne d'Gaos...we need all of him."

When the Adhipan leader only clicked at me, giving me a level stare that told me exactly what he thought of that idea, I flung out a hand in frustration.

"'Dori...think about it! We have thousands of seers out there, newly released from camps with nowhere to go. We have the Lao Hu holding rebels and members of the Seven hostage, and Voi Pai on some kick to take control over all remaining seers...maybe even to use them to take out China's competition in the human world.

"...We have a disease that kills humans, that no one seems to be able to find. Seertown is rubble. We still haven't found half the seer children who were supposed to be hidden in the mountains. The Pamir is a disorganized mess with most of the Adhipan gone. We've got Black Arrow and the traders getting ready to strike back at us, and America is still a quasi-military zone with more than half of its seers in concentration camps. Hell...there are probably a dozen other things I'm not even aware of! Are you seriously going to look at me right now, and tell me we don't need him?"

"He is a walking time bomb, Allie," Balidor said. "He always will be."

"He *won't* always be! Damn it, 'Dori...have a little faith in him. And a little respect. He's been through more than most seers would even survive. And that's the guy we *need*, 'Dori...'"

Balidor just looked at me.

For once, though, I saw past the shield I normally couldn't see much past, the near-armor he habitually wore around his light. I saw the seer who was over 500 years old, who had watched history unfold in different ways throughout that time.

I saw the military man in him, the one who tracked Revik all over Germany and Eastern Europe, the one who still saw him as quarry, as something to be eliminated. I saw the defender of the Council, who saw his charge as fighting the Dreng from the light of his fellow seers, even if that meant killing them...or dying himself. And I saw the man I'd known briefly in those tunnels under Seertown, the one who'd given me back to Revik for a chance at taking down the Rebellion and hated himself for it. The one who blamed himself for everything that had happened between us since...the one who was still trying to protect me, even now.

I saw all of this in his light, and when he spoke, I almost heard it in his voice.

"Do you seriously want to risk thinking along these lines?"

"I can't afford not to!"

"Alyson..." he began, clicking tiredly.

"Balidor." I clasped his arm, and he looked at me, meeting my gaze directly. Swallowing at the expression in his eyes, I relaxed my hold on him, stepping back.

"Look," I said. "I know why you feel this way, I do. But I'm telling you... we need him. And he can beat this. I know he can. We just have to give him more time..."

He continued to hold my gaze, his gray eyes holding more now, a kind of frustrated empathy along with a more personal reaction I could almost feel.

"I know you want to believe it, Allie," he said. "I know how badly you want to believe it. Unfortunately, that is the part that worries me..."

"Dori'," I began, frustrated.

Another voice broke in before I could finish.

"Hey, guys?" Jon looked between us, his hazel eyes faintly worried above the hard line of his mouth. He stood by Dorje over the security console, one arm folded over his chest while his other hand pointed down at something on one of the smaller organic screens.

"I hate to break up the weekly 'fight about Revik' ritual," he added. "... But maybe you could come over here, take a look at this..."

After a faint pause where I bit my lip, I gave Balidor another glance, then walked over to where Jon stood.

"What?" I said.

"That," he said simply, pointing. A transcript was scrolling down the screen in black script over a pale gray background.

Leaning over him, Balidor and I read the words, Balidor voicing them aloud.

"...in addition to inviting them to stay as guests, as a sign of my continued goodwill towards the Esteemed Bridge, as well as my fealty to her and her husband, Syrimne d'Gaos...I have asked them to remain in the Imperial Suites until such time that I can hear the substance of the Esteemed Bridge's request for transfer of the rebel traitors and following my obligation to apologize to my lords and intermediaries in person..."

Balidor looked up at Jon, his eyes holding a faint puzzlement. "Is this from the Chinese?"

Jon nodded, his mouth still grim. "Voi Pai's emissary. Keep reading."

I picked up roughly where Balidor had left off.

"...I also greatly desire to know more of the work that is occurring in the West, related to a weapon that I had been heretofore told was only under development by the American warlords and their servants. I have since learned that operatives working under your name have taken it upon themselves to destroy the main stores of this organism...after procuring samples with which to threaten our human hosts. As all of our people were privy to a demonstration of the power of this weapon in Hong Kong, I wish to know what your intention is with this sample of the disease, and what your intended response to the American warlords will be, when speaking to them of our mutual interests in noninterference with the larger population of the world's humans..."

I looked up at the two of them in bewilderment, before returning my eyes to the screen.

"...I am told that you lost a brother in this operation, as well...for that you have my genuine condolences. It is possible I can help you to exact revenge for this *brutal transgression, particularly if I were to receive adequate assurance that my host families are not intended targets for this weapon you now are in sole possession of, and further, that you only procured a sample as a means of insurance against threat from personal harm and to further the goal of peace among all of our peoples. Although I recognize that the Bridge does not concern herself naturally with regional or factional differences among our brethren, much less our cousins, I would expect some concessions in this matter, as it clearly transcends a simple dispute over borders or economic rights to individual states and could bring about an untimely start to the war that all of us are intent on guiding to its highest evolutionary potential since Her arrival among us..."*

I looked up again, trailing on that last line.

"Do either of you know what the hell she's talking about?"

Balidor shook his head, gesturing 'no' in seer in the same beat.

Still, I saw something in his eyes that made me pause.

"'Dori?" I said. "Do you know anything about the op she's talking about?"

"No." Meeting my gaze, and then Jon's he frowned, pursing his lips. "...Not exactly. I did have an operative looking for the disease in the States. It's possible she found it. I didn't authorize destruction of the disease...but I would have, most certainly."

"Would this operative have taken a sample of the disease?" I asked, hearing my voice sharpen a little.

He hesitated again, then shrugged with one hand. "Possibly. Again, I didn't authorize it, but I can see the sense in it." He met my gaze. "An antidote could be developed, for one."

I felt something in my shoulders relax. "So Voi Pai might be right. We might have the only sample of this disease..."

"Possibly."

I felt my fingers tighten again. "Do you trust them?" I said. "This operative?"

He met my gaze directly, his eyes holding a faint guilt. "It's Chandre."

It took another few seconds for this information to penetrate. "What?"

Again, Balidor shrugged with one hand. "She's been working for me. I couldn't tell you before..."

Jon burst out into a laugh, even as I shook my head, unsure if I should laugh like Jon, or hit Balidor in the face.

"So she's been with you, this whole time?"

"Well..." Balidor glanced at Jon, then at Dorje, before looking back at me. His expression remained uncomfortable. "...Yes."

"And she might have a sample of this disease?"

"I will try to contact her..." Balidor's eyes were scanning the text again though, running over it with his eyes. "...I don't have another operative on this now, though," he added. "And she is specific that it is a 'brother' of ours who was killed..."

"Who do you think it is?"

He shrugged, one handed. "Possibly someone Chandre aligned with. Someone she was working with, to look for the disease...?"

"Uh, guys?" Jon broke in, pointing at the top of the message. "Did you miss this part? On top? Not only has refused your request for negotiation on the rebels without an in-person audience...but she's holding Cass and Baguen captive..."

I frowned, re-reading the transcript. "She's holding Cass prisoner? Are you sure?"

Balidor also pointed to the relevant lines of text. "It says right here they are being held as 'guests.' You don't suppose Cass decided to simply remain in the Forbidden City, perhaps to relax for a few weeks, while you complete your work with your husband?"

My frown deepened. "Jeez," I muttered. "I must be tired. How long have they been there?"

"You have to get her out of there, Al," Jon said, looking at me.

My eyes rose to his. Before I could answer, Balidor spoke up, gesturing more strongly in the negative.

"Out of the question," he said. "For multiple reasons. There are about a hundred bounty hunters out there looking for you, for one..."

Jon gave him a disbelieving look. "It's *Cass*, Balidor."

"I don't care who it is." Turning from Jon, Balidor looked at me, a complete lack of compromise in his gray eyes. "You're not going anywhere. Not until we've stabilized your mate."

I looked at him. "I'll have to go there, sooner or later."

"Perhaps," he conceded. "But we've discussed this, Allie. The bounties on you are astronomical right now. There's also the question of Wreg...and the rest of the rebels. Once we've stabilized Dehgoies, fine, we'll go. In fact, we can all go. But, Allie..." His eyes flickered up, meeting mine grimly.

"...You can't leave here and expect to come back. You can't. The second you pop up on the grid anywhere, you will definitely be tracked. That means no more tank...which means no longer will we be able to shield Dehgoies from the Dreng, either. That will bring the Rebels here, in days, I would imagine, if not hours...as well as anyone out there looking to collect on those bounties. This message went out through our main channels. That means there's a good chance that anyone watching the Adhipan...anyone looking for you...might also have picked it up..."

"She can't just *leave* Cass there, Balidor!" Jon said, exasperated. "We have no idea how long it will take for this thing to play out with Revik..."

"No," I said, giving both of them warning looks. "I can't leave her there, not for that long." I turned my eyes to Jon then. "...But Balidor is right, too, Jon. I can't just show up there, wearing my 'I am the Bridge' t-shirt. We need to negotiate a safe way to settle this. If Voi Pai won't do that for some reason..."

Balidor finished the thought for me.

"...Then we can assume Voi Pai is colluding with one or more of the bounty hunters," he said. "Or worse, that she has no intention of giving up the Rebels, and intends to declare war on us once they are trained as members of the Lao Hu..."

"So what about Cass?" Jon repeated, looking between us.

I sighed, folding my arms.

Exhaling, I glanced into the tank, looking at Revik. He was asleep, lying on his back on the pallet I'd had set up for him in the past week. His bare feet faced towards the window, one of his arms lay on his stomach while he cushioned his head with the other. I watched his chest rise and fall, his face taut as he slept.

"She wouldn't mess with him," I mused, barely aware I'd spoken aloud. "She'd never admit it, but she's afraid of him...I saw it when he came to get me that time."

"No, Allie," Balidor said.

When I turned to look at him, his eyes were flat.

"Allie," he said. "Even you must admit...it is too soon for that. He's not ready. Not for something like that. You're talking about a military exercise..."

Jon spoke up next to him. "He's right, Al. That's not a good plan...not now."

Sighing, I looked back at the tank, refolding my arms.

"Yeah." I sighed again, suddenly feeling more tired than I'd felt in weeks. "Yeah...I know. Just wishful thinking."

Pulling out of where my head wanted to go, I forced myself to snap back, to level out my light. Once I had, I looked at Balidor.

"Get the Adhipan on it," I said. "I want scenarios...at least two...in the next 24 hours. And get ahold of Chan. Find out if she's really got a sample of that disease...and where she is, if so. If what Voi Pai claims is true, I want her in a safe location as soon as possible. Send some people over there, and to get her out of the country. We might be able to use the disease as a bargaining chip with the rebels, assuming Voi Pai intends to let them go at all..." I hesitated, then added, "...And see if you can find out who got killed. Voi Pai seems to think I knew him, whoever it was. We'll regroup after my next session, come up with a response..."

"Allie," Jon said. "Aren't you going to get some sleep first?" He glanced at Revik, then back at me. "You just got out of there..."

"I'll sleep in a few hours," I told him. "It's easier to go in when he's sleeping. He fights me when he's awake...he doesn't mean to a lot of the time, not anymore, but he can't help himself. I don't want to miss an opportunity..."

"You're exhausted," Balidor said.

I turned to look at him, hearing the seriousness in his tone. I found him appraising me with narrow eyes, scanning my light. A pulse of worry left him in the same instant, even as I felt him kicking himself for not having noticed before.

"Allie," he said. "You cannot continue at this pace. You will break yourself, before you break him..."

"I'm all right," I told him, waving it off dismissively.

At Balidor and Jon's exchanged glances, I clicked at them a little.

"...I'm all right," I said, sharper. "I mean it. I'll sleep tonight."

"It is three a.m. now," Balidor said.

"Then I'll sleep in the morning."

They were still looking at one another when I turned back towards the door, walking up to it and keying in the combination that lived in the security side of the construct, where it changed at random intervals from five seconds to every thirty minutes.

Neither of them spoke again as I unlocked the hatch, stepping through the door and closing it behind me. But I heard the seal catch as one of them must have swung the wheel shut on the other side, re-locking the mechanism that kept the Barrier seal in place.

I did my best not to make a sound as I crossed the long, green, organic-paneled room, and when I laid down on the pallet next to his, I didn't touch him. He didn't seem to move where he lay, either, but I felt his light envelop mine in a pale cloud, exuding that same, faint pulse of relief it always did when I rejoined him inside the tank.

Even so, I felt a twinge of...something...as I settled on my back. I didn't dwell on it though; I closed my eyes, willing the Barrier to pull me back into that other place.

In any case, it didn't slow my fall.

Fifteen
Laren

AND THEN THE SKIES GO DARK OVERHEAD, ONLY NOW HE IS OUTSIDE.

Time has passed. Not a lot, but some.

He is home again. There is a familiarity in where he steps, even in the dark, a purpose as he thinks about where he might go before he heads for his bed. It crosses his mind to practice, while everyone else is drinking or asleep, when he can use the fields and no one will notice him. He has the cloak as back-up, which he can use to disguise his appearance if required, to keep the curious whispering only of the confusing and shifting appearances of their intermediary cousin, Syrimne. But his uncle warns him of the danger of relying on this, when some day he will be cornered and unable to get away.

And he is tired...more tired than he wants to admit.

He ran field exercises most of the day, with Wreg and the others. After, he spent more time with Menlim, working on manipulation, as well as some of the more subtle work in strategy for which he needs the higher structures in his light...the structures he cannot let the other seers see him access, even for something other than manipulation.

He finished the second round of work well after dinner, only to end his evening with a fight in the long cowshed belonging to the Rutghers.

He did the last solely for the money, since he knows they will be moving again soon. He still feels safer with his own stash of coin, despite how unnecessary his uncle tells him it is. He continues to fight and earn money, without arguing with his uncle outright...nodding without answering when his uncle tells him he will not need for anything for very much longer.

He is climbing down a path, a shortcut over a small hill that separates the fields beyond, and the forest beyond that. His face is cut on one side, and he wears a new bruise that will bloom into a black eye. The monster they put with him got in one lucky punch, but it was his last before he got him on the ground.

He is about to make the turn that leads to a shortcut path that winds its way through the trees to his home...when he feels them.

He realizes too late that they've been waiting for him...and that they already surround him.

He glances around at the dark forms, reading them swiftly with his light. They are partly shielded, so he doesn't get all of it, but he gets enough to understand. He does not want to understand though, and stares around at them again, feeling a kind of clutching pain in his chest as it sinks in, a near disbelief.

"Hullo there," the first one says, stepping directly into his path.

Nenzi scans his options. He cannot use his sight. He might not be able to push so many without witnesses anyway...but they have a seer with them.

She told them to bring a seer. She told them what he is.

His breath comes shorter, even as he looks around, counting, taking in sizes and faces and the way they move. Using the telekinesis is out of the question. And there are many of them, he realizes...many more than he first noticed when he realized they had him trapped. The seer obscured their numbers before they had him surrounded; he now counts at least eight forms standing around the small clearing, none of them small.

"What have I done?" he asks in German. "Please tell me...I have not wronged you."

The one who first spoke to him smiles, moving closer.

"That's not how we heard it," he says.

Nenzi digs a hand into his pocket, pulling out the bills half-sweated together inside his pants. He holds them out, keeping his voice steady.

"Is it this you want?" he says, knowing it is not. "Take it. It is yours."

"Keep your money, ice blood," another says, his voice thick, some of it from drink. "You're going to need it to pay the doctor when we're done..."

He finds himself sliding into a fighting stance, but looking around him, he knows some of these men. Some he's even seen in dirt rings in different parts of the city. They know who he is, too. They came expecting a fight.

Finally, picking out the one he knows to be a mediocre fighter at best, he slides around behind him, trying to force the human between himself and their leader.

But he stood there too long, looking at them. He let them get too close to him before he acted. Three of them dart up from behind, force him to turn. He catches one in a cross after dodging a hit from the larger of the two. Weaving under another series of hits, he manages to drive two of them back with hits to the temple, but he is not fast enough, he can feel it.

Twisting to get the largest of the four with an elbow to the face, he misses a block to a hit from the other side, and staggers a little from the blow. Again he slides his body sideways, tries to get someone between himself and the others, but he is too slow...his body too tired.

Adrenaline has him forcing another off him with a sharp side kick to the ribs, but he feels his own desperation now. He connects, knocking a man backwards, but he kicks too high. Again, it slows his reactions, and one of the men behind him hooks his arm, round-housing a punch to the side of his head. It's a solid hit, and it dazes him...enough to make him pause before twisting his weight to free his arm. When they catch hold of him again, he head-butts the man directly in front of him, breaking his nose.

Then someone has his chest in a vise grip. He wrenches himself backwards, feels a pain in his back and gasps as the knife slides between his ribs.

Two more hits to his face and one to his throat, and they have him on the ground.

He's made them angry...not from fighting back so much as from getting in too many hits.

So once they've knocked him down, they start by taking turns kicking him.

Things get foggy after that.

He wakes, gasping, when someone throws water on him.

Pain eclipses any awareness of where he is, or who is with him. He lets out a cry when someone grabs his arms, hoisting him up. He barely hears the words from the men under him.

"Another farmer's wife, Nenz...?" the voice under him smiles.

He hears the teasing in the tone, but also the hardness underneath. He can't fight back. He can't even pretend to be who he normally would. The arms under him are strong, and other than jostling every bruised and cracked bone in his body, they don't seem to be trying to hurt him. When they start walking, he grips hold of those arms, though, letting out another cry.

"Where are you taking me?"

"Home, runt," a second voice answers, to his left. "I'd think you'd want a bed about now...if not a bath and a few stiff drinks..."

He realizes he knows the new voice. His fingers loosen on the man holding him, and looking down, he realizes he knows him, too.

Kandash. Wreg.

And to the other side of him, he sees another youngster, only a few decades older than him, and another beside him.

Tardek. Raddi.

They are from his uncle. They are from his unit.

He relaxes, fighting a relief profound enough to close his throat. They don't like him, but they won't hurt him. He almost forgets he's not supposed to like them, either.

"I thought they had killed me, brothers," is all he says.

Wreg chuckles from beside him, glancing at the other three.

"From the looks of your face...they tried."

Kandash grunts a laugh from where he is carrying him, slung over his shoulder.

Nenzi nods, but can't force himself to speak again, not without emotion. It is the last thing he remembers before he is out.

He wakes, his tongue dried to his mouth, his lungs hurting with each breath. His clothes feel stuck to his skin, but he is sweating, lying under a thin blanket on a cot across from a larger wooden bed against the far wall.

He knows at once it is not his uncle's house, and while he knows this place, well enough to recognize the blanket on him, and the heavy wood beams of the ceiling, painted with a blue and white sword and sun, it takes him a moment to place it.

Then it clicks...barracks. Under the inn with the red door.

He is in one of their rooms.

He has been in this catacomb of rooms before, although perhaps not in this room exactly. He has come to their common space for meetings and trainings with the other seers, with briefings from his uncle, and even religious ceremonies and other more social things.

He has always been an outsider here, though. More than that, he knows the other seers dislike him...those who don't hate him outright. Most of this is his own doing, of course.

Pushing aside the thought, he focuses back on his body.

His jaw hurts, more than the rest. Wincing as he raises his arm, he touches it gingerly, feeling the swell of a bruise...maybe more than a bruise. It pulls at the skin of his face. He touches his face and jaw a few more times with his fingers, to get a sense of the breadth of it, and at the same time feeling something off in his mouth, a harder, more ragged pain that is muted somehow. It tells him they likely fed him something to dull the pain, maybe the *guland* he's seen the seers use when they've injured themselves in the field.

"Guland, yes," a voice says, in heavily-accented German.

When he looks up, he finds himself meeting the eyes of Wreg again. The thick-armed seer painted with body art motions towards his own mouth, laying down a few pieces of wood from where he entered through the door behind Nenzi's head.

He stacks the wood by the fire at one side of the room, then brushes off his hands, looking at him. Nenzi still hasn't spoken when Wreg gestures at his own mouth, roughly where Nenzi's injury is.

"They broke three of your teeth," he says, matter of fact. "We had to pull them."

Nenzi feels a cold kind of fear, irrational in that what he fears has already passed. He wonders what he looks like then, and decides he doesn't want to know, and is thankful for the lack of mirrors. The older seer gestures in reassurance.

"The teeth will grow back, Nenz...and they didn't scar your face. What it looks like now, doesn't matter."

Nenzi nods, forcing his shoulders to relax, and the other seer smiles.

"Did you forget you are not human, runt? Only the worms are gifted with one set of teeth." He grins wider. "...We are more like the sharks, yes?"

"Yes." Nenzi speaks awkwardly and forces himself to nod, if only to distract himself from the pains he is still cataloguing. Glancing around him once more as the older seer begins stacking wood by the hearth, he closes his eyes, fighting back a reaction in his light as he realizes again that he is not in his own room. He has never been permitted to sleep elsewhere...certainly not around other seers. Even in Serbia, he shared a tent with his uncle and Turek, one of his uncle's closest seers. He was never allowed to be alone with Wreg or the others while unconscious.

"Not that I'm not grateful, brother..." he says after another pause. "But why am I here?"

Wreg tosses a small log on the fire, waving away the sparks that rise. Straightening from a crouch, he grunts a little, looking at the younger seer.

"They must have hit you hard in the head," he says. "That was almost polite."

Seeing the younger seer's face twist in a half-scowl, stopped by the pain in his jaw and mouth, he smiles wider, shaking his head.

"...Not that I'm complaining," he adds.

He pauses, still assessing the other with his eyes and light.

"The truth is, they did hit you pretty hard, runt," he says. "Your uncle was not happy about this. He wanted some of our people to discuss this problem...with the humans who did this."

Nenzi feels his heart beating harder, almost hurting his chest. When he grips the side of the wooden frame though, struggling up to a seated position, Wreg abruptly holds up a hand, clicking as he walks closer to the cot. He gestures sharply for him to remain where he is, using the command form, rather than the polite one. Sending a pulse of his light to emphasize the point, he continues to stand over him until he feels the younger seer's acquiescence in his light.

"...You're to stay here, Nenz," Wreg adds. "At least a few weeks. Boss' orders. He wants you off the street for awhile..." He gives him an apologetic shrug. "...And I'm afraid your fighting days may be over. You'll have to find another way to earn extra coin."

When Nenzi doesn't answer, Wreg sighs a bit, wandering back to the other bed, against the opposite wall. Still, Nenzi doesn't feel him relax until he gestures his understanding.

"You *can* take orders, then," Wreg smiles. "Just not from me."

Nenzi doesn't answer that either.

He hopes this will discourage the other from talking, but it doesn't.

"...So you slept with the Franzin girl," Wreg says after another brief pause. "She's pretty Nenz. Very pretty."

The other speaks before he knows he intends to.

"She's a fucking bitch," he says, wincing at his jaw. "Her brother. He was with them...at least one of them. Maybe more."

Wreg chuckles at this, resting his arms on his knees as he leans against the wall, sitting on the blankets covering his wider bed.

"Yes," he says. "We know. What did you do to her, runt, to make her so angry?"

"I broke it off with her."

"Really?" Wreg grins wider. "And she did not take this so well?"

Nenzi gestures at the blood-stained shirt he still wears, the lump on his jaw, the gash in the side of his pants where another of them cut him.

"...Apparently not," he says.

Wreg chuckles a little again. His eyes continue to watch him though, holding that vague humor, but with something else shining brighter underneath. Nenzi feels it before he sees it, a cold calculation under the more surface guise of camaraderie. He is being scanned, he knows. Probed. He suspects he knows the reason why, even before the other speaks.

"She knew what you were, Nenz," Wreg says.

Nenzi gives him a hard look. "That was an accident," he says.

"An accident?"

"Yes."

"What kind of accident?"

"What kind do you think?" he growls back.

Wreg just looks at him for a moment, his eyes holding a kind of irritated impatience. When he breaks the silence again, he is shaking his head, his mouth hard.

"You know, Nenz," he says softly. "You are quickly becoming more work for me than all of my other seers combined. Not a one of your brothers under my command pains me so often, nor so deeply."

Nenzi doesn't answer that.

When the silence stretches, he fights to turn himself slowly on the bed, gripping the edges to try and lower his body to the thin mattress. His arms are weak, however, and he grips until his knuckles are white, fighting his own breaths. When he lands on his back on the padding, he gives a low gasp of pain, unable to make himself move further for a moment, once he is there. He lays with his eyes closed instead, fighting back the image of the woman's face.

"Why didn't you erase her, Nenz?" Wreg asks.

"I was going to."

"When?"

"I was going to," he repeats stubbornly.

"But you didn't."

"No, I didn't."

"Again I ask you...why?"

"Why do you think?" he says, opening his eyes just long enough to glare at the other seer. "She got off on it. She sucked me off...I liked it."

Wreg grimaced a little, averting his gaze.

"You're pathetic, Nenzi."

The younger seer only smiled, but that hurt his face, too. Wincing, he lay an arm over his eyes, avoiding the worst of the bruises, and resting it there gingerly.

"Fuck you, Wreg."

"...I'm not even talking about your obsession with human pussy," Wreg adds, as if he doesn't hear him. "...Although that is pathetic, too. I am talking about your complete lack of self control...no matter what the cost to others of our kind. I am talking about your seeming *inability* to put the needs of the cause before your own dick..." His voice grows harder. "If they hadn't done such a job on you, I'd be taking a strap to you myself...do you know that, little Nenz? I don't give a fuck who your uncle is...I would beat you if only in the hope that it might finally be the thing to reach you..."

Nenzi laughs at this, he can't help it. But the words depress him, too.

"Give it your best shot, Wreg," he says.

Wreg clicks at him a little, shaking his head.

"Again, you miss the point," he says, his voice now holding a thread of disgust. "Did it not occur to you, young brother, that you put all of our lives and identities at risk, with your love of this woman's mouth on you? And now I have to hunt down those fuckers...eliminate them and whoever they've bragged to. Including the brother seer they hired to help them bring you down..." His voice hardens more. "I do not like killing my own kind, Nenz. I do not like it at all. Not for any reason...but certainly not for your stupidity."

At this, the younger seer can't help but look at him.

After studying his eyes for a moment, Wreg clicks softly, but his eyes hold a fainter thread of satisfaction.

"Yes, brother Nenz...what did you think we would be doing, to clean up this mess? Or did you presume that we could simply let it be known that we have seers here in Dresden, masquerading as humans? That we are armed, and skilled in hand-to-hand combat...and that we like to seduce German girls when we are not drunk and shooting at Serbs?" Clicking again in annoyance, he folds his fingers together.

"To do this killing risks us, too...but then you knew that. And it can't be helped."

Nenzi feels his jaw harden more, despite the pain.

"And the girl?" he says finally. "Gretchen?"

Wreg frowns at him, his eyes holding a faint disbelief.

"The girl is dead, Nenz," he says, clicking almost to himself. "What do you think? That we would let her tell *more* people about your dick?"

Nenzi feels something cold in his stomach, even as he opens his eyes, staring up at the ceiling. For a moment he sees her face again, her eyes and lips laughing. He sees her as he first knew her behind his eyes...then forces it out of his light. He fights to feel nothing about this, then to simply pretend he feels nothing at all about anything.

"Do you want food?" Wreg asks.

After a faint pause, Nenzi gestures a yes.

Wreg climbs off of his bed, long enough to walk to the fire and pull a pot off the hearth that Nenzi had not seen sitting there. He watches as the ink-covered seer ladles broth into a deep wooden bowl, then brings it over to where he lays. He struggles once more to sit up, but the other seer holds up a hand to relax him. Then, sitting by him on the cot, he slides an arm under his shoulders and back, moving him up with surprising care.

"Mind the ribs," Nenzi says. "I think some are broken."

"Four," Wreg acknowledges with a gesture.

Letting him rest against his side until he is resting on his own legs instead, Wreg hands him the bowl once he is situated. Nenzi takes it with a gesture of thanks.

"Anything else?" he says, meaning his body.

"You have a concussion," Wreg says. "A fracture on your hip...the ribs and the teeth. A stab wound in your side that nicked your liver. The one on your leg is less serious...as is the one in your shoulder. Your jaw is fractured, too...but there was not a clean break, which is good. It is already starting to heal, according to Josef." Making another vague gesture with one hand, he puffs out his cheeks with a sigh. "Those are the serious things. Mostly you are bruised, Nenz...pretty much everywhere, from what Josef told us last night. But no internal bleeding, and no arteries cut. It is lucky for you, that they did not know seer physiology. If you were human, they would have ruptured at least one organ...possibly more than one. It is good for us that the brother they hired only did what they paid him for..."

"And you cannot spare him?" Nenzi says, looking up as he swallows a spoonful of broth.

Wreg makes a concessionary hand gesture, but his eyes lose some of their coldness.

"That is up to your uncle."

Nenzi nods slowly, sipping the soup after bringing the spoon carefully to his mouth once more. His jaw hurts, even with the guland, and the holes where the teeth were pain him with every mouthful, but he drinks it down anyway, laboriously slow. The pull of his stomach is more than any of the pains in his mouth, even then.

They do not talk again until he finishes the entire thing.

"Go back to sleep, Nenz," the other seer says then, taking the empty bowl from his fingers, along with the spoon.

For the first time, Nenzi hears genuine sympathy in the other's voice.

Wreg winks at him. "...We will talk more about your sins later."

Sliding his shoulder back under his, Wreg helps him ease slowly back into a prone position on the cot, even helping him adjust his shoulders so they are laying almost flat. No matter what side he lies on, it hurts, but his back seems to be doing less damage to the rest of him.

When he looks up, he finds that Wreg has not moved away.

He sits there, watching him silently, until Nenzi closes his eyes and once more lets himself drift back into the Barrier's folds.

He wakes again. Wreg is the only one there once more.

The Chinese-looking seer is crouched by the fire, his long, dark hair in a thick braid down his back, his muscular arms resting on his thighs. The seer is barefoot, his hair is wet...but it is the smell coming from the cooking pot hanging beside him that draws Nenzi's eyes. Wreg periodically stirs the contents in that iron pot while Nenzi fights to focus his eyes, to remember where he is. When another whiff of the smell reaches his nose, however, his stomach growls loudly, even as he feels a kind of longing pain envelop his light.

Wreg glances up at him, smiling a bit, his eyes almost friendly.

"I thought food might be the thing to wake you," he says.

"How long have I slept?"

Wreg gives him another nod. "Over a week. Almost two. You shut down...went into *ungrat*. The stasis. Josef has been here daily...he told us you would be fine."

Nenzi thinks about this. He knows about the comas seers can put themselves into to heal, of course, but as far as he knows, his body has never done this before. It is an odd feeling, to realize he has been out for so long.

"It feels it," he acknowledges finally.

"You are better then?" Wreg says, as he ladles stew into a deep wooden bowl that now sits in the palm of his hand.

Watching him, Nenzi feels his tongue thicken in his mouth. Swallowing with an effort, he closes his eyes, wincing as he fights to sit up.

"I'll tell you after you give me some of that," he responds, grunting a little as he rests his weight on his legs. "...If you don't, I may have to fight you, and then I'll feel worse."

Wreg laughs, even as Nenzi holds the edge of the cot, fighting a rush of dizziness once his body is more or less vertical. He can't remember the last time he's felt so weak...or so completely at another's mercy. He watches the other seer pull up from his crouch in a single, fluid motion, closing the distance to the cot in only a few strides.

"There is plenty," Wreg tells him, watching with hands on his waist as the other shovels chunks of potato and carrot and beef into his mouth, his eyes almost glazed. "...The others have eaten, so the rest is yours." He glances at the pot, as if calculating. "...Four more bowls, anyway. If you want."

"I want," Nenzi says.

Wreg smiles again, sitting down as he watches him eat. He brings him a second bowl a few minutes later. Nenzi is nearly finished with that one as well, before he speaks again.

"You still do skin art, Wreg?" he says, motioning at him with the spoon. "The inks?"

Wreg gives him a puzzled look, then a smile.

"Ceremonial inks, you mean?" He holds up his own arm, showing a pattern with multiple colors, adorned with symbols the other recognizes from books, along with images of twisting snakes and clouds filled with fire. "Like these?"

"Yes," Nenzi nods, handing him the bowl for another refill. He watches as the seer regains his feet, walking easily back to the fire. "I am told you did Rajan's....the sea creatures."

Wreg acknowledges this with a dismissive gesture from by the pot.

Filling the bowl a third time, he straightens, bringing it back to the younger seer.

"Yes," he says simply. "I did that one."

"It is good work," Nenzi says.

Surprise blossoms faintly in the older seer's eyes, but it doesn't reach his expression. "Are you buttering me up for something, Nenz?" he says only. "Or should I simply say, thank you, brother...and hope for the best?"

Nenzi ignores the other's smile.

"Would you do some for me?" he says. "I can pay."

Wreg's eyes turn faintly predatory in the pause, but there is a wariness there too, just visible above the softer smile.

"Some?" he says, still watching the other eat. "Just how many do you want, little brother? Are you looking to recreate the pantheon on your back?"

"I want two," he says, again ignoring the other's sarcasm. "Two of the colored drawings. I want them to be with seer ink...the ones that remain."

Wreg's eyes grow appraising once more.

"What are these inks you want, young brother?" he says. "What are the symbols?"

Nenzi looks around the low-ceilinged room, still eating the stew, although much slower now, savoring the pieces of meat. Swallowing what is chewed and in his mouth, he gestures around the room with one hand.

"Do you have the Second Codex?" he says.

Wreg gives him a faintly surprised smile, then nods, once.

Rising to his feet, he walks to a cabinet not far from the foot of his bed, one obscured in shadows that lay outside the circle of firelight. Nenzi watches him open the wooden doors, revealing a number of shelves holding leather-bound books and papers tied with thongs and even rolled and fastened with heavier weights.

Glancing over spines, Wreg uses the tips of his fingers to tug out one of the larger volumes. A few inches in thickness, it wears a thick, leather cover, dyed forest green.

He brings it over to the younger seer, who watches as he places it on the cot, only about a foot from his leg. Nenzi's eyes don't leave the book as he sets his bowl on the wooden floor, wiping his hands carefully on his shirt until they are completely dry.

He leans over the book, opening its cover gingerly before sliding his fingers between pages to reach somewhere in the middle of the book. Once in the rough section he wants, he flips through pages, scanning the numbers on the sides.

Wreg grunts, watching him.

Nenzi hears something in his voice that almost sounds impressed.

"You can find it without the key?" he says, his voice musing. "I must admit, I would never have guessed you would know the Commentaries so well, runt...even with who your uncle is."

Nenzi ignores this, flipping two more pages before his fingers rest on the segment he is looking for. He points at the passages, waiting for Wreg to move himself so that he is seated on the cot on the other side, so that the book lies between them.

"Here," he says, unnecessarily. "Can you do this one?"

"The whole segment? 1023 - 1055?"

"Yes."

Wreg reads it, squinting somewhat in the dim light. When he finishes, he raises an eyebrow, but doesn't comment, and Nenzi feels the other seer keeping the bulk of his reaction out of his light, where he might see it.

"Can you do it in the original language?" he says. "The old tongue, I mean?"

Wreg gestures assent, as though this were a detail. Looking up from the book once more, where he is apparently reading the passage again, he gives Nenzi a neutral look.

"And where do you want this thing?" he says.

Nenzi points to the upper part of his left arm.

"There?" Wreg frowns. "You want the text to circle there? Are you sure?"

"Yes."

There is a silence where Wreg only looks at him. Then he gestures at him again, his eyes once more neutral.

"And the other? You said there are two you want?"

Nenzi gestures a yes. "I want the Sword and Sun...the old version. I want the one with the high flames, with the gold center. Blue, white...gold."

Wreg's eyes narrow again slightly. "And where do you want this one, my friend?"

He points to his left shoulder. "I'd like it to be big," he adds. "Can you do that, brother?"

Wreg only looks at him again for a moment, his arms folded, his dark eyes unwavering. Finally, he sighs at whatever he sees in the other's face, clicking a little under his breath.

"Are you sure you don't have the placements backwards, runt? You know what you are asking for, don't you?"

Nenzi nods. "I am sure."

But Wreg's eyes remain unconvinced.

"The left shoulder," he says finally. "You know what this place means?"

Nenzi gestures another yes. "Yes, brother. It is what I will live for."

"And the left arm?"

"It is what I will die for."

Wreg frowns a bit, still looking at him, as if trying to read past his eyes, without reaching out directly with his light.

"It is not tradition, Nenzi," he says. "You know we wear the Sword and Sun there...on the arm. It is where we all wear it. All of us...and it is so in the old texts..."

Nenzi nods. "I know," he says. Meeting his gaze, he lets Wreg feel him, something he almost never does. He opens his light, holding his gaze, so that the other seer will feel his truth.

"It is not disrespect, brother," he says then. "It is not."

Wreg only looks at him, but it is clear from his face that he has felt what Nenzi showed him. He grunts a little, his eyes still assessing as he studies his face.

"Okay," he says. "Yes, I see that. I just do not understand..." Trailing, he shrugs again, as if not sure what to add to this.

"Do you need to?" Nenzi asks.

Wreg frowns at him. After another pause, he sighs again, clicking.

"No, brother...I do not." He continues to look at him though, that frown on his lips. "And you want *seer* ink, Nenz? Those do not come off so easily, runt...and while I may believe you that there is no disrespect in this, others may not..."

"I don't care about the others," he says.

"You should," Wreg says, quieter. "They are your kin."

"Then they should respect my will," he says, looking up at Wreg. "It is not for them I do this...not for them, nor against them."

After another pause, Wreg nods again, his eyes grudging.

"Yes," he says. "I see this, too."

"...And I do not want these to come off," Nenzi adds, his voice hard for the first time. "I want them deep, Wreg. As deep as you can make them."

After another pause, where the older seer seems to be trying to read his face once more, he nods...decisively this time.

"Yes," he says. "I can do that."

"Now?"

"Yes, now."

Wreg is already standing.

He walks back to his bed as Nenzi watches, kneeling down to pull a wooden box out from under the frame. He unlocks the iron latch with a key he keeps around his neck, then opens the top and rummages through clothing and other belongings inside. Nenzi continues to watch as he pulls out a hand-held device of some greenish-colored metal. He has seen it a few times, in this set of barracks...and even on the field, as seers used it to tally their human kills on their skin. Wreg then shuffles more items around, and pulls out a number of smaller glass jars. Several of these are filled with some clear liquid, but three of them carry colors so bright they seem to glow in the dim, fire-lit room.

Anticipation prickles his skin as the seer rolls all of this up in a stretched skin, grabbing a bag out of the top of the bin and bringing all of it over to him.

"Take off your shirt," he says then, gesturing matter-of-factly.

Nenzi barely hesitates before he starts to pulls the thing over his head, wincing as it sticks to dried blood from cuts on his skin. He shifts his weight on the cot as he pulls it off, exposing his left arm and side to the older seer as Wreg lays out his tools on the cot.

"Do we need to cover the sheets?" Nenzi says. "There will be a lot of blood, right?"

But Wreg doesn't answer him.

When Nenzi glances back, he sees the seer staring at his back, his eyes holding an open disbelief. Grief replaces the bewilderment in the older seer's eyes as Nenzi watches, bringing an odd pain to his chest once he realizes what it is from. He tries to find words, to explain this away somehow, but his throat closes around any he might have had.

"*Gaos d'argulem...*" Wreg says finally. "What happened to you, runt?"

Nenzi's throat tightens more.

He shakes it off, gesturing dismissively.

"Can you work around it?" he says. "Is there room for what I want?"

Wreg frowns when Nenzi looks at him again, but it is clear from his eyes that he hears the evasion in the other's voice, the unwillingness to discuss it.

After another pause, he gestures back, just as dismissively.

"Yes. It will not get in the way." He pauses then, his eyes returning to his tools as he lays out the jars in a row on the cloth he has spread. He glances again at the younger seer's back, and his eyes hold something for a moment, enough to make him pause. Then Wreg carefully blanks his face again, pulling a stack of clean rags from the bag down by his feet on the floor.

"I do not mean to question your judgment, Nenz," he says into the silence. "I only want you to be sure. It takes a lot to scar a seer. To really scar them. We tend to heal...unless it is too deep to grow over..."

Nenzi nods, hearing the second meaning behind this, too.

"I know," is all he says, his voice neutral.

He is walking down an alleyway behind the same bar, hours later.

It is dark outside now. He had less trouble talking Wreg into letting him go than he thought he would. He promised him he would not stay out of doors for long, or let anyone see him on the street...but he is still surprised the other let him leave.

His shoulder hurts, and his arm, but he feels exhilarated, knowing what lives under the bandages Wreg bound to his freshly-inked skin. The work is good, better even than he envisioned, and he looked at it in the mirrored glass in awe when Wreg showed him the final product. Even with parts of it bleeding still, the shocking bright of the colors overwhelmed him, and the dark permanence of the words on his flesh feel like an ongoing prayer.

Or a promise, perhaps. To himself, as much as her.

If he can't be with her down here, he will meet her in that other place. He will die for her. Eventually, everything he does will have been for her.

His aleimi vibrates with the knowledge of where his feet take him now.

When he first told his unit leader where he wanted to go, Wreg gave him a hard look.

"What are you asking me, runt?"

Nenzi's face warmed as he looked at the dark eyes of the elder seer. Still, the wanting keeps him asking, keeps him from backing down from that stare.

"Do you know of any, Wreg?" he says. "In town. I have heard rumors..."

"You should not be frequenting such places," the older seer warns. "You should not pay money to support such a thing. It is slavery, Nenz. It is wrong."

To this Nenzi can only look at him, feeling his jaw hurt like razor blades in his mouth when he bites his lip. The swelling had gone down while he slept, but his teeth and bones still hurt, enough that he blinks back a gasp when he clenches them out of habit.

Wreg just looks at him for a moment, as if assessing him again.

Nenzi knows enough to know that the other has been trying to get closer to him in some way, to find some means of connecting with him...of reaching him perhaps, in the hopes he might influence his behavior, maybe. He sees the difficulty of it for the older seer, enough to feel some element of gratitude, even compassion for his attempt. He sees this in the other's eyes even now, in the other's light, but he cannot let himself comment on it. He cannot let the other seer be overly successful, either. The thought brings another wave of that near-grief, but makes him want to be generous to the other, at least in the ways he can.

And yet, he wants this thing. He wants it badly enough that Wreg must see some indication of the hunger on his face.

"You haven't before, have you?"

Nenzi feels his jaw start to harden again. He stops it before it would hurt, but can't stop the flush that creeps over his cheeks.

"No," he says, blunt.

Wreg sighs then, clicking. Shaking his head, he walks to where Nenzi stands by the door, one of Wreg's clean shirts thrown around his shoulders over the fresh bandages, a pair of Wreg's pants hanging too big on his hips.

"Are you sure you're up for this?" he asks him, once he is nearer.

Nenzi nods. "I'm sure, brother."

Wreg smiles. "You think you are, anyway."

Still the smile is not unkind, nor even overly condescending, and Nenzi finds himself relaxing a little when he reads the other's light.

"You'll let me go?" he asks.

"How much money do you have?"

Nenzi hesitates, then walks back to the cot, where his torn and bloody pants lie on the floor.

Lifting them by one end, he feels for the correct pocket, and pulls out his winnings from the fighting he did the night Gretchen's brothers beat him into the dirt. They had been honest in that, at least...they had left him the money. He hadn't been too sure he would find it there.

Perhaps they'd only done it so the police would not come after them, accusing them of theft, but even so, Nenzi felt a brief pulse of gratitude that they had left it.

Pulling it out, still feeling that relief, he tosses the bundle to Wreg, who catches it easily and flips through the stack of marks. After he has, he frowns slightly, gazing up at the low ceiling as if thinking, or perhaps counting. Once he has, he shoves his hands into his own pocket, and pulls out another stack of bills. He tosses both of them back to the younger seer.

"If it is your first time," he says only. "You might need more."

Nenzi feels a flush of warmth. Half of it is from shock at the generosity of the gesture, the rest is embarrassment at the other's words.

"Thank you, brother. I have money at my uncle's...I can pay you back. I know I still owe you for the inks..."

"It is nothing. Pay me back when you are better." Wreg grunted then, raising an eyebrow at him. "...You'd do me a kindness, actually, if you kept the money and *listened* to me now and then, as payment instead..."

"Yes, brother, I will."

Clicking softly at this, Wreg folds his arms then, gauging his eyes.

"You will stay off the street?" he says.

"I vow it, yes."

Wreg grunts again. "Tell your uncle, and I'll skin you, runt...I really will."

Nenzi shakes his head, gesturing no in seer. "I won't tell him."

Wreg nods, smiling a little, as if in spite of himself.

"All right," he says. "Well, listen then...and look for the markers in my light. You can get to this place by alleys, so follow the way I show you. You know the little blue house, behind the general store run by those Jews?"

Nenzi nods. "Yes. I know it."

"Behind there, there are trees. And behind that, a garden. Cross the fence on the other side of that garden, and you will find a row of smaller places... built together in a long row. It goes far back, with the shoemaker having his workshop and apartment on top. They are green and white...do you know this?"

Nenzi nods again, picking up impressions off the other's light.

"I have passed that way," he says.

"Third door down from the stairs," Wreg says. "The blue door. Ask for Nina. Send her my regards...and tell her that I have not forgotten, and still intend to return that favor to her." His eyes turn openly warning. "...And be polite, runt."

"I will."

"You had better. Or I'll take that money out of you in ways you can't imagine."

Nenzi meets his gaze, and nods again, opening his light enough that the other can feel that he hears him, and that he understands. "I will be polite." He hesitates, then says it anyway. "Thank you, brother Wreg. I won't forget this..."

The older seer looks at him, his eyes once more holding a near amazement. Still, the pleasure in his smile is genuine, or feels it.

"You should get the tar beaten out of you more often, runt," he says, slapping his good shoulder affectionately. "It makes you much more agreeable..."

"That is probably true," he concedes.

"And watch the inks, brother," Wreg adds, as Nenzi turns back to the bed, picking up his boots and socks and carrying them with him to where he can sit to put them on. "...One of them digs their claws into that, and you'll feel it, trust me. Tell them to take it easy..."

"I will."

Even so, he is already buttoning the front of his shirt, casting around for his coat as he pulls the suspenders up over his shoulders. He sits on the edge of the cot, still running over the path Wreg has shown him in his light as shoves his feet into socks and then boots, lacing the latter with jerking pulls once he's stomped his heel all the way in.

He is out the door pretty much the instant he finishes and shoves the money, both his own and what Wreg gave him, into his pockets.

Now, a half-hour later, which is as long as it's taken him to cross town in the circuitous route Wreg mapped out for him through backyards and alleys, he finds his steps slowing before a low green building with an upstairs workshop. He scans the four doors which are painted white, then his eyes stop on the third door from the stairs, which is painted a sky blue. He touches his arm lightly where the new bandage covers it, feeling a ripple of nerves even as it occurs to him that he has scanned too deeply; they already know he is outside.

Picking up his feet, he moves quickly to the door before they can decide he is not friendly, or perhaps before he loses his nerve.

He reaches the covered porch, and is standing in front of the blue door, about to knock, when it opens, and he finds himself looking at a pair of bright blue eyes, nearly opaque they are so filled with color, and brighter than the deepest blue of the sky...brighter than the painted door. He has never seen eyes of such a color, and can only stare at first, watching them glint in the light from inside the dwelling. She smiles then, and he notices only then that she is wearing an exotic-looking robe that leaves her legs and knees bare, and that her hair is coal black. She looks foreign, like Wreg...as if she comes from the place on the other side of the mountains.

He finds his eyes riveted to her bare legs, which he's never seen before, not on a woman he hasn't undressed himself.

Her eyes swivel to someone behind her, even as she laughs.

"You've got one, all right, Nina. He looks ready to burst, this one..."

Stepping back, she lets the door swing open, gesturing in seer for him to enter.

His eyes are still on hers as he crosses the threshold, knowing he is blushing from her words, but lost once more in the color of her irises. It occurs to him he hasn't seen a seer female since he was a child, and pain slides through his light, strong enough that he has to fight to control it as he follows her past the foyer and into a low-ceilinged hallway beyond.

The woman walks in front of him, her strides casual, athletic, and he notices her feet are bare. She turns left at a lit doorway, the first he sees, and he follows her warily, only to stop at the entrance to the room, watching her as she walks directly to a couch upholstered in dark blue, and sits beside another female, this one with hair that is a honey-blond. Her eyes are not human either, but they are closer; a pale brown, they are almost the same color as her hair, but for gold flecks that shine from them, visible even where he stands.

"And what do you want, young sir?" A voice asks, to his left.

He turns his head, and finds himself looking at a small female, much shorter than the others. She looks Asian, as well, and her eyes burn a dark violet color that seems to turn crimson, depending on how they catch the light.

He clears his throat, glancing around. He realizes there are eight of them, and that he is the only one standing. Fighting his expression still, he holds out his hands, a peace gesture in seer, following it with a more polite gesture of greeting. The smallish female smiles, her eyes following his hands with a faint amusement.

"Yes," she says. "We will not attack you, brother. What is it you want?"

"One of you is Nina?" he says finally.

"I am Nina," the small one says, her eyes turning slightly more appraising. "But I do not know you," she adds, her voice not unfriendly.

"You don't," he affirms. "I am Nenzi...of Outer Reach. I asked a brother for directions here, and he gave me your name..."

"And what is his name? This brother of yours?"

"Wreg." Nenzi hesitates, realizes he has no other name for Wreg, nor a clan affiliation. He speaks over his own pause. "...He said to tell you that he remembers he owes you...that his gratitude remains, and that he has not forgotten his debt."

"I know brother Wreg is good for his debts," she says, smiling below the appraising look in her eyes. "Did you come all this way, in the night and the rain, to tell me that? If so, I think brother Wreg owes you something, as well..."

Nenzi feels his face tighten, even as he remembers not to clench his jaw. It hasn't occurred to him he would have to explain why he had come. He is about to try and speak again, when the female who answered the door laughs.

"Nina, you will give this youngster a heart attack..."

A quiet coil of laughter whispers around the room. Most of it is in his light, not audible to his ears, but it is good-natured, not derisive. He feels himself relax slightly, even as his eyes return to Nina, who he assumes is in charge.

"You have money?" she asks politely.

"Yes, sister."

"Well," she smiles, gesturing around the room. "Then choose. Unless you have enough for all of us...?"

He feels his skin warm again, but his eyes follow the direction of her hand. He finds himself looking at faces, feeling less comfortable letting his eyes stray much lower than that, given that none of them are dressed the way he is used to human females dressing. He pauses on a few of those faces, golden eyes and deep black irises.

Then he sees one of them sitting off by herself, in a corner by the window. She is wrapped in an Asian-looking robe like the first one, but her face is less Asian, despite the high cheekbones and faint slant to her eyes. Her skin is a tawny brown, darker than he is used to in the humans, and her hair is nearly black. Her eyes are hazel in color, green with gold and brown flecks. But it is her stillness he finds himself drawn to, the faint tinges of gold and white he sees in her light. She is looking at him, too, but not smiling like the others. She looks at him as if trying to figure him out, her large eyes serious.

"I think we have our answer," the seer with the blue eyes says, her voice a hard smile.

Nina is smiling too when Nenzi turns his eyes back to the rest of the room, but on her it seems more genuine. Instead of him, she looks at the female in the corner.

"Will you have him, Laren?" she says.

"I will," the other says easily.

She stands up when Nenzi turns, moving almost like a cat coiling out of a repose, and his eyes drift down involuntarily. She is tall, as tall as him, with legs that are muscular, as if she does mulei daily, like the seers in his unit. He watches her walk towards him, and doesn't move as she takes his arm. With scarcely a pause, she tugs him with her towards the darkened hallway, and his feet move before he's let himself think about it too clearly, distracted when he feels her light already exploring his.

As they reach the door, she glances back at the room a last time.

"I will take the blue room," she says. "Let me know if one of you would like him, as well."

He feels his face flush hot at this. He glances at the other seers before he can stop himself. A few of them are looking at him as well, their eyes also appraising.

"Let us know if he is worth it, first," the blue-eyed one says.

"Elan," Nina says softly. "...Manners."

But he barely hears this.

Turning his eyes from the others in the room, he follows the one they called Laren down the hall. She takes him past four more closed doors before her hand falls on the handle of the fifth, and he realizes the building is longer than it appeared from the outside. She glances back at him as he thinks it, and from her eyes, he can see that she has heard him.

"Yes," is all she says. "There is an underground component as well. It is a seer building, brother...only built to appear human."

He nods, swallowing a little when her light is in him again, pulling on his.

They don't speak again until after she has led him to a low couch. Sitting beside him, she starts to take off his shirt and he just sits there, half-leaning on velvet cushions. He is uncertain for the first time he can remember...maybe the first time in years...but doesn't know how to tell her that, or even ask her.

He feels her notice, but she doesn't laugh at him. Instead her eyes study his as she finishes with the shirt, sliding it and the suspenders off his shoulders. Looking at his body, she touches one of the bruises on the side of his ribs, lightly with one hand.

"Humans?" she asks only.

"Yes."

Sliding closer to him, she coils a hand into his hair before he's finished reacting to how close she is. He is still looking at her face when she pulls him down to kiss her mouth. He does as her fingers and light ask, tensely at first, then gradually he begins to relax. It hurts a little in those first moments, but he forgets that after awhile, too. Her light helps this along, until his breath begins to clutch in his chest, until he is tense for a different reason. Once she feels his shoulders unclench, she is touching him more intimately, caressing his neck and chest, sliding a bare leg between his, until he gasps against her mouth. Her light is in his now, pulling on it gently, coaxing it open, and when he notices he has to fight to maintain control.

He remembers his uncle's warning, his caution to leave his sisters alone...

But she has her hand in his pants and he groans, pushing the warning from his mind. He doesn't move as she touches him, following her light as it asks him to be still, letting her push him back on the couch. She uses her light and her hand until he is fully extended, half out of his head when she starts caressing the end of him.

"Stop," he manages after a moment of this. "Sister...stop..."

His fingers are gripping her hair, and he gasps when she complies, laying her hand back on his chest. She sits astride him, and now she is looking down at his face, her own eyes glazed slightly with light. Looking at her, he feels desire in her, a dense wanting that coils into him, pulling at him.

Pain floods his light, enough that he sees her expression change.

Her face tightens as her own pain meets his. He has his hand under the robe then. He slides his fingers inside her, watches her face as she gives a surprised gasp, and the pain worsens, nearly blinding him.

But he can't...not fully extended. He knows he can't, but he can't do anything about it. He doesn't know how to even begin pulling it back.

He can feel her waiting. She is wet, ready for him. After another moment, he groans again, removing his fingers from her, gripping her hair in his hand.

"Please," he says. "I haven't done this..."

Her eyes flicker with surprise.

"You haven't had sex? Intercourse?"

He shakes his head. "Only with humans."

Her eyes change. At first, he can't read the difference in her expression or her light. When her lips purse, pain sliding through his light in another pulse, he realizes he has startled her...and turned her on. His hand clenches her hip, hard enough that she arches against him, her hand on him once more.

He grips her wrist, crying out as he tries to stop her.

"Please," he says. "Please...I won't last..."

She smiles, and again, he sees empathy in her look. He realizes it bothers her, too, that he hasn't been with one of his own. She doesn't voice it, though.

"A little faith, brother," she says only. "I can hold you off."

"I doubt that," he says, looking at her.

She smiles, and her eyes light up when she does, making him hurt again.

Then she is kissing him, and her hand is still on him, her light flooding his, coaxing out his pain, pulling at him.

He groans, louder when she doesn't stop, half-pleading with her as she explores him with her fingers, undressing him as she goes. She avoids the bandages, and her fingers are light on the bruises and cuts that still litter his body. When his hands begin to explore her skin in return, sliding up under the embroidered robe, she lets him at first. A few minutes later, she pulls them off her though, pinning his wrists to the couch. Then she is tugging the pants off his legs, and he is under her once more, only naked this time, and half out of his head again.

He can't look at her anymore. It feels like he won't last beyond another touch, another sensual pull of her light, but her light is doing something else to him, and somehow, even with the other, it is holding him back.

He groans louder when she has ahold of him once more. She uses her light to calm him down. He can barely move when she presses at the base of the head, her voice and fingers firm.

"Retract, brother," she says. It is soft, but a command nonetheless.

"I can't..." he groans. He can feel what she's doing, but his light and body refuse to obey, are having none of it. His fingers wind into her hair, trying to pull her mouth to his, but she resists, her other hand firm on his chest.

"You can. Do you want me?"

"Yes." Pain overwhelms his light. "Yes. Gods, please..."

"Then retract...or you'll hurt me, too."

"I can't..."

"Retract, brother, or you'll have to be content with my hand...or my mouth. You could get either from a human, so I suspect it's not why you're here..."

He is fighting to concentrate then, gripping her arms.

Her light slides through his, showing him, coaxing him into a thinly contained calm, showing him what to do with his light. It takes another endless stretch of minutes, then he feels that part of him pulling back. It doesn't lessen his erection any; it almost hurts as the harder end pulls back into softer flesh. He is panting then, sweating as she moves further up on his body, still holding him with her light, her hand on his chest.

"Don't move, brother," she cautions him.

He fights to hold his light, to keep from losing it again...and then she has maneuvered him inside her. He cries out, his voice weak as she grips his hair.

She is talking to him though, coaxing him calm once more with her light.

"Not yet," she says, caressing his face and chest. "Not yet, brother..."

He realizes there are others in the room, that they are not alone. He feels their light in his, their eyes on his face, and he holds Laren over him, his arm clamped around her waist, pulling himself deeper inside of her. He is fighting her then, fighting for control, when she begins sending to him more sensually once more, using her light to control his.

He has his face against her shoulder, half sitting up, when she is showing him what to do, where to angle his body inside hers.

He groans when she helps him arch his way into the correct slot. He is panting again then, closing his eyes against her skin, sick with pain.

He grows conscious of the others once more, but he doesn't look at them.

"They wanted to see," Laren says. "...I told them it was your first...it is all right?"

"Yes," he manages.

"Are you all right, brother?"

"Yes," he manages again, his face against her neck.

He sinks his teeth into her shoulder when she angles him further against her, pressing down on the end of him deliberately. She still won't let him go all the way in. She holds his light, controlling his body through his aleimi, and he is sweating, half-lost in her.

Currents of pain spark through every vein in his light, and he is groaning almost without realizing it, half-begging her again.

When he looks up, her fingers clench in his hair.

For an instant, he sees her eyes, sees his own reflected in hers. His back is to the others, but he sees the rings of jade in her hazel, and it confuses him.

Shock filters rapidly over her expression...and it takes him another beat to recognize what it is from. Fear glides through his light, the realization that it is him.

His eyes are glowing.

Before he can move away, or even think, she lowers her face to his, speaking softly into his ear, lower than a whisper.

"Close your eyes, Illustrious brother," she says softly. "Close your eyes, or they will see, too. I won't tell them...I promise I won't..."

He lets out another groan, but does what she tells him.

He barely has time to think about this, even to fear what he's done, before she wraps her legs around him, and slides down hard on him, pressing against the end of him again, and releasing her stranglehold on his light.

He is fully extended before he knows what she's done.

He lets out a thick groan.

The hard end slides out of him and into her, and then he is clutching at her, crying out as his arm clamps roughly around her back. He arches deeper into her involuntarily, but she is still teaching him, still trying to show him. He cries out again, half-fighting her even as he tries to do as she says, gripping her tightly as she starts to move over him, sliding her body differently for how they are connected. Within moments, he is sweating again, and he feels the other seers watching him, their light coiling into his.

"Don't let him come," says another voice.

He didn't feel her approach. When he looks up, he sees the blue-eyed seer looking at him, her arm around Laren's waist. Another seer stands next to her, with dark auburn hair. They are both looking at him, and he clutches the woman on top of him tighter.

"I want him, sister," Elan says. "Let me have him before he finishes..."

Nenzi feels another low pull of pain. He looks at Laren.

"I want to come inside you," he says. "...Only you."

Laren's eyes react to his words; a softer emotion reaches her expression. They kiss until he is sweating, holding her tightly again, fighting to get deeper inside her.

When they part, though, she looks at him then, her eyes a question.

She says, "My sister Elan wants you, brother...there are others here who want you, too..."

He looks at the blue-eyed woman, feels pain on her, sees desire in her face. "Yes." He gestures with one hand, feeling another surge of pain as he looks back at Laren, fighting a different pain in his chest. "Yes...but..."

"I heard you, brother. We all did..." Elan smiles, but he sees her give the other woman a faintly irritated look. "I won't let him finish," she assures Laren. "Do not worry."

She kisses Laren, using her tongue. As she does, she starts pulling her up off of him gently, just enough that he groans. When Elan looks back at him, her eyes are predatory once more, assessing his face.

"I think he has a crush, Laren," she says.

Laren acquiesces to the other's hands, sliding off him completely and he cries out, clutching at her as she goes. When she is gone, the other one, Elan, is in his light, forcing him to retract again. Her light is stronger, more insistent, and he finds himself doing as she says. When he tries to touch her, she forces his wrist back to the couch, until he lets his body go soft under hers. He lies back, and she massages him, her eyes on his face.

"He is pliable, this one," Elan says, still exploring his body with her hands. She continues to stare at his face as she touches him.

When he cries out, she closes her eyes, holding his wrist.

"Are you going to do as I tell you, little brother? All of it?"

"Yes."

She smiles, glancing up at Laren. "I like this one. Is his cock sharp, too?"

"Yes," Laren says.

He looks over at her answer.

Laren meets his gaze, her own faintly hard.

Then Elan is tugging at his hair, pulling him up off his back. He winces a little from the new ink on his shoulder, but follows her hands willingly enough. "I want you to go down on me, first," she says. "Come on, brother. You've likely done that with your humans...?"

"Yes."

"Show me."

She lays back on the couch, and he follows her, putting his mouth on her before she's fully resting on her back. She is specific at first, directive, but he gradually gets her to let that go, until he can feel her starting to lose control of her light. He brings her to an orgasm...slow, pulling on her, experimenting when she isn't telling him what to do. She is clutching his hair then, crying out when he uses his fingers.

"Stop," she says finally, when he starts to build her again. "Stop...little brother...stop."

Laren is pulling him back then, holding his hand, and he turns, kissing her, wrapping his arm around her waist, pulling her flush against him from where he kneels on the couch. When they part, she is looking at him, her eyes glazed.

Elan slides her arms around him from behind.

"Your boy knows how to give head," Elan says to her, massaging him until his eyes close. "Won't need to teach him much there..."

Tugging him away from Laren, she guides him to the couch once more. Once he is lying on his back, she climbs on him, and he finds himself looking up, focusing on Laren's face. He sees her react when the other woman positions herself over him. He is still looking at her when he arches up as Elan's light requests...until he extends fully once more, letting out a startled cry.

"Gods..." Elan cries out.

Laren clutches his wrist. Still leaning over him, she kisses him, putting light into her tongue. He loses himself in the kiss, groaning against her mouth as the other woman fucks him. Laren helps her calm him down when he starts to lose control again, kissing his throat, caressing his arm above the bandage.

He closes his eyes. When he opens them again, Laren is watching his face. He sees a flicker of pain in her...it takes him a moment to recognize the look as jealousy. The understanding brings another low groan, and then he is kissing her again.

When they part, she looks at him, then points at her own eyes, briefly, right before she kisses his, using her tongue to close them. He closes them tighter as it occurs to him why she's done it. Both women are pulling at him again, hard enough that he loses control, nearly yelling when the Asian seer climaxes, grinding against his hips.

He is kissing Laren again, even as Elan climbs off him.

The red-headed one gives him head until he is begging her, too, then another one is on him as well, and by then, he is so close to orgasm he is literally crying. The minute the last one finishes, Laren is pushing her off, almost angrily now, pulling him up by the arm.

She lies on her back on the couch, guiding him to follow until he is on top of her. When he enters her that time, she cries out, digging her nails into his back. He nearly hurts her, starting to extend before he's all the way against the right part of her. He manages to stop it, mostly, then he is so far in her he nearly blacks out. She is still controlling his light, still holding him back even as she urges him harder, until he is barely aware of where he is.

The first time she climaxes, he is so far in her and the Barrier that all he can do is cry out, feeling her legs tighten around him. When she finally lets him do the same, he loses awareness completely, unable to make a sound as his body convulses in a hard angle against hers. He is whimpering as he continues to let go, gripping her hair, his forehead pressed against hers. She is still talking to him, but he can't understand her words, can't do anything but throw his light and body into hers, gasping in pain. He feels pain in her too, along with something else, a kind of bewildered emotion as she feels his light, as she remembers who he is.

"Gods," she murmurs, even as he feels it on her. "Gods...Illustrious Sword...I want you again...I want you again..."

He finds himself coming a second time. His back arches violently; he calls out her name. She digs her hands into his lower back, and he forces his way as far into her as he can, nearly losing his mind when he feels her climax with him. For a long moment, he hangs there, his mind lost in hers.

It isn't until moments have passed, until he realizes they are alone once more, that the others left, that he finally lets his arms relax, resting his weight on her heavily. He realizes she is naked then, that he can feel her belly and her breasts and thighs; the robe is gone, but he doesn't remember taking it off her.

She is caressing his back, his hair, his face, and he realizes he is sweating on her, too, still fighting his breath back to normal. He is still gasping a little, still trying to slow his heart rate, when he laughs, kissing her mouth.

"...I owe brother Wreg," he says, kissing her throat. "Gods. More than he owes your mistress. Perhaps I should come to work for her...pay off his debt for him..."

Laren smiles at him, kissing his face, then his mouth.

Her kiss deepens when his does, until he can feel himself hardening again, his light coiling almost desperately into hers. Her light affects his more than he can catalogue with his mind, more than he can think past.

When he breaks off the kiss, he is gasping again.

"I'm going to need all of the money he lent me," he says, softer, kissing her ear, then her face. "I think I'm going to need a lot more money from now on, sister..."

She caresses his face, using light in her fingers. When he raises his head though, smiling, her eyes are serious. She frowns at him while he watches, biting her lip.

"What?" he says, worried. "Did I say something?"

"You need no payment," she says quietly. "The Sword's money is no good here."

He tenses, staring down at her. She only smiles, her voice low again, lower than a whisper. Her hand massages his chest, working her way down to his stomach, then below it, to just above his groin. He closes his eyes as she massages him there, her fingers sliding light into his skin.

"You can have me whenever you want, Illustrious Syrimne," she says, her voice soft. "I want you again now...I'll want you for days, if you let me..."

His face hardens, even as his body reacts to her words, and her fingers. He opens his eyes, frowning a little as he looks at her, but he is touched too, so much so he can't answer her at first. When he finally does, he has to look away from her liquid gaze.

Even so, he already knows. He can't come back here. He can't come back here ever again. Even Wreg seemed to have known that.

"You can't tell anyone, Laren," he says, soft. He caresses her face with his. "...You should not use that name, even if you are shielding us...even in jest. You cannot tell anyone who I am...that I have been here...you should forget what you saw tonight..."

"Forget that I just deflowered the Sword?" she whispers back, smiling. "I do not think that is likely to happen anytime soon, brother..."

She kisses his neck, using her light until he softens, letting his body rest back into the curve of hers. She smiles at him, caressing his chest once more.

"You're going to be an amazing lover, brother," she says. "...you already had half my house wanting you. I thought Elan might actually fight me for you. And you aren't even to your full height yet...or your full size..."

He feels his face tighten again, even as his body reacts to her words.

"I only did what you told me," he reminds her.

She laughs, kissing his mouth lingeringly. "You will make her a good mate, brother," she says, teasing him in a softer voice, caressing his arms. "She will be so grateful for you...she will pull on you all the time...she will do everything she can to coax you into her bed..."

Realizing who she means, he closes his eyes, feeling a sharp pain in his chest. It is more than he can handle briefly, and he grips her hair, resting his face on hers.

"Don't talk about that," he says.

"Why not? Is that why you waited? Were you waiting for her, brother?"

He doesn't answer this, either. Pain eclipses his sight as he thinks about her words, making it hard for him to see her, to even think about where he is.

Then he shakes his head, clicking softly. "You must forget who I am," he insists. "I mean it, Laren...it is very important."

He looks down at her, remembering his uncle's words about this, about what he is doing. Understanding the old man's warning now, in retrospect, isn't enough to make him regret any of it. Not yet, anyway. But he knows that could change.

"It's not...safe," he says. "Knowing that. You must realize..."

"I won't tell anyone," she assures him.

"You cannot," he says. "Please promise me, Laren...promise you won't even think of it...not once, after I am gone."

"I promise, Illustrious Sword."

Before he can answer, she moves her hips up, spreading her legs so that he is further inside her again. He groans weakly; his eyes close, longer than a blink. "Laren, gods...sister..."

"You can trust me, Syrimne...I will help get you ready for her..."

Pain envelops him when she slides her body under his, changing the angle. It nearly doubles him over when she pulls at him harder, almost possessively with her light. He realizes she is pulling at him with that part of her body, as well, until it feels like her mouth is on him there, and he groans louder, letting his weight grow heavy on hers once more. He is begging her again in seconds, his arms clasping her back.

At the same time, he thinks of her words, and the tight feeling in his chest worsens.

"Please, sister...don't tell anyone..."

"You can trust me, brother," she whispers again.

"Promise me..." he says. "Promise me you won't..."

Sixteen
Finished

I COULDN'T MOVE.

I lay on my back, staring up at a green-mirrored ceiling. I didn't remember coming out of it. I couldn't think about how long I had been inside that place, with him...I couldn't make myself think about what I'd seen.

My heart hurt, more than I could suppress, or keep out of my light... that pain I remembered, faintly, from long ago, from thinking he was dead. I remembered that pain well enough, but this ache in my heart was new, almost more than I could bear without voicing it somehow. I clutched at my chest protectively, fighting to breathe, unable to see for what felt like a long time.

I knew the truth behind it, though. I'd finally seen more than I could handle. Other things hurt, scared me maybe...or scarred me, maybe even more than I realized. Other things made me wonder if he'd ever be okay, if he was so far lost in insanity and death that he might never come back. But I couldn't handle what he'd just shown me. I couldn't even articulate to myself why, but that didn't really matter, either.

I could feel my light closing, pulling away.

I even knew the story. He'd told me some of this before, in that rebel compound in the mountains, as the Sword. But I hadn't seen it in technicolor before, and in his version, he'd left out the part about the prostitutes. He'd also left out the part about how he'd given up...on me, anyway. On having love in the flesh, at least in this life. He'd decided he would be dead before we met again. He'd decided not to wait anymore.

I didn't look at him.

I felt his eyes on me though. I felt his pain as he looked at me, but I couldn't let myself think about whether it was aimed at me. I remembered how he felt, with that other seer, and the pain in my chest worsened.

Elan had been there. Elan Raven, Maygar's mother, had been there when he lost his virginity in a whorehouse. She'd practically molested him.

I covered my eyes with a hand, trying to fight the image out of my light.

I needed a break. Balidor was right; so was Jon. I could feel it now, my gradual loss of control, the inability to keep my mind running in straight lines. I felt my own exhaustion. It wasn't lack of sleep...not the part that hurt me, anyway. I fought it out of my light, that desperation, that pain that wasn't just separation pain, or even regret or fear or confusion at some of the more violent things he'd shown me.

I didn't know if I could handle much more of this.

The thought brought another hard pain in my chest, a tightness that cut off my breath. I fought back tears, fought back whatever wanted to manifest on my face.

I was losing it. I wasn't going to be able to help him much longer. I would have to call in Vash...or Tarsi. I had to believe that I'd been right in what I'd told him, that they could do it without me. I wasn't going to be any good to him much longer. Better to go now, before I lost control of my light altogether, and caused him to withdraw, or worse...to slide backwards into that fortress he'd built around himself.

I had been doing it for weeks now, fighting back everything I felt, every reaction I had to what I saw...anything that hit me that was personal. It wasn't denial...not all of it, anyway. I knew what I had to do. I had to be a kind of mirror. There was no way in hell I could remain objective, but I had to at least seem objective. For him.

Whatever his words said, I knew he was sometimes consumed with guilt, or maybe just shame...to the point where he couldn't look at me after. I didn't know if those feelings were personal to me, or the mere fact of having any witness at all...or if it came just from having to see it all again himself. Whatever his reasons...and I didn't probe them because I didn't have to...I knew he was looking for any excuse, any reason to fight me more than he already was.

I struggled to bring my light under control, breathing.

The pain gradually ebbed to a bearable throbbing, somewhere in the near background. It always did, eventually...but it took longer each time. Each time, it felt a little closer, even after it had receded. Each time, it bit into me harder.

I fought to swallow, lying there a few minutes more.

I waited for it to go back more, to recede further into the background. When it didn't, I waited until I could handle that. Or until I could at least keep it off my expression.

I wondered how long that time had been.

Going under, time distorted. That had felt like days...but I knew it had likely been hours. Ten at most. More likely, it had been seven or eight.

I grew conscious of my own fingers clenched in my shirt over my chest, and I loosened those too, taking my hand away from the sweated fabric. I laid it on the blanket by my side, and tried not to react to the fact that he'd seen me do that, as well.

I still felt his eyes on me, from where he lay only a few feet away.

It made it easier to connect, to be so close. But it made everything harder, too.

I was still trying to make up my mind to turn, to look at him, try to ascertain what lay behind his stare. I preferred to do it by reading his expression, without reaching out, without violating him inside the collar unless I absolutely had to. My own paranoia wasn't a pressing enough reason to take advantage of the disparity between us. In fact, I couldn't really think of a good reason to do it anymore. I suppose there had to be one, if I thought hard enough.

I still couldn't make myself look at him.

"Allie."

His voice was soft, almost a whisper.

I didn't turn. His voice slid through my light, bringing the pain back in a thick pulse, strong enough it probably showed on my face.

"Allie, look at me."

I swallowed again. But his words got me to turn, to shift my head on the hard pillow.

Meeting his gaze, I felt a kind of pit form in my stomach. I tried to keep it off my face, studying his expression. He looked at me, and I saw something like fear in his eyes.

"Allie," he said, softer. He touched my face.

"Are you all right?" I asked him.

His eyes shone back at me, conflicted, shimmering briefly with things I couldn't pin down long enough to identify. But whatever it was, it was more than he could handle, too. His clear eyes changed again as I watched, morphing until I could no longer see him through them.

The softness left his face. His clear irises held mine, holding an empty scrutiny that didn't reflect any of the things I fought in my own light...or that I'd felt in his, seconds before. All that remained was that emotionless appraisal, almost an infiltrator's stare.

I forced myself to hold that clear gaze. I couldn't force myself to speak, though.

He looked away from me a few seconds later, frowning. I saw his eyes narrow at the wall. Thoughts clouded his colorless irises while I watched, cycling forward and back as he pursed his lips. His expression didn't move really, but I saw flickers around his mouth and forehead, enough that I didn't buy his stillness.

I knew that look...sort of. But I didn't know what he was thinking. Some scenario was taking shape in his head, and he was feeding it, gearing up for something. I was still fighting to understand what I saw in his eyes when he spoke.

"So that's it, then?" he said. "We're done...aren't we?"

I swallowed. It wasn't an auspicious start.

Still, I couldn't lie to him. Swallowing, I shook my head.

"No," I said. "I just need a break. A few days..." Seeing his jaw harden, I touched his arm, fighting not to react when he flinched. "It would be good for you. To spend some time in someone else's light. Vash's...or Tarsi's. Someone who's not going to take things so personally." I fought to swallow again, shaking my head. "Revik. I'm just tired."

His eyes met mine, holding an anger on the surface. He didn't answer me though.

Still studying his eyes, I touched his face. "There's more going on," I said. "We just got a message from China, and I need to act on it. Voi Pai is trying to – "

"Spare me," he cut in. "I don't need to hear it, Allie." For a moment he only stared at the wall. Turning, he gave me a cold look. "You shouldn't be sharing intel with me anyway. You know damned well if I ever got free – "

"Revik," I cut him off, caressing his arm. "Don't. Please don't. It's not you. It's me."

He let out an angry laugh, shaking his head. "Yeah."

He stared at me. For a brief pause, he seemed to see me again. Then his eyes hardened more. I flinched at the anger that shimmered off his light.

"Just fucking go, Allie. Leave."

"Revik," I said, clicking softly. "Please. What do you want me to do?"

He shook his head. "I told you what I want. I want you to go, Allie. I want you to go and never come back...just stop explaining and leave..."

I fell silent at the pain that flared off his light.

He was breathing harder, his skin flushed, his mouth curled in anger. I saw that coldness in his eyes, but more lay behind it, so much more that I couldn't make sense of it. Neither could he, apparently. Confusion wove into the fury I could feel. Whatever it was, he barely seemed able to hold it back. His hands clenched on his thighs, and I felt pain on him, but it wasn't separation pain, at least not all on its own.

Looking at his face, it crossed my mind to leave...come back and talk to him about this later, after we'd both slept. Take a shower. Let him cool off. Maybe I would feel differently then, too. Maybe I would be able to convince myself I really could finish this.

But somehow, I didn't leave.

I should have left.

When I didn't move, pain came off him in a cloud. Then tears were running down his cheeks as he stared sightlessly at the wall. But most of what I felt on him was anger still...a rage so intense I couldn't get close enough to it to understand what it was about. I tried to touch him, but he didn't just flinch that time...he moved out of my reach, wiping his face with one hand.

"Revik," I said, soft. "I love you."

He shook his head, but didn't answer.

"Revik..." I began.

"Just stop, Allie," he said. "Stop. It's done. I want this to be done..."

"The sessions?" I felt a panic rise in my chest. "But we're so close. Please, just get some rest, Revik, and it'll feel different, I promise. I'll feel different – "

But he only shook his head, his voice deadened. "Not the sessions."

"Then what?"

"The marriage," he said, turning on me.

I flinched. I couldn't help it.

That time, his eyes reacted to my flinch. I felt him hesitate, then he looked away again. He covered his face with a hand, closing his eyes.

"I know we can't be severed," he said, still not looking at me. "I know all that, Allie. But I'm done. I don't want to be married to you anymore. I want to find some way to work around the bond...to have lives apart from one another..." He shook his head, his voice holding that pain still. "...I know it won't be easy, but it's got to be better than this."

I just looked at him, unmoving. I was lost again...lost in that place I'd woken up in, that place without hope, without anything. The pain turned in my gut, throbbing a low, dead pulse. I felt a part of me starting to shut off, to close down.

I couldn't handle this conversation, not now...maybe not ever.

But it was already here.

"I think we should formalize an agreement," he said. "Ground rules about how to use our light, and when to shield from one another." He met my gaze, his eyes empty. "And I want you to bring me someone to fuck. Anyone, Allie. Hire someone. All of this will be easier on both of us if we start taking other sexual partners...as soon as possible..."

Pain hit me, more than I could keep off my face.

"Don't," he growled. "Don't fucking start crying...I mean it, Allie...I can't take that right now. I really can't. You know I'm right about this...don't make me out to be the prick, just because I'm the one willing to say it out loud..."

I shook my head, but I still couldn't speak.

"I'm trying to make this easier for you," he said. "For both of us. The sooner we stop pretending, the better..."

I shook my head, but I still didn't look at him. "You can have whatever you want, Revik. I just...can we talk about this later..."

"You want to talk about this later?" He turned to stare at me. "Allie... there is no 'later.' I want us to come to an agreement, then I don't want to see you again. I want Vash and Tarsi to help me with the rest, and for you and I to go our separate ways..."

I didn't turn my head.

He stared at me for a moment longer. I felt his eyes on me, felt the pain coming off him, mixing with that colder anger, fighting its way out of him.

He wanted to hit me. He wanted to hurt me for real. I could feel that, too.

Even as I thought it, he lowered his voice, speaking in a kind of thick frustration.

"I can't stand it, Allie...I mean it...I can't fucking stand it anymore." His voice grew softer, holding so much pain I flinched. "I need you to go. I don't want to hurt you, and I don't trust myself not to if you stay. I never want to see you again, Allie...I mean it..."

"You said you wanted it to be me."

My voice came from far away, almost from someone else.

"...I could have made it someone else, Revik..." I said. "I offered..."

He grabbed my wrist in his fingers, squeezing tight enough to hurt. I felt him pulling at me, even through the collar, trying to force me to look at him.

"I tried to rape you," he said. "What the fuck are you doing, lying next to me?"

I shook my head, fighting for words. None came.

He released my wrist, half-throwing it back at me. I felt him fighting it again, pulling back at his light, fighting to control it. I watched this from far away, but I couldn't feel it anymore.

The pain was gone. I couldn't feel anything.

Even so, it took me longer to sit up than it should have. I looked down at my clothes, at my body, almost confused by their outlines. I tugged at the fabric of my pants, and they didn't look familiar to me. I realized I was still lost in the clothing of that other place, that other time I'd lived. As I acknowledged that much, his words hit me again.

It wasn't my life. I'd never been to those places. I'd never met those people.

Even the pain of it had been a voyeur's pain.

"I'm sorry," was all I said.

"Sorry?" he said. "For what? Are you fucking *apologizing* to me for raping you?"

"No," I said, shaking my head. "No. Not for that."

My voice sounded far away again, unfamiliar to me.

I felt another pulse of anger off his light, sharp enough that I closed my eyes, blocking it. Once I'd closed my light that much, I found I couldn't make myself want to open it again.

"Allie," he said, his voice tired. "Why do you even care? You married me when I wasn't me. We don't even know each other now..."

I couldn't make myself speak.

"Alyson!" he said. "Goddamn it. Are you going to give me what I'm asking for?"

I turned, meeting his gaze. I paused, silent when I saw him flinch at whatever he saw in my face. I continued to look at him, unable to take my eyes off his. As I did, I felt something in my mind phase out. Even in that, there wasn't nothing at all.

Thoughts formed pictures, despite the overlapping silences.

They hung there, in the dark, devoid of meaning, of any dialogue or story, but the themes woven through weren't difficult to understand.

I saw it again, what happened in DC. The way he'd looked at me on the plane...what he'd said to me when he thought I was in love with Balidor. What he'd said to me when I'd first entered the tank, all those weeks ago. Even as far back as the ship, and everything I'd done since to try and force us to be together. It had always been me, from the start. He'd pursued me as Syrimne, but only because of what I was, not because of me. He'd been waiting for the Bridge. Some mythical being...not me.

Until he wasn't waiting for her anymore, either.

I didn't have it in me to fight him anymore. Vash had warned me. So had Balidor. Even Jon in his own way, cautioned me about expecting too much. Remembering their words, I didn't move for a long moment.

Then I reached up behind my neck. It took a moment for my fingers to find the right spot on the chain. Unclasping the latch to the necklace I'd worn for almost two years, even while I'd been a captive of Terian, I caught it in my hand when it fell. I saw his eyes follow my fingers as I coiled it in my palm... as I held it out to him.

He didn't move at first. I motioned again with my hand for him to take it.

When he still didn't move, my voice grew impatient.

"Take it, Revik," I said. "Please. I need you to take it."

He met my gaze. I couldn't read him at all now, but it no longer mattered.

"I'll shield my light," I said. "I'll do whatever you ask. But I need you to take this back."

Reaching out almost cautiously, he held his hand under mine. With barely a hesitation, I dropped the chain and the ring into his fingers.

"Is there anything else you want?" I said. "Anything else of yours I have?"

For a long moment, he only looked at the ring in his hand.

I watched him look, then realized I didn't want to wait to hear what else he had to say. Before he could look up, I moved away from him, pulling my stiff legs under my body. Climbing to my feet, I didn't pause. I walked directly to the door.

I knew I was too calm, that something was wrong with me. I couldn't feel anything, even with him in the room, emanating light.

I also knew that someone was probably out there, listening, but I didn't care about that, either. Banging on the metal with my palm, I raised my voice for the microphones.

"Open the door."

"Allie..." Revik said. "Wait."

I only hit the metal again, harder. Hard enough to hurt my hand.

Revik raised his voice, pulling on me with his light. "Allie! Goddamn it. Come back here. Right now..."

I banged on the metal again.

His voice rose angrier. "Don't you dare pretend you aren't relieved... or that you won't run right into his arms again, now that I've given you permission..."

I didn't look at him. I knew I was crying, if only because I couldn't see; my light snaked and sparked around me, but nothing lay before my eyes but a wash of blurred green. I still didn't feel anything. The weight in my chest dulled all of it.

"Open the fucking door," I said, louder, my voice harsh.

Before I could bang on it again, someone did.

Jon looked at Dorje, feeling something in his hands go cold. Dorje seemed almost to be in pain, as if feeling something sympathetic through his light...but he couldn't have felt anything, not through the thick walls of the tank, or even the collar.

Allie's eyes, more than Revik's words, brought a kind of sickness to Jon's stomach, something he found he couldn't really think past. He saw the anger in Revik's face, the hardness of his mouth as he tried to get her to react, maybe to yell at him in return.

But Jon barely heard their words after her face changed like that.

Then he saw her hand back the ring.

She was on her feet then, and he moved even as she did, taking the handful of strides to the door at a near jog. He was still working on the combination lock at the front of the door, putting in symbols as Dorje read them to him from the terminal, when he heard her voice turn into a near snarl through the loudspeaker.

"*Open the fucking door!*"

Just then, the lock caught, and he heard the mechanism roll backwards, moving all of the cylinders back into place on the back of the door. Twisting the wheel on the outside of the thick piece of green organic, he heard the seal give with a faint sucking sound. He was still pulling it open when she was already past him and through the opening.

She probably would have walked out of the room altogether, before he could get the thing closed and locked again, but he stopped pushing at its weight once it met the seal, raising his voice to stop her.

"Allie!" he said.

She paused on one foot. Then she turned, her expression entirely empty. Staring at the mask of her face, Jon swallowed a little.

"Al," he said, at a loss. "What are you doing?"

She didn't seem to understand the question.

Her eyes went almost blank in the pause, just before they shifted to Dorje. Then she looked back at Jon. The calm on her face unnerved him, more than any expression he'd seen in her eyes before, even when they'd glowed at him with that alien, pale-green light.

"Give him whatever he wants," she said in Prexci.

Her voice remained as flat as her expression.

"If you need money, let me know," she said. "...otherwise, I'll cover it afterwards. Or he can, if you're willing to wait. It's going to take me a few days to get my name off all of the relevant accounts. You're going to want to set up some kind of terminal so he can access some of his funds, without – "

"Al!" Jon cut into her words. "What the hell are you talking about?"

Her eyes grew cold, the color of a frozen stream. Jon felt his breath catch. He didn't recognize anything he could see there...anything at all.

"I said to give him whatever he wants," she said.

"You really want us to put a prostitute in there?"

Her mouth rose in a half-smile. Again, he didn't know it, or the look in her eyes that came with it. She just looked at him, her expression unmoving.

"Which part of 'whatever he wants' isn't clear?" she said. "You'll have to pay to transport them here...and to keep the location secret. But if he likes a few of them, you can probably board them in the caves for awhile. Hell, I'm sure you can order them from the network channels, Jon. Give him a terminal...let him pick whatever flavor he wants."

"Al, that's completely nuts," Jon said. "You know that, right? Let him calm down, all right? Both of you need to just calm down...you're exhausted..."

She shook her head though, her eyes unchanging.

Jon tried again. "Allie..."

"Just do it," she said. "I need to go and talk to Balidor about the Cass thing. I don't have the time or the inclination to deal with this, too."

Jon started to shake his head, but her voice grew dangerously quiet.

"That's not a fucking request."

When he started to speak, she held up a hand, her eyes sparking faintly with greenish light.

"...And don't bother me with it again. Talk to Poresh if you need help with the logistics...or one of the others, I don't care who. Just leave me out of it."

Before Jon could think of a reply, she had already turned away.

He watched as she disappeared back into the corridor leading to the common areas and the residences housed inside the caves. It wasn't until she was completely gone, that he glanced at Dorje. The seer was looking at him, sympathy in his brown eyes.

After a pause, Dorje gestured towards the organic door.

"Lock the hatch, cousin," he said softly.

Jon realized he still hadn't locked the door. He held the handle, and the door was shut, but he hadn't activated the new code, or spun the wheel to reengage the seal. He stared at the thick door, his mind still moving somewhere, sluggishly in the background, without being connected to the rest of him. He looked past Dorje then, staring at the organic window into the tank. Through the green-tinted pane, he saw Revik sitting against the wall, his forearms resting on his knees.

His clear eyes stared at the ceiling, his expression unreadable. The silver chain with the ring dangled from the fingers of one hand.

Staring at him for another blink of time, Jon felt his hands clench into fists.

Before the thought fully formed, he jerked at the handle of the door.

"Cousin!" Dorje said. "No!"

Ignoring him, Jon stepped in to the green tiled room. Turning around once he was inside, he slammed the heavy door behind him, hitting the key for the lock.

He saw Revik look up, but didn't meet his gaze. Without pausing, he walked directly to where the seer sat on the floor.

"Jon." Revik watched him approach, his eyes startled. "Jon, what – "

Jon kicked him, hard, in the leg. Without a pause, he kicked him again, bending down to hit him in the mouth as hard as he could with his fist. Kicking him again, in the ribs that time, he grabbed his shoulder, slamming him against the organic metal of the wall. Revik only cowered away from his blows, throwing up his arms.

"Jon! Cousin! Please...please!"

He hit him again, slamming his fist against the left side of his head. It hurt his hand, but it must have hurt Revik more, because he let out a gasp when it knocked him sideways. He held up his hands then, protecting his temples.

"Cousin!" he said. "Please! Stop!"

"*Jon! Stop!*" Dorje's voice came over the loudspeaker, sounding worried, strangely far away. "*Stop, cousin...please! I'll have to gas both of you if you don't!*"

Jon found himself standing over the dark-haired seer, breathing hard, every muscle in his arms and shoulders tensed. He stared down at the man who had been his friend, and the fury in his heart nearly exploded out of him when he saw the other staring at the wall, wiping his bleeding lip with the back of his hand.

"You just couldn't help yourself, could you?" he spat. "You couldn't fucking *help* it, right?"

"I did her a favor."

"Did you? Was that supposed to be a mercy killing?"

Revik stared at him. His mouth hardened.

"We don't belong together," he said.

"No *shit!*" Jon shouted at him.

Revik winced, staring up at him.

Jon took a step closer, fighting not to hit him again.

"What the *hell* do you think everyone's been telling her for the past year?" Jon said. "What do you think she's been hearing from *every single person*...anyone she tries to convince you're worth giving a damn about? Do you think the other seers have been supportive? That they've all been giving her high fives, for half-killing herself in here with you? Every goddamned one of them would *shoot you in the head,* if you weren't bonded to her..."

Revik's mouth hardened more.

"And you think she needs it from you, too?" Jon said. "You self-centered prick! She asked for a break. A fucking *break* is all. You couldn't give her that?"

Revik shook his head, his eyes cold.

"That's not the point..."

"Then what is, exactly? What *was* the point of that?"

"Maybe they're right, Jon," he said. "All of those people."

"What?"

"Maybe I should die. Maybe we both should. I don't see how we've done a hell of a lot of good for anyone since we got together..."

"Jesus H. Christ. So it's a suicide pact? You're back on that kick again?"

"She's the Bridge isn't she? Maybe she shouldn't be here. Maybe it's not her time yet. Maybe us being here at the same time is only making everything worse..."

"Just what the hell kind of monster are you?"

"Monster?" Revik clicked at him in irritation, touching his temple with his fingers and wincing. He looked up at Jon. "That's probably the most selfless thing I've done with her since I met her..."

"The most cowardly, you mean."

"What's your problem, Jon?"

"What's my *problem,* man?" he said. "Did you really just ask me that?"

Revik's eyes met his. "You know I'm right. You said as much. She's better off without me...hell." He gave a short laugh. "Everyone thinks so. You said that, too."

Jon just looked at him, clenching his hands in frustration.

"What did she ever do to you, man?" he said. "Seriously. That wasn't some brush off. It wasn't even you trying to hurt her enough that she'd leave. You wanted her to *stay,* just so you could keep lobbing those fucking bombs at her. You were *trying* to hurt her..."

Revik shook his head, clicking louder.

"I wasn't trying to hurt her."

"Yes," Jon snapped. "You were. Why? What did she do?"

"She didn't do anything, Jon," he said. "She just tends to need to hear things in strong words...or she ignores them. I've tried being subtle with her. It doesn't work. She needs to be hit with a two-by-four or it's like I didn't say anything..."

"Really?" Jon said. "*That's* your excuse? So she's just a little thick then, I guess? Dim-witted?" When the seer wouldn't look at him, his voice grew openly angry. "I'm not *her,* Revik. I'm not Allie...you can't sell me the 'Allie's stupid' crap and expect it to fly. Hell, I think she's smarter than you are... about everything but *you,* that is..."

"Jon," he said, looking up. "I don't have to explain myself to you."

"Okay. Fine." Jon held up his hands. "So let's just have a conversation then...since you're so reasonable about all this."

Revik's jaw hardened more, but he didn't speak.

"So tell me," Jon said, fighting his own anger. "...what about the *bond*, man? The fact that the two of you literally can't separate your light, or you'll die? What do you plan to do about that? Or do you think if you're a big enough prick to her, that will go away, too?"

Revik frowned. He clasped his fingers between his knees, the chain and ring still dangling between them. His eyes focused on the ring, expressionless.

"I don't know," he said.

"You don't know."

"No, Jon," he said. "I don't. But we'll figure something out. You heard her. We can shield. We can find some way to – "

"Shield?" Jon said, incredulous. "You're just going to shield your light, while you go back to buying sex...or selling it, or whatever it is you do? You can't be serious, man."

"What the *fuck* do you want from me?"

When Revik looked up, Jon froze, staring at the tears in the other man's eyes. He could only gape at the seer's face, sure he was hallucinating at first, but Revik looked away, gripping his own hair in his hand. For a long moment, Jon didn't move, watching him sit there, his knees up, his hands in his hair as his body hitched under his breaths. He wiped his eyes as Jon watched.

"I fucking raped her, Jon."

Jon frowned. "I know, man...I saw."

Revik winced, clutching his hair harder.

"Then what do you want from me?" he said. "Why won't you leave me alone?"

"Because that's not what this is, man," Jon said.

"What is that supposed to mean?"

"You didn't do this for her. You *are* angry at her...why?"

The seer didn't move for a long moment. He sat there, staring out over the dark green room, his eyes out of focus. Tears still ran down his face as Jon watched, but the look in his eyes was anger again, an anger that was seemed to darken the longer Jon looked at it. Revik wiped his cheek with the palm of his hand, his eyes hardening more.

"She'll never forgive me, Jon."

"She might not now," he said mildly.

Revik looked up, his eyes flashing with anger.

"You don't know how she *looked* at me," he said. "Every time, Jon. After every session...she looked at me different. I could see it on her face. Not just the people I killed...whoever I slept with, whatever I did to the seers in my unit...what I did to those human women, in the town..."

"Revik, man." Jon sighed. "What do you expect?"

"I don't expect anything! But I don't *need* that shit, Jon! It's bad enough, her seeing all this...it's bad enough having to remember it myself. I won't keep explaining it to her for the rest of my life. I'm not going to do it! I won't!"

Jon just watched him, his eyes holding a faint incredulity. "Seriously, man? That's pathetic."

"She'll never let it go," Revik said, wiping his face again. "She'll look at me, and she'll think I'm a murderer, a whore-monger, a little runt fuck, like I was when I was a kid. She'll never see me the same, Jon. Never. And I'll never be right...not with her around, reminding me of what I was, every time I do anything..."

When the seer looked away, his eyes angry once more, Jon sighed.

"Jesus, man. You've got to give her time to deal with this stuff. You've got to give yourself time, too. And you're wrong about her, anyway...that's not what's bothering her. She's exhausted, Revik. And she's worried about you...and Cass...and about a million other things. She's doing her damnedest to be the good little soldier, to not get upset..."

Revik gave a hard laugh, his fingers in his hair again.

There was another silence.

In it, Jon found himself looking at the other seer with new eyes. Something clicked as he stared, until he found himself letting out a kind of understanding exhale.

"That's still not all of it, man," he said, quieter. "Come on. Let's have it."

The seer shook his head, staring at the floor. His hand shook when he wiped his face with his knuckles, using his fingers on his cheeks.

"I'm not mad at her," he said.

Jon whistled softly. "Yeah. You are. And not for any of the reasons you just gave. Tell me the truth...seriously. I'm not leaving until you do."

Revik clicked in annoyance. "You're making up stories, Jon."

"I don't think so. Come on. What's this really about?"

Revik shook his head, not answering.

Jon waited, watching the angular face as thoughts clouded those clear eyes, as he frowned down at his own feet. After a pause, Revik shook his head. A thick laugh left his throat, even as he gripped his hair, clicking to himself. Or maybe at himself.

"It doesn't matter. It doesn't make any sense. It's not *real*, Jon..."

"What isn't?"

"I told you, it – "

"...Doesn't matter, I know," Jon said. "So why not just tell me then?"

"There's nothing to say."

"Revik, jesus. You accuse her of acting like a child – "

"She fucking left me here!" Revik snarled.

Jon flinched. He stared at Revik's face, watching the seer breathe harder as he glared up at him. The anger in his face only worsened though, until he was fighting clutching breaths, his eyes flashing with sparks of light, enough to make Jon nervous. The seer's skin flushed, even as his long fingers clenched on his thighs.

"Just drop it, all right!" he said.

Jon swallowed, but he held his ground, folding his arms.

"What do you mean? *When* did she leave you?"

"Drop it, Jon!"

"No, I'm not going to drop it. When did she leave you? Because as long as I've known you, it's been you pushing her away..."

"Bullshit."

"Revik, for God's sake..."

"Just fucking leave it alone, Jon!"

When Jon only stared at him, his arms folded, the seer glared up at him, his eyes shining once more, but this time with tears. Anger hardened his mouth, even as he gestured with one hand, wiping his face as he growled out words.

"For years," he said. "For fucking years, Jon. Do you understand? She left me to rot. She left me with them. For *years*...and now she's going to judge *me* for how I am? She leaves me in...that...and she's going to judge *me*?" He wiped his face with his other hand, gesturing shortly. "Letting go of her, of that whole bullshit story...it was the only thing that helped. I was better after that, Jon. I was *better*..."

"Revik," Jon looked at him, now at a loss. "What, man? What are you talking about?"

"I don't have to listen to *any* of that crap...not from her! Not from someone who never had to deal with *anything*...who never bothered to show up, to even just be there, if only to help me with it. She can just go back to her fucking gods and her golden goddamned light ocean or whatever the fuck she wants..."

Jon just stared at the seer's face, bewildered.

He saw the anger there, but also something else, a kind of desperate hurt, something that he'd seen in the male Elaerian's face before, but not in a long time.

And not like this. Or maybe he'd just never really connected the dots to what he knew about him now, what he could see in him now.

"She doesn't get it," the seer said. "She'll *never* get it, Jon...and I don't even care anymore. If she wanted me to be with her here, she needed to get it...at least a *little* bit..."

"Get what?" Jon said. "What do you need her to get?"

Revik closed his eyes, resting his head back on his hands.

He gave a short laugh while Jon watched, shaking his head.

"I told you it didn't matter," he said. "Just forget it."

Jon continued to look at him, frowning.

After the faintest pause, he let his knees bend, coming down to a cross-legged position in a single fluid fall. Still watching the seer's face, he moved closer to where he sat, so that their legs were almost touching. When the silence stretched, he laid a hand on his arm.

"What are you talking about, man?" he said.

Revik shook his head, his eyes closed. "You wouldn't understand."

"Try me."

Revik only shook his head again. He wiped his eyes again while Jon watched, still clutching the silver chain in his fingers where they wound into his hair. Jon found himself thinking about his words then, turning them over in his mind. After another moment where the seer just sat there, not looking at him, Jon sighed, louder that time.

"Revik. Are you angry at her that she wasn't *born* until now?"

The seer's jaw hardened. He didn't look up.

After another pause, he exhaled, shaking his head, clicking.

"That's not the point. I'm not a better person with her around," he said. "I'm worse. And so is she..."

Watching his face, Jon shook his own head, feeling a sharp wave of unreality, mixed with a kind of exasperated compassion as he looked at the other man.

"Revik." He sighed again, leaning his back against the wall next to him. "You think when she was born was her fault somehow? That she didn't come soon enough?"

"Forget it, Jon. You're not a seer. You wouldn't understand."

"No...I get it."

"I said *forget* it, Jon."

"But that's it, isn't it?" he said. "You think she abandoned you down here. Left you with uncle Menlim and Merenje because she couldn't be bothered to come get you?" Jon watched the other's face, seeing it tighten under his scrutiny. "...Or maybe it's some intermediary thing?" he said. "Some grand, cosmological scheme that just didn't factor you in? Or deem you as all that important, maybe?"

"Jon...please. Just drop it, okay?"

Jon couldn't help but stare at him though, his eyes and voice incredulous.

"That's deeply crazy, man. You know that, right?" He caught hold of the seer's arm again, squeezing his shoulder. "I don't give a damn what race you are. That is some seriously crazy shit, Revik...to blame her for something like that..."

"I don't blame her."

"The hell you don't!" Jon gave a short laugh. "You do, Revik. Flat out."

"I said it didn't make sense. Anyway, that's not the point..."

"But it still pisses you off."

Revik exhaled, clicking as he continued to stare at his feet. After another pause, he closed his eyes. Jon watched his face tighten again, just before he nodded.

"Yeah. It still pisses me off."

"Did you actually *tell* her that?"

"No."

"Don't you think you should?"

"Why, Jon?" Revik met his gaze, his jaw hard. "What good would that do? It doesn't change anything, does it? It doesn't *fix* anything. And I don't want to get on this fucking merry-go-round with her again. I told you...it doesn't make me better. *She* doesn't make me better. I should be alone...or with someone who doesn't make me crazy. She should be, too..."

Jon leaned against the wall, shaking his head. "You need to tell her, man.

You can't just end a marriage and not tell a person why."

"That's a courtesy, Jon. Not a reason."

"Isn't it reason enough?" Jon said.

Revik's eyes clouded briefly, then he shook his head.

"I don't want to talk to her, Jon. I really don't."

"Well, that's good, man...because I don't think she's going to be coming back here for awhile."

At the other's irritated clicking, Jon sighed, closing his own eyes as he leaned his head against the wall. "Jesus, Revik. Do you really want her out of your life totally?" He looked at him, turning his head. "She told me to get you a prostitute. As many as you wanted, actually."

Revik gave him a narrow look. "She said that?"

"Yeah, man. She said to give you your choice...'let him pick a flavor,' she said. She authorized funds and everything..." He paused, watching the Elaerian's eyes cloud again as he stared at the floor. "If you think she's sticking around for that, you're high, Revik. My guess is, you won't be seeing her for awhile, man. If ever."

There was another silence.

Then Revik shook his head, clicking under his breath.

"She's better off."

Looking at the seer's closed face, Jon felt a sudden swell of anger.

"Bullshit she's better off," he snapped. "I *knew* her before, man. You might have been creepy stalker guy...but you obviously missed a lot." His voice sharpened when the other only shook his head. "And bullshit that you're better off, too. You were half of who you really are. That might be easier, but it's hardly better..."

"Really, Jon?" Revik looked up, his mouth hard. "You remember me before the op in DC, don't you? Tell me...was I 'better' then? Was that the lighter, more forgiving and rational part of my nature you saw? You can't even blame it all on the Syrimne thing...she made me insane *before* I shot that kid. I was already falling...even before. You know it. I know you do..."

Jon stared at him, his mouth pursed. After another pause, he shook his head.

"Revik, man. You must have known it would be hard...dealing with all of this. You can't blame that on Allie. You can't." The anger left his voice somewhat though, as he saw the tired, empty look return to the other's face. "...And anyway, it wasn't all the marriage. Having that kid uncollared and so close...that had to be affecting you. You probably were already dealing with the Syrimne part of yourself. Even before you shot him..."

Revik's eyes were distant once more. Gesturing vaguely, he rubbed his face with his hand, leaning his head against the tile wall.

"It doesn't matter now anyway, Jon," he said, his voice hollow. "She can't be gone for that long...not while I'm in here. Like you said, we're bonded. She leaves for a few weeks, and we're both going to feel it. More than feel it, if it's anything like last time..."

Jon just looked at him for a moment.

Then he sighed, leaning his head on the wall next to Revik's.

"I'm sure she can find a way around that, man," Jon said. "Her 'dim-wittedness' aside, she's always been pretty good at making things happen that she wants to have happen."

The seer shrugged with a hand.

"She can't beat the bond, Jon."

"No, man," Jon said, looking at him. "But she can probably beat you."

The seer looked over at that, his clear eyes narrow.

"I'm not trying to 'win' anything, Jon." He focused back on the far wall. "I knew I wouldn't be able to handle being married again. I knew it as far back as the ship. I did it anyway. You're right, it's not her fault, but that doesn't change anything either..."

Jon smiled humorlessly, shaking his head without taking it away from the wall.

"Revik," he said. "...you're lying to yourself. And you don't know her as well as you think. You can convince yourself she's a doormat or whatever as much as you like, but you're stupid if you really believe that. You have no idea how fast she cut Jaden out of her life, once she knew it was over." His voice grew warning when he looked at the seer. "I haven't seen that look on her face in a long time...but I saw something a lot like it today."

"Great." Revik gave a low grunt, clutching his hair in his hands again. "Now I rank with some human punk she was fucking..."

"Yeah," Jon said, clenching his jaw briefly. "A human she was in love with...for longer than she's known you. When she was done...she was *done*, man."

Revik clicked to himself softly, giving a humorless laugh.

"She tried to cut his new woman," he grunted.

"Yeah," Jon said. "...She did. She did do that. And then, a week later, she got out of jail, and she had that look on her face I saw today. She cut him out of her life...I mean totally. They were friends for like ten years, even before they got together, but it didn't matter. He tried repeatedly to apologize, to at least keep her as a friend. She didn't want to hear it. She never spoke to him again, as far as I know. He was *still* trying when you showed up and took her out of there. She moved out of their place while he was out of town, and that was it..."

Revik looked at him, his expression cold.

"Is that supposed to scare me, Jon?"

"It should, man. Yeah."

"Well, it doesn't. It's good. She needs to move on...the sooner the better."

For a moment, Jon only looked at his face, watching the seer's expression close. Realizing the conversation was over, he removed his hand from the other man's arm, sliding backwards on the tile, using his arm for leverage.

"Okay, man." Leaning against the wall for balance, Jon regained his feet. "Fine. Let me know how that works out for you..."

The seer's mouth curled into a frown.

Jon thought for a moment he might be angry enough to answer, but he didn't.

Instead he stared back at the green-tiled floor, the silver chain still clutched in his hand.

Seventeen
Resigned

I DON'T USUALLY GET MOTION-SICKNESS.

It's rare for me, even when everyone around me is puking their guts out, like the one and only time I went deep sea fishing with Jon and Jaden and a few of Jaden's band buddies. Everyone else on that tugboat-like fishing boat turned a kind of greenish color and hung their heads over the side more than once. I got sicker watching them than from the motion of the boat...and I probably drank as much as they did the night before. Well, all but Winters and Drake, who seemed to make a point of destroying as many brain cells as they could on any given evening. But even thinking about them now, and Jaden, and Jaden's band, felt pretty unreal. That whole life seemed so distant from me I could barely believe it had been mine.

So I don't normally get motion-sickness. But I had it pretty much that entire flight to Beijing. Before that, I felt sick all during the drive to Amritsar, and the shorter flight from Amritsar to Tai Pei.

Granted, the roads through the mountains were narrow and rough and wound in sharp loops for miles, but I'd made similar trips before and been fine.

Those last days I spent in the compound weren't my finest, but at least they went by quickly, and somewhat in a blur.

I had business to take care of first, which helped. I did all of the logistical things before I spoke to anyone, before I even let any of them try to talk to me.

Balidor tried anyway, of course...so did Jon. It surprised me more when Vash showed up and knocked on my door, and after him, Tarsi.

I didn't sleep much. I'm not even sure I tried. I knew I was in an endurance push at the end, just trying to force myself through, to make it out before something in me collapsed for real. I was running on that exhausted adrenaline again, and there was something wrong with my light still, but I couldn't think about that overly either. I did wonder if it had gotten worse since I'd started those Barrier sessions with Revik.

It felt like I wrote a lot, during those days.

I wrote out instructions, passwords to bank accounts, advice, observations. Most of it was probably worthless, or close to it. Vash and Tarsi had taken their hands off the steering wheel with the Revik thing a few weeks in, once I no longer needed their help in holding the connection open between us. They still kept an open line to him, Vash told me, so that they could help me exploit any openings that occurred in his aleimi.

Even so, I knew they didn't really need my help in understanding where he was at, or my inexperienced thoughts about what might be going on with him at that point. Between them, they probably had about 800 or even 1000 years' worth of experience in working with seers' light; there wasn't anything new I could tell them.

They knew Revik's light, too, a lot better than I probably did.

I did it anyway. Maybe in the hopes that it would make it easier to let go, to pretend some kind of handoff or transition had taken place to make it all clean. I took care of all of Revik's money, like I told Jon I would, and handed all of that stuff over to Jon and Dorje to manage. Jon said Dorje would work out some sort of single-entry terminal system if Revik needed to access any of it for some reason, meaning before they let him go.

I also set up everything I needed for when I left. I worked with Tenzi to get skin patches, prosthetics, contact lenses, clothes…weapons. By all rights, I probably owed them a ton of money by then, but I didn't argue when Balidor and Vash insisted I simply take whatever I needed. I couldn't afford to argue, given that my total assets pretty much equalled what they'd handed me. By the time I finished packing all of that, it took up more than half of my luggage.

I'd shed a lot over the past few years.

Even before then, I'd never really owned much. I'd never really invested in *things*. Instead, I spent my money on fleeting, impractical wants, like going out with my friends and trips to New York to visit my cousins and band equipment for Jaden. I'd never owned much even before I left everything behind in San Francisco.

Then again, I never had much money, which probably contributed to the not owning anything thing.

Now I had a few t-shirts left from that time, my combat boots, and a couple of half-filled sketchbooks. I didn't have much in the way of jewelry... nothing but what Cass bought me in the markets of Seertown when she and Jon first got there. I didn't even have the stuff Mom and Dad left me, because I hadn't been wearing any of it the night I left with Revik. Whoever I'd been before all this...even before Revik became Syrimne and everything changed again...was pretty much gone.

I felt stripped clean, but it didn't make me feel light.

Instead, I was left wondering if anything remained. I also felt afraid, for my survival I guess...although I didn't share that with them, either. Nothing seemed left to mourn those things I'd thought were me, beyond the people I cared about. I had no idea who was left, or if I thought much of her, when it was all said and done. I also had no idea how I would survive as a seer in the world, since I'd never done it on my own. Since I'd known what I was, someone had always been around to take care of me, to feed me, give me things...buy me plane tickets.

I'd forgotten what it meant to be on my own in that way, too.

The conversations had been harder.

It started off as strategy, of course. Someone had to go and deal with the Cass thing, and Voi Pai had asked for me. No one seemed surprised when I said I would go and handle it myself. It wasn't until Balidor repeated that I couldn't come back to the caves once I left, not until they'd stabilized Revik, that we really got into it.

Jon seemed less surprised than the rest of them, but he was the one who cried, and who tried the hardest to get me to stay, at least for awhile longer. Vash said very little. Balidor hadn't seemed to comprehend what I was telling him. I tackled him, Vash and Tarsi as a group, and he just stared at me while I told the three of them what I intended to do after I left Beijing. Through most of the time I was talking, Balidor's arms were folded over his chest, his lips pursed. But the look in his eyes had been close to bewilderment, or maybe disbelief.

"You're...what?" he'd said when I finished.

"It's pretty clear, 'Dori," I told him. "I don't know how I could be clearer."

He just stared at my eyes, his own holding that dense aggregate of shock and confusion.

"In no way is this clear to me, Allie," he said.

"I'm quitting, 'Dor," I said. "You need to appoint a new boss. I'm done."

"You're quitting...what?" he said. "Being the Bridge?"

"I guess so, yeah."

He continued to stare at me, his gray eyes just blurred enough that I had to assume he was scanning me...maybe to determine if I was serious.

"But what does that mean?" he said.

"It means I'm leaving, 'Dor. I'm not just laying low for awhile with your people while Tarsi and Vash finish with Revik. I'm actually leaving... dropping out." When he opened his mouth again, I held up a hand. "Look," I said. "Please...at least try and be logical about this. I'm not any good to you anymore. Half the seers on the planet want me dead. I have no battle experience, no political experience...hell, I wasn't even raised seer, so even half of *your* people think I'm brainwashed. It's better if I just lay low for awhile. Disappear."

"What about what you said to me before?" he said. "About the refugees? The Chinese?"

"I'm going to try and deal with the Chinese," I said. "We've already covered that. I've got a meeting set up with Voi Pai. I'll at least see if I can negotiate Cass and Baguen's release...I think I have a way to do it safely. And I won't be coming back here, like I said, so I won't put any of you at risk."

"How much leverage do you think you will have with Voi Pai," he said flatly. "...As the 'non'-Bridge?"

My jaw firmed a little. "I don't plan to tell her that, actually. As far as she knows, I'm negotiating on behalf of the Seven. She's seen me in that role, so it may actually help you...although with Voi Pai, you can never tell. In any case, she didn't seem to be wiling to speak to anyone but me."

"And the refugees?"

I looked at him for a moment, then shook my head, clicking softly.

"Alyson," he said. "You have an obligation."

My eyes flashed up at this.

"Spare me, 'Dor," I said. "I've heard enough guilt trips on being an intermediary to last me a lifetime...I've just spent months listening to that crap, in fact...from Menlim and whoever else. It's not the right argument to try on me right now..."

"What about simple compassion then?" he said. "You used to care what happened to your people, Allie!"

"I still care!" I said angrily. Seeing his frown, I folded my arms, feeling my anger deflate back into that heavier tiredness. "...Did you not hear me on the part that over half of 'my people' want me dead?" I said. "Those refugees would be a big chunk of that half. I'm thinking Chan might be able to help you with that. She spent time in the camps...and you said she's got connections to SCARB now, she can probably help you sidestep the Sweeps until you get most of them relocated. I don't really see a lot I could contribute to that end, honestly."

Pausing as I thought about this, I shrugged.

"...Anything, really," I added.

Balidor's frown deepened, but I saw that scrutiny trained on me again.

"And you will go...where?" Balidor said.

"I don't know."

"You don't know?"

"No, 'Dor, I don't." I sighed. "I'll need to find a place to hide, obviously... and find a job, some way to make money where they won't know who I am. Or at least won't connect it to *what* I am. I'm sure I can find somewhere to hunker down for awhile...I've been talking to Poresh, and some of your other seers, and I know there are places in the mountains..."

"Which mountains...?" he said, still staring at me in disbelief.

"I don't know yet. Not exactly." Seeing his disbelief deepen, I threw up my hands. "I'll send you a postcard when I find it, okay? In the meantime, I've been offered a few safe houses, just to get me on my feet..."

"Where?"

I just looked at him, my eyes flat. "Balidor...let it go, okay?"

"Let *what* go?" he said. For the first time, anger reached his voice. "Alyson...you can't possibly believe that it's safe for you out there! That you will actually find some mythical location where you can just 'blend'?" His voice burst out louder. "A fucking *job*? Are you seriously listening to yourself?"

"Look," I said. "I've made my decision." Glancing around at the rest of them, I opened my mouth to say more, then shut it. Looking at Balidor, I realized the conversation was going nowhere. "Just...deal with it. Okay? I'm not going to fight you on this, 'Dori. I'm not."

Pushing back my chair, I regained my feet and walked out of the room.

I barely got ten yards before I heard him coming up behind me.

"Allie! Wait..."

I didn't slow until he caught hold of my arm. Reluctantly, I turned.

"What?" Seeing his expression, I sighed. "'Dori...I heard you, okay? I heard you, and you're right, and it doesn't change anything. I'm a liability to you now. You've got to see that. You don't need mythical beings starting riots every time they show up in a major city. You need a new government. Hell... elect someone. Someone half the seer community doesn't hate. Someone who can reason with the humans...and with the other seers. You need a new leader. Someone who can help you rebuild Seertown and mend fences with the rebellion..."

"This is because of him," he said, his voice openly angry now. "You are going to go out there, and commit suicide...because of him."

"I have no intention of committing suicide," I said. When the fury in his eyes worsened, I threw up my hands, letting out a humorless laugh. "Jesus, 'Dor. It's over, okay? You can blame him or me or call me a coward...it's not going to make any difference! There's nothing more I can do here...not with him, and not with this Bridge bullshit. All it ever does is get people killed. And I'd rather not *do* that if it's all the same to you..."

"So you will...what?" he said. "Be a waitress again?"

A low coil of anger hit my gut. Feeling my jaw clench, I started to turn away, but he grabbed my arm, forcing me to face him.

"Allie. Do not let him make this decision for you!"

I wrenched my arm away, angry for real then. "I'm not. Christ...you're as bad as he is!"

"Why are you leaving, Allie?" he said. "Why?"

When I tried to walk away again, he grabbed my arms, pulling me towards him.

"Allie!" he said. "We need you!"

Meeting his gaze, I just looked at him for a moment. His eyes filled with emotion while I watched, a kind of desperate anger that didn't feel aimed at me. I'd seen the look before, since everything happened in China and with the rebels, but I'd never seen it so completely on the surface of his face. I watched him look at me, as if fighting with words, or maybe with the feelings warring behind them. Then I saw his eyes drift to my mouth. Seeing his expression change again, I shook my head, feeling something in my light close even as I pushed him away.

"No, 'Dor."

He caught my arm. "Allie, wait..."

I jerked my arm away. "I said *no*, Balidor. I'm not in the market for a replacement. You'll have to find some other way to cock fight with Revik..."

"Alyson!"

I came to a stop, hearing a kind of desperate hurt in his voice. It was so unlike his usual tone that I closed my eyes; I felt something in me give, making my throat tighten. Covering my face with a hand, I fought my voice under control, my light. Turning, I forced myself to exhale.

"I'm sorry, 'Dor," I said. "I really am...that was out of line. I didn't mean it."

"Don't blame me for this!"

"I don't. I really don't."

"Take me with you, Allie..." he said. "Please. Let me go with you."

I stared at him, unable to believe my ears.

When his expression didn't change, I gave a short laugh, shaking my head.

"You're the leader of the Adhipan, Balidor...you're not going to tell me you think they could get along without you?"

"As a bodyguard, Allie...not a lover. Just let me help you!"

"You're the head of the *Adhipan*, Balidor!"

"And you are the Bridge...whether you want to be, or not."

Seeing the look on his face, I felt the pain slide somewhere deeper in my chest. I knew he meant his words, that he would just walk away from all this, from the Adhipan and everything else. He would probably even tell himself it was his sacred duty, but that wouldn't be the only reason he would do it. I didn't think before I moved. Walking to him, I threw my arms around him, enveloping him in a hug. He clasped me in return, but I felt pain on him, a kind of desperate panic in his hands and light as he pulled me into and against his chest. I felt the anger there, too, although if it was at me or Revik or himself at that point, I honestly didn't know.

When I started to draw away, he clutched me tighter, holding me against him.

I was still caressing the back of his head when I felt his light in mine. I felt him trying to weave into my light, pulling on me even as he asked me, as his heart opened to mine. When he started breathing harder, caressing my hair, kissing my face, I disentangled myself gently, pushing his light off as carefully as I did his hands.

I kissed him on the cheek, and he kissed me back, on the mouth. It turned into a real kiss as soon as I let it, and then he was crushing me in his arms again, caressing my face. His arm circled my waist, even as his light wound into mine once more.

I didn't let that last very long either.

Pulling away, I forced myself to hold his gaze.

"I love you, 'Dori," I said. "Remember that, okay?"

"Allie." His pain hit out at me. "Don't leave. Don't say goodbye to me, please..."

I couldn't hold his stare. "'Dori...please. Please try to understand. I really can't stay here. I know that probably doesn't make sense to you, but..."

"It doesn't," he cut in, caressing my face again. Stepping closer, he kissed me again, pulling me back into his arms. "It doesn't, Allie...but it doesn't matter. You don't have to stay here. But you don't have to go alone. You don't have to leave all of us...I'll go with you."

I gave a humorless laugh. "No," I said. "No, 'Dori...you won't."

"Why, Allie? Why not?"

"Because you're the head of the Adhipan," I repeated. I still couldn't make myself look at him. I felt my own pain rise. "Please, Balidor...don't make this harder. Please."

When I started to pull away, he caught my arm again.

"Allie...I love you. I really love you." His eyes met mine, and I felt my throat close when I saw tears in them. "Please. Please don't walk away. I know you're bonded to him, Allie. I know you are...but I want you to be with me."

The pain in my light worsened, enough that I couldn't answer him.

His fingers tightened on my arms. He pulled me closer to him.

"Please, Allie," he said. "Please. I swear to the gods...it doesn't have to be now. You can take all the time you need...all the time you want..."

I shook my head, feeling a kind of futility wash over me.

"I can't, 'Dori," I said. "I'm sorry. I wish I could, but I really can't."

"Why?" His pain wound back into my light, worsening as we stood there. He was pulling on me then, kissing my face. "Why, Allie? You just said you loved me."

"I do, 'Dori," I said. I bit my tongue. "I do love you...but not the way you mean."

Seeing the look that came to his face, I shook my head, more in a feeble attempt to clear it. Averting my eyes, I wiped my cheek, feeling my jaw harden as I realized I'd hurt him now, too. Nothing like spreading the pain around, when I hadn't even faced my own yet.

Disentangling my arm from his fingers, I took a step back from where he stood, my hands shaking. I couldn't look at him at all.

"'Bye, 'Dor," I said. "I'm sorry. I really am."

I walked away from him, faster than I should have. Faster than he deserved.

That time, he didn't try to follow me.

He wasn't there when the truck took off for Amritsar, either.

Jon and Dorje drove me, all three of us sitting in the front seat of a rust bucket monster that seemed to claw its way down the roads as much as ride over them. I had to climb up on one of the large, all-terrain tires just to get into the cab.

We didn't talk a whole lot on the way down, but I was shocked to see Dorje crying a few times. I figured it had to do with the Bridge thing, as much as me personally. Or maybe he just anticipated having to deal with Jon being upset once I'd gone. Seeing Jon's stony expression, even where he sat next to me, holding my hand, I didn't want to ask.

I should have felt better on the plane, being away from all that.

I didn't, even though I flew first class, which was enough of a novelty that I couldn't help but play with all of the gadgets in my individual cubicle, ordering every manner of drink and food item I could think of on the way to Beijing. I didn't end up eating most of it though, or drinking more than a few swallows.

I had to wonder about my disguise, too, when I saw the limousine waiting for me on the curb. The seer standing there looked directly at me, opening the door as soon as I left the sliding glass doors to the international terminal. In the same pause, I felt more infiltrators behind me, and realized they'd flanked me all the way from the door of the airplane. I wasn't sure if their presence was meant to be reassuring...or a veiled threat.

None of them talked to me, other than to acknowledge the forms. I climbed into the back, only pausing to return the countersign for the hand signal the driver gave me.

Honestly, all I could think on the drive from the airport to the Forbidden City, was that I wanted this part over with. I didn't think about the rebels really...or even Cass.

I just wanted to finish this thing, this last job as the Bridge.

I figured once I knew what Voi Pai wanted from me, I could just give it to her and be done with it. My guess was, she wanted to bargain with me personally. She just wanted to do it on her terms, holding all the cards, and at the biggest possible hassle to all concerned.

Mostly, she just wanted me to jump when she said jump.

So I'd dance for her. I figured I really didn't have much to lose, giving her that little power rush she seemed to crave. I didn't need any authority over her, or the Lao Hu, especially not now. I didn't even want it.

Really, all excuses of uselessness and death threats aside, all I really wanted to do was go back to being nobody. I wanted to disappear, to be swallowed by the faceless hum of humanity until none of these people even remembered I existed.

Especially Revik.

Revik stared down at the folded square of paper.

He didn't pick it up. He didn't make a move towards the section of floor where the human dropped it, but continued to use flat naan bread to scoop up the curry he was eating. He looked up at Jon, shoving another portion into his mouth and chewing. He swallowed the mouthful before he spoke again.

"A letter?" he said. "Seriously? Where is she?"

"Just read it, Revik."

"What's in it?"

"How would I know that?" Jon said, not looking at him.

Revik gave him a tight-lipped smile, shaking his head.

"Well, I know you've been talking to little sis," he said a second later, resting his arms on his knees as he stared up at him narrowly. "...Or you wouldn't be so pissed off at me again." He watched the human, studying his expression. "What did she say, Jon?"

"She didn't say anything. Look. Just read it...or don't. I've got things to do."

But Revik shook his head, clicking.

Stepping on it carefully, he pushed the note away with his bare foot.

"No," he said, picking up the curry dish once more and resting it on his thighs. "Tell her no, Jon. Forget it. I'm not reading a goddamned note. Tell her I want to talk to her. I want her to come back here, Jon...now. We have things we need to discuss."

Jon stopped in his tracks from where he'd been heading for the door.

Turning, he gave Revik a disbelieving look.

"Jesus, man...you just don't get it."

"Don't get what?"

"She's gone, Revik. She left. She asked me to give you that after she left. So you get the note...or you get nothing."

Revik stared at him, feeling his jaw harden. For a moment he wondered if the human was yanking his chain. But his face didn't look like a lie. He looked upset.

Like she might really have left.

Fighting the anger that wanted to coil back into his light, he shook his head, clicking sharply. Still, he found himself replaying the human's words. The longer he did, the more the anger worsened, shifting and combining with something denser, a kind of confused disbelief. He felt the food begin to turn in his stomach.

"When is she coming back?" he said.

Jon let out an incredulous laugh. Shaking his head, he turned away without answering, heading for the door again with rapid strides.

"Jon!" Revik said. "Wait a minute!"

But the human didn't turn.

Dorje waited for him by the heavy green door, and held it open for him as Jon exited through to the corridor beyond. Dorje didn't look at him, either, not directly anyway, but Revik saw the anger on the smaller seer's face.

Frowning as it occurred to him that Jon had literally only come inside to give him the note, Revik looked down at the folded squares of paper, still sitting by his foot.

After a longer pause, he stepped on it again, pulling it closer with his toes.

Holding the metal dish, he used the bread to scoop up another mouthful of curry. He ate for another handful of minutes, but his eyes never left the square of paper.

She couldn't be gone long. She couldn't be.

Even so, he remembered the human's laugh. Taking another bite of coconut curry and spices, he chewed on the chicken without tasting it.

Finally, he put down the metal plate, wiping his hands on the rag they'd given him. Reaching down, he picked up the note. He stared at it without opening it for another couple of minutes before he felt his jaw harden again.

Opening it and flattening the paper against his thigh, he began to read.

Revik, it said.

There was no other greeting. Staring at where she'd written his name, he almost felt her hesitation. Swallowing, he let his eyes return to the top.

Revik,
I know a note isn't the best way to do this. There didn't feel like any ideal way to do this, though, honestly, and I felt like I should tell you a few things before I left...

He felt his jaw harden, but read on.

Firstly, in regards to your finances. You had given me access to a number of your accounts...I didn't want you to worry about me doing anything with those without your consent, so I took the liberty of pulling my name off all of them. They let me do so at all of the banks except... His eyes skipped ahead, skimming lines. *...where they need your signature, or some key code confirmation, I guess. They said you would understand. I sent them everything they needed on my end. So you just need to talk to Jon...or maybe Dorje. He was going to set up a terminal to let you reach them directly. For obvious reasons, I couldn't do anything with your will, and I can't yet return the property Voi Pai stole from you, but I'm going to try to get at least some of it back if I can...*

Revik felt his jaw harden more. Skimming through more details around the accounts, his eyes shifted to the next paragraph.

...I also spoke to Vash, and Tarsi. They've agreed to help you with whatever else you might need in the way of the Barrier sessions we'd done, or any light work more generally. I know this isn't exactly freedom, to push this on you, but I got them to agree to release you once you'd gotten to a point with all this where you could handle yourself on your own. Meaning, without needing any assistance from either the Seven or the Dreng. They agreed that any work you wanted to do beyond that, you could handle on your own...but Vash said he'd make himself available to you for as long as you wanted.

I asked them not to draw this out, and they promised they wouldn't. I didn't want you being forced into something with monks in caves again, either, but Vash didn't seem to think that would help you much at this point anyway. I asked them to unchain you, too, but Balidor wants to wait until Vash and Tarsi give the okay...

"Where the fuck are you?" he growled under his breath.

...As far as your people are concerned, I'm going to do what I can. I can't promise anything, but I have some hope that Voi Pai might trade with me. The request we got from her most recently seemed to imply that if I came in person, she might grant me what I want, or at least discuss real terms. So I'm going to Beijing first. I'll see if I can find out what happened to Wreg while I'm there, and send word back with Cass and Baguen...

He flipped to the back of the letter, scanned a few more lines, then returned to where he'd left off on the front. His mouth tightened until he realized he was biting the inside of his cheek, hard enough to taste blood.

"Where are you Allie?" he muttered.

...If you get uncomfortable anytime in the next few weeks, tell Jon. I asked them to work on a collar that would make you difficult to locate, for security reasons for the Adhipan and the others...but that shouldn't cut you off from the Barrier totally. Vash also agreed to try and help you, in terms of anything you want to do to try and address the worst effects of the bond. Anything you figure out on your own, I'd appreciate it if you could share with them, as I will likely be in contact with them periodically for a few months at least...

He stared at the words, re-reading the last line a few times. Biting his cheek again, he forced his eyes to continue on down the page.

...I know I probably don't need to ask you this, as it's kind of a redundant request at this point, but I'd appreciate it if you didn't come looking for me, Revik. For any reason. You'll probably agree that we've both said enough in terms of apologies and explanations and accusations and so forth between us, that we really don't need to go over it all again. I am genuinely sorry for any pain I've caused you...not just in these last few weeks, but since we met. I know I'm at least partly responsible for what happened to you over these last two years, and I don't just mean drugging you on that plane...I mean all of it.

He stared at the words. Pain started somewhere in his light, seemingly in his chest, but he forced it back.

As he did, the anger returned, sending a pulse of heat through his light.

...That being said, I'm especially sorry for deceiving you while I was staying with you those months in the mountains. It's really difficult for me to sort out how I feel about some of that now, in terms of my motives and how I acted...as well as where things happened between us that felt more genuine. I realize now that I was living a fantasy there too, in a way. I knew you had that idea of us pounded into you by Menlim...and that it left you with a pretty mythologized idea of who we were to one another. I knew it wasn't realistic, in terms of who I really am. I'm not angry about that, Revik...I'm really not. I guess I've known for awhile that things might not work out for us, once that myth held less power over you.

I have no idea if you understand or even care at this point why I thought it needed to be done...taking you out of there...but I want you to know that I never intended to impede your free will permanently in that regard. I wanted to give you the chance to view the Dreng and Salinse in a more objective light...without the strain of needing them because of what Menlim did to you when you were a kid. What you choose to do with that information is completely up to you. I have no intention of going after you again, or sending anyone to stop you if you decide to pick up where you left off with Salinse or whoever else. It's not sentimentality on my part...or guilt. The thing is, I know you can do a lot of good in that role, Revik. It was never the what so much as the how...although maybe I didn't fully understand that myself until the end. I've never questioned your motives though, Revik...I really didn't. I knew what you were fighting for. I'm just not sure the Dreng will actually help you attain the ends you want. I know you understand this, better than I ever will, but I'm realizing that sometimes it's better to fight and lose, than it is to win for the wrong side. But that's something I've always respected about you, that you fight for things, even if I don't always agree with how you do it, or for whom.

There's a part of me that hoped we would come out of this on the same side again, that we'd see the important things the same, or close enough to work together. The truth is, I liked working with you, Revik. You're a great leader, and a compassionate one. Despite what I said before, I know that wasn't all the Dreng...it's who you are. You inspire people. You understand them, too.

You don't know how tempting it was to just stay there...to just forget everything else and be your wife there forever. But it would have been the worst thing I could have done to you, to join you in that lie. It would have meant compromising on our marriage, on who you really are. The sex was fantastic, Revik...it always was with *you. But even you might see some day that it was a little empty when we were with the Dreng, compared to how it was when it was just us. I think you felt it, too. If you hadn't, I don't know if you would have tried so hard to tie me to you in other ways.*

But I'm also realizing more and more, even without the Dreng, I'm just not a part of your world. Everything I've witnessed about seers' day-to-day lives, I've done as an outsider, as a newcomer in whatever way...maybe even a tourist. I'll never know what it was like, growing up the way you did. I think maybe the gap there, between us, is just too big to make a marriage work. I think it's also too big for me to make a very effective leader of our people. I'm tired of pretending, too, Revik...about a lot of things.

His jaw tightened as he re-read the last line. He found himself staring at it for a few seconds more before his eyes slid down the page.

...As much as I'd hoped we might come out of this intact, I really did always know that this was just as likely. I certainly knew nothing would ever be the same with us again, no matter whether you came to forgive me for what I did, or understand it, or not. So believe me when I tell you, I don't blame you for anything. I'm not bitter things turned out this way. I also don't feel as though either of us didn't try. But I'd be lying if I said it didn't hurt. It does hurt. It hurts a lot. I never cared that you were the Sword. I didn't grow up in the mythology, so I honestly don't give a damn about any of that. But I lost a husband in this...and I love you, Revik, more than I can tell you. I loved you before I knew you were Syrimne and I loved you after, even when I was trying to reach you through the Dreng and whatever else. I still love you, despite everything we've done to one another...so much so I couldn't make myself give you this note in person. I know it's cowardice, but I couldn't handle seeing you again, knowing it was goodbye.

He felt his jaw harden again, even as he stopped. His fingers tightened on the page, but he continued to read.

...Tell Wreg I'm sorry, too. About Nikka, and about shooting him, and everything else.

I don't know how to close this, other than to say, I really do hope your life turns out the way you want. You deserve something real with someone...something that isn't just about sex or mythology or whatever else. You deserve to be happy after everything you've been through. I know you think I judge you for all of that, too, but I really don't. You may not believe this, but if anything, it makes me respect you more. Through all of it, no matter how bad things got, it seemed to me that you at least tried to do what was right...or at least what was less wrong.

And despite what I've said above, if you ever really do need me for something, I'm here, Revik. That goes for your people, too.

...Allie.

He stared at the signature.

For a long moment, he couldn't think at all.

Then he forced his eyes to move, then his fingers. He flipped back to the first page, reading the whole thing again, this time poring over even the details in the logistics he'd skimmed before. He read every word, twice, then he leaned his head against the wall.

For a long moment, he only sat there, staring at the overhead light.

Then he turned his head.

Focusing on the wall, he spoke loud, nearly shouting into the microphone.

"I want to talk to Vash!" he said.

When no one answered, he pounded his hand on the floor, raising his voice.

"Do you hear me, Jon? Dorje? Whoever the fuck is out there...get me Vash, now!"

Eighteen
Payment

"Hold up your arms, Esteemed Bridge," the seer said politely, gesturing towards my body.

Sighing a little, I did as he said, opening my jacket and turning around slowly. He felt me over for weapons, not invasively, but unnecessarily. I knew their organics would have picked that up already, even if I'd whittled a gun out of wood.

I'd decided before arriving that I'd go along with whatever hoops Voi Pai threw up for me to jump through. I knew she intended to see me eventually, and also that it would probably go a lot faster if I just refused to react, or get impatient.

At least three hours had passed since I'd first entered through Tian'anmen Gate.

"This way, Esteemed Bridge," the seer murmured, keeping his eyes below mine.

I followed him, only sparing a glance upwards at the high walls of Meridian as we approached one of the arched entrances.

Snow covered the fields outside the gate, powdering the branches and twigs of the wet-limbed trees. Lanterns hung from poles on chains along the long path between the trees leading to the u-shaped walls of Meridian itself. It was cold, but they had given me a furred cloak, and now more torches and lanterns followed our procession inside. As we passed through, and the five bridges crossing the canals grew visible, I felt a pang of...something...when I saw how bare the city was, compared to how it had been in the spring. Some part of me wanted to read more into that, somehow. Or maybe it was the lanterns swinging from the hands of robed seers, sparking something else in me, some flicker of memory, even if it wasn't mine.

"I sent word ahead," I said softly to my seer guide in Prexci. "Is she amenable to seeing me on this night? Or would we wait for morning now?"

The seer looked up at me. He walked beside me in full ceremonial robes, but in a version that seemed to be much thicker in layers and fabrics. His eyes shone at me in the lamplight, a pale blue the color of glacial ice.

"Mistress Voi Pai would very much like to see you now, Esteemed Bridge," he said cordially. "She apologizes profusely for the delay...a military matter arose unexpectedly, and she was forced to secure the grounds prior to accepting your audience." He gestured respectfully to me in the pause, still bent at that odd angle as he walked, to keep his eyes below mine. "...The security measures invoked upon your entrance are a part of that protocol, Esteemed One. It seemed too much of a coincidence, with your arrival...we did not wish to take chances."

I gave him a slightly sharper look, one that was more appraising.

It took me another moment to realize I looked at him that way because it felt like he was telling the truth. Of course, that only really meant that *he* believed it.

"Thank you for your explanation, brother," I murmured. "I confess, I worried my person may have fallen out of favor with your most honorable mistress..."

He smiled. Again, the smile appeared genuine. "Not at all, Holy One."

I winced a little, but managed to keep the smile on my face, bowing to his words and giving the countersign with my hand. Some of my honorifics I found easier to stomach that others. He'd just voiced probably my least favorite of the bunch.

"You have been here before," he said, a moment later.

I nodded, then, realizing he might not understand the human gesture, given where he lived, I gestured yes in seer. "I have had this honor before, yes," I said.

"You were collared then," he said.

I turned my head, but I only saw puzzlement in his eyes, a kind of genuine curiosity. I realized I liked this seer with the blue eyes. I couldn't have said why, exactly.

"I was," I said. "It is a complicated story, brother."

"I assumed it must be so."

"What is your name, if I may ask?" I said, meeting his gaze again. "Have we met before, brother?"

He gestured in negative, smiling. "No, Esteemed One, but everyone who lives in the City was aware of your visit. We watched you walk the grounds. Every day you walked...for a very long time. Sometimes into the night, you walked, too."

He paused, smiling wider.

"...And my name is Ulai, Esteemed One."

I smiled back at him, acknowledging his words with a wave of my hand. "Please call me Alyson...or Allie."

"Yes, Est..." He laughed, correcting himself. "Allie. And thank you for that honor."

"And you are remembering right, brother Ulai," I said, glancing around us as we entered the tree-filled lane along the first of the winding canals. The trees looked rather huddled and afraid without leaves and blossoms, and with the dark black sky above.

"I did walk," I said. "...Every chance I could while I was here. I had spent much time indoors prior to that, mostly in caves, in fact, and had no intention of wasting my time in the City by neglecting to witness every one of its charms."

"And it was spring...err...Allie."

"Yes. It was spring." I sighed, smiling at him. "It is a kind of paradise here, in the spring, in my mind. All of the trees were blooming. All of the birds were nesting. I remember the tiger cubs in the back pens with particular fondness..."

He was taxing my limited knowledge of formal Prexci, but he didn't seem to notice, or mind. I was trying to decide what else to say, when he spoke up again.

"And the screens by the queen's entrance to the Royal Gardens?" he said. "Do you remember those, Esteemed...Alyson?"

I thought for a moment. "The dragons? Green and blue, with peacocks... and an image of the intermediaries of Wisdom and Folly?"

His smile turned almost childishly pleased. "Yes," he said. "Exactly right, Esteemed One!" At my smile, he added, "...Allie. Those are mine, if you'll permit me to boast."

"You made those?" I didn't keep the wonder from my voice. "It is very, very beautiful work, brother. I am deeply impressed..."

He smiled wider at that, so that it reached his eyes.

I found myself remembering that from the last time, how proud the seers here were of their City inside a city. That pride had been justified, from what I'd been able to tell. From the numerous works of art to the cleanly ordered beauty of the daily rituals along the lit pathways and sun-filled gardens, the City felt more like a lost, ancient world than even an oasis from outer Beijing. A silence hung over it that spoke of a profound concentration and stillness, and yet I remember it feeling very happy, too. Children ran through the inner markets and played. When they weren't working, adult seers walked and laughed and threw parties in the different gardens, rode horses or visited one of the many artisan shops or indoor theaters. The seers seemed at ease in the security and safety of the high walls, and the humans seemed content to live and work alongside them, even in the role of quasi-servants.

The abuse, beatings, collars, slavery and degradation of seers at the hands of humans that I witnessed in the States...and even in India, despite its large seer population...didn't seem to exist in the City at all.

Even now, in the ice and snow, I could feel that peculiarly subtle and complex construct that hung over the Lao Hu enclave.

In addition to its security features, which were likely unparalleled outside of the Pamir, the construct also maintained the inner purity of the light of the Inner City. It created a true sanctuary from the confusion of lights just outside the City gates, and maintained a "frozen in time" flavor that instantly caused something in my aleimi to relax. It also evoked an alien nostalgia for some particular time period or flavor of history that I couldn't quite name, but that didn't seem wholly Chinese, either. Whatever it was, it always hovered just outside of my reach; I couldn't pin down anything specific to me, much less remember.

In addition to the physical buildings of the City, the construct housed probably a few thousand Barrier rooms and spaces that could be accessed if one had the proper permissions. I'd been allowed to roam through some of these, including reconstructions of the old human City, before the time of the seers...all the way back to when the humans lived as nomads in this part of the world. Some of the constructs were imaginary places, things dreamed up by their seer creators. Some were views into possible futures and distant pasts, including one where one could sit and watch dinosaurs, even picnic among them as the sun set...and several that reconstructed pieces of history in the time of the greatest of the high seer civilizations, both of the First Race and the Second Race.

Remembering all of this now, I couldn't help thinking that the City existed as the last, true refuge for seers. The Pamir was mostly gone, an echo of what it once had been.

Although officially its guardians and protectors, there was no question that the seers had claimed the City as their own. The Lao Hu paid for that privilege by providing the Chinese human government with the largest, most highly-trained, disciplined and loyal group of infiltrators that existed anywhere else in the world. Even at the peak of the Seven, the Lao Hu's numbers had been greater than those the Council commanded. Now, with the near decimation of the Seven's Guard during the attack on Seertown, as well as the loss of many in the Adhipan through that same fight and its aftermath, the disparity was even greater.

Revik had been the only one who came close to challenging the strength of the Lao Hu, and compared to the Chinese infiltrators, his camp had consisted largely of half-trained, undisciplined misfits looking for a fight. Of course, that fighting force had been in its infancy; even in the time that I spent with them, I saw that beginning to change.

Revik had been grooming and training them as soldiers...and he had been looking to grow their numbers, too, both through freeing ex-infiltrators from the slave camps and human prisons, and by recruiting from among the ranks of free seers.

Thinking about this, it struck me again how naive I'd been.

I should have realized that Voi Pai would view Revik and his armies as a threat. Maybe she was even right, to see the danger there, in terms of the direction things were going. It was likely why she courted Balidor, as well; she'd been looking for a closer relationship with the Adhipan, the only group besides the Lao Hu really qualified to train the growing rabble of free seers.

In any case, I should have realized she'd take the opportunity to wipe her rivals out...before they were "grown up" enough to be a real threat.

Revik was right. I had been stupid. Or at the very least, incredibly naive.

My companion pulled me once more from my thoughts.

"Is the Esteemed Bridge hungry?" Ulai asked politely.

I glanced at him. I considered a polite lie, then smiled instead. "Starving, actually," I said, using the more common version of Prexci. "Is there any chance you have a pizza waiting for me in there, brother?"

He laughed at this, delighted by my informality. "The food on the human planes..."

"Is cardboard and ash, yes, brother...agreed. But due to my low-brow upbringing, I can't help but crave their cardboard now and again. Especially when I'm truly hungry."

He laughed again.

"We can find you much more agreeable food, Esteemed One. I have our chefs working on something now I hope you will like...although perhaps it will not be quite what you have imagined with your American-style pizza..."

I found myself remembering my favorite pizza joint in San Francisco, and smiled. I didn't realize he'd felt the memory until he gestured in appreciation.

"That helps, Esteemed One..." He smiled again in faint embarrassment. "...Allie. It helps a great deal in fact. Our cook expresses his appreciation for the impression..."

I had to chuckle at this, clasping my hands behind my back as I walked. "I will be very interested to see what they come up with, brother..."

"As will I," he affirmed sincerely.

"You will have to taste it with me," I teased him. "Ensure it passes muster."

His eyes grew serious. "I will taste it anyway, Esteemed Bridge. To ensure it is safe to eat before risking your person." His eyes grew troubled, and far-seeing. "...Particularly in these dangerous times, where you are being unfairly marked by militants and fanatics, Esteemed One."

I smiled wanly at this. "...Allie," I reminded him.

"Allie. Yes, of course, Esteemed One."

I raised an eyebrow at this, and both of us laughed.

I realized I missed this, just talking to other seers. Seers who didn't yell at me for being stupid, or try to force me to make decisions that meant other people's lives. I'd forgotten that all of the seers in the world didn't view me as the devil...even if most of those in the West currently did. It occurred to me in the same breath that I'd forgotten, while holed up in that mountain, just how many of those others really did want to kill me. It was possible, of course, that some here might as well.

"You are safe here, Esteemed sister Allie," Ulai said, seeming to find a compromise with my name and title that he felt comfortable with.

He said it with a vehemence I found comforting.

"Thank you, brother," I replied, tipping my hand respectfully. "That is a reassurance I very much appreciate at the moment."

We were passing the third set of gates inside the outer wall of Meridian.

I had lost my previous land markers to some extent, but I was fairly certain we had passed inside the segment that had belonged to the private quarters of the Imperial family, back in the days when the City was occupied solely by humans. I recognized some of the building fronts, and although the gardens were bare of most plants, the rock formations I remembered remained, along with several pieces of art that withstood the weather well enough to remain outdoors. One of these, a stone sculpture of a turtle with the world under one foot, I remembered.

Sighing a little, I pulled the coat more tightly around my chest. I fought to keep my mind clear, but something about being here brought the previous year more sharply into relief. Remembering how I'd felt when I first saw Revik in that courtyard, waiting for me under the trees, I had to fight back a low surge of pain.

For a moment then...for just the barest moment...he'd looked like Revik to me again. The look in his eyes, the way he'd studied my face. The way his light felt.

It came back, now and then, while we stayed in those caves with Salinse. Glimpses of him, through the fog of the Dreng. Just enough to confuse me, to make me want to reach him all the more. I think I could have gotten him out earlier. I think a part of me waited to see if he would want to go with me, without my even having to ask. But that day never came, and the longer we stayed with his people, the more I realized that was just a fantasy, too.

Now, of course, I understood. He'd known he couldn't survive without them. Not intact anyway. He might not have known that consciously, but on some level he knew...well enough to return there after they reunited him with that part of him that was Syrimne. Well enough to stay, even after he could probably tell I wanted us both to go.

Pushing those memories further from my light, I glanced again at Ulai. I was going to try and engage him in conversation again...anything to get my mind off of Revik and how I'd left him...when he smiled at me, gesturing towards a building to our left.

I hadn't noticed at first, since a wall separated us from its windows, but now that we reached an opening in the white stone, I could see that the building he indicated was awash in lights.

"Our mistress waits for you there, Esteemed sister," Ulai said.

I nodded, slowing my steps without realizing I did it. I noticed only because Ulai paced me, and I saw him correct. Taking a breath, I walked the stone path directly towards a sliding door that stood open. It hadn't been open a moment before, so I had to assume they'd felt us approach. I simply hadn't noticed them scanning me...which wasn't all that unusual here, given the complexity of the construct. I often couldn't feel other seers in it, or even humans.

Usually they could feel me, though, like Ulai had, so I had to assume it had to do with varying levels of access granted to those living inside.

"Exactly, right, Esteemed Allie," Ulai said, smiling.

I followed his hand as he indicated up the stairs and into the entryway beyond. There stood a darkened throne I remembered vaguely, and a collection of sculptures of birds and fish and even a dragon. Tall trees stood behind and beside it as well, reaching almost to the high ceiling, where wooden tiles had been cut and hand-painted in bright gold and red, creating an illusion of depth, almost like pyramids inverted inside each piece of wood. Tapestries fell down the far and side walls, along with tiered kites and lanterns. The inside seemed more richly decorated than I remembered...perhaps from much of the art having been moved indoors.

"This way, Esteemed Bridge," Ulai said, again indicating the direction I should walk, which was out of the candlelit entrance and towards the more brightly lit chambers beyond.

We walked through a circular opening cut into dark wood, the outer edges carved in great detail to appear like two trees grown together at their roots and highest branches. I blinked into the light as we entered the high-ceilinged room beyond, then scanned it in reflex. When my light told me little, other than to show me more holes and crevices in the construct itself, I used my physical eyes. At the first face my eyes focused on directly, I startled. I nearly jumped back in fact, bumping Ulai behind me.

The face was Wreg's.

He stared at me with equal surprise.

Then his expression hardened into a mask. That mask projected so much hatred I looked away before I'd fully taken it in. Even so, seeing him was a shock, and not only because of how I'd left him on the plane. After all that time in the Barrier with Revik, I felt like I knew him in a way I never had before. Some of that knowing made me like him more, some less, but the level of intimacy in my own light was disconcerting.

My eyes found Voi Pai a second later. She sat on a chair that also resembled a throne, but a significantly less ornate one than the remnants of the old human audience chambers of the outer hall. Voi Pai's seat stood at least five feet above the lower segments of the room. Made of padded silk cushions and hand sewn round pillows, it stretched out almost to the length of a couch and looked like a Chinese version of a love seat.

I studied her face long enough to remember its details. Her porcelain skin looked the same, her high cheekbones. Those strange, yellow eyes with the vertical, cat-like pupils focused on my face as well, as if she were doing a similar inventory. Her sleek, black hair stood in a traditional, high bun, adorned with jeweled combs. Two long, curved pieces of hair like bangs framed her oval face, accenting her cheekbones while seeming to point to her blood-red mouth.

I glanced around the rest of the room, and realized it was almost full.

I flinched again when I saw Garensche and Holo, standing not far from me, wearing the servant caste clothing of the City. Frowning when I saw the two of them standing in a slight alcove, Garensche nearly crouched due to his enormous height next to what looked like a small cooking area, I glanced away, taking in the rest of the room if only to keep the reaction off my face. Most of the seers lining the walls were Lao Hu...infiltrators, from the black sashes they wore. I also saw Cass and Baguen sitting at a bench to the left of Voi Pai's elevated chair. Next to them stood Jax and Mila, two more infiltrators who had worked for Revik.

Along with Wreg, five other seers knelt at the edge of the inner floor. I noticed only then that they were bound, and collared. Garensche, Holo, Jax and Mila wore collars as well.

Feeling my jaw harden, I looked back at Voi Pai.

"I am here," I said, throwing out every word of my carefully-rehearsed formal greeting. "You wished to speak to me in person?"

She smiled faintly, raising one penciled eyebrow. Even so, I heard the chiding in her softly clicking tongue.

"Is that how we shall greet one another, Esteemed Bridge?" she said softly. "I admit, sister, your words wound me..."

"As clearly this display is meant to do for me," I said.

Fighting back my anger, I gestured around at the seers on the floor, not looking at Wreg as I let my hand shift from his team to Garensche and Holo in the back room, finishing on Jax and Mila where they stood next to Cass and Baguen.

"What is the point of this, otherwise? Treating our brothers and sisters in this manner?"

"I treat then as what they are."

"Slaves to the Lao Hu?"

"Those whose lives belong to our people...yes."

I folded my arms, forcing my light to retract, to calm down. She'd done this on purpose, to rattle me, and it had worked. I was too exhausted to play it cool, and I'd just spent three hours getting the runaround besides.

Even so, I could see that my reaction pleased her...hell, I could almost feel it, despite the stranglehold of the construct. Somehow, I couldn't quite stop myself from reacting anyway. Finally, I glanced at Ulai, who remained standing beside me. I could see from his face that the tone of our exchange distressed him. I also realized for the first time how tall he was. He had maybe an inch on Revik even.

Sighing in a clicking kind of purr, I looked back at Voi Pai, bowing as graciously as I could.

"I apologize, most respected Voi Pai, leader of the Lao Hu," I said, holding my hand up in the polite manner. "Perhaps we could start again. I was told you wished to speak to me?"

The female seer smiled, but it did not reach her eyes.

"Yes, Esteemed Bridge."

"Would it be possible for us to continue this conversation in private?" I said, once more aware of Wreg's eyes on me. I gestured around vaguely. "This hardly seems a conducive environment for a civil negotiation."

"I disagree, Esteemed Bridge," Voi Pai returned smoothly. She smiled at me when I gave her a hard look. "I prefer to negotiate openly...where the parties retaining an interest are able to hear the discussion of their own worth..."

"Is this what you wished to say to me?" I said, biting my lip once more.

"No, Esteemed Bridge...of course not."

"Then perhaps," I said evenly. "We could begin there. Since you wish this to be publicly aired, please do share with me whatever words could not be communicated through my emissaries. Then, I also," I added. "...Would like to speak to you. About the request I sent, for which I have still heard no reply, as to terms you would find acceptable...despite the long stay of my two friends."

Briefly, I considered raising the issue of the human-killing disease, as well...which obviously bothered her enough that I'd read a real reaction in the words of that one message we received.

But I dismissed it from my mind a second later.

I'd let her bring that up, since it was clearly some kind of sticking point with her. And anyway, it wasn't why I was there.

Still watching me narrowly, Voi Pai leaned back in her chair, bowing her head politely, as if my request had been spoken with no anger at all. I felt my patience ebbing as she leaned over a small table, pouring herself a cup of tea from a dark clay tea pot etched with some kind of subtle design and fitted with a bamboo handle. Setting the pot down on the same brightly lacquered tray where she'd found it, she leaned back on her couch, pausing to sniff her cup before taking a gentle series of sips. I bit my lip, but didn't move.

"I wished only to apologize, first," the Lao Hu leader said. Smiling at me, she made her voice cajoling. "I wished things to be cordial between the two of us once more, Esteemed Intermediary...so much so that I risked your displeasure at my lack of reply."

"A rather flawed approach," I said sourly.

"Perhaps. And yet, my regrets are very real."

"Of that I have little doubt. Are you ready to talk business, respected Voi Pai?"

"I have not yet apologized, beloved intermediary."

I waved away her words, using every effort to keep the gesture polite, even as I bit my lip to keep the irritation off my face.

"No apologies are necessary, I assure you," I said. "An answer to my request, however, is, if you would like things to remain friendly between us."

She leaned back once more on her long chair and lit a hiri as I watched, one of the black-skinned, expensive ones I remembered her smoking when I stayed here before. I didn't take my eyes off her as she fitted the hiri's end into a filter made of what looked like real ivory.

"Perhaps you could remind me of the exact nature of your request?" she said, exhaling a plume of dark smoke. "...The details of this note have escaped me, I admit," she added, smiling. "...And my attention on this day has been taken up almost entirely by the difficulties we experienced, warding off yet another attack by these rebels with whom you are suddenly so enamored... whom you continually assure me are not a threat to the Lao Hu..."

Hesitating at this, I glanced at Wreg, almost before I could stop myself.

Letting my gaze trail down his body, I realized only then that he was wearing body armor, and that two holsters around his person were empty. His long hair was tied back, and he wore boots on his feet with spikes at the edges for climbing. The seers with him were all dressed similarly, all without the external armor coats I remembered, but clearly disarmed recently and dressed for a military operation. I wondered if they had actually tried to climb one of the newer walls...the higher ones erected sometime after World War II.

Still avoiding Wreg's eyes, I looked back at Voi Pai.

"You would call them dangerous," I said, letting a faint derision touch my voice. "...For doing what any of us would do in their position? Trying to free their brothers and sisters from this illegal 'ownership' you claim?"

I glanced at Cass, who smiled at me faintly. She looked angry too, however. So did Baguen, which made me like him a lot more for some reason.

Voi Pai's voice pulled my eyes off the two of them as well.

"There is nothing illegal about it," she said smoothly. Her voice had changed however, I heard an open warning in it that time, what sounded like real anger. "I would bid you caution, Esteemed Bridge...we honor you, but you are still a guest in my home..."

"A guest who has been repeatedly insulted, lied to and dishonored, well before I arrived in your home," I said shortly. I gestured towards Cass and Baguen, my face hard. "...What crime have I committed, that you see fit to imprison my friends? Very dear friends of mine, in fact, who came here only at my request, for honest parlay...?"

"I told you, Esteemed Bridge," Voi Pai warned. "I wished only to speak to you in person – "

"So you say," I cut in. "But I would have responded much more favorably to this request had it come without the illegal detention of my people. You could have requested the same, and returned my friends to me...along with an answer to my request that you name whatever price the respected Voi Pai would like for the purchase of her 'legitimately owned' seers..."

I felt Wreg turn, staring at me. I did my best to ignore it.

Voi Pai only smiled at my words, exhaling a perfect ring of smoke.

"I have heard no price quoted," she said, draping an arm over the back of the couch.

"I quoted one before," I returned, a little more sharply than I intended. "Instead of refusing this price, and bargaining one that was acceptable to us both...you simply pretended to agree and then extracted your own price, one that is clearly not acceptable to me..." I felt my jaw harden slightly. "How is that *friendly*, Voi Pai?"

She shrugged, gesturing vaguely with the hand that held the hiri.

"I was not aware the rebels were so precious to you. You seemed less interested in their welfare before..."

"Bullshit," I said, before I could stop myself. "I was crystal clear about the stipulations of this little 'partnership.' I said no fucking hostages, Voi Pai...apart from Salinse..."

"I could not find Salinse."

"So you take every other goddamned seer in the compound?"

As I bit back my fury, I heard the silence in the room.

I felt Wreg's eyes on me once more, along with Garensche's and Jax's. Really, every seer there was looking at me, but those were the ones whose eyes seemed to bore into me hardest. I avoided Cass' face as well, not sure if I was ready to know what she thought about all of this. I wasn't sure if I was ready to know if they'd been mistreating her here, either. I felt Baguen hovering over her protectively, enough that I knew they'd likely been separated before this.

Right then, that was more than enough to anger me.

Voi Pai smiled again, letting her eyes drift over the length of my body. Realizing she was enjoying my anger, that she was enjoying the conversation in general, I looked away, clicking sharply under my breath. Once more, I spoke before I had my anger under control.

"I would have thought the respected Voi Pai would have more interesting amusements," I said, folding my arms tighter. "...Than inviting guests for the sole purpose of insulting them. I would have hoped you would not be so *bored* as to risk a war with me, simply for the purpose of entertaining yourself on my displeasure..."

Voi Pai smiled wider, inclining her head.

"I still have not heard an offer as to price..." she purred softly.

"I have put that ball in your court, respected Voi Pai," I replied, my voice equally level. "As you surely must know by now. Since you have a tendency to say 'yes' when you mean 'no,' I thought it more likely I'd get a real quote if you named it yourself." Biting my lip again, I gestured towards her a bit sharply.

"...Clearly you have something in mind. Name it."

Voi Pai's smile turned predatory.

"I would like the Sword," she said.

"Fucking bitch," Wreg snarled.

Before I could turn my head, he got cuffed across the head, hard, by the guard standing behind him. I glanced at him just long enough to see him recover, kneeling once more at the edge of the square carpet.

Seeing the mark forming on his face, I bit my tongue. I returned my eyes to Voi Pai, my voice cold.

"He's not for sale," I said. "That is non-negotiable."

"Then we have no deal, Esteemed Bridge."

"I find that hard to believe," I said. "That you would ask for what is so clearly unreasonable, expecting anything but a 'no' in response. Clearly, you want war with me."

"But you are wrong, Esteemed Bridge," she said, her eyes serious. "I do not wish war. I wish a fair price, in exchange for what I would be giving up."

"Why do you want him?" I said, blunt.

For a moment she only looked at me, her yellow eyes unmoving.

Then she smiled, taking another drag of the hiri before exhaling another perfect ring.

"Why do you think?" she said, smiling wider at whatever look must have come to my face. "...He is valuable to me. He can work off the debt of these other seers you wish to rid me of. Far faster than anything you can offer. And I do not like trading in gold."

"So you would not take market price for these seers?"

"I would not. And you could not afford it...Esteemed Bridge."

I felt my jaw harden again, as I tried to think through this.

There was something she wasn't saying. I could feel it, but I couldn't quite grasp what it meant.

She knew I wouldn't give her Revik.

She hadn't shown a flicker of surprise when I said no...and yet, I could tell the door wasn't closed on our negotiation, either. Her price of Revik wasn't as firm as she pretended, but if she wouldn't take money, I didn't know what she was angling for...other than to know without a doubt that she was angling for something.

"Why him, though?" I said again.

"He is an intermediary," she said, gesturing as if this were obvious.

I felt my jaw harden more. Suddenly, I knew exactly what she wanted... and why she'd insisted that I come here in person. Shaking my head, I gave a low laugh. Then I looked at her, meeting her gaze directly.

"I, too, am an intermediary," I said. "...most venerable Voi Pai."

She froze, her hand poised with the hiri not far from her mouth. I didn't know how much of it was pure bullshit theatrics, but the effect worked well enough. It also left time for every seer and human in the room to swallow what I'd said.

After that pause, a smile slid carefully over Voi Pai's red mouth. I knew I'd been right when I saw that covetousness I'd seen in her before, what seemed like a million years ago in that square in the spring sun. She stared at me like she wanted to pin me to the wall with her eyes, like some kind of exotic bug for her collection.

"He is not for sale," she purred softly. "...But you are, Esteemed Bridge?"

I felt my jaw harden, even as every eye in the room seemed to turn and bore into me once more. I avoided all of them, focusing only on the seer on the silk-cushioned love seat.

"Can we finish this discussion alone, Voi Pai?"

"No," she said, her eyes still on mine. "I wish an answer to my question, Esteemed Bridge."

I glanced at Cass, almost without my willing it. Seeing her staring at me, shaking her head vehemently, I looked away again. Feeling a kind of tiredness come over me, I remembered again what I'd said to Balidor, and to Vash...and what I'd written to Revik. Did it really matter what I did for the next however-many months? I had nowhere to go. Chances were, I'd stay alive with the Lao Hu. At least until Revik resurfaced and everyone stopped assuming I'd murdered him.

Looking back at the Lao Hu leader, I gestured in a conciliatory way.

"I am willing to discuss a term of...repayment," I said, deliberately avoiding Cass' eyes, as well as those of the other seers. "If that is agreeable to you. You must know that security is a concern for me of late...and that my effectiveness as a leader is hampered as a result. Your timing appears well calculated in that regard, at least..."

I saw that look of near greed rise more prominently to her eyes.

"As you say," she said softly. "I am open to negotiation on that point."

"Then tell me what terms you would be willing to accept," I said.

She paused for a moment, looking up at the ceiling, as though thinking. I felt every seer in the room hold their breath, watching her. I felt Cass looking at her, too. Voi Pai's eyes narrowed slightly as she stared upwards, just before she glanced at an older seer to her right, one who appeared to be an advisor of some kind based on his age and the different cut of his robe.

Whatever she thought at him, he raised his eyebrows slightly, then bowed in acquiescence, as though he approved of whatever she'd sent.

"Eighteen million," she said, looking back at me. "That's half a million for each infiltrator ranked above a six...plus a quarter million for those who are ranked less. That is fair market price." She gave me a conciliatory bow. "...It is also rounded in your favor."

"You would have me work off their market price?" I raised an eyebrow, glancing at Ulai. I saw that he had paled, and that he stood closer to me, hovering almost protectively. For a moment, I felt a pulse of warmth for him, strong enough that he seemed to feel it.

"It is a fair offer," Voi Pai said. "And it is final. I would want the same from the Sword. I ask only for what is due me...in terms of payment for his rescue..."

"What about the others?" I said. "Those in the work camps?"

She waved dismissively. "Make it an even twenty million. For all of them."

I felt my jaw harden once more.

"And you will of course include all of those seers captured tonight?"

"Then it is twenty-two million," Voi Pai said curtly. "That one alone," she added, pointing at Wreg. "He is worth half that. It is a fair price."

"And how do I know you will keep our bargain this time?" I said, gesturing around at the others without looking at them. "How can I be sure you won't simply kidnap them again, and auction them off at your whim...?"

Voi Pai clicked softly. "The Esteemed Bridge has a poor opinion of her servant..."

"...Because I do not kid myself for one moment that that's what you are," I retorted, my hands clenching. "I need assurances, Voi Pai. They must be real assurances. I need to know they are free...before I will let you own me."

"We can provide that," she said, her eyes hard on mine. "You must agree to be collared, for at least a portion of your time under my employ..."

I thought about this, then was forced to concede, realizing I couldn't expect otherwise with the telekinesis. I gestured as much, avoiding Cass's eyes again.

"Agreed."

"And work at whatever work I deem you fit for."

I conceded to this as well, albeit more reluctantly. "Agreed." I hesitated. "In return, I would ask for training while I am here..."

"Training?" Her eyebrow lifted again humorously.

"Full infiltration training. Whatever you provide to your normal recruits."

Her eyes measured mine, then she nodded. "Agreed."

"Will I be a formal member of the Lao Hu?"

"Through the duration of the contract, yes," she said. Her eyes narrowed further. "Which means you will be bonded to the group...that is non-negotiable, Esteemed Bridge."

I hesitated at this. Unfortunately I didn't know enough about what she was saying to know if it was unreasonable or not, or what the effects would be long-term. There was no one there I could ask, obviously. After another longish pause, I gestured a yes.

"Agreed."

"The terms will begin, including the collar, once I have provided you these assurances to your satisfaction?"

"They must be to my satisfaction," I warned her. "You will not own me, in any way, until I am sure they are all away..."

"Sister...!"

I jumped, turning my head.

It wasn't that someone had spoken so much as who.

Wreg stared at me, his eyes stricken, like his voice. His face held a kind of bewilderment, like he didn't know me, but there was grief there too. From the look on his face, it seemed he wanted to say more, but he didn't move as I returned his gaze, probably as much in surprise as anything else. Finally, I swallowed, turning back to Voi Pai. I pointed at Wreg without looking at him, my jaw hard once more.

"I would request a moment alone with brother Wreg," I said. "No guards, no construct...I need to speak to him privately." Glancing briefly at Ulai, I added, "If you need one of your representatives there, I will accept brother Ulai as a chaperone...but no one else."

Voi Pai gestured dismissively. Despite the ease of the gesture, her eyes on mine were harder, examining my face as though looking for some kind of trick.

"You may go," she said. "Use the gardens past the antechamber...and brother Ulai."

Taking my arm gently, Ulai led me out the way we'd come in.

Before I turned, I glimpsed Cass' face once more, almost by accident. In that one look, I saw that she'd gone sheet white, her eyes wide as she shook her head in another silent 'no' to me, if anything more adamantly than before. My eyes flickered up to see Jax and Mila giving me equally stunned looks, but theirs were closer to what Wreg's had been, like they couldn't believe what they'd just heard. I saw a guard prod Wreg to his feet then, and followed Ulai into the candlelit dimness of a room past the throne room we'd walked through before.

We passed another set of doors, and then we were outside, in a lantern-lit patch of snow filled with stone landscapes. The creek that used to run through here was dry, but the cherry trees still stood, their bases wrapped with padding against the cold.

Wreg joined us a moment later. The guard shoved him out the door, so that we all stood in the new snow. He stumbled a little as he came to stand near Ulai and me, then looked up, his eyes narrow as he stared into mine.

"What the fuck are you doing?" he hissed. "Is this some kind of joke?"

Ulai spoke up before I could answer, his voice openly worried.

"You should not speak to her in this way," he said to Wreg. He gave me a worried look though, with some measure of apology. "...But he is right, Esteemed sister," he added. "Voi Pai is not positing this as an idle offer...she will take ownership of you, and she will employ you however she deems it most profitable..."

Swallowing, Ulai looked down at me nervously, letting his gaze grow meaningful as it trailed down to my feet.

"...You must know there are possibilities with that," he added. "Things which you might not wish to have done to you." Clearing his throat, he looked away again, his skin darkening slightly. "...Indignities, Esteemed Bridge. Not befitting your stature..."

I looked up at Ulai, reading the meaning in his light blue eyes.

Nodding, I realized I *had* known that.

Clearly, Voi Pai wanted me to know it, just as she'd wanted me to offer myself instead of just telling me outright what she wanted. I still didn't see a whole lot of options. I didn't exactly have the clout or the manpower to declare war on the Lao Hu...even if I managed to pull some kind of army together with the refugees from those camps, it would take too long, and anyway, half of them wouldn't even be trained. It would be months if not years before I would have any leverage with her that way.

Even Revik would need at least a year to plan such an operation, if not more.

I knew Voi Pai likely had her own reasons for wanting me out of the picture. More than simply humiliating me and playing her own stupid power games, that is. Maybe she was even trying to lure Revik back here. Maybe she wanted her own paired set of telekinetic seers.

Or maybe she was just hedging her bets again, protecting the hegemony of the Lao Hu by making sure we never became a threat to her. In any case, I got the feeling she was more than a little disappointed that I hadn't killed Revik following his capture. She'd likely go out of her way to humiliate me, in the hopes it would bring Revik here faster.

But it wouldn't work. Not anymore.

Feeling something in my chest tighten, I looked at Wreg. As soon as I had, I wished I hadn't. The same understanding that Ulai voiced seemed to have reached him as he studied my face.

"You knew," he said, his voice an accusation. "You are whoring yourself... you are doing it on purpose." His voice grew angry. "Why?"

I shook my head, clicking sharply. "I don't have to answer to you, Wreg, even when you shout. And no, I *didn't* know. I came here to make a deal. This is the deal she will accept."

"You are a liar!"

"Am I?" I bit my lip, remembering Revik accusing me of the same. "I suppose you're right. Being the mastermind that I am, I planned all of this. I coerced Voi Pai into demanding this ridiculous price of me...right after she asked me to sell her my husband..." I swallowed, almost correcting myself on that last, then shrugged, giving Wreg a flat look. "You've got me, brother Wreg. The jig is up..."

"You laugh. This whole thing could be a charade..."

"And you would never know if it were," I retorted. At his angry look, I threw up my hands. "Gods, Wreg. Would you rather I sold Revik? Or do you think there is someone else she would accept in either of our places?"

He shook his head, clicking at me angrily.

When I didn't say anything else, he looked away. I watched him thinking about my words, his eyes narrowed as he kicked a booted foot at the snow. I felt emotion pulse off him, but I couldn't read any of it, apart from his anger at me.

"You came here to sell yourself," he said. "...to martyr yourself. It is an indignity, to do such a thing...even for you. You are still an intermediary..."

"What I do isn't really any of your business, Wreg."

"Did you kill the Sword then?" he said, his voice bitter. "Is that what this is about? Penance for your crimes?"

I gave a disbelieving laugh, shaking my head. "What *is* it with you two? He asked me the same about you. No, I didn't kill him...he's fine, Wreg."

"Where is he?"

"You know I can't tell you that," I said, impatient. "But I don't need to. He'll be free, soon enough, and I have no doubt you'll be the first one he contacts..."

"Free?" Wreg stared at me. "You will release him?"

"I have ordered him released, yes. He'll be out in a month. Possibly less...possibly more. There is some discretion there, but it won't be very long, I promise you..." Sighing a little at his skeptical look, I rubbed my face with one hand. "I'll let him explain what happened when he sees you. I was trying to help him. He will likely describe it differently...but I never meant him any harm, Wreg..."

"Just the rest of us," he growled.

"Clearly, yes...I wished you all enslaved. And tortured."

"Then you are simply a fool," he said angrily.

I didn't answer that. I just stood there, my arms folded.

After I took a breath, I looked at Ulai.

"Can we trust that she will let me honestly verify that they are gone?"

Ulai nodded, slowly, his eyes still flickering between me and Wreg. They rested on Wreg more warily, pausing for a beat before he looked back at me.

"Yes," he said. "She is sincere in her price. I think she will not risk war by refusing your conditions. She would have to kill too many otherwise...and she fears the Sword."

"He won't come for me," I told him bluntly.

Wreg gave a low laugh at this.

"Are you sure of that, Esteemed Bridge?" Ulai asked nervously.

"I'm sure. He won't come...not unless someone gives him a reason to." I bit the inside of my cheek. "So if that's her game, it won't work."

Ulai gave me a puzzled look. "Her...game, Esteemed Bridge?"

"Is this still about him? About bringing him here?"

Ulai's eyes grew more thoughtful. Realizing he was in the Barrier space, I didn't speak, and a few seconds later, his eyes clicked back into focus.

"No," he said. "I do not think so. Her attention seems to be solely on you, Esteemed Bridge. She has some concern that he may come, actually...it does not seem to be her desire. She seems to be hoping the contract will be fulfilled before he does, or that she can force you to tell him to stay away, if you are in her employ and bonded to her infiltrators..."

Feeling my jaw harden, I turned on the other seer.

He was staring at me now, too, a new understanding in his eyes.

"You can't tell him, Wreg," I said. "...Where I am."

There was a silence where he just looked at me. Then he let out a snort, right before the expression in his eyes turned disbelieving once more.

"I can tell him whatever I want...*Bridge*."

I took a step closer to him, feeling my jaw harden more.

"No, you can't," I said. "I'm afraid I'm going to have to insist that you give me your blood oath that you won't...or I'll go in there and tell her you're not part of the deal. In fact, I may throw Jax and Mila in, as well. Clearly you don't value your own life much, if you were dumb enough to try and climb these walls..."

He stared back at me, his eyes holding a faint surprise, right before they narrowed.

"You would not do that."

"Believe me, brother Wreg," I said. "I would. As far as I'm concerned, it's one less million I have to work off...maybe two, with Jax and Mila..."

His dark eyes remained on mine a beat longer.

Then, as if seeing something in my face, he nodded slowly.

"You mean it?" he said. "You do not want him to know?"

"I do mean it."

"A blood oath?"

I gestured a sharp yes. "I figure that way I have a prayer of you keeping it."

"I will keep it."

He looked up at Ulai.

"A knife, brother?"

Ulai glanced at me, his eyes a question.

When I nodded, he flipped back his coat, pulling a knife from a leather scabbard at his right hip. He held the blade out towards the other male, hilt-first, but Wreg shook his head, indicating his hands bound behind his back.

"You'll have to do it, brother."

Ulai nodded, once, then walked around behind Wreg.

I followed, watching as Ulai pulled one of Wreg's hands flat gently below the cuffs. In one clean motion, he cut the seer's hand across the palm, making me wince. Turning to me, Ulai held a hand out politely, gesturing for me to take it. After a bare hesitation, I placed the same hand as he'd cut on Wreg in his, palm up. Without waiting, he cut mine across the palm, just as cleanly.

I winced again, but more at the sight of it; I barely felt it.

When he indicated, I clasped Wreg's hand over the cut, palm to palm.

"You will not tell him," I said to Wreg.

"I will not tell him."

"Where I am, or how you got away...you'll make up a story, one that does not involve me."

"I will not tell him...I will do exactly as you said."

"You did not see me here. You have not seen me since I shot you on the plane."

"I have not seen you."

"Promise me, Wreg!"

"I vow it," he said. "He will hear nothing of this, or of you...not from me, or from any of my people. I vow this, Esteemed Bridge."

"And you will tell the Wvercian...Baguen...to do the same," I added. "...You will tell him it is my wish, as his intermediary, that he forget this thing, that he speak of it to no one." I swallowed, fighting back a pain in my chest as it occurred to me that she might not forgive me. "...And tell him to erase Cass. Make her forget I was here. Give her whatever story you intend to give the Sword...or have her remember nothing at all. Whatever is more effective..."

"Yes," he said, after a pause. "If Baguen is unable to do it, one of my people will. We will remove the memory from her...or create a new one, Esteemed Bridge."

I nodded, almost to myself.

I tried to decide if there was anything I'd forgotten, then realized if he wanted to find a loophole, he probably could. I had to trust he would do as I'd asked, and not lie to me about it. Maybe it was dumb, but I *did* trust him, even then. I trusted him to keep his word, anyway; I still wouldn't trust him not to shoot me on sight if he got the opportunity.

When I released him, I saw his shoulders relax.

Walking back around to the front of where he stood, I met his gaze. His eyes had narrowed again. Even so, I saw that my words had affected him somehow, too.

"You said he would not come for you," he said.

I gestured a yes. "He won't."

"Why the secret, then?"

I gestured a seer's shrug, keeping my face carefully blank.

"I am telling the truth," I said. "He wouldn't come *only* for me, Wreg... but I don't want him to feel obligated. He might come out of a sense of debt, if he knew I'd freed you. I know how you seers value your honor in such things." I folded my arms. "I only want to keep this clean. I don't trust Voi Pai, and I don't want her using me to get to him."

Pausing again, I looked him in the face.

"Keep him safe," I added. "Do what you do best, Wreg, and be loyal. Don't give him a reason. If he doesn't know about you and the others, he won't care about the rest."

He continued to stare at me, his dark eyes openly skeptical.

Rolling my own a little, I clicked impatiently, saying it again. "Believe me on this. He wouldn't come only for me, Wreg. And he won't care what I do. I promise you that..."

For a long moment, Wreg only looked at me.

Then he averted his eyes, clicking to himself.

"I think you are lying to yourself, princess," he said softly.

His words startled me, more for his use of the old nickname he'd teased me with before. I didn't think about the rest of what he'd said until later.

"Well, you'd be wrong," I said only.

"...But I have made the oath," he added, as if I hadn't spoken. "I will keep it."

Hearing his words, I nodded, feeling my shoulders unclench.

I realized I believed him. I really believed him.

"Thanks, Wreg."

I felt a tightness come unexpectedly to my throat. Before he could see my expression, I looked away, forcing my face still as I looked again at Ulai. The taller seer's eyes and mouth remained pinched as he met my gaze. He seemed almost as if he wished to speak, too...but he didn't.

Squeezing Wreg's hand briefly, I let it go.

Not looking at either of them, I cleared my throat, speaking levelly.

"We can go back in now," I told them.

Nineteen
Contest

JON FROWNED A LITTLE, STARING AT HIS EIGHT FINGERS SPLAYED ON THE TABLE IN front of him. The table itself, an organic and therefore tinged green like all the rest, glowed faintly under his hands, exuding a pale light. Despite the sun-replicating lights around the rim of the room, it created a ghostly glow in every face ringing the long, oval table.

Jon's hands looked whiter to him, too...whiter even than they had before, when they'd been on the run for months from Revik and his people in India and Nepal.

He was getting pretty tired of living underground, like some kind of mole.

Despite the more irritated musings filtering through his mind around this, he couldn't help but listen as Vash continued to speak. The ancient seer directed his words to the whole room, in that same, calm voice he always used, the one that remained both gentle and melodious no matter what was going on around them...or what he was saying.

"...Therefore," he summarized serenely, completing a discourse involving inter-dimensional Barrier spaces that went over Jon's head entirely. "...I believe it is possible we have reached the limits of what we can do with him in this way." His words grew slightly somber, despite the inherent cheerfulness of his tone. "...We continue to see scenes of war, but the images are no longer impacting him in a manner that would be helpful to our purposes...at least not sufficiently to open whatever it is he is protecting in his aleimi..."

"Protecting in his aleimi?" Jon muttered. He looked up, his hands still splayed on the table. "What does that mean, exactly...?"

"It means, young cousin," Vash responded politely, looking directly at Jon. "...That we cannot access the part of his light that is broken off from the rest. He is protecting it. And without that part of his light repaired, he will remain broken." He made a more or less gesture with one hand. "...For all intents and purposes. It is preventing us from healing the main rift."

"He threw up a few times," Dorje added into the pause, glancing at Balidor. The other seer didn't appear to acknowledge him, so Dorje looked around at the others in the room, his voice turning explanatory. "...I had thought that indicated an emotional response of some kind. It seemed tied to the sessions..."

"Indeed," Vash conceded agreeably. "There is shame, yes...and self-hatred. He is not devoid of emotion, witnessing these scenes. But they do not hit at the core of what he is protecting. Shame alone is not sufficient to reach whatever it is that Alyson had been leading him towards."

"You think she was on to something?" Jon looked up at the old seer. "Allie, I mean."

The seer met his gaze just as seriously. "Most definitely. We both do, cousin. Tarsi and I believe that is the primary reason he drove her away so vehemently..."

Before Jon could fully absorb this, Vikram spoke up from the other side of the table. "What do you think it was?" he said. "Something about the war?"

Vash made a polite gesture with one hand, but one that obviously meant 'no.'

"Something more personal than that, I suspect, brother," he said. His dark eyes shone in the glow of the table as he turned his head, looking at Tarsi. After a pause where something seemed to be communicated between them, he shrugged with one white hand, almost a seer apology.

Tarsi spoke up when they broke eye contact.

"He won't show us anything personal," she said curtly. "He distracts us with the war...with his killing. Ironically, it is a part of himself he finds safer. He has, on some level, come to terms with the image of himself as a killer..."

"I thought he was just being a prick," Jon muttered, staring back at his hands. "Showing her all that crap...about the women he seduced, and that teacher..."

"He killed the teacher," Tarsi interjected, causing all of them to turn. "He didn't tell her that, did he?"

At the silence around the table, Tarsi shrugged, her clear eyes showing a different kind of understanding than Vash's. Jon continued to watch her, briefly unable to look away from her eyes, which were so much like Revik's sometimes it was unnerving.

"He didn't tell us that, either. We had that before," she said, matter-of-fact. "...Before these sessions I mean. There are records of Ewald Gottschalk with the authorities of the time. Just very few." Leaning back in her chair, she met Jon's gaze. Her oddly smooth skin didn't take away from the age he could feel on her, an almost timeless quality, especially with her dark hair, only faintly streaked with gray, and the teeth that looked like those of a twenty- or thirty-year-old human.

"...He went to find her, like he told the Bridge. But it was on his uncle's orders. He killed her...and when her husband came home, he killed him, too. The difference is, that time, the local authorities caught him. They found him sitting on a stump outside their house, covered in blood...holding a gun." She glanced back at Jon. "The blood was hers. He shot her at point-blank range. In the face. Then again in the chest..."

Jon swallowed, feeling sick.

He saw Tarsi glance at Balidor, her clear eyes almost blue in the odd lighting.

"It's one of the only records we have of him from that time," she added. "...From the humans, anyway. He was charged in the double-homicide that time, and spent a few weeks in jail before his uncle got him out for 'health reasons,' promising he wasn't a flight risk. Before the trial could happen, his uncle faked his death...masked it as a political attack by the French, paid for by enemies of Germany. Then he set fire to the police station where they had his photograph and fingerprints...and the bloody shirt as evidence, of course. There'd be no record of the event at all, but one of the policemen had taken the hard-copy file of the incident details to another township...to check it against other unsolved crimes. That human...he was pretty industrious, for the time. In his own words, something about the crime made him think it hadn't been the first..." She paused, looking once more at Jon.

"...He thought him a monster. A kind of remorseless animal."

"A serial killer," Jon clarified.

"That would be the modern term...yes," she conceded. She went on in the same voice as before, glancing around the table. "...They had a partial of the police file as a result. But no evidence, no way to positively identify the killer, other than by appearance, which might have been good enough back then, but they couldn't try a corpse..."

Tarsi shrugged, holding her hands almost flat, level with her shoulder.

She continued seconds later, her voice just as matter-of-fact.

"His death ended the inquiry," she said. "...The policeman in question died not long after. I don't know how the partial record escaped Menlim's notice...but it did. Ewald Gottschalk's remains were interred in a family plot, and that name never resurfaced again."

There was another silence.

Jon looked up somewhere inside it, glancing at the other faces. He couldn't tell from their eyes if they were speaking to one another in the Barrier or not. They all looked faintly unhappy...all but Balidor, who wore no expression at all.

"Did he lie to her on purpose?" Jon asked Tarsi finally.

Tarsi shrugged again, her eyes unmoving once they turned to his.

"Don't know," she said. "Could be either. But it's significant, either way."

Jon nodded, returning his gaze to his hands on the table. When no one broke the silence for another stretch of time, he glanced around at faces once more.

"Has anyone heard from her?" he said then. "Did she even make it to China?"

"She did," Vash acknowledged, smiling at Jon. "She made it there...and left shortly after. She said the others had already been released...including Cass and Baguen. Some agreement was struck between the Lao Hu and with the remnants of the rebels, who are now under the command of Wreg. Whatever it was, Voi Pai seemed content with the result."

Alarmed, Jon looked up. "Did she run into Wreg there?"

"No." Vash gesturing reassuringly, smiling again. "They had left well over a week before she got there, she said."

"So where is she?" Jon said. "Did she say where she was going?" He paused, looking around at all of them. None would meet his gaze, none except Dorje, who squeezed his hand. Disengaging their fingers, Jon continued to look around the table. "Are we really just going to let her go?"

"What would you have us do, cousin?" Balidor asked quietly from the corner.

Jon turned, looking at him in surprise. It occurred to him only then that it was the first time he'd heard the Adhipan leader speak.

"Go after her...track her at least!"

When he looked around at the others, Vash raised an apologetic hand.

"She is the Bridge, young cousin. It is not right that we do such a thing...

and even more, it is not practical. Brother Balidor taught her shielding well."

Jon frowned, then bit it back, looking back at the table.

"So where's Cass?" he said, his voice neutral once more. "Baguen?"

"We do not yet know," Vash said.

When Jon looked up at this, he met Vash's calm eyes.

"...For obvious reasons," the old seer added. "They cannot come here, Jon...surely the rebels would follow them. Wreg, in particular, would not pass up such an opportunity...he would hope they would provide a trail leading directly to the Sword. We could not even tell them the location of this site, in the event they might be captured. Both she and Baguen knew this when they left. They have likely gone to one of the several safe zones we outlined for their use."

But Jon was already nodding, waving off the old seer's explanations.

"Yeah," he sighed, rubbing his face with his mutilated hand. "Got it."

"So what must we do?" Tenzi asked, from near Balidor. He looked first at Vash, then at Tarsi, who seemed to command his eyes for longer. "The Bridge may not return. We cannot wait for her, to rid the Sword of the Dreng. Eventually, they will find us here..."

"Yes," Vash agreed. "Both of these things are true."

"And?" Jon said, staring at both of them now as well. "Is there no solution, is that what you're saying? What is the purpose of this stupid meeting, then?"

Tarsi clicked softly, but somehow, it got Jon to pull back his anger. Looking at those clear eyes, he remembered again that she had once been in Balidor's role, as head of the Adhipan. Unlike Vash, who had always been more of a spiritual and occasionally political leader, she had been their top infiltrator.

"We are advocating a different strategy," Tarsi said. "It is one with which we would need assistance...possibly one or more volunteers."

"What kind of strategy?" Vikram said.

Tarsi made a 'more or less' gesture with one hand. "We believe a more... aggressive approach might be more effective at this stage."

"Meaning what?" Jon said. A kind of wariness came over him as he studied the eyes of the ancient female. "Like, beat him up, aggressive?"

He'd meant it as a not-so-funny joke, but the old seer's eyes grew thoughtful, just before she shrugged in Vash's direction. He, too, merely raised an eyebrow, as if conceding a point.

"You're serious?" Jon said.

"Not precisely that," Vash said, holding up a hand in a calming gesture. Then, thinking for a moment, he made another of those 'more or less' gestures with one hand. "...Well, more or less. We believe he will be less able to block the two of us if he is sufficiently distracted..."

"Distracted?" Jon gave an incredulous laugh. "You're serious?"

Vash went on just as smoothly. "If we distract him long enough from his attempts to block us, we might be able to circumvent them. The connection his wife created remains quite intact...and quite strong, really...surprisingly so, considering her absence. We are able to reach his light, so the problem is not the same as the one we had with him before, when we attempted to reach him in the Pamir. We believe with the proper...distraction...we might be able to get past his defenses." Vash paused, glancing around the table at all of them once more. "...It would have to be sufficiently strenuous for him..." he added.

"You mean...uncuff him?" Jon said.

"It would be better, yes, young cousin," Tarsi said.

There was another silence.

Then Jon gave a low laugh.

"Who would be stupid enough to do that?" he said. "Did you not *see* the footage of him with Allie? Or did you imagine we'd take him in turns, until he's killed half of us, or we've somehow managed to tire him out?"

"I'll do it," a voice said.

Jon turned, realizing who had spoken even as he looked at the Adhipan leader's face. Again, he'd barely noticed his silence until he'd broken it.

Everyone else stared at Balidor, too.

"'Dori," Jon said, exasperated. "You remember how Revik fights, right? You remember Maygar...how it took about ten of your guys to get him down?"

"I said I'll do it," Balidor said to the rest of the table, ignoring Jon as he met Vash's gaze.

The two older seers glanced at one another. Then they looked at Balidor somberly, their eyes serious. Recognizing that look, Jon gave another disbelieving laugh. No one joined him in it.

Instead Vash looked at Tarsi, as if deferring to her judgment.

"I think he is the perfect choice, yes," Tarsi said, answering a question that Jon, and likely no other seer at the table heard. Her eyes sharpened on Balidor.

"You cannot kill him," she warned.

Balidor gave a short laugh. "Understood."

"There is some risk. Your cousin is not wrong..."

Balidor dismissed this with a gesture.

Then Tenzi spoke up from where he sat beside Balidor, making Jon jump.

"What about the prostitutes?" he said.

At Jon's irritated look, the seer gestured apologetically.

"...I just meant, if we wished to distract him. Wouldn't that work just as well? He asked for some, didn't he? The Bridge approved the request. We would not need to risk brother Balidor then..." He gave Jon another apologetic look. "...And he is less likely to be suspicious. He asked for them, after all. He is expecting them, yes?"

Another silence fell, this one uncomfortable.

In it, Jon felt every pair of eyes on him, as if waiting for him, personally, to approve that approach.

After a pause, Jon sighed, clicking softly with his tongue.

"He's refused them, since then," he said, clearing his throat. "I think he was just trying to piss off Allie. Or maybe he got nervous when she left...but he hasn't exactly been cooperative on that point since he read her letter." Jon gave a low grunt. "Hell, I almost think it would be a good idea. He's been a serious asshole since she left...and that's saying something..."

When he glanced up, he found Vash smiling at him, his eyes holding a kind of understanding.

His smile grew warmer when Jon met his gaze.

"He said what he had to say," the old seer nodded. "...To get her to leave. It is a shame, really, that it worked. But perhaps she, too, had reached the limit of what she could accomplish on her own, without a different set of tactics to aid her."

Everyone looked at Balidor again, as the silence once more stretched.

"So when do we begin?" the Adhipan leader said.

Jon leaned over Dorje's seat, peering through the green-tinted window.

Like the others, he found himself glued to the contents of the tank, unable to take his eyes off the window...at least not without shifting his gaze to one of the monitors ringing the security station, giving him different perspectives on the same view.

Imaging devices covered every segment of the rectangular room. Monitors displayed around him in a single, crescent-shaped pane, as thin as glass. They paused on Revik at different angles, and on Vash and Tarsi, who were already inside, sitting in the far corner of the room on thick prayer mats. The latter two both wore heavy robes, their eyes closed, faces smooth. Between them and the rest of the tank stood a thin, organic wall...not a Barrier shield, but a physical one, to keep them from being hurt by what came next, Jon supposed. Dorje, who had put it in place the night before, told Jon it performed some energetic function too...amplifying something, or maybe keeping the two of them somewhat apart from Revik's light. Whatever it was, Jon hadn't really understood how it would help, but apparently Tarsi provided the design.

Either way, neither of them would be much help in a fight. Not a physical one, anyway.

The camera angles shifted again, moving to the opposite ends of the room, including the hatch-like door and the corner across from it, which had only a toilet and shower. Dorje programmed both for use by Allie, along with a spigot for water and a partition she could pull out to change.

Jon had watched Revik stare at her when she retreated behind it, his eyes unmoving until she came back out again. Thinking about Vash's words, about how he'd driven her away on purpose, after showing her more than he seemed willing to show anyone else, Jon frowned a little, looking at the chained man in the green-tinted room.

It was hard to imagine that on some twisted level, to Revik, showing his wife scenes of him molesting women and whoring could be considered a sign of trust.

Jon turned when the other seers did, following Balidor's approach to the outside hatch. Balidor entered without preamble, Tenzi and Vikram unlocking the door and opening it for him, then shutting it behind him. He wore the same thing he always seemed to wear, what Jon was beginning to think of as the Adhipan uniform...dark pants, a gray-green shirt that probably had some kind of organic in the fabric, a heavier vest over that. He wore all but the boots, which were absent; he wore what looked like black slippers instead, separated out for each toe, with what looked like grips on the bottom.

Jon watched the monitor as the Adhipan leader stopped about midway into the tank, still about ten feet outside the protective circle drawn around Revik. He stood there, silently, waiting for Revik to acknowledge him.

Jon saw the Elaerian's eyes focused on Balidor, unwavering.

But he didn't speak. Not before Balidor addressed him, anyway.

"Nenzi," the Adhipan leader said. His voice was toneless, as if he were instructing a class. "I'm going to unchain you. You will have as long a time unchained as you can earn for yourself. In whatever way you earn it..."

Revik stared at him, his clear eyes narrow.

If he hadn't worn the collar, Jon would have thought for certain he was scanning him.

Revik glanced at Tarsi and Vash, who didn't move.

"They sent *you* to unchain me?" Revik said then, his voice openly disbelieving. "Just how fucking stupid do you think I am?"

"Do you really want me to answer that?"

Revik didn't lower his eyes.

After a pause, Balidor clicked softly, his hands on his hips. His voice remained matter-of-fact. "Vash and Tarsi seem to think the usual methods are no longer working to reach through that cloud of fantasies and delusions you call your mind," he said. "Therefore, I'm going to untie you. You may try to kill me...if you can. But I believe the purpose here will be an education for you, brother." He paused, his expression and his voice unmoving. "Make no mistake...I think they are wasting their time. I think there is nothing of you to reach. If it were my choice, I would simply gut your mind altogether...leave you with only enough to keep your wife alive."

His voice grew openly contemptuous, enough to make Jon wince a little.

"...I will do you the favor of recommending you exercise some caution, Nenzi," he added. "You have been sitting there for quite a long time. I would not be so sure you can best me so easily without some reasonable effort on your part...all arrogance aside..."

Revik's face hadn't moved, not once throughout the course of Balidor's speech. Jon saw something in his eyes at Balidor's last words though, a thread of harder caution. He didn't shift his gaze, but Jon could almost feel him sizing the other seer up, even as he continued to look for a lie in the other's face.

"Yes," Balidor said, softer. "...You are trying to remember if you have ever seen me fight before now. If maybe you haven't miscalculated, assuming so quickly that you would have the advantage over me. You wonder if maybe you aren't the only seer in existence who might have some skill at this sport... or at the very least, some formal training beyond scuffle fights in the yards at Seertown..."

Revik's eyes narrowed further, but his expression didn't shift. Balidor held his gaze, studying him right back. He hardened his voice more.

"...You are wondering if fighting humans and untrained punks has really made you as good as you think you are. In any case, you are remembering it has been awhile since you have had to fight for your life. You are remembering that before you became the mighty Syrimne, it had been *you* who had his face in the dirt, more often than not...that you were hardly born such a God as you imagine yourself to be now..."

He smiled, his eyes predatory, an infiltrator's eyes.

"...Perhaps you should try a good fight, eh? Against a seer with some real training under their belt? With a few more years on you...? Perhaps this would be a fun challenge for you...or a way to get some much-needed exercise at least?"

Revik shook his head, clicking softly.

"You do like to listen to yourself speak, Adhipan," he said, quiet.

"Do you wish me to unchain you?"

Revik watched him warily. "And the collar?"

Balidor laughed, shaking his head. "Now you take me for a fool... Illustrious *Syrimne*. No, I'm afraid the collar stays. In fact, I would not expect to lose that anytime soon."

Revik nodded, his face impassive.

His forearms rested on his knees. It crossed Jon's mind, looking at him, that he wanted a smoke. But more than anything, he was watching the Adhipan leader look at him, wondering how much of what he'd just said was pure bullshit, meant to rattle him. Jon knew such head games himself. It was part of fighting really, part of any martial art.

When Balidor continued to stand there, Revik gave him a wry smile, inclining his head and hand in a polite form of invitation for him to approach.

"Come then...brother Adhipan."

"We will fight," Balidor warned. "No games. No bullshit, thinking you might get out...they will not release you for me. If you try any of that crap on my people, *brother* Nenzi...you will be gassed, at once. I will leave you in your cage with your chains, and my elders will have to find some other way to keep you alive...or not. Believe me when I tell you, I am in no hurry to see you unchained. I do this only as a favor to my elders…and my Ancestors."

Revik continued to measure the other with his eyes. Then he gestured him forward again, this time using his fingers, a faint smile on his lips.

"I won't hurt you, brother." He smiled wider. "…I promise."

"You'd better hurt me," Balidor said. "…When the chains are off. Or you won't last long."

"Looking for an excuse to put me down, brother?"

Balidor didn't return the smile. His eyes remained flat, filled with loathing.

"I don't need any more excuses, Nenz."

Revik face tightened slightly. It struck Jon that he didn't like being called by his birth name, not by Balidor anyway.

Balidor noticed the same thing.

"Do you prefer your nickname, runt?" he said. "Or the name bequeathed you by a dead seer? One who never managed to commit any of the harm you did?"

"He was a child," Revik said, smiling, his eyes hard. "Perhaps he simply didn't have time."

"Shall we do this thing then?" Balidor said, his voice bored. "Will we dance today? Or not? Would you rather I came back tomorrow?"

Revik moved forward from the wall, holding his arms out behind him, so that the chains stood out in a line from the wall.

"Do you need to be close?" he said.

"No," Balidor said. "Not if you cooperate."

"Pity," Revik said.

Balidor only smiled, his eyes still on Revik's. "Are you ready, runt? Or would you rather banter some more…until I run out of patience?"

"No. I am ready."

Balidor smiled. Glancing at the window, he signaled to Dorje, who looked up at Jon.

"Do it," Jon said, his jaw hardening. "Balidor acts like he knows what he's doing. Let's see if he does." Muttering under his breath, quieter, he added, "…Just be ready with the gas. It's going to be an awfully short fight, if he doesn't."

Dorje hit in the sequence. They all watched the cuffs fall open on Revik's wrists and ankles. Jon winced a little when he saw the red marks there. He knew the cuffs weren't like metal, despite how strong they were. They were supposed to minimize chaffing and the normal sores one would get from wearing metal for so long. Even so, his wrists and ankles looked raw, like a welt had developed there from the weeks they'd held him in the tank.

Revik didn't move quickly, like Jon had expected.

He straightened slowly instead, stretching out all of his limbs.

"Going to do a bit of yoga, first?" Balidor said, smiling faintly.

"Just making sure everything is intact, brother," Revik said. "You know how it is."

Balidor clicked a little, gesturing him forward with a brusque movement. "Come on, Rook. I haven't got all day..."

"Jesus," Jon muttered. "Are they serious?"

Dorje looked up at him, smiling. "Haven't you witnessed seer machismo before?"

"Enough to last me a lifetime, cousin," Jon retorted.

He was still watching them, frowning a little, when Revik swung his arms in a few circles, then focused on Balidor. He began walking towards him, barefoot.

Jon watched his feet, then his hands. He seemed relaxed, but watching him, Jon could tell he wasn't really. His muscles were as taut as guitar strings; he nearly bounced on his feet as he approached the other seer. He was still testing his body though, too, Jon realized. He was figuring out where he would be weaker from the captivity, how he might have to compensate.

The methodicalness of it kind of unnerved Jon.

"He's done this before," Dorje agreed, next to him. "He's had to fight straight out of captivity before...he's not stupid enough to think he's physically the same as he was before he went in. He's making sure Balidor doesn't knock him off balance with it." He frowned a little, clicking softly. "What I don't understand is – "

"Why Balidor is letting him," Jon finished for him. "Yeah, I know. He should have gone after him as the cuffs were coming off him." Jon glanced down at the seer. "Have you seen Balidor fight before, Dorj?"

Dorje shook his head. "No. I was not Adhipan before...I was in the Seven's guard. I imagine they did their initial training in the Pamir." He glanced back at the seers lining the wall behind him. "They don't seem worried though..."

Jon followed his eyes to the Adhipan seers, and realized Dorje was right.

If anything, they looked slightly smug. Jon had seen money exchanging hands earlier that day, in the mess hall and in the common rooms. Bets on how long the fight would last, who would pin who first, who would get in the first hit...who would be the first to draw blood. Most of those bets had been exchanged with laughter. In fact, the whole Adhipan seemed to approach this exercise with a renewed good humor, most of it at Revik's expense.

Jon hoped their confidence was warranted.

"He would have had to keep it up, right?" he asked Dorje, still looking at the other seers. "His training, I mean...they keep it up, even down here?"

Dorje shrugged. "They have their own training area...I wouldn't know." He glanced up at Jon. "The Adhipan train in secret, Jon. It's their way. That's been true for thousands of years."

Jon nodded, his eyes back on Revik as he circled Balidor slowly.

The Adhipan leader motioned towards him again, his eyes impatient.

"Come on, runt. I've given you your space. Do you not know your body well enough to have assessed it by now?"

"I'm ready," Revik said, his eyes still on the other's. "I'm still trying to figure out why you're doing this, Adhipan Balidor."

"Are you afraid of me, now? I thought you were going to kill me when you got free of those things. You threatened it often enough..."

But Jon saw the wariness remain on Revik's face. He glanced at the segment of organic wall where the one-way window lived. He obviously sensed a trick, and didn't like it.

"She's not there, Dehgoies," Balidor said. "She left, remember?"

Revik flinched slightly. Even Jon saw it.

He covered it with a shrug.

"Who's out there?"

"Everyone else." Balidor smiled, making a vague gesture with one hand. "They wanted to see a good fight, too. Gets boring down here, you know. Watching you whine and moan about what an evil prick you've been." He mirrored Revik's steps, moving just as casually.

"But not your wife," he added. "...your wife left, remember?"

"I remember," Revik said. He gestured towards Balidor, the motion brusque. "I'm surprised she didn't take you with her, Balidor. Protection, you know. She always did seem to like fucking her bodyguards..."

Balidor smiled, but his eyes remained even.

"Yes, I suppose that's true," he conceded. "But maybe she wanted to start fresh...you know, get some new blood."

Revik shrugged with one hand, the parody of a seer apology.

"Sorry, brother," he said. "Better luck next time, I guess."

Balidor continued to smile at him easily, still studying the other's face. "She kissed me before she left," he said. "...it was a good kiss, Dehgoies. A really good kiss. I kind of wish now that I'd let it be more than that..."

Revik paused in a step. The falter was barely perceptible, but Jon saw it.

"Christ. Here we go," he muttered.

Balidor gauged his eyes, but Revik's expression didn't shift.

"She told me she loved me, runt," he added. "...did she tell you that, before she left you?"

Jon saw Revik's jaw tighten. More than that, a flicker of tautness went over his expression, enough to tell Jon that he was in pain. Balidor noticed it, too. He probably felt it, since they shared the construct of the tank.

"That separation starting to hurt yet, runt?"

"You want me to kill you, 'Dori?" His voice came out thick, almost low.

"So far, I'm just hearing a lot of words, Dehgoies."

"What do you want from me?" he said, angry. "Why are you doing this? I've cooperated with Vash...with Tarsi. Why won't you leave me the fuck alone?"

"Because I don't like you," Balidor said. His voice remained hard, yet close to indifferent. "I think you're a sick, dangerous animal, Dehgoies. I think you're a rapist...and a murderer. And I think you'll bring nothing but pain to anyone unfortunate enough to give a damn about you, no matter what you tell yourself...so no, I won't leave you alone." Pausing a beat, he went on without changing inflection. "...So what *did* she say to you before she left? I know she wrote you a note. No kiss though, I guess?"

Revik darted forward, so fast, Jon started when he moved.

He threw his weight forward and to the side, twisting his body in a hard arc behind a punch. He slid out of range of Balidor's hands even as he threw it, hooking another at his ribs. He didn't pause, aiming a kick at the knee of his opposite leg, trying to trip up his legs.

Balidor somehow managed to escape all but the hit to the ribs, and that he slid away from, missing most of the force. He moved differently than Revik, Jon noticed at once. His moves were slight, more like shifts of weight and angle. But those moves came fast...faster than they appeared. Before Revik had finished his combination, Balidor had moved his body around his and back, sliding half behind him, and forcing Revik to turn. Revik did turn, seemingly without a pause, using his weight to knock into Balidor before grabbing his hips. He tried to trip-throw him, but Balidor smashed him in the head with his elbow, moving quickly enough that Jon flinched.

Revik disengaged, but only for a heartbeat.

It was long enough for Balidor to get further away from the wall, where Revik wanted him.

Jon watched, his eyes riveted as they exchanged blows, some of them faster than his eyes could follow. Revik got in a few good hits, but he was still testing him, Jon realized, trying to get a feel for how he fought. Some of it was misdirection, but he fought with the same, economical, single-purpose style Jon remembered.

He went for shins, knees, ankles, using low kicks even as he hit out with his upper body at sensitive areas...throat, temple, mouth, eyes, kidney, solar plexus. He moved fast, using combinations that varied quickly, that could be any from three to sixteen hits at a time. He'd hit high and kick low, then hit high maybe five more times, until Balidor got him good enough to force him to back off.

Balidor still seemed relaxed, even when Revik got him hard, directly in the face, with a sideways, descending blow that reminded Jon of things he'd learned in San Francisco. It nearly knocked the older seer off his feet, but his stance was well-grounded; he only slid under the next hit, moving behind him once more.

Balidor's mouth was bleeding after that. Jon saw money exchange hands behind him, and heard a few laughs and additional bets, but none of the infiltrators seemed fazed. Watching the fight once more, Jon noticed Balidor hadn't slowed at all.

He wondered suddenly, if Balidor had given him that hit.

It struck him in the same moment, Balidor was anticipating a lot of what Revik threw at him. He slid two inches back to avoid kicks, angled his body to deflect the impact of punches. He moved swiftly around behind Revik when he feinted right, moving left so that the taller seer had to compensate. He seemed almost to be waiting for him to move, then reacting, getting out of the way and hitting him while he was extended.

Jon saw Revik shift to avoid the force of a hit, then Balidor use that same shift to punch him hard, in the side, winding him. Revik managed to compensate, deflecting part of the blow, but he was behind the other seer, just enough that Jon could almost see it.

"He's using his sight," Jon muttered. He glanced at Dorje. "That's why he wasn't worried. He knows Revik can't see."

Dorje nodded. "It is why Tarsi cautioned him...it is a large advantage."

Jon was still watching Balidor, though.

The Adhipan leader was anticipating, yes, but he was doing it strategically, not defensively. He was letting Revik set the pace, saving his strength and testing the range of the other's repertoire...maybe even trying to give him a false sense of confidence. The fact that he did so seemingly without effort told Jon another thing. Balidor was good. Better than good. In fact, Jon suspected the Adhipan leader would be holding his own even without the collar, if he was going all out.

He was certainly better than he was pretending to be in there.

Jon doubted he was fooling Revik, though.

Even as he thought it, Revik seemed to be gauging the other's face more cautiously.

His eyes were focused, deadly still, but he was thinking again.

He dropped the next time the other seer came near him, barely missed sweeping his legs...it occurred to Jon that Revik wanted him on the ground, where Balidor's sight would matter less. Balidor sidestepped the attempt, and before Revik slid out of the way, the older seer punched him hard, the hardest he had yet. He hit him high in the cheek, almost at his eye. He hit him again immediately in the throat with the hard end of his hand, and then the ear with his other fist. When Revik ducked a fourth blow, Balidor kicked him in the solar plexus before he could adjust.

Revik staggered a little, moving back to keep his stance. From his face, at least one of those had hurt him, if not all four.

"You all right, runt?" Balidor asked, wiping blood off his mouth. "Come on...you're not even out of breath yet. I thought you were going to kill me..."

Revik swallowed, his face taut enough that Jon wondered if the older seer had hurt his throat with the hit.

"Can't you talk?" Balidor said.

"What do you want from me?" Revik said. "What's the point of this?"

"What is wrong? Is all of this not fun anymore?"

"Where is Allie?" he said. It came out of him angrily, almost like he didn't mean to say it. Once he had though, his jaw hardened. "Where the fuck *is* she, 'Dori? Half the world wants her dead, from what Jon told me. Why did you let her leave?"

"*Let* her leave?" Balidor gave him a scornful look. "What makes you think any of us 'let' her do anything? Since when do we have control over what she chooses? Or who she chooses to do it with? She is the Bridge, Dehgoies..."

Balidor shrugged then, with one hand.

"...Well, she was, anyway."

"What the hell is that supposed to mean?" Revik growled. "Where *is* she, Balidor?"

"You know, Jon told me a few things too," Balidor said, gesturing towards him. "He told me about your whining about how she left you down here...about how she didn't incarnate in time to save you from turning into a murderous monster..."

Revik's eyes turned to glass. He glanced at the window again.

Jon found himself clicking under his breath, irritated in spite of himself.

"I didn't tell him that," Jon said to Dorje.

"He listens to all the records," Dorje said. "Everything is recorded Jon... audio and visual. Balidor watched them all again, before this...he's been watching them for days, all of the sessions with Allie, too...her transcripts, the notes she left for Vash and Tarsi..." He paused, clasping Jon's fingers briefly with his. "He knows what he's doing, Jon. Trust him, okay?"

"Yeah, okay," Jon muttered, but his eyes didn't leave the monitors.

Balidor continued studying Revik's eyes. "What is it with you and women, Dehgoies?"

Jon saw Revik's body tense once more, his shoulders clench.

"...You just don't like them very much, is that it?" Balidor said. "Mommy didn't love you enough, is that the problem? Or is it something else? Maybe she loved you too much?"

Revik lunged at him again. That time, he got the front of his shirt, fought to trip him and lost his balance. He nearly fell, but slammed Balidor into the wall instead, hard enough to shake the organic window. Jon stiffened when he saw Revik pinning him there, his legs holding him against the organic metal, his hand around his throat.

"...Do we gas him?" Jon said.

Dorje held up a hand, cautioning him to wait.

"He may have let him do that," he said, but his eyes never left the two of them.

Balidor laughed, gasping a little against the hold Revik had on his throat. "Touched a nerve there, did I runt?"

Revik squeezed his throat tighter. Tight enough that the older seer's complexion darkened. Jon didn't see him struggling for his life though, and realized he still had an arm between Revik's body and his, that Revik couldn't get his other hand around his throat.

When Revik finally loosened his hold with the other hand, Balidor laughed again, still gasping as he met the Elaerian's gaze.

"Why did you tell her to leave, Nenzi?"

"I didn't...she left..."

"Crap. I saw you with her. You did everything but punch her in the mouth."

Revik loosened his hold on his throat, but not by much. He stared into the other seer's eyes.

"Still jealous, 'Dori? Worried she'd have me if she could?"

"Yes," Balidor said. "But that's not why I'm asking. I want to know why you drove her away...why you all but forced her to leave you...when you're clearly still so in love with her you can barely stand to hear her name."

Revik's eyes changed.

Jon saw them flicker in a kind of startled expression, right before his mouth hardened once more.

"Bullshit," he said.

"Now who's lying...?"

"What the fuck do you want from me?"

"Why did you show her all those memories of you with whores, Revi'? Why bludgeon her with all the rapes...all the murders of your lovers...?"

Revik's jaw hardened more. "Fuck you."

"You could have shown her other things about your past, surely...things with just as dramatic of an impact. Why did you keep bringing her back there? Why torture her with that? Did you really expect sympathy from her...?"

Revik shook his head, clicking angrily. The coldness was back in his eyes though.

"What is it with you and my sex life, 'Dori?"

"Is that what you'd call it?" Balidor said. He gave a contemptuous laugh. "I know about Pirna, Revi'. I know what you did to her...and to her husband." His eyes grew cold. "What? Didn't like the way she looked at you, after all those years? Or did you think she would have *forgiven* you for raping her...for making a public display of her, when she was only trying to help you? I guess that wasn't enough for you, though. You had to kill her for her crime of feeling some compassion for the runt in school. The blow-job king of Bavaria..."

Revik slammed his head against the wall, hard. His fingers tightened again, turning white as he fought to squeeze them around the other's throat. Balidor's arms remained in his way, refusing him the leverage he would need to close them all the way. Revik strained against those arms, fighting to break their hold, but he couldn't.

Eventually, he had to relax, and Balidor laughed.

"Truth hurts, does it, Nenz?"

"Fuck you!"

"Did you think it would impress Allie? All of your conquests?"

Revik's eyes brightened, all at once. "I didn't mean to show her..."

"Bullshit. You didn't show Vash and Tarsi any of that juvenile crap... any of your perversions. You must have some control over what you show to whom..."

"No." He lunged his weight against the wall again, fighting again to break the other's hold, to squeeze his throat. His eyes were brighter now though, even past the anger in his face. "I don't...I didn't want her to see that..."

"You're lying to yourself, runt...what, did you hope to scare her away then, too?"

Jon saw emotions grow confused on Revik's face. He glanced at Dorje.

"Are Vash and Tarsi doing that?" he said, quiet.

Dorje nodded. "They are helping a lot, yes...I went over the plan with them last night. They are feeding some of this to Balidor, too...what he should say..."

Balidor's voice grew harsh in the other room, becoming close to a snarl.

"What happened to Laren, Nenzi? Did you kill her, too?"

Revik cried out, slamming him harder against the wall.

"You did, didn't you? But you already knew that would happen, yes? You knew she'd end up dead before you stuck your cock in her. You just couldn't control yourself, could you?" Staring up at the taller seer's face, he clicked at him in disgust. "Wreg was right. You couldn't stop, even when you knew it meant others would pay for it...even when you knew you were risking their lives..."

Revik's jaw hardened, his eyes overly bright. "Shut up!"

"Is that what your uncle did to you, runt, depriving you of affection all

415

those years?" Balidor clicked in mock admiration. "...If so, I have to hand it to him. It's brilliant really. He makes you into an affection-needy infant, then punishes everyone else for your lack of self control. Nothing like a little self-loathing to prime a perfect killing machine for the Dreng..."

Revik loosened one of his hands, punching the older seer hard in the face.

As soon as he did, Balidor shoved him, using the wall as leverage as he propelled his whole weight forward behind his hands, his leg hooked on his. He knocked Revik to the floor...hard. Landing on his chest in the same forward momentum, he pinned him down as he punched him in the face, also hard...hard enough to stun him. He kept hitting him until Revik began fighting back, twisting out from under him. Wrenching his weight to the side and over, he got enough leverage that they were struggling, side by side, each trying to get advantage. Revik kicked him, hard, in the shin. He fought to knee him in the crotch, but Balidor punched him in the head again and Revik flinched, protecting his head.

It was enough that Balidor was able to grab his shoulders, slamming his head against the floor, hard enough that Revik cried out.

That time, the blow did daze him. While he lay there, Balidor managed to pin him, face down, his arms twisted behind his back.

"I told you you'd only remain free as long as you could," Balidor said.

The organic reconfigured, looping a cuff around one of his arms, solidifying around his left wrist. Revik cried out, struggling, but another had already caught his left ankle. It created a kind of panic in him that Jon recognized...that fear of being caged.

He managed to break free of the seer's hold, enough to hit Balidor, hard in the face with his unchained hand. He flipped to his back in the same moment, lunging against the two chains that held him, glaring up at the older seer.

"Come on!" he snarled. "Come *on!*"

Balidor regained his feet, backing off a few paces.

"Not having fun anymore, 'Dori?" Revik said, lunging against the chain again.

"You're the one who looks like he's not having much fun," Balidor observed, motioning towards his own face.

Mirroring the gesture, Revik touched his mouth, which was bleeding, moving his fingers to his cheek, which had already started to swell. Turning his head, he spat out a mouthful of blood, wiping his lips with his free hand. The expression in his eyes didn't change.

"You think you can get me to say uncle, 'Dor?"

"Interesting choice of words, runt." Balidor smiled. "You need a new uncle, is that it? Just don't trust yourself without someone holding your leash?"

Revik gave a short laugh, but there was so much pain in it, Jon flinched.

"Gods," he said, his accent thick once more. "Why don't you get a real hobby, 'Dor? Other than fucking other men's wives..."

"What happened to Laren, runt? Are you going to tell me?"

"Go fuck yourself."

Balidor pointed at the chains. "You want to go back to your cage?"

"Go ahead," Revik said, holding up his shackled wrist. "Finish it. You want to give me a beating...so do it. Why pretend to make things even?"

Balidor clicked softly. "No, Nenz. I think you would like it too much. It's your comfort zone, isn't it? Getting beaten down?"

"Oh, shut up with the headfuck crap!" Revik snapped. "Jesus! Just shoot me already!"

"Why did you tell Allie to go?"

"I didn't..." At the other seer's amused look, Revik's eyes darkened in anger. "Maybe it's just not that complicated, 'Dori. Maybe I don't want her anymore..."

Balidor gave a disbelieving laugh. "Who do you think you are fooling? You're in so much pain you can barely stand, runt...and it's been only a week. I can feel you wondering about her even now...it's like an obsession with you, who she sleeps with when you push her away. Or are you really as worried about her safety as you pretend?"

Revik bit his lip. He seemed about to speak, then looked away, his eyes hard.

"Ah, maybe there is some of that, too. Is it her you are worried about, though, I wonder? Or your own sorry skin you'd like to protect?"

"You think I'm afraid to die?" Revik stared up at him. When the other seer didn't answer, he gave a hard laugh, motioning him forward. "Trust me on this, 'Dor. I honestly don't give a fuck. Come on...kill us both. Do the world a favor..."

Straightening, Balidor kicked him in the face, hard.

In the same instant, the chains around Revik's wrist and ankle retracted.

Revik staggered to one side, planting his hands on the floor, then he was on his feet again, backing away from the other seer, his legs taut as he slid back into a fighting stance.

"Why didn't you kill her, runt?" Balidor said, watching him. "If you want to die so badly...I would think that would be the easy way, yes? You are so good at killing women, after all..."

Revik tensed noticeably again, even as that pain touched his expression. Watching his face, Balidor smiled, but it didn't touch his gray eyes.

"Come," he said. "Don't be modest, my friend. You must admit to your expertise in this. Indirectly or directly, you have killed...what? Just about every woman you've ever been involved with for more than a fortnight, yes? Your mother...your sister. Your friend, Kuchta. Pirna. That human who had you beaten up when you left her...Gretchen. The poor prostitute they tortured for you, probably for years, yes? Gisele. Then there is Laren...who was decent enough to take your virginity. And let's not forget your first wife, Elise..."

Balidor stood there, his eyes on Revik's. He threw out his hands, as if in a question.

"Am I missing anyone? Surely there were more, Nenz...?"

Revik just stood there, unmoving.

For a moment, Jon thought he'd gone somewhere else, that he'd phased out somehow. His expression looked almost blank as he held up his hands, his eyes on the floor. His clear irises blurred, as if some part of him had retreated back into the Barrier.

"Is that why you wanted her to go?" Balidor said. "You knew you'd kill her too, eventually, didn't you? You'd already raped her...let her get kidnapped by Terian, tortured...nearly killed. After you picked her up in China, you pretty much treated her like a whore, from what she told me, the whole time you were with her in those mountains..."

Revik stared at him, his eyes lost, almost confused.

"She told you that?" he said.

Balidor walked closer to him, his face and eyes openly angry. Jon found himself thinking it was less of an act that time. In fact, he wondered if any of the anger was really an act.

"Yes...she did," he said. "Exhibitionism, Nenz? Really? With your *wife?*"

Revik stared at him, that confusion still in his eyes.

"Did you have some childish need to make sure everyone knew she was yours?" Balidor said, his voice openly contemptuous. "...Or were you just looking for a excuse to see her like a whore...the way you viewed the others? Some way to make her less than your mate, in case she ended up dead? Or did it just turn you on, seeing what she would do for you?"

Revik grabbed the front of his shirt, swinging him around and slamming him against the wall again. He held him there, his whole body taut, as if fighting to control himself.

"Watch your fucking mouth," he growled.

"Why? Have I offended you?"

Tears came to Revik's eyes, so quickly Jon nearly flinched.

"Don't fucking talk about her like that!"

Balidor laughed, gripping his wrists. "You can't be serious! Didn't you *rape* her the other day? In front of a room full of seers? Oh, and her brother...I'm sure he really appreciated seeing her like that, Nenz. Down on the ground, begging her husband to stop..."

Revik slammed his back against the wall again.

Jon couldn't take his eyes away from Revik's face. He seemed to be struggling, fighting to control his expression, maybe even his light. Jon saw that pain on his face again, forcing a tautness to his eyes, tightening his jaw. He glanced at a different monitor, at the image of Tarsi and Vash sitting on the floor behind that wall. Neither of their faces moved.

"What do you want?" Revik said. "What do you want from me?"

"Did you kill Laren, Nenz?"

"Yes." He spat the word. "You know I did."

"How did you do it? Did you shoot her, like Pirna?"

Revik's jaw hardened, even as he closed his eyes. He shook his head, as if fighting something out of his light.

"My uncle..."

"Yes? He told you to do it, is that it? So what else is new? Do you think that *absolves* you somehow?"

"He didn't tell me..."

"He didn't?"

Revik met his gaze, his eyes bright once more. His expression hardened, turning into a mask. "I woke up...in the basement. They had her there."

Balidor met his gaze. After a bare pause, he nodded.

His eyes showed a heavier understanding.

"What about the telekinesis? You were active then, weren't you?"

"Drugs."

Balidor nodded again. "So how long? How long did they torture her before you killed her?"

Revik gasped. Pain flashed across his expression again, a kind of lost, angry look. "They didn't feed her...beat her. Raped her...for hours every day..."

"How *long*, Nenz?"

"Two weeks." He looked at Balidor like he hated him. "Two weeks..."

"Then you what?"

"I strangled her." His eyes filled with tears again. He couldn't seem to breathe. "She...she asked me to...begged me..."

"So it was missionary work, is that it? You're a holy man now, Nenz?"

Revik hit him, in the mouth, hard enough that he slammed the older seer's face into the wall. Balidor turned on him in seconds though, his eyes still filled with contempt.

"Come on!" Balidor said, shoving back at him. "Stop bullshitting me, Nenzi! It's not like we don't know what kind of man you are."

Revik hit him again, harder.

"You like to kill women...so what?"

Revik picked him up, taking his feet of the floor. He slammed his back and head into the wall so hard it shuddered the window.

Jon looked at the monitor showing their faces, gripping Dorje's shoulder.

"Jesus...he could kill him..." he muttered.

"No," Dorje said. "I don't think so."

Balidor hung there, gripping the taller seer's arms.

"You sent her away so you wouldn't kill her," Balidor said, breathless, still half off the floor. "Just admit it, Nenzi..."

"Yes," Revik said.

"You want to kill her. Is that it?" he said, still holding his gaze. "Or are you still afraid of your uncle, even after his death?"

Revik hit him in the stomach, doubling him over. Letting him drop back to the floor, he hit him in the face again, then square in the temple. Balidor threw up his arms, protecting his head, but Revik kept hitting him, kicking him until Balidor grabbed his wrists, pulling him closer. After a pause, Revik stopped moving. He stood there, breathing hard, his body still taut. To Jon he looked almost paralyzed now though. He stared at the floor, his face close to blank.

He was still standing there, when Jon realized he was crying again. Nothing seemed to penetrate his expression, however.

Balidor grabbed his hair, forcing him closer. Anger filled his expression. Words seemed to come out of him unwillingly, even as he met Revik's gaze.

"Nenzi," he said, his voice harsh. "You were a goddamned child."

"No." Revik shook his head, his face blank. "No. Not for all of it..."

"You blame yourself for Laren? I would have done the same, my brother..."

"Not only her...you said it yourself. All of them..."

"You blame yourself for your mother? Your sister?"

Revik closed his eyes, trying to push the other seer away. He didn't struggle very hard though, and Balidor grabbed his arms, right before he kicked Revik's legs out from under him. Both of them ended up on the floor. Jon flinched when Balidor punched Revik in the face, hard enough to rock his head on his neck. He hit him again, but Revik didn't fight back. He raised his arms when Balidor hit him a third time, still lying on his back on the floor.

"Don't let him!" he gasped, when Balidor hit him again.

"Don't let him?" Balidor gripped the front of his shirt, his voice harsh. "Don't let who, Nenzi? Your uncle?"

Revik didn't answer him, shaking his head, his eyes confused.

Balidor hit him again, hard enough that Jon flinched.

Revik gasped, holding up his arms. "Gods...'Dori...don't let me." Tears filled his eyes. "I can't...you're right. I can't stop it..."

Balidor stared down at him, his gray eyes flickering between Revik's. For a moment, he only looked at him, his expression stone.

"You really do believe it, don't you, runt?" he said finally. "You really believe he's out there somewhere still, that he controls you..." Disbelief colored Balidor's words, warring with the anger that still lived there. "...You think he'll rise from the grave to force you to kill her, is that it? Or is it Salinse you fear? Is it even real, Nenz, this belief in your uncle's shadow...or is he just a voice in your head? Is it just an excuse?"

The confusion returned to Revik's face, right before he shook his head. Tears once more ran down his cheeks. Balidor hit him again, but the empty, lost look never left Revik's eyes. He didn't fight back when Balidor hit him again, that time knocking his head against the floor. Revik stared up at the other seer, his face unmoving.

"Kill me," he told Balidor.

For a second, the older seer hesitated, staring down at him.

"Kill me," Revik said again. "Please, brother...kill me. Kill me..."

The anger returned to Balidor's voice.

"It's too late to kill you, Nenz. She'll die without you. You know that."

Revik shook his head. The words penetrated that time, though. Jon saw his expression crumple, just before he looked away, wiping his eyes with his hand.

"No, brother..."

"Yes, Nenzi. She will."

He shook his head. "We should never have been married. I didn't know who I was."

Again, Jon saw something in his words penetrate the mask of Balidor's face. Or maybe less the words. Maybe it was the openness in Revik's face, the lost note in his voice as he lay there, refusing to fight back. Balidor stared down at him, as if warring with his own feelings. Finally, he shook his head, clicking sharply.

"It doesn't matter now. You know it doesn't."

"It does matter."

Balidor's voice grew angry. "You can't *change* it, Nenz. It's too late."

Revik shook his head again, but his jaw clenched, even as he stared at the floor.

"You know I am right," Balidor said, his voice surprisingly gentle. "... You will remember this now. Even if you do not want to, you will remember."

Revik didn't answer, his eyes still focused on the green tiles of the floor.

Jon just stared at the two of them in the monitor, looking between their faces even as he wondered why they were no longer fighting. He flinched then, almost shocked when Balidor lowered his hands with a sigh, glancing at Tarsi and Vash, as if to confirm something he'd heard only in his head. Jon saw him gesture an acknowledgement, probably to that same message, right before he climbed easily up off the younger seer. Jon watched in disbelief as the Adhipan leader leaned down once he was up, offering a hand to help Revik up, too. After a pause, Jon saw Revik respond, if only by looking at him. As much in confusion as anything, Revik took the offered hand almost tentatively.

He let Balidor pull him to his feet, then stood there, unmoving, while Balidor gauged his face, his own still taut.

Balidor seemed as unsure how to react as Revik did.

"You feel better, brother?" he said finally.

Revik looked at him, his eyes incredulous. "No."

Something in his response broke the tension on Balidor's face. He laughed.

The laugh even sounded real, Jon thought.

"You're sure?" Balidor said.

"Yes, I'm fucking sure."

"Are you hungry?"

Revik rubbed his mouth, staring at the blood that came away on his pale hand. He looked at the other seer, his eyes still holding that confused disbelief. Then he seemed to be thinking about his words, and Jon saw a frown furrow his brow.

"Yes," he said finally.

Balidor laughed again, even more genuinely than before. Clapping Revik on the shoulder, he turned his head to look towards the organic window.

"Bring us food, my friends," he said, louder. "As much of it as you can... and make sure it is something I can eat. None of that damned human crap."

"Curry," Revik spoke up. "I want curry. Jon...tell them what kind..."

Balidor amended, "Except curry. But not for me..."

"And hiri," Revik added.

"Bourbon also would not be amiss."

Revik gave a low snort, almost a grudging laugh.

Folding his arms around his chest, he winced, looking at one of his hands. The knuckles on it were swelling, already bruising under the bright red. It looked like he might have broken it.

Turning away from the window, Jon gave Dorje an incredulous look.

But the Tibetan-looking seer only smiled at him, patting his arm. Jon found himself a little alarmed when he saw tears in the other's eyes. Dorje wiped them away, smiling wider, even as Jon glanced back over his shoulder at Vash and Tarsi, who were also smiling.

"What the fuck just happened?" he said, to no one in particular.

Tenzi, who stood next to him, laughed.

Revik leaned against the wall of the tank, a plate balanced on his legs.

Chewing on a piece of bread, he winced when it hit the part of his mouth still sore from getting hit in the face. His hand hurt the worst, even more than his jaw, where Balidor had clocked him harder than he'd been hit in at least a few years...apart from his time with Terian, anyway.

He found himself studying the face of the other seer warily.

Balidor leaned against the wall beside him, his posture totally at ease. He took a large bite of an *iresmic* wrap while Revik watched, chewing contentedly as his light coursed over and into that of the food. Revik couldn't see the light of course, but he could see the difference in the other's expression, even before he sighed, turning towards him.

"You like curry when you're blind?" Balidor said.

Revik nodded, almost before he realized he was still staring. Forcing his eyes away, he returned them to his plate.

"What?" Balidor said. "You want to ask me something...what is it?"

Revik felt his jaw stick in the bread. Without looking up, he took another bite, chewing about half as long as he should have before swallowing. He kept his eyes on the organic plate.

"She said she loved you?" he said, his voice neutral.

Balidor laughed, a little bitterly though.

"Nice," he said, resting the wrap back on his plate. His voice held a trace of his previous anger. "Feigned nonchalance. Very good, brother..."

"Did she?"

Balidor gave him a sideways look. After a pause, he clicked in irritation.

"Yes," he said, blunt.

Revik felt his chest tighten. He didn't look up.

"Why didn't you go with her?" he said finally.

"I wanted to. I asked her." Balidor gave him another look, his face briefly hard. "Hell, I begged her, brother...right before I kissed her. And after, too..."

Revik felt his jaw harden more. Taking another bite of the curry, he didn't speak.

"Nenz," Balidor said. Anger sharpened his voice, forcing Revik to turn. "She told me she didn't love me like that. She was clear about it." Giving a low snort, he took another bite of the wrap. Chewing, he looked at Revik again, his gray eyes holding a denser irritation. "...Hell, she's always been clear about it. I was the one who wanted more."

Revik didn't answer. It took him a moment to realize he was staring at his plate, holding bread in his hands without moving. Forcing himself to focus his eyes, he scooped up another chunk of the green curry, nodding without looking at the other man.

"I understand."

"No," Balidor said, his voice angrier. "You don't."

When Revik looked over, the older seer's expression was hard once more.

"She's never been unfaithful to you, Nenz. Never. That whole thing with me...it was an op. I may have lied about manipulating her into it...but the op part was true. She felt like crap about it afterwards. I'm kind of amazed she went through with it at all, to be honest."

Revik just looked at him, studying his face. Then he nodded, inclining his head, a seer's concession without real agreement.

"She told me differently," he said.

"Did she?" Balidor's voice was skeptical.

"Yes." He looked back at the Adhipan leader. "She said she had feelings for you. She told me she didn't sleep with you again because she was afraid of what might develop between the two of you if she let it..." Swallowing, he averted his gaze, pushing the bread through the curry without seeing it. "She also said it was intimate. The sex."

Balidor didn't answer for a moment.

Then he sighed, a near purr of clicks, leaning his head back against the green tile.

"Gods above, Nenz." He stared at the far wall. "She can't control her light. She'd never been with anyone but you before...she opened to me as if I were you. She didn't know any different. She didn't even realize she was making love to me, when we could have just had sex..."

Revik felt his jaw harden more, until it hurt again. He felt his body tense along with it, but didn't let himself look up, or think too much about the other's words.

"You know what I mean," Balidor said, exasperated. "Why didn't you teach her anything?"

"Teach her anything?" Revik stared at him. "Like what?"

"Like about her light. Like about *sex*, Nenz...how it's different for seers."

Revik felt his jaw clench again. "You think I should have taught her how to fuck other men?"

"No." Balidor clicked softer, but more irritated. "But you could have shown her *something*. I nearly had a heart attack when she did that to me..."

Revik held up a hand, turning on him sharply. "Enough."

"I just mean..."

"Enough!" Revik growled. "I don't want to hear any more about this, brother! Unless you want me to start hitting you again..."

Balidor raised an eyebrow. Then he looked away, clicking softly with a smile.

"I don't think I came out the worst in that fight," he said.

"The hell you didn't."

"I let you have those on the wall."

"Sure you did."

"I had you on the ground first."

"I'm *blind*, brother Balidor..."

Balidor chuckled loudly, raising a hand in a peace gesture as he leaned back against the wall.

"Always there is an excuse..." he said jokingly.

There was a longer silence, where the two of them just ate.

Then Balidor shifted his eyes back to his face, the humor in his expression gone.

"Where would she go, brother Revik?" he said.

Revik turned, staring at him before he could stop himself. "What?"

"Where do you think she is? Where would she go, if she wanted to disappear?"

Revik continued to look at him, almost blank, feeling something in his chest stop. It occurred to him, studying the other seer's face, that he hadn't really believed them before, when they told him they didn't know where she was. Looking at Balidor now, it felt true.

"I don't know," he said finally. "Have you checked the States?"

"As well as we could, with the contacts we have there."

"San Francisco? What about her family? She has an aunt she was close to."

"We have looked, brother."

"No one has heard from her?"

Balidor gestured a short no, then modulated it slightly with the same hand.

"She called Vash...once," he amended. "To tell him she was leaving China. That was it." He looked away, resting his shoulders and back against the wall. After a pause, he gave a humorless chuckle. "She quit you know... before she left."

"Quit?" Revik looked at him. "Quit what?"

"Being the Bridge."

Revik frowned at him. "What the hell does that mean?"

Balidor shrugged with his free hand, taking another bite of the thick wrap. Once he'd finished chewing what was in his mouth, he turned his head again.

"Honestly, brother," he said. "I have no idea. She said she was 'tired of pretending.'"

Revik winced at the words. Staring down at the curry, he realized he was no longer hungry. After a pause, he moved the plate, setting it on the floor beside him, then shoving it further away with one bare foot. He stared at the floor a second longer, trying to think before he gave up, resting his head on his arms. He tried to relax, but couldn't.

"Gods," he said after a moment. "Can't you track her? Vash or someone?"

Balidor shook his head. "We've tried. No one can find her. We lost her not long after she got to the Forbidden City."

"Well, the shields there would hide her," Revik said, raising his head. "It is no wonder you would lose her there. No one saw her leave?"

"No," Balidor said. He met his gaze uneasily. "I taught her to shield well, brother. She is very good at it...better than me. She might know we would watch for her exit."

"She has to go into the Barrier sometime."

"Perhaps she has found a construct. Someone to shelter her."

"Like who?"

"I don't know, brother. Any ideas?"

Revik frowned, staring at the far wall. For a moment he didn't speak. Then he turned, looking at the other seer, his arms still crossed over his knees.

"Jon said she would never speak to me again," he said.

Balidor raised an eyebrow. "Jon doesn't understand seers as well as he thinks."

Revik didn't feel reassured. He gestured with one hand, again not really agreeing.

"He knows Allie," is all he said.

Twenty
Unfeeling

"I DON'T WANT TO DO THIS." I LOOKED AT ULAI, FEELING MY FACE TIGHTEN AS I GAZED up at his pale blue eyes. "Seriously. Do I have to do this?"

Voi Pai answered me before he could. I looked over, saw her staring at me with those vertical pupils from where she stood in the middle of the square room. I recognized the room, even...it was the same kung fu palace chambers I'd woken up in when I landed here the last time. I remembered the bed with the wooden frame and the detailed carvings. Even with how old it was though, and how beautifully constructed, it still reminded me of a fort I would have created with Jon and Cass out of blankets and couch cushions when we were kids.

"What is the problem, Esteemed Bridge?" she said, her voice steel. "You agreed to this. You agreed in front of witnesses, I might add, to bond with the group..."

I glanced at her, but Ulai spoke up before I could answer.

"She'd rather not be in the open construct for this."

"She must."

"Why, venerable Voi Pai? Can we not simply allow an open scan of her light? That would bond her to the group just as well, would it not?"

"It will take too long," Voi Pai sniffed. "It won't open her light enough..."

"You have allowed it for the younger seers..." Ulai began, but Voi Pai cut him off.

"She will be taking her clothes off for strangers soon enough. It is best to rid her of any false modesty now..." Voi Pai turned, staring at me when she saw me wince. Her odd pupils narrowed to lines inside dark gold irises. "I recognize that this is awkward, Esteemed sister...particularly given your soul's age...but we have interested parties already. I cannot refuse them forever. Nor can you delay putting off repaying your debt for as long as you seemingly desire. Further, you are now a member of the Lao Hu. You cannot live in my home and use our constructs and not be bonded to the rest of your brothers and sisters..."

"But why like this," I said, not hiding my irritation. "Can't you train me for other work? I'm telekinetic for the gods' sakes. Doesn't this seem a little..."

"Low born?" Voi Pai said, smiling.

"Wasteful, I was going to say." Looking again at Ulai, I bit my lip. "If you think you're going to draw Revik here, playing some stupid game – "

"The Esteemed Bridge perhaps does not understand the relative issues involved in training an infiltrator versus training a concubine," Voi Pai interjected, her voice sharper. "One takes years, to do it properly...and we have already begun you in this, as per our agreement. The other, Esteemed Bridge, takes weeks. Months at most. In addition, given who you are, one pays significantly better than the other..." She smirked a little.

"...Sadly, it is not infiltration."

Gesturing with one manicured hand, she exhaled with a kind of exaggerated patience.

"Your husband, I could use as an infiltrator. He is highly ranked, experienced, and male concubines are far less interesting to most of my clients...even the Sword." Those predatory eyes returned to mine. "...You, on the other hand, have garnered a list as long as my arm, and that is only from a few, discreet inquiries."

I folded my arms. "I would have thought a female prostitute would be a bit...common," I said. "It seems like you can't go anywhere in America without tripping over a few dozen of them, standing on the streets..."

"This is not America," she said with a harder smile.

"You have planes," I grumbled.

"You are missing the point," Voi Pai said. "The Lao Hu do not sell it, Esteemed Bridge...and you are, for want of a better term, a unique product."

I felt my jaw clench more. I looked at Ulai, but his face was serious, almost drawn.

Voi Pai gestured towards him, then between us.

"I have given you your favorite pet as a handler," she said, exasperated. "I am using your training as a means of bonding via the construct...I'm not even requiring a group session of you with my senior infiltrators, as I have with adult recruits in the past. What more do you require of me, Esteemed sister? You have none of even the usual markers in your light...so I must assume you have no idea how to control your aleimi, much less any schooling in the more sophisticated arts. Ulai will teach you. So will the others we keep here for this purpose..."

"What if I don't want to be 'taught?'"

"Then you will begin seeing clients tonight," Voi Pai said coldly. "We will tie you down for the experience, if necessary. You won't fetch as high of a price, but we can pair you with experienced professionals who will at least help to redeem the experience somewhat..." Voi Pai's expression remained porcelain smooth, but for the first time I heard some semblance of sincerity in her voice. "...You would do well to take up our offer, Esteemed sister. If you allow clients to access all of your light, it will be much more of a violation. If you are trained, you choose which areas they touch in you..."

I felt my throat close again. It occurred to me in the next instant that this was likely Voi Pai trying to be nice to me. Even as I thought it, Ulai squeezed my shoulder with one hand.

"...She is not wrong, Esteemed Bridge," he said, soft.

Looking up at him, I found myself nodding. I looked at the female seer, feeling a kind of resignation steal over me.

"So it's rape or professional whoring," I said.

Ulai winced a little. His hand grew heavier on my shoulder. "I will not let you get hurt, Esteemed Bridge. She has given me discretion in this."

"Discretion in what?"

"In your clients, Esteemed Bridge. As well as your sessions with them."

"So you're my pimp, Ulai?" I said, giving him a hard stare.

He gave Voi Pai a kind of helpless look, but the female seer chuckled.

"Yes," Voi Pai said, folding the ends of her sash over in a tighter knot before reaching inside to the pocket of the dress. I watched her extract a hiri, that smile still on her red-painted lips. "That is precisely what he is, Esteemed Bridge." She motioned towards the bed, clicking her fingers at Ulai. "Begin now. I will remain, to oversee the bonding..."

"I don't want you here," I said, blunt.

"I don't much care what you want in this, Esteemed sister."

"Leave," I said. "Please."

The woman only rolled her eyes at me, clicking in that odd, accented purr.

Ulai looked at Voi Pai, seeming to measure her expression. Then he looked back at me, leaning down somewhat to speak more quietly to my face.

"You will have witnesses at times, Esteemed Bridge," he said, his voice quiet once more. "It is probably best that you grow accustomed to that, too... and she is right, about the bonding..."

"Nice. So you're going to loan me out for orgies?"

"Sell...not loan," Voi Pai corrected me. "And do not worry, Esteemed Bridge. Most will not be able to afford it."

I tried to fight the anger out of my voice, and didn't succeed. "You can drop the 'Esteemed' bit, sister," I said. "Why are you keeping up this stupid pretense?"

Voi Pai smiled at me wanly, then tilted her hand in a shrug, holding a gold lighting coil to the end of the dark-skinned hiri.

"Because it's the difference between charging five thousand yuan for you and one hundred and five thousand yuan," she said calmly, exhaling smoke as she finished lighting the hiri. She motioned again at the bed, speaking to Ulai. "Proceed. Force her, if you have to. I am not spending my day here, watching you educate a toddler about sex..."

Ulai paled at this, but I rolled my eyes, clicking loudly.

"Fine," I said. "Whatever."

Before Ulai could steer me over there with his hands, I walked the five paces deeper into the room and sat on the edge of the low-built bed. Leaning back on my palms on the mattress, I planted my feet in the hanfu dress, waiting for him.

His brow furrowed, making a series of fine wrinkles on his forehead. I found myself wondering how old he was. With his short-cropped black hair and tanned skin, it was difficult to tell. Like most male seers, he was attractive, at least.

"I am three-hundred-and-forty-six, Esteemed Bridge," he said, sitting down beside me. "Is there anything else you would like to know about me?"

I glanced at Voi Pai, then shrugged a little, human-fashion, as I looked back at him.

"Maybe later, Ulai."

His ice-blue eyes studied mine. I thought at first he might kiss me, but he reached up, fingering the collar around my neck instead. Seeing the question there, I swallowed again.

"Okay, yeah. Of course. That needs to come off." I glanced at Voi Pai. "One benefit of this little job, I guess...although I don't suppose you collar your infiltrators, either?"

"Not generally, no," she said, rolling her eyes.

I turned around, fighting nerves as I pulled my hair off my neck, allowing Ulai to reach the thumbnail latch that opened the retinal scanner in the back of the collar.

I glanced again at Voi Pai. "You're not afraid I might just make your head explode?"

She gave me another disdainful look. "I am working on the assumption, Esteemed Bridge, that you do not wish to die before you reach the halfway point to the first wall of my City...and," she added sweetly, exhaling smoke. "...If I'm not mistaken, having your husband the Sword die a slow death not long after you crumple to the dirt."

I felt my jaw harden again. Turning away, I conceded her point with a gesture.

"Fair enough."

The retinal scanner clicked off a second later, after running a bright red beam over Ulai's eyes. I felt the being inside the organic collar clench and then relax, unravelling swiftly from around the bones in my spine. The sensation made me shudder.

Grimacing a little, I glanced up at Ulai.

"Thanks," I said. "I think."

Only one person could remove a particular collar. As far as I knew, they could only hold one retinal imprint at a time, by design. Anyone else had to cut the damned things off, rendering them useless. Apparently, since the collar was still intact, Ulai was my one guy.

My light filtered slowly back around me. My nerves rose once it had, when I realized he was already turned on, that his light already felt charged and warmer as it coiled around parts of me, exploring my limbs. He let me feel that he wanted me and how much.

Fighting not to react, I flinched a little when I felt a sharp pulse of pain off him. My light flared, opening almost without my willing it.

Immediately, his eyes widened. He'd been about to lower his mouth to mine, but instead he paused, meeting my gaze.

"No, Esteemed Bridge," he said firmly. "Control your light."

"Meaning what?"

He pushed at the center of my chest lightly with his fingers. It made me wince, but he was showing me something with his aleimi as he did it.

"You are opening too much," he said. "Pull back...pull back, sister..."

I felt myself flush slightly. Then I was focusing on what he was showing me. After a few seconds, I could see what he wanted me to do.

"Oh," I said, my eyes still out of focus as I looked at my light through his in the Barrier. "So that's...wrong?"

"Not wrong. But not for this." He smiled, caressing my face. "That is for your mate, Esteemed Bridge...no one else."

I met his gaze, feeling my jaw harden a little. I knew better than to argue the point, but a part of me wanted to. Instead, I found myself following his light again with mine, studying what it did, even as he began caressing the side of my neck. He was pulling on me, coaxing me to pull on him. When I did, I felt his approval, just before he slid deeper into my light, showing me another way to do the same thing, until I was fighting to keep my breathing steady.

They hadn't been kidding, I realized.

This wasn't just some test ride to make me feel like a jerk, or even to bond me with the group, or try and break me out of my inhibitions. I was actually going to be trained in this.

Voi Pai must have heard some part of my thoughts through the construct...because she laughed, exhaling smoke.

"Your husband," she said derisively. "...No wonder he left you."

I felt my jaw harden more. Pain hit me at her words, but I didn't look at her.

I forced my eyes back to Ulai's instead, and the look there reassured me a little. He didn't want to hurt me, at least. I could feel it in his light, he wanted to make this okay for me, at least as much as he could.

"All right." My voice came out gruffer than I intended, but I fought it out of my expression, holding out my hands in a seer gesture of surrender. "...Train me. What the hell."

Ulai smiled. I saw a flicker of something like empathy before he leaned down, kissing my mouth, taking his time as he continued to explore my light with his, tugging at it in slow pulls. His mouth on mine made it difficult to not react as I tried to do as he prodded me, gently at first, then more insistently as he started to respond to my hands on him. His pain worsened when I tried to comply...I found myself fighting to follow his light, unable to focus on the kiss, until I realized suddenly that he was untying the front of the dress.

At the same time, I felt Voi Pai in my light, and realized she was doing that bonding thing, somewhere in the middle of all this. I didn't feel as exposed as I had with Revik in those caves with his rebellion seers, but it was a close second. I felt the attention of most of the construct on me, even as I felt flavors of the other members of the Lao Hu.

A kind of panic hit me, but I fought that, too.

Ulai pushed me back on the bed, gently, but he was big enough that I found myself panicking slightly at that, too. His light blew over mine once more, and in the next instant, I felt his pain pulse higher. I felt myself starting to open again, but he laid his hand on my chest.

"No," he said, quiet. "Stop." He switched to my mind. *I want that, Esteemed Bridge...I want it very much...but do not give it to me. Or the others. You must learn...it is important for you.*

His pain made the pulling worse, but I fought back my light, struggling again for control. He had his hands inside the dress then, which didn't exactly help. I was starting to undress him then, but he stopped me halfway through it, pinning me to the bed. Pausing, he looked down at me, his pale blue eyes shining faintly, lighter than his tanned face in the shadows.

"How many seers have you been with?" he said.

I stared up at him. "Is that strictly relevant?"

He pulled on my light again, sending a pulse of reassurance through me that melted my limbs. But his eyes never left my face, and his expression stayed serious.

"How many, Esteemed Bridge?" he said again. "Please. I need to know."

I tried not to remember Voi Pai was listening to this only a dozen or so feet away...or that the rest of the construct might even hear it by now. I kept my eyes on his as I shrugged a little, fighting my voice nonchalant.

"Three," I said.

He gave me a faintly skeptical look.

"Two, really," I said, feeling my face warm. "One of the three was a rape. The other was only one time. Really, mostly just Revik. You know...Syrimne. The Sword, I mean..."

I felt another flicker of pain on him, just before he rested his weight heavily on me, enough to make me react again. Sliding his light through mine in soft tendrils, he eased my legs apart with his. His pain worsened when my light started to respond again, but he pushed it back gently, pushing me to use other structures in my light to control it.

"Ease off, Esteemed Bridge...you are doing it again..."

"I'm sorry..."

"Don't be sorry," he said, his voice a gasp. "It is for you I do this...not me."

He looked at me then, his blue eyes on my mouth, then back on mine. I felt another pulse of pain on him, even as he pressed his weight down on mine, showing me how to pull back my light when I started to react again. His weight was a lot like Revik's...too much. Even the length of his body confused me. Ulai kissed my throat, pressing down on me again...showing me again how to control it when my light began to respond as if he were Revik.

"And he won't kill me for this?" he murmured. "...Your Sword?"

Glancing up, I smiled a little at his expression. I shook my head. "No."

"You are sure about that?"

Realizing he was teasing me a little, I smiled again. "I'm pretty sure, yeah."

"Pretty sure?"

"Yeah."

"Pretty sure is...not that reassuring, Esteemed Bridge..."

He was pushing the dress higher on me as he spoke, caressing my thighs and hips, then my belly. I closed my eyes as he started pulling on my light again, showing me how to respond with mine. I fought to focus on what I could feel him showing me, to not think about...

His fingers slid inside me and I jumped, opening my eyes.

He met my gaze, his eyes serious. Before I could speak, he was showing me more with my light, until I was pulling on his fingers, sliding light down his legs, to his feet. He nodded when I pulled it higher, up his back. When I pulled harder, he closed his eyes, giving a low groan. I felt him showing me where to move my hips then, and suddenly I was panicking again. He sent more light, calming me, until I clenched my fingers in his short hair, fighting to relax.

"I'm going to enter you now," he said quietly.

It felt too soon, but I bit my lip, nodding. "All right."

He moved his body up over mine, and then he had his hand on mine. Taking my fingers, he slid them down between his legs. I fought not to react, touching him when I felt his light ask for it. I felt him over cautiously, feeling my face grow hot even as I looked down at his prompting.

"You are not used to sex with strangers?" he said. "Not even humans?"

"Not without a lot more alcohol involved," I said, still looking at his body. I glanced up at him at his silence. "...I'm all right, Ulai...really."

He groaned when I slid my hand down him again. He was different than Revik...more like Balidor, in that it was curved slightly differently. Still big though, bigger than most humans. I wondered if the shape was an age thing, too, or some race thing, meaning Sark versus Elaerian. It honestly kind of freaked me out. I'd barely gotten used to Revik.

I looked up at him again, and saw his eyes on my face.

"It's all right?"

"Do I have much choice?" I joked.

"Yes," he said, frowning. "Of course."

I met his gaze, feeling my chest tighten a little. "It's fine, Ulai. Sorry."

I felt him pulling at me again, and then he was kissing me, holding my wrist in his hand. He did something to my light, hitting me in the chest and then in the belly almost urgently, in a way that nearly paralyzed me, forcing most of my muscles to relax. As soon as he'd done it, I realized he was inside me. He did it while I was completely open...my body anyway.

I cried out, half startled and half from the pain that rose in me abruptly.

He helped me control my light again, and then he was groaning, arching into me with long thrusts of his hips and back. After another moment, I had my arms and legs coiled around his, but I could barely move.

"You are shielding us," he said, looking at me as I gasped, holding his arm. "Why?"

"The Sword," I told him.

I saw understanding reach his eyes. He arched into me harder, making me cry out.

"You are blocking Voi Pai, too...and the others...she doesn't like it, it will make the bonding more difficult..."

"Tough shit," I said. My voice came out angry, half from his words and half from what he was doing to my body. "She'll like it less if he shows up here, pissed off because I can't keep my light to myself..."

"You can't do it all the time, Esteemed Bridge. You can't always shield. There will be times when – "

"We'll cross that when we come to it," I said.

Hesitating, he nodded.

Then, lowering his head, he arched into me again, harder, forcing my back into a curve with his hands. I felt his pain worsen as his light relaxed, as he lost himself in the motion. He built a slow rhythm as I coiled my light into his, until both of us were gasping. I had my legs wrapped around him tighter as he pulled me into a different angle again. He was still showing me things with his light. He coaxed me into subtleties of motion and friction in my body and then groaned when I got it right...only to show me more, trying to get me closer to the exact thing he wanted me to understand.

By the end, he was sweating, holding me under him as I fought to answer his mind's pull, to shift my body where he wanted it, to tense or relax where he wanted me.

By the time he came, he actually seemed to lose control. He cried out as he held me under him, extended all the way as his back spasmed in jerks under my hands.

I lay there, fighting off an almost paralyzing feeling of...I don't know. Guilt maybe. Regret. Maybe it was some form of self-disgust. Either way, it stayed with me, lingering in the background while he slowly brought his breathing under control.

I would have to do this again, I realized.

With other people I didn't know.

It struck me again that, bravado aside, I wasn't sure if I really *could* do it. I knew the feeling was irrational. Seers did it all over the world, male and female. Hell, it was pretty much commonplace...almost every seer I'd met had done at least a short stint, apart from the monks and those seers who'd been raised in the Adhipan. Even Dorje told me he'd been forced to 'sell it' for awhile, as the seers generally phrased it, when he'd first entered the human world and desperately needed the money.

I didn't think I was better than them. I just didn't want it to be me.

Maybe it was the human-raised part of me, thinking that way. Or maybe they all felt like that at first. Maybe humans and seers really weren't all that different.

For a long time, that was the only real cycle of thoughts that penetrated.

It wasn't until afterwards, when I was alone and having what amounted to a delayed reaction to all that Ulai had shown me about my anatomy in that hour or so, that I realized that Revik hadn't told me anything. Like, basic things, about angles...and friction, and what females could do to slow down males, and where to pull on them to hold them at the edge, closer than I'd ever gotten Revik, even when I'd thought I was doing something similar.

He'd done some of those things himself, of course...on the male side, anyway...but he'd never shown me anything about what I could do for him. I tried not to think about what it meant, in terms of how Revik viewed me... if it meant anything at all.

The longer I thought about it, the more my head started to pound.

Even foreplay. From what Ulai had shown me, a lot of "foreplay" happened during intercourse for seers...meaning before the males, at least, had extended all the way inside.

What had felt too soon to me was, essentially, a human reaction to what he'd wanted to do to get me turned on. He hadn't actually built to an orgasm for another thirty or so minutes.

Some of my own gaps in education I'd already figured out, of course, watching Revik with those prostitutes in the Barrier. But the reality of it hit me again, harder in some ways, in those few hours of being alone after Ulai and I finished.

At the time, however, I was more stunned, I think.

For a long moment, I just lay there on my side, trying not to think and still half in pain as Ulai caressed my back, running his fingers through my hair. I didn't know how tense I was until Ulai pulled me against him. Glancing at him over my shoulder, I peered through the curtains a second later. A kind of relief rippled my light when I realized Voi Pai had disappeared.

Ulai kissed my cheek, still massaging the front of my body.

"She left, yes," he said, quietly. "The bonding is mostly complete. The rest will happen tonight, while you are sleeping..."

I realized he was hard again, even as his hands roamed lower, less cautiously than before.

"...And yes, I want you again..." he added, softer.

I felt my face warm. I knew it was stupid to blush at that point, but I couldn't help it. "So...lay it on me," I said. "How bad was I?"

I tensed a little when he paused before answering.

Then he laughed, gripping my hair, tugging on it with one hand. Not answering me, he laughed again, pulling me against him, pressing his erection against the back of my thighs. His pain worsened as he did, and then he was kissing my neck, pulling me to my back, sliding a hand between my legs.

"Your light is unbelievable," he told me, kissing me again. "Gods... Esteemed Bridge...learn to keep your light in control. Or we'll have seers fighting over you, even humans..."

"But what about the rest of it?" I said, pushing at his chest.

He shrugged with one hand, dismissive. "The rest you'll learn. The light part...you can't learn that." He kissed my shoulder lingeringly, caressing my breast with one hand. "Can I teach you more?" he said, smiling a little as he leaned on me. "I want to show you something else...in fact, I want to show you a couple of something elses'..."

I fought not to care that he'd basically told me I didn't know what the hell I was doing. I'd already guessed that, but it didn't make it any easier to hear. I felt another pulse of anger at Revik, but I couldn't have articulated to myself why, so I forced it out of my light. The truth was, it didn't really matter anymore, what I did.

I couldn't really think clearly about what came after this...meaning after I left the Lao Hu. Images of myself waiting tables in Bratislava tended to come to mind, and I wasn't ready to go there yet. Although the thought of approaching Ullysa in Seattle for a job didn't exactly appeal to me, either. I'd asked for the infiltration training. Hopefully, if I studied hard enough at that, and managed to earn even a low-level sight ranking, I'd at least have some options when I left.

It was easier to just focus on that exact moment, push the rest to the background. Eventually I would have to pick up the pieces of my life...figure out what was left.

Somewhere in all that I'd have to think about the fact that I was broke again, that I probably couldn't go back to the States easily, that I had even less to my name than I had in San Francisco, and now I was a wanted criminal and hated by most of the seer community to boot. I'd also have to think about the fact that seers with no money usually ended up doing exactly what I was doing now.

I would have to think about all of that, and decide which of the twenty or so crappy options I had seemed the least unpalatable.

But now wasn't that time.

I had a cool twenty million to work off before then.

Given that I had no idea what that meant, in terms of either time or people, there was no point in getting worked up over what came after. Anyway, I'd finally done what I'd told Revik I didn't know how to do.

I'd had casual sex with another seer.

I looked up at Ulai.

He was watching my face, and I saw that empathy in his eyes once more.

After a pause, I slid my arms around his neck. I felt him react as I did, pain rippling off him as he coiled his light carefully back into mine.

"Okay," I said, shrugging. "Go ahead. Teach me everything."

They didn't let me see any actual clients for another few weeks.

Which probably should have been a relief, but actually just stressed me out more, maybe because it built the whole thing up into my head until I was barely eating after a few days.

I tried to keep my brain in kind of a 'static' place with the whole thing... meaning, one foot in front of the other, not thinking about what I was doing, but just going with it, like I would with any new job or project. I definitely avoided thinking about what I 'was' now, technically-speaking...much less what any of my friends back home would say if they ever found out.

In particular, I tried not to think about my parents, or how my mother would probably cry for about six months straight if she knew where I was right now.

I didn't want to go there, so I just deleted that part of my thinking. I deliberately focused on the trees, doing my best to completely ignore the forest...even when it was trying to bludgeon me in the face. Voi Pai, in particular, seemed to find my human-like take on all of this either funny, painfully naive, or 'human-religio-prudish,' all in about equal measure.

Strangely, I got the feeling that some of this was even driven by compassion.

She at times resorted to ridiculing me to force me to cut it out. Once or twice my depression about the whole thing even seemed to make her angry... or possibly offend her, if such a thing were possible. In any case, her reactions were enough to convince me that, at some point, she'd taken her own turn at this time-honored tradition.

Either that, or someone close to her certainly had.

Oddly, the whole thing seemed to make her like me more, too. Maybe because it leveled the playing field between us...or maybe it was some sisterhood thing I only halfway understood. Maybe it was simply because she viewed me as 'one of hers' now, and therefore falling under her protection. Since my first night at the compound, I couldn't help noticing that I felt differently towards the other Lao Hu seers, and they felt far less like strangers. I'd dreamt about most of them that night, and while I couldn't remember a lot of the specifics the next morning, I found I knew a lot about the seers I met...and they all looked vaguely familiar to me, even when I was reasonably certain I hadn't met them before. I also knew most of their names.

Most of my basic freedoms were returned to me within the first two weeks. I was also given access to a lot more of the construct...far more than I ever had while staying in the City as a guest the year before. Voi Pai assigned me my own living space, gave me access to all of the gardens and open spaces, and essentially treated like any other resident of the City.

There were exceptions. Most of those had little to do with me, personally, and everything to do with either my new role for the Lao Hu, or the additional security measures required to keep me alive. No one, from the highest ranking members of the Lao Hu on down to the lowliest human servant, had access to me without extensive security screens.

I found this out almost by accident, actually. I went for a walk in the Imperial Gardens and happened to notice one of the human gardeners I recognized from before. Strangely happy to see the old guy, who'd always had a kind word for me, I waved in hello. He approached me a moment later, smiling, and holding a trowel.

I thought nothing of it until the six Lao Hu guards I hadn't known were following me had guns on the poor guy, forcing him to his knees on the stone path. I watched, mortified, as they conducted invasive scans of his light and person before they let him go...and couldn't help but notice that the old guy had peed himself he'd been so afraid of the Lao Hu guards.

After that, I didn't wave to people.

During most of that period, I spent the majority of my "training" hours with Ulai. He ended up sleeping at my place a lot of the time as a result...often enough that I got sort of used to having him around. He had me practice on a few others as well, letting me take my pick of a group of infiltrators and guards who had apparently volunteered. I don't know if it was more or less disturbing that there didn't seem to be a lack of volunteers.

Voi Pai had a few of the other female consorts spend time with me, as well.

Unlike with Ulai, she didn't specify how I was supposed to spend that time, which I admit was a relief. Being around them wasn't as strange as I might have thought. In fact, it was a lot like hanging around any other group of female seers, only the consorts were a lot friendlier than the majority of infiltrators I'd met.

I picked up a fair bit through listening to them talk.

Looking at it objectively, I guess we were all supposed to get along, too. Maybe Voi Pai was trying to soften things for me with that, if nothing else by reminding me I wasn't the only seer in the City working in a similar capacity, despite myths to the contrary.

Three of these consorts decided to adopt me, in a manner of speaking. They came by my place just about every morning to talk. Within a few days, they were also inviting me out for walks, for meals, for winter garden parties of various kinds...even to see a movie in the main theater of the Imperial residency.

"Charlie" spoke almost perfect English. She had some kind of Chinese name, too, which I heard Ulai mention, but no one else seemed to use it.

Charlie was cool, but definitely quirky. Her hair hung long down her back, framing a face as flawless as Voi Pai's, but significantly more Asian-looking. She didn't wear her hair up in any of the traditional styles used by a lot of the other girls, and her make up and clothing were generally Western. Her eyes were dark, with flecks of green the color of new pine needles. They stood out against her pale skin, large and innocent-looking inside a baby-round face.

She also had a pet snake named Gulag that a human servant named Ugi carried around for her. A python of some kind, "Gulag" maxed out at about a fourteen to sixteen inch diameter in his middle, and looked capable of swallowing small children whole.

I didn't ask her if she knew the meaning of her snake's name in English... or if he ever came along with her while she was seeing clients. I didn't really want to know the answer to either question, to be honest...and anyway, most of the time when we hung out, she wanted me to tell her all about the United States. Specifically, Charlie was obsessed with American movies... male action stars in particular. She also liked pro wrestling, which she grilled me on endlessly every time I saw her, no matter how often I told her I knew absolutely nothing about it.

Miao, Charlie's best friend and sometimes-partner, was a lot more quiet.

Even so, I felt like I got to know her a little better, maybe because her light was a little more accommodating and open, so it was easier to get a feel for who she was under the more obvious things. Small and elfin in appearance, Miao had a cultured quality that contrasted well with Charlie's gregariousness. Her Prexci reminded me of Vash's, as if she'd learned to speak it during a different historical age.

Funnily enough, rather than Charlie, she was the favorite of many of the American and European men who came to China for commerce or government business. She did a better job of maintaining the illusion of exotic other; as a result, she kept a fairly stable list of clients to whom she, as she told me with a wry smile, gave "the Ancient China treatment" on a regular basis.

Although seer prostitution was technically illegal in China, it was considered a "favor" or "gift" from the Lao Hu to offer a consort as a token of goodwill to select individuals and representatives of countries or industries. Because of the interdependent relationship of the Lao Hu and the Chinese Communists, they often extended these "favors" to those persons deemed important in stature to the Chinese government on request.

In return, they were compensated well by the government for the service.

It was also considered "impolite" for those *receiving* such a gift to not provide some measure of compensation directly to the Lao Hu, as well. Part of this was meant to indicate that the particular gift had pleased whoever it was. But, more importantly from the Lao Hu's perspective, the client's compensation also signified a gesture of mutual respect. The Lao Hu, as well as the Chinese humans themselves, were extremely sensitive in regard to any hint that this gift had not been freely given, or that it resulted from some version of seer slavery that even remotely approximated the Western versions.

As these gifts were acknowledged to be a great honor for the recipient, to not provide some sort of compensation in appreciation was tantamount to a direct insult. As a result, any future gifts would not be granted to that particular person...or company, for that matter, if they represented an organization rather than an individual.

The whole thing was b.s., of course.

Like a lot of things in the City, I couldn't help but see it as an elaborate and ritual-laden cover for business as usual for seers and humans. I admit, it disappointed me a little, given that the Lao Hu and the Chinese had a rep outside of Asia of treating seers more as equals than their less-enlightened cousins in the West.

Like most myths though, some truth existed in the b.s., too.

For one thing, I was the only consort I saw collared. In fact, I was the only *seer* I saw collared, anywhere in the City...and the reasons were pretty obvious, given the telekinesis and the need to keep my exact location somewhat unclear to seers even within the City.

I also heard both Miao and Charlie talk about refusing clients.

In the cases I heard them discuss, the refusals had occurred for different reasons...but the fact that they could refuse at all struck me as significant. Consorts or not, they still had some discretion around who they let into their bed. Their handlers did as well, for reasons they didn't even have to share with the clients. A no was a no from the Lao Hu. They didn't have to give a reason for the answer, or even listen to a petition to have that answer changed...which also happened on occasion.

Ulai had already mentioned this to me, that I had rights of refusal, as long as I didn't abuse them. He told me that he would likely refuse some too, either for security reasons (the security protocols around me were ridiculous when it came to clients), or because he picked something up in their thoughts that made them "unworthy."

I didn't ask what he meant by this exactly.

I did find it somewhat comforting though, when I heard Miao talk with enormous distaste about a client who had been thinking about the female seers in subhuman terms and had been refused out of hand, with no rights to re-petition. Being an ignorant, racist jerk was enough to get you the boot, apparently.

I admit, after my experience in the White House, I found that gratifying.

I tried to do my best to tune out most of the sex trade stuff, though, to be honest. I kept my focus on infiltration instead. I'd officially joined a group of Lao Hu apprentice seers, and I let those lessons consume my thoughts pretty much 24/7, at least when I could. To my enormous relief, I didn't have to push Voi Pai for this part of our contract at all. A pair of guards simply showed up at my door and led me and Ulai to my first class...and when I arrived, Ulai uncollared me. The three of them picked me up later that same day when the class ended. Since the classes were daily, and around four hours long...and I wasn't seeing clients yet...that left me a lot of time to practice on my own. I used every minute of it, at least that I could.

Truthfully, they were the first real infiltration classes I'd ever been given. Revik had always been reluctant to train me outside of the basics. He said he wasn't "qualified" to teach straight infiltration...that he'd been trained too haphazardly himself to know how to break it down into the appropriate steps. The truth was, I realized after awhile, he'd been trained by being beaten when he made mistakes.

He never came out and said it, but I got flashes, here and there, of him using a similar method himself, training new recruits under the Rooks. As a result, the whole idea of training me, even without that as motivation, rubbed him the wrong way.

Balidor focused all of his efforts on teaching me how to shield. He, too, seemed somewhat reluctant to teach me a lot, in terms of the more offensive skills. Tarsi taught me a few things, but mostly she'd just been testing me for my potential rank...and trying to educate me about my husband, although I hadn't known it at the time.

Wreg and the others gave me pointers when I lived with Revik as the Sword. Even Dorje, Maygar and Chan taught me a few tricks, when I asked them point blank.

But I'd never actually been given *lessons*.

Now, I found my brain close to bursting following every session with the Lao Hu trainees. Sitting with them in a circle around our teacher, an old female seer by the name of Cilap, could be a little embarrassing at times. Most of the other students looked like kids compared to me, although truthfully, I probably only had about five to ten years on any of them in actual age. Due to my more adaptable aging pattern as an Elaerian, I looked closer to my human age...but to most seers, I looked closer to fifty or sixty, if not older.

In contrast, my classmates ranged in age from their late teens to mid-twenties, so looked anywhere from ten to sixteen years of age to my eyes, which still couldn't help counting age in relation to humans.

After the first day or two, I forgot to care. I was too busy trying to memorize all of the technical tricks Cilap taught us, or that I learned from the other students. Cilap had me focusing on the tracking mostly and blocking and Barrier-sparring with other seers, which I'd never really done apart from haphazardly in the mulei ring. The concept was familiar to me, as I'd watched Revik engage in these kinds of battles a number of times with Rooks, but other than a few tricks I'd learned in mulei, I'd never tried any of it myself.

Straight Barrier sparring with other seers, I'd never done at all.

It proved to be fun, if really difficult...closer to chess than sparring in the physical, even using sight tricks...and confusing from the multidimensionality of fighting inside the Barrier. The first time I tried it, I basically got my ass handed to me by a kid who looked about thirteen. He looked a little sheepish when the fight ended so fast, but then both of us were laughing and I promptly asked him to fight me again.

Within a few days of this, I was hooked.

In terms of shielding and concealing, Cilap had me show the other students a few things I'd learned from Balidor...and then a few things I'd figured out on my own.

She didn't touch the telekinetic stuff at all, which truthfully, was a relief.

I still hadn't gotten a straight answer on what Voi Pai knew about the human-killing disease that those terrorists had demo'd in Hong Kong. The most Voi Pai would tell me was that there had been some kind of hit at a lab in the United States that wiped out the disease and its antidote, all but for a small sample. When I asked who'd died in the attack, she pretended like she didn't know what I was talking about. As soon as I arrived in the City, Voi Pai seemed to realize I didn't know anything about it and mostly pretended like she hadn't asked me in the first place. When I pressed, I got the equivalent of "don't worry your pretty little head, Esteemed Bridge," and "we have experts looking into it."

When I pressed harder, she retorted that she thought I'd "quit" so what did I care?

I tried asking Ulai, but he genuinely didn't seem to know any more than I did. In fact, he'd seemed surprised when I told him about the hit on the lab in the States.

I tried not to care too much about any of that...it wasn't like I could do much with the information anyway. Voi Pai and I were at least in total agreement that it was better that the Adhipan not know my current whereabouts or any of the specifics of our agreement. As a result, I made one call to Vash to tell him I'd left China...and that was it.

It was better if they thought I was off "finding myself" or whatever. The way I'd left things, I figured they would probably head for America, and not look in China at all. As long as Wreg kept his mouth shut, that is...and as long as Cass didn't remember anything about seeing me.

I tried not to think about Revik much at all.

It was surprisingly easy...or, maybe just easier than it had ever been before. It was as if some part of me had just closed shop. It left me in an odd kind of limbo when it came to sex, or even just everyday relating with the seers around me, many of whom in the Lao who seemed to be trying to befriend me, or at least get to know me, now that I was living with them.

A large part of me just didn't care...about any of it. I knew, somewhere in all of that, that I *should* care, that the numbness I felt wasn't exactly healthy.

The problem was, I didn't really care about that, either. It was as if that whole part of me had gone on vacation, and didn't leave a forwarding address.

I wasn't depressed though...not actively anyway. I wasn't even *trying* to kill my feelings. I simply rested in a flatline of indifference...about everything but infiltration, which pretty much consumed my waking thoughts, and even a lot of my dreams. I enjoyed little things, like a hot bath, or a foot rub from Ulai, or the snow falling at night over the reddish lanterns. I watched the birds in the winter gardens, and watched Ulai design and paint more screens. I even painted a few canvasses myself, which I hadn't done once since I'd left San Francisco.

But in some undefined way, I was gone. Not home.

On that level, the whole selling sex thing didn't even bother me.

The truth was, I'd just stopped caring.

About all of it.

Twenty-One
Working

They started me off with a human. Which made sense, when I thought about it, but it surprised me. After the seers I'd trained with, facing a human struck me as almost...easy. But I suppose that was kind of the point.

I think Ulai was more nervous than I was.

Well, maybe not. But he hovered over me through the whole lead-up process to the event and stood just inside the door during, so at least I didn't feel alone through any of it.

I'd spent more than four days with the wardrobe people the week before. The process probably would have made a lot of my girlfriends back in San Francisco really happy, but I found myself looking at the ornate clock on the high table by the window approximately every thirty seconds, waiting for the few hours I would be released for infiltration training.

The wardrobe team, which consisted of three female seers and two males, seemed to find me almost superfluous, anyway...more so when I did such a terrible job of hiding my indifference around their endless tugging and pulling and wrapping and tying and hooking and buttoning and knotting and untying and mussing and playing. They dressed me up the way a child would dress a doll...or, really, how a department store staff probably dresses mannequins.

They would put me into dresses and skirts and shoes and wraps and scarves and various kinds of underwear only to take me out of them...I spent as much of the day naked as I did clothed. I stopped caring about that, too. When it was clear they'd gone back to the drawing board for this or that, half the time I didn't even bother to put the robe back on, which was hot in the heated rooms anyway. Instead I just plunked myself down on the plush chair, my legs crossed as I sighed as loudly as I could at the ceiling.

Once they realized I didn't give a damn, they talked amongst themselves more than they spoke to me, finding styles and colors that flattered my body and face, and that mixed with what they knew of client preferences...as apparently a preliminary list had already been provided, to everyone but me. They also discussed which clothes would be most compatible with the expectations of the sex itself, in terms of how they came off.

I suppose if I'd been in a different frame of mind, it would have had its fascinating moments...anthropologically speaking. The psychology of the whole thing had more to it than I'd ever really given much thought around before. By the end of the first day, I even found myself listening to them, here and there. I realized by mid-morning on day two that I was fighting to understand this for real.

Some of it might have been pride.

Jaden, my boyfriend of six or so years in San Francisco, told me once that I had no awareness of the male fondness for female clothing. He accused me of being a bit of a killjoy around that, actually. I knew all about the stereotypes around women manipulating men with that kind of thing, of course...but it was a power I'd never really learned how to wield, one that I'd frankly never had anything but contempt for.

But the reality was, this was my *job* now.

I could remain as contemptuous as I wanted in the background, but the truth was, I *needed* to understand something about this, and take it more seriously if I was going to do this work for real. Maybe it was stupid, but I intended to not embarrass myself with my new crap job, at least not more than absolutely necessary.

I knew how dumb it was to get on a pride kick around that, but there it was.

Also, it was easier in some ways to think of it as a job...like acting, or even waiting tables. I knew something else lived there, too...something different than just pride on its own, or even an attempt to distance myself. Something a little too close to how I'd left things with Revik than I really wanted to admit to myself fully.

Despite the part of me that listened whenever the information struck me as useful in any way, when it came to watching them sew and assemble combinations of colors and swatches, I was bored out of my mind. I couldn't keep my thoughts from wandering to infiltration. I even talked them into taking off my collar so I could practice while I waited. I guess for a female, even a female seer, I really was hopeless.

I tried not to let my mind draw the inevitable conclusions about that, either...or to think too hard about the fact that the only two serious boyfriends I'd ever had both cheated on me with women who understood those games all too well.

The wardrobe team seemed as unimpressed with my indifference as I was with their artistic vision. Instead of dealing with me directly, they had servants ply me with tea and little noodle dishes, fruits and finger-length cakes, picture books and antique kaleidoscopes and virtual reality devices of various kinds...just to keep me out of their hair, most likely. When I asked them if I could work on infiltration, all of them seemed relieved. The lead costumer even went personally to get special permission from Voi Pai to uncollar me for the duration of the fittings.

They discussed me and my body without bothering to soften their voices, including what they saw as my "flaws" and my need for just about every beauty treatment under the sun. One of them seemed particularly affronted in regards to my hair, which shouldn't have surprised me, I guess, given my lack of any real hair cut in the past year or so.

They set their team of beauticians to work on me with gusto the following day, even as they retreated back into the racks to continue the work of designing and creating clothing and accessory combinations for me once they deemed my actual body presentable. I had my eyebrows plucked, my legs and bikini area waxed. I got multiple facials, a pedicure, a manicure, my hair cut and styled, about two dozen make up combinations applied to my face, some of which I found positively frightening.

In the plus column, I also got a few massages.

I had my skin buffed and covered in towels and hot rocks by four different seers. I was scrubbed and moisturized and finally rubbed raw and set in a steam room for over an hour...I had my feet rubbed.

Then they returned me to wardrobe yet again.

I suppose they all had their jobs to do. Pride and competition and saving face seemed as integral to the City as it was to anyone presenting their work on a runway in New York.

They wanted the clients to at least be wowed by the presentation... whether or not they had their private doubts they'd be wowed by me. The problem was, they wanted an ecstatic, squealing, overjoyed client...blown away by the transformation they visited upon my previous shabbiness.

Instead, ironically I suppose, I found my mind aligning more with theirs. I looked at myself critically, standing outside of myself. I noted flaws, tried to decide if they would make me unique or be detracting. I tried to imagine the various reactions my appearance might evoke, depending on how I carried myself, how I held my arms and legs. I tried to predict how different styles might impact most male humans.

I tried also to see myself from a male seer's perspective...or even a female seer's. Imagining seer reactions to me was harder. I'd never known Revik's thoughts on my looks really, except through observation. The Revik I married hadn't said much, in terms of what attracted him to anyone, much less me. He'd told me I was beautiful once, but he'd also been trying to get me into bed. Syrimne had been more flattering, but it was all so caught up in his myth of the Bridge it never felt as personal as maybe it should have. I knew he was attracted to me, of course, but I had no idea what happened within that spectrum, or where I fit overall.

Anyway, I had no idea if he'd been attracted to me before we fell in love.

I had less experience with seers in general, at least those who would tell me the truth. From what Ulai told me, their reactions were invariably more complex anyway.

And, well...better hidden.

In any case, I saw my body and face as props, and as I looked around at the other props in the warehouse, I realized I wasn't in a very good state of mind when I didn't feel like I measured up to most of them.

Ulai told me I was being ridiculous. It actually seemed to anger him...he thought Revik had done a number on my self esteem.

Eventually, one of the wardrobe seers seemed to pick up on how I was viewing the whole thing. A female named Wahlu, she began speaking to me almost as a colleague. The others followed her lead, and by the third day, I could ask any one of them questions like what they were going for exactly with a particular color or style, what order I should undress in, how to hold my arms or where to stand to show off certain aspects of my body through the clothes. What male seers looked for, in terms of physical characteristics, and whether it was roughly the same as human men.

Wahlu spent hours explaining how they designed the looks of different costumes, which pieces I should leave on, when and where I should discard others, what colors to use near my hair and skin. She told me a lot about male seers, even going over my body specifically, telling me what they would appreciate about it most...where I was still immature in some ways, in terms of how old I looked without clothes, and how to use that to my advantage or hide it, depending on the particular male.

She approached me where I was at...which was closer to how I approached the infiltration training.

The truth was, I didn't really care how I looked, per se. I just wanted to know what the hell I was doing. I knew I would have to make this personal, at least to a degree, or I'd never be convincing to either the humans or the seers...but even that struck me as something that could be learned. If it wasn't faking precisely, I could at least use my light selectively to evoke that feeling of intimacy without letting it happen on its own.

Something about me made the other seers sad.

I suppose it was the bond thing, what they could feel through me. I noticed it with Ulai first, but saw it a few times in Wahlu's eyes, too, and even some of my classmates in infiltration class.

At some point, they must have taken Revik out of the tank. The separation pain had worsened gradually over the weeks I'd been there, until there was no way to hide it from the other seers. It got to the point where I was having trouble sleeping. I'd started dropping weight by week three or four. I could see from Ulai's eyes, and even from a frown I caught from Voi Pai, that they'd started to worry.

Then, one morning it eased.

Somewhat, anyway...enough that I could keep food down. My breathing improved, and my light seemed to remember it belonged to my body. I even overslept that morning, probably because for the first time in over a week, the separation pain hadn't woken me up off and on throughout the night, so I got a chance to catch up.

My light grew easier to control again too, which seemed to reassure Ulai. He told me, only after of course, that he'd been worried about whether I would be able to see clients at all in that state. He and Voi Pai had met a few times to discuss what they would do, in the event I got worse. They'd even discussed attempting to bond me to another seer, as that was the only partial solution that had ever been found to the problem.

Since that was a new one on me, I was a little surprised. I'd been told there was no cure at all for the bond.

Ulai confirmed that was essentially true. Re-bonding was risky as hell, and often didn't take. Even when it did, it wasn't always enough to keep the other seer alive. They'd only ever attempted it before when a bonded seer's mate had actually died, and they were trying to save the life of the other half of the bonded pair.

When the pain eased, everyone around me relaxed.

It didn't go away entirely, of course.

I knew it would probably remain about the same amount of bad indefinitely, at least if our previous periods of separation were any indication. It might even get worse, depending on what he started doing with his light on the other end.

But it did stabilize. I could even control it when I concentrated.

It also meant I was given the okay to start working.

My first real client, meaning the first person I slept with that the Lao Hu received actual payment for, was Yin Bao Xi, the current President and General Secretary of the Communist Party of the People's Republic of China.

I guess maybe that shouldn't have surprised me.

It did surprise me, though. In fact, it completely threw me when Ulai told me who he was.

I'd seen his picture on the feeds, of course...in avatar form, anyway...but the avatar resembled him closely enough in the flesh that I had to fight a bout of nerves when they first led him to the door of my room.

He was surprisingly charming though, and not very demanding, in terms of the sex itself. The most difficult part had been holding him off. I got the impression he wasn't used to seers...maybe not even to prostitutes... because he got so excited once I started taking his clothes off that most of my light was spent keeping him from climaxing before we'd done anything.

Afterwards, he was all smiles, and bowed to me so many times I had to fight not to smile.

He flattered me with his words, and also with his unwillingness to leave...and finally by asking me permission if he could submit his name to Voi Pai a second time.

I told him sure, and I meant it.

All I could think was, if every time was like him, I could definitely handle this. Maybe not forever, but long enough to pay off what Voi Pai decided I owed her.

I saw Ulai wink at me from the doorway as I finally showed him out. I could tell from the dense flush of pride and other emotions I felt in the pulse of warmth he sent my way that...at the very least...I hadn't embarrassed him. Two days later, I received a bouquet of hothouse flowers. With it came a long velvet-covered box containing an emerald bracelet that probably cost more than my mother made in a year, working for the Post Office in San Francisco. Probably more than I made in two as a waitress in that crappy diner. It also included a note offering me a house in Beijing, if I ever grew tired of being a consort of the Lao Hu.

The whole thing kind of freaked me out, honestly. Even knowing it had more to do with what I was, not who, it just struck me as the most bizarre form of make-believe imaginable. The guy didn't know me at all, and he was trying to buy me houses. I couldn't even get Jaden to do the dishes when I had a cold.

Voi Pai seemed satisfied, though. She gave me access to the indoor pool in one of the buildings outside Meridian Gate, and offered me a horse of my own, a pure-blooded, white Arabian stallion named Ri, which I was told meant "intelligence." It was the most beautiful horse I'd ever *seen* before, much less ridden, so I didn't hide my disbelief when they led him out of the barn and put him through paces in front of me.

Again, their world struck me as this bizarre light show of delusion.

Still, people paid well for their delusions, I guess.

I knew I had it easier than probably anyone in this line of work on the planet, seer or human, but it didn't change the fact that I was letting people have sex with me for money. They could try and make it seem like some expensive "date" and ply me with million dollar horses afterwards, but it didn't change the reality of any of it. Anyway, that kind of thing had never really worked on me...the whole 'wow her with money' thing, I mean. I ended up feeling like I was acting even when I was just talking to others in the Lao Hu, pretending enthusiasm about things that struck me as almost childishly shallow.

Just having to be that "on" all the time was kind of exhausting. As soon as they were all gone, it was like the puppet strings got cut. I'd just lay there, usually without bothering to turn on the lights, relieved at the silence.

The rooms where they housed me had actually once been part of, and modified from, the original concubine's quarters in use when the human Royal Family ruled the city. Instead of one of these rooms, however, we seer consorts generally received two...one for clients, and one for ourselves. The client's room didn't really belong to us in any real sense. Presentation artists made up the client-facing side...theatrically, of course. Following every meeting, that room, including all sheets, towels, blankets and dishes, was cleaned by servants I never saw, but who seemed to conduct their work with an almost obsessive attention to detail.

I actually had been granted three of these rooms, to provide padding between my clients and the outer walls...for security purposes, of course. I saw clients in the middle room, linking the other two. That was only one of the differences between me and the other consorts.

With the exception of their regulars, most of the other consorts only brought their clients back for sex after they'd been chosen from a line up, often assembled in a larger audience chamber. That audience chamber stood outside the gated security segment of the old concubine's quarters, so they never actually had to bring anyone into their space until they were working. Further, if they *weren't* chosen, they either waited for the next round, or went home for a few hours to chill out and live life.

Not so with me.

I had no regulars. I also didn't get picked from a choice of other consorts.

I saw clients by appointment only.

As all of my clients were also heavy hitters in some way, either politically or economically, they didn't come in through the front gates. They also expected more of an overall "experience," and therefore required more than the usual courtesies. As part of the whole foreplay thing, this was often couched more like a date and took a lot longer. I was expected to serve tea and entertain them...give them an opportunity to talk to me and to spend time with me in the pre-show sense. I also followed the client's timeline, at least within reason.

As a result, I usually spent at least half a day with each client. I think my shortest was around three hours...the longest closer to seven. I knew they paid handsomely for the privilege, but it wore me out by the time they left. It also often meant no infiltration training that day, which frankly bothered me more. I got catch up sessions at night sometimes, from Cilap and some of the others, but it wasn't the same; I wanted to be with my class.

Given my unique set up, I also had to learn more than just sex. For the whole tea ritual thing alone, I'd spent a few hours every day for weeks. Even then, Ulai still badgered me about elements of my delivery being not 'traditional' enough.

I had a seer's memory now, so that part didn't worry me so much as the small talk that was also required as part of the pre-game show. Both Voi Pai and Ulai warned me to be polite, but said that otherwise, I could essentially be myself. The problem was, I wasn't entirely sure they knew what this actually meant, in regards to me. Most of my social skills were learned in human bars in San Francisco, and while I'd adapted to Seertown and even older seers like Vash and Balidor well enough to squeak by, I still got a head tilt and puzzled looks often enough to know I didn't act like your average Asian seer.

The Lao Hu, Voi Pai in particular, educated all of the clients to expect an American, and a young one to boot. Since that was part of my marketing appeal in many cases, no one expected me to know the traditional forms of conversation or etiquette like the other consorts. But still, I didn't exactly feel like I could just kick up my heels and "be myself" either.

So I did the best I could with what I had. Apart from making Ulai laugh aloud at one of my comments to a tech mogul from California, I think I did okay. But so far, I'd mostly been given humans to entertain, so I could read them for when I stepped too far out of line.

I think Voi Pai let me off the hook as well because, technically, all of the old forms said I should be the one *receiving* deference. The humans probably wouldn't know this, but my seer clients certainly would...and while I didn't expect anywhere near as many seers as humans, due to the financial constraints of hiring me, Ulai already told me a few made it relatively high on the list. High enough that I could expect to see the first of them within the next four weeks to two months, depending on scheduling constraints.

I didn't find out until a number of months later just how much they charged for each of those little half-day visits, but even in the beginning, clearly it was a lot.

The order of my list changed almost daily, too. More important clients bumped down less important clients. Political situations shifted in the outside world, and at times, my list followed, depending on who the Communists wished to please at any given time.

No one came out and told me, but at times I felt the pressure of this through Voi Pai. Ulai told me later that Voi Pai intended to widen the client base only if it seemed appropriate...or necessary. Until then, it was rich friends of the Chinese government, business moguls and Head's of State.

That was pretty much it.

Also, despite the individualized nature of those invitations, whoever came to my client room had to go through about two hours' worth of security protocols in order to gain access...in addition to the hour or so they had to endure to even get that far into the Imperial City.

Those were the "friends" of the Lao Hu, by the way.

Strangers, which usually meant friends of friends of the Lao Hu, pretty much had to wait all day before seeing me sometime in the evening...or most of the previous night to see me the following morning.

According to Miao, the waiting list for me already numbered in the hundreds by the time I'd actually seen my first client...and that included only those names for which they'd already conducted basic security screening. The original set of invites numbered only about fifty, but word apparently spread fast that the Bridge was in the City and being auctioned off to the highest bidders. Within a week, according to Miao, that list ballooned into three times its original size. A few hours with me was apparently the new cachet, at least amongst those living within the high-floating networks of the rich, unimaginative and chronically bored.

None of this flattered me, by the way.

From the beginning, it was pretty clear I was purely a trophy conquest in 98% of these cases...often simply a check mark in some power-freak's bucket list. Or even more trite, dinner party fodder for their other rich friends, who of course immediately wanted their own names added to the list to keep up with the Joneses.

Nothing about that basic routine really changed until I got a good look at my third seer client.

The first two seers I saw were pleasant enough.

One, a high-ranking official in the Party, had left the Lao Hu's formal ranks and essentially lived full-time among humans. Having sex with him was strange only because he was a seer, but he kept things light between us. I think curiosity about my Bridge status brought him there as much as anything, and other than liking the sex okay, he seemed disappointed I wasn't more "mythic." Still, he was polite. He also sent me a gift...a golden statue of the Bridge symbol that I plunked down on my bureau, unsure what else to do with it.

The second of the two was a middle-aged infiltrator named Surli, and the first person I saw who didn't feel so much like a client. He'd been put on the list as a reward for thwarting an attempt at cyber-terrorism against the Republic, one that could have cost the state billions.

He'd come in informally, wearing the usual infiltrator black, and glanced around like he was in a museum. Then, finding me with his eyes, he stared at me, seer fashion...then grinned so wide I couldn't help but smile back.

We only made it about halfway through tea before he asked me to take off my clothes and pulled me into his lap. Despite this, I had more real conversation with him than I did with perhaps anyone who came into that room, client or otherwise. He wanted to talk to me during breaks between sex, during sex, after sex...he even asked me out afterwards, wanting to know if I had free time to see seers socially, apart from clients.

He was also the only one to ask me directly about Revik.

He wanted to know if I was still bonded to him, if the rumors about me killing him were true, why I was being unfaithful to him, and if that meant I was open to bonding to someone else. After stammering at him in shock for a few seconds, I tried to tell him I wasn't really supposed to talk about any of that, but he pushed me until I told him more or less the truth.

In fact, at one point, he made me cry, pushing me to open to him.

We ended up having sex on the floor almost roughly, him reading me while I fought my way through the worst case of pain I'd had since I'd gotten there. He'd wanted me to call him by Revik's name, if only to get my reaction. I hadn't been able to do that...but he opened me enough that both of us lost control...I only managed to talk him down long enough that he lasted past the worst of it. And even through that, he was talking to me, cursing Revik even as he continued to try and get me to feel it...to move past the thing between us, maybe.

I didn't know how to tell him that that probably wasn't going to happen.

He left reluctantly, about eight hours later, and I found myself making out with him in the doorway, and telling him I'd try to find some way to see him again.

When I asked Ulai, he'd seemed amused at first.

Then, after reading my light for a few minutes, he actually got jealous. He did ask Voi Pai on my behalf if I could see Surli again, and she'd agreed to it with her usual dismissive wave, as long as it was on my own time and didn't interfere with clients.

When I passed a message to him, however, he had mysteriously been redeployed in the States. He messaged me back at once, promising to visit once he was back in town. We ended up communicating at least every few days after that, via the secure network, but he soon got so busy that it got pushed out to once every week.

I distinctly got the impression that we were being kept apart by someone...or possibly several someone's. I didn't know who was behind it, but I suspected Voi Pai, despite her surface indifference to my personal life. I wasn't sure if she was trying to keep me focused on work, or if there was some other reason, but it was a little depressing.

In addition to the rest, Surli was funny...and charming. I'd liked him.

He'd also been good with his light. Really good, and he'd liked mine, enough to try and coax me to open more, well past where Ulai warned me not to go with any of my clients. The one time he got me part of the way there, I'd seen it in his eyes, right before he pulled on me harder, groaning as he let me into more of his. He'd climaxed not long after that, but he spent the rest of our time together trying to get me to go there with him again.

With Surli gone, it was back to the usual parade of...nothing.

Most of my clients were fine, not jerks or anything. I got a lot of presents...a fair number of which I gave to the other consorts, or my wardrobe people, at least once I found out I couldn't trade them in as any part of my debt to the Lao Hu. I kept the jewelry, and the gold and jade...and the few pieces of fine art I received. It wasn't a vanity thing; I like art, sure, but on a certain level, it also constituted a bunch of junk I couldn't really move easily if I needed to.

I kept them so I'd have something when I got out of there. Insurance, I guess.

Certain things Revik had told me about the reality of most seers' lives kept reverberating through my head, including what he said about the dangers of being poor and a seer. He was obsessive about having savings of some kind...preferably a lot of savings, spread over multiple accounts and in different currencies. He did it partly so he wouldn't be forced to do work he didn't want to do, but mostly I suspected he kept it as bribe money, in case he or anyone he cared about ever got into trouble and he needed to pay their way out.

Very few problems couldn't be solved in the human world with enough money.

I'd never really felt comfortable relying on other people for that kind of thing...including the Seven, who, like Revik, also assured me I would never need to worry about money. Maybe it was watching my mother rapidly go broke due to an insurance policy "glitch" when my father got MS...after he'd worked his whole life and had savings and paid his premiums and all the rest of it. Or maybe I'd just learned a long time ago that people said a lot of things that didn't always pan out, no matter how good their intentions.

So when Voi Pai refused to take any of my "gifts" in lieu of hours worked, I didn't argue. I hoarded my stuff. And when I got enough of it, I asked Ulai to help me open a bank account and I sold a bunch of it. From that point on, I started hoarding cash, too.

Ulai seemed to approve of my approach. He elected himself my financial advisor, and even helped me invest some of it, utilizing some of the market experts in the Lao Hu. He also helped me spread it around a bit, like Revik did, so I wouldn't be overly reliant on the Chinese economy in case something happened.

My mother would laugh if she knew I had a Swiss bank account, but I found the knowledge oddly reassuring. I also had money in the United States, and in England.

In terms of "what next" after this, I'd already been offered a few positions in China, both within the Lao Hu and for the government directly, doing something like what Surli did. I found myself taking those offers seriously. For one thing, I'd be safe in China...relatively speaking. Despite the debacle in Hong Kong, most of the Chinese seers seemed to have come to peace with me. And, of course, the Chinese human government very much wanted me to stick around, as a permanent, willing and loyal member of their seer family. They wanted my title, I suppose. They also probably hoped I'd propagate little baby telekinetic seers.

More than anything, they wanted me as leverage against the West. There was still a lot of fear around telekinetic seers. Thanks to the image captures on the Registry job, all speculation as to whether I could use my powers to kill had been handily laid to rest.

There was some chance they'd force the issue, of course, when it got time for me to leave, but I kind of doubted they'd throw me in a cell and start experimenting on me. Too many seers would get pissed off...and in the City, at least, most now seemed to believe me that Revik was alive and well and would soon be rejoining seer society. Revik's rumored good health went a long way towards calming down a lot of the seer-traitor and mate-traitor crap I would probably have to deal with in the West for the next several decades.

Seers in the West were just more pissed off...and really, with good reason.

All in all, my life moved forward. I worked off the debt to the Lao Hu, and managed to keep my mind almost totally off how I was doing it. I saved money. Every now and then, I tried to think about what I might do when I got out, where I might go. I was friendly to the other seers, and rode my horse when I had free time, or talked to Surli on the network.

Then, on a day finally warm enough to make me think wistfully about the approach of spring, Voi Pai called me into her receiving room, and I got a good look at my third seer client.

Twenty-Two
REFUSAL

I DIDN'T EVEN KNOW I WAS GOING IN TO SEE A SEER.

I assumed it was a human...some head of state, or someone the Chinese were particularly nervous about for some reason.

They never brought me to the reception room to meet clients. All of that business stuff was normally handled behind the scenes; they never included me in any of it. My clients were all screened, questioned and scanned long before they got anywhere near me. It actually annoyed me at times, how little they involved me in my own "list."

So when the wardrobe team made a big fuss and told me I had to be in the reception hall at four p.m. sharp, dressed to kill and using every single one of the correct forms of the formal manners I'd been taught..I was a little nonplussed. The one guy, their boss, I guess, kept slapping my fingers away from my face and hair as he worked, until finally I just stood there, hands at my sides, feeling again like some kind of dog being groomed instead of a person.

Trying to get anything specific from them proved impossible, so I resigned myself to the fact that I was meeting some head honcho bigwig... someone Voi Pai didn't trust me to meet on my own. Apparently he or she was important enough that Voi Pai wanted to grease the wheels and make sure I didn't inadvertently insult anyone, or embarrass the Lao Hu. So when I finally entered the reception area, I was more than a little stunned at who waited for me.

A group of Wvercians stood there, in their full, semi-Viking regalia.

I counted five of them before cycling around to look at each individual in more detail. The one in front was probably the largest seer I'd ever seen in real life. The ones standing behind him appeared to be closer to Baguen's size, which I would have termed "huge" before seeing the seer in the center. He clearly held the place of honor, as he stood right before Voi Pai's chair, where most in the Lao Hu normally bowed, or even knelt.

Turning towards her, I tried to keep the incredulousness off my face.

She raised an eyebrow at me, but I saw the warning in her eyes.

I found myself looking back at the leader.

I wore a backless, flowing white dress with no sleeves and only a single, thin neck strap on top...presumably to emphasize the collar around my neck. The dress was nearly transparent, showing parts of my body depending on the angle of the light, especially in the sunlight-filled reception hall. It was one I hated, actually, in that it made me feel naked, and on display. It struck me as cruder than the majority of the wardrobe team's creations...and one that invariably put me in a bad mood when I was forced to parade it in front of a crowd.

Staring up at those broad, windburned faces, and the dark eyes trained on my body through the thin material, I had even less of a sense of humor about it than usual. This was starting to look like some kind of gang rape scenario, which was definitely not cool with me.

As I made a second pass through the room, I paused again on the leader. That time, I looked at his face.

I found myself staring at him then, lost in his countenance...the black eyes above sunburned and blotchy cheeks, skin like some of the plains humans got from eating too much meat. His eyes were dead-looking, empty. A murderer's eyes. More than that, I couldn't help but see the familiarity in them...a familiarity I realized, horribly, that I shared.

My gaze dropped to his throat, where a jagged white scar stood out on his darker skin, visible above the collar of a coarse-spun cotton shirt, open at the neck.

Moving from the scar, my eyes shifted upwards once more, without my willing it. I stared at his face, still unable to believe what my mind told me, what I already knew, despite the activated collar around my neck. He was smiling now, but that dead look never left his eyes. I saw the hunger there. I saw it, and I feared it...but I couldn't tear my gaze off his.

I couldn't believe he was alive.

Staring at his face again, I found myself looking sharply at Voi Pai.

"No," I said, blunt. "I refuse."

I didn't wait for her reaction.

I turned on my heel, walking out of the room.

After the barest pause, where I'm sure Ulai exchanged some kind of communication with Voi Pai, he hurriedly followed me, half-jogging to catch me in the corridor outside the cavernous reception hall. Gripping my arm in his large hand, he ignored my attempt to jerk it angrily from his fingers, steering me firmly into a side chamber. He closed the door behind us, probably so we wouldn't be overheard.

"What?" I said, finally managing to free my arm. I glared up at him. "I've never once exercised my right of refusal. Not once."

"I am aware of that, Esteemed Bridge – "

"Well I am now! It's non-negotiable...and I don't have to say why."

His blue eyes held a glint of frustration, but it was more than that. I found myself staring up at that gaze, half in disbelief when I found I recognized the look there.

He was afraid. But more than that...

"I don't have any choice," I said, blunt.

"Normally, you would, Esteemed Bridge," Ulai said. "Normally, the right to refuse is inviolate – "

"Except when it really matters."

"This is not a usual situation, Esteemed Bridge – "

"And what makes this *not* usual, Ulai?"

"There are..." He hesitated, meeting my eyes. "...Political considerations, Esteemed Bridge."

I gave him a disbelieving look. "Are you telling me that the Lao Hu is so desperate for favors from the Wvercians that they would sell the Bridge against her will?"

He winced, but his eyes held mine, and the expression in them didn't change.

"It is not all of them, Esteemed Bridge..." Ulai's voice held a thread of fear, along with a cajoling plead that made me stare up at him again, trying to read behind his words. "You are not being asked to service all of them. It is only their leader. I know he is not attractive, but – "

"His looks aren't the issue, Ulai."

"Then what?"

"I said no. I also said it's non-negotiable...I meant it."

"But why?" he said, frustrated. "He is one man. You have been with others, less of physical specimens than he – "

"He is the exact one I'm refusing," I snapped. "I won't sleep with him, Ulai. I won't."

"But you cannot refuse!" Ulai said, his voice rising somewhat. "This is one client you *cannot refuse*, Esteemed Sister...you cannot!"

"Why?" I said. I stepped back, still fighting to free myself of his hands... but most of all his light, which was both attempting to pull on me and calm me at the same time. "Cut it out!" I snapped. "Just talk. Stop treating me like animal. *Why* can't I refuse?"

"He is an emissary of important allies of the Lao Hu..."

"What allies would those be?"

"I cannot tell you who they work for," Ulai said, pleading again. "But it is most important, Esteemed Bridge. They wish to know you are being cared for...and that you are docile. They want to know you are safe with us..."

"Cared for?" I said. "Docile? You make it sound like I belong to them."

"All of us belong to them, Esteemed Bridge...even you."

"Really? And who are they, that I owe them so much? Who are they to *me*, Ulai?"

"Please, Esteemed Bridge! Please! Voi Pai will not accept a refusal for this..."

Seeing the look on his face, I felt my jaw harden. "Why don't you lay it out for me, Ulai? Brother? For we are all in the same family of Lao Hu, are we not?"

He didn't answer at first, but I felt a pulse of pain in his light.

For a moment we only stood there. I watched him stare into the darkness of the hallway. Even with the collar, I could feel how much my words bothered him. I felt pain on him again, distant through the collar's shield, but tangible.

"You know what she will do," he repeated, looking at me with that pained look still in his eyes. "Please, Allie. *Please*. Do not make me do it! I do not want to."

I felt my light lash out in a furious pulse. It activated the collar's shock, forcing me to stop, to pull it back before it hurt for real. Wincing, giving a near gasp, I clasped my neck, fighting for self-control. I couldn't control the anger, but I managed to dim my light.

He noticed, and his face reflected that pain once more. "We have made no demands on you of this kind before now. Voi Pai has treated you as an equal...as a sister..."

"Even though I outrank her..."

"We have made no demands! You *owe* the Lao Hu, and we have gone out of our way to ensure your dignity! To treat you fairly..."

"And I have refused no one before now. *No one,* Ulai. I haven't raised a protest to a single person you've brought through my door..."

"Allie...it is done! He is under orders, and so are we."

I bit my lip. After a longer pause, where I turned this over in my mind, I faced him once again. At his stone-faced look, I gestured angrily at the closed door.

"*Who* has bought me, Ulai?" I said. "Who would send *him* to me, to assess my well-being? Who would trust that piece of shit with a job like that?"

But Ulai was staring at me now, understanding in his eyes.

"You know him? You know this Wvercian, Esteemed Bridge?"

I felt my jaw harden more. Folding my arms tighter, so that they cinched my ribs, I stared back at the door leading to the hallway to the reception room.

Ulai hesitated, and I felt a pulse of grief off him. Nothing else in his light wavered.

"Allie. I cannot disobey her," he said. "I cannot."

I didn't answer, but I felt my light grow dense, vibrating the collar.

"Alyson!" He caught hold of my arms, forcing me to look at him. "Please! Do this thing. Just do it...and then it will be over! He will not hurt you! We have received the utmost in assurances that he will not harm you in any way..."

I stared up at him, but my mind remained blank...back in that flatline place.

I knew he was telling the truth. I studied his eyes, trying to think past what I knew, but nothing came. I saw the regret on his face. He knew what this would do to how I felt about him, even as a friend. None of these things mattered. None were enough to sway him.

Even with all of my cynicism, I'd been deluding myself. Whatever I told myself I had in the way of safety, of friends, of dignity here, was nothing less than a complete illusion.

I looked at Ulai, unable to feel...anything.

I knew full well, who I was dealing with in Voi Pai. I thought about the reality of that, how things might go if I called her bluff, if I let them drag me in there, tie me up or drug me like one of those females I'd seen in the work camps. I also thought about what I would have to do, if I went into that room willingly. I wondered if I could even pull it off. Honestly, it might be worth the bruises and the humiliation, just to avoid that.

Then something else occurred to me.

It took another few seconds for that thought to fully penetrate my mind. Once it had, I nodded, once.

"Fine," I said. My voice came out abrupt. "Fine. I'll do it."

I looked at Ulai. He stared back at me in surprise. The bewilderment was so intense in his expression that I worried he might have read my thoughts. My jaw hardened.

"She'll drug me if I refuse?" I said. "Tie me up, whatever?"

Ulai hesitated, then nodded reluctantly.

"Then I'll do it," I said, my jaw hardening once more. I folded my arms. "But I want four times the credit for it. Towards my debt."

There was a silence.

I waited, knowing Ulai was checking my terms with Voi Pai. His irises clicked back into focus a few seconds later.

"She agrees."

I nodded, once. "Then bring me back to my room. I'll wait for him there."

Relief expanded off Ulai's light. He caressed my face with his fingers, but I jerked away from his touch, feeling my mouth harden. He barely seemed to notice.

"Thank you." He touched my hair, murmuring, his light still exuding relief. "...Thank you, beautiful Bridge. The Lao Hu owes you a debt, Esteemed sister. The venerable Voi Pai thanks you, too. She is most grateful...she will ensure that you are rewarded beyond your asking price, in such a way that you deem fair, that is worthy of your concession..."

I bit my lip at that, but didn't meet his gaze.

"Whatever," I muttered.

Still smiling, still exuding relief, he only nodded, as if he hadn't heard me at all.

I followed him back to my client chamber sandwiched between the two rooms they'd given me for myself, and we didn't talk. I don't remember thinking much, either. My mind remained partly focused on the fact that I would soon be alone with the Wvercian leader, but I kept those thoughts vague as well...other than my overall opinion about the situation, which was hardly a secret. Mostly, I just let my mind go blank.

I didn't have to wait long. Ulai barely had time to resume his usual place by the door, following his routine security scan and the removal of my collar for the client.

I didn't sit. With the collar gone, I could already feel him.

I tried to see pieces of the missing story I'd glimpsed through Ulai and Voi Pai...and even in the worried and frantic light of my wardrobe seers. But Wvercian light had always been strange to me, difficult to read. I could rarely get real thoughts from it, even from Baguen, who never shielded overtly in my presence. Instead I got a kind of thick flowing feeling, sometimes with emotions, but more often with a feeling of separation...as if I studied their aleimic bodies through a deep pool of water.

This one's presence did not hide from mine, either. I felt his anticipation under that heavier fog, that feeling of disconnection inherent to Wvercian light. He looked forward to this, and my clear unwillingness didn't put a dent in that anticipation at all; for all I could tell, it may have heightened it. I felt a broader knowing in his light as well...kind of an 'on mission' feeling I recognized from the Adhipan and even from Revik. With that, I also felt a flavor of reverence. This duty had a religious component to it, for him anyway. That didn't mean it did for whoever hired him. Yet, it made a perverse kind of sense, too.

I stood by the largest of the couches, next to a waiting pot of steeping tea and two cups. I didn't move from that spot as the giant, near-albino seer entered through the main door. He was greeted with a deep bow from Ulai, but barely seemed to notice.

In the same instant, Ulai gave me a faintly encouraging look, before he darted out through the cloth-covered door, standing on the other side of its round, wooden entrance.

That was new, too. No guard. I guess that was part of the agreement.

I turned my head, fighting all expression out of my light as I faced the Wvercian.

He walked into the room and glanced around at the furnishings, but not like Surli had. He did it more like a caretaker looking over his owner's property. His black eyes, when they met mine, looked at me the same way.

Almost. The difference shone behind those black irises, barely discernible in the flat density of that gaze. He walked towards me without speaking, not seeming to care that I hadn't spoken. I studied his thick face, trying not to let my eyes drift down to the scar on his throat.

He stepped right up to me, so there would be no mistaking the height discrepancy between us. I couldn't help myself calculating roughly what that was. I'd never measured Revik or anything, but I guessed him at somewhere just over six and a half feet. The Wvercian in front of me had to be over seven feet, easy.

He seemed to enjoy watching me estimate his size. A bare smile touched his thick lips, right before his eyes flickered down my body. For the first time, I felt arousal off him. It pulsed off his aleimi, thick and dense, like the rest of his light.

"They treating you all right, girl?" he said.

His voice came out surprisingly soft.

I didn't let my expression move. While he waited for my answer, he looked down at me again, focusing on my bare feet with the twin circlets of bronze anklets.

Meeting his gaze, I unfolded my arms.

"What difference does it make?" I said. "...Boy?"

His heavy gaze flickered up.

For an instant, I saw surprise there, a faint thread of something darker. He smiled then, looking from one of my eyes to the other.

"You don't want my cock in you?" he said. "Why, sister?"

The question sounded oddly genuine. Fighting back my surprise, and his attempt to engage me in eye contact again, I shrugged, not returning his gaze.

"I'd prefer not to rut with barn animals," I said.

A silence fell over the room. I didn't look at him through it.

Then he surprised me, laughing aloud.

"What made you change your mind?" he said.

"What makes you think I did?" I retorted.

His smile widened. I felt warmth on him then, a pulse of feeling that made me flinch.

"I am glad they have not broken you, Esteemed Bridge," he said, softer once more.

That reverence touched his voice, just audible enough that I glanced over at him, in spite of myself. His gaze was heavy again, looking at me through the thin fabric.

"I'm going to enjoy fucking you," he said then, his voice thicker. "More than I can tell you...I hope I can help you to enjoy it, as well, sister..."

I heard the cajole in his voice, and looked away again, clicking softly to myself. I could tell he was trying to win me over in his own way. It more angered than confused me, but I felt enough of both that I couldn't quite meet his gaze.

"Were you unsure before?" I retorted. "Am I not your type, brother?"

He smiled again, unperturbed by my words.

"I volunteered, Esteemed Bridge," he said. "And believe me when I tell you...I am very glad that I did."

Shaking my head, I clicked at him again, louder that time.

He only laughed. He moved then, faster than I would have credited him, given his size. His hand reached out in the same moment. Before I could step out of his reach, he caught hold of my breast, sliding his fingers over the thin fabric of the shift I wore. I forced myself to remain where I was, but my whole body stiffened.

"You like that, Esteemed Sister?" he said, his voice thicker.

I gave him an incredulous look, pushing his hand away in irritation.

"Are you going to be able to get it up?" I said. "Now that I've agreed?"

He smiled. I saw that predatory glint sharpen in his eyes, though, even as they darted once more between mine.

"I'm up, girl," he said. "Talking to me like that is only making it harder..."

Pain rippled through my light at his words.

For a moment, I couldn't think clearly about why. Then I realized Revik had said something similar to me, that first day in the tank. Fighting the feeling out of my light, I avoided his eyes as I stepped back towards the table with the pot of tea.

"You're sure?" I said coldly, reaching for the bamboo handle of the pot. I poured a cup for him, and then another for myself. "After all, I'm a little old for you for your usual tastes."

"Are you, now?" His voice was amused. "Is that what they tell you?"

"It is," I said. "Is that why you keep calling me 'girl'?"

I straightened as I said it, handing him a cup of the tea I'd just poured.

He didn't take it, but stared at me, his eyes sliding between mine once more. I watched his face grow wary, just before he stepped up to me again. That time, he slid his hand under the collared top of the dress, yanking it off my neck roughly, nearly making me lose my balance. Biting my lip, I just stood there, holding the cup of tea as he gripped my breast again. His fingers tightened when I wouldn't look at him, twisting enough that I winced, still holding the tea.

"You want to see, Esteemed One?" he said, his voice soft.

I forced my eyes to the floor, not answering.

Then I shrugged, my voice bored.

"If it makes you feel better. Sure."

He laughed, startling me again.

Before I could turn my head, he knocked the cup out of my hand, breaking the china and spilling the tea in a splash across the wooden floor. His other hand grabbed hold of one of my wrists in the same motion, yanking me towards him.

I half-stumbled into his bulky form. Before I'd regained my balance, he took my hand, pressing my palm and fingers against his crotch and forcing them to squeeze.

Pain rippled off him when I complied.

His fingers gripped mine harder, his other hand caressing my breast.

"How's that, little girl?" he said. His voice came out slightly gruff. "Big enough for you?"

I met his gaze. "Does it make *you* feel big...?"

"Is that why you refused me? Afraid of Wvercian cock?"

I bit my lip, averting my gaze. I heard him smile.

"You haven't been broken in by one of my family yet, have you, girl?"

I met his gaze, my eyes flat.

He smiled wider. "I'll be good to you, girl. Promise. I'll treat you real good..."

"Sure you will."

His eyes hardened a little, but the smile never faltered. "You seem awfully angry, given that you suck cock for a living. Did I do something to you I don't know about? Did one of my family hurt you? Or is this just a general hatred for all of your brothers?"

I didn't look at him at first.

Then the images came, fast enough that I couldn't block the feeling that rose behind them. Feeling a kind of pain hit my chest, I forced my eyes back up to his, even as I felt his light trying to probe mine, to find an answer to his questions. It struck me that I might be as difficult to read for him as he was for me. He felt some of it though.

Enough that I saw a harder look come to his face.

"You *do* know me...or think you do, anyway." The smile on his lips didn't soften the look living in those black eyes. "All right. If we've got such a sordid past together...what's my name, girl?"

I stared at the floor, fighting back the pain, feeling a kind of heat in my chest.

"What is it?" he said. "Come on. You think you have something to say to me...so say it." He made a thick sound, nearly a grunt. It might have been a laugh, but for the irritation in it. "I haven't even *been* to your part of the world since before you were born...so whatever you think you know, it's not about me."

The pain in my chest worsened. I knew it was irrational. I knew.

I also knew I might end up regretting what I was about to do.

But I didn't care.

I really didn't give a rat's ass.

"I know your name," I said. My eyes fell, staring at his hands on me.

"Do you now? Tell me, then. I'm starting to get bored of this fight, girl."

The lightness had returned to his voice, almost masking the deeper irritation underneath. I felt the pain under that though, his impatience with talking. He wanted to do what he'd come here to do; he was sick of our back and forth, and no longer cared what I thought.

"Tell me," he said. He softened his voice again, caressing my breast under the dress. I felt his erection grow under my hand and winced, but didn't try to pull away. His voice turned gruff once more, even as he pressed my palm tighter against him.

"Tell me my name, girl. For you to be so angry, you must know that at least. And tell me what wrong I did to you, to make you despise me so..."

I looked up, feeling nothing now.

"Your name is Gerwix," I said.

His fingers froze on my skin. So did his face, which had been lowering to mine.

For a long moment, he didn't move. He stood there, poised, where he'd been about to try to kiss me. We stared at one another, our faces only about a foot apart.

Through that silence, though, he barely seemed to comprehend what I'd said. The blank look on his broad face appeared confused more than angry.

For the barest instant, I thought maybe I'd been wrong, that I was imagining things.

Then my eyes shifted to the scar on his throat, and I knew I wasn't wrong. He didn't even look that different, despite the age that creased his skin, and darkened the circles under his eyes, flaring crow's feet from wind and sun.

As he stared at me, his dark eyes widened.

For an instant, I thought I saw fear there...but I may have imagined it.

Whatever it had been, it swiftly morphed into anger. The depth of that anger, the confusion of things I felt behind it, probably would have frightened me under normal circumstances...or maybe just if I'd really cared anymore, what happened to me. I felt the animal there again, the predator, and I knew I hadn't been wrong.

His words, when he finally spoke, seemed to burst out of him.

"Where did you hear that name, girl?" he said.

When I didn't answer, his thick, red fingers grabbed my shoulders. He shook me hard, roughly, enough to rattle my teeth.

"Who the *fuck* told you that name?" he demanded, his voice rising, growing more harsh. "Where did you hear it, bitch? Where?"

I looked up, gasping a little from his hold on me.

He held me higher, to stare into my face; my feet barely touched the ground. For a long moment, I could only look at him, trying to understand what rattled him so much, what he thought he had to be afraid of.

"Do you know who I work for?" he said. "Do you?"

For some reason, I smiled.

"Gerwix," I said softly. "...Nenzi says hi."

His eyes widened more, lost in a kind of blank disbelief.

"What?" he said. "What the *fuck* did you – "

He didn't get any further.

Something in me let go, relaxing every muscle in my body.

In the same breath, I released the fist coiled around that part of my light.

The folding sensation came without warning. Strong, like a drug. It rippled through me, so rapidly I barely exhaled before it exploded out of me...so dense I choked on my own breath. It had been so long since I'd done that...it felt even longer than it had been in reality. I hadn't even let myself think about using it, or what I'd done with it in the past, working with Revik and his rebels. The sensation brought up a near-pain, a longing as it pulsed out of me. It fought its way through darkened structures in my aleimi, a rush of heat that sang in my light, wanting nothing more than to do what I willed it to do.

I felt that sense of belonging, of pulling the Barrier into myself... projecting it out onto the world. I felt the difference in my body, bringing that fire into the grayer light of the mundane.

I felt that wanting to go back.

It was almost a wanting to die.

Atoms vibrated around me, rushing like crystals through a wash of insubstantial matter. Spaces peered between the flecks and I lived in those spaces. I belonged here. I belonged with everyone here, even the Wvercian standing across from me. We were family, in that light...and what I was doing for him...

...It was a gift. An act of love.

It was over so fast I found myself gasping.

I had to fight to pull it back, to not make it go further...spread further... touch others...spread that warmth and love to them. A part of me wanted to throw that heat over the whole City, to wash away all of the gray around me, to make it one with the fire of those clouds over my head...

I wanted it...enough that it hurt...

I wanted it so badly.

But I remembered...I remembered Revik's words.

I remembered what happened before. Not only to him.

I remembered the Registry, the burning bodies, the smell of singed hair and flesh, a barbecue smell, melting organics that smelled darker, like decay and rubber and plastic burning in a hotter, darker fire...the coil of smoke bursting out through a broken window...

Forcing it back, I gasped it in like breaths, swallowing it almost.

I jerked out of the space, and...

...heard a loud crack.

It was loud. Too loud.

I winced, throwing my body backwards when those giant hands released me. I was still fighting my way back into the room as my vision clicked into focus.

He collapsed, a broken doll.

He fell on me, directly on me. His weight crashed into mine so fast I barely had time to slide my own body out of the way. Turning on one leg in reflex, as if I were fighting him in mulei, I shifted my weight to the right, pulling my shoulders as his thick body crumpled. He hit the floor hard. Hard enough that I worried I'd hurt him.

...Until I remembered that he didn't feel anything anymore.

For what felt like a long time, I could only stand there, paralyzed, light-headed from the telekinesis. I looked down at his collapsed form, which seemed smaller somehow. I watched the light dissipate from around the meat like smoke. I stared at his blank eyes, watching those lose light, too. The only sound I heard came from my own breathing, which seemed to hitch out of me in uneven pants.

Then Ulai stood beside me.

I heard him shouting, from somewhere inside all of that silence, overlain with my shifting and jerking breaths. Then he was holding my shoulders, shaking me like that giant had only moments before. Shaking me and yelling, and fear stood out plainly in his eyes.

I couldn't hear him though. I was the one trapped underwater now.

An odd ringing filled my ears. Minutes passed that felt like hours before I felt the presences, sliding and whispering in my light. It wasn't until then that I realized how far in that other place most of my light remained.

I knew where I was.

I was there again. I was in the golden valley...

Tears came to my eyes. Feeling sank me to my knees. I was lost there, unable to dig my way out. I felt the waves of light, the ocean pooling at my waist, tugging at my feet in the current. I looked down at my bare toes, saw them glowing under that clear water, digging into pearl-white sand. But he wasn't there. He wasn't with me.

I was alone, staring up at that golden valley in a wash of hot sunlight, feeling the ocean's waves lap my sides...the sun reflecting gold and white diamonds on its rippling surface below red and orange-tinged clouds. I stood there, and I didn't want to leave. It occurred to me, for the first time maybe, that I could just end it, like he'd offered in that green-tiled room. I could end it, and in time, he'd be there with me. I wouldn't have to do this anymore.

It could be over. Really over.

I thought about that from a concubine's room inside the Forbidden City...still far away.

Security flooded through the doors on all sides.

I stared at the ring of guns on me, and all I could think was, it's okay.

Whatever they did to me now, it would all be okay.

Twenty-Three
Rynak

R EVIK LAY ON THE FLOOR, STARING UP AT A DARK GREEN CEILING. EVEN WITH THE collar, it felt different being outside the tank, almost disorienting... and not only from the lack of chains. His light was still adjusting, as was his body. As if in reminder of that, he winced a little when he sat up, enough that the man next to him noticed.

"Your ribs bothering you?"

A thread of humor underlay his words.

Revik rolled his eyes. "You wish."

"You sure about that?" Balidor said. "Not feeling a bit tender?"

Revik shook his head, snorting in spite of himself. "I don't know how you've managed not to be fragged in the last three hundred years. For such an old seer, you're a juvenile shit."

Balidor chuckled, slapping him on the shoulder. "Takes one to know one."

Despite his words, Revik felt the Adhipan leader continue to study his face, his gray eyes holding a thread of something else.

"Is it bothering you again?" he said finally.

Revik didn't meet his gaze.

Unwinding the cloth wraps from around his hands, he fought back the pain in his light. The collar protested a little as he expended his aleimi in order to control it, but not enough to deter him.

Even so, his jaw tightened at Balidor's question. He glanced at the other seer.

"She's got a boyfriend," he said.

Balidor blinked a little, staring at him. "How can you be sure?"

Revik gave him a hard look.

Balidor held up his hands, exuding a pulse of regret. "Sorry. I just meant..." He hesitated. "It might not mean anything. It might just be sex, Nenz."

Revik didn't answer at first. Slowly, he pulled himself to his feet, focusing on his body instead. He stretched his arms over his head, and winced again. That time, it was because of the shot he'd gotten to the ribs, but Balidor either didn't notice, or chose not to comment due to the other's mood. Finally, Revik looked at him again.

"Well, either she's fucking a lot of people...or she has a boyfriend," he commented finally.

Balidor winced, but didn't argue that time. He continued to study the Elaerian's face. "Sorry, Nenz."

Revik shrugged it off, but didn't say the obvious. Instead he found himself staring at the wall, his hands on his waist. He still couldn't feel where she was...much less who she was with. He just got sick. The kind of sick he couldn't think past, couldn't fully suppress, maybe with or without the collar. The feeling was new to him; he'd never felt anything like it the one other time she'd been unfaithful to him. He'd never felt it with anyone else, either.

It was worse than separation pain...more like being forced to share light with someone he didn't know. So there was a feeling of being violated, but it was worse than that, too...the foreign light actually made him ill. He knew a lot of it was simply from having someone other than her in his light. Even happening through her, it still felt wrong, like the other light didn't belong there. Worse, although he couldn't see any of it, he could still feel her. It felt like being forced to watch, only he couldn't actually see anything...the only way he could deal with that side of things was to blank out his mind altogether.

He'd thought before that if he'd been able to see her with Balidor, it might not have hurt so bad afterwards; he'd assumed that being forced to rely on his imagination made everything worse. He didn't believe that anymore.

He could tell she was shielding. It just wasn't really working. Not enough anyway.

He wondered if Allie had ever felt that same feeling. In DC. On the ship. He didn't voice any of that to Balidor, though.

They were in one of the larger residency rooms in the underground caverns. They'd converted the space into Revik's new "cell," following his graduation from chains and the tank, but everyone treated it like his quarters.

The Adhipan guards remained outside his door, but had a tendency to hang out inside the room with him just as often. While Revik occasionally felt their scans of his light, and more often, Tarsi and Vash adjusting things in his aleimi...they mostly left him alone. Inside the caves, his options were limited, but he still appreciated it.

Anyway, he supposed Balidor had taken it upon himself to guard him, in a way.

"Are you hungry?" the Adhipan leader asked.

Forcing back another thread of pain that tried to creep into his throat, he shook his head. Nausea overwhelmed him briefly, but he forced it out of his light, bringing another faint jolt from the collar. He fought to ignore it, stretching his back.

"No," he said.

Balidor stared at him, his eyes showing him at a loss. "Nenz."

"Does anyone know where she is yet?" he said, ignoring the concern in the other's voice. "Have any of your people found her?"

"No." Balidor shook his head, his eyes going more flat. "We may have to wait for you, my friend. All of the leads my people and our contacts have chased have died."

Revik bit his lip. He fought to suppress the emotion that rose, but didn't succeed.

"You're the fucking Adhipan, aren't you?" he said. "Why can't you find her?" It came out of him before he knew he meant to speak. At the compassion he saw in the other's eyes, he looked away, fighting the impatience out of his voice with an effort.

"Did Vash give you a date yet?"

"No, not yet."

"Just uncollar me, damn it!" he said. "Jesus, 'Dor. You know I won't hurt you."

Balidor laughed a little, turning his head to show him the bruise on his jaw.

"You know what I mean." Frustration leaked further into his voice. "What is he waiting for? Does he really think I'm going to go on a killing spree?"

Balidor clicked softly. "No. I don't think that's what concerns him."

"Then what?"

Balidor gestured vaguely, about to answer...

...when another voice answered from the doorway.

"He might be worried about me," the voice said flatly.

Revik turned his head, staring at the seer standing there.

He knew the voice...knew the face and eyes he met even better, but for a moment he only stood there, in the middle of the high-ceilinged room, unmoving. He couldn't quite make up his mind whether to believe his eyes... not until they found the gun in the man's hand. It wasn't pointed at him, but at the seer on the floor behind him.

Revik moved his body, placing it between the two men.

"No." He looked the armed seer in the face, shaking his head, once. "Wreg. Don't."

"Don't?" Wreg turned his eyes back to his, and for an instant, Revik saw a flicker of emotion there. "This son of a bitch has you *collared*, boss."

Revik couldn't help but smile.

His eyes never left the seer in front of him. The broad-chested, tattooed male with the long, black ponytail looked almost exactly as he'd last seen him. Even so, something about having him standing right in front of him brought up a rush of feeling, more than he knew what to do with precisely. Memories coalesced behind his eyes, trading this version of the seer with the one who'd given him the tattoo all those years ago. He'd remembered a lot of these things with Salinse, too, but all of it felt different now. More real. The man in front of him felt more real, too.

Unable to express any of this, he averted his gaze.

Clicking softly, he glanced at Balidor, then back at his second in command.

At a loss briefly, he gestured vaguely with one hand.

"How the hell did you get in here, Wreg?" he said.

The Chinese-looking seer stared at him, his expression nearly blank.

Revik felt a whisper of worry. "Your people. They aren't – "

"No one's dead, Nenz...yet." Wreg continued to stare at him, his eyes showing him to be at a loss, too. "What the hell is going on here? A picnic? I thought we were rescuing you..."

Revik's smile turned into a grin. Without thought, he walked directly up to the muscular seer and pulled him into a rough bear hug. Still seemingly at a loss, Wreg accepted the embrace, clapping him on the back with his free arm.

"And I can't shoot this Adhipan prick?" he said, his voice still bewildered.

"No," Revik said. He laughed, releasing the other seer. "Are you all right, brother?"

"Am *I* all right?"

"We'd heard rumors...about the Lao Hu."

"No." Wreg continued to stare at him for a moment. Then, clicking, he shook his head. He amended his words. "Well...yes. But we worked something out with them."

"Yeah," Revik said, studying his eyes. He had to suppress another flood of feeling, and managed it only by grinning wider. "We heard that, too."

"I really can't shoot this fucker, Nenz?"

Revik laughed. "No. I owe him my life...so I'd prefer it if you didn't. Anyway, we need him. We're not exactly in a position to be disposing of high-ranked seers..."

"Can I take the fucking collar off at least?"

Revik glanced at Balidor, who was looking between the two of them, a vague tension around his eyes. It faded as he returned Revik's gaze, but it crossed Revik's mind that Balidor really hadn't been sure he wouldn't kill him...not until that moment.

At the thought, Revik found himself staring at the Adhipan seer, thinking about this for the first time. Whatever else, Balidor really was no coward. He'd not been sure what he'd do, but he'd stayed with him anyway. He could just as easily have left, as soon as he'd completed his work with Revik in the tank. Hell, he could have been out looking for Allie.

At the thought, Revik frowned.

But the Adhipan leader was trying to answer Wreg's question. After another pause, where his eyes fell slightly out of focus, Balidor nodded.

"Yeah. Vash agrees. I'll take it off him..."

"Wouldn't want to waste the tech," Wreg muttered. His expression remained puzzled, aimed at Revik's face. But Balidor answered him, his own voice grim.

"No, brother...we wouldn't. Not considering how they're harvesting it these days."

Wreg grunted, his eyes unmoving, but his hand conceded the point.

His gun came down for real then. Wreg still looked annoyed, and more than a little confused, but he holstered the Mateba semi-automatic revolver as Revik watched. Revik remembered the gun; Wreg had carried that damned thing for years, even though he'd switched to the more standard Beretta M9 for most military ops, when he wasn't carrying an organic-modified M16 or G36. Revik smiled a little looking at it, strangely comforted by the familiarity, even with this. Balidor watched him put it away, too, and Revik saw the sharpness in his eyes fade. His shoulders visibly relaxed, too.

Wreg likely noticed as well. Clearly, Balidor meant him to.

Even so, Revik noticed a thread of nerves still in the Adhipan leader's light. He smiled a little wider, unable to help himself.

"You sure about that, 'Dori?" he said. "Taking it off? I owe you a few good hits."

"Like hell you do."

"Maybe I'm still holding a grudge from the other day..."

"I guess we'll find out," the older seer grunted.

He pulled himself somewhat stiffly to his feet as he said the last. Motioning with his fingers for Revik to turn around, he closed the gap between them. When Revik only stood there, Balidor cleared his throat in some amusement, tapping at his shoulder from behind and motioning for him to bend his knees so he could reach the back of the collar.

Revik complied, still watching Wreg as Balidor activated the thumbnail switch. The rebel commander folded his thick, tattooed arms, staring at Revik as if perhaps trying to determine if he'd lost his mind...or perhaps if he really had some plan in all this, and would kill Balidor once he was free. Or maybe he was wondering if they had brainwashed him in some way, or doped him up on heavy narcotics. In any case, Revik could feel himself being scanned, although the collar made it impossible for him to pick up anything specific. Again, for some reason, this touched him more than annoyed him, and caused him to give Wreg another reassuring smile.

Balidor activated the retinal scanner as Revik continued to watch the other seer.

A faint vibration trembled the skin at his neck, and then it was over. Revik gasped a little, feeling the organic coils unwrap from around the bone at the top of his spine.

The sensation filled him with relief, even as the nausea violently spiked. Fighting with it, he clutched at his chest.

He'd forgotten how long it had been until the mechanism clunked open around his neck. He barely had a chance to enjoy the freedom of his light, however. Within seconds, as his light filtered back around him, the wave of sickness nearly overwhelmed him. Fighting back a surge of bile in his throat, he closed his eyes, leaning a hand against the wall.

Balidor caught one of his arms. Wreg caught the other, and Revik found himself in the almost humorous position of standing between the two men.

"I'm all right," he said, avoiding both of their eyes.

"You sure about that?" Balidor said.

"Yeah, I'm sure."

"You should sit a moment. I should have had you sit...I am sorry. Vash warned me...it was part of why he was waiting to uncollar you. He wanted to come up with some solution before you were forced to deal with it without filters..."

The concern was audible in his voice, and Wreg stared at the Adhipan leader, that incredulousness back in his eyes.

"What the *fuck* is going on?" he burst out.

His anger barely masked his frustration. He'd finished scanning Revik. Not finding anything wrong with him only seemed to anger him more.

"What have you been doing here, *laoban?*" he said. "We thought we were here to rescue you...to break you free of being their damned captive... likely to lose lives in the process. Then we get offered tea by that human brother of your wife...and that Seven fossil is inviting us to stay for dinner. Now shithead here is acting like your wet nurse..."

Revik burst out in a laugh, glancing at Balidor, who clicked at him, smiling ruefully, an eyebrow raised. "You weren't here earlier," Revik said to Wreg. "When I kicked his ass...even with a collar on. He begged me before he tapped out..."

Balidor rolled his eyes. "You are so completely full of shit, Illustrious Liar..."

But Wreg only looked between them, his anger worsening.

"Nenz!" He slammed a hand against the organic wall. "What is going on? Are you all one big happy family now...? With this asshole who seduced your wife?"

Revik gave him a hard look.

Then he glanced at Balidor.

The Adhipan seer shrugged, giving him a flat look in return, as if to concede Wreg's point. At the same time, he opened his light deliberately, letting Revik in past his shields, allowing him to feel whatever he wanted. Getting a glimmer of the intent behind that, too, even without probing for specifics, Revik felt his shoulders relax a little more. He realized he hadn't really let it go. Maybe he never would, really...but it was enough.

To be able to feel the other seer's light, to really feel it, for the first time since he'd been there...was enough.

Glancing at Wreg again, he couldn't help but smile a little, shaking his head.

"Yeah," he said. "I guess so."

Revik sat in the control room, his feet propped on the organic console. He still felt strange, being there, but he found his light adjusting to the surrounding folds of the Seven...and even the Adhipan...in a way that let him relax for the first time in what felt like months.

Scanning Wreg's light another time, he glanced at Mila, then at Loki.

He frowned a little, feeling the faint flavor of silver light still woven into their aleimi. It clung strongest of all to Wreg, which wasn't surprising, but bothered him the most. He wondered if it would be enough, even if the older seer agreed.

Wreg seemed to understand him the best, but he also seemed the most irritated by what he'd asked of them.

"But why, *laoban*? They've given us everything we've ever wanted... resources past anything these kneelers can offer you..."

Revik shook his head. "I'm sorry, brother. It's non-negotiable." He hesitated, then made a conciliatory gesture with one hand. "...And anyway, it will unite the two factions of seers..."

"And break it into three factions..." Wreg muttered.

"Four, really," Revik replied. "The Lao Hu will not likely join us, either. Whatever agreements you have made with them." He paused again, his voice holding a faint reproach. "And those same four existed before, Wreg."

"But Salinse and the others..."

"Will be against us, yes," Revik said. "Which is why I'm making it voluntary. You can go whichever way you want. I mean it, Wreg...I'm simply telling you where I am going, and what I would require if you want to come with me."

Wreg gave him an irritated look. "Because I would follow some old man, instead of the Sword? I swore my loyalty to you, *laoban*."

Revik met his gaze. He opened his light to the other man, knowing he wouldn't be able to reach him at this point, not fully anyway, but letting more of himself shine through anyway. At the same time, that emotion came back, coloring his words.

"It is for you I do this, Wreg," he said, quoting the words quietly. "Trust me, brother. We don't need them. We never did...but we definitely don't now. Once I find Allie, we can..." He saw the other flinch and this time he stopped, staring at his light.

"What?"

Wreg shook his head, gesturing dismissively. Revik noticed he didn't quite meet his gaze. As he thought it, Wreg's jaw hardened.

"What makes you think you will find her, *laoban?*" he said.

"What makes you think he won't?" Balidor asked, from the other side of the room.

Wreg gave him a hard look, before shifting his gaze back to Revik. "I just mean...if she left here, and has refused to take her post as Bridge, what is there to discuss?"

"She left under a misunderstanding," Revik said, not looking at him.

"Did she? And whose misunderstanding was it?" Wreg said. He glanced at Balidor long enough to frown. "Does she know you are pals with her lover now?"

Revik flinched at his words, but didn't manage to pull the anger out of his voice.

"Wreg, you've heard my condition. You can stay or go...but we need you to decide within the next twenty-four hours. Anyone who will not agree must leave by then."

"Ute is already gone," Wreg said.

Revik acknowledged this with a wave of one hand. "You are still here."

Wreg stared at him. Then he shook his head, giving Balidor another angry look. "I still don't like that fucker, Nenz..."

Balidor chuckled. Revik merely smiled, his eyes still on Wreg's.

"I can live with that, my brother. Please stay...if you would."

Wreg sat down then, taking the seat next to his.

"Do it then," he said, sighing. "Have your witch doctor perform his operation."

Revik pinged Vash in the other room, hiding his relief badly as he glanced at Balidor, and then back at Wreg. Wreg studied his face for a moment.

Snorting then, he smiled, seemingly in spite of himself.

"You feared fighting on opposite sides with me, *laoban?*" He grunted again, clicking softly. "I suppose I should be flattered by that." He paused, still assessing Revik's eyes. Nodding then, almost to himself, he leaned back in his chair, opening his light. "Or were you only afraid you would have to kill me, runt?"

Revik didn't answer. Part of his light remained focused on the higher structures in the other seer's aleimi, watching Vash unravel what had been put there by the Dreng and by Salinse. He glimpsed the flickering of the other's light, saw Wreg feel the shift too. For an instant, fear shone in his near-black eyes. Seeing it, Revik held his gaze, laying a hand on his muscled shoulder.

"Your light will be stronger for this," he assured him. "We do not need the Dreng to fight our battles for us."

"And the gods of the Seven?" Wreg grunted, giving him a wry look.

"Only if you pray to them, my brother," Revik quoted, smiling back.

"And if I don't?"

Revik shrugged with one hand. "There is no contract here. No one here will force your light to conform to their need. I won't permit it."

Wreg clicked again, softly, a faint skepticism in his eyes.

But Revik continued to watch the other seer's light, noticing subtle changes as the silver sheen of the Dreng began to dissipate slowly...as even more slowly, the harder structures began to dissolve. Seeing Wreg's outline grow both softer and yet somehow more clearly defined, he smiled, unable to stop himself. He glanced up at Jax and Holo, who had just entered the organic-paneled, octagon-shaped room.

"And you? What will you decide?"

Jax laughed, shoving playfully at his arm even as Jon entered through another doorway, holding what was probably a mug of coffee. Holo shook his head at the same time, clicking at Revik sharply, as though deeply offended.

Revik saw the humor in the shorter seer's eyes, however.

"We go with the Sword," he said. "It is already done in us, can you not see it?"

"Really, brother," Jax said, going along with Holo. "We thought we would register on your scale of recruits a little more than that!"

Smiling faintly at the humor in their eyes, Revik gave Jon a brief nod in welcome, gesturing in seer sign language that he wanted a coffee, too. Jon rolled his eyes, then handed him the one he'd brought, as if to say, "D'uh." He then gestured back that food was coming for all of them. It couldn't help but amuse Revik a little, that Jon knew sign language so well. He knew it a lot better than Allie, actually...or at least better than she had when he'd last spent time with her.

Taking a sip of the coffee after nodding a thanks, he focused back on the light of Jax and Holo. He fell into the Barrier briefly, just enough to see the truth of their words. Scanning them a few more times, in admiration of Vash's thoroughness as much as anything, he smiled as the two of them began talking to Jon, relaxing still more. He noticed then that Mila and Loki were in the Barrier too, and watched briefly as Vash began working on their light as well.

Revik found his light relaxing still more. With Jax and Holo and Wreg, that was five in under an hour. Hardly everyone, but certainly not nothing.

Glancing at the door again, he nodded to Dorje as he entered, but the Tibetan-looking seer was looking only at Balidor, his face slightly pinched.

Revik didn't think about the expression at first. Instead, he found his mind drifting to Ute, and to Yarli, who had left earlier that same day, pretty much the moment they understood that Revik intended to work with the Adhipan and the Seven, and not butcher them wholesale. Rigor and Tan had left as well.

He knew many of the rebels would do as they had, and leave rather than lose their connection to the Dreng. He'd expected it, braced for it...but not losing Wreg had almost compensated for losing the other four. He'd been afraid to hope that the older seer's loyalty might extend that far, but he couldn't suppress his relief that it had.

To have the four younger seers throw in with him so easily heartened him even more. More than he could really express, at least in words. Smiling wider at Jax and Holo when they looked over, he nodded, folding his arms across his chest and leaning back in the padded chair.

"That is good you are staying," he said in formal Prexci. "...very good. I thank you."

"Jesli is staying, too," Holo offered. "She is with that old seer now...along with Garensche and Silwa."

Smiling wider, Revik nodded. "Eight. So half of you, then."

"It will be more than half," Holo said, confident. "Once we reach out to the others."

"You do not mind the stink of the Adhipan?" Poresh said teasingly.

Holo answered him more seriously. "Not if you mean it...that the Sword is in charge."

Dorje looked faintly surprised at this. "The Bridge is in charge, you mean."

Holo looked at Revik. So did Jax.

Revik acknowledged this with a gesture of his fingers, not quite meeting either gaze. "Where is she, then?" Jax said.

Revik hesitated.

He glanced at Balidor, pausing at the hard look on the other's face. He realized then, that the older seer wasn't listening to any of them, and perhaps hadn't been for some time. Ever since Dorje entered the room and said something to him, he'd seemed distracted. Now he appeared to be doing something in VR, and watching one of the feeds. Without interrupting him, or answering Jax, Revik called up a duplicate channel on the screen closer to his hand.

Reading the feed signature, he frowned.

"Rynak," he muttered. He glanced at the Adhipan leader again.

Balidor didn't seem to notice he'd duplicated his feed.

"'Dor?" Revik said to him. "What are you doing?"

The older seer didn't look up, but Revik saw his frown deepen at whatever he was looking at. His gray eyes moved back and forth across the screen, as if reading one of the entries there. Revik saw his eyes move again a second later, as if he'd either re-read what he'd read before, or had scrolled down the page. But the image on Revik's screen didn't move.

"Balidor!" Revik said.

Balidor turned his head, meeting his gaze. When he saw who called him, his expression changed, holding less anger and more of a heavier reluctance. Revik saw a glimmer of guilt in his eyes as well, mixed with...something else. It occurred to him in the same instant that the other was shielding him, blocking him from pieces of his light.

It was the first time he'd noticed him doing so since he'd taken off the collar.

Revik glanced at Dorje, who wouldn't return his gaze, either. His eyes returned to Balidor. "What?" he said, sharper.

Balidor gestured at Wreg, not quite looking at him with his eyes.

"They did not quite tell you the truth, brother," he said quietly. "About how they got out of China. They had help."

The room grew deathly quiet.

Revik saw Wreg glance at Holo, then at Jax, as if threatening them with his eyes.

Studying their reactions briefly, Revik concentrated his focus back on Wreg, who was standing by the console again, his black hair hanging down to the middle of his back in a long braid. Revik studied the Chinese seer's light, feeling where Balidor indicated.

He felt a pulse of pain even before Wreg's eyes met his. Wreg's nearly black eyes held their own sort of reluctance, and the guilt there was stronger than it had been in Balidor. With the silver light gone, Revik saw more of him, as well. He saw pockets of his light that had been chambered off...places where he'd hidden things suddenly exposed. He saw enough that he could feel what Balidor was talking about, and kicked himself for not seeing it before.

Wreg was hiding something from him. He'd chambered it off in such a way that it had to be something pretty important. Revik remembered where Balidor had been looking on the feeds then, and returned his gaze to the screen.

He knew this particular feed, of course.

The Rynak was infamous.

It was shorthand for the market feed. The seer's black market, that is, and it was well-trafficked, particularly by those in trading and smuggling, but also among those with enough money to purchase rarer items. The Rynak had its own regulars, but its clientele was varied enough that it remained accessible to most seers without overt fear of reprisal from SCARB or the other authorities. The World Court pretty much ignored it, in fact.

Even so, it wasn't exactly common knowledge, either. One needed to know how to read it, and what they were looking at...and sometimes, for.

Entries in the Rynak were generally written in old Prexci only, which only the scholars and ancients still spoke, even though it continued to be taught in seer schools, sort of like how Latin or Sanskrit was for some human disciplines. Moreover, the Rynak's feed lines were constructed in a specific form, usually coming across as flowery if somewhat cryptic prose. The combination tended to confuse anyone who stumbled across it unknowingly.

Most adult seers could read it, of course, even outside the various hierarchies. The majority of pre-first contact seers knew how to read Old

Prexci...and could speak it even, under duress. Humans who traded in those markets, who lived professionally off the seer black markets, knew of the Rynak too, of course. Most required translation of the old-form Prexci, but there were humans who could read that, as well. For those who couldn't, any seer could be hired for a fee to translate it live.

Revik focused on the entry in front of him.

His eyes had skimmed over it before, perhaps unconsciously...perhaps because some part of him knew. Perhaps because he'd felt it already, in Balidor and Wreg's and Dorje's light. Now he forced his eyes to take in each word, to understand.

"...*Rare and exquisite jewel...over the water and with eyes of fire. Invitation by the white cat only, but requests to see her unique shine now considered for invite's extension. Limited time, buyer pending. For private showing, contact the gold wire and ask for the jade bird...*"

Something in his chest clenched. He stared at it, reading it again.

A voice over his head made him jump...making him wonder how long he'd sat there, silent.

"Gods." It was Wreg. "That bitch put it on the Rynak."

Revik forced his eyes up.

Seeing the hard, almost furious look on the other's face, he felt the pain in his chest worsen, growing into something closer to a clenching inside his ribs. It made it hard to breathe for a moment, almost to see.

He glanced at the others, as if for someone to refute what his mind was telling him. He saw Holo and Jax paling, staring at the same piece of screen, which Balidor had projected to the main monitor for the others' benefit. None of Wreg's people looked as surprised as they should. Least of all Wreg. Revik looked at Jon, whose eyes held only confusion...and Dorje, whose skin looked almost gray as he stared up at the same block of text. Jon finally looked back at Dorje, frowning.

He hit a key for translation while Revik watched, but his expression didn't clear.

"What is it?" he said. "Why is everyone freaking out? What is the jade bird?"

Holo looked at Jax. For a second, one or both of them seemed about to answer.

Then Balidor spoke up from the corner, his deeper voice heavy.

"Allie never left China, Jon," he said.

"What? What do you mean?"

"The Lao Hu have her."

"How the hell do you know that?"

Jon's voice sounded angry though, and Revik looked away, realizing the human already understood, at least in part.

"Because they're selling her, Jon," Balidor said simply.

"Selling her?" Jon looked at Revik, pressing his lips together. The puzzlement remained in his eyes, but Revik saw something else flare there. "Selling her how? In what way?"

"What way do you think, worm?" Wreg growled. "Are you soft in the head, cousin? Or do you want me to draw you a goddamned diagram?"

But Revik was on his feet before the seer finished speaking. He didn't know what he intended to do, hadn't thought a single word in his mind when he caught hold of Wreg by the front of his shirt. He punched him in the face, hard, knocking the heavier seer backwards. Wreg's legs slammed into the organic console, his fingers clutching the sides. Revik hit him again and Wreg held up a hand, trying to block it.

Everyone rose to their feet, backing away.

Revik barely noticed.

Wreg stared up at him, his eyes widening in disbelief. "Nenz..."

"What the fuck did you do?"

"Nenzi...brother Syrimne...gods..."

Revik was over him before he could finish, his hand gripping his shirt. He slammed him back against the console, then stood there, panting, barely able to make himself stop. "You let my wife *sell herself* to the Lao Hu?"

"Let her?" Wreg gasped. "I didn't do anything of the kind, brother! I was there on the ground...in chains. I didn't do anything..."

"You walked away! *You walked away and left her there...*"

The room fell silent.

Jax and Holo froze, staring at Wreg where Revik held him.

Revik couldn't breathe, couldn't force out more words. He gripped the seer tighter, slamming him against the computer station again, using more of his strength. He felt eyes on him, but the only face he could see was the one in front of him, the dark eyes rounding in fear as they stared up at his, taking in his expression. He saw his own eyes reflected there, shining a pale green in the darkness of Wreg's irises, and fought it back, even before he felt others approaching him from behind.

"Revik..." Jon said, breathless. "Revik, Jesus...calm down, man..."

"Deghoies..." Balidor's voice held an open caution. "Brother...please! Do not kill him. We need to know what happened...if you kill him we won't know what happened to her..."

Revik didn't take his eyes off the seer in front of him. He heard the words, somehow, well enough that he fought harder to force it back, to gain control of his light. Wreg stared up at him, his eyes sliding between the glowing pulse in Revik's.

"Nenzi...gods...I'm sorry...I'm so sorry brother..."

"Explain this to me!" he burst out. "Fucking explain it!"

"It was her decision..."

"It was her decision to *sell herself*? To turn herself over to the Lao Hu?"

His voice came out hoarse, thick enough that it sounded foreign in his own ears. Gripping Wreg harder in his hands, he slammed the broad-shouldered seer against the platform again, hard enough to shake the walls of the rounded room. He had to fight not to do it again.

"You let her *prostitute* herself?" Tears came to his eyes, hot enough to blind him. "She's the Bridge. If you don't care about me – "

"Nenz...gods...it wasn't like that! I *tried* to talk to her. I told her not to do it. Even thinking she had you somewhere, that she had hurt you, I *still* tried to talk her out of it. She wouldn't listen to reason...she was adamant..."

"Why? Why did she do it? Did she tell you?"

"She said it was to make things right...for what she did..."

"Did she do it because of me? Was she angry at me?"

Wreg stared up at him. Slowly, his eyes bled into a deeper understanding. Swallowing, he shook his head, grabbing the taller seer's arm.

"Nenz...no. She didn't say that. She didn't say anything like that..."

"Then why? Why would she accept those terms? She never wanted that...never!" Pain swallowed his sight as he remembered what he'd said to her, the look on her face. "Why did she do it, Wreg? She must have told you why..."

Wreg shook his head, once, but it wasn't a no. His gaze turned inward, but the look there grew almost angry as he seemed to be remembering.

"That Lao Hu bitch wouldn't take any other terms," Wreg growled after a pause. "Damn it, Nenz...she set her up...lured her there. Hell, the only other terms she offered were if Alyson was willing to sell *you* to the Lao Hu. They knew damned well she wouldn't agree to that..."

Seeing the look that rose to Revik's face, Wreg gripped his arm harder, his voice holding fear once more.

"...It was a *ruse,* Nenz. Your wife thought so, too. Voi Pai wanted her. She was like a cat with the cream when Alyson finally agreed..."

Revik felt his jaw harden more. He fought to speak, gripping the other's shirt tighter in his fingers. He knew he was probably hurting him, but Wreg's expression barely moved. The Chinese-looking seer didn't move where he half-lay against the console, his face wary as he stared up at him.

"Nenz," he said. "She's stubborn, your wife. She wouldn't listen to me."

"How hard did you try, Wreg?"

The other's eyes narrowed. For a moment, the look in them was almost angry. Then he averted his gaze, his voice low as he shook his head.

"They agreed on terms. It was legal, Nenz...and I was in cuffs. What could I do?"

"Why would you let her?" Revik growled. "Why did the others? You just let her trade herself for you, and you leave, just like that?"

"Voi Pai wouldn't take anything else..."

"You left her there! You *left* her there!"

"What else could we do?" Wreg snapped. "I obeyed the Bridge!"

Revik just stared at him for a moment, trying to make sense of his words.

"Your wife did not *want* us to refuse, Nenz," Wreg said. He looked up at him again, almost at a loss, right before his jaw hardened. "Gods, man. Are you listening to me at all? She made up her mind...she demanded that we go. She demanded that I take a blood oath not to tell you. She threatened to sell me back if I didn't agree to her terms..."

"You should have let her!"

Wreg gave him a disbelieving look.

"Why, Nenz? What good would it have done? I was a prisoner of the Lao Hu when she arrived...I had no pull with them! My only hope was to get out, and to find you. She would still have done it if I refused...she made that clear enough. Hell, even if all of my people refused, she would have done it anyway, for the ones in the camps. They wouldn't even have known *why* they were being let go..."

Seeing the Elaerian's eyes focus back on his, Wreg lowered his voice, speaking almost angrily. He showed him his palm as he spoke, and Revik stared at the red line there, a scar that had mostly healed.

"She made me vow it, Nenz...hell, we took a blood oath, right there in that damned garden. She made me swear not to tell you, to not let any of my people tell you." Swallowing, he stared up at Revik's face, as if he barely recognized it.

"...Jesus, Nenz...she told me you wouldn't care!"

"And you believed her?"

"Hell, yes, I believed her! *She* believed it, Nenz...and the last time I'd seen her, she had you collared and tranked like an animal. Right before she shot me..."

Revik's jaw hardened more.

Before he could speak, the other went on, his voice sharper.

"She even let me scan her, so I'd know you were all right. She convinced me that you were alive, that the Adhipan would let you go...and that you wouldn't care what she did...that you'd only come out of some sense of religious obligation..."

"And you believed her?" he said again.

"I did," Wreg answered without hesitation. *"She* believed it, Nenz...I'd swear to it."

Revik released him, stepping back. His hands were shaking. Forcing himself to look away, to take another step from the other seer, he leaned his weight against the other side of the console. Holding himself up by his palms, he fought to breathe again, unable to move for a moment as he stared sightlessly at the controls.

He fought to restrain his light, keeping his hands flat so he wouldn't move.

He felt the others' eyes on him, but no one spoke.

"How long has she been there?" he said finally.

There was another silence.

"Goddamn it," he said. "How long, Wreg? Since she left here?"

"Nenz..." Wreg approached, looking almost as if to touch him.

Revik stared at him, hard enough that the other backed off, holding up his hands.

"I don't know when she left this place." He exhaled then, and his voice turned businesslike, as if he were giving an ops report. "...She got us out about four months ago. I used the old rebel code to speak to her a last time, once we were away. Allie requested that they let us call in once we were away, as insurance that Voi Pai had been true to her word. Even so, I could tell she was worried that Voi Pai only pretended to agree to terms...and would pick us up before we got away. Sell us maybe, or throw us all in another work camp..."

When Revik didn't answer, Wreg lowered his hands.

Sighing, he leaned against the wall, rubbing his face with a tattooed hand. "...After we left, I checked with some of our contacts, got wind of a few of the invitations to high-end clients..." Feeling Revik's eyes on him, he swallowed, then glared up at the screen, his dark eyes flashing in the organic lights. "...I never thought that bitch would put it on the Rynak."

When Revik's gaze didn't move, Wreg averted his.

Glancing around at the others, he shrugged his broad, tattooed shoulders.

"I assume she's been there since," he said. "It took us awhile to find you...your wife promised you'd be going free. She said it would only be a few months at most, before they released you, but when we didn't hear from you..." He trailed, as if seeing something on Revik's face. "I honestly assumed they were treating her well, Nenz. From what I heard, it was a simple debt contract, nothing more. I knew they'd train her...but the Lao Hu are supposed to be decent in that, compared to most. Their consorts are supposed to be well cared for...and to have at least basic rights of refusal. I figured if she didn't care, and the two of you weren't together..."

He trailed, maybe seeing something in Revik's eyes once more.

His own darkened, right before he looked back at the monitor.

"...But if she's on the Rynak," he said.

Not finishing the thought, he shrugged, his eyes cold as he stared at the feed.

Revik's jaw hardened. He looked at Balidor, but the Adhipan leader didn't return his gaze. His eyes were more difficult to read than Wreg's, staring at the same lines of text projected over the console. His anger looked colder than the rebel's, too.

Wreg glanced at all of them again, but seemed to be speaking to no one in particular. "...We hoped that human of hers might lead us back here," he added. He focused on Jon, exhaling in a rolling set of clicks. "...But she didn't. She and that Wvercian went back to the Americas somewhere. Really, we only found this place through sheer luck...a fluke. One of the seers we've been working with in SCARB must have run a trace on you..."

"Who?" Balidor said, staring at Wreg again.

Wreg shrugged. "No one I know. We only found it because she didn't call it in. She'd tried to bury the signal in her records. We have a program for any tampering. So we got a flag that showed she talked to someone here..."

"Chan," Jon said, speaking up from by the door. He looked at Balidor, then at Revik. "He means Chandre. She warned me we'd better move...that we were at risk. She found me through my implant. Some SCARB bullshit, where she had my illegal ident on file..."

Wreg shrugged with one hand, neither agreeing nor arguing.

"Well, we assumed she was a traitor," he said only. "We sent someone after her, too. They should be halfway to DC by now."

"Call them back," Revik said. "Now, Wreg."

He didn't look up from the console, but his words silenced the room.

When the other didn't move right away, Revik lifted his gaze.

For a moment, Wreg continued to stare at him, a wary measurement in his dark eyes. Then, seeming to understand his words belatedly, he nodded, gesturing an additional affirmative in seer before he turned to look at Jax, clicking his fingers to get his attention before signing a command. The younger seer made an affirmative gesture in return, bowing before he removed himself swiftly from the room, half-jogging down the long, green corridor.

Revik barely followed any of it.

He continued to stare at the console, but he could feel all of them now, even when he tried to shut them out. He fought to think, to move his mind past this...past the images that wanted to rise, that wanted to connect to what he'd been feeling off her off and on for the past weeks...

"Revik?"

He turned before he could stop himself.

Jon stood there. The human paled a little, seeing the look on his face, but his eyes remained on his. "Revik, man," he said shakily. "...it's all right. We can get her out. We know where she is now, so we can get her out. Right?"

Revik didn't answer.

When the silence stretched, Balidor spoke into it.

"Not without starting a war with the Lao Hu," he said.

"But they have the Bridge," Jon said. He glanced at Revik. "...Allie. Are you going to tell me the rest of the seers are going to stand by and let her be a..." Hesitating, he reddened, waving a hand vaguely. "...You know. To do that?"

Balidor gave him a grim look. The smile at his lips didn't touch his eyes.

"Does she seem particularly popular to you in the seer world these days, cousin?" he said. "I think right now, it would not help us to look for support from within the seer community..."

Revik turned, and saw the Adhipan leader's eyes on his, too.

Balidor's gaze was warier though, than Jon's had been...as if measuring Revik's face, the vibrations in his light. He looked at him as one might look at a wild animal, trying to determine what it might do.

"So," Jon said. "Then we risk war."

Still looking at Revik, Balidor sighed.

"It may not be that simple, cousin..." he said.

"What choice do we have? We can't *leave* her there!"

"The human is right," Wreg said. "We cannot leave her, Nenz. It says they've sold her. That means they've broken the original deal with her..." He looked at Balidor, as if finding his gaze easier to hold than Revik's. "...She was under contract before. There was a specific sum involved, and then she was to be set free. If they've sold her, something's changed."

"What was the sum?" Jon said.

"Does it matter?" Balidor asked dryly.

"It does if we have to pay it," Jon shot back.

"Twenty-two million. American." Wreg looked at Jon as he said it, then, as if feeling something off Revik, he glanced at him as well. "It was a steep price...an unfair price. But that Voi Pai cunt would not negotiate the amount. She wanted a quarter to a half mil for each of the infiltrators, even those with very little formal training. She charged more for me and some of the others... and the work camp was a set price."

Revik barely heard this, either.

He stared at his own hands, fighting the rest of it out of his head. What he'd felt off her, for weeks now...long before he voiced it aloud to Balidor.

He should have known what it meant. He should have figured it out.

Balidor must have noticed something. He must have picked up on something in Wreg...maybe one of the others. Balidor had known something was off in their story, and he'd made the connection to Allie, long before it even occurred to Revik to go that direction in his own mind. He'd been so sure she'd taken up with someone else. He'd assumed that she'd simply found another lover more quickly than he would have expected...maybe even to forget about him. Or to get back at him, maybe.

He should have considered it might be something else. She'd never done anything like that before.

Not even when he'd given her cause...she still hadn't. Even the thing with Balidor hadn't been what he'd thought. They might have been friends. She might have loved him even, in her own way. But according to Balidor, she hadn't let herself love him romantically. She hadn't been looking to replace him, or even to hurt him.

Hell, she'd never even *threatened* to sleep with someone else. Even that time in Delhi, when she'd been so angry at him she'd looked at him like she hated him, she'd thrown his past indiscretions in his face, but hadn't threatened him with the same.

This time had felt different, though. Even Jon convinced him it had been different, that he'd have to work just to get her to talk to him. Jon told him she probably *wouldn't* talk to him, at least not anytime soon. It hadn't occurred to him she might have been in danger, that something might have happened to her. It should have occurred to him.

Hell, half the free seers in the Western hemisphere wanted her dead. According to Balidor, there'd been a price on her head...and not only from Wreg's people. He'd been too worried about what he would have to do to get her to come back.

But he knew he was distracting himself, still. He couldn't think past that distraction, or what wanted to cycle back to the forefront of his mind.

Anger rose in his light. It was at himself, he could feel that much...but he couldn't contain it, and it wasn't enough to aim it inward. So he lifted his eyes, staring at Balidor.

"How could you be so stupid?" he said. "You let her walk right into it..." Fighting his voice, he gripped the console harder in his hands. "Goddamn it! What was she *doing* there? She's the Bridge, damn it! Are you all fucking stupid, to have forgotten what that means?"

Everyone stared at him again.

Revik saw the fear in their eyes. He knew from his blurred, ghosted vision that his own were probably glowing again. He tried to bite back his anger, to control himself, but he couldn't seem to stop the words from exploding out of him.

"Voi Pai *asked* her to come!" he said. "She wouldn't negotiate with anyone else...she took one of Allie's oldest friends! What did you *think* she wanted? Did you really think she'd let her just walk out of there?" He glared at Wreg. "That she'd *ever* let her out? That she'd honor a contract...even one for twenty-two mil?"

None of the seers moved. Jon glanced between Wreg and Balidor, then swallowed, gesturing in affirmative.

"Yeah, about Cass," he said. "Why *didn't* Cass get word to us? Not inside. I mean when she got out. Why didn't she tell us Allie was there?"

There was another silence.

Wreg clicked softly, still looking at Revik, although his words aimed at Jon. "That was part of it," Wreg said. "My vow to the Bridge."

"*What* was part of it?" Jon said.

Wreg shrugged, one handed. "I erased the human. Her Wvercian said he'd take care of it from there...keep an eye on her. Make sure none of it came back."

Jon stared at him, his eyes showing incredulity.

"Jesus," he said. "Her own boyfriend?"

Wreg gave him a hard look. "He's loyal to the Bridge. He knew how to follow orders. Believe me, I was grateful of that...I would have had to kill a lot of Wvercians in that situation. Most of them have no loyalty. Except to money, or their dicks..."

Revik shook his head, still staring down at the console. He didn't speak though, and didn't look up when he felt the others watching him once more.

"We can't leave her there," Jon said again, looking at Revik. "We can't, man."

"We're not leaving her there, Jon," Balidor said.

Revik felt something in his chest start to tighten again, even as the others' words sank in. Raising his head, he straightened abruptly, taking his hands off the organic metal.

"No," he said, his voice cold. "No. We're not leaving her."

"So we're going, then?" Jon said, relief in his voice. "When, Revik?"

The Elaerian glanced at Wreg, then at Balidor, whose eyes looked wary once more.

"We're going now, Jon," Revik said flatly. "Right now."

Twenty-Four
Compensation

I SAW MORE CLIENTS NOW.

The type and variety of clients changed, too. The variety, in particular, made me wonder, but I figured that was Voi Pai's attempt to shame me, since the whole status thing and saving face was big for her. I'm fairly sure she threw a few slave traders into the mix...and others she likely invited to demean me in whatever way.

The security protocols didn't seem to have grown any more lax; in fact, on my end, they tightened considerably.

Voi Pai claimed I'd cost her around forty million US dollars, for what I'd done, killing Gerwix. She said I owed her for that. She also said she didn't intend to wait another decade or so before she could collect the full amount.

I didn't argue with her...mostly because she didn't give me the opportunity.

But the thought of working off sixty million kept me up at night. I had no idea how much she charged for each of those sessions, but it couldn't be the same ten or twenty thousand she charged that original set of heavy hitters and government bigwigs. Even among that high-end group, the price varied significantly between 'friends of the Republic' and their more flush business partners from the West.

Even if I commanded the same high price for every single one of them, I'd done the math. Sixty million, even at forty thousand a pop, was still around 4 a day for over a year. And there was no way I was making forty thousand a pop...not even for half of these. Nor was I seeing four clients a day. The reality was closer to two...three, tops.

At ten thousand a client, that was four years of four clients a day. Or eight years of two clients a day. And that was at ten thousand a client. I doubted I was making that with any but the high end guys, and they usually booked me for an eight hour bloc. So that meant one of those guys a day, given the security constraints.

Broken out hourly and daily like that, it meant doing this gig for longer than I could bear to think about. My mind couldn't really go there, in terms of what that would look like for me...but I figured I was looking at three or four years, minimum.

Realistically, more like six to eight.

None of this had been negotiated with me directly, though...and I wasn't really sure what that meant, either. It could mean that killing Gerwix put me more in the status of prisoner than "contract employee," so Voi Pai no longer felt the need to negotiate terms with me directly. It could also mean that she was still negotiating with whoever had been at the other end of Gerwix's leash. In any case, the silence made me nervous, too.

I was beginning to hate the work. I still tried to stay numb, but either it wasn't working as well, or something else was forcing me to face things more directly. I probably would have drank myself stupid, in another environment, but Voi Pai forbade that, too. The one time she found me drunk had been enough...after that, I wasn't allowed anything alcoholic at all, even when I was off-duty.

Other things changed. I was bumped up in infiltration classes, and those got more intense, too. I now spent five or six non-working hours a day with an older set of seers, working hard with my aleimi, mostly at tracking and sparring. Only one of my former classmates joined me in that new group, a youngster with the highest potential rank in the bunch, something like a ten or eleven. Since the classes were daily, that cut into the number of clients I could see in any given week, too, even though they shifted the times of class to suit my schedule. In any case, they were now training me at some considerable expense to themselves.

Which, of course, made me wonder why.

Ulai wouldn't tell me.

For some reason, his silence and the infiltration lessons made me nervous, too, even if I was glad for the lessons themselves. I even tried to bring it up with Voi Pai, but she only dismissed my questions with a wave of her manicured hand. It was essentially the same answer I got when I asked her if she really expected me to work off forty million dollars for a piece of excrement like Gerwix. I imagined the fact that there was no way she'd willingly get me to agree that Gerwix's life was worth that much contributed to her unwillingness to make formal terms with me. She refused to discuss anything regarding my situation, in fact. When I insisted, she claimed I could not negotiate the value of something of which I knew nothing.

She did tell me once, in her first bout of anger about what I'd done, that mostly she would be forced to pay 'respect' money...as well as additional compensation for the sentimental value Gerwix commanded for his many years of loyal service.

The latter might have made me laugh under different circumstances.

They still had to take the collar off me for me to work...and for the infiltration classes, of course. I honestly didn't know whether my having murdered one of my clients was common knowledge in the City, but I assumed it had to be. I didn't know if it was communicated to my clients, either, whether for insurance/liability reasons or as a matter of courtesy. I also didn't know if that information would make me worth more or less. But I did know that more of them appeared to be afraid of me.

It probably didn't help that I now had a cadre of Lao Hu guards surrounding my apartments during the length of every consort appointment... or that at least a half-dozen of them held high-powered trank guns that looked more like assault rifles. Following the incident with Gerwix, my client compartment was also fitted with gas.

A part of me couldn't help but find that sort of karmically fitting.

A sense of foreboding remained with me, regardless. I couldn't get a read on what it meant, or why it clung to my light with such tenacity. I woke up feeling worried...beyond the sickness at the job, or the increasing anger at feeling trapped. I stayed up too late at night, too, staring at my ceiling, either alone or with Ulai lying next to me.

More of those nights, lately, he wanted to sleep beside me. I let him, and even had sex with him some of those nights...but I couldn't say his presence provided any true comfort. I distracted myself, wondering about him, and about Voi Pai, but the truth was, neither of them really factored into my mind's true preoccupation. I spent more time practicing for infiltration classes than I did thinking about anything else in my increasingly small world.

I was waiting for something.

I didn't know what it was, exactly, but it made Ulai more clingy with me, and caused Voi Pai to avoid my eyes whenever I looked at her directly. It might have been my imagination, but it felt like my friends among the consorts were distancing their light from mine, too.

The only people who seemed oblivious were the other seers in my infiltration group, most being too young to be in the know on much of anything going on at the higher levels of the Lao Hu. So I probably talked more to them, despite Ulai's efforts to get closer to me.

I didn't find out until later that I'd already been sold.

It was a lot longer after that before I knew who I'd been sold to.

Jon shoved his hands in his pockets, looking nervously around at the line of infiltrators that ringed the walls of the high-ceilinged room. Most of them held assault rifles of one kind of another, and didn't seem shy about aiming them at the seers in their party. He noticed the majority pointed at Revik, however.

It was pretty different from the last time they'd all been under this roof.

Revik had done surprisingly well, keeping his cool. That was in spite of the three days' wait they'd had, at the gates of the Forbidden City, and the following ten hours in a holding area outside the first, and largest, of the inner walls...the one able to be breached only through the Meridian Gate. Then there had been another day of security checks of various kinds, cups of tea, ceremonial greetings of one kind or another, tours of the gardens, puppet shows.

Despite how he'd reacted when he first discovered Allie's situation... Revik remained polite. He adhered to every one of the protocols requested of him, even when they bordered on ridiculous. He'd even sent gifts to Voi Pai... expensive gifts, from what Jon could discern...in an attempt to impress upon her the friendliness of his intent.

He'd been quiet, but he'd also been calm.

Jon still found himself staring at the Elaerian when the other man wasn't looking.

It wasn't just that he looked different than he had for the last year or so... although the physical and facial expression differences themselves could be startling at times. It wasn't even that he'd gotten quieter again, to the point where he didn't speak much at all now, even in strategy sessions, unless he had something specific to contribute. This was in spite of the fact that he was ostensibly leading most of those sessions and had the final call on any real decisions that resulted. He led with a light hand, even given the potential disaster of throwing together some of the angrier individuals among the motley crew of the Seven, the Adhipan and the rebel infiltrators who now fell under his command.

Jon stared at him in those silences, as if trying to convince himself that the change he saw in the Elaerian's eyes was real.

Dorje told him it was. He said he could see it in his light, ever since that day with Balidor and Vash and Tarsi in the tank. According to Dorje, they'd healed some kind of break that had lived there, a rift that kept his aleimi in pieces, rather than whole.

Following that day...as well as whatever Allie had done to him prior to that...the very expressions on Revik's face had altered. The odd, disjointed look of his gaze faded, leaving a more subdued and often shielded stillness. The underlying anger seemed to have faded, too, most of it anyway...along with that flavor of arrogance that irritated Jon in the Sword.

He felt like a different person...again.

What threw Jon more, though, was how much he felt like the old Revik... the one he'd gotten to know in that prison cell under the Caucasus Mountains.

Jon had mentioned the same to Vash once, in passing. Instead of getting a blank look for his troubles, the old seer favored him with a surprisingly warm smile, and nodded emphatically at Jon's observations.

"Indeed," he said. "It seems that without the blocks caused by the trauma, his surface personality is much like it was when we removed the traumatized pieces of his aleimi altogether..." Vash smiled again cheerfully. "...This is good for us, yes? He could have been anyone, really, in terms of surface traits. And I quite liked him as Dehgoies Revik..."

Jon felt his own flare of hope at this, but the old seer gave him a warning look.

"...But he is not really the same man, Jon," Vash said gently. "Half of a person can never contain as much as the whole...and those other parts of him are still there, living inside of him. They are simply not broken as they were. As a result, they are no longer covering over the rest of him...or forcing him to hide in the light of the Dreng to escape the feelings associated with them. But he is not the same, Jon. He never will be."

Jon had thought about the seer's words at the time, glancing at Revik, who had been sitting on the edge of a table, listening to Wreg and Balidor argue with an intent look on his face.

"So what does that mean?" he had asked Vash finally, shoving his hands back in his pockets.

Vash smiled that wide smile of his, so that Jon could only smile back.

"I do not know, young cousin," Vash said cheerfully. "...But I imagine we will find out. In the meantime, it is good to see him in a more peaceful state, is it not?"

Jon nodded, swallowing a little as he looked at Revik.

The Elaerian's eyes narrowed faintly as he stared down at something on a VR screen that stood on the table between Balidor and Wreg. From his expression, Jon could tell he was scanning, but a bare frown touched his lips as he clicked out, and he still didn't speak, not even to break up the argument between the two seers standing in front of him.

"He's just so much like he was," Jon said, speaking almost to himself. "It's like seeing someone rise from the dead. I can't help but think..."

But he cut that thought off, looking away from Revik's face. He wasn't really ready to think about Allie yet, or how she might react to any of them, much less Revik, given where she was. Swallowing again, Jon shrugged, looking up at Vash.

"...It's a good thing, what you did," he finished lamely.

Vash smiled at him, but there was a sharper knowing in his eyes.

"You helped too, cousin," he said. "More than you know."

Jon had turned back to the three seers, watching Wreg and Balidor again. He saw Balidor fold his arms as he rolled his eyes at something the more muscular seer said, right before Wreg pointed emphatically at something on the VR screen, clicking loudly as his skin flushed on his high cheekbones. Seconds later, Balidor was clicking in return, gesturing a negative with one hand as he began speaking rapidly in Prexci, aiming his finger at the same screen.

"The real question is," Jon muttered. "Are the two of them ever going to stop bickering?"

Vash chuckled, patting Jon on the back.

"...Only time will tell on that account, too, young cousin," Vash replied, still cheerful.

Jon pulled himself out of the memory, staring again at the walls of the enormous audience chamber draped in silk tapestries over brightly painted walls. He tried to avoid the Lao Hu infiltrators with his eyes. Allie had called much of the Forbidden City the 'kung fu palace' while they'd been staying there a year previous. Glancing around at the antique-looking, enameled furniture, along with the swords and the silk kites streaming from the ceiling in tiers, he found himself agreeing with her. He would have agreed with her more if it wasn't for the panels morphing on several flat surfaces that spoke of VR feeds, and the organics on the assault rifles trained at their significantly smaller party.

He'd thought maybe they'd brought too many with them, coming in.

Twelve...maybe thirteen infiltrators. Looking around at the thirty or so Lao Hu he could see now, and remembering the dozens they'd passed on their way through the gates and through the gardens outside the room's walls, he revised his opinion belatedly. Revik had said he wanted to remind Voi Pai that they represented more than simply his personal interests, and now Jon found himself thinking that maybe they'd undershot.

Revik's eyes remained emotionless, apparently calm as he held the Lao Hu leader's gaze.

"We cannot speak with her directly?" he said again.

Jon watched him narrow his eyes at the female seer, lifting the tea cup that sat on the lacquered table in front of him. He took a sip of the likely-lukewarm tea, his gaze steady as he sat easily in a wooden chair with embroidered cushions. He gazed up at the elevated seat of Voi Pai, his expression unreadable. Jon knew that her being seated above him broke protocol too, severely enough that it had to be deliberate.

If it bothered Revik, that did not show on his face, either.

"She is working, Illustrious Sword," Voi Pai replied smoothly.

Jon knew that had to be deliberate, too.

Not a ripple touched Revik's face.

"When will she be finished, sister?" he said. "We are willing to wait."

"It will not be anytime soon, I'm afraid."

"We are willing to wait," he repeated. "We will wait here, if necessary. For as long as you require us to."

Voi Pai continued to measure his gaze, her expression also difficult to read. Jon found himself wondering if the Lao Hu leader noticed the changes in him from their last encounter, or if she noticed any hint of the differences in his light.

As far as Jon knew, she'd only ever encountered him as Syrimne.

"You are imposing on me for overnight hospitality, Illustrious brother?"

she said then, lifting an eyebrow, a smile teasing her lips. "Is that polite, I wonder?"

"No less polite," Revik replied, his voice as calm as a windless lake. "...Than asking an intermediary to wait on an audience with his wife. Or refusing him the basic courtesies of his rank."

Voi Pai sighed, as if bored. Clicking softly, she tilted her face towards the ceiling.

"I was under the impression from her that your marriage to her was terminated," she said, blowing by his second point without comment. "...Perhaps there is a communication problem in more than one area, Illustrious Sword...?"

"There is a miscommunication," he conceded. "It is true."

"Illuminate me, dear brother."

Revik shrugged with one hand. "I have, sister. Repeatedly. I am here declaring myself in need of forgiveness from her. I wish reconciliation...and an opportunity to make amends. Under every recognized seer law, including the initial Codes and the common law of the Lao Hu, I have the right to be heard by her in this..."

"And if she does not wish to grant that right?"

"I have the right to hear the refusal from her directly."

"And if she refuses to grant that right, as well?"

Revik gestured again politely, if vaguely, with one hand.

"I would need to see her in person to know that as well, loyal Voi Pai," he said, his face unmoving. "I would not be willing to leave until I had been granted this right."

His Prexci sounded different from the common tongue Jon had grown accustomed to hearing most seers use. At times, Jon even had trouble understanding him through the accent, although the style was slow enough, and enunciated enough, that he could usually stay at least only a beat or two behind. The more formal cadence was one that Jon had never heard from Revik before; it came out practiced, however, enough to sound almost like Vash's manner of speaking, or Balidor's when he was particularly annoyed.

But Revik didn't sound annoyed. He sounded completely at ease, in fact.

He also sounded absolutely immovable, which Jon supposed was the point.

Again, the Lao Hu leader's eyebrows rose, cartoonish under their dark paint over the white powder of her face.

Her red-painted lips pursed over a pointed chin.

At her prolonged silence, Jon felt himself sigh internally.

This particular ping-pong match had been going on all morning and for most of the afternoon already...through tea and a number of odd dances, two epic-long poems and other entertainments that were likely seer in origin...not to mention all the b.s. they'd encountered at the gate and in each subsequent courtyard following their initial entrance through the high walls around Tian'anmen.

They'd gotten here not long after dawn the day before, and it was dark outside again.

Jon glanced at Wreg and Balidor, who stood side by side, wearing similar postures despite the different expressions on their faces. Wreg looked angry, and Jon knew without being told that he was likely furious at Voi Pai's blatant disrespect to Revik, both overt and implied. Balidor wore a similar expression as Revik, actually...like a rock that did not intend to budge, no matter how long it took, or how many distractions were put in front of him.

The older seer's patience surprised Jon less than Revik's, however.

Revik leaned back in the wooden chair, even as Jon thought it. He didn't noticeably shift to adjust his weight, despite his probable discomfort from sitting in the hard-looking chair for so long. Jon himself had struggled with being forced to stand for a similar amount of time, but he didn't bother trying to hide his body's lack of ease.

He nearly jumped when Voi Pai spoke into that silence, even before he heard her words.

"Very well," she said, as though it was the first time Revik had asked. "She will be brought up presently."

Revik did not flinch. He continued to look up at the Lao Hu leader, a layer of impenetrable silence over the clear irises of his eyes.

Jon knew his own expression was probably a lot more transparent.

When he glanced at Balidor and Wreg, neither of their expressions had changed, for the better or the worse. Only Garensche, on the other side of Balidor, let a flicker of relief reach his broad, scarred face. His hair had grown longer too, since Jon had last seen him, and he wore it similarly to Wreg's, making him look even more of a pirate than he had before, with his thick girth and near-Wvercian height and chest proportions. The scar running along one side of his face to his hazel eyes only added to the image. Still, Jon knew him as one of the softer souls among the rebel seers...and one who had a particular fondness for Allie.

Jon found his open emotions a relief.

He watched Revik lean back in the red-silk lining of the wooden chair, a chair that might be several hundred years old, or only carved to appear as such. His eyes never left Voi Pai's face, even when the configuration of infiltrators shifted slightly around them, presumably to prepare for Allie's arrival.

Jon felt his own heart constricting in his chest, and wondered again at Revik's completely flatline appearance. The look went past the infiltrator's mask Jon had grown accustomed to when he knew him before. His very light seemed to exude a kind of calming glow, as if he were merely there to mediate a discussion between foreign parties...on a topic that interested him only peripherally. Jon watched his face minutely, but he could not penetrate that demeanor. Nor could he hide his own increasing anxiousness at the thought of Allie walking in there any minute, in gods only knew what condition.

It didn't escape his notice either, that Voi Pai hadn't given them any kind of time frame for her arrival.

"And what do you intend," she said as Jon thought it, still staring at Revik as if the rest of them weren't present. "...In the event your wife is amenable to reconciliation?"

Revik laid an arm on the hard wood of his chair, his eyes still focused on Voi Pai's.

"I intend to buy her from you," he said.

Voi Pai smiled, her thin lips twitching. "She is not for sale, Illustrious Sword."

"She is under debt contract," he said, his cadence unchanging. "Her debt can be bought, even if she cannot."

"You are doing well indeed, to afford a debt of this kind," Voi Pai remarked wryly. "Perhaps you are not aware of the full amount?"

"I am aware of the twenty-two million agreed upon at the onset of the contract," Revik said, his tone implying he heard none of the condescending humor of hers. "I assume she would have worked off a portion of that amount in the time since..."

"That amount is no longer relevant," Voi Pai broke in coldly.

"Is it not?" Revik settled more deeply into the chair. "And why is that?"

"She murdered one of her clients," Voi Pai replied, smiling once more.

For the first time, Jon saw Revik's face flicker with a shadow of reaction.

It was gone almost before he saw it, but he knew Voi Pai would have seen it, too. She smiled wider, as if in answer to Jon's thoughts, waving a manicured hand.

"...Penalties were demanded. The client she saw fit to kill was one who belonged to an important friend of the Lao Hu. There is more than simply the matter of blood money..."

"How much?" Revik said, his voice polite.

Voi Pai tapped a red-lacquered nail against her tea cup. "I was quoted a price for penalty. It was beyond our means, frankly...and the wronged party's patience, in terms of her ability to work it off within a reasonable timeframe. I was therefore required to offer ownership of your wife's debt to the wronged party..."

"How much?" Revik repeated, as if she hadn't spoken.

"Forty million, Illustrious Sword...in addition to the eighteen million she still owed the Lao Hu." Smiling at Jon when he choked out a sound at the amount, she let her eyes flicker back to Revik's. "...The money is merely a courtesy. They require service of her, to compensate for their loss. They were unspecific as to the nature of that service."

"Was their loss so great?" Wreg asked, from the back of the room.

She didn't honor him with a glance, but continued to look at Revik.

"The man she murdered was a favored pet of our friends. And he had certain...historical knowledge...that they claim is impossible to duplicate." She paused, tapping her nail quietly. "...Although they claim your wife is able to supply some of that history..."

"What is the name of her alleged victim?" Revik said.

"This is important to you?" Voi Pai smiled again, quirking just one of those painted brows. "Have you not heard me on the relevant details, Illustrious Sword?"

"I listen to all words that come from the leader of the Lao Hu," Revik said, his voice as unchanged as the air of the room. "...I merely wish to know the nature of the knowledge that is said to be carried by my wife. After all," he added, gesturing in polite deference. "...At her young age, historical knowledge is not her specialty. Unless you imply it is something from a previous incarnation...?"

Jon caught some flicker of a taunt in this.

He knew the politics around reincarnation were complicated in the seer world. He also knew that the Lao Hu's official stance was that such a thing didn't exist, since it conflicted directly with the Chinese doctrines around religion and communism. How they reconciled that with Allie being here and wearing her religious title had never fully made sense to Jon, but he figured there was some political subtlety there that he was missing. In any event, Revik's comment seemed to irritate Voi Pai.

"His name was Hulen, Illustrious Sword...but your wife called him by another name."

"She knew him?" Jon spoke aloud before he realized he intended to.

He saw Balidor give him a faintly warning look.

Revik didn't turn his head. He continued to watch Voi Pai, his clear eyes unmoving.

"I would repeat my question, most venerable Voi Pai," he said.

Voi Pai shrugged elegantly, but her eyes never left Revik's face.

"I do not remember the name she called him, Illustrious Sword...but if you are adamant about knowing, we record all of our sessions with our consorts..." Again, she lingered on the word, watching Revik's face. "...I could have one of my people call up the meeting in question, if such a trivial thing is indeed of such interest to our beloved intermediary?"

Revik bowed his head to her, his face still polite.

"I would appreciate that very much, sister..."

He trailed, for the first time losing his words.

Jon saw a struggle in his eyes, brief but visible. He stared at a side entrance to the room, seemingly unable to speak, or tear his eyes off the small procession entering through the round wooden opening. Jon hadn't noticed the newcomers until that moment. They walked past the raised platform where Voi Pai sat, moving so silently that he hadn't caught the change in the air until Revik paused to stare. Now Jon felt the other seers stiffening around him. Jon's own eyes followed Revik's, even as a sinking feeling in his stomach told him that he knew exactly who had just entered the room.

He didn't recognize her at first.

The thought terrified him briefly, especially since he could make out only one form not dressed in the hanfu clothing and black sashes of the Lao Hu infiltrators.

Initially, it was the only clue he had to which of them was her.

It wasn't only the clothes...although those were enough to make his jaw drop. Her face looked different, partly from the make up she wore, which was probably twice what he'd ever seen on her...but also from the way they'd styled her hair, in a complicated system of braids and dark strands hanging on either side of her high cheekbones. Her green eyes stood out sharply against black kohl make up, and she looked thinner than he remembered. He stared down at her body, flushing a little at the amount of skin showing, and pausing on the thin chains connecting her wrists to her ankles.

She wore a collar of ornately carved, organic metal, barely visible on her throat over the clothing.

The outfit itself looked more Indian than Chinese to him, but it had touches that made him wonder if it had been designed more from a seer style than anything human. It showed her midriff all the way up to a beaded top that hooked at her throat and had no sleeves. The collar at her throat emphasized the slave look, as did the draping cloth of the skirt below, slit to the tops of her thighs, and her bare feet underneath. Her feet had been painted, too, wearing designs that reminded him of Indian henna tattoos.

She stared around at all of them, the same way they must be staring at her.

The look on her face told Jon, if nothing else, that she hadn't been told who they were bringing her to see. She couldn't hide her shock as she looked at each of them in turn. Her eyes paused on Jon himself, then moved to Balidor, then to Wreg. She paused again, looking between the two of them, before her eyes found Garensche, then Jax and Holo...until finally, she seemed to put the pieces together, and Jon saw a near fear in her eyes. The look worsened when her eyes finally found Revik.

For a moment, the two of them only stared at one another.

Revik had his expression under control again, but he didn't take his eyes off her face. Jon thought he saw the Elaerian scanning her briefly, but he didn't do it for long. Instead, his eyes clicked back into focus abruptly, almost as if he'd been burnt, or startled by what he'd found. The expression on his face didn't change, but he didn't move his eyes off hers either.

Allie, on the other hand, seemed to be struggling to breathe. She stared at him, almost as if she'd never seen him before. Then her eyes shifted to Voi Pai.

"What is this?" she said. "I demand an explanation."

She spoke the same formal Prexci Revik had.

Jon flinched a little at how different her voice sounded. He also noticed the tall, blue-eyed seer standing behind her, right before he laid a possessive-seeming hand on her bare shoulder. He pulled her closer to where he stood, and Jon glanced involuntarily at Revik. He saw the Elaerian male staring at the same blue-eyed seer.

"What is this?" Allie demanded again. "What am I doing here?"

Voi Pai smiled. Clearly she was enjoying the show, which shouldn't have surprised Jon, given everything he'd seen, but managed to anger him to the point he had to bite his lip to remain silent. His fury flared to a blinding hatred when the Lao Hu leader spoke.

"Be silent, Esteemed Bridge," Voi Pai said, as casual as a blown kiss.

Jon looked at Allie, unable to help wondering if she would heel like Voi Pai clearly expected her to. He saw the tall seer with the blue eyes squeeze her shoulder a second time, as if in warning. Allie was staring at Revik again, though. She bit her lip, as if to prevent herself saying more, then averted her gaze. After another pause, she bowed slightly to the raised chair of the Lao Hu leader, gesturing in acquiescence to Voi Pai.

Jon felt his anger turn into something closer to disbelief.

Revik seemed to have to work harder to pull his eyes off her.

He turned eventually, looking back up at the Lao Hu leader. She smiled at him, leaning deeper into the cushions of her chair before quirking an eyebrow at him again. Her voice held an open thread of humor.

"Would you still wish to see the recording, Illustrious Sword?"

After a bare pause, he gestured an assent.

Leaning back in his chair, he took a sip of tea while Jon watched, and he had to give the seer props. Jon had no idea what Revik was thinking right then; his face looked almost like it had for most of the day. But Jon seriously doubted whatever it was, it was even remotely as calm as his expression portrayed.

Jon knew Voi Pai likely could perceive that much, as well.

He also understood something else. She'd waited to bring up the image-capture she had of Allie until Allie herself was in the room.

Even as Jon thought it, the seer clicked her fingers, motioning to one of the infiltrators who stood beneath a blank-looking stretch of wall. Jon had already determined that flat stretch behind her 'altar' or throne or whatever it was must house one of those large organic screens, masked to be near to invisible when not activated.

When the image rose, it seemed overly large.

Jon flinched, in spite of himself. It didn't help when he saw Allie standing there, in another slave-girl outfit, this one a filmy white that barely concealed her outline underneath its folds.

...Or the fact that a seer that made Cass' boyfriend, Baguen, look small, had ahold of her breast through that same material.

The male's giant hand squeezed while Jon watched, making him turn away.

"You like that, Esteemed Sister?" he said, his voice thick.

Allie, to her credit, didn't sound the least bit intimidated when she spoke.

"Are you sure you're going to be able to get it up?" she said, her voice cold. "Now that I've agreed...?"

Jon glanced up in time to see the giant smile at her. He could only see part of the broad face, as most of the image-capture seemed to be focused on Allie herself. Jon saw the brute staring at her though, his hand still massaging her breast.

"I'm up, girl," he said. "Talking to me like that is only making it harder..."

Jon glanced at Revik, again, unable to stop himself.

The male Elaerian remained in the chair, focusing up at the screen, his face immovable. His eyes flickered to Voi Pai as Jon watched, even as he raised an eyebrow.

"You expect our sympathies, sister," he said, below the sound of the recording. "That the Esteemed Bridge defended herself from an apparent rape?"

Voi Pai clicked at him mildly, rolling her eyes.

"He pawed at her, Illustrious Sword. That hardly constitutes a rape. Don't be so naive as to assume this wasn't a part of her act in seducing him, either...she is quite schooled in the arts now, brother..."

Jon felt his jaw harden, even as he glanced back up at the screen. He couldn't force himself to look at Allie herself, not with her image right there.

"You're sure?" the Allie on the screen said, her voice equally cold.

Jon found himself a little thrown by her calm as she turned her back on the massive seer, reaching for the bamboo handle of a tea pot sitting on a low table behind her. She poured two cups of tea, lifting them both after she'd returned the pot to its heating stone on the table.

"After all," she added, her voice still removed. "...I'm a little old for you for your usual tastes."

"Are you, now?" The giant's voice was amused. "Is that what they tell you?"

"It is," she said. "Is that why you keep calling me 'girl'?"

She straightened as she said it, handing him one of the cups of tea. Again, Jon found himself thinking about Voi Pai's words...but no, there was nothing coy or teasing in Allie's eyes as she looked up at the broad face of the Wvercian. In fact, the look on her face reminded him more of images he'd seen of her in the Registry, when she'd...

He glanced at Revik again, realizing why he recognized the look.

She'd intended to kill him. It hadn't been spontaneous. She'd planned it.

He wondered if Revik knew that, too.

When Jon glanced back at the screen, the giant was ripping off the top of her filmy dress. Allie let him, still holding the tea cups, but she nearly lost her balance when he yanked at the cloth. Jon looked away when the giant started feeling her up again, but he couldn't help noticing that Revik continued to stare up at the screen.

"You want to see, Esteemed One?" the giant asked Allie on the screen.

She didn't answer at first, but Jon saw her jaw harden.

Then she shrugged, her voice bored.

"If it makes you feel better. Sure."

The giant only laughed at this. Jon jumped as he knocked the tea cups out of her hands. The china smashed on the floor, even as he grabbed hold of one of her wrists, yanking her towards him so that she stumbled. She was still regaining her balance when he grabbed her hand, forcing it between his tree-trunk like legs.

The giant let out a low gasp, still feeling her up with his other hand.

"How's that, little girl?" he said. His voice came out gruff again. "Big enough for you?"

She met his gaze, her eyes still holding that cold look. "Does it make *you* feel big...?"

"Is that why you refused me? Afraid of Wvercian cock?"

She looked away, and Jon saw that hard look on her face again, a colder anger. Oblivious, the Wvercian only smiled.

"You haven't been broken in by one of my family yet, have you, girl?"

Allie didn't answer, but Jon saw that unwavering look in her eyes.

"I'll be good to you, girl. Promise. I'll treat you real good..."

"Sure you will."

Jon felt sick. He wanted to tell yell at them to to turn it off, but he found himself listening to the conversation on the VR screen, unable to stop himself.

"...You seem awfully angry, given that you suck cock for a living. Did I do something to you I don't know about? Did one of my family hurt you? Or is this just a general hatred for all of your brothers?"

Jon winced again, unable to keep from looking at Revik again. The Elaerian's face hadn't moved. Nor had his body, where he perched on the wooden chair. Jon couldn't tear his eyes off his expression anyway, though, and missed part of the back and forth before his attention found its way back to the organic screen.

"...I know your name," he heard Allie say.

"Do you now?" The giant replied. "Tell me, then. I'm starting to get bored of this fight, girl." He stepped closer to her, softening his voice. Whatever he was doing out of view of the image made Allie wince, disgust flickering over her expression, but she didn't pull away. "...Tell me my name, girl. For you to be so angry, you must know that at least. And tell me what wrong I did to you, to make you despise me so..."

She looked up, her eyes unusually pale, dead-seeming.

"Your name is Gerwix," she said.

Jon felt his heart stop in his chest. He looked at Revik, but the Elaerian didn't move. Jon's eyes followed Revik's back to the screen.

The giant was staring at her, as if paralyzed.

For a long moment, the Wvercian didn't move. He stood over her, almost as if he'd been about to kiss her, but the look on his face was more like some kind of surprised beast. Then, his mouth curled into an angry frown.

His words, when he finally spoke, seemed to burst out of him.

"Where did you hear that name, girl?" he growled.

When Allie didn't answer, his thick, red fingers grabbed her bare shoulders. He shook her hard, roughly, enough to probably hurt her...or disorient her at the least. She held up her hands, almost as if to ward him off, but essentially, she endured it.

"Who the *fuck* told you that name?" His voice rose to a near shout. "Where did you hear it, bitch? Where?"

He lifted her off the floor, gripping her until his fingers whitened, until the skin of her shoulders must have been bruised.

"Do you know who I work for?" the giant demanded. "Do you?"

There was a pause.

Then Allie looked down at him again. She smiled, but the look in her eyes was so cold Jon didn't recognize her in it at all.

"Gerwix," she said softly. "...Nenzi says hi."

Jon felt Revik flinch.

The giant seer's eyes widened visibly on the screen.

"What?" he said. "What the *fuck* did you – "

Before he could go on...

...A loud, cracking sound made half the seers in the room jump.

Gerwix crumpled. As he did, he brought Allie's feet to the floor, dropping her as his fingers abruptly loosened. He continued to fall, his weight bringing him down fast...forcing her to move nimbly, almost gracefully out of the way to avoid being crushed. She slid sideways with a kind of dancing step and a gasp, her face no longer calm but flushed...

Then she was just standing there, breathing hard, her fists clenched as she stared down at the giant's broken body.

The screen went dark.

There was a silence where everyone in the room just seemed to stare at the blank screen. Then Jon looked up, feeling as much as hearing some kind of commotion at the front of the room. At first he had no comprehension of what he was seeing.

He saw Voi Pai's head back, saw her fingers at her throat, almost like she was scratching at her own neck. Her body appeared to be pressed too far into the silk cushions, sliding down the seat in an awkward position that partly splayed her legs. Her chin and head tilted so far upwards, she appeared to be staring at the ceiling. It looked almost like someone held her there...

Then Balidor cursed, jerking Jon's eyes sideways.

Glancing at his pale face, Jon found comprehension reach him. He stared back at the Lao Hu leader, and realized suddenly, that Revik was on his feet, breathing harder, staring up at the high chair, his hands open at his sides.

"Dehgoies!" Balidor said. "Dehgoies...calm yourself, brother!"

"Nenzi..." Wreg said, also stepping towards the front of the room. "Nenzi...don't kill her, *laoban!* Do not!"

Jon realized then that Voi Pai wasn't dead.

Revik had some kind of stranglehold on her throat, and she was choking, her fingers fighting to remove invisible fingers from around her pale skin. Her eyes widened, even as she gestured to other seers in the room. Revik's eyes darted sideways, then around at the other infiltrators.

"I feel anyone's light move, and she's dead," he said.

His voice was almost soft.

"...Guns, gas, anyone move towards me or try to take me down in the construct...and she's dead," he said, glancing briefly around for emphasis. "...Obey me, and she'll come through this just fine. All I want is my wife..."

Jon glanced at Allie, for the first time since they played that godawful recording.

She was staring at Revik, disbelief in her eyes that bordered on shock. When she spoke, he heard both in her voice, along with a near-anger that held enough grief that Jon flinched.

"Revik! What are you doing?"

Revik glanced at her. His expression didn't move, but Jon saw a flicker of pain there, enough that he felt almost like he shouldn't be looking at the two of them.

"You'll start a war," she said, that pain in her voice, too. "What are you doing? I told you not to come for me...I asked you..."

Revik's jaw hardened, but his eyes didn't move from hers.

"You said I could come if I needed you," he said.

"Revik..."

"I need you. I'm not leaving here without you, Allie...so if you stay, I'll stay. I'll work the other half of the contract. I'll work the whole goddamned thing..."

She stared at him, her eyes lost, like she couldn't believe what he'd said.

"Revik...it's not just about us. The Lao Hu..."

"...Aren't our friends," he said. "The war is already happening, Allie... they're just lying about it. Your being here won't make any difference...you're not keeping the peace, you're just giving them leverage." He swallowed, and for the first time, the infiltrator's mask wavered. "Gods, baby. Please. *Please* come with me..."

Her expression wavered as his did. Jon saw her eyes brighten.

Finally, she nodded.

Looking at the blue-eyed seer behind her, she motioned at her collar.

"Take it off," she said.

He shook his head, once. "No, Esteemed Bridge. No."

Jon was surprised at the emotion he heard in the tall seer's voice, even before he turned, glaring openly at Revik.

"Not for him, Alyson. I won't free you for him..."

Clicking at him angrily, Allie started to move away, to walk towards the rest of the rebels and Adhipan, when the blue-eyed seer caught her by the arms. Turning her around, he pulled her against him, kissing her before Allie seemed to realize what he was doing. Jon saw her kiss him back, briefly, just before her hand raised to his chest, pushing on him to separate them.

Revik's voice rose even as she turned her face away from the blue-eyed seer.

"Brother!" he said. "Brother...stop!"

The Lao Hu seer let Allie push him back. He glared at Revik, still holding her arms. "She told me what you did to her," the other said. "You don't deserve her...intermediary or no. She will only leave you again..."

"That's probably true," Revik said. "But she wants you to let her go. If you don't take your hands off her, I'm going to have to hurt you..." His voice held pain again. "...Please, brother. Whatever you think of me...you're hurting me right now...and her."

The Lao Hu seer released her, after staring a long moment into her face. He only stood there, his eyes pained as he watched Allie pull her arms around herself. She barely glanced at the rest of the Lao Hu seers, some of whom were looking at her with as much emotion in their faces as the one who had kissed her.

Without looking directly at any of the Adhipan or Rebels, either, she walked deeper into the room. She paused a few yards from Jon, then seemed to hesitate, uncertainty in her eyes when she didn't go any further. Feeling a tightening in his throat, Jon took the remaining steps to close the gap between them, and grabbed her hand, clutching her fingers tightly in his.

He wanted to give her his jacket...his shirt...something to cover her up, but he knew it would probably only make her feel worse. He could still see her avoiding all of their eyes, holding herself upright as her jaw hardened. Finally, she stared at Revik, who still had his back to them from where he stood in the front of the room. His eyes paused on the blue-eyed seer another beat, then he looked around at the rest of the Lao Hu seers, his clear eyes narrow. His voice came out soft, calm once more.

"I won't hurt your leader," he said. "...If you give me no reason, she will come out of this completely unharmed. I give you my word, as your intermediary..."

The Lao Hu infiltrators traded looks. Jon could feel more information passing in the space, even being a non-seer, but the looks on their faces were pretty easy to read. They didn't believe him. Not for a second.

"I will not harm her," Revik repeated. "I realize it is war with us, either way, but you must know I would not risk my people being hurt...my wife being hurt. Your mistress' life is insurance for me, as much as it is for you. But I will take it, if need be. Do not test me on this, please. I will leave here with my wife...the easy way, or the hard way..."

Hearing his words, Jon swallowed, and realized Revik meant every one. If he had to leave here by leveling half of the City, he would.

Jon couldn't help wondering who would come out of that little contest alive. He would have placed higher bets on Revik if Allie wasn't wearing a collar. Especially after what he'd seen of her in those recordings in São Paulo, and now on the screen, with that Wvercian.

He felt the infiltrators surrounding them thinking about this too, maybe realizing the same thing. Revik might not win, but he just might kill more than half of them trying. He also might manage to get Allie free of the collar... and all of them had seen the tapes of her, too. Not just the one they'd shown a few minutes before, but Allie during the Registry job, exploding guns with her mind and throwing seers through organic windows that were supposed to be able to withstand the impact of a small plane hitting them from outside.

Not only that, Jon could tell they didn't want to kill Allie. Whatever else she'd done here, some of them appeared to be loyal to her, too.

Jon glanced back up at the silk-upholstered chair, and realized that Revik had knocked Voi Pai unconscious. She lay slumped on the long, divan-like chair, her black hair bunched up in the odd angle of her head and throat, her cat-like eyes with the vertical pupils closed. Without that predatory stare, her face appeared strangely soft, yet older somehow, too...almost peaceful.

"I will take her with us, to ensure our safe passage," Revik added. "Only as far as I need to, my brothers and sisters. I promise I will not hurt her, if you give me no cause. I want no war with your people, not that kind of war...I only want my wife. I came only for my wife..."

"You will never make it out of Beijing alive," one of the infiltrators said.

Revik's eyes swiveled, meeting his.

"You'd better hope I do, brother," he said softly, his eyes a touch colder. "Your mistress' life depends on it..."

Twenty-Five
Transit

J ON FOUND HIMSELF WALKING BACK THROUGH THE CITY IN A NEAR-DAZE.
He gripped Allie's hand, but neither of them really looked at the other as they made their way back through the successive gates. Even after they'd left the Meridian Gate and reached the wide gardens on the other side, there was a odd, impenetrable silence over the entire procession.

Allie walked easily in the flowing material, despite the chill of the evening air. Garensche had offered her his shirt, but she'd declined politely, smiling at him as she pointed out that it was warm enough that she could make it to the front gate at least. Even her feet remained bare as she walked the stone paths, jangling slightly as the chains moved with each step. No one really looked at her, or at what she wore, but Jon found himself acutely aware of it.

He knew she wasn't messing with them; she really didn't seem to care all that much, about what she wore...but more than that, he could feel her urgency around their leaving. She didn't want to waste time with clothing when they had Voi Pai captive, not with all of those seers following after them as they made their way back towards the main city of Beijing.

He felt her awareness of all of their lives, even as she gripped his hand tighter.

Her feet must have been cold, much less her legs and arms, but when Jon glanced at her face, she only stared around at the seers circling her in a protective ring, as if she still wasn't sure any of them were real.

He saw her eyes pause on Balidor and Wreg again, as if unable to reconcile seeing them walking side by side, only to swivel back to Garensche, Dorje, Jax and Poresh. She paused again on Vikram and Tenzi, her eyes reflecting a similar confusion, only to look back at a few more of the rebels, ones with names Jon hadn't yet learned.

Lao Hu infiltrators followed them every step of the way through the City grounds. Some followed them openly, walking alongside only a dozen or so paces to either side of their huddled procession. Most seemed to keep their eyes on Revik, who brought up the rear, his gaze fixed straight ahead although Jon had no doubt he continued to operate in a number of different levels of the Barrier.

Wreg held Voi Pai. The Lao Hu leader remained unconscious, but she now wore a collar. Balidor had fitted it around her neck, locking it there at Revik's instruction once they'd been provided one of the devices by the Lao Hu infiltrators...also at Revik's command. Wreg held her carefully, and visibly, so that the infiltrators could see that she remained unharmed, but none of that seemed to relax a single one of the seers following them.

Jon didn't realize just how tense he was until Allie squeezed his fingers.

He nearly jumped out of his skin before he turned his head, gasping a little as he met her gaze. She smiled up at his expression, but her green eyes remained measured...distant.

"Cass?" she said softly.

Jon hesitated, then shook his head. "She's all right. We're going to her," he added. "After this, I mean."

She nodded slowly, then glanced around them once more.

"How did he find me, Jon?" she asked.

Her voice had a faint note of accusation in it.

Frowning, Jon shook his head, clicking softly as he pulled her closer to him. "We'll talk about that later, Al."

She let him tug her closer, walking beside him carefully with her bare feet.

It was cold in the dark, but Jon could see the flowers on the trees, and remembered it was spring again, that the winter had finally passed. He'd spent so much of the last few months underground, he found himself inhaling the blossoms in spite of himself, feeling an odd sort of relief in the simple fact of life exploding out around him. His shoulders relaxed slightly in the same moment, and he held her hand tighter, against his side, giving Dorje a bare glance where the seer walked closely on her other side.

All of the seers were looking at her, Jon realized suddenly.

It occurred to him in the same moment that he wasn't the only one who felt guilty.

After what felt like another long silence, they reached the front gate.

Seers stood in a line at the edge of it, parting as they got closer, all of them staring either at Allie or at the collared Voi Pai being carried by Wreg. Jon noticed a number of the seers seemed emotional. He saw a few bow as they passed, and not only to Voi Pai; most made the symbol of the Bridge with one hand when Allie reached them, too.

Instead of touching him though, it angered him, and reminded him again that he might never understand all the weird-ass ritual and "respect" crap of seers. That they'd kept here here like an animal, forcing her to work off some stupid debt, and yet still had the temerity to act like Revik and the rest of them were stealing some precious artifact from their city.

Dorje touched his shoulder, gently, from the other side of Allie.

Jon felt the reassurance of his touch, but the tightness remained in his chest anyway. He hadn't let himself think about any of this too much. For one thing, like everyone else, he'd been afraid Revik might lose his shit for real if they didn't hold steady for him. But he'd also been in denial too, he supposed. He was so sick of this degrading crap with seers.

"It is over now, cousin," Dorje said softly.

"For now," Jon muttered.

Allie looked up at him, her eyes studying his silently. Realizing his eyes were leaking somewhat, he brushed it away angrily, giving her a taut smile.

"I'm sorry," she said, her voice low.

He gave a humorless snort, squeezing her hand again. "Shut up, sis," he said. "Or I'm going to have to kick your ass."

She didn't answer, but he didn't see her smile, either.

They made their way through the last gate as silently as they had all of the others.

Jon felt himself stiffen though, preparing himself for the worst as they left the main construct of the Lao Hu. It was too late at night for them to see tourists outside, but passing through that gate still brought up an exposed feeling...he wondered if it came from him or the other seers, either theirs of the Lao Hu watching them from the high walls.

It occurred to him that they could just shoot Revik from there, hit him in the back of the head and everything would be over.

A second later he thought, if it was that easy, they would have done it already...likely before he made it out of the reception chamber. He must have some direct line to their construct, either through Allie or through Voi Pai herself. It was the only thing that made sense.

He remembered all of those muttered sessions with Balidor and Wreg in the planning room while they were still in that odd, underground maze on the border of Russia. He remembered pieces of some of the louder arguments they sometimes overheard, and wondered if that had anything to do with this. But Wreg and Balidor seemed just as surprised as the rest of them when they saw Revik holding Voi Pai, so Jon doubted this had been the original plan, other than the part about Allie leaving there with them.

He glanced at her again, watching her wince as they reached the road, picking her steps carefully on the uneven sidewalk. She blinked against the lights of the high buildings, raising a hand in bewilderment to shield her eyes from the headlamps of passing cars.

Most of the latter were almost as far away as the buildings. Routed away from the circle of road nearest to the Tian'anmen gate, the public street only passed by the higher security checkpoints that led to the main circle, even with the long stretch of sidewalk and the smaller park intervening. They were close enough that the honk of horns reached them, however, and the lights looked bright, even to Jon, who hadn't been sequestered inside the oddly timeless space of the Forbidden City for the past however-many months.

He tugged harder on her hand, pulling her insistently down the stone pathway that wound between trees in the small park that stood between them and the road. The other seers closed around them tighter as he walked with her, and he found himself glancing at her bare feet as his hand and legs urged her to hurry. He glanced at Dorje, who nodded, once, and then picked up the pace even more. They reached the curb right as three stretch limousines pulled up, one after the other. The doors seemed to be open before they'd come to a complete stop.

Jon followed when Garensche and Dorje led Allie towards the middle car. He glanced back in time to see Revik disappear into the rear car with Wreg and Balidor and Vikram. Revik spared him a quick look, then glanced at Dorje before he disappeared. Jon looked at the smaller, Tibetan-looking seer as well.

"He's not riding with us?" Jon said, quiet, as Allie got into the car in front of him.

Dorje shook his head, once, giving him a look that said he'd explain later.

Then they were all in the car and speeding down the road.

Jon didn't feel relaxed, even then, shoved into the rear seat of the limo with Dorje on one side and Allie on the other. Garensche sat at the door, and now he had a gun in his hand. Others were also being passed around the small car. Jon accepted a handgun that Holo handed to him, and then a few magazines, which he shoved into his jacket pocket. Everyone seemed to be armed then, except Allie herself. For a long moment, no one in the car spoke.

Then Allie seemed to be looking around, as if coming out of a kind of daze.

Dorje answered the question she never bothered to voice aloud.

"He's behind us, Esteemed Bridge," he said. "He is helping the others read Voi Pai, while they have the opportunity..." At Allie's blank look, Dorje tapped his temple. "Intelligence, Esteemed Bridge...we'll need it. Especially now."

"Intelligence on what?" she said.

"Who bought you," Dorje replied, his voice unflinching. "Who hired the Wvercian you killed. They wanted also to determine more information about the disease Chandre found in the United States...Voi Pai's communication to you previously does not correlate with our own intelligence." At Allie's questioning look, Dorje elaborated, "...Chandre has no sample of the drug as Voi Pai accused, Esteemed Bridge. There is some concern that someone else may have custody of this sample instead. Voi Pai was not forthcoming when your husband questioned her in the hours prior to our audience with you..."

Allie flinched a little at how Dorje referred to Revik. Jon wondered if anyone noticed but him. When Dorje finished speaking, however, she only nodded, leaning her head against Garensche's thick arm.

"Yeah," she said, sounding tired suddenly. "She wasn't all that forthcoming with me on that subject, either." She turned her head, looking at Dorje directly. "How did he find me, Dorje? Did one of these lugs tell him?"

She rolled her eyes up, indicating Garensche behind her.

The large seer laughed, jostling her back.

Then a muscular arm stole around her, hugging her from behind, hard enough that her eyes widened a little. He hugged her again when Allie glanced up, smiling at him wanly. He gripped her bare shoulder from behind with one hand, holding her tightly against his side. Jon couldn't help but smile when he felt the warmth flood the car, almost like an exhaled breath. Holo and Jax moved closer on their seats, perching on the end of them to be closer to her.

"You're going to lose that hand, Gar," Holo said, but he grinned at Allie as well, touching her leg and then her arm almost tentatively.

"Yes," Ike said, the other tattoo-covered seer who looked almost like a young version of Wreg to Jon. "...Wait until the boss sees you groping his wife."

He caressed her fingers though, smiling at her from the opposite seat.

Jax wiped his eyes, touching her other leg as well, then her hand.

"Are you all right, Esteemed Bridge?"

She smiled around at the three of them. "I'm fine."

Poresh shoved closer to her as well, moving Jon out of the way. He slid an arm around her from the other side, as did Yumi next to him, her tattooed face wrinkling under her smile. She caressed Allie's face with long fingers, then kissed her cheek, elbowing Poresh when he laughed. Even the solemn-faced seer from the rebels, the one who looked like he came from a desert somewhere in the Middle East, Loki, moved closer to touch her leg. For a long moment, Jon watched them look at her, as if assuring themselves that she was all right.

Finally, it seemed to get a little too awkward for Allie.

She glanced around at all of them, still leaning against Garensche's bulk.

"So is anyone going to tell me?"

"Tell you what, Esteemed Bridge?" Dorje said.

"Why Wreg and Balidor haven't killed one another yet?"

All of them broke out in laughter around her.

Something about that made Jon relax even more, even as the tightening in his throat briefly worsened. Even feeling like hell, like she probably did right now, something about having her back lifted the mood of everyone in the car. Most of them leaned back from where they'd hovered around her, still laughing amongst themselves as they gave each other knowing looks. Garensche was the first to answer her in actual words.

"They've tried a few times..."

"You should have heard them in the first planning sessions we tried to have," Poresh added, laughing. "It was, 'I'll stab you in your sleep, kneeler...' and 'are you done trying to kill the Sword, you ink-covered Dreng addict?'"

"...I think Wreg might have punched him at the very least," Jax added. "But your husband wouldn't allow it to go much further..."

"You should've seen them talking about who should accompany him in here..." Dorje began, shoving at Loki's arm, who only smiled at him thinly, his dark eyes unmoving from Allie's face.

"...and Wreg's face when the Sword first told them he intended to combine infiltration teams..." Ike added.

"I'm not sure Wreg will ever forgive the Sword for not letting him gun Adhipan Balidor down on the spot," Holo said, grinning. "He complains under his breath every time the boss isn't listening..."

"We've joked we should assign tasters for their food, so one of them doesn't show up dead. At this point we need all the infiltrators we can get..."

Allie looked around at all of them, a vague wonder still in her eyes.

"How did this happen?" she said. "How are you all here?"

Garensche laughed again, squeezing her against him, tightly enough that she grabbed his arm. "The boss gave us a choice. We could follow him, or Salinse and the Dreng...but not both. He told us we were going to ally with the Seven, which meant the Adhipan too...and no killing one another once we'd taken that vow..."

"...He said we had to stop fighting amongst ourselves," said Holo. "That we have to start rounding up the seers who are out there, from the work camps, before Salinse makes them dependent on the Rooks. He wants to rebuild a seer economy..."

"...He wants to start a new colony, too," Poresh added. "And rebuild Seertown...maybe also rebuild the colony in the Pamir. He's talked about freeing the remaining seers from work camps...forcing new terms with the humans once we have the leverage..."

Allie looked around her again, her mouth firming.

But the bewilderment in her eyes remained, Jon noticed. He saw her willfully shove some of her own thoughts...or doubts maybe...from her mind.

"But not everyone?" she said. "How many from the rebels took his terms?"

"Thirty-eight of us, so far," Jax answered promptly. "...In Asia anyway. A few more in South America. He hasn't approached everyone yet. We were still in the process of contacting people, when..." He colored a little, looking down at her clothes, then shrugged with one hand.

"...I don't know how many of us are left," he finished lamely.

"How many went back to Salinse?" she said.

The others looked at one another, and again Jax's expression grew uncomfortable.

"Closer to seventy, Esteemed Bridge," he explained apologetically. "...

Ute left first. She contacted a bunch of the others. Salinse commanded a lot of loyalty before the Sword returned. Many of them owe him their lives..."

Allie nodded, but Jon saw a shadow pass over her eyes.

"How many infiltrators?" she said.

"Only about forty of a rank above four or five," Garensche said reassuringly, rubbing her shoulder from where he held her against his side.

"And on our side?" she said.

He shrugged, smiling down at her. "You're looking at them...and those in the other cars. We pretty much all came along when the Sword told us where he was going. There are a few deployed in the States, and in Europe... another half-dozen in South America..."

Nodding, she smiled back, glancing around at all of their faces once more.

Jon wondered if she was counting as her eyes passed over each one.

He'd already counted the same. It was maybe fourteen total, of the rebels who were with them in Asia. Maybe they had Chan with them now, in America...plus the six Revik spoke to in Brazil. So around twenty...twenty-five if they were lucky. Half of what had opted to go to Salinse at the outset, and who knew how many of those were working both sides of the fence.

The numbers hadn't seemed to bother Revik though. Jon got the impression he'd been so relieved at Wreg's answer that anyone after him had been a kind of bonus.

He was still thinking about this, when Loki fished a tool out of the side pocket in the car's door. Jon had seen one like it before, the last time they were in China. Thick organic metal blades stood on either side of a heavy handle with dark grips. It reminded Jon of a nutcracker, or heavy wire cutters. After showing the tool to Allie, Loki asked a question with one hand.

She answered with a returning gesture of her fingers, and he fit the grooved edges of the blade around the collar at her neck.

He squeezed the handles and she gave a short gasp as the ring around her neck opened with a faint sucking sound. Jon knew that the coils of organic material were likely unraveling from around her neck. She was pulling it off when Loki caught hold of her other wrist, making another questioning motion with his hand.

She nodded that time, instead of using seer hand-language. Jon and the others watched as he fit the tool under the chains around her wrist, cutting through the metal in a series of three or four squeezes of the thick handles.

He moved immediately to the one at her ankle...then to her other wrist...then her other ankle.

Another seer's hands reached out, pulling the chains off her, tossing them to the floor on the other side of the car, by the opposite door.

Jon watched the chains disappear, swallowing. He didn't look away from her bare wrists and ankles until he felt Allie's eyes on his face.

He saw embarrassment in her eyes, but her jaw hardened while he watched, as if she was daring him to say something about it.

"What about Chan, Jon?" she said. "Has anyone talked to her recently?"

Jon hesitated.

For a moment, he wondered how much he should say about that before she'd recovered from the rest of it...and given the high spirits of everyone in the car. Finally, he just shrugged, smiling at her with as much cheerfulness as he could muster.

"She's fine," he said. He checked his watch, glancing at Dorje as he fought the worry from his voice. "She should be on a plane to South America right about now..."

"South America?" Allie said, dumbfounded.

Jon nodded, again looking at Dorje, maybe for help.

"She's gone to Argentina, Esteemed Bridge," Dorje added reassuringly. "A reconnaissance mission. She is working with a few other seers...under the command of the Sword."

"A few other seers?" Allie said, still bewildered. "Who?"

For a second, Jon and Dorje only looked at one another, hesitating again.

"They have her," Chan confirmed, speaking loud above the sound of the plane's engines and whatever she listened to in her headset. "...She is all right."

Chandre glanced at the three seers who sat next to her in the middle row of commercial seats on the plane. Padded on either side with two empty seats, they had the row to themselves. They had only just left the air conditioned confines of the Albuquerque International Airport and been seated in the first class compartment of the Boeing 747-8.

"Any news on Eddard?" Varlan asked her.

Chandre, still listening on the other end, shook her head.

"...Nothing on Maygar, either." She glanced at Varlan, then past him, to Rex and Stanley on his other side. "They haven't told them yet. The Bridge... or the Sword."

Varlan didn't answer, but his indigo eyes flickered slightly.

Chandre didn't bother to try and figure out what that meant.

They'd headed south and east by car, not risking any of the Bay Area airports after blowing up the lab and electrical substation near Hayward, California. They'd settled on Albuquerque finally, as it was one of the smaller international airports in the area, far smaller than Denver or Phoenix. The op had gone fine, or so they thought up until the end. They managed to place all of the explosives, to find the exit through the ventilation shafts, just like Eddard had shown them. They also managed to round up and identify all of the head scientists for the project. It had been necessary, of course, to make sure those who could even possibly reconstruct the formula from memory went up with the equipment. That hadn't been Chandre's favorite part of the job, but she recognized the necessity for it; she didn't argue when Varlan gave the order.

Everything had gone as smoothly as could be expected, really, considering that they'd tripped the construct alarms a good thirty minutes before they'd planned. Yet somewhere in the course of that op, while Chandre had been working with Stanley, Rex and Varlan to lay the charges in the main lab, Eddard and Maygar had vanished.

Varlan and his people and Chandre spent months looking for them in the time since. They'd searched all over California, then widened that search to include most of the west coast when they still didn't turn up. Varlan had insisted on accompanying and aiding Chandre when she proposed a search. She wondered why at first, but then Varlan told her he had 'concerns' about Eddard and the samples of the human-killing virus he'd intended to remove from the lab.

It hadn't occurred to Chandre until then that Varlan likely hadn't intended the human to succeed in that goal, as it directly violated the terms of his contract with his client, 'Shadow,' which had been to destroy the disease in totality. In fact, Chan realized, Varlan likely intended to put a few well-placed bullets in Eddard's brain before they'd left the lab, and after he'd ceased to be useful in terms of getting them in and out safely.

But none of that occurred to her until the job was finished.

They hadn't waited to find Maygar and Eddard to detonate the lab of course...they couldn't afford to, no matter what the odds that the human and the young seer had been left inside. Even in the wake of the attack, however, they hadn't found any evidence that the two had remained underground. Nor, really, had they found any evidence that they'd escaped, other than the fact that they searched the entire lab before leaving and saw no sign of either of them. Eddard had disappeared to collect his samples of the disease and the antidote. Maygar left to look for the exit through the cooling and ventilation shafts, as per Eddard's instructions. While Chandre and the others were halfway through setting the charges in the underground lab, Maygar had pinged them all to tell them that he'd found the way out.

Then nothing. Neither of them had been heard from since.

Varlan, however, had been relatively sure that he could sense imprints of the two of them, leaving out through the ventilation shafts ahead of them. Chandre knew it was possible he'd only said that, of course, to get the rest of them to leave when the clock started to run down, to keep them on schedule for the job...but for some reason, she believed him.

Of course, with an infiltrator of Varlan's rank, she couldn't trust that feeling either.

It bothered her more than she wanted to admit, that Maygar, little shit that he was, could have been trapped and killed down there. She knew it was still a strong possibility, that he had been missed somehow in their sweep and died in the explosions and cave ins that followed. The whole scene had gotten so chaotic once the Barrier alarms went off...Chandre had no way of pinning down an exact moment when she knew for certain that either Maygar or Eddard had no longer been with them.

"...She is already out of the main city," Chandre added, pulling her mind back to the present. "It looks like they got away cleanly..."

Varlan's expression remained unchanged at Chandre's news, but something in the dark-skinned seer, Stanley's, visibly relaxed. He adjusted his narrow body in the cloth seat, looking off to the side to peer through the nearest of the distant oval windows. Chandre noted the male seer's expression though, and with some relief. Whoever he worked for, he didn't entirely hate the Bridge. Moreover, he was likely religious. The thought comforted her, especially since she had to trust the three of them, at least for the next leg of their journey.

Balidor was footing the bill for this little venture, which was strange enough, but stranger still, Varlan had accepted his offer, despite the clear conflict of interest it posed with his client. Chandre couldn't help wondering what Balidor had said to him to convince him to accept. She also couldn't help wondering if the Adhipan leader had other things on his mind, in asking the ex-Rook to help them. Like perhaps recruitment...which wasn't so much of a stretch these days really, especially given the rank of the seer sitting directly beside her. Given the fact that it looked like Dehgoies now led military operations, as well as the shit storm they'd just stirred by picking a fight with the Lao Hu, they would need all the infiltrators they could get.

In any case, when Chandre told Balidor about the mysterious client of Varlan's, Balidor had jumped at the chance, offering Varlan and his people more than twice their usual rate to allow Chandre to accompany them to their meeting with this 'Shadow' person. Varlan balked at first, for predictable reasons, claiming he couldn't afford to misuse his contacts or his clients in such a way, but Balidor managed to persuade him somewhere in the course of their conversation. Chandre didn't know how, exactly, but she suspected it hadn't only been with money. She still found it interesting Balidor hadn't told Dehgoies any of this, but maybe the Sword had enough on his mind, given what Allie had been up to for the past few months.

That whole story, however, was something Chandre herself still had trouble believing.

As if reading her thoughts, Rex, the mammoth seer who sat between Varlan and Stanley, leaned around the older seer to look at her.

"Did they really sell her through the Rynak?" He kept his voice low, even as he darted a look at an airline stewardess as she passed in the aisle.

Chandre nodded, aiming it in two directions at once when she caught the eye of a second airline steward, who frowned at her, tapping the side of his head to indicate her headset. Pulling the device from around her ear, Chandre clicked it off, giving the human an apologetic smile as she shoved it into her bag underneath the seat in front of her.

She glanced up at Rex as she straightened, and found Stanley looking at her, too.

"She seems to be fine," she said. "They say she is changed..."

"Changed?" Varlan raised an eyebrow, giving her a pointed look.

Chandre merely shrugged, her eyes shifting towards the far window, where Stanley's attention seemed to be focused once more.

"Changed how, sister Chandre?"

Considering for a moment, Chandre turned. There was no reason she could think of to withhold this information, so after another pause she shrugged, giving the older seer a humorless smile.

"How do you think? They trained her...in several different arts. Her light is changed, brother." She averted her eyes at his frown, fighting her own expression still. "...Apparently they trained her in more than simply those things which one might expect. Something to do with the transfer of rights over her person...an agreement they made with her new owners. They say they may have to give her a number now." Her voice lowered still more as she watched the steward pass on the aisle next to Stanley. "...A real rank," she added, soft. "Actual, instead of simply a guess at her potential."

Varlan stared at her, his dark eyes holding nothing as he processed all of her words.

"They had avoided that before," he said finally.

She nodded, using the human version of saying yes.

Despite the contacts she wore, she'd already received a number of stares from other passengers, particularly in the boarding areas for the plane, so she wasn't sure how many people she was actually fooling. Still, to make them at least pause, to question whether she was one thing or the other, was all they really required for this trip. The place where the plane landed did not exclude her people, so to obscure her race was more of a convenience than a necessity.

"They may have no choice now," she answered him.

"Will they register her? Formally, I mean?"

Chandre merely shrugged. "I do not know. He said they will determine that later...after they have done a more systematic assessment of what it is about her that has changed."

"Who said this?"

"Adhipan Balidor."

Varlan didn't blink. "Did you speak to any others?"

She shook her head, knowing what he was asking. Like the rest of them, he wanted information about the Sword, about what the Sword was thinking, about what he would do next. Chandre couldn't have told them that even if she wanted to. In the same set of heartbeats, however, it occurred to her that using Revik's name likely had a lot to do with why Varlan had agreed to their arrangement in the first place.

Tucking a stray braid behind her ear, she only blew out her cheeks before she glanced at him. "Right now, they are still questioning the woman they brought with them from the city. They only have a few more minutes with her, before they must depart..."

"To go where?"

Chandre gave him a warning look, glancing around them pointedly.

"That will be determined, brother."

Varlan nodded at her words, but the slight frown never left his face. Chandre had focused back on her bag, trying to remember if she'd brought an actual paper book, when Rex spoke up from Varlan's other side, his voice holding a low humor.

"The Sword is a lucky man," he said, whistling softly.

Chandre tensed, even as she'd been about to grab a magazine from the rack in front of her. She almost didn't ask it. Then, after biting her lip, she did anyway.

"Why do you say that?" she said stiffly.

When she glanced up, Rex's brown eyes smiled along with his lips, but she felt the pulse of arousal there, a faint flare off his light.

"The Lao Hu consorts are famous," he said, smiling at her, winking. "You have no idea what I'd give to have a wife trained in those arts...but maybe an arm." He nudged Stanley, who only grunted, his eyes still focused out the window. Rex laughed, adding, "...Maybe even a foot. I bet he doesn't let her out of their room, now that he has her back in his bed." His smile turned into a leer. "...Are you sure it was an accident she ended up there, sister Chandre?"

Chan felt her mouth and jaw turn to granite. She stared at him, fighting the urge to punch him in the face, using the knuckles of the stronger of her two hands, maybe blinding him in one eye with her fingers. Instead she forced her gaze sideways, looking out the window to her left. She was still staring out, unseeing, when Varlan spoke from her other side.

"Could he tell us anything?" he said. When Chandre turned, the anger still warring in her light, Varlan clarified, "Balidor. Did he say anything else? Anything that will help us, where we are going?"

Biting her lip, she shrugged, one handed, forgetting to use the human version.

"He said whoever they are, our friends in the East appear to have sworn allegiance to them, as well." She gave Rex a hard look, but the muscular seer seemed unfazed. "...She had been sold to them, to pay for her crime against one of theirs. Someone they sent to assess her, to ensure her good health and progress in the areas in which they wished to see her grow."

"Crime?" Stanley jerked out of his silence, turning. "What crime is that?"

Chandre met his gaze, biting her lip in anger once more. "She killed him. The messenger."

"Why?"

"That, I do not know...precisely. Balidor implied it was something personal."

"Personal?" Rex grunted. "Doesn't her line of work preclude the personal...?"

She gave him a cold look. "Something to do with her husband."

Rex stared at her, his eyes holding an open surprise. Before he could speak, Varlan's voice rose from his left, and Chandre felt the calming influence he threw lightly over both of them.

"How did they know it was the same person?" he said softly. "...As my client?"

Chandre shrugged. "Whoever it was, they used the same call sign. It was the only real ID they could get off their friend from the East." At Varlan's raised eyebrow, she added, "Shadow. She, too, referred to their leader as Shadow...nothing else."

"...Any other news from our friends in the East?" he said. "Anything relevant to the meeting we will be attending down there?"

Hesitating, she shook her head, but her hand gesture was more noncommittal.

"They are still with the woman," she said. "He said he would contact me again, once we land. They will be in transit themselves by then..." She looked at her watch, then at him directly. "...He seemed to think that it is not Salinse, however."

"Not Salinse?"

"At least not on his own."

"Meaning...what?"

"Meaning there are indications to them as well, of a larger group behind this," she said, lowering her voice as the stewardess walked by, her dark navy dress brushing the sides of the aisle. Chandre waited for her to disappear past the curtain dividing the two sides of the cabin, then spoke again, her voice lower than a whisper.

"...It seems our friends in the East," she added, making the symbol of the Lao Hu in the stale air of the cabin. "...Also received news of the destruction of this disease. No one on our side told them of this op, since no one I work for in Asia knew anything about it until well after the fact. Yet this woman knew...and assumed Alyson would know of this thing, too. They thought, in fact, that it was our side who took the samples that Eddard claimed he wanted..."

"And this worried them?" Varlan asked emotionlessly.

"Yes. I mean...apparently it did. I do not know precisely why."

"Yet they claim this group as allies? Claim allegiance to them, so you say?"

Hesitating, Chandre looked back at Varlan. "Yes. But Balidor is unsure about the truth behind this. It is also possible that our Eastern friends are being played...as much as those in the West appear to have been. Balidor seems to think so. He thinks they are all pawns...the rebels, the tiger people. He thinks there are those in Washington who are being toyed with as well. It is creating a great deal of fear. More than that, it is puzzling to all of them why they would want this disease destroyed...when it seems likely the same group may have had a hand in its creation. Balidor is quite relieved that was the case, of course, but it is puzzling..."

Varlan's expression remained immobile.

After a moment's thought, he shrugged. It was a human shrug.

"So we continue our journey," he said. "And we see what we shall see."

Chandre glanced at Rex, then at Stanley. The latter's chiseled face looked just as grim as she felt. Returning her eyes to Varlan's, she nodded, once, just as matter-of-fact.

"Yes, brother," she said, gesturing subtly in respect. "...We do."

Twenty-Six
Ring

I SAT IN THE FRONT ROW OF SEATS ON THE PLANE, FEELING AN ODD SENSE OF DÉJÀ VU.
It wasn't a commercial plane...in fact, it was unmarked plane, a lot like the one I'd ridden in the last time I'd left Beijing with Revik and Wreg and the rest of his people.

We were brought on board first...meaning me and Jon and the others I rode with in the limousine. I sat at the front and to the far starboard side of the plane without thinking about it much. I found myself surrounded by other seers within minutes, this time including some who had ridden in the other cars from the City. It felt like forever that I sat there trying as graciously as I could to field greetings and well-wishes, hand clasps and caresses and even kisses. Meanwhile, I felt my hands clutching the armrests between waves, conscious that we were all sitting in a plane that stood on the tarmac of a private airport just outside of Beijing.

The fact that the engines were gearing up for take-off relaxed me only marginally.

And still I didn't see him.

Since that initial greeting, the other seers had all drifted off to other parts of the plane, leaving me and Jon alone. Even Dorje sat behind us somewhere, talking to Jax and some of the other rebel seers. It seemed they were still bonding, in terms of working together...still getting to know one another. I wondered how many had known each other before Salinse started recruiting among the Seven's guard and even the Adhipan.

But I couldn't really think about any of that clearly.

I couldn't really get my mind to work at all, not yet.

After a few more minutes that seemed to take hours, I watched Wreg, Balidor and Revik board the plane with Vikram and a few others.

All of them looked at me but Revik himself.

None of them stopped though, and only Balidor raised a hand in greeting, his mouth touched by a faint smile below grim eyes. They passed by that front row of seats, moving down the aisle without pausing. I could feel from the Barrier space around them that some kind of conversation continued between them as they made their way to some other segment of the plane, further back and out of earshot of that front bulkhead.

I tried not to react to the silence I could feel, or the infiltrator's mask I saw on his face as he passed. Even so, when I turned my head, I saw Jon watching him pass, too.

Once they were gone, I felt Jon's fingers tighten on my arm.

"Go easy on him, sis," he said softly. "He's not ignoring you."

I smiled at his words, but failed to keep the bitterness out of my voice entirely. "He's just doing his usual, bang-up job at *pretending* to ignore me... is that it?"

"Pretty much, yeah."

Glancing over at Jon's serious tone, I fought to push the rest of it from my mind. I looked down at my hand, realizing my brother still held it in his, realizing his fingers held mine tightly enough to whiten his knuckles. I still felt numb, even my hands. I was about to open my mouth again, to try and change the subject, but he spoke before I could.

"Go talk to him, Al," Jon said. "Seriously."

There was a silence while this penetrated. Then I looked up, meeting his gaze.

"Why, Jon?"

"Because you want to," Jon answered, his eyes unwavering on mine. "And because he's different now. And because he's worried as hell about you, no matter what you think. He's not ignoring you...he's probably terrified of you, Allie..."

"Terrified of me?" I smiled. "I seriously doubt that."

He hesitated, as if wrestling with what he was about to say next.

"...Al," he said, quieter. "I know it's going to sound crazy, but he's like..."

He paused, his eyes holding a strange kind of light, almost a kind of hope as they met mine.

"...He's like *Revik* again, Al. Like how he was. He's so much like him, it's almost disturbing. It's like the exact same guy almost, like how he was before...before all..." Jon waved a hand, as if struggling with words. "...You know. The Syrimne thing."

I felt myself frowning, even as my heart tightened briefly in my chest. But I couldn't go there with Jon on this. I wasn't ready to even consider his words, much less to believe them. I was about to make a joke of some kind, anything to shift the subject, when I found myself remembering the look on Revik's face when he'd first seen me in that audience chamber in the City. After a pause, I shook that off, too.

"He's not the same, Jon. He'll never be the same as he was then...it's impossible."

"I know that," Jon said. He sounded frustrated, and when I looked at him, I realized he'd followed my shifting thoughts across my face. "But I'm telling you...he's different. I'm not the only one who's noticed. We've all talked about it...all the seers, too."

I shook my head, feeling my jaw harden more. "It's not possible."

"Okay," he said, his voice still carrying that frustration. "Fine. It's not possible. But you should still talk to him, Al...decide for yourself, okay?"

My jaw remained hard, almost painfully so.

Then I shrugged, pulling at the fabric of the long skirt I still wore.

"I'm different too, Jon," I said finally.

When I glanced up at him that time though, his eyes looked angry.

"Bullshit," he said.

I raised an eyebrow at him. "I see. So you're the expert now, are you?"

The anger in his eyes worsened. "You're not really going to hide behind *that*, are you?"

"Hide?" I said, feeling my face flush. "What's that supposed to mean?"

"You know exactly what I mean. If you want to martyr yourself, make yourself over into slave girl or whatever the fuck you let them do to you in there, go for it. But don't expect me to buy it. I know who you are, Allie...I'll *always* know who you are. And so will he...and Balidor. And Cass. And Chan. Maybe even Wreg. Just because you're too much of a coward to face any of us for real, don't expect us to go along with your little charade..."

I stared up at him.

I tried to be angry, to feel something about his words. But I couldn't quite do that, either. I remembered everything that had happened in the past few months, everything I'd told myself when I left them in that cave in those mountains. But I didn't have it in me to explain myself to them anymore. I'd been doing it for months now...longer. The Sword thing, taking Revik.

The deal with Voi Pai. What I'd let Revik do to me in that tank. The endless sessions, pushing him until both of us were near exhaustion. Now it would be the leaving. Agreeing to Voi Pai's conditions for letting the rebels go.

I guess I should have expected anger about that, too. Somehow, it hadn't occurred to me I'd have to hear about it so soon.

I don't know if I was too sick of it all to fight him, or if it just seemed pointless. I looked away, staring out the window of the plane. I don't know what my face looked like, either, but he gripped my hand, hard enough to hurt.

I didn't turn my head, but I felt a kind of resignation fill my light.

"Do we have to do this now?" I said finally. "Can it wait until I've slept?" I glanced at him, my face unmoving. "I'm tired, you know. Long day of playing slave girl...then there was the whole starting a war thing, which kind of ruined my evening plans..."

He gripped my hand, tighter.

"Stop it," he said. When I looked up, tears shone in his eyes, enough to make me wince. "Just cut it out, okay? We love you. We all love you. Don't you dare pretend we don't. There's no way we would have let you do that, if any one of us had known. I still want to kick your ass. I don't care how noble you thought you were being..."

"I didn't think it was *noble,* Jon. Jesus."

"Bullshit. You think I don't know what you were doing? You were trying to disappear. To erase yourself. You decided no one gave a damn about you. You found the first cross to nail yourself to, and you handed Voi Pai the hammer..."

I shook my head, clicking in irritation.

"Allie." He shook my hand, forcing my eyes back to his. "We don't judge you for anything you did! We were *worried* about you...about what you seemed willing to do to yourself in order to make him better. That whole thing with you going after him when he was with the rebels...the thing in the tank. That's all it was. We didn't think you did the *wrong* thing, exactly...we were afraid you would both end up dead...or worse. Don't you get that?"

I shrugged, trying to lighten my voice.

"Well, at least Tarsi and Vash were able to help him."

"Bullshit...they said *you* did it, not them. They said the reason he drove you off was because you'd gotten so close to the real problem. It took Balidor going in there and nearly getting himself killed before Revik finally seemed to snap out of it. But he was a bastard after you left, Al. I don't think he believed you'd really leave...he accused us of lying for weeks."

I shrugged. "I'm sure the hookers softened the blow."

"He didn't do that, either," Jon said, gripping my hand tighter again. "And it wasn't because of us. He came close to hitting me when I offered that to him..."

I looked back out the window, trying to think about this, to make it mean something to me. It did, of course...but I couldn't feel anything about my role in it, or about whatever Revik had decided about me and him after I'd gone. I could barely remember what we'd done all those weeks in the tank. I knew Jon wouldn't lie to me deliberately, but I also knew, when it came down to it, it didn't really matter who finally helped Revik. It didn't really matter how it happened at all.

"Well, I'm glad he's all right," I said finally. "I really am, Jon."

I turned again, looking out the window. Then I sighed, returning my eyes to his. I squeezed his hand in my fingers, tugging gently on his arm.

"Seriously. It's okay, Jon. Really. Can we just let it go for now? I meant it about being tired."

"Al," he began, frustrated.

"...I'm just embarrassed. I never wanted any of you to see me like that. I know this may not make total sense to you, but honestly, I thought I'd just do it, and no one would even have to know. I thought I'd be out of there before it ever got back to any of you. The initial contract didn't seem like that big of a deal..."

"Well, you're stupid," he said angrily.

"I'm pretty sure we've established that," I sighed. "Can you please just yell at me more later?"

But he barely seemed to hear my words.

"...And you're cruel," he said. "None of us deserved that. Not even him."

I looked up at the anger in his voice. But that time, his words penetrated. My voice held a kind of blank incredulity.

"I didn't do this to *hurt* him, Jon," I said.

Jon gave a humorless laugh, shaking his head. "Yeah. Okay."

"I didn't!" I said. "I went there to get them free. To get *Cass* free! Remember Cass? Who Voi Pai took prisoner? I thought it was just some power play, her wanting me to come in person. I wasn't going to stay there...I didn't intend for any of this to happen!"

"Really?" Jon said. "So what was the plan, Al? What were you going to do? Where were you going to *go*? And for that matter, how stupid are you, to not realize the craziness of going to the Lao Hu alone, given who you are?" His anger worsened, even as he gripped my hand tighter, tugging on it when I turned away. "How long are you going to pretend that you aren't the Bridge? That you're just some waitress chick from San Francisco who designs tattoos? You can't just do anything you want anymore, Al! You can't!"

"Jon," I said, my voice warning. "Cut it out."

"...Last time I checked, half the seers in the West wanted you dead! Were you just going to hang out until a group of them stoned you to death? Hide in the mountains somewhere, eating goat meat and living in a cave for a few decades, like Tarsi?"

I stared at him, unable to hide my incredulity.

"You're pissed at me?" I said. "You're really *pissed* at me for this? For trying to help Cass? For leaving when Revik told me to leave?"

"You're damned right I'm pissed at you!" he snapped. "Jesus, Al! You didn't just leave him...you left all of us! You could have been killed! What if we hadn't found you before that group of seers came and took you from the Lao Hu?"

I stared at him, unable to come up with an answer to that, either.

Then I looked away, staring around at the rest of the cabin. If any of the other seers heard us, I couldn't see it on their faces. They all seemed to be talking amongst themselves. Even so, I found myself remembering Balidor's face when I left, and even Dorje's. I remembered Balidor's grim smile just now, and the look on Revik's face as Ulai and the other Lao Hu infiltrators led me into that audience chamber in the Forbidden City. Forcing it all out of my head, I rose to my feet, disentangling my fingers from Jon's.

I didn't feel guilt exactly, but I guess I figured he was right about the cowardice part.

More than anything, I was tired.

Maybe I was just hoping to get the inevitable over with.

I stood there for probably a few seconds before any of them noticed me. They sat together, the four of them, Revik between Wreg and Balidor as they and Vikram looked down at something on a screen in Revik's lap. It occurred to me a second later that they appeared to be speaking to someone in VR, too. I saw Revik's lips move, in that subtle speech that was almost a subvocalization, that kept people from yelling aloud when they were communicating via a link on the network.

I didn't try to read his lips, or even watch his face all that closely once I knew what they were doing. I did wonder who they were talking to.

Given everything, I figured they'd tell me that...or not.

Truthfully, I had no idea if I figured into their plans at all in that regard anymore. I'm not sure I cared really, either. Not then, anyway.

Balidor looked up first.

His eyes widened when he saw me standing there, at the end of the aisle. He was still looking at me when he laid a hand on Revik's arm, likely using a pulse of his light to get his attention. Revik looked at him first, his eyes showing him to be faintly startled. Then he followed Balidor's gaze to me. Glancing at the men sitting and crouching around him, I realized that all of them were staring at me now.

I fought not to move. Part of me wanted to cover my bare belly with an arm, or maybe cross both arms over my chest. I didn't. Instead I stood there, feeling my jaw tighten slightly.

Then Revik ripped the headset from around his ear. He did it so quickly it fell to the top of the VR screen sitting between them, but he didn't look away from me.

He also didn't speak. When they all continued to stare at me, I finally averted my gaze, still holding onto a seat back on either side of the narrow row where they sat.

"Could I, uh..." I let my eyes meet Revik's again. "...Borrow you? Just for a minute."

Feeling the silence deepen, I forced myself to hold his gaze.

"...If it's a bad time," I began.

"No."

He stood, as rapidly as he'd taken off the headset. I saw Wreg rescue the VR monitor before it could fall onto the floor, even as he exchanged a faint smile with Balidor. Balidor was looking at my face though, his own expression inscrutable. When Revik turned his body sideways to edge down the aisle, Balidor grabbed his arm briefly, stopping him. Some communication passed between them in the Barrier.

Whatever it was, Revik waved it away, frowning silently. His returning gesture looked like something along the lines of, "I know, I know."

I wondered what exactly Balidor had reminded him of.

But I pushed that out of my mind, too.

Revik reached the end of the row of seats, looking tall to me again. Even so, I found myself studying his face briefly, just before he made a polite motion with one hand, indicating that I lead him wherever I wanted him to go.

Turning, I aimed my feet for the curtain separating the front and back compartments of the plane. I passed through the heavy material, then hesitated, looking at the rows of seats. My eyes found the odd-shaped bulkhead at the back then, and I realized that both sides had been curtained off in regular lengths along the windows of the main passenger cabin. I didn't see anyone else, but I knew there might be others in there.

Walking the rest of the way through, I made my way up a few rows of seats, then stopped, standing by the end of a row without sitting down. Turning, I faced Revik, still standing in the aisle as I leaned my weight against one of the seat backs.

He stood there, looking uncomfortable, but didn't move away, or avert his gaze. I noticed he was wearing a jacket I recognized, from when I stayed with him in that rebel compound.

"The plane?" I said, glancing around. "Is it from before?"

He hesitated, then nodded. "They took most of it. Salinse and the others."

I nodded again. For a moment, I found myself struggling with words. I didn't want to be coy though, so I just looked up at him.

"I don't really need you," I said. He flinched a little, but I didn't let my light dwell on that either, plowing on as I gestured with one hand. "...Right now, I mean," I clarified. "I just...I guess I just wanted to talk to you."

He nodded, his face still wearing that infiltrator's mask.

He didn't fold his arms, but I saw him shift his weight when I didn't go on immediately.

Finally, I sighed, fingering my hair out of my eyes.

"I do need a shower," I said, glancing around vaguely behind me. "Jon said there are showers here...and beds..."

Revik followed my eyes to the rear of the cabin. I felt a kind of relief on him once I gave him something actionable, something he could help me with.

"Yes," he said. "There are showers. I can find you a bunk, Allie..."

"I don't have any clothes," I said. I felt my cheeks flush slightly, but I didn't look down at what I was wearing. "...Could I borrow some?"

"From me?" He stared at me blankly.

I felt my face grow hotter. "It doesn't have to be you, Revik."

He shook his head, clicking a little. "No, it's fine. I just meant..."

He glanced down at me, his eyes lingering on the long skirt I wore. His skin colored a little, and I found myself staring up at his face when I noticed. I hadn't seen him blush at anything when I lived with him as Syrimne. Not once. In fact, I hadn't seen him do that since...

"...I just don't have anything...feminine, Allie." He cleared his throat, avoiding my eyes. "I could ask one of the other infiltrators. Yumi, or..."

I shook my head though, gesturing a negative.

"It doesn't need to be feminine, Revik." I hesitated again. "...But you can ask whoever you want. Or I could," I added. "I could ask them. I just didn't think of it until now..."

He gestured another negative, shaking his head. Before I could really decide what that meant, he motioned for me to follow him, making his way down the aisle towards the back. Reaching the section where the bulkhead seemed to curve outwards, he undid the latch to a rounded, organic-looking door that said 'vacant' over a green light that reminded me of toilets I'd seen on commercial planes.

When he opened the door, however, I was a little bewildered by the space on the other side. It looked more like a locker room bathroom in a gym back in San Francisco than it did one of the cramped, odd-shaped bathrooms found on most planes.

"Shower's in here," he said. He glanced at me, then let go of the handle. "I'll be right back...wait here, Allie...please..."

I found myself watching as he walked back down the aisle. Wrapping my arms around my waist in the pause, I saw him pull a bag out of the overhead bin. Kind of a sophisticated duffle, it had handles on the side that he pulled, opening a flat panel on the widest of the storage segments.

I looked away as he rifled through the contents inside, glancing through the partway open door at the bathroom itself. As I did, I fought a wave of pain, seemingly out of nowhere. I forced it out of my light without trying to figure out what it was from, and off my face as he walked back towards me down the aisle. By the time he reached me again, I smiled at him, taking the proffered stack of clothes, folded neatly in his hands.

Pulling them against me, I fought to smile again. "Thanks."

He hesitated, looking at me.

I felt him wanting to speak, so I didn't say anything. Even so, I had to fight not to stare at him, especially his eyes. I found myself noticing what Jon had seen, what he'd told me about how Revik was now. But I couldn't let myself go there, even then. I knew all about that kind of delusional thinking...I'd engaged in it for months when I'd lived with Syrimne before. I'd engaged in something similar in the tank with him, too, well after I should have known better.

I wasn't sure I had it in me to be broken by that particular fantasy again.

Forcing my eyes off his when he noticed me staring, I looked back at the bathroom.

"Do you want me to wait?" he said.

I looked back at him, hiding my surprise. I answered before I'd really thought about it.

"Yes," I said. Feeling my cheeks warm a second later, I fumbled to soften my answer. "But if you're busy...with the others..."

He shook his head, once. "I'm not."

I moved towards the door to the shower, but he caught hold of my arm.

I froze. Glancing back at him, I tried to hide the confusion in my light.

"Allie," he said. He winced a little, meeting my gaze. "There is one more thing. Well...two," he amended. "Two more things."

I continued to look up at him, unmoving. I watched his eyes study my face. After another pause, he released my arm. He gestured vaguely as he averted his gaze.

"...There are remnants," he said. "In your light. Balidor thought..." Clearing his throat, he wiped his face with one hand, still not looking at me. "We don't want them following us. Salinse and his people. Or the Lao Hu..." He gestured again. "...Voi Pai seem to be allied with whoever was going to take you. We've felt the Dreng on them, too..."

But I already understood. I nodded, then gave the hand-language version of yes.

"It's fine, Revik. Whatever you have to do."

"It's not much," he said, looking me in the face again. His voice grew apologetic. "It's from me, Allie...not from anything you did. It's my fault it's there..."

"It's fine," I said. "Really." I held the folded clothes more tightly against my body, covering my bare skin self-consciously, despite what I'd told myself earlier. I gestured back towards the other side of the plane, beyond the curtain, using a brief wave with my fingers.

"Can you do it now?" I said. "Or do you need the others?"

"I can do it." He continued to hold my gaze.

I was still looking up at him when his irises blurred faintly. I felt a part of him leave...his expression grew blank even as his mouth firmed somewhat in concentration.

Then his light flooded mine. I gripped the handle of the bathroom door, fighting not to panic as I felt him there. He only remained in the lower parts of my light briefly. I felt him start to scan me more thoroughly, emotion stripped from his light. The process felt methodical, almost clinical as he made his way through different layers in my aleimi. That part of him moved systematically up and through the lower segments of my light, until I felt him working high above my head, somewhere in the structures I used to perform the telekinesis and more complicated types of sight-work. The parts of my light I'd used when working with him in the tank, too.

I felt a sharp jolt then...a jerk right before...

...not really pain. It was like he'd broken something. Broken something on me...or maybe broken it *off* me, like a gardener cutting off a dead branch.

For a long moment, I just stood there, feeling him scan me, as if checking me for anything more. I held onto the bathroom door, gripping it tighter as a feeling of vulnerability came over me, so intense I was nearly shaking. He scanned me again. Then he did it a third time, cleaning off a few smaller things he found along the way.

Out of nowhere, heat hit my light, pooling in the middle of my chest.

I fought it, but it spread rapidly down my torso and through my limbs, making me breathe harder, worsening that vulnerability until it grew into a near panic. I tried to block what came with it, the emotions that rose up, nearly blinding me as I lost myself in that initial flush of light. But I couldn't block it. It was as if a bandaid had been ripped off without warning...or maybe more like Novocain wearing off all at once, leaving nothing but heat and raw pain. I'd lost my ability to live in that blank space, where nothing mattered.

I felt Vash with me again, and Tarsi.

I felt Revik, too...still searching my light. This time, I felt the grief on him, the worry as he scanned me a fourth time. Then a fifth. Unwilling to risk leaving anything in me that he'd put there, that the Lao Hu or anyone else had put in me...

...The pain behind it made me gasp.

I gripped the door tighter. Clutching the clothes against my body, I fought to pull myself back, to control my light. I was fighting tears then, too.

I tried to push it away, to hold it in...even before I felt him coming back, returning to where we stood at the rear of the plane by the door to the shower.

I pulled myself upright, standing almost straight when I saw his eyes click back into focus. Still, he must have seen something in my face. He caught hold of my arm, pulling me to him. His eyes held that same worry, and now I could feel his light, all around me. I felt him noticing the difference in mine too, and pain rippled off him again, even as he pulled me closer.

"Allie. Gods. Are you all right?"

I clutched his arm with my free hand, still holding the bundle of his clothes against me. I tried to speak, then didn't want to risk it and nodded instead. I looked away from him when my throat tightened, unable to meet that clear gaze.

He caressed my hair, kissing my cheek.

I flinched, even as I felt my light respond...more so when he opened his so close to mine. I fought not to just open to him in return, to merge into him again...but it was difficult, almost impossible when I felt another curl of emotion off his light. That part of me felt starved, half out of control when he opened more, letting me closer to him.

Finally, I averted my gaze from his, looking towards the shower.

His fingers loosened on me, but he didn't let go.

"Allie," he said.

I looked up, biting my lip.

I saw his eyes study mine. His expression looked almost the same as it had before, only now, I saw clearly behind the infiltrator's mask. Pain lived there, a kind of longing that hurt to look at, especially when I felt another curl of his light. He caressed my hair again, pushing it back from my face, his throat moving in a swallow.

I was trying to force out words when he looked away, still holding my arm as he shoved his other hand in a front pocket of his pants.

I watched him pull something out.

My throat closed when I saw the silver chain, even before I saw what it held. Pain clenched my chest, worsening when he cleared his throat, when my eyes rose back to his. His were bright. Too bright.

"Allie," he said, his voice thick. "You don't have to wear it. You can throw it away..." He pressed it into my hand, closing my fingers around it. "It's yours, Allie. Please. Please don't try to give it back to me again..."

I stared up at him. Then, forcing myself to move, I nodded. Still staring at my fingers wrapped around the silver chain, I nodded again dumbly.

My eyes found his fingers then. I focused on the band of silver around his index finger, not quite believing it was real. A shock touched my heart when he squeezed my hand tighter, and I saw the ring dimple the flesh around the bone. I stared at it...too long. Long enough for Revik to notice.

"Is it all right?" he said, caressing my fingers. His voice was lower than a whisper. "Can I wear it again, Allie?"

Another flicker of pain reached me. That time I didn't know if it was his or mine. Unable to speak, I only nodded.

I don't think I looked at him again as I stumbled through the rounded door into the shower area, clutching the ring in one hand and his clothes in the other.

He sat in one of the cloth airline seats, fighting not to feel what was going on in the rest of the plane. He occasionally saw one of the others look through the curtains from the other cabin, but no one bothered him, or tried to speak with him directly, which was a relief.

He kept his light from hers, too, in the adjacent room. He'd found her a place to sleep...it turned out only a few of the bunks were taken, and all of those were the smaller ones, closer to the front of the main cabin.

He remembered having the plane refitted for longer combat trips. They'd spent so much time in the air, those first few months he'd been with the rebels...

...but all of that seemed so long ago now.

His mind tried to toy with what they'd found out from Voi Pai in their scans of her between the Forbidden City and the small airport where his pilots guarded his plane. He couldn't concentrate on that, either. Not enough concrete information lived in her mind to really distract him from the person on the other side of the rounded door.

Voi Pai knew enough about Gerwix's patrons to know they could harm the Lao Hu. She hadn't exactly sworn allegiance to them, not like one had to swear allegiance to the Rooks in the time of the Pyramid, or even the rebellion less than a year ago. It was more like a tribute relationship, it seemed. The Lao Hu paid protection tribute to these people...like they owed them some kind of debt. What they got in return still wasn't clear; the blocks on the female seer's light had been extensive, and well-constructed. Too well constructed for Balidor or any of the others to crack them before they made it to the airport. He would have liked to take her with them, to find out more. But that had been impossible, too.

As it was, Allie hadn't been wrong, when she said this would mean war. The Lao Hu would never forgive him for taking their leader from them, for holding her captive, removing her from the City...even for so short a time. It would definitely mean war.

It would also mean that the Lao Hu might see fit to ally with their enemies, which was another development they couldn't really afford.

But he couldn't say he regretted it, either.

He just wished they'd been able to discover who pulled Gerwix's leash. He didn't know of any group of seers powerful enough that the Lao Hu would fear them. But someone was out there, and it wasn't Salinse and his seers. If it had been, Voi Pai would never have attacked them.

In fact, he almost got the impression from her light that she'd been acting under orders with that, too...and with luring Allie to the City. He wondered if they would have found some other pretext to take her before her contract terms expired. He even wondered if they'd known how Allie would react to Gerwix...if they'd sent him as a test, to see if she would kill him. Feeling a pain sliver through his light, he gripped the armrests of the economy chair.

She'd killed Gerwix. He knew he shouldn't feel touched by that, or feel as much emotion as what rose in him at the memory...but he couldn't help it. The fact that she'd cared enough to even react that way brought enough feeling that he could barely breathe.

It also gave him a flicker of hope.

He jumped when the door opened behind him.

Turning his head, he didn't stand up until he saw her outline in the backlit opening. She wasn't looking at him, but down at her feet as she fumbled with the handle of the door. She turned her back to him as she shut it more firmly, twisting the mechanism until it caught.

Then she looked at him. He stood in the same moment, still holding the back of the plane seat where he'd been sitting.

Her hair hung down her back now, wetting the dark blue t-shirt he'd given her. Her brown legs stuck out below shorts he normally slept in, which came down to about the middle of her muscular thighs. She must have been doing mulei in the City, as well.

He stared at her legs, unable to stop himself from staring, then felt her eyes on him and looked up. He knew he was reacting, even before pain slid through his light, making it difficult to hold her gaze.

"Better?" he said, a little lamely.

She nodded, arranging the bundle of clothes she clutched in her arms. He noticed then, that she was wearing the chain around her neck, and the pain worsened, nearly blinding him as he felt his body react, too. He forced his eyes off where the ring hung almost to the top of her breasts, hating himself for staring, especially when he could see from her face that she felt where his eyes were trained. When she didn't speak, he tried again, clearing his throat.

"Do you want me to take those?" he said, holding out a hand for the clothes.

She looked up at him, and he stared at her pale green eyes, fighting the reaction out of his light once more.

"Where do they go?" she said.

Vulnerability wafted off her light, which made his tongue thicken more.

Gods. He could barely control his light, and he wasn't even standing next to her. He gestured vaguely for a bin set into the wall, a push door that stood flush with the bulkhead. Feeling his face warm, he motioned towards the same with his head and chin.

"You can put it in there," he said.

She followed the prodding of his light, pushing open the flap and then shoving the clothing she'd been wearing before into the bin on the other side. He watched her do it, felt her noticing his eyes on her again, but he couldn't make himself look away. When she turned, she wrapped her arms around her front once more...not quite folded, but almost.

"You said there's a place I could lie down?" she said.

He nodded, still fighting reactions out of his light as he indicated to one of the bunks to the left of the row of seats. She followed his pointing finger with her eyes.

"The bottom one?" she said.

He cleared his throat again. "Either, Allie. Any one you want."

She turned then, looking at him. He found himself glad of the seat between them again, when her eyes focused seriously on his. That vulnerability grew prominent in her light once more, enough that he found himself averting his gaze.

"Are you tired, Revik?" she said.

Realizing what she was asking him, he felt his skin flush with heat. Pain rippled through him, enough that he couldn't answer her at first, or look at her. His voice came out soft when he finally spoke, low enough that he fought to make it louder so she could hear him.

"Allie," he said. "The plane...the whole plane...it's a construct..." He forced himself to look at her. "We can't. I want to...gods. I want to, Allie...so much. I can't even..." He shook his head. "But we can't...not here..."

There was a silence.

She didn't move, didn't change expression, but he realized his mistake the instant before she looked away, her jaw hardening. He raised a hand in apology, speaking quickly, feeling his shoulders tense even as he took a step towards her.

"Allie," he said. "Allie, I'm sorry...I don't mean you, Allie. I wasn't accusing you..."

"I wasn't offering you sex," she said. Her voice was dull now, almost tired.

"I know. I'm sorry..."

"I wasn't offering that," she said again. "I wasn't, Revik."

She met his gaze, and his heart hurt, forcing him silent briefly.

"I didn't mean you, Allie," he said finally. "I swear to the gods I didn't..."

He stepped towards her, and she backed off, towards the bunk that he'd indicated for her earlier. Her face looked openly wary now.

"Allie," he said. "I'm sorry. Gods, I'm sorry. Please..."

She stared at him, her green eyes glowing faintly.

He knew she didn't believe him, even before her gaze narrowed slightly. She looked away, off somewhere to the side, her eyes unfocused as she seemed to be pulling back her light. He watched as she folded her arms tighter in front of her chest.

He could barely feel her at all now.

"Goddamn it, Allie," he said, his voice thick. "It's not you! It's me."

She shook her head, closing her eyes, longer than a blink.

"Forget it," she said. "It's okay. I'm just tired."

She looked at him then, and he felt that vulnerability on her again. He forced himself to hold her gaze, to not look away.

"I wanted you to stay," she said slowly. "I was asking you to stay. I wasn't going to do anything. I won't even touch you, if you don't want..." Seeing him flinch, she reddened again. "Revik. I mean your hand, anything. I didn't mean – "

"I know," he cut in. "I know what you meant, Allie."

For a moment, they only looked at each other.

He realized then, that she'd forced herself to say it, to admit she wanted him there. His pain worsened, enough that he couldn't speak.

He watched, unmoving, as she turned towards the bunk set into the outer bulkhead. He felt another coil of pain reach his light when she walked away from him. She pulled the curtain aside, bending down to peer into the low-ceilinged bunk. There was a pause where he felt her scan the space, both with her eyes and her light. He continued to watch her as she crawled inside, her movements still almost cautious.

She closed the curtain a moment later.

He couldn't see her once she had. He could still feel her though. He felt the embarrassment on her, what bordered on shame, a kind of frustration that lost itself in the vulnerability he'd felt before. But it was more than that, too...a denser kind of sadness that hurt him with its intensity, that felt connected to him. Along with that, he felt a flush of anger she aimed at herself.

He felt whispers of her time with the Lao Hu in that.

He felt the other on her as well, those added structures in her light, what he'd felt when he'd looked for what had been left behind in her by the Dreng. He'd seen those structures before that, of course; he'd seen them in that reception room of the Lao Hu, from the moment he set eyes on her. He felt them the moment he'd touched her with his light. He knew the other seers reacted to the same thing in her...not only the males, but the females, too. The clothing in which the Lao Hu dressed her only made it worse.

He remembered the other, then...what he'd said to her before she left those caves. He remembered the look on her face, the resignation he'd felt in her then, too.

She probably thought...Christ.

Pain reached him again, intense enough that he clutched his shirt.

He crossed the space to the bunk where she was. He didn't speak to her, not even through the curtain, but kicked off his shoes while he stood outside. He took off his jacket once he had, flipping it off his shoulders and leaving it on the nearest airplane seat. He felt eyes on him and glanced to his left, saw Garensche watching him through the curtain. The giant seer winked at him, gesturing a sign of encouragement that made Revik's jaw harden again.

Taking a breath, he pulled the curtain back with one hand.

He saw her flinch, jumping a little before she glanced over her shoulder at him. Her face reflected a kind of startled surprise, white against the dark blue of his shirt. She'd been curled up on her side, her knees drawn up where she faced the windows of the bulkhead. Only one of the window shades was open, but it shed enough light that he could see all of her.

"Can I?" he said, gruff.

She looked up at him, her eyes still holding that bewilderment.

He saw her frown then, saw her wanting to argue with him...

He didn't wait. He crawled inside on his hands and knees, pausing only to close the curtain behind him. He knew Garensche had probably told the others he'd come in here with her, but he didn't care about that, either. Crawling deeper into the low space, he shifted his weight so that he was lying on his side. Then he settled onto his back, lying almost flat on the dense mattress and blanket, only a few feet away from her. His eyes never left hers.

He held out a hand when she continued to look at him, an invitation.

She didn't move, but he saw her eyes shift to his fingers. He saw her looking at the ring he wore again, and pain slivered through his light, enough to force his eyes closed.

"Please," he said. He couldn't keep the pain out of his voice. "Please, Allie...I won't do anything. Please come here...please..."

When he could focus on her again, he saw doubt in her eyes.

He was about to try again, when he saw the doubt fade, replaced by what looked like resignation once more. He was still watching her face when she turned over, until her body faced his. Hesitating another beat, she slid closer to him. Close enough that he could wrap his arm around her shoulders, draw her the rest of the way to where he lay. He pulled her up against his chest, sliding his other hand over her arm where she wrapped it around him, then into her hair. For a moment, he couldn't make himself breathe. He fought back another reaction in his light, holding her tighter.

"Thank you," he said.

"Revik, it's okay," she said. "You don't have to stay...I mean it."

"I know."

There was another silence. He fought for words through it, trying to sort through the several hundred things he'd wanted to say to her for most of the time she'd been gone.

"I'm sorry," he said finally. "I'm so sorry, Allie."

She shook her head against his chest. He felt more in her light, but she didn't speak.

"I wanted to stay," he said. "I want to talk to you. I just don't want to..."

He hesitated, looking down as he caressed her hair.

"I want to be alone with you, Allie," he said. "Really alone."

There was another pause, then she nodded. He felt something in her light relax into his.

"I love you," he said, feeling the pain in his light worsen. "I love you, Allie. I'm so sorry. I'm sorry about everything I did..." He fought for words again, holding her tighter. He pulled her into the curve of his body, until his light was fighting to coil into hers once more. "Everything you did for me...in the tank, before that. I don't know how you can forgive me...but I need you to, Allie. Gods, I know how unfair that is...but I need it so badly..."

She tensed in his arms. He had to fight not to react at first, then he felt her fighting her own light, trying to control her reaction to his words. Her fingers gripped his arm, grasping at the fabric of his shirt. Kissing her, he held her tighter.

"I've missed you," he murmured, caressing her face. "...So much. I don't want to be away from you...not even here. It's not you...it's me I don't trust... please believe me..." He hesitated. "...All those things you saw about me. They're still there, Allie..."

Pain wafted off her, enough that he clutched at her tighter, feeling something in his light flare, fighting to get at hers as his self-control slipped. Remembering the others in the next cabin, he forced that back as well, caressing her hair as he kissed her head, caressing her shoulders with the same hand, then her bare arm past the t-shirt, her fingers. Pain fought its way over his skin, but he ignored that, too, touching her face.

After another moment, she raised her head, looking at him. His pain worsened, pretty much as soon as her eyes met his. If she noticed, it didn't show on her face.

"Revik..." she began. He watched her think, saw her seem to be fighting with words, too. After another pause, she shook her head, caressing his face with her fingers. "...I can't stay here," she said, softer. "With you. Not until..." Feeling him flinch, she gripped his hair in her hand, shaking her head as she forced him to look at her. "No...I don't mean it like that. I just mean. I can't... unless we clear this up. Unless we can get past this. I can't be a part of your team. Not if we're not..." She trailed, right before her skin darkened. Closing her eyes, she shook her head again, clicking softly. "I can't handle us fighting about this forever, Revik. I really can't. I understand if you're angry...I do. I wouldn't blame you if you can't get past it. But I need to know you're sure this time...as much as you can be. I need to know you can let this go..." Hesitating, she met his gaze. "...If we're going to do this, I mean. Any of it."

He was still looking at her, trying to understand, when she shook her head again, averting her eyes from his. Revik felt pain dart through his skin, nearly paralyzing him. He tried to replay her words, to make sense of them, but he couldn't be sure in either direction. She was shielding him again and he couldn't make himself look away from her face. He felt another whisper of pain on her, as she caressed his hair.

"You don't have to answer now," she said. "I know I probably shouldn't have said it now – "

"What if we got married?" he said, abrupt.

Her eyes drifted up. He saw the puzzlement there, and shook his head, clicking softly.

"I mean a ceremony, Allie," he said, softer. He caressed her face, putting light into his fingers. "What if we started over...for both of us." Hesitating, he added, "...Vash said we might have to anyway, in some respects. Our light... it's different. Parts of yours are awake that weren't before. And mine..." He trailed as he saw understanding reach her eyes. "...It won't erase everything," he said. "I know that. But we could start over..."

Her hand slid under his shirt, caressing his chest. He felt her merging into him tentatively as her fingers explored his skin. Briefly, he couldn't move.

After another moment, he brought his light under control again.

"Allie," he said. "Is that what you were asking me?"

Her eyes rose to his once more. After a pause, she nodded. "Yes."

"Do you still want..." His fingers tightened on her again. "Allie, is that a yes? To what I asked?"

After another bare pause, she nodded. He felt her light relax again, despite the tension he could still feel sparking through both of them.

"Yes," she said.

Something in his chest let go, leaving him lying there, unable to move again. Her hands were still exploring his skin, and he could only close his eyes, fighting for control as her fingers slid over his shoulder. His own hand found its way under her shirt, massaging her back, but he still couldn't make himself look at her. His light was coursing through his hands, pulling at hers, growing more urgent when she leaned into his side. He knew he was hard... more than hard, he was fully extended, in more pain than he could remember being since he was a kid, but he couldn't make himself let go of her. He coiled a hand around her side under the shirt, pulling her arm around him, if only to keep her from touching more of his bare skin.

"Is this all right?" he said, gruff. "Is it all right, Allie?"

After another pause, he felt her nod again.

He was trying to decide if he should say more, when her light began opening tentatively to his. Not just on her hands and body...he felt the other part of her open that time, the light in her chest and heart and throat. It nearly made him groan, but he fought that too, forcing himself to relax into her as she did it, feeling something in his chest open in response. He kept ahold of his own aleimi, feeling it gradually grow easier to control as her heart opened to his. Once he could, he was pulling on her gently, coaxing her to wind her light deeper into his. He tugged at her leg with one hand, pulling her by the knee until he had it partly around him as well. She didn't fight him. He felt an almost debilitating relief when she slid her leg between his, resting her body deeper against his chest and side, her arm wound partway around his back.

He felt her close her eyes, her light still open, warm in his chest.

After another pause, he closed his own eyes, willing his body to relax into the mattress. Another stab of pain caught him off-guard as his back unclenched against the dense foam...then he was just lying there, in pain, but feeling so much relief it almost brought tears to his eyes.

A few more seconds passed before he realized he felt the same on her.

Epilogue
Shadow

The oldest of the six stood at the edge of the stone balcony. He balanced an angular hip against the moss-green carvings of flowers, his face half-hidden by the hooded cloak that covered his head with its close-cropped, iron gray hair.

In the mountains it was cold as fall began to turn into winter, but he didn't shiver as he stood there, despite wearing only light pants and a linen shirt under the cloak. He stood perfectly still, as if carved from stone, looking down over the valley below.

The servant couldn't see the elder's expression, but he could imagine it held some element of satisfaction, if not outright triumph.

None of them spoke as he unloaded the tray for their supper.

The servant glanced up, here and there, arranging the table with hand-painted china, adjusting silver spoons and forks, wiping his own fingerprints from the bases of glasses blown in the furnaces of the small town below the stone gates of the chateau on the mountain. He wondered if the ancient seer looked down on that town now, watching the sun glint off the water shining on cobblestone streets, listening to the lowing of cows as they were brought in from the fields, the triangular copper bells clanking from leather collars around their necks.

Evening crept over the green mountains ringing the ancient stone building, pulling long fingers across the valley. The last of the indigo light faded from the horizon at either side. The servant could see the other side of the colonial-built structure from the Barrier...the ocean lapping against the coastline, craggy rock shores guarded by bluffs, pock-marked by infrequent beaches. Most of the sand-covered stretches lived further south and north of the high grasslands and mountains overseen by the chateau and its owners.

No one came to this part of the world to indulge in beach tourism. In fact, very few came to this part of the world at all, as most of the land for almost a thousand miles belonged to a handful of private owners who did not encourage visitors of any kind.

The town, in most respects, was not dissimilar to the previous peasant, or *campesino* village that had once been situated outside those gates. The previous landowner had lived a few hundred years earlier, but the relationships remained almost the same as those of the original colonials...or even as it did during the middle ages in Europe's own history. In this part of the world, such an arrangement had once formed the keystone of the *hacienda* system. Servants and workers of a particular *patron* would cluster outside his gates, pretending a kind of freedom and loyalty that grew more out of the disparity in class distinctions and interdependence than anything else.

In Europe, it was called feudalism.

Still, the servant knew the arrangement was not terrible for those in the village, either. In the modern day, it fed their families, and gave them a sense of belonging they might not otherwise have enjoyed. It also freed them from many of the worst excesses of city life. Here, the barter system remained intact, although those on both sides of the stone gates used modern currencies, as well. Headsets and feed terminals were in short supply in the township, but the world remained accessible in all ways inside the gates of the chateau and its guest compartments.

More importantly, they would be safe here. They would survive the coming storm.

As none of the humans were permitted to tend to the personal needs or bodies of either the *patron* or his guests, the servant felt little about this. He knew none of the villagers personally. Well, apart from the occasional whore sent up for a business partner, but those rarely remained in his presence other than to exchange one or two words.

He, himself, had been trained at a much higher level than his current position might suggest to an untrained eye. His loyalty to the six ancient seers in the room made the position an honor, however. Further, and more importantly, the servant knew they meant it as such.

They proved it every day, by not censoring their conversations around him.

The servant, having spent most of his life masquerading as a human, knew the value of discretion. He had been forced to hide his true race not only from his human cousins, but also from other seers...which had been difficult at times, to say the least, particularly around his more highly-ranked brothers and sisters. Still, he'd had help...and help of the most expert kind. He managed to go years undetected with the help of his patrons, including the four ancient seers now in the room, as well as those others who served them.

The servant's success at such a difficult task, given the years involved, had earned him a honored place under his patrons. He could not help but be proud of that place...nor did he fail to appreciate the perks and privileges associated with it.

He listened to them now, he knew, as a result of what he had earned for himself over those years. Much of their conversation, of course, occurred elsewhere in the Barrier's folds. The construct over the estate and its grounds housed so many layers and mini-constructs that it constituted more of a maze than the underground caverns and catacombs beneath the aboveground structures on the same lands.

Still, words leaked out, here and there.

They switched back and forth, and he caught enough to understand.

"...It will be soon, sister," the youngest of the six said, answering a question that likely originated in one of those high currents. His eyes flashed as the lamps around them ignited, responding to the light-level cue written into the sensors living in the organic walls.

"...We must wait for the right moment. We have discussed this..."

"...Is the message being sent?" the oldest of the females asked. Turning to another, she raised an eyebrow, her face unsmiling. "We can count on her, can we not?"

"She has agreed," another affirmed, from his corner by the wall. "She will approach the Sword directly, once they reach their final destination..."

"They cannot know what is coming," another murmured, his narrow body encased in a forest green chair. "We should do it now, before they begin to suspect what we have. It was sloppy, letting them know that a sample of the virus would remain. It would have been better, if they thought all of it was destroyed...that the operation came off clean..."

The servant heard the rebuke in these words and winced, even though the seer did not look at him, or change expression.

The others did not seem to notice.

"It is important to get the time right," the first one intoned a second time. "...Even if it means delay."

"But why delay?" the eldest female questioned again. "They are off balance now. They have no forces to speak of...a rabble of untrained refugees along with a handful of ranked infiltrators, and now the Lao Hu tracking them, seeking vengeance. Most of her followers still want her dead. The humans will soon be after her, as well...and him, too, once they know he is alive. Further, they know they are vulnerable. The fear itself could work to our advantage..."

"We need more than that, sister," the other cautioned.

"Will we try again to retrieve them both?" the quietest of the six asked. "What if she comes with him? Will we try to bring them both with us...?"

"We have our people on the inside..."

"But none of that will likely be enough, to bring him here," the old female insisted. "Raven *must* convince him. She must convince him of the truth..."

"Will it matter to him, if she does?" another male asked, his voice containing doubt. "Do they not have a history of fighting over the female...or rivalry, even apart from this...?"

The old female smiled thinly, her eyes sharp as they flashed to their leader on the balcony. "It will matter to him, brother," she said softly. "Believe me, it will matter. He is a seer. Intermediary or not, this will matter to him a great deal, no matter what their past history..."

"In any case, the male will be harder to control now..."

"Perhaps," said the other female, who had been quiet up until then. Her voice was thoughtful, her light picking impressions off the others as she spoke. "...But perhaps not. We can still use her to get to him. They are as vulnerable together as they are apart..."

"They are still Intermediaries..."

"We do not even know if they will survive the virus," another male reminded them. "We have only tested it on Sarks..."

"They will survive it...she was in Hong Kong during the demonstration..."

"Indoors," the first male clarified. "Not in the kill zone..."

As the other five of them spoke, the servant felt their attention remain primarily on the eldest standing at the railing of the stone balcony, who had not yet said a word. Each of them connected to him in some way, touching his light, waiting for him to end the disagreement, or to make a statement that would change the direction of their discussion. The servant watched him, too, listening to the others in a different part of his light.

"...He still can be found. He will always have our mark on him..."

"But will it matter now, if he is under her protection? She might sense a trap. She might not let him come here...not alone. There is also the Adhipan leader, as well as the old man. They will help her. The old man still has a hold on him, too..."

At this, the leader finally turned his head.

They all fell silent, looking at him, waiting for him to speak. His eyes stood in shadow from the encroaching darkness outside, but they all could see them somehow, shining from the depths of a skull-like face.

"The elder will not last much longer," the leader commented softly. "We have nothing to fear in the Council, my friends. Once the elder is dead, they will cease to be..."

All of them paused on this, thinking over his words.

As per usual, it was his second who spoke first into the silence.

"And what of her? She will not want him to come here...not for any reason."

The elder smiled. "She will not fight him. Not on this. Once he has spoken to Raven, the rest will fall into place...I promise you. He will come here, and then I will speak with him..."

"When, sir?" she said. "When will the next phase begin?"

Thinking for a moment, he nodded to his second-in-command before he looked around at the others.

"You are correct, sister. We must not wait. We must do it now. Before they organize. Once this has begun, and the ramifications are clear to all of them, Raven will approach him. She will bring him here. If the virus is already active, it will give him added incentive..."

"And the female, sir?" another asked, his voice cautiously reverent.

The eyes swiveled to his, boring into his face.

"That can wait," he said. "We must diminish their numbers first. They must be isolated...even more than they are now. We must ensure the alliances are all broken..." He smiled at them, but it was an odd expression on that face, pulling the skin higher around his angular forehead. "...They are halfway there already, even without our intervention."

"Then you no longer want him with us?" another asked, his voice also cautious.

The elder turned, meeting his gaze. A fire shone in his eyes, cold and utterly without compromise.

"We will never abandon our intermediary to the enemy," he said. "Never."

"But to let his light be manipulated and changed by those kneelers," another said, his voice openly contemptuous. "It is not fitting, for a creature of his stature..."

The second in command never took her eyes off the elder.

"What will we do with him...if he will not change?"

The elder smiled, but it didn't touch more than his pale lips. "Then we will kill him, my beloved sister. Allow him another life to serve those who truly love him..." He gave a regretful shrug with one hand. "Sadly, it would be the only gift left for us to give."

"Will that not kill her, as well?" the youngest said.

The elder gestured dismissively. "What need have we of the Bridge? Are we not making our own evolutionary stand? Creating our own futures?"

He paused, looking over at the rest of them.

"...But for that, too, we must wait," he added. "There is one more thing our Intermediaries can give us, I think, before we send them back to the lands of their Ancestors..." That flicker of a smile returned, even as he held out his hands in a gesture of supplication. "But friends...brothers and sisters...I have not given up on him yet. I would advise you not to do the same. And she may yet be willing to follow, if we provide her enough incentive..."

Silence fell over the other five. It was the female again who broke it.

"Where?" she said, her eyes sharp as they stared into his. "Once the ground is laid, how would you have us deploy the sickness, father...and where? Do you intend that we deploy globally at the outset, to prevent them from redesigning a cure? Or would you rather start in a few key cities first...?"

His voice grew thoughtful. "A cure is not a viable option for them. Not anymore." He glanced at her. "I think...I think we will start in a single location."

"In the land of our ancestors?" she said. "If it works as we had planned, it will spread quickly. Quick enough that we will no longer need to work with the humans in Beijing..."

Clicking softly, he gestured in the negative with one pale hand.

"No," he said softly. "I would like a more dramatic beginning, I think. The Western mind is more useful for this...the East handles things differently..."

"New York?" one of the seers suggested.

"Rio, father?" another said. "We could use Paris as well...their water supply would lend itself easily..."

"How about Rome?" another said.

"Berlin?"

The oldest seer smiled faintly, staring around at each of their faces, his own still in shadow from where he stood outside the ring of interior lights.

"No," he said softly. "I think we will get the Bridge's attention far more easily if we deploy the first wave where she is most likely to know at least a few rats in the lab..." He clicked gently at their expressions, pausing only on the knowing look from his second-in-command. "We will start it in her home town. It is fitting, do you not think?"

"San Francisco," one of them breathed.

"America," another said. "Yes. It is right. It is brilliant, father...perfect..."

His lieutenant did not speak. The servant could tell that she had already drawn the obvious conclusion the other four only reached following the elder's words. But then, she, like the servant himself, had worked far more closely and directly with the Bridge and her mate than the other seers in the room.

The servant watched as the five lights coiled in odd tangents over their heads. Each of them thought through the implications of the elder's words, and what it would mean for them personally in the coming months.

The servant knew in a sudden flash; this was a historic moment.

The world was changing once again. And this time, he had witnessed the very words that would set that change in motion.

Continue reading the ALLIE'S WAR Series with
KNIGHT: ALLIE'S WAR BOOK FIVE

If you enjoyed the book please consider leaving a review on the vendor site where you purchased it. A short review is fine and greatly appreciated. Word of mouth is essential for any author to succeed.

THE ALLIE'S WAR SERIES is a dark, unique and gritty apocalyptic psychic romance involving a young woman grappling with her role in bringing about the end of one world and the start of a new one. Follow Allie Taylor and her antihero partner in crime, Dehgoies Revik, as they fight terrifying enemies and one another in a passionate story spanning centuries, and filled unpredictable twists, turns and betrayals.

THE ALIEN APOCALYPSE SERIES is a post-apocalyptic dystopian romance about a tough girl named Jet Tetsuo who grew up on Earth following an alien invasion. Forced into living among her conquerors, she must learn to navigate a treacherous world full of enemies who pose as friends, even as she becomes their most famous fighter in the Rings, their modern day version of the coliseum where she must fight just to survive.

For more books by JC Andrijeski, visit www.jcandrijeski.com

"Seeking Truth in Made-Up Worlds"

ABOUT THE AUTHOR

JC Andrijeski writes contemporary and urban fantasy, dystopian, paranormal romance and science fiction, most of it with a metaphysial twist. Current works include the new adult urban fantasy series, *Allie's War,* post-apocalyptic and dystopian series, *Alien Apocalypse,* and the *Gate Shifter* series, about a shape-shifting alien and a tough-girl PI from Seattle.

Her work has been featured in anthologies, online literary, art and fiction magazines as well as print venues such as *NY Press* and holistic health magazines. JC travels extensively and has lived abroad in Europe, Australia, Asia and North America.

To learn more about JC and her writing, please visit jcandrijeski.com.

If you want to get an automatic email when JC's next book is released, join THE REBEL ARMY at tinyurl.com/JCAndrijeski. Your email will be kept private, never sold and you can unsubscribe at any time.

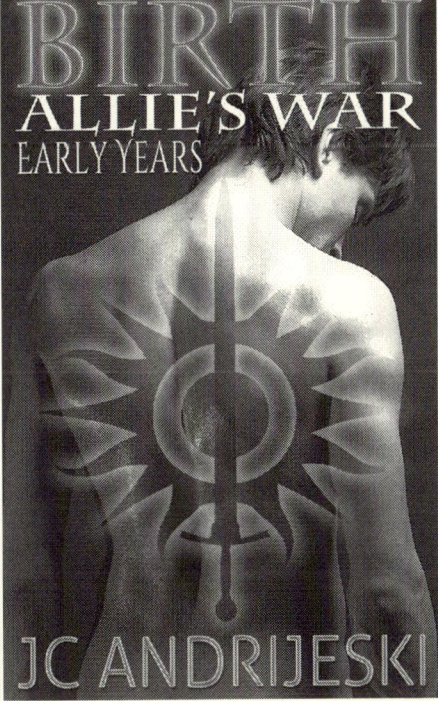

Made in the USA
Middletown, DE
12 December 2014